# COLLECTED
# STORIES 2

# ruth
# rendell

## COLLECTED
## STORIES 2

HUTCHINSON
LONDON

Published by Hutchinson in 2008

1 3 5 7 9 10 8 6 4 2

First published in Great Britain in 2008 by
Hutchinson
Random House, 20 Vauxhall Bridge Road,
London SW1V 2SA

www.rbooks.co.uk

Addresses for companies within The Random House Group Limited can be found at:
www.randomhouse.co.uk/offices.htm

The Random House Group Limited Reg. No. 954009

A CIP catalogue record for this book is available from the British Library

ISBN 9780091796839

**Mixed Sources**
Product group from well-managed
forests and other controlled sources
www.fsc.org  Cert no. TT-COC-2139
© 1996 Forest Stewardship Council
FSC

The Random House Group Limited supports The Forest Stewardship Council (FSC),
the leading international forest certification organisation. All our titles that are printed
on Greenpeace approved FSC certified paper carry the FSC logo.
Our paper procurement policy can by found at www.rbooks.co.uk/environment

Typeset by Replika Press, India

Printed and bound in Great Britain by
Mackays of Chatham plc

# Conte

# The New Girl Friend

*For Paul Sidey*

# The New Girl Friend

'You know what we did last time?' he said.

She had waited for this for weeks. 'Yes?'

'I wondered if you'd like to do it again.'

She longed to but she didn't want to sound too keen. 'Why not?'

'How about Friday afternoon, then? I've got the day off and Angie always goes to her sister's on Friday.'

'Not *always*, David.' She giggled.

He also laughed a little. 'She will this week. Do you think we could use your car? Angie'll take ours.'

'Of course. I'll come for you about two, shall I?'

'I'll open the garage doors and you can drive straight in. Oh, and Chris, could you fix it to get back a bit later? I'd love it if we could have the whole evening together.'

'I'll try,' she said, and then, 'I'm sure I can fix it. I'll tell Graham I'm going out with my new girl friend.'

He said goodbye and that he would see her on Friday. Christine put the receiver back. She had almost given up expecting a call from him. But there must have been a grain of hope still, for she had never left the receiver off the way she used to.

The last time she had done that was on a Thursday three weeks before, the day she had gone round to Angie's and found David there alone. Christine had got into the habit of taking the phone off the hook during the middle part of the day to avoid getting calls for the Midland Bank. Her number and the Midland Bank's differed by only one digit. Most days she took the receiver off at nine-thirty and put it back at three-thirty. On Thursday afternoons she nearly always went round to see Angie and never bothered to phone first.

Christine knew Angie's husband quite well. If she stayed a bit later on Thursdays she saw him when he came home from work. Sometimes she and Graham and Angie and David went out together as a foursome. She knew that David, like Graham, was a salesman or sales executive, as Graham always described himself, and she guessed from her friend's life style that David was rather more successful at it. She had never found him particularly attractive, for, although he was quite tall, he had something of a girlish look and very fair wavy hair.

Graham was a heavily built, very dark man with a swarthy skin. He had to shave twice a day. Christine had started going out with him when she was fifteen and they had got married on her eighteenth birthday. She had never really known any other men at all intimately and now if she ever found herself alone with a man she felt awkward and apprehensive. The truth was that she was afraid a man might make an advance to her and the thought of that frightened her very much. For a long while she carried a penknife in her handbag in case she should need to defend herself. One evening, after they had been out with a colleague of Graham's and had had a few drinks, she told Graham about this fear of hers.

He said she was silly but he seemed rather pleased.

'When you went off to talk to those people and I was left with John I felt like that. I felt terribly nervous. I didn't know how to talk to him.'

Graham roared with laughter. 'You don't mean you thought old John was going to make a pass at you in the middle of a crowded restaurant?'

'I don't know,' Christine said. 'I never know what they'll do.'

'So long as you're not afraid of what I'll do,' said Graham, beginning to kiss her, 'that's all that matters.'

There was no point in telling him now, ten years too late, that she was afraid of what he did and always had been. Of course she had got used to it, she wasn't actually terrified, she was resigned and sometimes even quite cheerful about it. David was the only man she had ever been alone with when it felt all right.

That first time, that Thursday when Angie had gone to her sister's and hadn't been able to get through on the phone and tell Christine not to come, that time it had been fine. And afterwards she had felt happy and carefree, though what had happened with David took on the colouring of a dream next day. It wasn't really believable. Early on he had said:

'Will you tell Angie?'

'Not if you don't want me to.'

'I think it would upset her, Chris. It might even wreck our marriage. You see . . .' He had hesitated. 'You see, that was the first time I – I mean, anyone ever . . .' And he had looked into her eyes. 'Thank God it was you.'

The following Thursday she had gone round to see Angie as usual. In the meantime there had been no word from David. She stayed late in order to see him, beginning to feel a little sick with apprehension, her heart beating hard when he came in.

He looked quite different from how he had when she had found him sitting at the table reading, the radio on. He was wearing a grey flannel suit and a grey striped tie. When Angie went out of the room and for a minute she was alone with him, she felt a flicker of that old wariness that was the forerunner of her fear. He was getting her a drink. She looked up and met his eyes and it was all right again. He gave her a conspiratorial smile, laying a finger on his lips.

'I'll give you a ring,' he had whispered.

She had to wait two more weeks. During that time she went twice to Angie's and twice Angie came to her. She and Graham and Angie and David went out as a foursome and while Graham was fetching drinks and Angie was in the Ladies, David looked at her and smiled and lightly touched her foot with his foot under the table.

'I'll phone you. I haven't forgotten.'

It was a Wednesday when he finally did phone. Next day Christine told Graham she had made a new friend, a girl she had met at work. She would be going out somewhere with this new friend on Friday and she wouldn't be back till eleven. She was desperately afraid he would want the car – it was *his* car or his firm's – but it so happened he would be in the office that day and would go by train. Telling him these lies didn't make her feel guilty. It wasn't as if this were some sordid affair, it was quite different.

When Friday came she dressed with great care. Normally, to go round to Angie's, she would have worn jeans and a tee shirt with a sweater over it. That was what she had on the first time she found herself alone with David. She put on a skirt and blouse and her black velvet jacket. She took the heated rollers out of her hair and brushed it into curls down on her shoulders. There was never much money to spend on clothes. The mortgage on the house took up a third of what Graham earned and half what she earned at her part-time job. But she could run to a pair of sheer black tights to go with the highest heeled shoes she'd got, her black pumps.

The doors of Angie and David's garage were wide open and their car was gone. Christine turned into their driveway, drove into the garage and closed the doors behind her. A door at the back of the garage led into the yard and garden. The kitchen door was unlocked as it had been that Thursday three weeks before and always was on Thursday afternoons. She opened the door and walked in.

'Is that you, Chris?'

The voice sounded very male. She needed to be reassured by the sight of him. She went into the hall as he came down the stairs.

'You look lovely,' he said.

'So do you.'

He was wearing a suit. It was of navy silk with a pattern of pink and white flowers. The skirt was very short, the jacket clinched into his waist with a wide navy patent belt. The long golden hair fell to his shoulders, he was heavily made-up and this time he had painted his fingernails. He looked far more beautiful than he had that first time.

Then, three weeks before, the sound of her entry drowned in loud music from the radio, she had come upon this girl sitting at the table reading *Vogue*. For a moment she had thought it must be David's sister. She had forgotten Angie had said David was an only child. The girl had long fair hair and was wearing a red summer dress with white spots on it, white sandals and around her neck a string of white beads. When Christine saw that it was not a girl but David himself she didn't know what to do.

He stared at her in silence and without moving and then he switched off the radio. Christine said the silliest and least relevant thing.

'What are you doing home at this time?'

That made him smile. 'I'd finished so I took the rest of the day off. I should have locked the back door. Now you're here you may as well sit down.'

She sat down. She couldn't take her eyes off him. He didn't look like a man dressed up as a girl, he looked like a girl and a much prettier one than she or Angie. 'Does Angie know?'

He shook his head.

'But why do you do it?' she burst out and she looked about the room, Angie's small, rather untidy living room, at the radio, the *Vogue* magazine. 'What do you get out of it?' Something came back to her from an article she had read. 'Did your mother dress you as a girl when you were little?'

'I don't know,' he said. 'Maybe. I don't remember. I don't want to *be* a girl. I just want to dress up as one sometimes.'

The first shock of it was past and she began to feel easier with him. It wasn't as if there was anything grotesque about the way he looked.

6

The very last thing he reminded her of was one of those female impersonators. A curious thought came into her head, that it was *nicer*, somehow more civilized, to be a woman and that if only all men were more like women . . . That was silly, of course, it couldn't be.

'And it's enough for you just to dress up and be here on your own?'

He was silent for a moment. Then, 'Since you ask, what I'd really like would be to go out like this and . . .' He paused, looking at her, 'and be seen by lots of people, that's what I'd like. I've never had the nerve for that.'

The bold idea expressed itself without her having to give it a moment's thought. She wanted to do it. She was beginning to tremble with excitement.

'Let's go out then, you and I. Let's go out now. I'll put my car in your garage and you can get into it so the people next door don't see and then we'll go somewhere. Let's do that, David, shall we?'

She wondered afterwards why she had enjoyed it so much. What had it been, after all, as far as anyone else knew but two girls walking on Hampstead Heath? If Angie had suggested that the two of them do it she would have thought it a poor way of spending the afternoon. But with David . . . She hadn't even minded that of the two of them he was infinitely the better dressed, taller, better-looking, more graceful. She didn't mind now as he came down the stairs and stood in front of her.

'Where shall we go?'

'Not the Heath this time,' he said. 'Let's go shopping.'

He bought a blouse in one of the big stores. Christine went into the changing room with him when he tried it on. They walked about in Hyde Park. Later on they had dinner and Christine noted that they were the only two women in the restaurant dining together.

'I'm grateful to you,' David said. He put his hand over hers on the table.

'I enjoy it,' she said. 'It's so – crazy. I really love it. You'd better not do that, had you? There's a man over there giving us a funny look.'

'Women hold hands,' he said.

'Only *those* sort of women. David, we could do this every Friday you don't have to work.'

'Why not?' he said.

There was nothing to feel guilty about. She wasn't harming Angie and she wasn't being disloyal to Graham. All she was doing was going on innocent outings with another girl. Graham wasn't interested in her new friend, he didn't even ask her name. Christine came to long for Fridays, especially for the moment when she let herself into Angie's house and saw David coming down the stairs and for the moment when they stepped out of the car in some public place and the first eyes were turned on him. They went to Holland Park, they went to the zoo, to Kew Gardens. They went to the cinema and a man sitting next to David put his hand on his knee. David loved that, it was a triumph for him, but Christine whispered they must change their seats and they did.

When they parted at the end of an evening he kissed her gently on the lips. He smelled of Alliage or Je Reviens or Opium. During the afternoon they usually went into one of the big stores and sprayed themselves out of the tester bottles.


Angie's mother lived in the north of England. When she had to convalesce after an operation Angie went up there to look after her. She expected to be away two weeks and the second weekend of her absence Graham had to go to Brussels with the sales manager.

'We could go away somewhere for the weekend,' David said.

'Graham's sure to phone,' Christine said.

'One night then. Just for the Saturday night. You can tell him you're going out with your new girl friend and you're going to be late.'

'All right.'

It worried her that she had no nice clothes to wear. David had a small but exquisite wardrobe of suits and dresses, shoes and scarves and beautiful underclothes. He kept them in a cupboard in his office to which only he had a key and he secreted items home and back again in his briefcase. Christine hated the idea of going away for the night in her grey flannel skirt and white silk blouse and that velvet jacket while David wore his Zandra Rhodes dress. In a burst of recklessness she spent all of two weeks' wages on a linen suit.

They went in David's car. He had made the arrangements and Christine had expected they would be going to a motel twenty miles outside London. She hadn't thought it would matter much to David where they went. But he surprised her by his choice of an hotel that was a three-hundred-year-old house on the Suffolk coast.

'If we're going to do it,' he said, 'we may as well do it in style.'

She felt very comfortable with him, very happy. She tried to imagine what it would have felt like going to spend a night in an hotel with a man, a lover. If the person sitting next to her were dressed, not in a black and white printed silk dress and scarlet jacket but in a man's

8

suit with shirt and tie. If the face it gave her so much pleasure to look at were not powdered and rouged and mascara'd but rough and already showing beard growth. She couldn't imagine it. Or, rather, she could only think how in that case she would have jumped out of the car at the first red traffic lights.

They had single rooms next door to each other. The rooms were very small but Christine could see that a double might have been awkward for David who must at some point – though she didn't care to think of this – have to shave and strip down to being what he really was.

He came in and sat on her bed while she unpacked her nightdress and spare pair of shoes.

'This is fun, isn't it?'

She nodded, squinting into the mirror, working on her eyelids with a little brush. David always did his eyes beautifully. She turned round and smiled at him.

'Let's go down and have a drink.'

The dining room, the bar, the lounge were all low-ceilinged timbered rooms with carved wood on the walls David said was called linenfold panelling. There were old maps and pictures of men hunting in gilt frames and copper bowls full of roses. Long windows were thrown open on to a terrace. The sun was still high in the sky and it was very warm. While Christine sat on the terrace in the sunshine David went off to get their drinks. When he came back to their table he had a man with him, a thickset paunchy man of about forty who was carrying a tray with four glasses on it.

'This is Ted,' David said.

'Delighted to meet you,' Ted said. 'I've asked my friend to join us. I hope you don't mind.'

She had to say she didn't. David looked at her and from his look she could tell he had deliberately picked Ted up.

'But why did you?' she said to him afterwards. 'Why did you want to? You told me you didn't really like it when that man put his hand on you in the cinema.'

'That was so physical. This is just a laugh. You don't suppose I'd let them touch me, do you?'

Ted and Peter had the next table to theirs at dinner. Christine was silent and standoffish but David flirted with them. Ted kept leaning across and whispering to him and David giggled and smiled. You could see he was enjoying himself tremendously. Christine knew they would ask her and David to go out with them after dinner and she began to be afraid. Suppose David got carried away by the excitement of it, the 'fun', and went off somewhere with Ted, leaving her and Peter alone together? Peter had a red face and a black moustache and beard and a wart with black hairs growing out of it on his left cheek. She and David were eating steak and the waiter had brought them sharp pointed steak knives. She hadn't used hers. The steak was very tender. When no one was looking she slipped the steak knife into her bag.

Ted and Peter were still drinking coffee and brandies when David got up quite abruptly and said, 'Coming?' to Christine.

'I suppose you've arranged to meet them later?' Christine said as soon as they were out of the dining room.

David looked at her. His scarlet-painted lips parted into a wide smile. He laughed.

'I turned them down.'

'Did you *really*?'

'I could tell you hated the idea. Besides, we want to be alone, don't we? I know I want to be alone with you.'

She nearly shouted his name so that everyone could hear, the relief was so great. She controlled herself but she was trembling. 'Of course I want to be alone with you,' she said.

She put her arm in his. It wasn't uncommon, after all, for girls to walk along with linked arms. Men turned to look at David and one of them whistled. She knew it must be David the whistle was directed at because he looked so beautiful with his long golden hair and high-heeled red sandals. They walked along the sea front, along the little low promenade. It was too warm even at eight-thirty to wear a coat. There were a lot of people about but not crowds for the place was too select to attract crowds. They walked to the end of the pier. They had a drink in the Ship Inn and another in the Fishermen's Arms. A man tried to pick David up in the Fishermen's Arms but this time he was cold and distant.

'I'd like to put my arm round you,' he said as they were walking back, 'but I suppose that wouldn't do, though it is dark.'

'Better not,' said Christine. She said suddenly, 'This has been the best evening of my life.'

He looked at her. 'You really mean that?'

She nodded. 'Absolutely the best.'

They came into the hotel. 'I'm going to get them to send us up a couple of drinks. To my room. Is that OK?'

She sat on the bed. David went into the bathroom. To do his face, she thought, maybe to shave before he let the man with the drinks see him. There was a knock at the door and a waiter came in with a tray on which were two long glasses of something or other with fruit and leaves floating in it, two pink table napkins, two olives on sticks and two peppermint creams wrapped up in green paper.

Christine tasted one of the drinks. She ate an olive. She opened her handbag and took out a mirror and a lipstick and painted her lips. David came out of the bathroom. He had taken off the golden wig and washed his face. He hadn't shaved, there was a pale stubble showing on his chin and cheeks. His legs and feet were bare and he was wearing a very masculine robe made of navy blue towelling. She tried to hide her disappointment.

'You've changed,' she said brightly.

He shrugged. 'There are limits.'

He raised his glass and she raised her glass and he said: 'To us!'

The beginnings of a feeling of panic came over her. Suddenly he was so evidently a man. She edged a little way along the mattress.

'I wish we had the whole weekend.'

She nodded nervously. She was aware her body had started a faint trembling. He had noticed it too. Sometimes before he had noticed how emotion made her tremble.

'Chris,' he said.

She sat passive and afraid.

'I'm not really like a woman, Chris. I just play at that sometimes for fun. You know that, don't you?' The hand that touched her smelt of nail varnish remover. There were hairs on the wrist she had never noticed before. 'I'm falling in love with you,' he said. 'And you feel the same, don't you?'

She couldn't speak. He took her by the shoulders. He brought his mouth up to hers and put his arms round her and began kissing her. His skin felt abrasive and a smell as male as Graham's came off his body. She shook and shuddered. He pushed her down on the bed and his hands began undressing her, his mouth still on hers and his body heavy on top of her.

She felt behind her, put her hand into the open handbag and pulled out the knife. Because she could feel his heart beating steadily against her right breast she knew where to stab and she stabbed again and again. The bright red heart's blood spurted over her clothes and the bed and the two peppermint creams on the tray.

# A Dark Blue Perfume

It would be true to say that not a day had passed without his thinking of her. Except for the middle years. There had been other women then to distract him, though no one he cared for enough to make his second wife. But once he was into his fifties the memory of her returned with all its old vividness. He would see other men settling down into middle age, looking towards old age, with loving wives beside them, and he would say to himself, Catherine, Catherine . . .

He had never, since she left him, worked and lived in his native land. He was employed by a company which sent him all over the world. For years he had lived in South America, Africa, the West Indies, coming home only on leave and not always then. He meant to come home when he retired, though, and to this end, on one of those leaves, he had bought himself a house. It was in the city where he and she had been born, but he had chosen a district as far as possible from the one in which she had gone to live with her new husband and a long way from where they had once lived together, for the time when he had bought it was the time when he had begun daily to think of her again.

He retired when he was sixty-five and came home. He flew home and sent the possessions he had accumulated by sea. They included the gun he had acquired forty years before and with which he had intended to shoot himself when things became unendurable. But they had never been quite unendurable even then. Anger against her and hatred for her had sustained him and he had never got so far as even loading the small, unused automatic.

It was winter when he got home, bleak and wet and far colder than he remembered. When the snow came he stayed indoors, keeping warm, seeing no one. There was no one to see, anyway, they had gone away or died.

When his possessions arrived in three trunks – that was all he had amassed in forty years, three trunkfuls of bric-à-brac – he unpacked wonderingly. Only the gun had been put in by him, his servant had packed the rest. Things came to light he had long forgotten he owned, books, curios, and in an envelope he thought he had destroyed in those early days, all his photographs of her.

He sat looking at them one evening in early spring. The woman who came to clean for him had brought him a bowl of blue hyacinths and the air was heavy and languorous with the sweet scent of them. Catherine, Catherine he said as he looked at the picture of her in their garden, the picture of her at the seaside, her hair blowing. How different his life would have been if she had stayed with him! If he had been a complaisant husband and borne it all and taken it all and forgiven her. But how could he have borne that? How could he have kept her when she was pregnant with another man's child?

The hyacinths made him feel almost faint. He pushed the photographs back into the envelope but he seemed to see her face still through the thick, opaque, brown paper. She had been a bit older than he, she would be nearly seventy now. She would be old, ugly, fat perhaps, arthritic perhaps, those firm cheeks fallen into jowls, those eyes sunk in folds of skin, that white column of a neck become a bundle of strings, that glossy chestnut hair a bush of grey. No man would want her now.

He got up and looked in the mirror over the mantelpiece. He hadn't aged much, hadn't changed much. Everyone said so. Of course it was true that he hadn't lived much, and it was living that aged you. He wasn't bald, he was thinner than he had been at twenty-five, his eyes were still bright and wistful and full of hope. Those four years' seniority she had over him, they would show now if they stood side by side.

She might be dead. He had heard nothing, there had been no news since the granting of the divorce and her marriage to that man. Aldred Sydney. Aldred Sydney might be dead, she might be a widow. He thought of what that name, in any context, had meant to him, how emotive it had been.

'I want you to meet the new general manager, Sydney Robinson.'

'Yes, we're being sent to Australia, Sydney actually.'

'Cameron and Sydney, Surveyors and Valuers. Can I help you?'

For a long time he had trembled when he heard her surname pronounced. He had wondered how it could come so unconcernedly off another's tongue. Aldred Sydney would be no more than seventy, there was no reason to suppose him dead.

'Do you know Aldred and Catherine Sydney? They live at number 22. An elderly couple, yes, that's right. They're so devoted to each other, it's rather sweet . . .'

She wouldn't still live there, not after forty years. He went into the hall and fetched the telephone directory. For a moment or two he sat still, the book lying in his lap, breathing deeply because his heart was beating so fast. Then he opened the directory and turned to the S's. Aldred was such an uncommon name, there was probably only one Aldred Sydney in the country. He couldn't find him there, though there were many A. Sydneys living at addresses which had no meaning for him, no significance. He wondered afterwards why he had bothered to look lower, to let his eyes travel down through the B's and find her name, unmistakably, incontrovertibly, hers. Sydney, Catherine, 22 Aurora Road . . .

She was still there, she still lived there, and the phone was in her name. Aldred Sydney must be dead. He wished he hadn't looked in the phone book. Why had he? He could hardly sleep at all that night and when he awoke from a doze early in the morning, it was with her name on his lips: Catherine, Catherine.

He imagined phoning her.

'Catherine?'

'Yes, speaking. Who's that?'

'Don't you know? Guess. It's a long long time ago, Catherine.'

It was possible in fantasy, not in fact. He wouldn't know her voice now, if he met her in the street he wouldn't know her. At ten o'clock he got his car out and drove northwards, across the river and up through the northern suburbs. Forty years ago the place where she lived had been well outside the great metropolis, separated from it by fields and woods.

He drove through new streets, whole new districts. Without his new map he would have had no idea where he was. The countryside had been pushed away in those four decades. It hovered shyly on the outskirts of the little town that had become a suburb. And here was Aurora Road. He had never been to it before, never seen her house, though on any map he was aware of precisely where the street was, as if its name were printed in red to burn his eyes.

The sight of it at last, actually being there and seeing the house, made his head swim. He closed his eyes and sat there with his head bent over the wheel. Then he turned and looked at the neat, small house. Its paint was new and smart and the fifty-year-old front door had been replaced by a panelled oak one and the square bay by a bow window. But it was a poor, poky house for all that. He sneered a little at dead Aldred Sydney who had done no better than this for his wife.

Suppose he were to go up to the door and ring the bell? But he wouldn't do that, the shock would be too much for her. He, after all, had prepared himself. She had no preparation for confronting that husband, so little changed, of long ago. Once, how he would have savoured the cruelty of it, the revenge! The handsome man, still looking middle aged, a tropical tan on his cheeks, his body flat and straight, and the broken old woman, squat now, grey, withered. He sighed. All desire for a cruel vengeance had left him. He wanted instead to be merciful, to be kind. Wouldn't the kindest thing be to leave her in peace? Leave her to her little house and the simple pursuits of old age.

He started the car again and drove a little way. It surprised him to find that Aurora Road was right on the edge of that retreating countryside, that its tarmac and grey paving stones led into fields. When she was younger she had possibly walked there sometimes, under the trees, along that footpath. He got out of the car and walked along it himself. After a time he saw a train in the distance, appearing and disappearing between green meadows, clumps of trees, clusters of red roofs, and then he came upon a signpost pointing to the railway station. Perhaps she had walked here to meet Aldred Sydney after his day's work.

He sat down on a rustic seat that had been placed at the edge of the path. It was a very pretty place, not spoilt at all, you could hardly see a single house. The grass was a pure, clean green, the hedgerows shimmering white with the tiny flowers of wild plum blossom which had a drier, sharper scent than the hyacinths. For the time of year it was warm and the sun was shining. A bumble bee, relict of the past summer, drifted by. He put his head back on the wooden bar of the seat and fell asleep.

It was an unpleasant dream he had, of those young days of his when he had been little more than a boy but she very much a grown woman. She came to him, as she had come then, and told him baldly, without shame or diffidence, that the child she carried wasn't his. In the dream she laughed at him, though he couldn't remember that she had done that in life, surely not. He jerked awake and for a moment he didn't know where he was. People talking, walking along the path, had roused him. He left the seat and the path and drove home.

All that week he meant to phone her. He longed fiercely to meet her. It was as if he were in love again, so full was he of obsessional yearnings and unsuspected fears and strange whims. One afternoon he told himself he would phone her at exactly four, when it got to

15

four he would count ten and dial her number. But when four came and he had counted ten his arm refused to function and lift the receiver, it was as if his arm were paralyzed. What was the matter with him that he couldn't make a phone call to an old woman he had once known?

The next day he drove back to Aurora Road in the late afternoon. There were three elderly women walking along, walking abreast, but not going in the direction of her house, coming away from it. Was one of them she?

In the three faces, one pale and lined, one red and firm, the third waxen, sagging, he looked for the features of his Catherine. He looked for some vestige of her step in the way each walked. One of the women wore a burgundy-coloured coat, and pulled down over her grey hair, a burgundy felt hat, a shapeless pudding of a hat. Catherine had been fond of wine-red. She had worn it to be married in, married to him and perhaps also to Aldred Sydney. But this woman wasn't she, for as they passed him she turned and peered into the car and her eyes met his without a sign of recognition.

After a little while he drove down the street and, leaving the car, walked along the footpath. The petals of the plum blossom lay scattered on the grass and the may was coming into green bud. The sun shone faintly from a white, curdy sky. This time he didn't sit down on the seat but left the path to walk under the trees, for today the grass was dry and springy. In the distance he heard a train.

He was unprepared for so many people coming this way from the station. There must have been a dozen pass in the space of two minutes. He pretended to be walking purposefully, walking for his health perhaps, for what would they think he was doing, there under the trees without a companion, a sketching block or even a dog? The last went by – or he supposed it was the last. And then he heard soft footfalls, the sound light shoes make on a dry, sandy floor.

Afterwards he was to tell himself that he knew her tread. At the time, honestly, he wasn't quite sure, he didn't dare be, he couldn't trust his own memory. And when she appeared it was quite suddenly from where the path emerged from a tunnel of trees. She was walking towards Aurora Road and as she passed she was no more than ten yards from him.

He stood perfectly still, frozen and dumb. He felt that if he moved he might fall down dead. She didn't walk fast but lightly and springily as she had always done, and the years lay on her as lightly and gently as those footfalls of hers lay on the sand. Her hair was grey and her

16

slenderness a little thickened. There was a hint of a double chin and a faint coarsening of those delicate features – but no more than that. If he had remained young, so had she. It was as if youth had been preserved in each of them for this moment.

He wanted to see her eyes, the blue of those hyacinths, but she kept them fixed straight ahead of her, and she had quickly gone out of his sight, lost round a curve in the path. He crept to the seat and sat down. The wonder of it, the astonishment! He had imagined her old and found her young, but she had always surprised him. Her variety, her capacity to astound, were infinite.

She had come off the train with the others. Did she go out to work? At her age? Many did. Why not she? Sydney was dead and had left her, no doubt, ill-provided for. Sydney was dead . . . He thought of courting her again, loving her, forgiving her, wooing her.

'Will you marry me, Catherine?'

'Do you still want me – after everything?'

'Everything was only a rather long bad dream . . .'

She would come and live in his house and sit opposite him in the evenings, she would go on holiday with him, she would be his wife. They would have little jokes for their friends.

'How long have you two been married?'

'It was our second wedding anniversary last week and it will be our forty-fifth next month.'

He wouldn't phone, though. He would sit on this seat at the same time tomorrow and wait for her to pass by and recognize him.

Before he left home he studied the old photographs of himself that were with the old photographs of her. He had been fuller in the face then and he hadn't worn glasses. He put his hand to his high, sloping forehead and wondered why it looked so low in the pictures. Men's fashions didn't change much. The sports jacket he had on today was much like the sports jacket he had worn on his honeymoon.

As he was leaving the house he was assailed by the scent of the hyacinths, past their prime now and giving off a sickly, cloying odour. Dark blue flowers with a dark blue perfume . . . On an impulse he snapped off their heads and threw them into the wastepaper basket.

The day was bright and he slid back the sunshine roof on his car. When he got to Aurora Road, the field and the footpath, he took off his glasses and slipped them into his pocket. He couldn't see very well without them and he stumbled a little as he walked along.

There was no one on the seat. He sat down in the centre of it. He heard the train. Then he saw it, rattling along between the tufty trees and the little choppy red roofs and the squares of green. It was bringing him, he thought, his whole life's happiness. Suppose she didn't always catch that train, though? Or suppose yesterday's appearance had been an isolated happening, not a return from work but from some occasional visit?

He had hardly time to think about it before the commuters began to come, one and one and then two together. It looked as if there wouldn't be as many as there had been yesterday. He waited, holding his hands clasped together, and when she came he scarcely heard her, she walked so softly.

His sight was so poor without his glasses that she appeared to him as in a haze, almost like a spirit woman, a ghost. But it was she, her vigorous movements, her strong athletic walk, unchanged from her girlhood, and unchanged too, the atmosphere of her that he would have known if he had been not short-sighted but totally blind and deaf too.

The trembling which had come upon him again ceased as she approached and he fixed his eyes on her, half-rising from the seat. And now she looked at him also. She was very near and her face flashed suddenly into focus, a face on which he saw blankness, wariness, then slight alarm. But he was sure she recognized him. He tried to speak and his voice croaked out:

'Don't you know me?'

She began walking fast away, she broke into a run. Disbelieving, he stared after her. There was someone else coming along from the station now, a man who walked out of the tree tunnel and caught her up. They both looked back, whispering. It was then that he heard her voice, only a little older, a little harsher, than when they had first met. He got off the seat and walked about among the trees, holding his head in his hands. She had looked at him, she had seemed to know him – and then she hadn't wished to.

When he reached home again he understood what he had never quite faced up to when he first retired, that he had nothing to live for. For the past week he had lived for her and in the hope of having her again. He found his gun, the small unused automatic, and loaded it and put on the safety catch and looked at it. He would write to her and tell her what he had done – by the time she got his letter he would have done it – or, better still, he would see her once, force her to see him, and then he would do it.

The next afternoon he drove to her house in Aurora Road. It was nearly half-past five, she would be along at any moment. He sat in the car, feeling the hard bulge of the gun in his pocket. Presently the man who had caught her up the day before came along, but now he was alone, walking the length of Aurora Road and turning down a side street.

She was late. He left the car where it was and set off to find her, for he could no longer bear to sit there, the pain of it, the sick suspense. He kept seeing her face as she had looked at him, with distaste and then with fear.

Another train was jogging between the tree tufts and the little red chevrons, he heard it enter the station. Had the green, the many, varied greens, been as bright as this yesterday? The green of the grass and the new beech leaves and the may buds hurt his eyes. He passed the seat and went on, further than he had ever been before, coming into a darkish grove where the trees arched over the path. Her feet on the sand whispered like doves. He stood still, he waited for her.

She slowed down when she saw him and came on hesitantly, raising one hand to her face. He took a step towards her, saying, 'Please. Please don't go. I want to talk to you so much . . . '

Today he was wearing his glasses, there was no chance of his eyes being deceived. He couldn't be mistaken as to the meaning of her expression. It was compounded of hatred and terror. But this time she couldn't walk on without walking into his arms. She turned to hasten back the way she had come, and as she turned he shot her.

With the first shot he brought her down. He ran up to where she had fallen but he couldn't look at her, he could only see her as very small and very distant through a red haze of revenge. He shot her again and again, and at last the white ringless hand which had come feebly up to shield her face, fell in death.

The gun was empty. There was blood on him that had flown from her. He didn't care about that, he didn't care who saw or knew, so long as he could get home and re-load the gun for himself. It surprised him that he could walk, but he could and quite normally as far as he could tell. He was without feeling now, without pain or fear, and his breathing settled, though his heart still jumped. He gave the body on the ground one last vague look and walked away from it, out of the tree tunnel, on to the path. The sun made bright sheets of light on the grass and long, tapering shadows. He walked along Aurora Road towards the car outside her house.

Her front door opened as he was unlocking the car. An old woman came out. He recognized her as one of those he had seen on his second visit, the one who had been wearing the dark red coat and hat. She came to the gate and looked over it, looked up towards the left a little anxiously, then backed and smiled at him. Something in his stare must have made her speak, show politeness to this stranger.

'I was looking for my daughter,' she said. 'She's a bit late today, she's usually on that first train.'

He put his cold hands on the bar of the gate. Her smile faded.

'Catherine,' he said, 'Catherine . . . '

She lifted to him enquiring eyes, blue as the hyacinths he had thrown away.

# The Orchard Walls

I have never told anyone about this before.

The worst was long over, of course. Intense shame had faded and the knowledge of having made the greatest possible fool of myself. Forty years and more had done their work there. The feeling I had been left with, that I was precocious in a foul and dirty way, that I was unclean, was washed away. I had done my best never to think about it, to blot it all out, never to permit to ring on my inward ear Mrs Thorn's words:

'How dare you say such a thing! How dare you be so disgusting! At your age, a child, you must be sick in your mind.'

Things would bring it back, the scent of honeysuckle, a brace of bloodied pigeons hanging in a butcher's window, the first cherries of the season. I winced at these things, I grew hot with a shadow of that blush that had set me on fire with shame under the tree, Daniel's hard hand gripping my shoulder, Mrs Thorn trembling with indignant rage. The memory, never completely exorcised, still had the power to punish the adult for the child's mistake.

Until today.

Having one's childhood trauma cured by an analyst must be like this, only a newspaper has cured mine. The newspaper came through my door and told me I hadn't been disgusting or sick in my mind, I had been right. In the broad facts at least I had been right. All day I have been asking myself what I should do, what action, if any, I should take. At last I have been able to think about it all quite calmly, in tranquillity, to think of Ella and Dennis Clifton without growing hot and ashamed, of Mrs Thorn with pity and of that lovely lost place with something like nostalgia.

It was a long time ago. I was fourteen. Is that to be a child? They thought so, I thought so myself at the time. But the truth was I was a child and not a child, at one and the same time a paddler in streams, a climber of trees, an expert at cartwheels – and with an imagination full of romantic love. I was in a stage of transition, a pupa, a chrysalis, I was fourteen.

Bombs were falling on London. I had already once been evacuated with my school and come back again to the suburb we lived in that sometimes seemed safe and sometimes not. My parents were afraid for me and that was why they sent me to Inchfield, to the Thorns. I could see the fear in my mother's eyes and it made me uncomfortable.

'Just till the end of August,' she said, pleading with me. 'It's beautiful there. You could think of it as an extra long summer holiday.'

I remembered Hereford and my previous 'billet', the strange people, the alien food.

'This will be different. Ella is your own aunt.'

She was my mother's sister, her junior by twelve years. There were a brother and sister in between, both living in the north. Ella's husband was a farmer in Suffolk, or had been. He was in the army and his elder brother ran the farm. Later, when Ella was dead and Philip Thorn married again and all I kept of them was that shameful thing I did my best to forget, I discovered that Ella had married Philip when she was seventeen because she was pregnant and in the thirties any alternative to marriage in those cirumstances was unthinkable. She had married him and six months later given birth to a dead child. When I went to Inchfield she was still only twenty-five, still childless, living with a brother-in-law and a mother-in-law in the depths of the country, her husband away fighting in North Africa.

I didn't want to go. At fourteen one isn't afraid, one knows one is immortal. After an air raid we used to go about the streets collecting pieces of shrapnel, fragments of shell. The worst thing to me was having to sleep under a Morrison shelter instead of in my bedroom. Having a room of my own again, a place to be private in, was an inducement. I yielded. To this day I don't know if I was invited or if my mother had simply written to say I was coming, that I must come, that they must give me refuge.

It was the second week of June when when I went. Daniel Thorn met me at the station at Ipswich. I was wildly romantic, far too romantic, my head full of fantasies and dreams. Knowing I should be met, I expected a pony carriage or even a man on a black stallion leading a chestnut mare for me, though I had never in my life been on a horse. He came in an old Ford van.

We drove to Inchfield through deep green silent lanes – silent, that is, but for the occasional sound of a shot. I thought it must be something to do with the war, without specifying to myself what.

'The war?' said Daniel as if this were something happening ten thousand miles away. He laughed the age-old laugh of the countryman scoring off the townie. 'You'll find no war here. That's some chap out after rabbits.'

Rabbit was what we were to live on, stewed, roasted, in pies, relieved by wood pigeon. It was a change from London sausages but I have never eaten rabbit since, not once. The characteristic smell of it cooking, experienced once in a friend's kitchen, brought me violent nausea. What a devil's menu that would have been for me, stewed rabbit and cherry pie!

The first sight of the farm enchanted me. The place where I lived in Hereford had been a late-Victorian brick cottage, red and raw and ugly as poverty. I had scarcely seen a house like Cherry Tree Farm except on a calendar. It was long and low and thatched and its two great barns were thatched too. The low green hills and the dark clustering woods hung behind it. And scattered all over the wide slopes of grass were the cherry trees, one so close up to the house as to rub its branches against a window pane.

They came out of the front door to meet us, Ella and Mrs Thorn, and Ella gave me a white, rather cold, cheek to kiss. She didn't smile. She looked bored. It was better therefore than I had expected and worse. Ella was worse and Mrs Thorn was better. The place was ten times better, tea was like something I hadn't had since before the war, my bedroom was not only nicer than the Morrison shelter, it was nicer than my bedroom at home. Mrs Thorn took me up there when we had eaten the scones and currant bread and walnut cake.

It was low-ceilinged with the stone-coloured studs showing through the plaster. A patchwork quilt was on the bed and the walls were hung with a paper patterned all over with bunches of cherries. I looked out of the window.

'You can't see the cherry trees from here,' I said. 'Is that why they put cherries on the walls?'

The idea seemed to puzzle her. She was a simple conservative woman. 'I don't know about that. That would be rather whimsical.'

I was at the back of the house. My window overlooked a trim dull garden of rosebeds cut out in segments of a circle. Mrs Thorn's own garden, I was later to learn, and tended by herself.

'Who sleeps in the room with the cherry tree?' I said.

'Your auntie.' Mrs Thorn was always to refer to Ella in this way. She was a stickler for respect. 'That has always been my son Philip's room.'

Always . . . I envied the absent soldier. A tree with branches against one's bedroom window represented to me something down which one could climb and make one's escape, perhaps even without the aid of knotted sheets. I said as much, toning it down for my companion who I guessed would see it in a different light.

'I'm sure he did no such thing,' said Mrs Thorn. 'He wasn't that kind of boy.'

Those words stamped Philip for me as dull. I wondered why Ella had married him. What had she seen in this unromantic chap, five years her senior, who hadn't been the kind of boy to climb down trees out of his bedroom window? Or climb up them, come to that . . .

She was beautiful. For the first Christmas of the war I had been given *Picturegoer Annual* in which was a full-page photograph of Hedy Lamarr. Ella looked just like her. She had the same perfect features, dark hair, other-worldly eyes fixed on far horizons. I can see her now – I can *permit* myself to see her – as she was then, thin, long-legged, in the floral cotton dress with collar and cuffs and narrow belt that would be fashionable again today. Her hair was pinned up in a roll off her forehead, the rest left hanging to her shoulders in loose curls, mouth painted like raspberry jam, eyes as nature made them, large, dark, alight with some emotion I was years from analysing. I think now it was compounded of rebellion and longing and desire.

Sometimes in the early evenings she would disappear upstairs and then Mrs Thorn would say in a respectful voice that she had gone to write to Philip. We used to listen to the wireless. Of course no one knew exactly where Philip was but we all had a good idea he was somehow involved in the attempts to relieve Tobruk. At news times Mrs Thorn became very tense. Once, to my embarrassment, she made a choking sound and left the room, covering her eyes with her hand. Ella switched off the set.

'You ought to be in bed,' she said to me. 'When I was your age I was always in bed by eight.'

I envied and admired her, even though she was never particularly nice to me and seldom spoke except to say I 'ought' to be doing something or other. Did she look at this niece, not much more than ten years younger than herself, and see what she herself had thrown away, a future of hope, a chance of living?

I spent very little time with her. It was Mrs Thorn who took me shopping with her to Ipswich, who talked to me while she did the baking, who knitted and taught me to knit. There was no wool to be had so we unpicked old jumpers and washed the wool and carded it and started again. I was with her most of the time. It was either that or being on my own. No doubt there were children of my own age in the village I might have got to know but the village was two miles away. I was allowed to go out for walks but not to ride the only bicycle they had.

'It's too large for you, it's a twenty-eight inch,' Mrs Thorn said. 'Besides, it's got a crossbar.'

I said I could easily swing my leg behind the saddle like a man.

'Not while you're staying with me.'

I didn't understand. 'I wouldn't hurt myself.' I said what I said to my mother. 'I wouldn't come to any harm.'

'It isn't ladylike,' said Mrs Thorn, and that was that.

Those things mattered a lot to her. She stopped me turning cartwheels on the lawn when Daniel was about, even though I wore shorts. Then she made me wear a skirt. But she was kind, she paid me a lot of attention. If I had had to depend on Ella or the occasional word from Daniel I might have looked forward more eagerly to my parents' fortnightly visits than I did.

After I had been there two or three weeks the cherries began to turn colour. Daniel, coming upon me looking at them, said they were an old variety called Inchfield White Heart.

'There used to be a cherry festival here,' he said. 'The first Sunday after July the twelfth it was. There'd be dancing and a supper, you'd have enjoyed yourself. Still, we never had one last year and we're not this and somehow I don't reckon there'll ever be a cherry festival again what with this old war.'

He was a yellow-haired, red-complexioned Suffolk man, big and thickset. His wide mouth, sickle-shaped, had its corners permanently turned upwards. It wasn't a smile though and he was seldom cheerful. I never heard him laugh. He used to watch people in rather a disconcerting way, Ella especially. And when guests came to the house, Dennis Clifton or Mrs Leithman or some of the farming people they knew, he would sit and watch them, seldom contributing a word.

One evening, when I was coming back from a walk, I saw Ella and Dennis Clifton kissing in the wood.


Dennis Clifton wasn't a farmer. He had been in the R.A.F., had been a fighter pilot in the Battle of Britain but had received some sort of head injury, been in hospital and was now on leave at home recuperating. He must have been very young, no more than twenty-two or three. While he was ill his mother, with whom he had lived and who had been a friend of Mrs Thorn's, had died and left him her pretty little Georgian house in Inchfield. He was often at the farm, ostensibly to see his mother's old friend.

After these visits Daniel used to say, 'He'll soon be back in the thick of it,' or 'It won't be long before he's up there in his Spitfire. He can't wait.'

This made me watch him too, looking for signs of impatience to return to the R.A.F. His hands shook sometimes, they trembled like an old man's. He too was fair-haired and blue-eyed, yet there was all the difference in the world between his appearance and Daniel's. Film stars set my standard of beauty and I thought he looked like Leslie Howard playing Ashley Wilkes. He was tall and thin and sensitive and his eyes were sad. Daniel watched him and Ella sat silent and I read my book while he talked very kindly and encouragingly to Mrs Thorn about her son Philip, about how confident he was Philip would be all right, would survive, and while he talked his eyes grew sadder and more veiled.

No, I have imagined that, not remembered it. It is in the light of what I came to know that I have imagined it. He was simply considerate and kind like the well-brought-up young man he was.

I had been in the river. There was a place about a mile upstream they called the weir where for a few yards the banks were built up with concrete below a shallow fall. A pool about four feet deep had formed there and on hot days I went bathing in it. Mrs Thorn would have stopped me if she had known but she didn't know. She didn't even know I had a bathing costume with me.

The shortest way back was through the wood. I heard a shot and then another from up in the meadows. Daniel was out after pigeons. The wood was dim and cool, full of soft twitterings, feathers rustling against dry leaves. The bluebells were long past but dog's mercury was in flower, a white powdering, and the air was scented with honey-suckle. Another shot came, further off but enough to shatter peace, and there was a rush of wings as pigeons took flight. Through the black trunks of trees and the lacework of their branches I could see the yellow sky and the sun burning in it, still an hour off setting.

Ella was leaning against the trunk of a chestnut, looking up into Dennis Clifton's face. He had his hands pressed against the trunk, on either side of her head. If she had ever been nice to me, if he had ever said more than hallo, I think I might have called out to them. I didn't call and in a moment I realized the last thing they would want was to be seen.

I stayed where I was. I watched them. Oh, I was in no way a voyeur. There was nothing lubricious in it, nothing of curiosity, still less a wish to catch them out. I was overwhelmed rather by the romance of it, ravished by wonder. I watched him kiss her. He took his hands down and put his arms round her and kissed her so that their faces were no longer visible, only his fair head and her dark hair and their locked straining shoulders. I caught my breath and shivered in the warm half-light, in the honeysuckle air.

They left the place before I did, walking slowly away in the direction of the road, arms about each other's waists. In the room at Cherry Tree Farm they still called the parlour Mrs Thorn and Daniel were sitting, listening to the wireless, drinking tea. No more than five minutes afterwards Ella came in. I had seen what I had seen but if I hadn't, wouldn't I still have thought her looks extraordinary, her shining eyes and the flush on her white cheeks, the willow leaf in her hair and the bramble clinging to her skirt?

Daniel looked at her. There was blood in his fingernails, though he had scrubbed his hands. It brought me a flicker of nausea. Ella put her fingers through her hair, plucked out the leaf and went upstairs.

'She is going up to write to Philip,' said Mrs Thorn.

Why wasn't I shocked? Why wasn't I horrified? I was only fourteen and I came from a conventional background. Adultery was something committed by people in the Bible. I suppose I could say I had seen no more than a kiss and adultery didn't enter into it. Yet I knew it did. With no experience, with only the scantiest knowledge, I sensed that this love had its full consummation. I knew Ella was married to a soldier who was away fighting for his country. I even knew that my parents would think behaviour such as hers despicable if not downright wicked. But I cared for none of that. To me it was romance, it was Lancelot and Guinevere, it was a splendid and beautiful adventure that was happening to two handsome young people – as one day it might happen to me.


I was no go-between. For them I scarcely existed. I received no words or smiles, still less messages to be carried. They had the phone, anyway, they had cars. But though I took no part in their love affair and wasn't even with accuracy able to calculate the times when it was conducted, it filled my thoughts. Outwardly I followed the routine of days I had arranged for myself and Mrs Thorn had arranged for me, but my mind was occupied with Dennis and Ella, assessing what meeting places they would use, imagining their conversations – their vows of undying love – and re-creating with cinematic variations that kiss.

My greatest enjoyment, my finest hours of empathy, were when he called. I watched the two of them as intently then as Daniel did. Sometimes I fancied I caught between them a glance of longing and once I actually witnessed something more, an encounter between them in the passage when Ella came from the kitchen with the tea tray and Dennis had gone to fetch something from his car for Mrs Thorn. Unseen by them, I stood in the shadow between the grandfather clock and the foot of the stairs. I heard him whisper:

'Tonight? Same place?'

She nodded, her eyes wide. I saw him put his hand on her shoulder in a slow caress as he went past her.

I slept badly those nights. It had become very hot. Mrs Thorn made sure I was in bed by nine and there was no way of escaping from the house after that without being seen by her. I envied Ella with a tree outside her window down which it would be easy to climb and escape. I imagined going down to the river in the moonlight, walking in the wood, perhaps seeing my lovers in some trysting place. My lovers, whose breathy words and laden glances exalted me and rarefied the overheated air . . .

The cherries were turning pale yellow with a blush coming to their cheeks. It was the first week of July, the week the war came to Inchfield and a German bomber, lost and off course, unloaded a stick of bombs in one of the Thorns' fields.

No one was hurt, though a cow got killed. We went to look at the mess in the meadow, the crater and the uprooted tree. Daniel shook his fist at the sky. The explosions had made a tremendous noise and we were all sensitive after that to any sudden sound. Even the crack of Daniel's shotgun made his mother jump.

The heat had turned sultry and clouds obscured out blue skies, though no rain fell. Mrs Leithman, coming to tea as she usually did once in the week, told us she fancied each roll of thunder was another bomb. We hardly saw Ella, she was always up in her room or out somewhere – out with Dennis, of course. I speculated about them, wove fantasies around them, imagined Philip Thorn killed in battle and thereby setting them free. So innocent was I, living in more innocent or at least more puritanical times, that the possibility of this childless couple being divorced never struck me. Nor did I envisage

Dennis and Ella married to each other but only continuing for ever their perilous enchanting idyll. I even found Juliet's lines for them – Juliet who was my own age – and whispered to myself that the orchard walls are high and hard to climb and the place death, considering who thou art . . . Once, late at night when I couldn't sleep and sat in my window, I saw the shadowy figure of Dennis Clifton emerge from the deep darkness at the side of the house and leave by the gate out of the rose garden.

But the destruction of it all and my humiliation were drawing nearer. I had settled down there, I had begun to be happy. The truth is, I suppose, that I identified with Ella and in my complex fantasies it was I, compounded with Juliet, that Dennis met and embraced and touched and loved. My involvement was much deeper than that of an observer.

When it came the shot sounded very near. It woke me up as such a sound might not have done before the bombs. I wondered what prey Daniel could go in search of at this hour, for the darkness was deep, velvety and still. The crack which had split the night and jarred the silence wasn't repeated. I went back to sleep and slept till past dawn.

I got up early as I did most mornings, came downstairs in the quiet of the house, the hush of a fine summer morning, and went outdoors. Mrs Thorn was in the kitchen, frying fat bacon and duck eggs for the men. I didn't know if it was all right for me to do this or if all the cherries were reserved for some mysterious purpose, but as I went towards the gate I reached up and picked a ripe one from a dipping branch. It was the crispest sweetest cherry I have ever tasted, though I must admit I have eaten few since then. I pushed the stone into the earth just inside the gates. Perhaps it germinated and grew. Perhaps quite an old tree that has borne many summer loads of fruit now stands at the entrance to Cherry Tree Farm.

As it happened, of all their big harvest, that was the only cherry I was ever to eat there. Coming back half an hour later, I pushed open the gate and stood for a moment looking at the farmhouse over whose sunny walls and roof the shadows of the trees lay in a slanted leafy pattern. I looked at the big tree, laden with red-gold fruit, that rubbed its branches against Ella's window. In its boughs, halfway up, in a fork a yard or two from the glass, hung the body of a man.

In the hot sunshine I felt icy cold. I remember the feeling to this day, the sensation of being frozen by a cold that came from within while outside me the sun shone and a thrush sang and the swallows dipped in and out under the eaves. My eyes seemed fixed, staring in the hypnosis of shock and fear at the fair-haired dangling man, his head thrown back in the agony of death there outside Ella's bedroom window.

At least I wasn't hysterical. I resolved I must be calm and adult. My teeth were chattering. I walked stiffly into the kitchen and there they all were, round the table, Daniel and the two men and Ella and, at the head of it, Mrs Thorn pouring tea.

I meant to go quietly up to her and whisper it. I couldn't. To get myself there without running, stumbling, shouting, had used up all the control I had. The words rushed out in a loud ragged bray and I remember holding up my hands, my fists clenched.

'Mr Clifton's been shot. He's been shot, he's dead. His body's in the cherry tree outside Ella's window!'

There was silence. But first a clatter as of knives and forks dropped, of cups rattled into saucers, of chairs scraped. Then this utter stricken silence. I have never – not in all the years since then – seen anyone go as white as Ella went. She was as white as paper and her eyes were black holes. A brick colour suffused Daniel's face. He swore. He used words that made me shrink and draw back and shiver and stare from one to the other of the horrible, horrified faces.

Mrs Thorn was the first to speak, her voice cold with anger.

'How dare you say such a thing! How dare you be so disgusting! At your age – you must be sick in your mind.'

Daniel had jumped up. He took me roughly by the arm. But his grasp wasn't firm, the hand was shaking the way Dennis's shook. He manhandled me out there, his mother scuttling behind us. We were still five or six yards from the tree when I saw. The hot blood came into my face and throbbed under my skin. I looked at the cloth face, the yellow wool hair – our own unpicked carded wool – the stuffed sacking body, the cracked boots . . .

Icy with indignation, Mrs Thorn said, 'Haven't you ever seen a scarecrow before?'

I cried out desperately as if, even in the face of this evidence, I could still prove them wrong, 'But scarecrows are in fields!'

'Not in this part of the world.' Daniel's voice was thin and hoarse. He couldn't have looked more gaunt, more shocked, if it had really been Dennis Clifton in that tree. 'In this part of the world we put them in cherry trees. I put it there last night. I put *them* there.' And he pointed at what I had passed but never seen, the man in the tree by the wall, the man in the tree in the middle of the green lawn.

I went back to the house and up to my room and lay on the bed, prone and silent with shame. The next day was Saturday and my parents were coming. They would tell them and I should be taken home in disgrace. In the middle of the day Mrs Thorn came to the door and said to come down to lunch. She was a changed woman, hard and dour. I had never heard the expression 'to draw aside one's skirts' but later on when I did I recognized that this was what she had done to me. Her attitude to me was as if I were some sort of psychopath.

We had lunch alone, only I didn't really have any, I couldn't eat. Just as we were finishing, I pushing aside my laden plate, Daniel came in and sat down and said they had all talked about it and they thought it would be best if I went home with my parents on the following day.

'Of course I shall tell them exactly what you said and what you inferred,' said Mrs Thorn. 'I shall tell them how you insulted your auntie.'

Daniel, who wasn't trembling any more or any redder in the face than usual, considered this for a moment in silence. Then he said unexpectedly – or unexpectedly to me, 'No, we won't, Mother, we won't do that. No point in that. The fewer know the better. You've got to think of Ella's reputation.'

'I won't have her here,' his mother said.

'No, I agree with that. She can tell them she's homesick or I'll say it's too much for you, having her here.'

Ella hid herself away all that day.

'She has her letter to write to Philip,' said Mrs Thorn.

In the morning she was at the table with the others. Daniel made an announcement. He had been down to the village and heard that Dennis Clifton was back in the Air Force, he had rejoined his squadron.

'He'll soon be back in the thick of it,' he said.

Ella sat with bowed head, working with restless fingers a slice of bread into a heap of crumbs. Her face was colourless, lacking her usual make-up. I don't remember ever hearing another word from her.

I packed my things. My parents made no demur about taking me back with them. Starved of love, sickened by the love of others, I clung to my father. The scarecrows grinned at us as we got into the van behind Daniel. I can see them now – I can permit myself to see them now – spreadeagled in the trees, protecting the reddening fruit, so lifelike that even the swallows swooped in wider arcs around them.

\* \* \*

In the following spring Ella died giving birth to another dead child. My mother cried, for Ella had been her little sister. But she was shy about giving open expression to her grief. She and my father were anxious to keep from me, or for that matter anyone else, that it was a good fifteen months since Philip Thorn had been home on leave. What became of Daniel and his mother I never knew, I didn't want to know. I couldn't avoid hearing that Philip had married again and his new wife was a niece of Mrs Leithman's.

Only a meticulous reader of newspapers would have spotted the paragraph. I am in the habit of reading every line, with the exception of the sports news, and I spotted this item tucked away between an account of sharp practice in local government and the suicide of a financier. I read it. The years fell away and the facts exonerated me. I knew I must do something, I wondered what, I have been thinking of it all day, but now I know I must tell this story to the coroner. My story, my mistake, Daniel's rage.

An agricultural worker had come upon an unexploded bomb on farm land near Inchfield in Suffolk. It was thought to be one of a stick of bombs dropped there in 1941. Excavations in the area had brought to light a skeleton thought to be that of a young man who had met his death at about the same time. A curious fact was that shotgun pellets had been found in the cavity of the skull.

The orchard walls are high and hard to climb. And the place death considering who thou art, if any of my kinsmen find thee here . . .

# Hare's House

A murderer had lived in the house, the estate agent told Norman. The murder had in fact been committed there, he said. Norman thought it very open and honest of him.

'The neighbours would have mentioned it if I hadn't,' said the estate agent.

Now Norman understood why the house was going cheap. It was what they called a town house, though Norman didn't know why they did as he had seen plenty like it in the country. There were three floors and an open-tread staircase going up the centre. About fifteen years old, the estate agent said, and for twelve of those no one had lived in it.

'I'm afraid I can't give you any details of the case.'

'I wouldn't want to know,' said Norman. 'I'd rather not know.' He put his head round the door of the downstairs bathroom. He had never thought it possible he might own a house with more than one bathroom. Did he seriously consider owning this one then? The price was so absurdly low! 'What was his name?'

'The murderer? Oh, Hare. Raymond Hare.'

Rather to his relief, Norman couldn't remember any Hare murder case. 'Where is he now?'

'He died in prison. The house belongs to a nephew.'

'I like the house,' Norman said cautiously. 'I'll have to see what my wife says.'

The area his job obliged him to move into was a more prestigious one than where they now lived. A terraced cottage like the ones in Inverness Street was the best he had thought they could run to. He would never find another bargain like this one. If he hadn't been sure Rita would find out about the murder he would have avoided telling her.

'Why is it so cheap?' she said.

He told her.

She was a small thickset woman with brown hair and brown eyes

33

and a rather large pointed face. She had a way of extending her neck and thrusting her face forward. It had once occurred to Norman that she looked like a mole, though moles of course could be attractive creatures. She thrust her head forward now.

'Is there something horrible you're not telling me?'

'I've told you everything I know. I don't know any details.' Norman was a patient and easy-going man, if inclined to be sullen. He was rather good-looking with a boyish open face and brown curly hair. 'We could both go and see it tomorrow.'

Rita would have preferred a terraced cottage in Inverness Street with a big garden and not so many stairs. But Norman had set his heart on the town house and was capable of sulking for months if he didn't get his own way. Besides, there was nothing to *show* Hare had lived there. Rather foolishly perhaps, Rita now thought, she had been expecting bloodstains or even a locked room.

'I've no recollection of this Hare at all, have you?'

'Let's keep it that way,' said Norman. 'You said yourself it's better not to know. I'll make Mr Hare the nephew an offer, shall I?'

The offer was accepted and Norman and Rita moved in at the end of September. The neighbours on one side had lived there eight years and the neighbours on the other six. They had never known Raymond Hare. A family called Lawrence who had lived in their large old house surrounded by garden for more than twenty years must have known him, at least by sight, but Norman and Rita had never spoken to them save to pass the time of day.

They had builders in to paint the house and they had new carpets. There were only two drawbacks and one of those was the stairs. You found yourself always running up and down to fetch things you had forgotten. The other drawback was the bathroom window, or more specifically, the catch on the bathroom window.

Sometimes, especially when Norman was at work and she was alone, Rita would wonder exactly where the murder had taken place. She would stand still, holding her duster, and look about her and think maybe it was in that room or that one or in their bedroom. And then she would go into the bedroom, thrusting her head forward and peering. Her mother used to say she had a 'funny feeling' in the corners of some houses, she said she was psychic. Rita would have liked to have inherited this gift but she had to admit she experienced no funny feelings in any part of this house.

She and Norman never spoke about Raymond Hare. They tended to avoid the very subject of murder. Rita had once enjoyed detective stories but somehow she didn't read them any more. It seemed better not to. Her next-door neighbour Dorothy, the one who had lived there eight years, tried one day to talk to her about the Hare case but Rita said she'd rather not discuss it.

'I quite understand,' Dorothy said. 'I think you're very wise.'

It was a warm house. The central heating was efficient and the windows were double gazed except for the one in the upstairs bathroom. This bathroom had a very high ceiling and the window was about ten feet up. It was in the middle of the house and therefore had no outside wall so the architect had made the roof of the bathroom just above the main roof, thus affording room for a window. It was a nuisance not being able to open it except by means of the pole with the hook on the end of it that stood against the bathroom wall, but the autumn was a dull wet one and the winter cold so for a long time there was no need to open the bathroom window at all.

Norman thought he would have a go at re-tiling the downstairs bathroom himself and went to the library to look for a do-it-yourself decorating manual. The library, a small branch, wasn't far away, being between his house and the tube station. Unable at first to find Skills and Crafts, his eye wandered down through Horticulture, Botany, Biology, General Science, Social Sciences, Crime . . .

Generally speaking, Norman had nothing to do with crime these days. He and Rita had even stopped watching thriller serials on television. His impulse was to turn his eyes sharply away from these accounts of trials and reconstructions of murders and turn them away he did but not before he had caught the name Hare on the spine of one of the books.

Norman turned his back. By a happy chance he was facing the section labelled 'Interior Decoration'. He found the book he wanted. Then he stood holding it and thinking. Should he look again? It might be that the author's name was Harc and had nothing at all to do with his Hare. Norman didn't really believe this. His stomach began to feel queasy and he was conscious of being rather excited too. He turned round and quickly took the book off the shelf. Its title was *Murder in the Sixties*, the author was someone called H. L. Robinson and the cases examined were listed on the jacket: Renzini and Boyce, The Oast-house Mystery, Hare, The Pop Group Murders.

Norman opened it at random. He found he had opened it in the middle of the Hare case. A page or two further on were two photographs, the top one of a man with a blank characterless face and half-closed eyes, the other of a smiling fair-haired woman. The caption said that above was Raymond Henry Montagu Hare and below Diana Margaret Hare, née Kentwell. Norman closed the book and replaced it on the shelf. His heart was beating curiously hard. When his do-it-yourself book had been stamped he had to stop himself actually running out of the library. What a way to behave! he thought. I must get a grip on myself. Either I am going to put Hare entirely out of my mind and never think of him again or else I am going to act like a rational man, read up the case, make myself conversant with the facts and learn to live with them.

He did neither. He didn't visit the library again. When his book had taught him all it could about tiling he asked Rita to return it for him. He tried to put Hare out of his mind but this was too difficult. Where had he committed the murder was one of the questions he often asked himself and then he began to wonder whom he had killed and by what means. The answers were in a book on a shelf not a quarter of a mile away. Norman had to pass the library on his way to the station each morning and on his way back each night. He took to walking on the other side of the street. Sometimes there came into his mind that remark of Rita's that there might be something horrible he wasn't telling her.

Spring came early and there were some warm days in March. Rita tried to open the bathroom window, using the pole with the hook on the end, but the catch wouldn't budge. When Norman came home she got him to borrow a ladder from Dorothy's husband Roy and climb up and see what was wrong with the catch.

Norman thought Roy gave him rather a funny look when he said what he wanted the ladder for. He hesitated before saying Norman could have it.

'It's quite OK if you'd rather not,' Norman said. 'I expect I can manage with the steps if I can find a foothold somewhere.'

'No, no, you're welcome to the ladder,' said Roy and he showed Norman the bathroom in his own house which was identical with the next-door's except that the window had been changed for a blank sheet of glass with an extractor fan.

'Very nice,' said Norman, 'but just the same I'd rather have a window I can open.'

That brought another funny look from Roy. Norman propped the ladder against the wall and climbed up to the window and saw why it wouldn't open. The two parts of the catch, a vertical bolt and a slot for it to be driven up into, had been wired together. Norman supposed that the builders doing the painting had wired up the window catch, though he couldn't imagine why. He undid the wire, slid down the bolt and let the window fall open to its maximum capacity of about seventy-five degrees.

On 1 April the temperature dropped to just on freezing and it snowed. Rita closed the bathroom window. She took hold of the pole, reached up and inserted the hook in the ring on the bottom of the bolt, lifted the window, closed it, pushed up the bolt into the slot and gave it a twist. When she came out of the bathroom on to the landing she stood looking about her and wondering where Hare had committed the murder. For a moment she fancied she had a funny feeling about that but it passed. Rita went down to the kitchen and made herself a cup of tea. She looked out into the tiny square of garden on to which fluffy snow was falling and melting when it touched the grass. There would have been room in the garden in Inverness Street to plant bulbs, daffodils and narcissi. Rita sighed. She poured out the tea and was stirring sugar into her cup when there came a loud crash from upstairs. Rita nearly jumped out of her skin.

She ran up the two flights of stairs, wondering what on earth had got broken. There was nothing. Nothing was out of place or changed. She had heard of haunted houses where loud crashes were due to poltergeist activity. Her mother had always been able to sense the presence of a poltergeist. She felt afraid and sweat broke out on her rather large pointed face. Then she noticed the bathroom door was closed. Had it been that door closing she had heard? Surely not. Rita opened the bathroom door and saw that the window had fallen open. So that was all it was. She got the pole and inserted the hook in the ring on the bolt, slid the bolt upwards into the slot and gave it a twist.

It had been rather windy but the wind had dropped. Next day the weather began to warm up again. Norman opened the bathroom window and it remained open until rain started. Rita closed it.

'That window's not the problem I thought it might be once you get the hang of using the pole,' said Norman.

He was trying to be cheerful and to act as if nothing had happened. The man called Lawrence who lived opposite had got into conversation with him on his way home. They had found themselves sitting next to each other in the tube train.

'It's good to see someone living in your place at last. An empty house always gets a run-down look.'

Norman just smiled. He had started to feel uneasy.

'My wife knew Mrs Hare quite well, you know.'

'Really?' said Norman.

'A nice woman. There was no reason for what he did as far as anyone could tell. But I imagine you've read it all up and come to terms with it. Well, you'd have to, wouldn't you?'

'Oh, yes,' said Norman.

Because he had his neighbour with him he couldn't cross the street to avoid passing the library. Outside its gates he had an almost intolerable urge to go in and take that book from the shelf. One thing he knew now, whether he wanted to or not, was that it was his wife Hare had murdered.

Some little while after midnight he was awakened by a crash. He sat up in bed.

'What was that?'

'The bathroom window, I expect,' said Rita, half-asleep.

Norman got up. He took the pole, inserted the hook into the ring on the bolt, slid up the bolt and gave it a firm clockwise twist. The rest of the night passed undisturbed. Rita opened the window two or three days later because it had turned warm. She went into their bedroom and changed the sheets and thought, for no reason as far as she could tell, I wonder if it was his wife he murdered? I expect it was his wife. Then she thought how terrible it would be if he had murdered her in bed. Hare's bed must have stood in the same place as their own. It must have because of the position of the electric points. Perhaps he had come home one night and murdered her in bed.

A wind that was more like a gale started to make the house cold. Rita closed the bathroom window. About an hour after Norman got home it blew open with a crash.

'It comes open,' said Norman after he had shut it, 'because when you close it you don't give the bolt a hard enough twist.'

'It comes open because of the wind,' said Rita.

'The wind wouldn't affect it if you shut it properly.' Norman's handsome face wore its petulant look and he sulked rather for the rest of the evening.

Next time the window was opened petals from fruit tree blossom blew in all over the dark blue carpet. Rita closed it an hour or so before Norman came home. Dorothy was downstairs having a cup of tea with her.

'I'd have that window wired up if I were you,' said Dorothy, and she added oddly, 'to be on the safe side.'

'It gets so hot in there.'

'Leave it open then and keep the door shut.'

The crash of the window opening awoke Norman at two in the morning. He was furious. He made a lot of noise about closing it in order to wake Rita.

'I told you that window wouldn't come open if you gave the bolt a hard enough twist. That crashing scares the hell out of me. My nerves can't stand it.'

'What's wrong with your nerves?'

Norman didn't answer. 'I don't know why you can't master a simple knack like that.'

'It isn't me, it's the wind.'

'Nonsense. Don't talk such nonsense. There is no wind.'

Rita opened the window in order to practise closing it. She spent about an hour opening and closing the window and giving the bolt a firm clockwise twist. While she was doing this she had a funny feeling. She had the feeling someone was standing behind and watching what she did. Of course there was no one there. Rita meant to leave the window open as it was a dry sunny day but she had closed it for perhaps the tenth time when the phone rang. The window therefore remained closed and Rita forgot about it.

She was pulling up weeds in the tiny strip of front garden when a woman who lived next door to the Lawrences came across the road, rattled a tin at her and asked for a donation for Cancer Research.

'I hope you don't mind my telling you how much I like your bedroom curtains.'

'Thank you very much,' said Rita.

'Mrs Hare had white net. Of course that was a few years back. You don't mind sleeping in that bedroom then? Or do you use one of the back rooms?'

Rita's knees felt weak. She was speechless.

'I suppose it isn't as if he actually did the deed in the bedroom. More just outside on the landing, wasn't it?'

Rita gave her a pound to get rid of her. She went upstairs and stood on the landing and felt very funny indeed. Should she tell Norman? How could she tell him, how could she begin, when they had never once mentioned the subject since they moved in? Norman never thought about it anyway, she was sure of that. She watched him eating his supper as if he hadn't a care in the world. The window crashed open just as he was starting on his pudding. He jumped up with an angry shout.

'You're going to come with me into that bathroom and I'm going to teach you how to shut that window if it's the last thing I do!'

He stood behind her while she took the pole and inserted the hook into the ring on the bolt, pushed the bolt up and gave it a firm twist.

'There, you see, you've turned it the wrong way. I said clockwise. Don't you know what clockwise means?'

Norman opened the window and made Rita close it again. This time she twisted the bolt to the right. The window crashed open before they had reached the foot of the stairs.

'It's not me, you see, it's the wind,' Rita cried.

Norman's voice shook with rage. 'The wind couldn't blow it open if you closed it properly. It doesn't blow it open when I close it.'

'You close it then and see. Go on, you do it.'

Norman closed it. The crash awakened him at three in the morning. He got up, cursing, and went into the bathroom. Rita woke up and jumped out of bed and followed him. Norman came out of the bathroom with the pole in his hand, his face red and his eyes bulging. He shouted at Rita:

'You got up after I was asleep and opened that window and closed it your way, didn't you?'

'I did *what*?'

'Don't deny it. You're trying to drive me mad with that window. You won't get the chance to do it again.'

He raised the pole and brought it down with a crash on the side of Rita's head. She gave a dreadful hoarse cry and put up her hands to try and ward off the rain of blows. Norman struck her five times with the pole and she was lying unconscious on the landing floor before he realized what he was doing. Norman threw the pole down the stairwell, picked Rita up in his arms and phoned for an ambulance.

Rita didn't die. She had a fractured skull and a broken jaw and collarbone but she would survive. When she regained consciousness and could move her jaw again she told the people at the hospital she had got up in the night and fallen over the banisters and all the way down the stairwell in the dark. The curious thing was she seemed to believe this herself.

Alone and remorseful, Norman kept thinking how odd it was there had nearly been a second murder under this roof. He went to the estate agents and told them he wanted to put the house back on the market. Hare's house, he always called it to himself these days, never 'my house' or 'ours'. They looked grave and shook their heads but brightened up when Norman named the very low figure he intended to ask.

Now he was going to be rid of the house Norman began to feel differently about Hare. He wouldn't have minded knowing what Hare had done, the details, the facts. One Saturday afternoon a prospective buyer came, was in raptures over Norman's redecorations and the tiles in the downstairs bathroom, and didn't seem to care at all about Hare. This encouraged Norman and immediately the man had gone he went down the road to the library where he got out *Murder in the Sixties*. He read the account of the case after getting back from visiting Rita in hospital.

Raymond and Diana Hare had been an apparently happy couple. One morning their cleaner arrived to find Mrs Hare beaten to death and lying in her own blood on the top landing outside the bathroom door. Hare had soon confessed. He and his wife had had a midnight dispute over a window that continually came open with a crash and in the heat of anger he had attacked her with a wooden pole. Not a very interesting or memorable murder. Robinson, in his foreword, said he had included it among his four because what linked them all was a common lack of any kind of understandable motive.

But how could I have tried to do the same thing and for the same reason? Norman asked himself. Is Hare's house haunted by an act, by a motiveless urge? Or can it be that the first time I looked into that book I saw and read more than my conscious mind took in but not more than was absorbed by my *unconscious*? A rational man must believe the latter.

He borrowed the ladder from Roy to climb up and once more wire the window catch.

'By the way,' he said. 'I've been meaning to ask you. It's not the same pole, is it?'

'Your one, you mean? The same as Hare's? Oh, no, I don't know what became of that one. In some police museum, I expect. You've got ours. When we had our window done we offered ours to Mr Hare the nephew and he was very glad to accept.'

Norman found a buyer at last. Rita was away convalescing and he was obliged to find a new home for them in her absence. Not that he had much choice, the miserable sum he got for Hare's house. He put a deposit on one of the terraced cottages in Inverness Street, hoping poor Rita wouldn't mind too much.

# Bribery and Corruption

Everyone who makes a habit of dining out in London knows that
Potters in Marylebone High Street is one of the most expensive
of eating places. Nicholas Hawthorne, who usually dined in his
rented room or in a steak house, was deceived by the humble-sounding
name. When Annabel said, 'Let's go to Potters,' he agreed quite happily.

It was the first time he had taken her out. She was a small pretty
girl with very little to say for herself. In her little face her eyes looked
huge and appealing – a flying fox face, Nicholas thought. She suggested
they take a taxi to Potters 'because it's difficult to find'. Seeing that
it was a large building and right in the middle of Marylebone High
Street, Nicholas didn't think it would have been more difficult to find
on foot than in a taxi but he said nothing.

He was already wondering what this meal was going to cost. Potters
was a grand and imposing restaurant. The windows were of that very
clear but slightly warped glass that bespeaks age, and the doors of a
dark red wood that looked as if it had been polished every day for
fifty years. Because the curtains were drawn and the interior not
visible, it appeared as if they were approaching some private residence,
perhaps a rich man's town house.

Immediately inside the doors was a bar where three couples sat
about in black leather chairs. A waiter took Annabel's coat and they
were conducted to a table in the restaurant. Nicholas, though young,
was perceptive. He had expected Annabel to be made as shy and
awkward by this place as he was himself but she seemed to have shed
her diffidence with her coat. And when waiters appoached with menus
and the wine list she said boldly that she would start with a Pernod.

What was it all going to cost? Nicholas looked unhappily at the
prices and was thankful he had his newly acquired credit card with
him. Live now, pay later – but, oh God, he would still have to pay.

Annabel chose asparagus for her first course and roast grouse for
her second. The grouse was the most expensive item on the menu.
Nicholas selected vegetable soup and a pork chop. He asked her if

she would like red or white wine and she said one bottle wouldn't be enough, would it, so why not have one of each?

She didn't speak at all while they ate. He remembered reading in some poem or other how the poet marvelled of a schoolmaster that one small head could carry all he knew. Nicholas wondered how one small body could carry all Annabel ate. She devoured roast potatoes with her grouse and red cabbage and runner beans, and when she heard the waiter recommending braised artichokes to the people at the next table she said she would have some of those too. He prayed she wouldn't want another course. But that fawning insinuating waiter had to come up with the sweet trolley.

'We have fresh strawberries, madam.'

'In November?' said Annabel, breaking her silence. 'How lovely.'

Naturally she would have them. Drinking the dregs of his wine, Nicholas watched her eat the strawberries and cream and then call for a slice of chocolate roulade. He ordered coffee. Did sir and madam wish for a liqueur? Nicholas shook his head vehemently. Annabel said she would have a green chartreuse. Nicholas knew that this was of all liqueurs the pearl – and necessarily the most expensive.

By now he was so frightened about the bill and so repelled by her concentrated guzzling that he needed briefly to get away from her. It was plain she had come out with him only to stuff and drink herself into a stupor. He excused himself and went off in the direction of the men's room.

In order to reach it he had to pass across one end of the bar. The place was still half-empty but during the past hour – it was now nine o'clock – another couple had come in and were sitting at a table in the centre of the floor. The man was middle-aged with thick silver hair and a lightly tanned taut-skinned face. His right arm was round the shoulder of his companion, a very young, very pretty blond girl, and he was whispering something in her ear. Nicholas recognized him at once as the chairman of the company for which his own father had been sales manager until two years before when he had been made redundant on some specious pretext. The company was called Sorensen-McGill and the silver-haired man was Julius Sorensen.

With all the fervour of a young man loyal to a beloved parent, Nicholas hated him. But Nicholas was a very young man and it was beyond his strength to cut Sorensen. He muttered a stiff good evening and plunged for the men's room where he turned out his pockets, counted the notes in his wallet and tried to calculate what he already owed to the credit card company. If necessary he would have to

43

borrow from his father, though he would hate to do that, knowing as he did that his father had been living on a reduced income even since that beast Sorensen fired him. Borrow from his father, try and put off paying the rent for a month if he could, cut down on his smoking, maybe give up altogether . . .

When he came out, feeling almost sick, Sorensen and the girl had moved farther apart from each other. They didn't look at him and Nicholas too looked the other way. Annabel was on her second green chartreuse and gobbling up *petit fours*. He had thought her face was like that of a flying fox and now he remembered that flying fox is only a pretty name for a fruit bat. Eating a marzipan orange, she looked just like a rapacious little fruit bat. And she was very drunk.

'I feel ever so sleepy and strange,' she said. 'Maybe I've got one of those viruses. Could you pay the bill?'

It took Nicholas a long time to catch the waiter's eye. When he did the man merely homed in on them with the coffee pot. Nicholas surprised himself with his own firmness.

'I'd like the bill,' he said in the tone of one who declares to higher authority that he who is about to die salutes thee.

In half a minute the waiter was back. Would Nicholas be so good as to come with him and speak to the maître d'hôtel? Nicholas nodded, dumbfounded. What had happened? What had he done wrong? Annabel was slouching back in her chair, her big eyes half-closed, a trickle of something orange dribbling out of the corner of her mouth. They were going to tell him to remove her, that she had disgraced the place, not to come here again. He followed the waiter, his hands clenched.

A huge man spoke to him, a man with the beak and plumage of a king penguin. 'Your bill has been paid, sir.'

Nicholas stared. 'I don't know what you mean.'

'Your father paid it, sir. Those were my instructions, to tell you your father had settled your bill.'

The relief was tremendous. He seemed to grow tall again and light and free. It was as if someone had made him a present of – well, what would it have been? Sixty pounds? Seventy? And he understood at once. Sorensen had paid his bill and said he was his father. It was a little bit of compensation for what Sorensen had done in dismissing his father. He had paid out sixty pounds to show he meant well, to show that he wanted, in a small way, to make up for injustice.

Tall and free and masterful, Nicholas said, 'Call me a cab, please,' and then he went and shook Annabel awake in quite a lordly way.

44

His euphoria lasted for nearly an hour, long after he had pushed the somnolent Annabel through her own front door, then climbed the stairs up to the furnished room he rented and settled down to the crossword in the evening paper. Things would have turned out very differently if he hadn't started that crossword. 'Twelve across: Bone in mixed byre goes with corruption.' (7 letters) Then I and the Y were already in. He got the answer after a few seconds – 'Bribery'. 'Rib' in an anagram of 'byre'. 'Bribery'.

He laid down the paper and looked at the opposite wall. That which goes with corruption. How could he ever have been such a fool, such a naive innocent fool, as to suppose a man like Sorensen cared about injustice or ever gave a thought to wrongful dismissal or even believed for a moment he *could* have been wrong? Of course Sorensen hadn't been trying to make restitution, of course he hadn't paid that bill out of kindness and remorse. He had paid it as a bribe.

He had paid the bribe to shut Nicholas's mouth because he didn't want anyone to know he had been out drinking with a girl, embracing a girl, who wasn't his wife. It was bribery, the bribery that went with corruption.

Once, about three years before, Nicholas had been with his parents to a party Sorensen had given for his staff and Mrs Sorensen had been the hostess. A brown-haired mousey little woman, he remembered her, and all of forty-five which seemed like old age to Nicholas. Sorensen had paid that bill because he didn't want his wife to find out he had a girlfriend young enough to be his daughter.

He had bought him, Nicholas thought, bribed and corrupted him – or tried to. Because he wasn't going to succeed. He needn't think he could kick the Hawthorne family around any more. Once was enough.

It had been nice thinking that he hadn't after all wasted more than half a week's wages on that horrible girl but honour was more important. Honour, surely, meant sacrificing material things for a principle. Nicholas had a bad night because he kept waking up and thinking of all the material things he would have to go short of during the next few weeks on account of his honour. Nevertheless, by the morning his resolve was fixed. Making sure he had his cheque book with him, he went off to work.

Several hours passed before he could get the courage together to phone Sorensen-McGill. What was he going to do if Sorensen refused to see him? If only he had a nice fat bank account with five hundred pounds in it he could make the grand gesture and send Sorensen a blank cheque accompanied by a curt and contemptuous letter.

45

The telephonist who used to answer in the days when he sometimes phoned his father at work answered now.

'Sorensen-McGill. Can I help you?'

His voice rather hoarse, Nicholas asked if he could have an appointment with Mr Sorensen that day on a matter of urgency. He was put through to Sorensen's secretary. There was a delay. Bells rang and switches clicked. The girl came back to the phone and Nicholas was sure she was going to say no.

'Mr Sorensen asks if one o'clock will suit you?'

In his lunch hour? Of course it would. But what on earth could have induced Sorensen to have sacrificed one of those fat expense account lunches just to see him? Nicholas set off for Berkeley Square, wondering what had made the man so forthcoming. A weak hopeful little voice inside him began once again putting up those arguments which on the previous evening the voice of a common sense had so decisively refuted.

Perhaps Sorensen really meant well and when Nicholas got there would tell him the paying of the bill had been no bribery but a way of making a present to the son of a once-valued employee. The pretty girl could have been Sorensen's daughter. Nicholas had no idea if the man had children. It was possible he had a daughter. No corruption then, no betrayal of his honour, no need to give up cigarettes or abase himself before his landlord.

They knew him at Sorensen-McGill. He had been there with his father and, besides, he looked like his father. The pretty blond girl hadn't looked in the least like Sorensen. A secretary showed him into the chairman's office. Sorensen was sitting in a yellow leather chair behind a rosewood desk with an inlaid yellow leather top. There were Modigliani-like murals on the wall behind him and on the desk a dark green jade ashtray, stacked with stubs, which the secretary replaced with a clean one of pale green jade.

'Hallo, Nicholas,' said Sorensen. He didn't smile. 'Sit down.'

The only other chair in the room was one of those hi-tech low-slung affairs made of leather hung on a metal frame. Beside it was a black glass coffee table with a black leather padded rim and on the glass lay a magazine open at the centrefold of a nude girl. There are some people who know how to put others at their ease and there are those who know how to put others in difficulties. Nicholas sat down, right down – about three inches from the floor.

Sorensen lit a cigarette. He didn't offer the box. He looked at Nicholas and moved his head slowly from side to side. At last he said:

'I suppose I should have expected this.'

Nicholas opened his mouth to speak but Sorensen held up his hand. 'No, you can have your say in a minute.' His tone became hard and brisk. 'The girl you saw me with last night was someone – not to put too fine a point on it – I picked up in a bar. I have never seen her before, I shall never see her again. She is not, in any sense of the words, a girlfriend or mistress. Wait,' he said as Nicholas again tried to interrupt. 'Let me finish. My wife is not a well woman. Were she to find out where I was last night and whom I was with she would doubtless be very distressed. She would very likely become ill again. I refer, of course, to mental illness, to an emotional sickness, but . . .'

He drew deeply on his cigarette. 'But all this being so and whatever the consequences, I shall not on any account allow myself to be blackmailed. Is that understood? I paid for your dinner last night and that is enough. I do not want my wife told what you saw, but you may tell her and publish it to the world before I pay you another penny.'

At the word blackmail Nicholas's heart had begun to pound. The blood rushed into his face. He had come to vindicate his honour and his motive had been foully misunderstood. In a choked voice he stuttered:

'You've no business – it wasn't – why do you say things like that to me?'

'It's not a nice word, is it? But to call it anything else would merely be semantics. You came, didn't you, to ask for more?'

Nicholas jumped up. 'I came to give you your money back!'

'Aah!' It was a strange sound Sorensen made, old and urbane, cynical yet wondering. He crushed out his cigarette. 'I see. Youth is moralistic. Inexperience is puritanical. You'll tell her anyway because you can't be bought, is that it?'

'No, I can't be bought.' Nicholas was trembling. He put his hands down flat on Sorensen's desk but still they shook. 'I shall never tell anyone what I saw, I promise you that. But I can't let you pay for my dinner – and pretend to be my father!' Tears were pricking the backs of his eyes.

'Oh, sit down, sit down. If you aren't trying to blackmail me and your lips are sealed, what the hell did you come here for? A social call? A man-to-man chat about the ladies you and I took out last night? Your family aren't exactly my favourite companions, you know.'

Nicholas retreated a little. He felt the man's power. It was the power of money and the power that is achieved by always having had money. There was something he hadn't ever before noticed about Sorensen but which he noticed now. Sorensen looked as if he were made of metal, his skin of copper, his hair of silver, his suit of pewter.

And then the mist in Nicholas's eyes stopped him seeing anything but a blur. 'How much was my bill?' he managed to say.

'Oh, for God's sake.'

'How much?'

'Sixty-seven pounds,' said Sorensen, 'give or take a little.' He sounded amused.

To Nicholas it was a small fortune. He got out his cheque book and wrote the cheque to J. Sorensen and passed it across the desk and said, 'There's your money. But you needn't worry. I won't say I saw you. I promise I won't.'

Uttering those words made him feel noble, heroic. The threatening tears receded. Sorensen looked at the cheque and tore it in two.

'You're a very tiresome boy. I don't want you on my premises. Get out.'

Nicholas got out. He walked out of the building with his head in the air. He was still considering sending Sorensen another cheque when, two mornings later, reading his paper in the train, his eye caught the hated name. At first he didn't think the story referred to 'his' Sorensen – and then he knew it did. The headline read: 'Woman Found Dead in Forest. Murder of Tycoon's Wife.'

'The body of a woman,' ran the story beneath,

was found last night in an abandoned car in Hatfield Forest in Hertfordshire. She had been strangled. The woman was today identified as Mrs Winifred Sorensen, 45, of Eaton Place, Belgravia. She was the wife of Julius Sorensen, chairman of Sorensen-McGill, manufacturers of office equipment.

Mrs Sorensen had been staying with her mother, Mrs Mary Clifford, at Mrs Clifford's home in Much Hadham. Mrs Clifford said, 'My daughter had intended to stay with me for a further two days. I was surprised when she said she would drive home to London on Tuesday evening.'

'I was not expecting my wife home on Tuesday,' said Mr Sorensen. 'I had no idea she had left her mother's house until I phoned there yesterday. When I realized she was missing I immediately informed the police.'

Police are treating the case as murder.

That poor woman, thought Nicholas. While she had been driving home to her husband, longing for him probably, needing his company and his comfort, he had been philandering with a girl he had picked up,

48

a girl whose surname he didn't even know. He must now be overcome with remorse. Nicholas hoped it was biting agonized remorse. The contrast was what was so shocking, Sorensen cheek to cheek with that girl, drinking with her, no doubt later sleeping with her; his wife alone, struggling with an attacker in a lonely place in the dark.

Nicholas, of course, wouldn't have been surprised if Sorensen had done it himself. Nothing Sorensen could do would have surprised him. The man was capable of any iniquity. Only this he couldn't have done, which none knew better than Nicholas. So it was a bit of a shock to be accosted by two policemen when he arrived home that evening. They were waiting in a car outside his gate and they got out as he approached.

'Nothing to worry about, Mr Hawthorne,' said the older of them who introduced himself as a Detective Inspector. 'Just a matter of routine. Perhaps you read about the death of Mrs Winifred Sorensen in your paper today?'

'Yes.'

'May we come in?'

They followed him upstairs. What could they want of him? Nicholas sometimes read detective stories and it occurred to him that, knowing perhaps of his tenuous connection with Sorensen-McGill, they would want to ask him questions about Sorensen's character and domestic life. In that case they had come to the right witness.

He could tell them all right. He could tell them why poor Mrs Sorensen, jealous and suspicious as she must have been, had taken it into her head to leave her mother's house two days early and drive home. Because she had intended to catch her husband in the act. And she would have caught him, found him absent or maybe entertaining that girl in their home, only she had never got home. Some maniac had hitched a lift from her first. Oh yes, he'd tell them!

In his room they sat down. They had to sit on the bed for there was only one chair.

'It has been established,' said the Inspector, 'that Mrs Sorensen was killed between eight and ten p.m. on Tuesday.'

Nicholas nodded. He could hardly contain his excitement. What a shock it was going to be for them when he told them about this supposedly respectable businessman's private life! A split second later Nicholas was left deflated and staring.

'At nine that evening Mr Julius Sorensen, her husband, was in a restaurant called Potters in Marylebone High Street accompanied by a young lady. He had made a statement to us to that effect.'

Sorensen had told them. He had confessed. The disappointment was acute.

'I believe you were also in the restaurant at that time?'

In a small voice Nicholas said, 'Oh yes. Yes, I was.'

'On the following day, Mr Hawthorne, you went to the offices of Sorensen-McGill where a conversation took place between you and Mr Sorensen. Will you tell me what that conversation was about, please?'

'It was about my seeing him in Potters the night before. He wanted me to . . .' Nicholas stopped. He blushed.

'Just a moment, sir. I think I can guess why you're so obviously uneasy about this. If I may say so without giving offence you're a very young man as yet and young people are often a bit confused when it comes to questions of loyalty. Am I right?'

Mystified now, Nicholas nodded.

'Your duty is plain. It's to tell the truth. Will you do that?'

'Yes, of course.'

'Good. Did Mr Sorensen try to bribe you?'

'Yes.' Nicholas took a deep breath. 'I made him a promise.'

'Which must carry no weight, Mr Hawthorne. Let me repeat. Mrs Sorensen was killed between eight and ten. Mr Sorensen has told us he was in Potters at nine, in the bar. The bar staff can't remember him. The surname of the lady he says he was with is unknown to him. According to him you were there and you saw him.' The Inspector glanced at his companion, then back to Nicholas. 'Well, Mr Hawthorne? This is a matter of the utmost seriousness.'

Nicholas understood. Excitement welled in him once more but he didn't show it. They would realize why he hesitated. At last he said:

'I was in Potters from eight till about nine-thirty.' Carefully he kept to the exact truth. 'Mr Sorensen and I discussed my being there and seeing him when I kept my appointment with him in his office on Wednesday and he – he paid the bill for my dinner.'

'I see.' How sharp were the Inspector's eyes! How much he thought he knew of youth and age, wisdom and naivety, innocence and corruption! 'Now then – did you in fact see Mr Sorensen in Potters on Tuesday evening?'

'I can't forget my promise,' said Nicholas.

Of course he couldn't. He had only to keep his promise and the police would charge Sorensen with murder. He looked down. He spoke in a guilty troubled voice.

'I didn't see him. Of course I didn't.'

# The Whistler

Jeremy found the key in one of the holiday flats while he was working for Manuel. The flats were being painted throughout in a colour called champagne and so far they hadn't found a machine to do this. Jeremy hoped they wouldn't until the job was done. Manuel was an American citizen though he came from somewhere south of the border – Cuba, Jeremy had always supposed. Jeremy himself came from somewhere a long way north of the border, England in fact, and he had been feeling his way around the United States for a couple of years now, always hoping for his luck to change. The key, he thought, might be a piece of luck.

It was up in a corner of the bedroom windowsill, under the blind. Manuel was in the living room, whistling country music. He whistled all the time he was working, never anything Spanish, always Western or country stuff, and he never played the radio which Jeremy would have preferred. The key had a label tied on its head with a piece of string. On the label an address was written. Jeremy started to say, or thought of saying, 'Hey, Manuel, look at this . . .' and then checked himself. The whistling went on unbroken. Whatever might be on offer at the address on the key label, did he want to have to share it with Manuel? Or, worse, did he want Manuel to take the key off him?

Finding things in the flats wasn't unusual. People were very careless. They rented these flats at Juanillo Beach for a couple of weeks in the high season and went off home to New Jersey or Moscow, Idaho, or wherever it might be, leaving their jewellery behind and their cameras, not to mention such trifles as books and tapes and so on. The company who owned the property were supposed to come in and check before Manuel started but they didn't make much of a job of it. Jeremy had found a roll of banknotes, over eighty dollars, in a kitchen unit, and in a gap between tiled floor and wall, a diamond ring. A jeweller in downtown Miami had given him $250 for the ring and that was probably a fraction of its value. It had been a mistake telling Manuel about it. Manuel hadn't cared about the banknotes but he had jibbed at the ring. It wasn't that he was more honest than the next man, but he had this contract with Juanillo Beach Properties Inc. and he didn't want to lose it. At any rate he had warned Jeremy off helping himself to anything he found in the flats – which was enough in itself to make Jeremy pick up the key and put it in the pocket of his jeans. In the next room the whistling continued, becoming very rollicking and Rocky Mountain.

It was starting to get hot and the air conditioning had broken down. Or Juanillo Beach Properties had taken the fuse out, Jeremy thought. He wouldn't put it past them. By noon it would be up in the nineties. Well, it was for the climate he'd come down here and for the climate he stayed. It is easier to be poor in a warm climate. He thought of England with horror, of being deported and having to go back there as his worst nightmare. It couldn't really be like that, it wasn't, but he remembered his native land as green and cold, full of rich elderly people who had log fires going all the year round, a land of joblessness and privilege where, though he had been born there, he had never felt welcome. Now the blind was up he could see the subtropical garden in which the apartment block was, palms and citrus and Indian paintbrush and oleander and here and there the sliced spear leaves of a banana. Yellow and black striped zebra butterflies flitted among the thick shiny leaves. And the sun blazed from a clear blue sky. It suited him here, or would if he had a bit of money.

In London he had had a very small room, for which he paid £25 a week, and had shared bathroom and kitchen two floors down with four other tenants. Here he had a motel room with bath – well, shower – for less than that. And he didn't need a kitchen because eating out was cheap. But sometimes he thought he'd come to the United States too late to seek his fortune, maybe fifty years too late. That was what Josh who owned the motel said. Josh didn't know he was there illegally of course. Or if he did he didn't say.

After work he and Josh sometimes had a beer together on the porch at the rear of the motel office building. The motel was in a rough area and was pretty shabby but if there was one thing Josh kept in repair it was the screens round that porch. All the mosquitos of the diaspora came down there, Josh said, driven out of more prosperous parts.

Jeremy remembered the address on the key. 'Where's Eleventh Avenue?'

There were two more cans of Coors on the table, sweating icy drops, and a bag of toasted pecans. A little brown lizard ran up the screen on the outside.

'What d'you mean, Eleventh Avenue? Eleventh Avenue where?'

'Miami.'

'There's not so many cities in this country you'll find the avenues numbered. Streets, yes. Why? What d'you ask for?' He didn't wait for an answer. 'Take L.A., take Philly – they don't have numbered avenues.'

'New York has.'

'New York's different,' said Josh which was something Americans always said, Jeremy had noticed.

'So how about Miami?'

'Sure Miami's got an Eleventh Avenue. Downtown. There's a street plan in the office.'

Jeremy had a look at it. The address on the key was 1562A Ave. 11. No city, no state. The label was rather smudged and there had been more of the address there, a couple of capital letters, in fact. The second letter was certainly a J or a Y. Y for York? J for Juanillo? He knew without enquiring that there was no First Avenue in Juanillo, let alone Eleventh. Come to that, could he be sure the writer had meant Eleventh Avenue? Ave. 11 was a funny way of putting it, more a European way, except that Europeans don't number their streets much.

It wasn't likely to be Miami. People from Miami wouldn't rent a flat at Juanillo Beach. But he could try. Burglary would be so simple, scarcely dishonest even, when you didn't have to break in. That evening he was going to eat out with Manuel and Lupe in a Thai restaurant out in posh Fort Cayne where Manuel lived. But first he'd make a little trip downtown and try the key on the front door of 1562A Eleventh Avenue.

The place wasn't guarded, all was quiet. He rang the bell, waited, rang again, tried the key. It didn't fit. In the taxi going out to Fort Cayne he thought about what Josh had said about not many American cities having numbered avenues. Of course Josh might be wrong, he had only named three cities . . . Wasn't it more probable anyway that the key opened an apartment in New York? What was Eleventh Avenue, New York, like and how far uptown would 1562A be? If it was 1562 Fifth they were talking about he'd have some idea. He imagined a gorgeous New York apartment full of treasures waiting for someone to walk in and take them. The trouble was that the fare to New York was something around $300 round trip.

The restaurant was called the Phumiphol and it was in one of those glossy malls. Jeremy got there first and ordered a vodka on the rocks. Put it on the check, please. It was going to be a bit awkward meeting

Lupe again. Nothing he couldn't handle, of course, but he did need that vodka.

Her real name was Guadelupe or Maria del Guadelupe or some such thing and she was an illegal immigrant like him. A small dark beautiful girl with the huge eyes and symmetrical features of those Mexican film stars of thirties Hollywood. She resembled a photograph he had seen of Dolores del Rio. Manuel was going to marry her and she too would become an American, as much a citizen as the President's wife or a Daughter of the American Revolution.

The vodka came and a little dish of something that looked like salted beetles but couldn't be. Jeremy had first met Lupe in Manuel's apartment. Not that she lived there with him. Manuel was very strict and very Spanish about that sort of thing. His affianced wife had to be a virgin and manifestly seen by all the world to be a virgin.

Oddly enough, Lupe had been. Jeremy had never actually come across one before. She lived in a room in a Cuban lady's house and every day she came to clean Manuel's apartment for him and iron his shirts. Manuel put his shirts through the washer himself but Lupe ironed them. Wherever she came from she didn't want to go back there and that, Jeremy had been sure, was why she was waiting on and obeying Manuel in the hope of marrying him. Manuel was an ugly devil, very thin and somehow spiderlike with a pockmarked hatchet face while Jeremy was tall, blond and good-looking which was partly, no doubt, why Lupe had fallen in love with him.

Or whatever you called it. At any rate she hadn't resisted much. Manuel had had to go home because his father was dying. He died before Manuel got there, so he was only away two days but that was enough. Jeremy and Lupe were making love in the apartment at Hacienda Alameda before Manuel got on the plane. Lupe's virginity was a surprise and bit daunting but after the third or fourth time it was all the same as if it had been gone five years.

The trouble was that they couldn't stop and at last Manuel found out. One stupid afternoon when Jeremy had the day off and Lupe was cleaning the apartment they forgot discretion and succumbed. They might so easily have gone to the motel, he thought afterwards. Manuel didn't find them, nothing so crude as that, he found a blond hair and a long chestnut wavy hair on the pillow where only a black-haired man slept.

Jeremy was finishing off his vodka when Manuel and Lupe came in. Manuel looked cheerful and pleased with himself, talking about the holiday he would take away from Florida when the really hot weather started. Make it a honeymoon, was what Jeremy would have said a few months back. They say Alaska's a great place in the summer. Something stopped him saying it now. Manuel hadn't mentioned marriage since that night.

They had some transparent soup with flowers floating in it. A jar of sake and a bottle of Perrier water. Neither Manuel nor Lupe drank much. Then came little pancakes, shredded vegetables, perfumed duck. It was all as if dolls had cooked it. Lupe ate daintily, chewing every mouthful twenty times, keeping her head bent.

'I want to act like a civilized man, ' Manuel had said, and pathetically, Jeremy thought, 'like an American gentleman.' He looked ridiculous when he was unhappy, a black crow with mud on its feathers. 'My ancestors would have killed you and her too.'

Jeremy had cast up his eyes at that. Oh, Christ . . .

'Times have changed. With me it will be as if it had never happened.' Manuel looked at Lupe. 'But it must never happen again.'

'It won't happen again,' said Lupe.

'Of course not.' Jeremy didn't want her any more anyway. All this fuss was enough to put one off more desirable women than Lupe Garcia.

'Then you stay working for me,' Manuel said to Jeremy, 'and bygones shall be bygones.' He smiled. He insisted on shaking Jeremy's hand. Then he went to the kitchen to open a bottle of wine, whistling 'The Tennessee Waltz' as he went. An apposite if tactless choice, Jeremy thought, but perhaps Manuel didn't know the words. Lupe tried to catch his eyes but Jeremy wouldn't look.

That had been two months ago and this was the first time since then that he had seen Lupe. It was archaic the feeling the whole set-up gave him that by that one initial act, let alone the others, he had spoiled her for Manuel, she was damaged goods. She had grown more subdued. She didn't look unhappy. They ate little cakes of dough in syrup sauce.

Manuel had his car, though he lived only round the corner. Jeremy was asked back for coffee. He went to the bathroom and saw unmistakable signs of Lupe's occupancy, a jar of skinfood, an eyeliner, a bottle of the cologne she used. It hadn't taken long for Manuel's principles to break down, Jeremy thought with a quiet laugh to himself.

'Yes, I've moved in,' she said to him.

He looked at her hand and she saw him looking. Not even an engagement ring.

Manuel drove him home. He had just taken delivery of this year's new car. Jeremy often wondered where the money came from. You didn't own a condominium at prestigious Hacienda Alameda and have a new car every year and fly home to see your family every couple of months out of painting ceilings. It was no business of his. He'd be moving on soon anyway. Maybe to California when he could raise the fare.

The coconut palms round Josh's Motel hummed with tree frogs as if they themselves were sensate things, an unbroken droning that twitched at the nerves. They kept Jeremy awake. He could go to New York instead and try out that key. There were two letters on that label after Ave. 11 and one of them could be a Y. Perhaps there were only two cities in the United States with numbered avenues – and perhaps there were dozens.

A couple of days later he and Manuel moved on into the next apartment. It was the same as the one they had finished except that no one had left a key on the windowsill. Manuel was whistling away in the next room, a song about the sunflowers of Kansas. He had taken off the fancy pale blue blouson he had been wearing and slung it down over the side of the bath. There was nowhere else to put it. Jeremy felt in the pockets. He had done this before when times were hard and hauled himself fifty bucks. Manuel was too careless about money to notice. The whistling continued, only the tune changing and going south to become 'The Yellow Rose of Texas'. Jeremy pulled out a wad of notes, all of them twenties, a lot of money.

He couldn't just pocket it, that was no good. He looked about him, thinking quickly. The bath plug was the metal kind, operated by a lever underneath the taps but nevertheless removable. Jeremy removed it and carefully poked the roll of notes inside. The roll expanded a little to fit the hole as he had known it would. He put the plug back.

Manuel or he usually went out at lunchtime and fetched back a couple of Whoppers, onion rings and two Cokes. It was Manuel who always paid. Cutting off the whistling, he went to the bathroom for his jacket and the six or seven dollars Jeremy would need at Burger King. This time he wasn't quite so philosophical about the loss of his money.

'I know you're not accusing me,' Jeremy said. 'I know you wouldn't do that, but for my own sake I'd like to show you.'

He pulled the empty pockets out of his jeans, stripped off his shirt, kicked off his shoes, handed Manuel his own denim jacket with just $8 in the pocket.

'I don't know how much you had on you, Manuel, but you were swinging that thing around when we got in the car at my place. It's a rough old area round Josh's . . .'

'And finding's keepings, eh?' Manuel used a lot of quaint old English expressions that sounded crazy uttered in his Spanish accent. 'There's worse things happen at sea,' he said. 'But you must pay for the lunch.' He laughed and patted Jeremy on the back.

Jeremy hooked the notes out of the plughole before he went home. There were sixteen of them, more than enough to get to New York on. But suppose the place the key opened wasn't in New York? He'd have wasted all that money. It was an expensive looking key, a *classy* key, he thought, shinier, heavier, more trimly cut, than the keys that opened Hacienda Alameda . . .

Manuel went off home the following week and Lupe was alone. There was no way Jeremy was going to get himself involved with her again. He intended to avoid Fort Cayne altogether for the four days Manuel was gone.

She came to him. He was sitting out on the porch with Josh when she drove on to the parking lot in Manuel's new car. There was something uncertain and vulnerable in the way she drove, the way she parked. She had the lowest self-image of anyone Jeremy knew. Because she thought of herself as dirt people treated her like it, though physically she was obsessively clean, had two showers or baths every day. It was Oriental not Latin girls that had been compared to little flowers but Lupe reminded one of a flower, a hibiscus maybe.

'I should be so lucky,' said Josh.

'Help yourself.' Jeremy shrugged. Lupe had opened the screen door and was coming hesitantly up the steps. 'There's a new rule here,' he said to her. 'No members of the opposite sex in guests' rooms after sunset,' and he laughed at his own wit.

Her face grew hot. Josh who usually had a great sense of humour didn't laugh for some reason but asked her to sit down and how about a drink on the house? Lupe said quietly that she'd have a Coke if there was one. Josh brought the Coke and asked where Manuel was. He had once or twice met Manuel.

'San José,' said Lupe.

That did surprise Jeremy. 'His mum lives in California? I never knew that.'

'Not California, Costa Rica,' Josh said. 'Isn't that right? The capital of Costa Rica?'

She nodded. Jeremy barely knew where Costa Rica was and cared less. Josh said he'd never been there but he'd heard it didn't have an army and it was the only real democracy in Central America. Lupe hadn't been there either. Nicaragua was where she came from. They were actually having a conversation. Let's keep it that way, Jeremy thought.

He didn't know if she was devoted to Manuel or only to his money and his citizenship. Whichever it was, she talked about him all the time. He was a devoted son to his mother, he'd bought her a house in the best residential suburb of San José. Lupe had photographs which she proceeded to show them of a bungalow covered in bougainvillea with gilded bars on its windows.

Jeremy looked at the photographs which had been done by a professional whose address was stamped on the back. Ave. 2, it said, San José, Costa Rica.


From a bookshop in downtown Miami he managed to get a street plan of San José. It was a city in which the streets or *calles* were numbered and so were the avenues or *avenidas*. 'Ave.', of course, could be short for *avenida* as well as avenue. A grid-plan city more or less, with the avenues running east to west and the *calles* north to south. At Juanillo Beach Properties they told him that one of the apartments had last been occupied by a couple from Costa Rica. A lot of Costa Ricans came to Florida for a week or a few days. Shopping was cheaper and better here. Electrical goods, for instance, were half the price they were in San José. But no, they couldn't give him the address. If he had found something in the flat let them have it and they'd send it on. Jeremy handed over a couple of rolls of film he'd bought just now at Gray Drug. The Juanillo Beach Properties girl looked at him as if he was out of his mind.

The travel agent he went to could get him a three-day package to San José for a lot less than he'd nicked off Manuel. Manuel was back by now and they were on the last apartment in the block. When Jeremy said he'd like next week off Manuel didn't put up any objections and seemed interested when he said he was going to New York. He smiled and patted Jeremy's shoulder and said something about the Big Apple and in a funny old-fashioned phrase, not to do anything he, Manuel, wouldn't do. Then he took a clean brush and the bucket of emulsion and went off into the bedroom whistling that song about a boy called Sue.

Jeremy got there in the late afternoon. There were more Costa Ricans than Americans on the flight and when the captain announced they were beginning their descent for San José they all clapped and cheered and drummed their feet. Evidently they were a patriotic lot. A bus the tour company had laid on took him into the city. It was four thousand feet up and cooler than Florida though a lot nearer the equator. There was a view of blue mountains behind coffee plantations and banana groves and the whole was dotted with flame-of-the-forest trees like points of fire. Jeremy had seen a bit of the Third World one way and another and immediately outside the city he expected to see the shantytowns of poverty, the huts made of tin and sacks and plastic bags, the rubbish tips and flies. Poverty didn't bother him, he never thought about it, but here in a kind of subconscious way he expected to see it just as in his native land he expected rain and Tudor mansions, but there was none to be seen. Only neat stucco bungalows and little houses like on an English council estate.

In case the plan had lied it was a comfort to see the *avenidas*. The Hotel Latinoamericana was on Avenida Central and if it wasn't exactly the Hilton it was the best hotel Jeremy had ever stayed in and about five stars up on Josh's. The dark came down at six o'clock. Carmen the tour guide had warned them about pickpockets in the city where thieves abounded. Jeremy thought he would have an early night. San José did anyway, the hotel bar closing at ten sharp.

In the morning he swam in the hotel pool. The water was icy. Outside in the Avenida Central the atmosphere was thick and stinking with petrol fumes. He walked downtown a bit but the pollution which hung as blue smog and obscured the mountains made him cough. Another thing Carmen had said was that if you took a taxi you should settle the fare with the driver first. Jeremy found a taxi and haggled a bit but he had no Spanish and the driver hardly any English and when he had seated himself in the back he was fairly certain he'd be ripped off. The driver was going to take him on a city tour.

First they went to that suburb on the road to Irazu where the finest houses were and the foreign embassies. It wasn't Avenida 11 nor was Manuel's mother's house to be seen. The driver pointed out places of interest that Jeremy wasn't interested in. He showed him the university and the museum of art and then, not far from the children's hospital, Jeremy did see a bungalow very like Manuel's mother's, perhaps indeed the very one, with orange bougainvillea swarming all over it, a golden grille to keep out the burglars and a little white dog peering out of one of the windows. At one point they actually drove along Avenida 11 but nowhere near number 1562. It wasn't far from the Latinoamericana though, he could easily walk there.

After dark? That might be best. Or should he watch the house or flat or whatever it was for the occupants to go out? He remembered that after all he had only two days. He paid the taxi driver – twice, it seemed to him, what they had fixed on – and walked up the Calle Central to Avenida 11. There were two branches of it, the street being broken rather ominously by the Central Prison.

When he found the house he was deeply disappointed. It wasn't even up to the standard of Manuel's mother's place, far below it in fact. He thought of where his parents lived in London, in North Finchley. This bungalow, standing alone on the side of the road, might itself have been in North Finchley but for the two palm trees in front of it and the thorn hedge with red flowers which divided it from the abandoned lot stacked with empty oil drums next door.

Lace curtains, none too clean, hung at all the windows. The paint was faded. It looked unoccupied but he didn't dare try the key. He walked across the oil drum lot and looked round the back. Everything shut up. An empty dog kennel and a broken rusty dog chain.

He found a Macdonald's and lunched there. The unaccustomed high altitude was tiring and after a few drinks in the hotel bar he slept. By six-thirty it was quite dark. He walked up the Calle Central on to Avenida 11 and back to the bungalow. It was in darkness, not a light on in the place. The traffic was beginning to thin and with it the smog so that it was possible now to see the stars and a wire-thin curve of moon. He stood on the opposite side of the street and watched the house. For a quarter of an hour he did that. He went round the back across the oil drum lot and looked round the rear. Nothing. No one. Darkness. There were fewer people on the street now. He walked away, as far as the zoo, back again along a nearly deserted street, breathing clean fresh air. The house looked just the same. He took the key out of his pocket, walked up to the front door and inserted it in the lock. The door opened easily.

He closed it behind him and stood in the small square hall. The place smelt dusty, stuffy, breath-catching as places do that have been shut up a long time in a warm dry climate. Not only was it unoccupied now, it had been unoccupied for months. A little light came in from the street but not enough. Jeremy switched on his torch. He pushed open a door and found himself in a bedroom, insufferably stuffy, smelling of camphor. By the marks on the walls he could see that pieces of furniture had been removed from it and only the big bed with carved mahogany headboard and white lace cover remained. The bungalow was a sizable house, much bigger than it seemed from outside. There were two more bedrooms, one empty of furniture. Either the traffic on Avenida 11 had ceased or you couldn't hear it in here. He moved through the rooms in dim musty silence, directing the torch beam across walls and floors.

The front room or parlour was also half-furnished. There had been a piano or chest of drawers up against one wall. Shabby wooden-armed chairs stood around. The wallpaper was stained and yellow, imprinted with small paler rectangles where framed photographs had once hung. One still remained, hanging crookedly, a family group.

There was nothing worth taking. The most valuable thing was probably the hand-crocheted lace bed cover which, when he looked at it again, turned out to be scored by the depredations of moths. He returned to the living room. There was a drawer in the table which he didn't expect to contain the family silver or wads of whatever they called their currency, *colones*, but he might as well look. It didn't. He was right. The drawer had two paper table napkins in it and a United States ten cent piece, a dime. Closing the drawer, he raised the beam of the torch and it fell on the single framed photograph. Something made Jeremy look more closely, bringing the light right up to the glass.

He gasped as if a hand had fallen on his shoulder. The picture was of an old wrinkle-faced man and a stout old woman with three young men standing behind them, one of them spidery thin, very dark, sharp-featured. Jeremy looked and shut his eyes and looked again. He thought, I have to get out of here and fast. It may be too late. There may be someone in the house now, he may have been here all the time, one of those brothers . . .

He put out the torch. He listened. There was only the dark dusty silence. He went out into the hall, his heart beating quickly, sweat standing on his forehead. When he opened the front door . . . But he dared not open it. A window? The back way was obviously the worst idea. It was dark, desolate, empty at the rear. Though Avenida 11 seemed deserted the front door was still his best bet. He ought to have a weapon. A poker? It was never cold enough in this country to have a fire. He groped his way into the kitchen, opened the door and yelled aloud, clamping his hand too late over his mouth.

Something tall and thin was standing in an embrasure of the wall between sink and cupboard. He didn't know what he'd imagined but when he shone the torch on it he saw it was a six-foot-tall houseplant in a tub, dried-up, brown, dead. There was a piece of iron pipe with a tap on it lying on the draining board. Jeremy took it with him.

Gripping his weapon in his right hand, he opened the front door with his left. There was no one there, no sound, no still or moving shadow. A car with only side lights on cruised slowly down Avenida

11 and turned into a side street. The ten minutes it took Jeremy to get out of the neighbourhood and find a taxi were some of the worst he had ever spent. He knew one of Manuel's brothers had to be lying in wait for him in a doorway or else following him until he reached a totally dark and secluded part of the road.

The house he had been in had obviously once been the home of Manuel's parents. It was probably now up for sale. Manuel had of course moved his mother somewhere more plush. Jeremy could see it all, how he had been led here, but he didn't let himself think too much about the ins and outs of it until at last a taxi came and he was safely in it. No haggling about fares this time.

Why had Manuel done it? Because Jeremy had stolen $320 from him, no doubt. Anyway, it hadn't come off. Perhaps he had gone to the house in Avenida 11 earlier or later than they'd expected or one of those brothers had got the date wrong. Or it might even be that Manuel's desire to get his own back would be satisfied by Jeremy's disappointment at finding nothing to steal in the house. For Manuel might only be hoaxing him, merely playing a *joke*.

Jeremy felt relieved at this idea. If Manuel's aim had simply been to teach him a lesson – well, that was OK with him. He'd been taught a lesson. If he ever saw another key lying about he'd leave it where it was. But his fear was ebbing with every turn the taxi took to bring him nearer the Latinoamericana. It was all right, he was safe now, he could even see the funny side of it – the irony of getting nothing out of the burgled house but an old iron tap.

At the desk he asked for his key. The reception clerk said Jeremy hadn't handed it in, so Jeremy felt in his pockets but it wasn't there. He had a hollow feeling first that he had had the key and his pocket had been picked, then that someone must have come into the hotel while he was out and taken the key from the pigeon-hole. It could very easily be done by reaching across the end of the counter while the clerk had his back turned or was attending to another guest.

The clerk found a second key to his room and sent the wizened old bellboy up with him. The door was locked. The bellboy bent over and picked something up from the floor, something that had been half-hidden by the bottom of the door.

'Here is your key, señor.'

Jeremy was beginning to hate the sight of keys. He sent the man away. Was it possible he had dropped the key there himself? As soon as he was inside he knew there was no question of that. The room had been turned upside down. What he had planned to do, he thought,

they had done to him. He sat down in the wicker chair and surveyed
the mess. His bedding was in a heap, the mattress doubled over and
half on the floor. All the drawers in the dressing table-cum-writing
desk had been pulled out. He hadn't brought much luggage with him,
a zipper bag only, but they had taken everything out of it and strewn
the contents, spare pair of jeans, sweat shirt, sponge bag, half-bottle
of duty-free Kahlua, across the floor. But nothing had been damaged
or destroyed. There was nothing missing – or was there?

An empty envelope lay half under the sweat shirt. Jeremy read what
was written on it and remembered. 'Fond thoughts from Lupe.' He
had told her that wasn't the way to write it. You should say 'love
from' or 'best wishes from'. Inside had been a cassette of Latin-
American love songs, awful stuff he'd never even bothered to take out
of the zipper bag he'd had with him that weekend at Hacienda Alameda . . .

And obviously he never had taken it out. He had re-packed the bag
with the cassette – wrapped in red tissue paper, he recalled, sealed in
this envelope – still inside. Well, if it was that tape they wanted they
were welcome to it. But why should they want it? Jeremy hauled the
mattress back on to the bed. He felt horribly uneasy, his hands shook
and a muscle twitched in his forehead. He could have done with a
drink but the bar closed at ten and it was past that. He pulled the
stopper off the Kahlua bottle and then thought: suppose they put
something in it?

Had the whole exercise been mounted simply to get back a tape
Lupe had given him? No, of course not. It wasn't being done because
he'd stolen the $320 either, he saw that now. It was because he'd stolen
Lupe. Manuel had probably *meant* him to steal the money, had indeed
set it up. It wasn't normal for a man, however well off, to be quite
so careless with cash as that or so indifferent to its loss . . .

Jeremy was too frightened now not to drink the Kahlua. It enabled
him to get some sleep. First, though, he pulled the heavy writing desk
across the door. A sound he thought came from in the room awakened
him and he jumped up with a cry, but it wasn't in the room, it was
outside in the corridor, the people next door coming in late. A Kahlua
hangover began to bash his head. He had no aspirin and dared not
leave the room to go and ask for some.

Thank God he was going back to Miami today. He didn't leave the
hotel. He breakfasted in the dining room, despite the cost, and sat for
the rest of the morning on the leather settee facing reception and reading
one of the few books in English the Latinoamericana had, a James M.

Cain paperback. Nothing untoward happened. He jumped out of his skin when a voice uttered his name into his ear. It was only Carmen, the tour guide.

'The bus for the international airport is going thirteen hundred hours. Have a nice day!'

Could he go back and work for Manuel again? The chances were Manuel wouldn't say a word, would want bygones to be bygones, in his own phrase. Jeremy thought he'd work for him just long enough to get the fare together for California . . . It was a long three hours before the bus came. He'd finished *The Postman Always Rings Twice* and was reduced to reading travel brochures. He didn't bother with lunch. It was only something else that cost money.

Nobody drummed feet or clapped when the aircraft began its descent for Miami. But Jeremy felt a lightening of his heart. For one thing, Immigration would doubtless allow him a further six months' stay in the United States. His last six months' allowance had long since expired but he'd torn the slip out of his passport and would say it had fallen out and got lost. That was a trick he'd used successfully coming over the border from Mexico once before. Feeling you were legal even for a little while gave you a sense of security.

He walked into Customs. They tended to search young people coming in after a short stay in Central or South America. Josh had told him. So he wasn't concerned when the Customs man took everything out of the zipper bag and only mildly surprised at the close examination his sponge bag was subjected to.

There was a split in the bottom seam. The Customs man put his fingers through, then his whole hand, and drew out from between cover and lining a package wrapped in red tissue paper. The red tissue, which he'd last seen round Lupe's cassette, unfolded to reveal its contents, a fine white crystalline powder.

Jeremy had never seen it before but he knew what it was. He thought briefly of the annual new car, of Hacienda Alameda, and then he thought of himself and how he need not worry about his stay in the United States being curtailed. He would be there a long time.

# The Convolvulus Clock

'Is that your own hair, dear?'

Sibyl only laughed. She made a roguish face.

'I didn't think it could be,' said Trixie. 'It looks so thick.'

'A woman came up to me in the street the other day,' said Sibyl, 'and asked me where I had my hair set. I just looked at her. I gave a tiny little tip to my wig like this. You should have seen her face.'

She gave another roar of laughter. Trixie smiled austerely. She had come to stay with Sibyl for a week and this was her first evening. Sibyl had bought a cottage in Devonshire. It was two years since Trixie had seen Sibyl and she could detect signs of deterioration. What a pity that was! Sibyl enquired after the welfare of the friends they had in common. How was Mivvy? Did Trixie see anything of the Fishers? How was Poppy?

'Poppy is beginning to go a bit funny,' said Trixie.

'How do you mean, "funny"?'

'You know. Funny. Not quite *compos mentis* any more.'

Sibyl of all people ought to know what going funny meant, thought Trixie.

'We're none of us getting any younger,' said Sibyl, laughing.

Trixie didn't sleep very well. She got up at five and had her bath so as to leave the bathroom clear for Sibyl. At seven she took Sibyl a cup of tea. She gave a little scream and nearly dropped the tray.

'Oh my conscience! I'm sorry, dear, but I thought that was a squirrel on your chest of drawers. I thought it must have come in through the window.'

'What on earth was that noise in the middle of the night?' When Sibyl wasn't laughing she could be downright peevish. She looked a hundred without her wig. 'It woke me up, I thought the tank was overflowing.'

'The middle of the night! I like that. The sun had been up a good hour, I'm sure. I was just having my bath so as not to be a nuisance.'

They went out in Sibyl's car. They had lunch in Dawlish and tea in

Exmouth. The following day they went out early and drove across Dartmoor. When they got back there was a letter on the mat for Trixie from Mivvy, though Trixie had only been away two days. On Friday Sibyl said they would stay at home and have a potter about the village. The church was famous, the Manor House gardens were open to the public and there was an interesting small gallery where an exhibition was on. She started to get the car out but Trixie said why couldn't they walk. It could hardly be more than a mile. Sibyl said it was just under two miles but she agreed to walk if Trixie really wanted to. Her knee hadn't been troubling her quite so much lately.

'The gallery is called Artifacts,' said Sibyl. 'It's run by a very nice young couple.'

'A husband and wife team?' asked Trixie, very modern.

'Jimmy and Judy they're called. I don't think they are actually married.'

'Oh my conscience, Sibyl, how can one be "actually" married? Surely one is either married or not?' Trixie herself had been married once, long ago, for a short time. Sibyl had never been married and neither had Mivvy or Poppy. Trixie thought that might have something to do with their going funny. 'Thankfully, I'm broad-minded. I shan't say anything. I think I can see a seat ahead in that bus shelter. Would you like a little sit-down before we go on?'

Sibyl got her breath back and they walked on more slowly. The road passed between high hedges on high banks dense with wild flowers. It crossed a stream by a hump-backed bridge where the clear brown shallow water rippled over a bed of stones. The church appeared with granite nave and tower, standing on an eminence and approached, Sibyl said, by fifty-three steps. Perhaps they should go to Artifacts first?

The gallery was housed in an ancient building with bow windows and a front door set under a Georgian portico. When the door was pushed open a bell tinkled to summon Jimmy or Judy. This morning, however, they needed no summoning for both were in the first room, Judy dusting the dolls' house and Jimmy doing something to the ceiling spotlights. Sibyl introduced Trixie to them and Trixie was very gracious towards Judy, making no difference in her manner than she would have if the young woman had been properly married and worn a wedding ring.

Trixie was agreeably surprised by the objects in the exhibition and by the items Jimmy and Judy had for sale. She had not expected such a high standard. What she admired most particularly were the small pictures of domestic interiors done in embroidery, the patchwork quilts and the blown glass vases in colours of mother-of-pearl and butterfly wings. What she liked best of all and wanted to have was a clock.

There were four of these clocks, all different. The cases were ceramic, plain and smooth or made in a trellis work, glazed in blues and greens, painted with flowers or the moon and stars, each incorporating a gilt-rimmed face and quartz movement. Trixie's favourite was blue with a green trellis over the blue, a convolvulus plant with green leaves and pale pink trumpet flowers climbing the trellis and a gilt rim round the face of the clock which had hands of gilt and blue. The convolvulus reminded her of the pattern on her best china tea service. All the clocks had price cards beside them and red discs stuck to the cards.

'I should like to buy this clock,' Trixie said to Judy.

'I'm terribly sorry but it's sold.'

'Sold?'

'All the clocks were sold at the private view. Roland Elm's work is tremendously popular. He can't make enough of these clocks and he refuses to take orders.'

'I still don't understand why I can't buy this one,' said Trixie. 'This is a shop, isn't it?'

Sibyl had put on her peevish look. 'You can see the red sticker, can't you? You know what that means.'

'I know what it means at the Royal Academy but hardly here surely.'

'I really do wish I could sell it to you,' said Judy, 'but I can't.'

Trixie lifted her shoulders. She was very disappointed and wished she hadn't come. She had been going to buy Sibyl a pear carved from polished pear wood but now she thought better of it. The church also was a let-down, dark, poky and smelling of mould.

'Things have come to a pretty pass when shopkeepers won't sell their goods to you because they're upset by your manner.'

'Judy wasn't upset by your manner,' said Sibyl, puffing. 'It's more than her reputation is worth to sell you something she's already sold.'

'Reputation! I like that.'

'I mean reputation as a gallery owner. Artifacts is quite highly regarded round here.'

'You would have thought she and her – well, partner, would be glad of £62. I don't suppose they have two half-pennies to bless themselves with.'

What Sibyl would have thought was never known for she was too out of breath to utter and when they got home had to lie down. Next morning another letter came from Mivvy.

'Nothing to say for herself of course,' said Trixie at breakfast. 'Practically a carbon copy of Thursday's. She's going very funny. Do you know she told me sometimes she writes fifty letters in a week? God bless your pocket, I said. It's fortunate you can afford it.'

They went to Princetown in Sibyl's car and Widecombe-in-the Moor. Trixie sent postcards to Mivvy, Poppy, the Fishers and the woman who came in to clean and water the plants in the greenhouse. She would have to buy some sort of present for Sibyl before she left. A plant would have done, only Sibyl didn't like gardening. They went to a bird sanctuary and looked at some standing stones of great antiquity. Trixie was going home on Tuesday afternoon. On Tuesday morning another letter arrived from Mivvy all about the Fishers going to see the Queen Mother open a new arts centre in Leighton Buzzard. The Fishers were crazy about the Queen Mother, watched for her engagements in advance and went wherever she went within a radius of 150 miles in order just to catch a glimpse of her. Once they had been at the front of the crowd and the Queen Mother had shaken hands with Dorothy Fisher.

'We're none of us getting any younger,' said Sibyl, giggling.

'Well, my conscience, I know one thing,' said Trixie. 'The days have simply flown past while I've been here.'

'I'm glad you've enjoyed yourself.'

'Oh, I have, dear, only it would please me to see you a little less frail.'

Trixie walked to the village on her own. Since she couldn't think of anything else she was going to have to buy the pear-wood pear for Sibyl. It was a warm sunny morning, one of the best days she'd had, and the front door of Artifacts stood open to the street. The exhibition was still on and the clocks (and their red 'sold' discs) still there. A shaft of sunlight streamed across the patchwork quilts on to the Georgian dolls' house. There was no sign of Jimmy and Judy. The gallery was empty but for herself.

Trixie closed the door and opened it to make the bell ring. She picked up one of the pear-wood pears and held it out in front of her on the palm of her hand. She held it at arm's length the way she did when she had helped herself to an item in the supermarket just so that there couldn't be the slightest question of anyone suspecting her of shop-lifting. No one came. Trixie climbed the stairs, holding the pear-wood pear out in front of her and clearing her throat to attract attention. There was no one upstairs. A blue Persian cat lay sleeping on a shelf between a ginger jar and a mug with an owl on it. Trixie descended.

She closed the front door and opened it to make the bell ring. Jimmy and Judy must be a heedless pair, she thought. Anyone could walk in here and steal the lot.

Of course she could just take the pear-wood pear and leave a £5 note to pay for it. It cost £4.75. Why should she make Jimmy and Judy a present of 25p just because they were too idle to serve her? Then she remembered that when she had been here with Sibyl a door at the end of the passage had been open and through that door one could see the garden where there was a display of terracotta pots. It was probable Jimmy and Judy were out there, showing the pots to a customer.

Trixie went through the second room and down the passage. The door to the garden was just ajar and she pushed it open. On the lawn, in a cane chair, Judy lay fast asleep. A ledger had fallen off her lap and lay on the grass alongside a heap of books. Guides to the management of tax they were and some which looked like the gallery account books. It reminded Trixie of Poppy who was always falling asleep in the daytime, most embarrassingly sometimes, at the table or even while waiting for a bus. Judy had fallen asleep over her book-keeping. Trixie coughed. She said 'Excuse me' very loudly and repeated it but Judy didn't stir.

What a way to run a business! It would serve them right if someone walked in and cleared their shop. It would teach them a lesson. Trixie pulled the door closed behind her. She found herself tiptoeing as she walked back along the passage and through the second room. In the first room she took the ceramic clock with the convolvulus on it off the shelf and put it into her bag and she took the card too with the red sticker on it so as not to attract attention to the clock's absence. The pear-wood pear she replaced among the other carved fruit.

The street outside seemed deserted. Trixie's heart was beating rather fast. She went across the road into the little newsagent's and gift shop and bought Sibyl a teacloth with a map of Devonshire on it. At the door, as she was coming out again, she saw Jimmy coming along the street towards the gallery with a bag of groceries under one arm and two pints of milk in the other. Trixie stayed where she was until he had gone into Artifacts.

She didn't much fancy the walk back but there was no help for it. When she got to the bridge over the stream she heard hooves behind her and for a second or two had a feeling she was pursued by men on horseback but it was only a girl who passed her, riding a fat white pony. Sibyl laughed when she saw the teacloth and said it was a funny thing to give someone who *lived* in Devonshire. Trixie felt nervous and couldn't eat her lunch. Jimmy and Judy would have missed the clock by now and the newsagent would have remembered a furtive-looking woman skulking in his doorway and described her to them and soon the police would come. If only Sibyl would hurry with the car! She moved so slowly, time had no meaning for her. At this rate Trixie wouldn't even catch her train at Exeter.

She did catch it – just. Sibyl's car had been followed for several miles of the way by police in a Rover with a blue lamp on top and Trixie's heart had been in her mouth. Why had she done it? What had possessed her to take something she hadn't paid for, she who when shopping in supermarkets held 17p pots of yogurt at arm's length?

Now she was safely in the train rushing towards Paddington she began to see things in a different light. She would have paid for that clock if they had let her. What did they expect if they refused to sell things they had on sale? And what *could* they expect if they went to sleep leaving their shop unattended? For a few moments she had a nasty little qualm that the police might be waiting for her outside her own door but they weren't. Inside all was as it should be, all was as she had left it except that Poppy had put a pint of milk in the fridge and someone had arranged dahlias in a vase – not Poppy, she wouldn't know a dahlia from a runner bean.

That would be just the place for the clock, on the wall bracket where at present stood a photograph of herself and Dorothy Fisher at Broadstairs in 1949. Trixie put the photograph away in a drawer and the clock where the photograph had been. It looked nice. It transformed a rather dull corner of the room. Trixie put one of the cups from her tea service beside it and it was amazing how well they matched.

Mivvy came round first thing in the morning. Before letting her in Trixie quickly snatched the clock off the shelf and thrust it inside the drawer with the photograph. It seemed so *exposed* up there, it seemed to tell its history in every tiny tick.

'How did you find Sibyl?'

Trixie wanted to say, I went in the train to Exeter and got out at the station and there was Sibyl waiting for me in her car . . . Only if you started mocking poor Mivvy where would you end? 'Very frail, dear. I thought she was going a bit funny.'

'I must drop her a line.'

Mivvy always spoke as if her letters held curative properties. Receiving one of them would set you up for the winter. After she had gone Trixie considered replacing the clock on the shelf but thought better of it. Let it stay in the drawer for a bit. She had read of South American millionaires who have Old Masters stolen for them which they can never show but are obliged, for fear of discovery, to keep hidden away for ever in dark vaults.

Just before Christmas a letter came from Sibyl. They always sent each other Christmas letters. As Trixie said, if you can't get around to writing the rest of the year, at least you can at Christmas. Mivvy wrote hundreds. Sibyl didn't mention the theft of the clock or indeed mention the gallery at all. Trixie wondered why not. The clock was still in the drawer. Sometimes she lay awake in the night thinking about it, fancying she could hear its tick through the solid mahogany of the drawer, through the ceiling and the bedroom floorboards.

It was curious how she had taken a dislike to the convolvulus tea service. One day she found herself wrapping it in tissue paper and putting it away in the cupboard under the stairs. She took down all the trellis work round the front door and put up wires for the clematis instead. In March she wrote to Sibyl to enquire if there was a new exhibition on at Artifacts. Sibyl didn't answer for weeks. When she did she told Trixie that months and months back one of those ceramic clocks had been stolen from the gallery and a few days later an embroidered picture had also gone and furniture out of the dolls' house. Hadn't Sibyl mentioned it before? She thought she had but she was getting so forgetful these days.

Trixie took the clock out of the drawer and put it on the shelf. Because she knew she couldn't be found out she began to feel she hadn't done anything wrong. The Fishers were bringing Poppy round for a cup of tea. Trixie started unpacking the convolvulus tea service. She lost her nerve when she heard Gordon Fisher's car door slam and she put the clock away again. If she were caught now she might get blamed for the theft of the picture and the dolls' house furniture as well. They would say she had sold those things and how could she prove she hadn't?

Poppy fell asleep halfway through her second buttered scone.

'She gets funnier every time I see her,' Trixie said. 'Sad, really. Sibyl's breaking up too. She'll forget her own name next. You should see her letters. I'll just show you the last one.' She remembered she couldn't do that, it wouldn't be wise, so she had to pretend she'd mislaid it.

'Will you be going down there again this year, dear?' said Dorothy.

'Oh, I expect so. You know how it is, you get to the stage of thinking it may be the last time.'

Poppy woke up with a snort, said she hadn't been asleep and finished her scone.

Gordon asked Trixie, 'Would you like to come with us and see Her Majesty open the new leisure complex in Rayleigh on Monday?'

Trixie declined. The Fishers went off to do their shopping, leaving Poppy behind. She was asleep again. She slept till six and, waking, asked Trixie if she had put something in her tea. It was most unusual, she said, for her to nod off like that. Trixie walked her back to the bus stop because the traffic whipped along there so fast you had to have your wits about you and drivers didn't respect zebra crossings the way they used to. Trixie marched across on the stripes, confident as a lollipop lady but without the lollipop, taking her life in her hands instead.

She wrote to Sibyl that she would come to Devonshire at the end of July, thinking that while there it might be best to make some excuse to avoid going near Artifacts. The clock was still in the drawer but wrapped up now in a piece of old flannel. Trixie had taken a dislike to seeing the colour of it each time she opened the drawer. She had a summer dress that colour and she wondered why she had ever bought it, it didn't flatter her, whatever it might do for the Queen Mother. Dorothy could have it for her next jumble sale.

Walking back from posting a letter, Mivvy fell over and broke her ankle. It was weeks getting back to normal. Well, you had to face it, it was never going to be *normal*. You wouldn't be exaggerating, Trixie wrote to Sibyl, if you said that obsession of hers for writing letters had crippled her for life. Sibyl wrote back to say she was looking forward to the last week of July and what did Trixie think had happened? They had caught the thief of the pieces from Artifacts trying to sell the picture to a dealer in Plymouth. He had said in court he hadn't taken the clock but you could imagine how much credence the magistrate placed on that!

Trixie unwrapped the clock and put it on the shelf. Next day she got the china out. She wondered why she had been so precipitate in pulling all that trellis off the wall, it looked a lot better than strands of wire on metal hooks. Mivvy came round in a taxi, hobbling up the path on two sticks, refusing the offer of the taxi driver's arm.

'You'll be off to Sibyl's in a day or two, will you, dear?'

Trixie didn't know how many times she had told her not till Monday week. She was waiting for Mivvy to notice the clock but at this rate she was going to have to wait till Christmas.

'What do you think of my clock?'

'What, up there? Isn't that your Wedgwood coffee pot, dear?'

Trixie had to get it down. She thrust it under Mivvy's nose and started explaining what it was.

But Mivvy knew already. 'Of course I know it's a clock, dear. It's not the first time I've seen one of these. Oh my goodness, no. The young man who makes these, he's a friend of my nephew Tony, they were at art school together. Let me see, what's his name? It will come to me in a minute. A tree, isn't it? Oak? Ash? Peter Oak? No, Elm is his name. Something Elm. Roland Elm.'

Trixie said nothing. The glazed surface of the clock felt very cold against the skin of her hands.

'He never makes them to order, you know. He just makes a limited number for a few selected galleries. Tony told me that. Where did you get yours, I wonder?'

Trixie said nothing. There was worse coming and she waited for it.

'Not around here, I'm sure. I know there are only two or three places in the country they go to. It will come to me in a minute. I shall be writing to Tony tomorrow and I'll mention about you having one of Richard's – no, I mean Raymond's that is, Roland's clocks. I always write to him on Tuesdays. Tuesday is his day. I'll mention you've got one with bindweed on it. They're all different, you know. He never makes two alike.'

'It's convolvulus, not bindweed,' said Trixie. 'I'd rather you didn't write to Tony about it if you don't mind.'

'Oh, but I'd like to mention it, dear. Why ever not? I won't mention your name if you don't want me to. I'll just say that lady who goes down to stay with Auntie Sibyl in Devonshire.'

Trixie said she would walk with Mivvy up to the High Street. It was hopeless trying to get a taxi outside here. She fetched Mivvy's two sticks.

'You take my arm and I'll hold your other stick.'

The traffic whipped along over the zebra crossing. You were at the mercy of those drivers, Trixie said, it was a matter of waiting till they condescended to stop.

'Don't you set foot on those stripes till they stop,' she said to Mivvy.

Mivvy didn't, so the cars didn't stop. A container lorry, a juggernaut, came thundering along, but a good way off still. Trixie thought it was going much too fast.

'Now if we're quick,' she said. 'Run for it!'

Startled by the urgency in her voice, Mivvy obeyed, or tried to obey as Trixie dropped her arm and gave her a little push forward. The lorry's brakes screamed like people being tortured and Trixie jumped back, screaming herself, covering her face with her hands so as not to see Mivvy under those giant wheels.

Dorothy Fisher said she quite understood Trixie would still want to go to Sibyl's for her holiday. It was the best thing in the world for her, a rest, a complete change, a chance to forget. Trixie went down by train on the day after the funeral. She had the clock in her bag with her, wrapped first in tissue paper and then in her sky-blue dress. The first opportunity that offered itself she would take the clock back to Artifacts and replace it on the shelf she had taken it from. This shouldn't be too difficult. The clock was a dangerous possession, she could see that, like one of those notorious diamonds that carry a curse with them. Pretty though it was, it was an *unlucky* clock that had involved her in trouble from the time she had first taken it.

There was no question of walking to Artifacts this time. Sibyl was too frail for that. She had gone downhill a lot since last year and symptomatic of her deterioration was her exchange of the grey wig for a lilac-blue one. They went in the car though Trixie was by no means sure Sibyl was safe at the wheel.

As soon as they walked into the gallery Trixie saw that she had no hope of replacing the clock without being spotted. There was a desk in the first room now with a plump smiling lady sitting at it who Sibyl said was Judy's mother. Trixie thought that amazing – a mother not minding her daughter cohabiting with a man she wasn't married to. Living with a daughter living in sin, you might put it. Jimmy was in the second room, up on a ladder doing something to the window catch.

'They're having upstairs remodelled,' said Sibyl. 'You can't go up there.' And when Trixie tried to make her way towards the garden door, 'You don't want to be had up for trespassing, do you?' She winked at Judy's mother. 'We're none of us getting any younger when all's said and done, are we?'

They went back to Sibyl's, the clock still in Trixie's bag. It seemed to have grown heavier. She could hear it ticking through the leather and the folds of the sky-blue dress. In the afternoon when Sibyl lay down on the sofa for her rest, the lilac wig stuck on top of a Poole pottery vase, Trixie went out for a walk, taking the clock with her. She came to the hump-backed bridge over the stream where the water was very low, for it had been a dry summer. She unwrapped the clock and dropped it over the low parapet into the water. It cracked but the trellis work and the convolvulus remained intact and the movement continued to move and to tick as well for all Trixie knew. The blue and green, the pink flowers and the gilt, gleamed through the water like some exotic iridescent shell.

Trixie went down the bank. She took off her shoes and waded into the water. It was surprisingly cold. She picked up a large flat stone and beat at the face of the clock with it. She beat with unrestrained fury, gasping and grunting at each blow. The green trellis and the blue sky, the glass face and the pink flowers, all shattered. But they were still there, bright jewel-like shards, for all to see who came this way across the bridge.

Squatting down, Trixie scooped up handfuls of pebbles and buried the pieces of clock under them. With her nails she dug a pit in the bed of the stream and pushed the coloured fragments into it, covering them with pebbles. Her hands were bleeding, her knees were bruised and her dress was wet. In spite of her efforts the bed of the stream was still spread with ceramic chips and broken glass and pieces of gilt metal. Trixie began to sob and crawl from side to side of the stream, ploughing her hands through the blue and green and gold gravel, and it was there that one of Sibyl's neighbours found her as he was driving home over the bridge.

He lifted her up and carried her to his car.

'Tick-tock,' said Trixie. 'Tick-tock. Convolvulus clock.'

# Loopy

At the end of the last performance, after the curtain calls, Red Riding Hood put me on a lead and with the rest of the company we went across to the pub. No one had taken make-up off or changed, there was no time for that before. The George closed. I remember prancing across the road and growling at someone on a bicycle. They loved me in the pub – well, some of them loved me. Quite a lot were embarrassed. The funny thing was that I should have been embarrassed myself if I had been one of them. I should have ignored *me* and drunk up my drink and left. Except that it is unlikely I would have been in a pub at all. Normally, I never went near such places. But inside the wolf skin it was very different, everything was different in there.

I prowled about for a while, sometimes on all fours, though this is not easy for us who are accustomed to the upright stance, sometimes loping, with my forepaws held close up to my chest. I went up to tables where people were sitting and snuffled my snout at their packets of crisps. If they were smoking I growled and waved my paws in air-clearing gestures. Lots of them were forthcoming, stroking me and making jokes or pretending terror at my red jaws and wicked little eyes. There was even one lady who took hold of my head and laid it in her lap.

Bounding up to the bar to collect my small dry sherry, I heard Bill Harkness (the First Woodcutter) say to Susan Hayes (Red Riding Hood's Mother):

'Old Colin's really come out of his shell tonight.'

And Susan, bless her, said, 'He's a real actor, isn't he?'

I was one of the few members of our company who was. I expect this is always true in amateur dramatics. There are one or two real actors, people who could have made their livings on the stage if it was not so overcrowded a profession, and the rest who just come for the fun of it and the social side. Did I ever consider the stage seriously? My father had been a civil servant, both my grandfathers in the ICS.

As far back as I can remember it was taken for granted I should get my degree and go into the civil service. I never questioned it. If you have a mother like mine, one in a million, more a friend than a parent, you never feel the need to rebel. Besides, Mother gave me all the support I could have wished for in my acting. Acting as a hobby, that is. For instance, though the company made provision for hiring all the more complicated costumes for that year's Christmas pantomime, Mother made the wolf suit for me herself. It was ten times better than anything we could have hired. The head we had to buy but the body and the limbs she made from a long-haired grey fur fabric such as is manufactured for ladies' coats.

Moira used to say I enjoyed acting so much because it enabled me to lose myself and become, for a while, someone else. She said I disliked what I was and looked for ways of escape. A strange way to talk to the man you intend to marry! But before I approach the subject of Moira or, indeed, continue with this account, I should explain what its purpose is. The psychiatrist attached to this place or who visits it (I am not entirely clear which), one Dr Vernon-Peak, has asked me to write down some of my feelings and impressions. That, I said, would only be possible in the context of a narrative. Very well, he said, he had no objection. What will become of it when finished I hardly know. Will it constitute a statement to be used in court? Or will it enter Dr Vernon-Peak's files as another 'case history'? It is all the same to me. I can only tell the truth.

After The George closed, then, we took off our make-up and changed and went our several ways home. Mother was waiting up for me. This was not invariably her habit. If I told her I should be late and to go to bed at her usual time she always did so. But I, quite naturally, was not averse to a welcome when I got home, particularly after a triumph like that one. Besides, I had been looking forward to telling her what an amusing time I had had in the pub.

Our house is late Victorian, double-fronted, of grey limestone, by no means beautiful, but a comfortable well-built place. My grandfather bought it when he retired and came home from India in 1920. Mother was ten at the time, so she has spent most of her life in that house.

Grandfather was quite a famous shot and used to go big game hunting before that kind of thing became, and rightly so, very much frowned upon. The result was that the place was full of 'trophies of the chase'. While Grandfather was alive, and he lived to a great age, we had no choice but to put up with the antlers and tusks that sprouted everywhere out of the walls, the elephant's foot umbrella stand, and the snarling maws of *tigris* and *ursa*. We had to grin and bear it, as Mother, who has a fine turn of wit, used to put it. But when Grandfather was at last gathered to his ancestors, reverently and without the least disrespect to him, we took down all those heads and horns and packed them away in trunks. The fur rugs, however, we did not disturb. These days they are worth a fortune and I always felt that the tiger skins scattered across the hall parquet, the snow leopard draped across the back of the sofa and the bear into whose fur one could bury one's toes before the fire, gave to the place a luxurious look. I took off my shoes, I remember, and snuggled my toes in it that night.

Mother, of course, had been to see the show. She had come on the first night and seen me make my onslaught on Red Riding Hood, an attack so sudden and unexpected that the whole audience had jumped to its feet and gasped. (In our version we did not have the wolf actually devour Red Riding Hood. Unanimously, we agreed this would hardly have been the thing at Christmas.) Mother, however, wanted to see me wearing her creation once more, so I put it on and did some prancing and growling for her benefit. Again I noticed how curiously uninhibited I became once inside the wolf skin. For instance, I bounded up to the snow leopard and began snarling at it. I boxed at its great grey-white face and made playful bites at its ears. Down on all fours I went and pounced on the bear, fighting it, actually forcing its neck within the space of my jaws.

How Mother laughed! She said it was as good as anything in the panto and a good deal better than anything they put on television.

'Animal crackers in my soup,' she said, wiping her eyes. 'There used to be a song that went like that in my youth. How did it go on? Something about lions and tigers loop the loop.'

'Well, *lupus* means a wolf in Latin,' I said.

'And you're certainly loopy! When you put that suit on I shall have to say you're going all loopy again!'

When I put that suit on again. Did I intend to put it on again? I had not really thought about it. Yes, perhaps if I ever went to a fancy-dress party, a remote enough contingency. Yet what a shame it seemed to waste it, to pack it away like Grandfather's tusks and antlers, after all the labour Mother had put into it. That night I hung it up in my wardrobe and I remember how strange I felt when I took it off that second time, more naked than I usually felt without my clothes, almost as if I had taken off my skin.

Life kept to the 'even tenor' of its way. I felt a little flat with no rehearsals to attend and no lines to learn. Christmas came. Traditionally,

Mother and I were alone on the Day itself, we would not have had it any other way, but on Boxing Day Moira arrived and Mother invited a couple of neighbours of ours as well. At some stage, I seem to recall, Susan Hayes dropped in with her husband to wish us the 'compliments of the season'.

Moira and I had been engaged for three years. We would have got married some time before, there was no question of our not being able to afford to marry, but a difficulty had arisen over where we should live. I think I may say in all fairness that the difficulty was entirely of Moira's making. No mother could have been more welcoming to a future daughter-in-law than mine. She actually wanted us to live with her at Simla House, she said we must think of it as our home and of her simply as our housekeeper. But Moira wanted us to buy a place of our own, so we had reached a deadlock, an impasse.

It was unfortunate that on that Boxing Day, after the others had gone, Moira brought the subject up again. Her brother (an estate agent) had told her of a bungalow for sale halfway between Simla House and her parents' home and it was what he called 'a real snip'. Fortunately, *I* thought, Mother managed to turn the conversation by telling us about the bungalow she and her parents had lived in in India, with its great colonnaded veranda, its English flower garden and its peepul tree. But Moira interrupted her.

'This is *our* future we're talking about, not your past. I thought Colin and I were getting married.'

Mother was quite alarmed. 'Aren't you? Surely Colin hasn't broken things off?'

'I suppose you don't consider the possibility *I* might break things off?'

Poor Mother could not help smiling at that. She smiled to cover her hurt. Moira could upset her very easily. For some reason this made Moira angry.

'I'm too old and unattractive to have any choice in the matter, is that what you mean?'

'Moira,' I said.

She took no notice. 'You may not realize it,' she said, 'but marrying me will be the making of Colin. It's what he needs to make a man of him.'

It must have slipped out before Mother quite knew what she was saying. She patted Moira's knee. 'I can quite see it may be a tough assignment, dear.'

There was no quarrel. Mother would never have allowed herself to be drawn into that. But Moira became very huffy and said she wanted to go home, so I had to get the car out and take her. All the way to her parents' house I had to listen to a catalogue of her wrongs at my hands and my mother's. By the time we parted I felt dispirited and nervous, I even wondered if I was doing the right thing, contemplating matrimony in the 'sere and yellow leaf' of forty-two.

Mother had cleared the things away and gone to bed. I went into my bedroom and began undressing. Opening the wardrobe to hang up my tweed trousers, I caught sight of the wolf suit and on some impulse I put it on.

Once inside the wolf I felt calmer and, yes, happier. I sat down in an armchair but after a while I found it more comfortable to crouch, then lie stretched out, on the floor. Lying there, basking in the warmth from the gas fire on my belly and paws, I found myself remembering tales of man's affinity with wolves, Romulus and Remus suckled by a she-wolf, the ancient myth of the werewolf, abandoned children reared by wolves even in these modern times. All this seemed to deflect my mind from the discord between Moira and my mother and I was able to go to bed reasonably happily and to sleep well.

Perhaps, then, it will not seem so very strange and wonderful that the next time I felt depressed I put the suit on again. Mother was out, so I was able to have the freedom of the whole house, not just of my room. It was dusk at four but instead of putting the lights on, I prowled about the house in the twilight, sometimes catching sight of my lean grey form in the many large mirrors Mother is so fond of. Because there was so little light and our house is crammed with bulky furniture and knick-knacks, the reflection I saw looked not like a man disguised but like a real wolf that has somehow escaped and strayed into a cluttered Victorian room. Or a werewolf, that animal part of man's personality that detaches itself and wanders free while leaving behind the depleted human shape.

I crept up upon the teakwood carving of the antelope and devoured the little creature before it knew what had attacked it. I resumed my battle with the bear and we struggled in front of the fireplace, locked in a desperate hairy embrace. It was then that I heard Mother let herself in at the back door. Time had passed more quickly than I had thought. I had escaped and whisked my hind paws and tail round the bend in the stairs just before she came into the hall.

Dr Vernon-Peak seems to want to know why I began this at the age of forty-two, or rather, why I had not done it before. I wish I knew. Of course there is the simple solution that I did not have a wolf skin before, but that is not the whole answer. Was it perhaps that until then I did not know what my needs were, though partially I had satisfied them by playing the parts I was given in dramatic productions? There is one other thing. I have told him that I recall, as a very young child, having a close relationship with some large animal, a dog perhaps or a pony, though a search conducted into family history by this same assiduous Vernon-Peak has yielded no evidence that we ever kept a pet. But more of this anon.

Be that as it may, once I had lived inside the wolf, I felt the need to do so more and more. Erect on my hind legs, drawn up to my full height, I do not think I flatter myself unduly when I say I made a fine handsome animal. And having written that, I realize that I have not yet described the wolf suit, taking for granted, I suppose, that those who see this document will also see it. Yet this may not be the case. They have refused to let *me* see it, which makes me wonder if it has been cleaned and made presentable again or if it is still – but, no, there is no point in going into unsavoury details.

I have said that the body and limbs of the suit were made of long-haired grey fur fabric. The stuff of it was coarse, hardly an attractive material for a coat, I should have thought, but very closely similar to a wolf's pelt. Mother made the paws after the fashion of fur gloves but with the padded and stiffened fingers of a pair of leather gloves for the claws. The head we bought from a jokes and games shop. It had tall prick ears, small yellow eyes and a wonderful, half-open mouth, red, voracious-looking and with a double row of white fangs. The opening for me to breathe through was just beneath the lower jaw where the head joined the powerful grey hairy throat.

As the spring came I would sometimes drive out into the countryside, park the car and slip into the skin. It was far from my ambition to be seen by anyone, though. I sought solitude. Whether I should have cared for a 'beastly' companion, that is something else again. At that time I wanted merely to wander in the woods and copses or along a hedgerow in my wolf's persona. And this I did, choosing unfrequented places, avoiding anywhere that I might come in contact with the human race. I am trying, in writing this, to explain how I felt. Principally, I felt *not human*. And to be not human is to be without human responsibilities and human cares. Inside the wolf, I laid aside with my humanity my apprehensiveness about getting married, my apprehensiveness about *not* getting married, my fear of leaving Mother on her own, my justifiable resentment at not getting the leading part in our new production. All this got left behind with the depleted sleeping man I left behind to become a happy mindless wild creature.

Our wedding had once again been postponed. The purchase of the house Moira and I had finally agreed upon fell through at the last moment. I cannot say I was altogether sorry. It was near enough to my home, in the same street in fact as Simla House, but I had begun to wonder how I would feel passing our dear old house every day yet knowing it was not under that familiar roof I should lay my head.

Moira was very upset.

Yet, 'I won't live in the same house as your mother even for three months,' she said in answer to my suggestion. 'That's a certain recipe for disaster.'

'Mother and Daddy lived with Mother's parents for twenty years,' I said.

'Yes, and look at the result.' It was then that she made that remark about my enjoying playing parts because I disliked my real self.

There was nothing more to be said except that we must keep on house-hunting.

'We can still go to Malta, I suppose,' Moira said. 'We don't have to cancel that.'

Perhaps, but it would be no honeymoon. Anticipating the delights of matrimony was something I had not done up till then and had no intention of doing. And I was on my guard when Moira – Mother was out at her bridge evening – insisted on going up to my bedroom with me, ostensibly to check on the shade of the suit I had bought to get married in. She said she wanted to buy me a tie. Once there, she reclined on my bed, cajoling me to come and sit beside her.

I suppose it was because I was feeling depressed that I put on the wolf skin. I took off my jacket, but nothing more of course in front of Moira, stepped into the wolf skin, fastened it up and adjusted the head. She watched me. She had seen me in it before when she came to the pantomime.

'Why have you put that on?'

I said nothing. What could I have said? The usual contentment filled me, though, and I found myself obeying her command, loping across to the bed where she was. It seemed to come naturally to fawn on her, to rub my great prick-eared head against her breast, to enclose her hands with my paws. All kinds of fantasies filled my wolfish mind and they were of an intense piercing sweetness. If we had been on our holiday then, I do not think moral resolutions would have held me back.

But unlike the lady in The George, Moira did not take hold of my head and lay it in her lap. She jumped up and shouted at me to stop this nonsense, stop it at once, she hated it. So I did as I was told, of course I did, and got sadly out of the skin and hung it back in the cupboard. I took Moira home. On our way we called in at her brother's and looked at fresh lists of houses.

It was on one of these that we eventually settled after another month or so of picking and choosing and stalling, and we fixed our wedding for the middle of December. During the summer the company had done *Blithe Spirit* (in which I had the meagre part of Dr Bradman, Bill Harkness being Charles Condomine) and the pantomime this year was *Cinderella* with Susan Hayes in the name part and me as the Elder of the Ugly Sisters. I had calculated I should be back from my honeymoon just in time.

No doubt I would have been. No doubt I would have married and gone away on my honeymoon and come back to play my comic part had I not agreed to go shopping with Moira on her birthday. What happened that day changed everything.

It was a Thursday evening. The stores in the West End stay open late on Thursdays. We left our offices at five, met by arrangement and together walked up Bond Street. The last thing I had in view was that we should begin bickering again, though we had seemed to do little else lately. It started with my mentioning our honeymoon. We were outside Asprey's, walking along arm in arm. Since our house would not be ready for us to move into till the middle of January, I suggested we should go back for just two weeks to Simla House. We should be going there for Christmas in any case.

'I thought we'd decided to go to an hotel,' Moira said.

'Don't you think that's rather a waste of money?'

'I think,' she said in a grim sort of tone, 'I think it's money we daren't not spend,' and she drew her arm away from mine.

I asked her what on earth she meant.

'Once get you back there with Mummy and you'll never move.'

I treated that with the contempt it deserved and said nothing. We walked along in silence. Then Moira began talking in a low monotone, using expressions from paperback psychology which I am glad to say I have never heard from Dr Vernon-Peak. We crossed the street and entered Selfridges. Moira was still going on about Oedipus complexes and that nonsense about making a man of me.

'Keep your voice down,' I said. 'Everyone can hear you.'

She shouted at me to shut up, she would say what she pleased. Well, she had repeatedly told me to be a man and to assert myself, so I did just that. I went up to one of the counters, wrote her a cheque for, I must admit, a good deal more than I had originally meant to give her, put it into her hands and walked off, leaving her there.

For a while I felt not displeased with myself but on the way home in the train depression set in. I should have liked to tell Mother about it but Mother would be out, playing bridge. So I had recourse to my other source of comfort, my wolf skin. The phone rang several times while I was gambolling about the rooms but I did not answer it. I knew it was Moira. I was on the floor with Grandfather's stuffed eagle in my paws and my teeth in its neck when Mother walked in.

Bridge had ended early. One of the ladies had been taken ill and rushed to hospital. I had been too intent on my task to see the light come on or hear the door. She stood there in her old fur coat, looking at me. I let the eagle fall, I bowed my head, I wanted to die I was so ashamed and embarrassed. How little I really knew my mother! My dear faithful companion, my only friend! Might I not say, my other self?

She smiled. I could hardly believe it but she was smiling. It was that wonderful, conspiratorial, rather naughty smile of hers. 'Hallo,' she said. 'Are you going all loopy?'

In a moment she was down on her knees beside me, the fur coat enveloping her, and together we worried at the eagle, engaged in battle with the bear, attacked the antelope. Together we bounded into the hall to pounce upon the sleeping tigers. Mother kept laughing (and growling too) saying, what a relief, what a relief! I think we embraced. Next day when I got home she was waiting for me, transformed and ready. She had made herself an animal suit, she must have worked on it all day, out of the snow leopard skin and a length of white fur fabric. I could see her eyes dancing through the gap in its throat.

'You don't know how I've longed to be an animal again,' she said. 'I used to be animals when you were a baby, I was a dog for a long time and then I was a bear, but your father found out and he didn't like it. I had to stop.'

So that was what I dimly remembered. I said she looked like the Queen of the Beasts.

'Do I, Loopy?' she said.

We had a wonderful weekend, Mother and I. Wolf and leopard, we breakfasted together that morning. Then we played. We played all over the house, sometimes fighting, sometimes dancing, hunting of course, carrying off our prey to the lairs we made for ourselves among the furniture. We went out in the car, drove into the country and there in a wood got into our skins and for many happy hours roamed wild among the trees.

There seemed no reason, during those two days, to become human again at all, but on the Tuesday I had a rehearsal, on the Monday morning I had to go off to work. It was coming down to earth, back to what we call reality, with a nasty bang. Still, it had its amusing side too. A lady in the train trod on my toe and I had growled at her before I remembered and turned it into a cough.

All through that weekend neither of us had bothered to answer the phone. In the office I had no choice and it was there that Moira caught me. Marriage had come to seem remote, something grotesque, something that others did, not me. Animals do not marry. But that was not the sort of thing I could say to Moira. I promised to ring her, I said we must meet before the week was out.

I suppose she did tell me she would come over on the Thursday evening and show me what she had bought with the money I had given her. She knew Mother was always out on Thursdays. I suppose Moira did tell me and I failed to take it in. Nothing was important to me but being animals with Mother, Loopy and the Queen of the Beasts.

Each night as soon as I got home we made ourselves ready for our evening's games. How harmless it all was! How innocent! Like the gentle creatures in the dawn of the world before man came. Like the Garden of Eden after Adam and Eve had been sent away.

The lady who had been taken ill at the bridge evening had since died, so this week it was cancelled. But would Mother have gone anyway? Probably not. Our animal capers meant as much to her as they did to me, almost more perhaps, for she had denied herself so long. We were sitting at the dining table, eating our evening meal. Mother had cooked, I recall, a rack of lamb so that we might later gnaw the bones. We never ate it, of course, and I have since wondered what became of it. But we did begin on our soup. The bread was at my end of the table, with the bread board and the long sharp knife.

Moira, when she called and I was alone, was in the habit of letting herself in by the back door. We did not hear her, neither of us heard her, though I do remember Mother's noble head lifted a fraction before Moira came in, her fangs bared and her ears pricked. Moira opened the dining-room door and walked in. I can see her now, the complacent smile on her lips fading and the scream starting to come. She was wearing what must have been my present, a full-length white sheepskin coat.

And then? This is what Dr Vernon-Peak will particularly wish to know but what I cannot clearly remember. I remember that as the door opened I was holding the bread knife in my paws. I think I remember letting out a low growl and poising myself to spring. But what came after?

The last things I can recall before they brought me here are the blood on my fur and the two wild predatory creatures crouched on the floor over the body of the lamb.

# Fen Hall

When children paint a picture of a tree they always do the trunk brown. But trees seldom have brown trunks. Birches are silver, beeches pewter colour, planes grey and yellow, walnuts black and the bark of oaks, chestnuts and sycamores green with lichen. Pringle had never noticed any of this until he came to Fen Hall. After that, once his eyes had been opened and he had seen what things were really like, he would have painted trees with bark in different colours but next term he stopped doing art. It was just as well, he had never been very good at it, and perhaps by then he wouldn't have felt like painting trees anyway. Or even looking at them much.

Mr Liddon met them at the station in an old Volvo estate car. They were loaded down with camping gear, the tent and sleeping bags and cooking pots and a Calor gas burner in case it was too windy to keep a fire going. It had been very windy lately, the summer cool and sunless. Mr Liddon was Pringle's father's friend and Pringle had met him once before, years ago when he was a little kid, but still it was up to him to introduce the others. He spoke with wary politeness.

'This is John and this is Roger. They're brothers.'

Pringle didn't say anything about Roger always being called Hodge. He sensed that Mr Liddon wouldn't call him Hodge any more than he would call *him* Pringle. He was right.

'Parents well, are they, Peregrine?'

Pringle said yes. He could see a gleam in John's eye that augured teasing to come. Hodge, who was always thinking of his stomach, said:

'Could we stop on the way, Mr Liddon, and buy some food?'

Mr Liddon cast up his eyes. Pringle could tell he was going to be 'one of those' grown-ups. They all got into the car with their stuff and a mile or so out of town Mr Liddon stopped at a self-service shop. He didn't go inside with them which was just as well. He would only have called what they bought junk food.

Fen Hall turned out to be about seven miles away. They went

through a village called Fedgford and a little way beyond it turned down a lane that passed through a wood.

'That's where you'll have your camp,' Mr Liddon said.

Of necessity, because the lane was no more than a rough track, he was driving slowly. He pointed in among the trees. The wood had a mysterious look as if full of secrets. In the aisles between the trees the light was greenish-gold and misty. There was a muted twittering of birds and a cooing of doves. Pringle began to feel excited. It was nicer than he had expected. A little further on the wood petered out into a plantation of tall straight trees with green trunks growing in rows, the ground between them all overgrown with a spiky plant that had a curious prehistoric look to it.

'Those trees are poplars,' Mr Liddon said. You could tell he was a schoolteacher. 'They're grown as a crop.'

This was a novel idea to Pringle. 'What sort of a crop?'

'Twenty-five years after they're planted they're cut down and used for making matchsticks. If they don't fall down first. We had a couple go over in the gales last winter.'

Pringle wasn't listening. He had seen the house. It was like a house in a dream, he thought, though he didn't quite know what he meant by that. Houses he saw in actual dreams were much like his own home or John and Hodge's, suburban Surrey semi-detached. This house, when all the trees were left behind and no twig or leaf or festoon of wild clematis obscured it, stood basking in the sunshine with the confidence of something alive, as if secure in its own perfection. Dark mulberry colour, of small Tudor bricks, it had a roof of many irregular planes and gables and a cluster of chimneys like candles. The windows with the sun on them were plates of gold between the mullions. Under the eaves swallows had built their lumpy sagging nests.

'Leave your stuff in the car. I'll be taking you back up to the wood in ten minutes. Just thought you'd like to get your bearings, see where everything is first. There's the outside tap over there which you'll use of course. And you'll find a shovel and an axe in there which I rely on you to replace.'

It was going to be the biggest house Pringle had ever set foot in – not counting places like Hampton Court and Woburn. Fen Hall. It looked and the name sounded like a house in a book, not real at all. The front door was of oak, studded with iron and set back under a porch that was dark and carved with roses. Mr Liddon took them in the back way. He took them into a kitchen that was exactly Pringle's idea of the lowest sort of slum.

He was shocked. At first he couldn't see much because it had been bright outside but he could smell something dank and frowsty. When his vision adjusted he found they were in a huge room or cavern with two small windows and about four hundred square feet of squalor between them. Islanded were a small white electric oven and a small white fridge. The floor was of brick, very uneven, the walls of irregular green-painted peeling plaster with a bubbly kind of growth coming through it. Stacks of dirty dishes filled a stone sink of the kind his mother had bought at a sale and made a cactus garden in. The whole place was grossly untidy with piles of washing lying about. John and Hodge, having taken it all in, were standing there with blank faces and shifting eyes.

Mr Liddon's manner had changed slightly. He no longer kept up the hectoring tone. While explaining to them that this was where they must come if they needed anything, to the back door, he began a kind of ineffectual tidying up, cramming things into the old wooden cupboards, sweeping crumbs off the table and dropping them into the sink. John said:

'Is it all right for us to have a fire?'

'So long as you're careful. Not if the wind gets up again. I don't have to tell you where the wood is, you'll find it lying about.' Mr Liddon opened a door and called, 'Flora!'

A stone-flagged passage could be seen beyond. No one came. Pringle knew Mr Liddon had a wife, though no children. His parents had told him only that Mr and Mrs Liddon had bought a marvellous house in the country a year before and he and a couple of his friends could go and camp in the grounds if they wanted to. Further information he had picked up when they didn't know he was listening. Tony Liddon hadn't had two halfpennies to rub together until his aunt died and left him a bit of money. It couldn't have been much surely. Anyway he had spent it all on Fen Hall, he had always wanted an old place like that. The upkeep was going to be a drain on him and goodness knows how he would manage.

Pringle hadn't been much interested in all this. Now it came back to him. Mr Liddon and his father had been at university together but Mr Liddon hadn't had a wife then. Pringle had never met the wife and nor had his parents. Anyway it was clear they were not to wait for her. They got back into the car and went to find a suitable camping site.

It was a relief when Mr Liddon went away and left them to it. The obvious place to camp was on the high ground in a clearing and to make their fire in a hollow Mr Liddon said was probably a disused gravel pit. The sun was low, making long shafts of light that pierced the groves of birch and crab apple. Mistletoe hung in the oak trees like green birds' nests. It was warm and murmurous with flies. John was adept at putting up the tent and gave them orders.

'Peregrine,' he said. 'Like a sort of mad bird.'

Hodge capered about, his thumbs in his ears and his hands flapping. 'Tweet, tweet, mad bird. His master chains him up like a dog. Tweet, tweet, birdie!'

'I'd rather be a hunting falcon than Roger the lodger the sod,' said Pringle and he shoved Hodge and they both fell over and rolled about grappling on the ground until John kicked them and told them to stop it and give a hand, he couldn't do the lot on his own.

It was good in the camp that night, not windy but still and mild after the bad summer they'd had. They made a fire and cooked tomato soup and fish fingers and ate a whole packet of the biscuits called iced bears. They were in their bags in the tent, John reading the *Observer's Book of Common Insects*, Pringle a thriller set in a Japanese prison camp his parents would have taken away if they'd known about it, and Hodge listening to his radio, when Mr Liddon came up with a torch to check on them.

'Just to see if you're OK. Everything shipshape and Bristol fashion?'

Pringle thought that an odd thing to say considering the mess in his own house. Mr Liddon made a fuss about the candles they had lit and they promised to put them out, though of course they didn't. It was very silent in the night up there in the wood, the deepest silence Pringle had ever known, a quiet that was somehow heavy as if a great dark beast had lain down on the wood and quelled every sound beneath under its dense soft fur. He didn't think of this for very long because he was asleep two minutes after they blew the candles out.

Next morning the weather wasn't so nice. It was dull and cool for August. John saw a Brimstone butterfly which pleased him because the species was getting rarer. They all walked into Fedgford and bought sausages and then found they hadn't a frying pan. Pringle went down to the house on his own to see if he could borrow one.

Unlike most men Mr Liddon would be at home because of the school holidays. Pringle expected to see him working in the garden which even he could see was a mess. But he wasn't anywhere about. Pringle banged on the back door with his fist – there was neither bell nor knocker – but no one came. The door wasn't locked. He wondered if it would be all right to go in and then he went in.

The mess in the kitchen was rather worse. A large white and tabby cat was on the table eating something it probably shouldn't have been eating out of a paper bag. Pringle had a curious feeling that it would somehow be quite permissible for him to go on into the house. Something told him – though it was not a something based on observation or even guesswork – that Mr Liddon wasn't in. He went into the passage he had seen the day before through the open door. This led into a large stone-flagged hall. The place was dark with heavy dark beams going up the walls and across the ceilings and it was cold. It smelled of damp. The smell was like mushrooms that have been left in a paper bag at the back of the fridge and forgotten. Pringle pushed open a likely looking door, some instinct making him give a warning cough.

The room was enormous, its ceiling all carved beams and cobwebs. Even Pringle could see that the few small bits of furniture in it would have been more suitable for the living room of a bungalow. A woman was standing by the tall, diamond-paned, mullioned window, holding something blue and sparkling up to the light. She was strangely dressed in a long skirt, her hair falling loosely down her back, and she stood so still, gazing at the blue object with both arms raised, that for a moment Pringle had an uneasy feeling she wasn't a woman at all but the ghost of a woman. Then she turned round and smiled.

'Hallo,' she said. 'Are you one of our campers?'

She was at least as old as Mr Liddon but her hair hung down like one of the girls' at school. Her face was pale and not pretty yet when she smiled it was a wonderful face. Pringle registered that, staring at her. It was a face of radiant kind sensitivity, though it was to be some years before he could express what he had felt in those terms.

'I'm Pringle,' he said, and because he sensed that she would understand, 'I'm called Peregrine really but I get people to call me Pringle.'

'I don't blame you. I'd do the same in your place.' She had a quiet unaffected voice. 'I'm Flora Liddon. You call me Flora.'

He didn't think he could do that and knew he would end up calling her nothing. 'I came to see if I could borrow a frying pan.'

'Of course you can.' She added, 'If I can find one.' She held the thing in her hand out to him and he saw it was a small glass bottle. 'Do you think it's pretty?'

He looked at it doubtfully. It was just a bottle. On the windowsill behind her were more bottles, mostly of clear colourless glass but among them dark green ones with fluted sides.

'There are wonderful things to be found here. You can dig and find rubbish heaps that go back to Elizabethan times. And there was a Roman settlement down by the river. Would you like to see a Roman coin?'

It was black, misshapen, lumpy, with an ugly man's head on it. She showed him a jar of thick bubbly green glass and said it was the best piece of glass she'd found to date. They went out to the kitchen. Finding a frying pan wasn't easy but talking to her was. By the time she had washed up a pan which she had found full of congealed fat he had told her all about the camp and their walk to Fedgford and what the butcher had said:

'I hope you're going to wash yourselves before you cook my nice clean sausages.'

And she told him what a lot needed doing to the house and grounds and how they'd have to do it all themselves because they hadn't much money. She wasn't any good at painting or sewing or gardening or even housework, come to that. Pottering about and looking at things was what she liked.

'"What is this life if, full of care, we have no time to stand and stare?"'

He knew where that came from. W. H. Davies, the Super-tramp. They had done it at school.

'I'd have been a good tramp,' she said. 'It would have suited me.'

The smile irradiated her plain face.

They cooked the sausages for lunch and went on an insect-hunting expedition with John. The dragonflies he had promised them down by the river were not to be seen but he found what he said was a caddis, though it looked like a bit of twig to Pringle. Hodge ate five Mars bars during the course of the afternoon. They came upon the white and tabby cat with a mouse in its jaws. Undeterred by an audience, it bit the mouse in two and the tiny heart rolled out. Hodge said faintly, 'I think I'm going to be sick,' and was. They still resolved to have a cat-watch on the morrow and see how many mice it caught in a day.

By that time the weather was better. The sun didn't shine but it had got warmer again. They found the cat in the poplar plantation, stalking something among the prehistoric weeds John said were called horse tails. The poplars had trunks almost as green as grass and their leafy tops, very high up there in the pale blue sky, made rustling whispering sounds in the breeze. That was when Pringle noticed about tree trunks not being brown. The trunks of the Scotch pines were a clear pinkish-red, as bright as flowers when for a moment the sun shone. He pointed this out to the others but they didn't seem interested.

'You sound like our auntie,' said Hodge. 'She does flower arrangements for the church.'

'And throws up when she sees a bit of blood, I expect,' said Pringle. 'It runs in your family.'

Hodge lunged at him and he tripped Hodge up and they rolled about wrestling among the horse tails. By four in the afternoon the cat had caught six mice. Flora came out and told them the cat's name was Tabby which obscurely pleased Pringle. If she had said Snowflake or Persephone or some other daft name people called animals he would have felt differently about her, though he couldn't possibly have said why. He wouldn't have liked her so much.

A man turned up in a Land-Rover as they were making their way back to camp. He said he had been to the house and knocked but no one seemed to be at home. Would they give Mr or Mrs Liddon a message from him? His name was Porter, Michael Porter, and he was an archaeologist in an amateur sort of way, Mr Liddon knew all about it, and they were digging in the lower meadow and they'd come on a dump of nineteenth-century stuff. He was going to dig deeper, uncover the next layer, so if Mrs Liddon was interested in the top, now was her chance to have a look.

'Can we as well?' said Pringle.

Porter said they were welcome. No one would be working there next day. He had just heard the weather forecast on his car radio and gale-force winds were promised. Was that their camp up there? Make sure the tent was well anchored down, he said, and he drove off up the lane.

Pringle checked the tent. It seemed firm enough. They got into it and fastened the flap but they were afraid to light the candles and had John's storm lantern on instead. The wood was silent no longer. The wind made loud sirenlike howls and a rushing rending sound like canvas being torn. When that happened the tent flapped and bellied like a sail on a ship at sea. Sometimes the wind stopped altogether and there were a few seconds of silence and calm. Then it came back with a rush and a roar. John was reading Frohawk's *Complete Book of British Butterflies*, Pringle the Japanese prison-camp thriller and Hodge was trying to listen to his radio. But it wasn't much use and after a while they put the lantern out and lay in the dark.

About five minutes afterwards there came the strongest gust of wind so far, one of the canvas-tearing gusts but ten times fiercer than the last; and then, from the south of them, down towards the house, a tremendous rending crash.

John said, 'I think we'll have to do something.' His voice was brisk but it wasn't quite steady and Pringle knew he was as scared as they were. 'We'll have to get out of here.'

Pringle put the lantern on again. It was just ten.

'The tent's going to lift off,' said Hodge.

Crawling out of his sleeping bag, Pringle was wondering what they ought to do, if it would be all right, or awful, to go down to the house, when the tent flap was pulled open and Mr Liddon put his head in. He looked cross.

'Come on, the lot of you. You can't stay here. Bring your sleeping bags and we'll find you somewhere in the house for the night.'

A note in his voice made it sound as if the storm were their fault. Pringle found his shoes, stuck his feet into them and rolled up his sleeping bag. John carried the lantern. Mr Liddon shone his own torch to light their way. In the wood there was shelter but none in the lane and the wind buffeted them as they walked. It was all noise, you couldn't see much, but as they passed the plantation Mr Liddon swung the light up and Pringle saw what had made the crash. One of the poplars had gone over and was lying on its side with its roots in the air.

For some reason – perhaps because it was just about on this spot that they had met Michael Porter – John remembered the message. Mr Liddon said OK and thanks. They went into the house through the back door. A tile blew off the roof and crashed on to the path just as the door closed behind them.

There were beds up in the bedrooms but without blankets or sheets on them and the mattresses were damp. Pringle thought them spooky bedrooms, dirty and draped with spiders' webs, and he wasn't sorry they weren't going to sleep there. There was the same smell of old mushrooms and a smell of paint as well where Mr Liddon had started work on a ceiling.

At the end of the passage, looking out of a window, Flora stood in a nightgown with a shawl over it. Pringle, who sometimes read ghost stories, saw her as the Grey Lady of Fen Hall. She was in the dark, the better to see the forked lightning that had begun to leap on the horizon beyond the river.

'I love to watch a storm,' she said, turning and smiling at them.

Mr Liddon had snapped a light on. 'Where are these boys to sleep?'

It was as if it didn't concern her. She wasn't unkind but she wasn't involved either. 'Oh, in the drawing room, I should think.'

'We have seven bedrooms.'

Flora said no more. A long roll of thunder shook the house. Mr

Liddon took them downstairs and through the drawing room into a sort of study where they helped him make up beds of cushions on the floor. The wind howled round the house and Pringle heard another tile go. He lay in the dark, listening to the storm. The others were asleep, he could tell by their steady breathing. Inside the bag it was quite warm and he felt snug and safe. After a while he heard Mr Liddon and Flora quarrelling on the other side of the door.

Pringle's parents quarrelled a lot and he hated it, it was the worst thing in the world, though less bad now than when he was younger. He could only just hear Mr Liddon and Flora and only disjointed words, abusive and angry on the man's part, indifferent, amused on the woman's, until one sentence rang out clearly. Her voice was penetrating though it was so quiet:

'We want such different things!'

He wished they would stop. And suddenly they did, with the coming of the rain. The rain came, exploded rather, crashing at the windows and on the old sagging depleted roof. It was strange that a sound like that, a loud constant roar, could send you to sleep . . .

She was in the kitchen when he went out there in the morning. John and Hodge slept on, in spite of the bright watery sunshine that streamed through the dirty diamond windowpanes. A clean world outside, new-washed. Indoors the same chaos, the kitchen with the same smell of fungus and dirty dishcloths, though the windows were open. Flora sat at the table on which sprawled a welter of plates, indefinable garments, bits of bread and fruit rinds, an open can of cat food. She was drinking coffee and Tabby lay on her lap.

'There's plenty in the pot if you want some.'

She was the first grown-up in whose house he had stayed who didn't ask him how he had slept. Nor was she going to cook breakfast for him. She told him where the eggs were and bread and butter. Pringle remembered he still hadn't returned her frying pan which might be the only one she had.

He made himself a pile of toast and found a jar of marmalade. The grass and the paths, he could see through an open window, were littered with broken bits of twig and leaf. A cock pheasant strutted across the shaggy lawn.

'Did the storm damage a lot of things?' he asked.

'I don't know. Tony got up early to look. There may be more poplars down.'

Pringle ate his toast. The cat had begun to purr in an irregular throbbing way. Her hand kneaded its ears and neck. She spoke, but not perhaps to Pringle or the cat, or for them if they cared to hear.

'So many people are like that. The whole of life is a preparation for life, not living.'

Pringle didn't know what to say. He said nothing. She got up and walked away, still carrying the cat, and then after a while he heard music coming faintly from a distant part of the house.

There were two poplars down in the plantation and each had left a crater four or five feet deep. As they went up the lane to check on their camp, Pringle and John and Hodge had a good look at them, their green trunks laid low, their tangled roots in the air. Apart from everything having got a bit blown about up at the camp and the stuff they had left out soaked through, there was no real damage done. The wood itself had afforded protection to their tent.

It seemed a good time to return the frying pan. After that they would have to walk to Fedgford for some sausages – unless one of the Liddons offered a lift. It was with an eye to this, Pringle had to admit, that he was taking the pan back.

But Mr Liddon, never one to waste time, was already at work in the plantation. He had lugged a chainsaw up there and was preparing to cut up the poplars where they lay. When he saw them in the lane he came over.

'How did you sleep?'

Pringle said, 'OK, thanks,' but Hodge, who had been very resentful about not being given a hot drink or something to eat, muttered that he had been too hungry to sleep. Mr Liddon took no notice. He seemed jumpy and nervous. He said to Pringle that if they were going to the house would they tell Mrs Liddon – he never called her Flora to them – that there was what looked like a dump of Victorian glass in the crater where the bigger poplar had stood.

'They must have planted the trees over the top without knowing.'

Pringle looked into the crater and sure enough he could see bits of coloured glass and a bottleneck and a jug or tankard handle protruding from the tumbled soil. He left the others there, fascinated by the chainsaw, and went to take the frying pan back. Flora was in the drawing room, playing records of tinkly piano music. She jumped up, quite excited, when he told her about the bottle dump.

They walked back to the plantation together, Tabby following, walking a little way behind them like a dog. Pringle knew he hadn't a hope of getting that lift now. Mr Liddon had already got the crown of the big poplar sawn off. In the short time since the storm its pale silvery-green leaves had begun to wither. John asked if they could have

96

a go with the chainsaw but Mr Liddon said not so likely, did they think he was crazy? And if they wanted to get to the butcher before the shop closed for lunch they had better get going now.

Flora, her long skirt hitched up, had clambered down into the crater. If she had stood up in it her head and shoulders, perhaps all of her from the waist up, would have come above its rim, for poplars have shallow roots. But she didn't stand up. She squatted down, using her trowel, extracting small glass objects from the leafmould. The chainsaw whined, slicing through the top of the poplar trunk. Pringle, watching with the others, had a feeling something was wrong about the way Mr Liddon was doing it. He didn't know what though. He could only think of a funny film he had once seen in which a man, sitting on a branch, sawed away at the bit between him and the tree trunk, necessarily falling off himself when the branch fell. But Mr Liddon wasn't sitting on anything. He was just sawing up a fallen tree from the crown to the bole. The saw sliced through again, making four short logs now as well as the bole.

'Cut along now, you boys,' he said. 'You don't want to waste the day mooning about here.'

Flora looked up and winked at Pringle. It wasn't unkind just conspiratorial, and she smiled too, holding up a small glowing red glass bottle for him to see. He and John and Hodge moved slowly off, reluctantly, dawdling because the walk ahead would be boring and long. Through the horse tails, up the bank, looking back when the saw whined again.

But Pringle wasn't actually looking when it happened. None of them was. They had had their final look and had begun to trudge up the lane. The sound made them turn, a kind of swishing lurch and then a heavy plopping, sickening, dull crash. They cried out, all three of them, but no one else did, not Flora or Mr Liddon. Neither of them made a sound.

Mr Liddon was standing with his arms held out, his mouth open and his eyes staring. The pile of logs lay beside him but the tree trunk was gone, sprung back roots and all when the last saw cut went through, tipped the balance and made its base heavier than its top. Pringle put his hand over his mouth and held it there. Hodge, who was nothing more than a fat baby really, had begun to cry. Fearfully, slowly, they converged, all four of them, on the now upright tree under whose roots she lay.

The police came and a farmer and his son and some men from round about. Between them they got the tree over on its side again but by then Flora was dead. Perhaps she died as soon as the bole and the mass of roots hit her. Pringle wasn't there to see. Mr Liddon had put the plantation out of bounds and said they were to stay in camp until someone came to drive them to the station. It was Michael Porter who turned up in the late afternoon and checked they'd got everything packed up and the camp site tidied. He told them Flora was dead. They got to the station in his Land-Rover in time to catch the five-fifteen for London.

On the way to the station he didn't mention the bottle dump he had told them about. Pringle wondered if Mr Liddon had ever said anything to Flora about it. All the way home in the train he kept thinking of something odd. The first time he went up the lane to the camp that morning he was sure there hadn't been any glass in the tree crater. He would have seen the gleam of it and he hadn't. He didn't say anything to John and Hodge, though. What would have been the point?

Three years afterwards Pringle's parents got an invitation to Mr Liddon's wedding. He was marrying the daughter of a wealthy local builder and the reception was to be at Fen Hall, the house in the wood. Pringle didn't go, being too old now to tag about after his parents. He had gone off trees anyway.

# Father's Day

Teddy had once read in a story written by a Victorian that a certain character liked 'to have things pleasant about him'. The phrase had stuck in his mind. He too liked to have things pleasant about him.

It was to be hoped that pleasantness would prevail while they were all away on holiday together. Teddy was beginning to be afraid they might get on each other's nerves. Anyway, it would be the last time for years the four of them would be able to go away in October for both Emma and Andrew started school in the spring.

'A pity,' Anne said, 'because May and October are absolutely the best times in the Greek Islands.'

She and Teddy had bought the house with the money Teddy's mother had left him. The previous year they had been there twice and again last May. They hadn't been able to go out in the evenings because they had no baby-sitter. Having Michael and Linda there would make it possible for each couple to go out every other night.

'If Michael will trust us with his children,' said Teddy.

'He isn't as bad as that.'

'I didn't say he was bad. He's my brother-in-law and I've got to put up with him. He's all right. It's just that he's so nuts about his kids I sometimes wonder how he dares leave them with their own mother when he goes to work.'

He was recalling the time they had all spent at Chichester in July and how the evening had been spoilt by Michael's insisting on phoning the baby-sitter before the play began, during the interval and before they began the drive home. And when he wasn't on the phone or obliged to be silent in the theatre he had talked continually about Andrew and Alison in a fretful way.

'He's under a lot of stress,' Linda had whispered to her sister. 'He's going through a bad patch at work.'

Teddy didn't think it natural for a man to be so involved with his children. He was found of his own children, of course he was, and anxious enough about them when he had cause, but they were little still and, let's face it, sometimes tiresome and boring. He looked forward to the time when they were older and there could be real companionship. Michael was more like a mother than a father, a mother hen. Teddy, for his sins, had occasionally changed napkins and made up feeds but Michael actually seemed to enjoy doing these things and talking about them afterwards. Teddy hoped he wouldn't be treated to too much Dr Jolly philosophy while on Stamnos.

Just before they went, about a week before, Valerie Wilton's marriage broke up. Valerie had been at school with Anne, though just as much Linda's friend, and had written long letters to both of them, explaining everything and asking for their understanding. She had gone off with a man she met at her Commercial French evening class. Apparently the affair had been going on for a long time but Valerie's husband had known nothing about it and her departure had come to him as a total shock. He came round and poured out his troubles to Anne and drank a lot of scotch and broke down and cried. For all Teddy knew, he did the same at Linda's. Teddy stayed out of it, he didn't want to get involved. Liking to have things pleasant about him, he declined gently but firmly even to discuss it with Anne.

'Linda says it's really upset Michael,' said Anne. 'He identifies with George, you see. He's so emotional.'

'I said I wasn't going to talk about it, darling, and by golly I'm not!'

During the flight Michael had Alison on his lap and Andrew in the seat beside him. Anne remarked in a plaintive way that it was all right for Linda. Teddy saw that Linda slept most of the way. She was a beautiful girl – better-looking than Anne, most people thought, though Teddy didn't – and now that Michael was making more money had bought a lot of new clothes and was having her hair cut in a very stylish way. Teddy, who was quite observant, especially of attractive things, noted that recently she had stopped wearing trousers. He looked appreciatively across the aisle at her long slim legs.

They changed planes at Athens. It was a fine clear day and as the aircraft came in to land you could see the wine jar shape of the island from which it took its name. Stamnos was no more than twenty miles long but the road was poor and rutted, winding up and down over low olive-clad mountains, and it took over an hour for the car to get to Votani at the wine jar's mouth. The driver, a Stamniot, was one of those Greeks who spend their youth in Australia before returning home to start a business on the money they have made. He talked all the way in a harsh clattering Greek-Strine while his radio played bouzouki music and Alison whimpered in Michael's arms. It was hot for the time of year.

Tim, who was a bad traveller, had been carsick twice by the time they reached Votani. The car couldn't go up the narrow flagged street, so they had to get out and carry the baggage, the driver helping with a case in each hand and one on his head. Michael didn't carry a case because he had Andrew on his shoulders and Alison in his arms.

The houses of Votani covered a shallow conical hill so that it looked from a distance like a heap of pastel-coloured pebbles. Close to, the buildings were neat, crowded, interlocking, hung with jasmine and bougainvillea, and the hill itself was surmounted by the ruins, extravagantly picturesque, of a Crusaders' fortress. Teddy and Anne's house was three fishermen's cottages that its previous owner had converted into one. It had a lot of little staircases on account of being built on the steep hillside. From the bedroom where the four children would sleep you could see the eastern walls of the fortress, a dark blue expanse of sea, and smudgy on the horizon, the Turkish coast. The dark came quickly after the sun had gone. Teddy, when abroad, always found that disconcerting after England with its long protracted dusks.

Within an hour of reaching Votani he found himself walking down the main street – a stone-walled defile smelling of jasmine and lit by lamps on iron brackets – towards Agamemnon's Bar. He felt guilty about going out and leaving Anne to put the children to bed. But it had been Anne's suggestion, indeed Anne's insistence, that he should take Michael out for a drink before supper. A whispered colloquy had established they both thought Michael looked 'washed out' (Anne's expression) and 'fed up' (Teddy's) and no wonder, the way he had been attending to Andrew's and Alison's wants all day.

Michael had needed a lot of persuading, had at first been determined to stay and help Linda, and it therefore rather surprised Teddy when he began on a grumbling tirade against women's liberation.

'I sometimes wonder what they mean, they're not "equal",' he said. 'They have the children, don't they? We can't do that. I consider that makes them *superior* rather than inferior.'

I know I shouldn't like to have a baby,' said Teddy irrelevantly.

'It's because of that,' said Michael as if Teddy hadn't spoken, 'that we need to master them. We have to for our own sakes. Where should we be if they had the babies and the whip hand too?'

Teddy said vaguely that he didn't know about whip hand but someone had said that the hand which rocks the cradle rules the world.

By this time they were in Agamemnon's, sitting at a table on the vine-covered terrace. The other customers were all Stamniots, some of whom recognized Teddy and nodded at him and smiled. Most of the tourists had gone by now and all but one of the hotels were closed for the winter. Hedonistic Teddy, wanting to have things pleasant about him, hadn't cared for the turn the conversation was taking. He began telling Michael how amused he and Anne had been when they found that the proprietor of the bar was called after the great hero of classical antiquity and how ironical it had seemed, for this Agamemnon was small and fat. Here he was forced to break off as stout smiling Agamemnon came to take their order.

Michael had no intention of letting him begin once more on the subject of Stamniot names. He spoke in a rapid violent tone, his thin dark face pinched with intensity.

'A man can lose his children any time and through no fault of his own. Have you ever thought of that?'

Teddy looked at him. Notions of kidnapping, of mortal illness, came into his head. 'What do you mean?'

'It could happen to you or me, to any of us. A man can lose his children overnight and he can't do a thing about it. He may be a good faithful husband, a good provider, a devoted father – that won't make a scrap of difference. Look at George Wilton. What did George do wrong? Nothing. But he lost his children just the same. One day they were living with him in his house and the next they were in Gerrards Cross with Valerie and that Commercial French chap and he'll be lucky if he sees them once a fortnight.'

'I see what you're getting at,' said Teddy. 'He couldn't look after them though, could he? He's got to go to work. I mean, I see it's unfair, but you can't take kids away from their mother, can you?'

'Apparently not. But you can take them from their father.'

'I shouldn't worry about one isolated case if I were you,' said Teddy, feeling very uncomfortable. 'You want to forget that sort of thing while you're here. Unwind a bit.'

'An isolated case is just what it isn't. There's someone at work, John Frost, you don't know him. He and his wife split up – at her wish, naturally – and she took their baby with her as a matter of course. And George told me the same thing happened in his brother's marriage a couple of years back. Three children he had, he lived for his children, and now he gets to take them to the zoo every other Saturday.'

'Maybe,' said Teddy who had his moments of shrewdness, 'if he'd lived for his wife a bit more it wouldn't have happened.'

He was glad to be back in the house. In bed that night he told Anne about it. Anne said Michael was an obsessional person. When he'd first met Linda he'd been obsessed by her and now it was Andrew and Alison. He wasn't very nice to Linda these days, she'd noticed, he was always watching her in an unpleasant way. And when Linda had suggested she take the children up to the fortress in the morning if he wanted to go down to the harbour and see the fishing boats come in, he had said:

'No way am I going to allow you up there on your own with my children.'

Later in the week they all went. You had to keep your eye on the children every minute of the time, there were so many places to fall over, fissures in the walls, crumbling corners, holes that opened on to the empty blue air. But the view from the eastern walls, breached in a dozen places, where the crag fell away in an almost vertical sweep to a beach of creamy-silver sand and brown rocks, was the best on Stamnos. You could see the full extent of the bay that was the lip of the wine jar and the sea with its scattering of islands and the low mountains of Turkey behind which, Teddy thought romantically, perhaps lay the Plain of Troy. The turf up here was slippery, dry as clean combed hair. No rain had fallen on Stamnos for five months. The sky was a smooth mauvish-blue, cloudless and clear. Emma and Andrew, the bigger ones, ran about on the slippery turf, enjoying it because it was slippery, falling over and slithering down the slopes.

Teddy had successfully avoided being alone with Michael since their conversation in the bar but later that day Michael caught him. He put it that way to himself but in fact it was more as if, unwittingly, he had caught Michael. He had gone down to the grocery store, had bought the red apples, the feta cheese and the olive oil Anne wanted, and had passed into the inner room which was a secondhand bookstore and stuffed full with paperbacks in a variety of European languages discarded by the thousand tourists who had come to Votani that summer. The room was empty but for Michael who was standing in a far corner, having taken down from a shelf a novel whose title was its heroine's name.

'That's a Swedish translation,' said Teddy gently.

'Oh, is it? Yes, I see.'

'The English books are all over here.'

Michael's face looked haggard in the gloom of the shop. He didn't tan easily in spite of being so dark. They came out into the sunlight, Teddy carrying his purchases in the string bag, pausing now and then to look down over a wall or through a gateway. Down there the meadows spread out to the sea, olives with the black nets laid under them to catch the harvest, cypresses thin as thorns. The shepherd's dog was bringing the flock in and the sheep bells made a distant tinkling music. Michael's shadow fell across the sunlit wall.

'I was off in a dream,' said Teddy. 'Beautiful, isn't it? I love it. It makes me quite sad to think we shan't come here in October again for maybe – what? Twelve or fourteen years?'

'I can't say it bothers me to have to make sacrifices for the sake of my children.'

Teddy thought this reproof uncalled for and he would have liked to rejoin with something sharp. But he wasn't very good at innuendo. And in any case before he could come up with anything Michael had begun on quite a different subject.

'The law in Greece has relaxed a lot in the past few years in favour of women – property rights and divorce and so on.'

Teddy said, not without a spark of malice, 'Jolly good, isn't it?'

'Those things are the first cracks in the fabric of a society that lead to its ultimate breakdown.'

'*Our* society hasn't broken down.'

Michael gave a scathing laugh as if at the naivety of this comment. 'Throughout the nineteenth century,' he said in severe lecturing tones, 'and a good deal of this one, if a woman left her husband the children stayed with him as a matter of course. The children were never permitted to be with the guilty party. And there was a time, not so long ago, when a man could use the law to compel his wife to return to him.'

'You wouldn't want that back, would you?'

'I'll tell you something, Teddy. There's a time coming when children won't have fathers – that is, it won't matter who your father is any more. You'll know your mother and that'll be enough. That's the way things are moving, no doubt about it. Now in the Middle Ages men believed that in matters of reproduction the woman was merely the vessel, the man's seed was what made the child. From that we've come full circle, we've come to the nearly total supremacy of women and men like you and me are reduced to – mere temporary agents.'

Teddy said to Anne that night, 'You don't think he's maybe a bit mad, do you? I mean broken down under the strain?'

'He hasn't got any strain here.'

'I'll tell you the other thing I was wondering. Linda's not up to anything, is she? I mean giving some other chap a whirl? Only she's all dressed up these days and she's lost weight. She looks years younger. If she's got someone that would account for poor old Michael, wouldn't it?'

It was their turn to go out in the evening and they were on their way back from the Krini Restaurant, the last one on the island to remain open after the middle of October. The night was starry, the moon three-quarters of a glowing white orb.

'There has to be a reason for him being like that. It's not normal. I don't spend my time worrying you're going to leave me and take the kids.'

'Is that what it is? He's afraid Linda's going to leave him?'

'It must be. He can't be getting in a tizzy over George Wilton's and Somebody Frost's problems.' Sage Teddy nodded his head. 'Human nature isn't like that,' he said. 'Let's go up to the fort, darling. We've never been up there by moonlight.'

They climbed to the top of the hill, Teddy puffing a bit on account of having had rather too much ouzo at the Krini. In summer the summit was floodlit but when the hotels closed the lights also went out. The moonlight was nearly as bright and the turf shone silver between the black shadows made by the broken walls. The Stamniots were desperate for rain now the tourist season was over, for the final boost to swell the olive crop. Teddy went up the one surviving flight of steps into the remains of the one surviving tower. He paused, waiting for Anne. He looked down but he couldn't see her.

'The Aegean's not always calm,' came her voice. 'Down here there's a current tears in and out like a mill race.'

He still couldn't see her, peering out from his look-out post. Then he did – just. She was silhouetted against the purplish starriness.

'Come back!' he shouted. 'You're too near the edge!'

He had made her jump. She turned quickly and at once slipped on the turf, going into a long slide on her back, legs in the air. Teddy ran down the steps. He ran across the turf, nearly falling himself, picked her up and hugged her.

'Suppose you'd fallen the other way?'

The palms of her hands were pitted with grit, in places the skin broken, where she had ineffectually made a grab at the sides of the fissure in the wall. 'I wouldn't have fallen at all if you hadn't shouted at me.'

At home the children were all asleep, Linda in bed but Michael still up. There were two empty wine bottles on the table and three glasses. A man they had met the night before in Agamemnon's had come in to have a drink with them, Michael said. He was German, from Heidelberg, here on his own for a late holiday.

'He was telling us about his divorce. His wife found a younger man with better job prospects who was able to offer Werner's children a swimming pool and riding lessons. Werner tried to kill himself but someone found him in time.'

What a gloomy way to spend an evening, thought Teddy, and was trying to find something cheerful to say when a shrill yell came from the children's room. Teddy couldn't for the life of him have said which one it was but Michael could. He knew his Alison's voice and in he went to comfort her. Teddy made a face at Anne and Anne cast up her eyes. Linda came out of her bedroom in her dressing gown.

'That awful man!' she said. 'Has he gone? He looks like a toad. Why don't we seem to know anyone any more who hasn't got a broken marriage?'

'You know us,' said Teddy.

'Yes, thank God.'

Michael took his children down to the beach most mornings. Teddy took his children to the beach too and would have gone to the bay on the other side of the headland except that Emma and Tim wanted to be with their cousins and Tim started bawling when Teddy demurred. So Teddy had to put up a show of being very pleased and delighted at the sight of Michael. The children were in and out of the pale clear green water. It was still very hot at noon.

'Like August,' said Teddy. 'By golly, it's a scorcher here in August.'

'Heat and cold don't mean all that much to me,' said Michael.

Resisting the temptation to say Bully for you or I should be so lucky or something on those lines, Teddy began to talk of plans for the following day, the hire car to Likythos, the visit to the monastery with the Byzantine relics and to the temple of Apollo. Michael turned on him a face so wretched, so hag-ridden, the eyes positively screwed up with pain, that Teddy who had been disliking and resenting him with schoolboy indignation was moved by pity to the depths of himself. The poor old boy, he thought, the poor devil. What's wrong with him?

'When Andrew and Alison are with me like they are now,' Michael began in a low rapid voice, 'it's not so bad. I always have that feeling, you see, that I could pick them up and run away with them and hide them.' He looked earnestly at Teddy. 'I'm strong, I'm young still. I could easily carry them both long distances. I could hide them. But there isn't anywhere in the civilized world you can hide for long, is there? Still, as I say, it's not so bad when they're with me, when there are just the three of us on our own. It's when I have to go out and leave them with *her*. I can't tell you how I feel going home. All the way in the train and walking up from the station I'm imagining going into that house and not hearing them, just silence and a note on the mantelpiece. I dread going home, I don't mind telling you, Teddy, and yet I long for it. Of course I do. I long to see them and know they're there and still mine. I say to myself, that's another day's reprieve. Sometimes I phone home half a dozen times in the day just to know she hasn't taken them away.'

Teddy was aghast. He didn't know what to say. It was as if the sun had gone in and all was cold and comfortless and hateful. The sea glittered, it looked hard and huge, an enemy.

'It hasn't been so bad while we've been here,' said Michael. 'Oh, I expect I've been a bore for you. I'm sorry about that, Teddy, I know what a misery I am. I keep thinking that when we get home it will all start again.'

'Has Linda then . . .?' Teddy stammered. 'I mean, Linda isn't . . .?'

Michael shook his head. 'Not yet, not yet. But she's young too, isn't she? She's attractive. She's got years yet ahead of her – years of torture for me, Teddy, before my kids grow up.'

Anne told Teddy she had spoken to Linda about it. 'She never looks at another man, she wouldn't. She's breaking her heart over Michael. She lost weight and bought those clothes because she felt she'd let herself go after Alison was born and she ought to try and be more attractive for him. This obsession of his is wearing her out. She wants him to see a psychiatrist but he won't.'

'The trouble is,' said Teddy, 'there's a certain amount of truth behind it. There's method in his madness. If Linda met a man she liked and went off with him – I mean, Michael could drive her to it if he went on like this – she *would* take the children and Michael *would* lose them.'

'Not you too!'

'Well, no, because I'm not potty like poor old Michael. I hope I'm a reasonable man. But it does make you think. A woman decides her marriage doesn't work any more and the husband can lose his kids, his home and maybe half his income. I mean if I were twenty-five again and hadn't ever met you I might think twice about getting married, by golly, I might.'

Their last evening it was Anne and Teddy's turn to baby-sit for Michael and Linda. They were dining with Werner at the Hotel Daphne. Linda wore a green silk dress, the colour of shallow sea water.

'More cosy chat about adultery and suicide, I expect,' said Teddy. Liking to have things pleasant about him, he settled himself with a large ouzo on the terrace under the vine. 'I shan't be altogether sorry to get home. And I'll tell you what. We could come at Easter next year, in Emma's school hols.'

'On our own,' said Anne.

Michael came in about ten. He was alone. Teddy saw that the palms of his hands were pitted as if he had held on to the rough surface of something stony. Anne got up.

'Where's Linda?'

He hesitated before replying. A look of cunning of the kind sane people's expressions never show spread over his face. His eyes shifted along the terrace, to the right, to the left. Then he looked at the palm of his right hand and began rubbing it with his thumb.

'At the hotel,' he said. 'With Werner.'

Anne cottoned on before he did, Teddy could see. She took a step towards Michael.

'What on earth do you mean, with Werner?'

'She's left me. She's going home to Germany with him tomorrow.'

'Michael, that just isn't true. She can't stand him, she told me so. She said he was like a toad.'

'Yes, she did,' said Teddy. 'I heard her say that.'

'All right, so she isn't with Werner. Have it your own way. Did the children wake up?'

'Never mind the children, Michael, they're OK. Tell us where Linda is, please. Don't play games.'

He didn't answer. He went back into the house, the bead curtain making a rattling swish as he passed through it. Anne and Teddy looked at each other.

'I'm frightened,' Anne said.

'Yes, so am I, frankly,' said Teddy.

The curtain rattled as Michael came through, carrying his children, Andrew over his shoulder, Alison in the crook of his arm, both of them more or less asleep.

'I scraped my hands on the stones up there,' he said. 'The turf's as slippery as glass.' He gave Anne and Teddy a great wide empty smile. 'Just wanted to make sure the children were all right, I'll put them back to bed again.' He began to giggle with a kind of triumphant relief. 'I shan't lose them now. She won't take them from me now.'

# The Green Road to Quephanda

There used to be, not long ago, a London suburban line railway running up from Finsbury Park to Highgate, and further than that for all I know. They closed it down before I went to live at Highgate and at some point they took up the sleepers and the rails. But the track remains and a very strange and interesting track it is. There are people living in the vicinity of the old line who say they can still hear, at night and when the wind is right, the sound of a train pulling up the slope to Highgate and, before it comes into the old disused station, giving its long, melancholy, hooting call. A ghost train, presumably, on rails that have long been lifted and removed.

But this is not a ghost story. Who could conceive of the ghost, not of a person but of a place, and that place having no existence in the natural world? Who could suppose anything of a supernatural or paranormal kind happening to a man like myself, who is quite unimaginative and not observant at all?

An observant person, for instance, could hardly have lived for three years only two minutes from the old station without knowing of the existence of the line. Day after day, on my way to the Underground, I passed it, glanced down unseeing at the weed-grown platforms, the broken canopies. Where did I suppose those trees were growing, rowans and Spanish chestnuts and limes that drop their sticky black juice, like tar, that waved their branches in a long avenue high up in the air? What did I imagine that occasionally glimpsed valley was, lying between suburban back gardens? You may enter or leave the line at the bridges where there are always places for scrambling up or down, and at some actual steps, much overgrown, and gates or at least gateposts. I had been walking under or over these bridges (according as the streets where I walked passed under or over them) without ever asking myself what those bridges carried or crossed. It never even, I am sorry to say, occurred to me that there were rather a lot of bridges for a part of London where the only railway line, the Underground, ran deep in the bowels of the earth. I didn't think about them. As I walked under one of the brown brick tunnels I didn't look up to question its presence or ever once glance over a parapet. It was Arthur Kestrell who told me about the line, one evening while I was in his house.

Arthur was a novelist. I write 'was', not because he has abandoned his profession for some other, but because he is dead. I am not even sure whether one would call his books novels. They truly belong in that curious category, a fairly popular *genre,* that is an amalgam of science fiction, fairy tale and horror fantasy.

But Arthur, who used the pseudonym Blaise Fastnet, was no Mervyn Peake and no Lovecraft either. Not that I had read any of his books at the time of which I am writing. But Elizabeth, my wife, had. Arthur used sometimes to give us one of them on publication, duly inscribed and handed to us, presented indeed, with the air of something very precious and uniquely desirable being bestowed.

I couldn't bring myself to read them. The titles alone were enough to repel me: *Kallinarth, the Cloudling, The Quest of Kallinarth, Lord of Quephanda, The Grail-Seeker's Guerdon* and so forth. But I used somehow, without actually lying, to give Arthur the impression that I had read his latest, or I think I did. Perhaps, in fact, he saw through this, for he never enquired if I had enjoyed it or had any criticisms to make. Liz said they were 'fun', and sometimes – with kindly intent, I know – would refer to an incident or portion of dialogue in one of the books in Arthur's presence. 'As Kallinarth might have said,' she would say, or 'Weren't those the flowers Kallinarth picked for Valaquen when she woke from her long sleep?' This sort of thing only had the effect of making poor Arthur blush and look embarrassed. I believe that Arthur Kestrell was convinced in his heart that he was writing great literature, never perhaps to be recognized as such in his lifetime but for the appreciation of posterity. Liz, privately to me, used to call him the poor man's Tolkien.

He suffered from periods of black and profound depression. When these came upon him he couldn't write or read or even bring himself to go out on those marathon walks ranging across north London which he dearly loved when he was well. He would shut himself up in his Gothic house in that district where Highgate and Crouch End merge, and there he would hide and suffer and pace the floors, not answering the door, still less the telephone until, after five or six days or more, the mood of wretched despair had passed.

His books were never reviewed in the press. How it comes about that some authors' work never receives the attention of the critics is a mystery, but the implication, of course, is that it is beneath their notice. This ignoring of a new publication, this bland passing over with neither a smile nor a sneer, implies that the author's work is a mere commercially motivated repetition of his last book, a slight variation on a tried and lucrative theme, another stereotyped bubbler in a long line of profitable potboilers. Arthur, I believe, took it hard. Not that he told me so. But soon after Liz had scanned the papers for even a solitary line to announce a new Fastnet publication, one of these depressions of his would settle on him and he would go into hiding behind his grey, crenellated walls.

Emerging, he possessed for a while a kind of slow cheerfulness combined with a dogged attitude to life. It was always a pleasure to be with him, if for nothing else than the experience of his powerful and strange imagination whose vividness coloured those books of his, and in conversation gave an exotic slant to the observations he made and the opinions he uttered.

London, he always insisted, was a curious, glamorous and sinister city, hung on slopes and valleys in the north of the world. Did I not understand the charm it held for foreigners who thought of it with wistfulness as a grey Eldorado? I who had been born in it couldn't see its wonders, its contrasts, its wickednesses. In summer Arthur got me to walk with him to Marx's tomb, to the house where Housman wrote *A Shropshire Lad*, to the pond in the Vale of Health where Shelly sailed boats. We walked the Heath and we walked the urban woodlands and then one day, when I complained that there was nowhere left to go, Arthur told me about the track where the railway line had used to be. A long green lane, he said, like a country lane, four and a half miles of it, and smiling in his cautious way, he told me where it went. Over Northwood Road, over Stanhope Road, under Crouch End Hill, over Vicarage Road, under Crouch Hill, under Mount View, over Mount Pleasant Villas, over Stapleton Hall, under Upper Tollington Park, over Oxford Road, under Stroud Green Road, and so to the station at Finsbury Park.

'How do you get on to it?' I said.

'At any of the bridges. Or at Holmesdale Road. You can get on to it from the end of my garden.'

'Right,' I said. 'Let's go. It's a lovely day.'

'There'll be crowds of people on a Saturday,' said Arthur. 'The sun will be bright like fire and there'll be hordes of wild people and their bounding dogs and their children with music machines and tinned drinks.' This was the way Arthur talked, the words juicily or dreamily enunciated. 'You want to go up there when it's quiet, at twilight, at dusk, when the air is lilac and you can smell the bitter scent of the tansy.'

'Tomorrow night then. I'll bring Liz and we'll call for you and you can take us up there.'

But on the following night when we called at Arthur's house and stood under the stone archway of the porch and rang his bell, there was no answer. I stepped back and looked up at the narrow latticed windows, shaped like inverted shields. This was something which, in these circumstances, I had never done before. Arthur's face looked back at me, blurred and made vague by the dark, diamond-paned glass, but unmistakeably his small wizened face, pale and with its short, sparse beard. It is a disconerting thing to be looked at like this by a dear friend who returns your smile and your mouthed greeting with a dead, blank and unrecognizing stare. I suppose I knew then that poor Arthur wasn't quite sane any more. Certainly Liz and I both knew that he had entered one of his depressions and that it was useless to expect him to let us in.

We went off home, abandoning the idea of an exploration of the track that evening. But on the following day, work being rather slack at that time of the year, I found myself leaving the office early and getting out of the tube train at Highgate at half-past four. Liz, I knew, would be out. On an impulse, I crossed the street and turned into Holmesdale Road. Many a time, walking there before, I had noticed what seemed an unexpectedly rural meadow lying to the north of the street, a meadow overshadowed by broad trees, though no more than fifty yards from the roar and stench of the Archway Road. Now I understood what it was. I walked down the slope, turned south-eastwards where the meadow narrowed and came on to a grassy lane.

It was about the width of an English country lane and it was bordered by hedges of buddleia on which peacock and small tortoiseshell butterflies basked. And I might have felt myself truly in the country had it not been for the backs of houses glimpsed all the time between the long leaves and the purple spires of the buddleia bushes. Arthur's lilac hour had not yet come. It was windless sunshine up on the broad green track, the clear, white light of a sun many hours yet from setting. But there was a wonderful warm and rural, or perhaps I should say pastoral, atmosphere about the place. I need Arthur's gift for words and Arthur's imagination to describe it properly and that I don't have. I can only say that there seemed, up there, to be a suspension of time and also of the hurrying, frenzied bustle, the rage to live, that I had just climbed up out of.

I went over the bridge at Northwood Road and over the bridge at Stanhope Road, feeling ashamed of myself for having so often walked unquestioningly *under* them. Soon the line began to descend, to become a valley rather than a causeway, with embankments on either side on which grew small, delicate birch trees and the rosebay willow herb and the giant hogweed. But there were no tansy flowers, as far as I could see. These are bright yellow double daisies borne in clusters on long stems and they have the same sort of smell as chrysanthemums. For all I know, they may be a sort of chrysanthemum or belonging to that family. Anyway, I couldn't see any or any lilac, but perhaps Arthur hadn't meant that and in any case it wouldn't be in bloom in July. I went as far as Crouch End Hill that first time and then I walked home by road. If I've given the impression there were no people on the line, this wasn't so. I passed a couple of women walking a labrador, two boys with bikes and a little girl in school uniform eating a choc ice.

Liz was intrigued to hear where I had been but rather cross that I hadn't waited until she could come too. So that evening, after we had had our meal, we walked along the line the way and the distance I had been earlier and the next night we ventured into the longer section. A tunnel blocked up with barbed wire prevented us from getting quite to the end but we covered nearly all of it and told each other we very likely hadn't missed much by this defeat.

The pastoral atmosphere disappeared after Crouch End Hill. Here there was an old station, the platforms alone still remaining, and under the bridge someone had dumped an old feather mattress – or plucked a dozen geese. The line became a rubbish dump for a hundred yards or so and then widened out into children's playgrounds with murals – and graffiti – on the old brick walls.

Liz looked back at the green valley behind. 'What you gain on the swings,' she said, 'you lose on the roundabouts.' A child in a rope seat swung past us, shrieking, nearly knocking us over.

All the prettiness and the atmosphere I have tried to describe was in that first section, Highgate station to Crouch End Hill. The next time I saw Arthur, when he was back in the world again, I told him we had explored the whole length of the line. He became quite excited.

'Have you now? All of it? It's beautiful, isn't it? Did you see the foxgloves? There must be a mile of foxgloves up there. And the mimosa? You wouldn't suppose mimosa could stand an English winter and I don't know of anywhere else it grows, but it flourishes up there. It's sheltered, you see, sheltered from all the frost and the harsh winds.'

Arthur spoke wistfully as if the frost and harsh winds he referred to were more metaphorical than actual, the coldness of life and fate and time rather than of climate. I didn't argue with him about the mimosa, though I had no doubt at all that he was mistaken. The line up there was exposed, not sheltered, and even if it had been, even if it had been in Cornwall or the warm Scilly Isles, it would still have been too cold for mimosa to survive. Foxgloves were another matter, though I hadn't seen any, only the hogweed with its bracts of dirty white flowers, garlic mustard and marestail, burdock and rosebay, and the pale leathery leaves of the coltsfoot. As the track grew rural again, past Mount View, hawthorn bushes, not mimosa, grew on the embankment slopes.

'It belongs to Haringey Council.' Arthur's voice was always vibrant with expression and now it had become a drawl of scorn and contempt. 'They want to build houses on it. They want to plaster it with a great red sprawl of council houses, a disfiguring red naevus.' Poor Arthur's writing may not have been the effusion of genius he seemed to believe, but he certainly had a gift for the spoken word.

That August his annual novel was due to appear. Liz had been given an advance copy and had duly read it. Very much the same old thing, she said to me: Kallinarth, the hero-king in his realm composed of cloud; Valaquen, the maiden who sleeps, existing only in a dream-life, until all evil has gone out of the world; Xadatel and Finrael, wizard and warrior, heavenly twins. The title this time was *The Fountains of Zond*.

Arthur came to dinner with us soon after Liz had read it, we had three other guests, and while we were having our coffee and brandy I happened to say that I was sorry not to have any Drambuie as I knew he was particularly fond of it.

Liz said, 'We ought to have Xadatel here, Arthur, to magic you some out of the fountains of Zond.'

It was a harmless, even rather sympathetic, remark. It showed she knew Arthur's work and was conversant with the properties of these miraculous fountains which apparently produced nectar, fabulous elixirs or whatever was desired at a word from the wizard. Arthur, however, flushed and looked deeply offended. And afterwards, in the light of what happened, Liz endlessly reproached herself for what she had said.

'How were you to know?' I asked.

'I should have known. I should have understood how serious and intense he was about his work. The fountains produced – well, holy waters, you see, and I talked about it making Drambuie . . . Oh, I know it's absurd, but he *was* absurd, what he wrote meant everything to him. The same passion and inspiration – and muse, if you like, affected Shakespeare and Arthur Kestrell, it's just the end product that's different.'

Arthur, when she had made that remark, had said very stiffly, 'I'm afraid you're not very sensitive to imaginative literature, Elizabeth,' and he left the party early. Liz and I were both rather cross at the time and Liz said she was sure Tolkien wouldn't have minded if someone had made a gentle joke to him about Frodo.

A week or so after this there was a story in the evening paper to the effect that the Minister for the Environment had finally decided to forbid Haringey's plans for putting council housing on the old railway line. The Parkland Walk, as the newspaper called it. Four and a half miles of a disused branch of the London and North-Eastern Railway, was the way it was described, from Finsbury Park to Highgate and at one time serving Alexandra Palace. It was to remain in perpetuity a walking place. The paper mentioned wild life inhabiting the environs of the line, including foxes. Liz and I said we would go up there one evening in the autumn and see if we could see a fox. We never did go, I had reasons for not going near the place, but when we planned it I didn't know I had things to fear.

This was August, the end of August. The weather, with its English vagaries, had suddenly become very cold, more like November with north winds blowing, but in the last days of the month the warmth and the blue skies came back. We had received a formal thank-you note for that dinner from Arthur, a few chilly lines written for polite-ness' sake, but since then neither sight nor sound of him.

*The Fountains of Zond* had been published and, as was always the case with Arthur's, or Blaise Fastnet's, books, had been ignored by the critics. I supposed that one of his depressions would have set in, but nevertheless I thought I should attempt to see him and patch up this breach between us. On 1 September, a Saturday, I set off in the afternoon to walk along the old railway line to his house.

I phoned first, but there was no answer. It was a beautiful afternoon and Arthur might well have been sitting in his garden where he couldn't hear the phone. It was the first time I had ever walked to his house by this route, though it was shorter and more direct than by road, and the first time I had been up on the Parkland Walk on a Saturday.

I soon saw what he had meant about the crowds who used it at the weekends. There were teenagers with transistors, giggling schoolgirls, gangs of slouching youths, mobs of children, courting couples, middle-aged picnickers. At Northwood Road boys and girls were leaning against the parapet of the bridge, some with guitars, one with a drum, making enough noise for a hundred.

I remember that as I walked along, unable because of the noise and the press of people to appreciate nature or the view, that I turned my thoughts concentratedly on Arthur Kestrell. And I realized quite suddenly that although I thought of him as a close friend and liked him and enjoyed his company, I had never even tried to enter into his feelings or to understand him. If I had not actually laughed at his books, I had treated them in a light-hearted cavalier way, almost with contempt. I hadn't bothered to read a single one of them, a single page of one of them. And it seemed to me, as I strolled along that grassy path towards the Stanhope Road bridge, that it must be a terrible thing to pour all your life and soul and energy and passion into works that are remaindered in the bookshops, ignored by the critics, dismissed by paperback publishers, and taken off library shelves only by those who are attracted by the jackets and are seeking escape.

I resolved there and then to read every one of Arthur's books that we had. I made a kind of vow to myself to show an interest in them to Arthur, to make him discuss them with me. And so fired was I by this resolve that I determined to start at once, the moment I saw Arthur. I would begin by apologizing for Liz and then I would tell him (without revealing, of course, that I had so far read nothing of his) that I intended to make my way carefully through all his books, treating them as an *oeuvre*, beginning with *Kallinarth, the Cloudling* and progressing through all fifteen or however many it was up to *The Fountains of Zond*. He might treat this with sarcasm, I thought, but he wouldn't keep that up when he saw I was sincere. My enthusiasm might do him positive good, it might help cure those terrible depressions which lately had seemed to come more frequently.

Arthur's house stood on this side, the Highgate side, of Crouch End Hill. You couldn't see it from the line, though you could get on to the line from it. This was because the line had by then entered its valley out of which you had to climb into Crescent Road before the Crouch End Hill bridge. I climbed up and walked back and rang Arthur's bell but got no answer. So I looked up at those Gothic lattices as I had done on the day Liz was with me and though I didn't see Arthur's face this time, I was sure I saw a curtain move. I called up to him, something I had never done before, but I had never felt it mattered before, I had never previously had this sense of urgency and importance in connection with Arthur.

'Let me in, Arthur,' I called to him. 'I want to see you. Don't hide yourself, there's a good chap. This is important.'

There was no sound, no further twitch of curtain. I rang again and banged on the door. The house seemed still and wary, waiting for me to go away.

'All right,' I said through the letterbox. 'Be like that. But I'm coming back. I'll go for a bit of a walk and then I'll come back and I'll expect you to let me in.'

I went back down on to the line, meeting the musicians from Northwood bridge who were marching in the Finsbury Park direction, banging their drum and joined now by two West Indian boys with zithers. A child had been stung by a bee that was on one of the buddleias and an alsatian and a yellow labrador were fighting under the bridge. I began to walk quickly towards Stanhope Road, deciding to ring Arthur as soon as I got home, to keep on ringing until he answered.

Why was I suddenly so determined to see him, to break in on him, to make him know that I understood? I don't know why and I suppose I never will know, but this was all part of it, having some definite connection, I think, with what happened. It was as if, for those moments, perhaps half an hour all told, I became intertwined with Arthur Kestrell, part of his mind almost or he part of mine. He was briefly and for that one time the most important person in my world.

I never saw him again. I didn't go back. Some few yards before the Stanhope bridge, where the line rose once more above the streets, I felt an impulse to look back and see if from there I could see his garden or even see him in his garden. But the hawthorn, small birches, the endless buddleia grew thick here and far higher than a man's height. I crossed to the right hand, or northern, side and pushed aside with my arms the long purple flowers and rough dark leaves, sending up into the air a cloud of black and orange butterflies.

Instead of the gardens and backs of houses which I expected to see, there stretched before me, long and straight and raised like a causeway, a green road turning northwards out of the old line. This debouching occurred, in fact, at my feet. Inadvertently, I had parted the bushes at the very point where a secondary branch left the line, the junction now overgrown with weeds and wild shrubs.

I stood staring at it in wonder. How could it be that I had never noticed it before, that Arthur hadn't mentioned it? Then I remembered that the newspaper story had said something about the line 'serving Alexandra Palace'. I had assumed this meant the line had gone on to Alexandra Palace after Highgate, but perhaps not, definitely not, for here was a branch line, leading northwards, leading straight towards the palace and the park.

I hadn't noticed it, of course, because of the thick barrier of foliage. In winter, when the leaves were gone, it would be apparent for all to see. I decided to walk along it, check that it actually led where I thought it would, and catch a bus from Alexandra Palace home.

The grass underfoot was greener and far less worn than on the main line. This seemed to indicate that fewer people came along here, and I was suddenly aware that I had left the crowds behind. There was no one to be seen, not even in the far distance.

Which was not, in fact, so very far. I was soon wondering how I had got the impression when I first parted those bushes that the branch line was straight and treeless. For tall trees grew on either side of the path, oaks and beeches such as were never seen on the other line, and ahead of me their branches met overhead and their fine frondy twigs interlaced. Around their trunks I at last saw the foxgloves and the tansy Arthur had spoken of, and the further I went the more the air seemed perfumed with the scent of wild flowers.

The green road – I found myself spontaneously and unaccountably calling this branch line the green road – began to take on the aspect of a grove or avenue and to widen. It was growing late in the afternoon and a mist was settling over London as often happens after a warm day in late summer or early autumn. The slate roofs, lying a little beneath me, gleamed dully silver through this sleepy, gold-shot mist. Perhaps, I thought, I should have the good luck to see a fox. But I saw nothing, no living thing, not a soul passed me or overtook me, and when I looked back I could see only the smooth grassy causeway stretching back and back, deserted, still, serene and pastoral, with the mist lying in fine streaks beneath and beside it. No birds sang and no breeze ruffled the feather-light, golden, downy, sweet-scented tufts of the mimosa flowers. For, yes, there was mimosa here. I paused and looked at it and marvelled.

It grew on either side of the path as vigorously and luxuriantly as it grows by the Mediterranean, the gentle swaying wattle. Its perfume filled the air, and the perfume of the humbler foxglove and tansy was lost. Did the oaks shelter it from the worst of the frost? Was there by chance some warm spring that flowed under the earth here, in this part of north London where there are many patches of woodland and many green spaces? I picked a tuft of mimosa to take home to Liz, to prove I'd been here and seen it.

I walked for a very long way, it seemed to me, before I finally came into Alexandra Park. I hardly know this park, and apart from passing its gates by car my only experience of it till then had been a visit some years before to take Liz to an exhibition of paintings in the palace. The point in the grounds to which my green road had brought me was somewhere I had never seen before. Nor had I ever previously been aware of this aspect of Alexandra Palace, under whose walls almost the road led. It was more like Versailles than a Victorian greenhouse (which is how I had always thought of the palace) and in the oblong lakes which flanked the flight of steps before me were playing surely a hundred fountains. I looked up this flight of steps and saw pillars and arches, a soaring elevation of towers. It was to here then, I thought, right up under the very walls, that the trains had come. People had used the line to come here for shows, for exhibitions, for concerts. I stepped off on to the stone stairs, descended a dozen of them to ground level and looked out over the park.

London was invisible, swallowed now by the white mist which lay over it like cirrus. The effect was curious, something I had never seen before while standing on solid ground. It was the view you get from an aircraft when it has passed above the clouds and you look down on to the ruffled tops of them. I began to walk down over wide green lawns. Still there were no people, but I had guessed it likely that they locked the gates on pedestrians after a certain hour.

However, when I reached the foot of the hill the iron gates between their Ionic columns were still open. I came out into a street I had never been in before, in a district I didn't know, and there found a taxi which took me home. On the journey I remember thinking to myself that I would ask Arthur about this curious terminus to the branch line and get him to tell me something of the history of all that grandeur of lawns and pillars and ornamental water.

I was never to have the opportunity of asking him anything. Arthur's cleaner, letting herself into the Gothic house on Monday morning, found him hanging from one of the beams in his writing room. He had been dead, it was thought, since some time on Saturday afternoon. There was a suicide note, written in Arthur's precise hand and in Arthur's wordy, pedantic fashion: 'Bitter disappointment at my continual failure to reach a sensitive audience or to attract understanding of my writing has led me to put an end to my life. There is no one who will suffer undue distress at my death. Existence has become insupportable and I cannot contemplate further sequences of despair.'

Elizabeth told me that in her opinion it was the only review she had ever known him to have which provoked poor Arthur to kill himself. She had found it in the paper herself on that Saturday afternoon while I was out and had read it with a sick feeling of dread for how Arthur would react. The critic, with perhaps nothing else at that moment to get his teeth into, had torn *The Fountains of Zond* apart and spat out the shreds.

He began by admitting he would not normally have wasted his typewriter ribbon (as he put it) on sci-fi fantasy trash, but he felt the time had come to campaign against the flooding of the fiction market with such stuff. Especially was it necessary in a case like this where a flavour of epic grandeur was given to the action, where there was much so-called 'fine writing' and where heroic motives were attributed to stereotyped or vulgar characters, so that innocent or young readers might be misled into believing that this was 'good' or 'valuable' literature. There was a lot more in the same vein. With exquisite cruelty the reviewer had taken character after character and dissected each, holding the exposed parts up to stinging ridicule. If Arthur had read it, and it seemed likely that he had, it was no wonder he had felt he couldn't bear another hour of existence.

All this deflected my thoughts, of course, away from the green road. I had told Liz about it before we heard of Arthur's death and we had intended to go up there together, yet somehow, after that dreadful discovery in the writing room of the Gothic house, we couldn't bring ourselves to walk so close by his garden or to visit those places where he would have loved to take us. I kept wondering if I had really seen that curtain move when I had knocked at his door or if it had only been a flicker of the sunlight. Had he already been dead by then? Or had he perhaps been contemplating what he was about to do? Just as Liz reproached herself for that remark about the fountains, so I reproached myself for walking away, for not hammering on that door, breaking a window, getting in by some means. Yet, as I said to her, how could anyone have known?

In October I did go up on to the old railway line. Someone we knew living in Milton Park wanted to borrow my electric drill, and I walked over there with it, going down from the Stanhope Road bridge on the southern side. Peter offered to drive me back but it was a warm afternoon, the sun on the point of setting, and I had a fancy to look at the branch line once more, I climbed up on to the bridge and turned eastwards.

For the most part the leaves were still on the bushes and trees, though turning red and gold. I calculated pretty well where the turn-off was and pushed my way through the buddleias. Or I thought I had calculated well, but when I stood on the ridge beyond the hedge all I could see were the gardens of Stanhope Road and Avenue Road. I had come to the wrong place, I thought, it must be further along. But not much further, for very soon what had been a causeway became a valley. My branch line hadn't turned out of that sort of terrain, I hadn't had to climb to reach it.

Had I made a mistake and had it been on the *other* side of the Stanhope Road bridge? I turned back, walking slowly, making sorties through the buddleias to look northwards, but I couldn't anywhere find that turn-off to the branch line. It seemed to me then that, whatever I thought I remembered, I must in fact have climbed up the embankment to reach it and the junction must be far nearer the bridge at Crouch End Hill than I had believed. By then it was getting dark. It was too dark to go back, I should have been able to see nothing.

'We'll find it next week,' I said to Liz.

She gave me a rather strange look. 'I didn't say anything at the time,' she said, 'because we were both so upset over poor Arthur, but I was talking to someone in the Highgate Society and she said there never was a branch line. The line to Alexandra Palace went on beyond Highgate.'

'That's nonsense,' I said. 'I can assure you I walked along it. Don't you remember my telling you at the time?'

'Are you absolutely sure you couldn't have imagined it?'

*Imagined it?* You know I haven't any imagination.'

Liz laughed. 'You're always saying that but I think you have. You're one of the most imaginative people I ever knew.'

I said impatiently, 'Be that as it may. I walked a good two miles along that line and came out in Alexandra Park, right under the palace, and walked down to Wood Green or Muswell Hill or somewhere and got a cab home. Are you and your Highgate Society friends saying I imagined oak trees and beech trees and mimosa? Look, that'll prove it, I picked a piece of mimosa, I picked it and put it in the pocket of my green jacket.'

'Your green jacket went to the cleaners last month.'

I wasn't prepared to accept that I had imagined or dreamed the green road. But the fact remains that I was never able to find it. Once the leaves were off the trees there was no question of delving about under bushes to hunt for it. The whole northern side of the old railway line lay exposed to the view and the elements and much of its charm was lost. It became what it really always was, nothing more or less than a ridge, a long strip of waste ground running across north London, over Northwood Road, over Stanhope Road, under Crouch End Hill, over Vicarage Road, under Crouch Hill, under Mount View, over Mount Pleasant Villas, over Stapleton Hall, under Upper Tollington Park, over Oxford Road, under Stroud Green Road, and so to the station at Finsbury Park. And nowhere along its length, for I explored every inch, was there a branch line running north to Alexandra Palace.

'You imagined it,' said Liz, 'and the shock of Arthur dying like that made you think it was real.'

'But Arthur wasn't dead then,' I said, 'or I didn't know he was.'

My invention, or whatever it was, of the branch line would have remained one of those mysteries which everyone, I suppose, has in his life, though I can't say I have any others in mine, had it not been for a rather curious and unnerving conversation which took place that winter between Liz and our friends from Milton Park. In spite of my resolutions made on that memorable Saturday afternoon, I had never brought myself to read any of Arthur's books. What now would have been the point? He was no longer there for me to talk to about them. And there was another reason. I felt my memory of him might be spoiled if there was truth in what the critic had said and his novels were full of false heroics and sham fine writing. Better feel with whatever poet it was who wrote:

I wept as I remembered how often thou and I

Have tired the sun with talking and sent him down the sky.

Liz, however, had had her interest in *The Chronicles of Kallinarth* revived and had reread every book in the series, passing them on as she finished each to Peter and Jane. That winter afternoon in the living room at Milton Park the three of them were full of it, Kallinarth, cloud country, Valaquen, Xadatel, the lot, and it was they who tired the sun with talking and sent him down the sky. I sat silent, not really listening, not taking part at all, but thinking of Arthur whose house was not far from here and who would have marvelled to hear of this detailed knowledge of his work.

I don't know which word of theirs it was that caught me or what electrifying phrase jolted me out of my reverie so that I leaned forward, intent. Whatever it was, it had sent a little shiver through my body. In that warm room I felt suddenly cold.

'No, it's not in *Kallinarth, the Cloudling*,' Jane was saying. 'It's *The Quest of Kallinarth*. Kallinarth goes out hunting early in the morning and he meets Xadatel and Finrael coming on horseback up the green road to the palace.'

'But that's not the first mention of it. In the first book there's a long description of the avenue where the procession comes up for Kallinarth to be crowned at the fountains of Zond and ...'

'It's in all the books surely,' interrupted Peter. 'It's his theme, his leitmotiv, that green road with the yellow wattle trees that leads up to the royal palace of Quephanda ...'

'Are you all right, darling?' Liz said quickly. 'You've gone as white as a ghost.'

'White with boredom,' said Peter. 'It must be terrible for him us talking about this rubbish and he's never even read it.'

'Somehow I feel I know it without reading it,' I managed to say.

They changed the subject. I didn't take much part in that either, I couldn't. I could only think, it's fantastic, it's absurd, I couldn't have got into his mind or he into mine, that couldn't have happened at the point of his death. Yet what else?

And I kept repeating over and over to myself, he reached his audience, he reached his audience at last.

# The Copper Peacock and Other Stories

*For Don*

# A Pair of Yellow Lilies

A famous designer, young still, who first became well-known when she made a princess's wedding dress, was coming to speak to the women's group of which Bridget Thomas was secretary. She would be the second speaker in the autumn programme which was devoted to success and how women had achieved it. Repeated requests on Bridget's part for a biography from Annie Carter so that she could provide her members with interesting background information had met with no response. Bridget had even begun to wonder if she would remember to come and give her talk in three weeks' time. Meanwhile, obliged to do her own research, she had gone into the public library to look Annie Carter up in *Who's Who*.

Bridget had a precarious job in a small and not very prosperous bookshop. In her mid-thirties, with a rather pretty face that often looked worried and worn, she thought that she might learn something from this current series of talks. Secrets of success might be imparted, blueprints for achievement, even short cuts to prosperity. She never had enough money, never knew security, could not have dreamed of aspiring to an Annie Carter ready-to-wear even when such a garment had been twice marked down in a sale. Clothes, anyway, were hardly a priority, coming a long way down the list of essentials which was headed by rent, fares, food, in that order.

In the library she was not noticeable. She was not, in any case and anywhere, the kind of woman on whom second glances were bestowed. On this Wednesday evening, when the shop closed at its normal time and the library later than usual, she could be seen by those few who cared to look, wearing a long black skirt with a dusty appearance, a T-shirt of a slightly different shade of black – it had been washed fifty times at least – and a waistcoat in dark striped cotton. Her shoes were black velvet Chinese slippers with instep straps and there was a hole she did not know about in her turquoise blue tights, low down on the left calf. Bridget's hair was wispy, long and fair, worn in loops. She was carrying an enormous black leather bag, capacious and heavy, and full of unnecessary things. Herself the first to admit this, she often said she meant to make changes in the matter of this bag but she never got around to it.

This evening the bag contained: a number of crumpled tissues, some pink, some white, a spray bottle of 'Wild Musk' cologne, three ballpoint pens, a pair of nail scissors, a pair of nail clippers, a London tube pass, a British Telecom phone card, an address book, a mascara wand in a shade called 'After-midnight blue', a chequebook, a notebook, a postcard from a friend on holiday in Brittany, a calculator, a paperback of Vasari's *Lives of the Artists*, which Bridget had always meant to read but was not getting on very fast with, a container of nasal spray, a bunch of keys, a book of matches, a silver ring with a green stone, probably onyx, a pheasant's feather picked up while staying for the weekend in someone's cottage in Somerset, three-quarters of a bar of milk chocolate, a pair of sunglasses and her wallet which contained the single credit card she possessed, her bank cheque card, her library card, her never-needed driving licence and seventy pounds, give or take a little, in five- and ten-pound notes. There was also about four pounds in change.

On the previous evening Bridget had been to see her aunt. This was the reason for her carrying so much money. Bridget's aunt Monica was an old woman who had never married and whom her brother, Bridget's father, referred to with brazen insensitivity as 'a maiden lady'. Bridget thought this outrageous and remonstrated with her father but was unable to bring him to see anything offensive in this expression. Though Monica had never had a husband, she had been successful in other areas of life, and might indeed almost have qualified to join Bridget's list of female achievers fit to speak to her women's group. Inherited money wisely invested brought her in a substantial income, and this, added to the pension derived from having been quite high up the ladder in the Civil Service, made her nearly rich.

Bridget did not like taking Monica Thomas's money. Or she told herself she didn't, actually meaning that she liked the money very much but felt humiliated as a young healthy woman who ought to have been able to keep herself adequately, taking money from an old one who had done so and still did. Monica, not invariably during these visits but often enough, would ask her how she was managing.

'Making ends meet, are you?' was the form this enquiry usually took.

Bridget felt a little tide of excitement rising in her at these words because she knew they signified a coming munificence. She simultaneously felt ashamed at being excited by such a thing. This was the way, she believed, other women might feel at the prospect of lovemaking or discovering themselves pregnant or getting promotion. She felt excited because her old aunt, her maiden aunt tucked away in a gloomy flat in Fulham, was about to give her fifty pounds.

Characteristically, Monica prepared the ground. 'You may as well have it now instead of waiting till I'm gone.'

And Bridget would smile and look away, or if she felt brave tell her aunt not to talk about dying. Once she had gone so far as to say, 'I don't come here for the sake of what you give me, you know,' but as she put this into words she knew she did. And Monica, replying tartly, 'And I don't see my little gifts as paying you for your visits,' must have known that she did and they did, and that the two of them were involved in a commercial transaction, calculated enough, but imbued with guilt and shame.

Bridget always felt that at her age, thirty-six, and her aunt's, seventy-two, it should be she who gave alms and her aunt who received them. That was the usual way of things. Here the order was reversed, and with a hand that she had to restrain forcibly from trembling with greed and need and excitement, she had reached out on the previous evening for the notes that were presented as a sequel to another of Monica's favourite remarks, that she would like to see Bridget better-dressed. With only a vague grasp of changes in the cost of living, Monica nevertheless knew that for any major changes in her niece's wardrobe to take place, a larger than usual sum would be required. Another twenty-five had been added to the customary fifty.

Five pounds or so had been spent during the course of the day. Bridget had plenty to do with the rest, which did not include buying the simple dark coat and skirt and pink twinset Monica had suggested. There was the gas bill, for instance, and the chance at last of settling the credit card account, on which interest was being paid at 21 per cent. Not that Bridget had no wistful thoughts of beautiful things she would like to possess and most likely never would. A chair in a shop window in Bond Street, for instance, a chair which stood alone in slender, almost arrogant, elegance, with its high-stepping legs and sweetly curved back; she imagined it gracing her room as a bringer of daily-renewed happiness and pride. Only today a woman had come into the shop to order the new Salman Rushdie and she had been wearing a dress that was unmistakably Annie Carter. Bridget had gazed at that dress as at some unattainable glory, at its bizarreries of zips round the sleeves and triangles excised from armpits, uneven hemline and slashed back, for if the truth were told it was the fantastic she admired in such matters and would not have been seen dead in a pink twinset.

She had gazed and longed, just as now, fetching *Who's Who* back to her seat at the table, she had stared, in passing, at the back of a glorious jacket. Afterwards she could not have said if it was a man or woman wearing it, a person in jeans was all she could have guessed at. The person in jeans was pressed fairly close up against the science fiction shelves so that the back of the jacket, its most beautiful and striking area, was displayed to the best advantage. The jacket was made of blue denim with a design appliquéd on it. Bridget knew the work was appliqué because she had learned something of this technique herself at a handicrafts class, all part of the horizon-widening, life-enhancing programme with which she combated loneliness. Patches of satin and silk and brocade had been used on the jacket, and beads and sequins and gold thread as well. The design was of a flock of brilliant butterflies, purple and turquoise and vermilion and royal blue and fuchsia pink, tumbling and fluttering from the open mouths of a pair of yellow lilies. Bridget had gazed at this fantastic picture in silks and jewels and then looked quickly away, resolving to look no more, she desired so much to possess it herself.

Annie Carter's *Who's Who* entry mentioned a book she had written on fashion in the early Eighties. Bridget thought it would be sensible to acquaint herself with it. It would provide her with something to talk about when she and the committee entertained the designer to supper after her talk. Leaving *Who's Who* open on the table and her bag wedged between the table legs and the leg of her chair, Bridget went off to consult the library's computer as to whether this book was in stock.

Afterwards she recalled, though dimly, some of the people she had seen as she crossed the floor of the library to where the computer was. An old man in gravy-brown clothes reading a newspaper, two old women in fawn raincoats and pudding-basin hats, a child that ran about in defiance of its mother's threats and pleas. The mother was a woman about Bridget's own age, grossly fat, with fuzzy dark hair and swollen legs. There had been other people less memorable. The computer told her the book was in stock but out on loan. Bridget went back to her table and sat down. She read the sparse *Who's Who* entry once more, noting that Annie Carter's interests were bob-sleighing and collecting netsuke, which seemed to make her rather a daunting person, and then she reached down for her bag and the notebook it contained.

The bag was gone.

The feeling Bridget experienced is one everyone has when they lose something important or think they have lost it, the shock of loss. It was a physical sensation as of something falling through her – turning over in her chest first and then tumbling down inside her body and out through the soles of her feet. She immediately told herself she couldn't have lost the bag, she couldn't have done, it couldn't have been stolen – who would have stolen it among that company? – she must have taken it with her to the computer. Bridget went back to the computer, she ran back, and the bag wasn't there. She told the two assistant librarians and then the librarian herself and they all looked round the library for the bag. It seemed to Bridget that by this time everyone else who had been in the library had swiftly disappeared, everyone that is but the old man reading the newspaper.

The librarian was extremely kind. They were about to close and she said she would go to the police with Bridget, it was on her way. Bridget continued to feel the shock of loss, sickening overturnings in her body and sensations of panic and disbelief. Her head seemed too lightly poised on her neck, almost as if it floated. 'It can't have happened,' she kept saying to the librarian. 'I just don't believe it could have happened in those few seconds I was away.'

'I'm afraid it did,' said the librarian who was too kind to say anything about Bridget's unwisdom in leaving the bag unattended even for a few seconds. 'It's nothing to do with me, but was there much money in it?'

'Quite a lot. Yes, quite a lot.' Bridget added humbly, 'Well, a lot for me.'

The police could offer very little hope of recovering the money. The bag, they said, and some of its contents might turn up. Meanwhile Bridget had no means of getting into her room, no immediate means even of phoning the credit card company to notify them of the theft. The librarian, whose name was Elizabeth Derwent, saw to all that. She took Bridget to her own home and led her to the telephone and then took her to a locksmith. It was the beginning of what was to be an enduring friendship. Bridget might have lost so many of the most precious of her worldly goods, but as she said afterwards to her aunt Monica, at least she got Elizabeth's friendship out of it.

'It's an ill wind that blows nobody any good,' said Monica, pressing fifty pounds in ten-pound notes into Bridget's hand.

But all this was in the future. That first evening Bridget had to come to terms with the loss of seventy pounds, her driving licence, her credit card, her chequebook, the *Lives of the Artists* (she would never read it now), her address book and the silver ring with the stone which was probably onyx. She mourned, alone there in the room. She fretted miserably, shock and disbelief having been succeeded by the inescapable certainty that someone had deliberately stolen her bag. Several cups of strong hot tea comforted her a little. Bridget had more in common with her aunt than she would have liked to think possible, being very much a latter-day maiden lady in every respect but maidenhood.

At the end of the week a parcel came. It contained her wallet (empty but for the library card), the silver ring, her address book, her notebook, the nail scissors and the nail clippers, the mascara wand in the shade called 'After-midnight blue' and most of the things she had lost but for the money and the credit card and the chequebook, the driving licence, the paperback Vasari, and the bag itself. A letter accompanied the things. It said: *Dear Miss Thomas, this name and address were in the notebook. I hope they are yours and that this will reach you. I found your things inside a plastic bag on top of a litter bin in Kensington Church Street. It was the wallet which made me think they were not things someone had meant to throw away. I am afraid this is absolutely all there was, though I have the feeling there was money in the wallet and perhaps other valuable things. Yours sincerely, Patrick Baker.*

His address and a phone number headed the sheet of paper. Bridget, who was not usually impulsive, was so immediately brimming with amazed happiness and restored faith in human nature, that she lifted the phone at once and dialled the number. He answered. It was a pleasant voice, educated, rather slow and deliberate in its enunciation of words, a young man's voice. She poured out her gratitude. How kind he was! What trouble he had been to! Not only to retrieve her things but to take them home, to parcel them up, pay the postage, stand in queue no doubt at the Post Office! What could she do for him? How could she show the gratitude she felt?

Come and have a drink with him, he said. Well, of course she would, of course. She promised to have a drink with him and a place was arranged and a time, though she was already getting cold feet. She consulted Elizabeth.

'Having a drink in a pub in Kensington High Street couldn't do any harm,' said Elizabeth, smiling.

'It's not really something I do.' It wasn't something she had done for years, at any rate. In fact it was two years since Bridget had even been out with a man, since her sad affair with the married accountant, which had dragged on year after year, had finally come to an end. Drinking in pubs had not been a feature of the relationship. Sometimes they had made swift furtive love in the small office where clients' VAT files were kept. 'I suppose', she said, 'it might make a pleasant change.'

The aspect of Patrick Baker which would have made him particularly attractive to most women, if it did not repel Bridget, at least put her off. He was too good-looking for her. He was, in fact, radiantly beautiful, like an angel or a young Swedish tennis player. This, of course, did not specially matter that first time. But his looks registered with her as she walked across the little garden at the back of the pub and he rose from the table at which he was sitting. His looks frightened her and made her shy. It would not have been true, though, to say that she could not keep her eyes off him. Looking at him was altogether too much for her, it was almost an embarrassment, and she tried to keep her eyes turned away.

Nor would she have known what to say to him. Fortunately, he was eager to recount in detail his discovery of her property in the litter bin in Kensington Church Street. Bridget was good at listening and she listened. He told her also how he had once lost a briefcase in a tube train and a friend of his had had his wallet stolen on a train going from New York to Philadelphia. Emboldened by these homely and not at all sophisticated anecdotes, Bridget told him about the time her aunt Monica had burglars and lost an emerald necklace which fortunately was insured. This prompted him to ask more about her aunt and Bridget found herself being quite amusing, recounting Monica's financial adventures. She didn't see why she shouldn't tell him the origins of the stolen money and he seemed interested when she said it came from Monica who was in the habit of bestowing like sums on her.

'You see, she says I'm to have it one day – she means when she's dead, poor dear – so why not now?'

'Why not indeed?'

'It was just my luck to have my wallet stolen the day after she'd given me all that money.'

He asked her to have dinner with him. Bridget said all right but it mustn't be anywhere expensive or grand. She asked Elizabeth what she should wear. They were in a clothes mood, for it was the evening of the Annie Carter talk to the women's group which Elizabeth had been persuaded to join.

'He doesn't dress at all formally himself,' Bridget said. 'Rather the reverse.' He and she had been out for another drink in the meantime. 'He was wearing this kind of safari suit with a purple shirt. But, oh Elizabeth, he is amazing to look at. Rather too much so, if you know what I mean.'

Elizabeth didn't. She said that surely one couldn't be too good-looking? Bridget said she knew she was being silly but it embarrassed her a bit – well, being seen with him, if Elizabeth knew what she meant. It made her feel awkward.

'I'll lend you my black lace if you like,' Elizabeth said. 'It would suit you and it's suitable for absolutely everything.'

Bridget wouldn't borrow the black lace. She refused to sail in under anyone else's colours. She wouldn't borrow aunt Monica's emerald necklace either, the one she had bought to replace the necklace the burglars took. Her black skirt and the velvet top from the second-hand shop in Hammersmith would be quite good enough. If she couldn't have an Annie Carter she would rather not compromise. Monica, who naturally had never been told anything about the married accountant or his distant predecessor, the married primary school teacher, spoke as if Patrick Baker were the first man Bridget had ever been alone with, and spoke too as if marriage were a far from remote possibility. Bridget listened to all this while thinking how awful it would be if she were to fall in love with Patrick Baker and become addicted to his beauty and suffer when separated from him.

Even as she thought in this way, so prudently and with irony, she could see his face before her, its hawk-like lineaments and its softnesses, the wonderful mouth and the large wide-set eyes, the hair that was fair and thick and the skin that was smooth and brown. She saw too his muscular figure, slender and graceful yet strong, his long hands and his tapering fingers, and she felt something long-suppressed, a prickle of desire that plucked very lightly at the inside of her and made her gasp a little.

The restaurant where they had their dinner was not grand or expensive, and this was just as well since at the end of the meal Patrick found that he had left his chequebook at home and Bridget was obliged to pay for their dinner out of the money Monica had given her to buy an evening dress. He was very grateful. He kissed her on the pavement outside the restaurant, or if not quite outside it, under the archway that was the entrance to the mews. They went back to his place in a taxi.

Patrick had quite a nice flat at the top of a house in Bayswater, not exactly overlooking the park but nearly. It was interesting what was happening to Bridget. Most of the time she was able to stand outside herself and view these deliberate acts of hers with detachment. She would have the pleasure of him, he was so beautiful, she would have it and that would be that. Such men were not for her, not at any rate for more than once or twice. But if she could once in a lifetime have one of them for once or twice, why not? Why not?

The life too, the lifestyle, was not for her. On the whole she was better off at home with a pot of strong hot tea and her embroidery or the latest paperback on changing attitudes to women in western society. Nor had she any intention of sharing aunt Monica's money when the time came. She had recently had to be stern with herself about a tendency, venal and degrading, to dream of that distant prospect when she would live in a World's End studio with a gallery, fit setting for the arrogant Bond Street chair, and dress in a bold eccentric manner, in flowing skirts and antique pelisses and fine old lace.

Going home with Patrick, she was rather drunk. Not drunk enough not to know what she was doing but drunk enough not to care. She was drunk enough to shed her inhibitions while being sufficiently sober to know she had inhibitions, to know that they would be waiting to return to her later and to return quite unchanged. She went into Patrick's arms with delight, with the reckless abandon and determination to enjoy herself of someone embarking on a world cruise that must necessarily take place but once. Being in bed with him was not in the least like being in the VAT records office with the married accountant. She had known it would not be and that was why she was there. During the night the central heating went off and failed, through some inadequacy of a fragile pilot light, to restart itself. It grew cold but Bridget, in the arms of Patrick Baker, did not feel it.

She was the first to wake up. Bridget was the kind of person who is always the first to wake up. She lay in bed a little way apart from Patrick Baker and thought about what a lovely time she had had the night before and how that was enough and she would not see him again. Seeing him again might be dangerous and she could not afford, with her unmemorable appearance, her precarious job and low wage, to put herself in peril. Presently she got up and said to Patrick, who had stirred a little and made an attempt in a kindly way to cuddle her, that she would make a cup of tea.

Patrick put his nose out of the bedclothes and said it was freezing, the central heating had gone wrong, it was always going wrong. 'Don't get cold,' he said sleepily. 'Find something to put on in the cupboard.'

Even if they had been in the tropics Bridget would not have dreamt of walking about a man's flat with no clothes on. She dressed. While the kettle was boiling she looked with interest around Patrick's living room. There had been no opportunity to take any of it in on the previous evening. He was an untidy man, she noted, and his taste was not distinguished. You could see he bought his pictures ready-framed at Athena Art. He hadn't many books and most of what he had was science fiction, so it was rather a surprise to come upon Vasari's *Lives of the Artists* in paperback between a volume of fighting fantasy and a John Wyndham classic.

Perhaps she did after all feel cold. She was aware of a sudden unpleasant chill. It was comforting to feel the warmth of the kettle against her hands. She made the tea and took him a cup, setting it down on the bedside table, for he was fast asleep again. Shivering now, she opened the cupboard door and looked inside.

He seemed to possess a great many coats and jackets. She pushed the hangers along the rail, sliding tweed to brush against serge and linen against wild silk. His wardrobe was vast and complicated. He must have a great deal to spend on himself. The jacket with the butterflies slid into sudden brilliant view as if pushed there by some stage manager of fate. Everything conspired to make the sight of it dramatic, even the sun which came out and shed an unexpected ray into the open cupboard. Bridget gazed at the denim jacket as she had gazed with similar lust and wonder once before. She stared at the cascade of butterflies in vermilion and purple and turquoise, royal blue and fuchsia pink that tumbled and fluttered from the open mouths of a pair of yellow lilies.

She hardly hesitated before taking it off its hanger and putting it on. It was glorious. She remembered that this was the word she had thought of the first time she had seen it. How she had longed to possess it and how she had not dared look for long lest the yearning became painful and ridiculous! With her head a little on one side she stood over Patrick, wondering whether to kiss him goodbye. Perhaps not, perhaps it would be better not. After all, he would hardly notice.

She let herself out of the flat. They would not meet again. A more than fair exchange had been silently negotiated by her. Feeling happy, feeling very light of heart, she ran down the stairs and out into the morning, insulated from the cold by her coat of many colours, her butterflies, her rightful possession.

# Paperwork

My earliest memories are of paper. I can see my grandmother sitting at the table she used for a desk, a dining-table made to seat twelve, with her scrapbook before her and the scissors in her hand. She called it her research. For years three newspapers came into that house every day and each week half a dozen magazines and periodicals. She was a diligent correspondent. Her post was large and she wrote at least one letter each day. She was a writer without hope or desire for publication. My grandfather was a solicitor in our nearest town, four miles away, and he brought work home, paperwork. He always carried two briefcases and they bulged with documents.

Because he was a man he had a study of his own and a proper desk. The house was quite large enough for my grandmother to have had a study too but she would not have used that word in respect of herself. She had her table put into what they called the sewing room, though no sewing was ever done in it in my time. She spent most of each day in there, covering reams of paper with her small handwriting or cutting things out of papers and pasting them into a succession of scrapbooks. Sometimes she cut things out of books and one of the small miseries of living in that house was to open a book in the library and find part of a chapter missing or the one poem you wanted gone from an anthology.

The sewing-room door was always left open. This was so that my grandmother might hear what was going on in the rest of the house, not to indicate that visitors would be welcome. She would hear me coming up the stairs, no matter what care I took to tread silently, and call out before I reached the open door, 'No children in here, please,' as if it were a school or a big family of sisters and brothers living there instead of just me.

It was a very large house, though not large enough or handsome enough to be a stately home. If visitors go there now in busloads, as I have heard they do, it is not for architecture of antiquity, but for another, uglier, reason. Eighteen fifty-one was the year of its building.

The architect, if architect there was, was one of those Victorians who debased the classical and was too cowardly for the innovations of the Gothic. White bricks were the principal building material and these were not really white but the pale glabrous grey of cement. The windows were just too wide for their height, the front door too low for the fat pillars which flanked it and the hemispherical portico they supported, a plaster dome shaped like the crown of my grandfather's bowler hat and which put me in mind, when I was older, of a tomb in one of London's bigger cemeteries. Or rather, when I saw such a tomb, I would be reminded of my grandparents' house.

It was a long way from the village, at least two miles. The town, as I have said, was four miles away, and anything bigger, anywhere in which life and excitement might be going on, three times that distance. There were no buses. If you wanted to go out you went by car and if there was no car you walked. My grandfather, wearing his bowler, drove himself and his briefcases to work in a black Daimler. Sometimes I used to wonder how my mother had gone, when I was a baby and she left me with her parents, by what means she had made her escape. It was not my grandmother but the daily woman, Mrs Poulter, who told me my mother had no car of her own.

'She couldn't drive, pet. She was too young to learn, you see. You're too young to drive when you're sixteen but you're not too young to have a baby. Funny, isn't it?'

Perhaps someone had called for her. Anyway, two miles is not far to walk and a denizen of that house would be used to walking. Has she gone in daylight or after dark? Had she discussed her departure with her parents, asked their permission to go perhaps, or had she done what Mrs Poulter called a moonlight flit? Sometimes I imagined her writing a note and fastening it to her pillow with the point of a knife. Notes were always being written, you see, particularly by my grandmother (to my grandfather, to Evie, Mrs Poulter, to the tradesmen, to me when I could read handwriting, thank-you notes and even occasionally notes of invitation) so I had experience of them from an early age, though not of knives at that time.

I used to wonder about these things, for I had plenty of time and solitude for wondering. One day I overheard my grandmother say to an acquaintance from the village, not a friend, she had no friends: 'I have never allowed myself to get fond of the child, purely as a matter of self-preservation. Suppose its mother decides to come back for it? She is its mother. She would have a right to it. And then where should I be? If I allowed myself to get fond of it, I mean?'

That was when I was about seven. A person of seven is too old to be referred to as 'it'. Perhaps a person of seven months or even seven days would be too old. But overhearing this did not upset me. It cheered me up and gave me hope. My mother would come for me. At least there was a strong possibility she would come, enough to keep my grandmother from loving me. And I understood somehow that she was tempted to love me. The temptation was there and she had to prevent herself from yielding to it, so that she was in a very different position from my grandfather who, I am sure, had no temptation to resist.

It was at about this time that I took it into my head that the scrapbook my grandmother was currently working on was concerned with my mother. The newspaper cuttings and the magazine photographs were of her. She might be an actress or a model. Did my grandparents get letters from her? It was my job or Evie's to take up the post and on my way to the dining room where my grandparents always had a formal breakfast together, I would examine envelopes. Most were typewritten. All the letters that came for my grandfather were typed letters in envelopes with a typed address. But regularly there came to my grandmother, every two or three weeks, a letter in a blue envelope with a London postmark and the address in a handwriting not much more formed than my own, the capitals disproportionately large and the 'g's and 'y's with long tails that curled round like the Basenji's. I was sure these letters were from my mother and that some of them, much cut about, found their way into the scrapbook.

If children are not loved, they say, when they are little, they never learn to love. I am grateful therefore that there was one person in that house to love me and a creature whom I could love. My grandparents, you understand, were not old. My mother was sixteen when I was born, so they were still in their early forties. Of course they seemed old to me, though not old as Evie was. Even then I could appreciate that Evie belonged in quite a different generation, the age group of my school-fellows' grandmothers.

She was some sort of relation. She may even have been my grandmother's aunt. I believe she had lived with them since they were first married as a kind of housekeeper, running things and organising things and doing the cooking. It was her home but she was there on sufferance and she was frightened of my grandmother. When I wanted information I went to Mrs Poulter who was not afraid of what she said because she did not care if she got the sack.

'They need me more than I need them, pet. There's a dozen houses round here where they'd fall over themselves to get me.'

The trouble was that she knew very little. She had come to work there after my mother left and what she knew – as, for instance, my mother's inability to drive – was from hearsay and gossip. My mother's name she knew, and her age of course, and that she had not wanted to marry my father, though my grandparents had very much wanted her to marry without being particular about whom.

'They called her Sandy. I expect it was because she had ginger hair.'

'Was it the same colour as the Basenji?' I said, but Mrs Poulter could not tell me that. She had never seen my mother.

Evie was afraid to answer my questions. I promised faithfully I would say nothing to my grandmother of what she told me but she wouldn't trust me and I daresay she was right. But it was very tantalising because what there was to know Evie knew. She knew everything, as much as my grandparents did. She even knew who the letters were from but she would never say. My grandmother was capable of throwing her out.

'She wanted to throw your mother out,' said Mrs Poulter. 'Before you were born, I mean. I suppose I shouldn't be telling you this at your age but you've got to know sometime. It was Evie stopped her. Well, that's what they say. Though how she did it when she never stands up for herself I wouldn't know.'

Basenjis are barkless dogs. They can learn to bark if they are kept with other sorts of dogs but left to themselves they never do, though they squeak a bit and make grunting sounds. Basenjis are clean and gentle and it is a libel to say they are bad-tempered. They are an ancient breed of hound dog native to Central Africa, where they are used to point and retrieve and drive quarry into a net. Since I left that house I have always had a Basenji of my own and now I have two. What could be more natural than that I should love above all other objects of affection the kind I first loved?

My grandparents were not fond of animals and Evie was allowed to keep the Basenji only because he did not bark. I am sure my grandmother must have put him through some kind of barking test before she admitted him to the house. Evie and the Basenji had a section of the house to live in by themselves. If this sounds like uncharacteristic generosity on my grandmother's part – you will not expect this from her after what I have said – in fact their rooms were two north-facing attics, the backstairs and what Mrs Poulter called the old scullery. All the time I was not at school (taken there and fetched by Evie in the old Morris Minor Estate car) I spent with her and the Basenji in the old scullery. And in the summer, when the evenings were light, I took the Basenji for his walks.

You will have been wondering why I made no attempt to examine those scrapbooks or read those letters. Why did I never go into the sewing room in my grandmother's absence or penetrate my grandfather's study in the daytime? I tried. Though my grandmother seldom went out, she seemed to me to have an almost supernatural ability to be in two places, or more than two places, at once. She was a very tall thin woman with a long narrow face and dark, flat, rather oily hair which looked as if it were painted on rather than grew. I swear I have stood at the top of the first flight of stairs and seen her at the dining-table which could seat twelve, the scissors in her hand, her head turned as she heard the sound of my breathing, have run down and caught her just inside the drawing-room door, one long, dark, bony hand on the brass knob, twisted away swiftly and glimpsed her in the library, taking from the shelves a book destined for mutilation.

It was all my fancy, no doubt. But she was ever alert, keeping watch. For what? To prevent my discovery of her secrets? She was a mistress of the art of secrecy. I think she loved it for its own sake. At mealtimes she locked the sewing-room door. Perhaps she hung the key around her neck. Certainly she always wore a long chain, though what was on the end of it I never saw, for it was tucked into the vee of her dark dress. The study was never locked up but all the papers inside it were. One day, from the doorway, I saw the safe. I saw my grandfather take down the painting of an old man in a red coat and with a wig, and move this way and that a dial in the wall behind it.

On Fridays Evie put all the week's newspapers out for the dustmen. She brought them out of the drawing room and she brought them downstairs, a sizeable pile which I sometimes went through in the hope of finding clues. Windows had been cut out of most of them, sometimes from the sports pages, sometimes from the arts section, from the home news and the foreign news. Once, in possession of a mutilated copy of *The Times*, I managed by great guile and considerable labour, to persuade Mrs Poulter to bring me an identical undamaged copy which she helped herself to from another house where she cleaned. But the cut-out pieces had been only a report of a tennis tournament and a photograph of a new kind of camellia exhibited at the Chelsea Flower Show.

You might think my grandparents would have wanted to send me to boarding school as soon as I was old enough to go. They didn't. I would have liked to go away to school, I would have liked to go away anywhere, but Mrs Poulter said they couldn't afford the fees. That house cost a lot to keep up. Evie went on driving me to school, four miles to the grammar school and back in the morning and four miles in and four miles back in the afternoon. She must have been in her seventies by then. She always brought the Basenji with her in the back of the car, for although she might have left him alone in that house she would never quite risk leaving him with my grandmother.

I used to badger and badger her about my mother but she would never answer. She told me frankly that she dared not answer. But at last, driven mad by my pestering, she must have said something to my grandmother, for one morning at the breakfast table after my grandfather had left, after I had brought the post in including one of the letters in the blue envelopes, my grandmother turned to face me in a slow portentous way. Her tone remote, she said, 'These letters which you have been so curious about for years come from a friend of mine I was at school with. Her handwriting is rather immature, don't you think?'

I think I blushed. I said quite feverishly, 'Tell me about my mother.'

The tone didn't change or the look. 'Her name is Alexandra. I seldom hear anything of her. I believe she has married.'

'Why didn't she have me adopted?' I said. 'Why didn't you?'

'Naturally I can't answer for her. I doubt if she ever knew what she was doing. I would have had you adopted if it had been in my power. The mother's consent is needed in these matters.'

'Why didn't she want me? Why did she go away?'

'I shan't answer any more questions,' my grandmother said. 'It would take too long and I should upset myself. You'll know one day. When we're dead and gone you'll know. All about your mother and what little is known of your father, about the murder, if it was murder, and everything else. And you can tell Evie from me that if she gives you any information about what is no business whatsoever of hers I shan't see it my duty to give her or that dog of hers houseroom any longer.'

I passed this message on to Evie. What else could I do? My grandmother always meant what she said, she was a fearful woman, a cold force to be reckoned with. But the murder – what was the murder? In the ten years before I was born there had been two in the part of the country where we lived. A woman had killed her husband and then herself. A young man, not a local, had been found dead at the wheel of his car which was parked at the edge of a wood. He had been shot through the head. They never found who did it. I didn't have to ask Mrs Poulter about these things, they were common knowledge, but I did ask her what they had to do with us.

'They weren't even near here, pet,' she said. 'The woman who killed her husband and gassed herself, she'd only been living in her house six months. And that young fellow – what was he called? Wilson? Williams? – he drove here from London, he was a stranger.'

She was more easily able to explain what my grandmother meant when she said I would know everything one day, when they were dead and gone.

'They're going to leave you this house and its contents. I know it for a fact. He got me in there to be a witness to their wills.'

'But they don't even like me,' I said.

'You're their flesh and blood. They like you as much as they like anyone, pet. Anyway it's no big deal, is it? Who'd want it? Great white elephant, it's not worth much.'

Not then, perhaps, not then.


When I was fifteen and the Basenji was twelve and Evie getting on for eighty, my grandfather went out into the wood with his gun one morning and shot himself. They said it was an accident. After the funeral my grandmother got a carpenter in from London and had him build her three cupboards in the sewing room. She had the kind of doors put on them which security firms recommend nowadays for the front doors of London flats, reinforced with steel and with locks that when turned caused metal rods to bolt into the doorframe. Into these cupboards she placed the contents of my grandfather's wall safe and all the documents that were in his study. She probably put her own completed scrapbooks in there too, for I never saw her at work with scissors and paste again and there was no more mutilation of books.

There were rumours, and more than rumours, that my grandfather had been in some kind of trouble. Converting his clients' money to his own use or persuading elderly women to make wills in his favour – something of that sort. I suppose that when he went out into the wood that morning it was because he was afraid of criminal proceedings. His death must have averted that. His secrets were in the papers my grandmother hid away. She changed after he was dead, becoming even more cold and remote, and the few acquaintances she had used to see, she shunned. It was a cold house, though she had never seemed to feel it. She did then. Evie began lighting a fire in the grate and for some reason unknown to me it was my grandfather's cigarette lighter she used to light it, a silver object in the shape of an

Aladdin lamp which stood in the centre of the mantelpiece. For a while my grandmother continued to leave the sewing-room door open and when I passed and looked in the fire would be alight and she would be writing. She was always writing. Memoirs? A diary? A novel?

Records of births, marriages and deaths were kept at Somerset House then. When I reached the age my mother was when I was born I went by train to London and looked her up in the appropriate great tome. Alexandra was her name, as my grandmother had said (she never told lies) and she had married, as she also said, a man called Jeremy Harper-Green. They had two children, the Harper-Greens, a boy of six and a girl of four. I think it was when I saw this that I understood I would never meet my mother now.

The Basenji was the first to die. He was fifteen and he had had a good life. Evie and I buried him at the bottom of the garden which was on the side of a hill and from which you could look across the beautiful countryside of Derbyshire and see in the distance the landscape Capability Brown made at Chatsworth. It was winter, the woods dark and the hillsides covered in snow. I dug the grave but Evie was there with me in the intense cold, the biting wind. She caught a cold that night which turned to pneumonia and a week later she was dead too.

There was nothing to keep me after that. I packed up everything I owned into two suitcases and went to the sewing room and knocked on the door. For the past year she had kept that door closed. She said, 'Who is it?' not 'Come in', though it could only have been me or a ghost, for Evie was dead and she had given Mrs Poulter the sack six months before for what she called 'filling the child's head with lies and scandals'.

I told her I was leaving, I was going to London. She didn't ask me if I had any money so I was spared telling her that I had taken all the money I found hidden in Evie's rooms, in old handbags and stuffed into vases and wrapped in a scarf at the back of a drawer. Evie had told me often enough she wanted me to have what she left behind. My grandmother didn't ask me but she did me the one good service I ever remember receiving from her hands. She gave me the name and address of that old school friend, the one who wrote the letters in the blue envelopes and who was part owner of an employment agency in the Strand.

After that she shook hands with me as if I were a caller who had dropped in for half an hour. She didn't get out of her chair. She shook her head in a rueful way and said, not to me but as if there were someone else standing in the doorway to hear her, 'Who would have thought it would have gone on for eighteen years?'

Then she picked up her pen and turned back to whatever it was she was writing.

That was nearly thirty years ago. The friend with the employment agency got me a job. I stayed with her until I found a room of my own. I have prospered. I am managing director of my own company now and if I am not rich I am comfortably off. My marriage lasted only a short time but there is nothing very unusual in that. Children I never wanted and I have none. Five Basenjis have been my companions through the years, one who lived to be twelve, a pair who reached ten and eleven years respectively, and the five-year-olds that are with me now. They have been more to me than lovers or children.

Mrs Poulter told me my grandmother had bequeathed the house to me in her will. The chance of this inheritance I believed I lost for ever on the day I left, closed the sewing-room door behind me and went down the stairs to the front door. I never heard from my grandmother again, wrote no letters and received none. By then, for she was something over sixty when I went, I believed she was very likely dead. I seldom thought of her. I have worked hard at blocking off the misery of my early years.

The solicitor's letter coming one Monday morning four years ago told me she had died and left me the house. The funeral had taken place. I wondered who had seen to the arrangements. The Harper-Greens? If they expected a legacy they were disappointed, for it all came to me, the house and everything in it, the grounds from which you could see the sweeping meadows and the woods of Chatsworth.

Now I should know the answers to all those questions, the solutions to many mysteries. I drove up there one morning in autumn, my Basenjis who were puppies then with me in the back of the estate car. Was the truth that she had loved me all along, valued me in her cold inexpressive way? Or had she simply not bothered to change her will because, though she cared nothing for me, there was no one else she cared for more? I inclined towards this view. As I drove through the shires and the dukeries, the keys to the house beside me on the passenger seat, I allowed myself to speculate about those things I had long forbidden myself to think of, my grandparents' strange loveless marriage, my mother's refusal to have me adopted, yet willingness to abandon me to a fate she had already experienced, the identity of my father. Which of those murdered men was he? Or was he neither? What then was my family's connection with a murder? What retribution would have caught up with my grandfather if he had waited and faced it instead of going out into the woods with his gun?

We let ourselves into the house, the dogs and I. It was dusty and the ceilings hung with cobwebs but the smell that met me as I walked up the stairs was the smell of paper, old paper turned yellow with time and packed away in airless places. The sewing-room door was not locked. There were ashes in the grate and the silver Aladdin's lamp lighter still on the mantelpiece. A sheet of paper lay on the blotter on the table that was big enough to seat twelve. There were nine or ten lines of writing on it, the final sentence broken off in the middle, a fountain pen lying where my grandmother had dropped it and a splutter of ink trailing from the last, half-completed word. It was a kind of awe I felt and a growing dismay. The miseries I thought I had succeeded in forgetting began to crowd back and those earliest memories.

With the keys from the bunch I held I unlocked the burglar-proof cupboard doors. It was all there, all the secrets, in fifty scrapbooks, in a thousand letters received and a thousand copies of letters sent, in a hundred diaries, in deeds and agreements and contracts, in unnumbered handwritten manuscripts. The smell of paper, or perhaps it was the smell of ink, was acrid and nauseating. The dogs padded about the room, sniffing in corners, sniffing along skirting boards and around chair legs, sniffing and holding up their heads as if in thought, as if considering what it was they had smelt.

I began emptying the cupboards. Everything would have to be examined page by page, word by word, and in this house, in this room. How could I take it away except in a removal van? I imagined the misery of it, the enclosing oppression as sad and dreadful things were slowly revealed. The tears came into my eyes and I began to weep as I knelt there on the floor with the piles of paper all round me. The dogs came and licked my hands as dogs licked the sores of Lazarus.

Presently I got up and went to the fireplace and took my grandfather's silver lighter off the mantelpiece. I struck it with my thumb and the flame flared orange and blue. The Basenjis were watching me. They watched me as I applied the lighter to the pile of paper and the flame began to lick across the first sheet, lick, die, smoulder, lick, crackle, burst into bright flame.

I picked up the dogs, one under each arm, and ran down the stairs. The front door slammed behind me. What happened to the keys I don't know, I think I left them inside. I didn't look back but drove fast away and back to London.

It had been insured but of course I didn't claim on the insurance. The land belongs to me and I could have another house built on it but I don't suppose I ever shall. Two years ago a tour company wrote to me and asked if they might bring parties to look at the burnt-out shell as part of a scenic Derbyshire round trip. So now, I am told, the coach that goes to Chatsworth and Haddon Hall and Bess of Hardwick's house, follows the winding road up the hill to my childhood home and shows off to tourists the blackened ruin and the incomparable view.

I will never forget the way the police told me my house had burned down. Later they hinted at arson and this is how the guide explains the destruction to visitors. But that same evening when I had only been back a few hours, the police came and spoke to me very gently and carefully. I must sit down, keep calm, prepare myself for something very upsetting.

They called it bad news.

# Mother's Help

The little boy would be three at the end of the year. He was big for his age. Nell, who was his nanny but modestly called herself a mother's help, was perturbed by his inability, or unwillingness, to speak. It was very likely no more than unwillingness, for Daniel was not deaf, that was apparent, and the doctor who carried out tests on him said he was intelligent. His parents and Nell knew that without being told.

He was inordinately fond of motor vehicles. No one knew why, since neither Ivan nor Charlotte took any particular interest in cars. They had one of course and both drove it but Charlotte confessed that she had never understood the workings of the internal combustion engine. Their son's passion amused them. When he woke up in the morning he got into bed with them and ran toy trucks and miniature tractors over the pillows, shouting, 'Brrm, brrm, brrm . . .'

'Say "car", Daniel,' said Charlotte. 'Say "lorry".'

'Brrm, brrm, brrm,' said Daniel.

One of the things he liked to do was sit in the driver's seat on Ivan's knee or Charlotte's and, strictly supervised, pull the levers and buttons that worked the windscreen wipers, the lights, put the automatic transmission into 'drive', make the light come on that flashed when the passenger failed to wear a seat belt, lift off the handbrake, and, naturally, sound the horn. All the time he was doing these things he was saying, 'Brrm, brrm, brrm.' The summer before he was three he said 'car' and 'tractor' and 'engine' as well as 'brrm, brrm, brrm.' He had been able to say Mummy and Daddy and Nell for quite a long time. Soon his vocabulary grew large and Nell stopped worrying, though Daniel made no attempt to form sentences.

'It may be because he's an only child,' she said to Ivan one evening when she came down from putting Daniel to bed.

'And likely to remain one,' said Ivan, 'in the circumstances.'

He kept his voice low. Charlotte had stayed late at work but she was home now, taking off her raincoat in the hall. Because Charlotte was there Nell made no reply to this cryptic remark of Ivan's. She tried to smile in a reproachful way but failed. Charlotte went upstairs to say good night to Daniel and in a little while Ivan went up too. Alone, Nell thought how handsome Ivan was and how there was something very masterful, not to say ruthless, about him. The idea of Ivan's ruthlessness made her feel quite excited. Charlotte was the sort of woman people call 'attractive', without meaning that they or any others in particular, were attracted by her. Nell guessed that she was quite a lot older than Ivan or perhaps she just looked older.

'I wish I'd met you four years ago,' Ivan said one afternoon when Charlotte was at work and he had taken the day off. He had been married nearly four years. Nell had seen the cards he and Charlotte got for their third wedding anniversary.

'I was only seventeen then,' she said. 'I was still at school.'

'What difference does that make?'

Daniel was pushing a miniature Land Rover along the windowsill and along the skirting board and up the side of the doorframe, saying, 'Brrm, brrm.' He got up on to a chair, fell off and started screaming. Nell picked him up and held him in her arms.

'You look so lovely,' said Ivan. 'You look like a Murillo madonna.'

Ivan was the owner of the picture gallery in Mayfair and knowledgeable about things like that. He asked Nell if it wasn't time for Daniel's sleep but Nell said he was getting too old to sleep in the daytime and she usually took him out for a walk. 'I shall come with you,' said Ivan.

It was August and business was slack – though not Charlotte's business – and Ivan began taking days off more often. He told Charlotte he liked to be with Daniel as much as possible. Unless they weren't put to bed till some ridiculously late hour of the night, children grew up hardly knowing their fathers.

'Or their mothers,' said Charlotte.

'No one obliges you to work.'

'That's true. I'm thinking of giving up and then we wouldn't need to keep Nell on.'

Nell couldn't drive. When she went shopping Ivan drove her. He came home specially early to do this. The house was a detached Victorian villa and the garage a converted coach-house with a door which pulled down rather like a roller blind. When the car had been backed out it was tiresome to have to get out and pull down the door but leaving the garage open was, as Charlotte said, an invitation to burglars. Nell sat in the front, in the passenger seat, and Daniel in the back. In those days safety belts in the rear of cars had scarcely been thought of and child seats were unusual.

It happened very suddenly. Ivan left the car in 'park' and the handbrake on and went to close the garage door. Fortunately for him, he noticed a pool of what seemed to be oil at the back of the garage on the concrete floor and took a step or two inside to investigate. Daniel, with a shout of 'Brrm, brrm!' but without any other warning, lunged forward across the top of the driver's seat and made a grab for the controls. He flipped on the lights, made the full beam blaze, whipped the transmission into 'drive', sent sprays of water across the windscreen and tugged off the handbrake.

The car shot forward with blazing lights. Nell screamed. She didn't know how to stop it, she didn't know what the handbrake was, where the footbrake was, she could only seize hold of laughing triumphant Daniel. The car, descending the few feet of slope, charged into the garage, slowing as it met level ground, sliding almost to a stop while Ivan stood on tiptoe, flattening himself against the wall.

Nell began to cry. She was very frightened. Seeing Ivan in danger made her understand all kinds of things about herself and him she hadn't realised before. He came out and switched off the engine and carried Daniel back into the house. Nell followed, still crying. Ivan took her in his arms and kissed her. Her knees felt weak and she thought she might faint, from shock perhaps or perhaps not. Ivan forced her lips apart with his tongue and put his tongue in her mouth and said after a moment or two that they should go upstairs. Not with Daniel in the house, Nell moaned.

'Daniel is always in the bloody house,' said Ivan.

When Charlotte came home they told her what Daniel had done. They didn't feel like talking, especially to Charlotte, but it would have looked unnatural to say nothing. Charlotte said Ivan should speak to Daniel, he should speak to him very gently but very firmly too and explain to him that what he had done was extremely naughty. It was dangerous and might have hurt Daddy. So Ivan took Daniel on his knee and gave him a lecture in a kind but serious way, impressing on him that he must never again do what he had done that afternoon.

'Daniel drive car,' said Daniel.

It was the first sentence any of them had heard him speak and Charlotte, in spite of the seriousness of the occasion, was enraptured. They thought it wiser to tell no one else about what had happened but this resolve was quickly broken. Charlotte told her mother and her mother-in-law and Nell confessed to Charlotte that she had told her boyfriend. Nell didn't in fact have a boyfriend but she wanted Charlotte to think she had. Their doctor and his wife came to dinner and they told them. Ivan knew he had repeated the story to the doctor (and the four other guests at the table) because it was an example of the intelligence of a child some people might otherwise be starting to think of as backward. When an opportunity arose, he told the two women who worked for him at the gallery and Charlotte told her boss and the girl who did her typing.

In September Charlotte took two weeks' holiday. Business hadn't yet picked up at the gallery and they could have gone away somewhere but that would have meant taking Nell with them and Charlotte didn't want to pay some extortionate hotel bill for her as well. She was going to stay at home with her son and Nell could have the afternoons off. Charlotte's mother had said that in her opinion Nell was stealing Daniel's affections in an indefensible way. Ivan took Nell to a motel on the A12 where he pretended they were a married couple on their way to Harwich en route for a weekend in Amsterdam.

Nell had been nervous about this aspect of things at first but now she was so much in love with Ivan that she wanted him to be making love to her all the time. Every time she saw him, which was for hours of every day, she wanted him to be making love to her.

'I shall have to think what's to be done,' said Ivan in the motel room. 'We can't just go off together.'

'Oh, no, I see that. You'd lose your little boy.'

'I'd lose my house and half my income,' said Ivan.

They got home very late, Ivan coming in first, Nell half an hour later by pre-arrangement. Ivan told Charlotte he had been working until eleven getting ready for a private view. She wasn't sure that she believed him but she believed Nell when Nell said she had been to the cinema with her boyfriend. Nell was always out with this boyfriend, it was evidently serious, and Charlotte wasn't sorry. Nell would get married and married women don't remain as live-in mother's helps. If Nell left she wouldn't have to sack her. She was having strange feelings about Nell, though she couldn't exactly define what they were, perhaps no more than fear of Daniel's preferring the mother's help to herself.

'He'll go to her before he goes to you,' said Charlotte's mother. 'You want to watch that.'

He was always on Nell's lap, hugging her. He liked her to bath him. It was Nell who was favoured when a bedtime story was to be read, sweet-faced Nell with the soft blue eyes and the long fair hair. He seemed particularly to like the touch of her slim fingers and to press himself close against her. One Saturday morning when Nell was cutting up vegetables for his lunch, Daniel ran up behind her and threw his arms round her legs. Nell hadn't heard him coming, the knife slipped and she cut her left hand in a long gash across the forefinger and palm.

## 2

The cut extended from the first joint of the forefinger, diagonally across to the wrist, following the course of what palmists call the life line. The sight of blood, especially her own, upset Nell. She had given one loud cry and now she was making frightened whimpering sounds. Blood was pouring out of her hand, spouting out in little leaps like an oil well she had seen on television. It dripped off the edge of the counter and Daniel, who wasn't at all upset by the sight of it, caught the drips on his forefinger and drew squiggles on the cupboard door.

Charlotte, coming into the kitchen guessed what had happened and was cross. If Nell hadn't encouraged Daniel in these displays of affection he wouldn't have hugged her like that and she wouldn't have cut herself. He should have been out in the fresh air hugging his mother who had a trowel, not a knife, in her hand. Charlotte had been looking forward to an early lunch so that she could spend the afternoon planting twelve Little Pet roses in the circular bed in the front garden.

'You'll have to have that stitched,' she said. 'You'll have to have an anti-tetanus injection.' What Daniel was doing registered with her and she pulled him away. 'That's very naughty and disgusting, Daniel!' Daniel began to scream and punch at Charlotte with his fists.

'Shall I have to go to hospital?' said Nell.

'Of course you will. We'll get that tied up, we'll have to try and stop the bleeding.' Ivan was in the house, upstairs in the room he called his study. It would be more convenient for Charlotte if she could get Ivan to drive Nell to the hospital, but unaccountably she felt a sudden strong dislike of this idea. It hadn't occurred to her before but she didn't want to leave Ivan alone with Nell again. 'I'll drive you. We'll take Daniel with us.'

'Couldn't we leave him with Ivan?' said Nell, who had wrapped a tea cloth tightly round her hand and was watching the blood work its way through the pattern, which was a map of Scotland. 'We could tell Ivan and ask him to look after Daniel. Perhaps', she added hopefully, 'we won't be very long.'

'I'd appreciate it if you didn't interfere with my arrangements,' said Charlotte very sharply.

Nell started crying. Daniel, who was still crying into Charlotte's shoulder, reached out his arms to her. With an exclamation of impatience, Charlotte handed him over. She washed the earth off her hands at the kitchen sink while Nell sniffled and crooned over Daniel. They took coats from the rack in the hall, Charlotte happening to grab an olive-green padded jacket her mother-in-law had left behind, and went out through the front door. The twelve roses lay in a circle along the edge of the flowerbed, their roots wrapped up in green plastic. Nell stood in the garage drive cuddling Daniel, the tea cloth not providing a very effective bandage. Blood had now entirely obscured Caithness and Sutherland. Looking down at it, Nell began to feel faint, and it was quite a different sort of faintness from the way she felt when Ivan started kissing her.

Charlotte raised the garage door, got into the car and backed it out. She took Daniel from Nell and put him on the back seat where he kept a fleet of small motor vehicles, trucks and tanks and saloon cars. Already regretting that she had spoken so harshly to Nell, she opened the passenger door for her. Pale, pretty Nell in a very becoming thin black raincoat, had grown fragile from shock and pain.

'You'd better sit down. Put your head back and close your eyes. You're as white as a sheet.'

'Brrm, brrm,' said Daniel, running a Triumph Dolomite up the back of the driver's seat.

Since Ivan was in the house there was no need to close the garage door. It occurred to Charlotte that, antagonistic towards him though she felt, she had better tell him they were going out and where they were going. But before she reached the front door it opened and Ivan came out.

'What's happened? Why was everyone yelling?'

She told him. He said, 'I shall drive Nell to hospital. Naturally, I want to drive her, I should have thought you'd know that. I can't understand why you didn't come and tell me as soon as this happened.'

Charlotte said nothing. She was thinking. She seemed to hear in Ivan's voice a note of unusual concern, the kind of care a man might show for someone close and dear to him. And, incongruously, that look of his which had originally attracted her to him, had returned.

More than ever he resembled some brigand or pirate who required for perfect conviction only a pair of gold earrings or a knife between his teeth.

'There's absolutely no need for you to go,' he said in the rough way he had lately got into the habit of using to her. 'It's pointless a great crowd of us going.'

Putting two and two together, seeing all kinds of things fall delicately into place, recalling lonely evenings and bizarre excuses, Charlotte said, 'I am certainly going. I am going to that hospital if it's the last thing I do.'

'Suit yourself.'

Ivan got into the driving seat. He said to Nell, 'Bear up, sweetheart, what a bloody awful thing to happen.'

Nell opened her eyes and gave him a wan smile, pushing back with her good hand the curtain of daffodil-coloured hair which had fallen across her pale tearful face. In the back, Daniel put his arms round his father's neck from behind and ran the Triumph Dolomite up the lapels of his jacket.

'The least you could do is close the garage door,' Charlotte shouted. 'That's all we need, to come back and find someone's been in and nicked the stereo.'

Ivan didn't move. He was looking at Nell. Charlotte walked down the drive to the garage door. With her back to the bonnet of the car, she reached up for the recessed handle in the door to pull it down. The green padded jacket went badly with her blue cord trousers and it made her look fat.

His hands on the steering wheel, Ivan turned slowly to look at her. Daniel was hanging on to his neck now, pushing the toy car up under Ivan's chin. 'Brrm, brrm, brrm!'

'Stop that, Daniel please. Don't do that.'

'Drive car,' said Daniel.

'All right,' said Ivan. 'Why not?'

He put the transmission into 'drive', all the lights on, set the windscreen jets spouting, the wipers going, took off the handbrake and stamped his foot hard on to the accelerator. As the car plunged forward, Charlotte, who had pulled the door down to its fullest extent and was still bending over, sprang up, alerted by the blaze of light. She gave a loud scream, flinging out her hands as if to hold back the car. In that moment Nell, her eyes jerked open, her body propelled forward almost against the windscreen, saw Charlotte's face as if both their faces had swung to meet each other. Charlotte's face seemed to loom and grimace like a bogey in a ghost tunnel. It was a sight Nell was never to forget. Charlotte's expression of horror, and the knowledge which was also there, the awareness of why.

The weak hands, the desperate arms, were ineffectual against the juggernaut propulsion of the big car. Charlotte fell backwards, crying out, screaming. The bonnet obscured her fall, the wheels went over her, as the car burst through the garage door which against this onslaught was as flimsy as a roller blind.

Fragments of shattered door fell all over the bonnet and roof of the car. A triangular shaped slice of it split the windscreen and turned it into a sheet of frosted glass. Nell was jumping up and down in her seat, making hysterical shrieks but on the back seat Daniel, who had retreated into the corner behind his father, was silent, holding a piece of the hem of his coat in his fingers and pushing it into his mouth.

Blinded by the whitening and cobwebbing of the glass, Ivan recoiled from it, put his foot on the brake and pulled on the handbrake. The car emitted a deep musical note, like a rich chord drawn from a church organ, as it sometimes did when brought to a sudden stop. Ivan lifted his hands from the wheel, tossed his head as if to shake back a fallen lock of hair and rested against the seat, closing his eyes. He breathed deeply and steadily, like someone about to fall asleep.

'Ivan,' screamed Nell, 'Ivan, Ivan, Ivan!'

He turned his head with infinite slowness and when it was fully turned to face her, opened his eyes. Meeting his eyes had the immediate effect of silencing her. She whimpered. He put out his hand and touched the side of her cheek, not with his fingertips, but very gently with his knuckles. He ran his knuckles along the line of her jaw and the curve of her neck.

'Your hand has stopped bleeding,' he said in a whisper.

She looked down at the bundle in her lap, a red sodden mass. She didn't know why he said that or what he meant. 'Oh, Ivan, Ivan, is she dead? She must be dead – is she?'

'I'm going to get you back into the house.'

'I don't want to go into the house, I want to die, I just want to give up and die!'

'Yes, well, on second thoughts it might be best for you to stay where you are. Just for a while. And Daniel too. I shall go and phone the police.'

She got hold of him as he tried to get out. She got hold of his jacket and held on, weeping. 'Oh, Ivan, Ivan, what have you done?'

'Don't you mean', he said, 'what has Daniel done?'

When he came back from his investigations underneath the car, Ivan knelt on the driver's seat. He brought his face very close to hers. 'I'm going back into the house. I was in the house when it happened. I came running out when I heard the crash and as soon as I saw what had happened I went back in to call the police and an ambulance.'

'I don't understand what you mean,' said Nell.

'Yes, you do. Think about it. I was upstairs in my study. You were alone in the car with Daniel, resting your head back with your eyes closed.'

'Oh, no, Ivan, no. I couldn't say that, I couldn't tell people that.'

'You needn't tell them anything. You can be in a state of shock, you are in a state of shock. Telling people things will come later. You'll be fine by then.'

Nell put her hands up to her face, her right hand and the bandaged one. She peered out between her two fingers like a child that has had a fright. 'Is she – is she dead?'

'Oh, yes, she's dead,' said Ivan.

'Oh my God, my God, and she said she was coming to the hospital if it was the last thing she did!'

'Closing the garage door was the last thing she did.'

He went into the house. Nell started crying again. She sobbed, she hung her head and threw it back against the seat and howled. She had completely forgotten Daniel. He sat on the back seat munching on the hem of his coat, his fleet of motor vehicles ignored. The people next door, who had been eating their lunch when they heard the noise of the car going through the garage door, came down the drive to see what was the matter. They were joined by the man from a Gas Board van and a girl who had been distributing leaflets advertising double glazing. It was a dull grey day and the front gardens here were planted with tall trees and thick evergreen shrubs. Trees grew in the pavements. No one had seen the car go over Charlotte and through the garage door, no one had seen who was driving.

The people next door were helping Nell out of the car when Ivan emerged from the front door. Nell saw one of Charlotte's feet sticking out from under the car and Charlotte's blood on the concrete of the drive and the scattered bits of door and began screaming again. The woman from next door smacked her face. Her husband, conveniently doing the best part of Ivan's work for him, said, 'What an appalling thing, what a ghastly tragedy. Who would have thought the poor little chap would get up to his tricks again with such tragic results?'

'Don't look at it, dear,' said the double-glazing girl, making a screen out of her leaflets between Nell and the body which lay half outside and half under the car. 'Let's get you indoors.'

Nell gave another wail when she saw the Little Pet roses all lying there waiting to be planted. The woman next door went into Charlotte's kitchen to make a cup of tea and her husband came in carrying Daniel who, when he saw Nell, spoke another sentence of sorts.

'Daniel hungry.'

'I'll see to him, I'll find something for him,' said the woman next door, dispensing tea. 'Bring him out here, poor little mite. He's not to blame, the little innocent, how was he to know?'

'You see,' said Ivan when they were alone.

'You can't mean to tell people Daniel did it. You can't, Ivan.'

'I can't, agreed, but you can. I wasn't there. I was up in my study.'

'Ivan, the police will come and ask me.'

'That's right and there'll be an inquest, certain to be. The coroner will ask you and police will probably ask you again and maybe solicitors will ask you, I don't know, a lot of different people, but they'll be kind to you, they'll be understanding.'

'I can't tell lies to people like that, Ivan.'

'Yes, you can, you're a very good liar. Remember all those lies you told to Charlotte. She believed you. Remember that boyfriend you invented and all the times you said you'd been to the cinema with him when you'd been with me? Besides, you don't have to lie. You only have to tell them what happened last time, only this time poor old Charlotte got in the way.'

Nell burst into sobs. 'Oh, I can't stop crying, I can't. What shall I do?'

'You don't have to stop crying. It's probably a very good thing for you to cry quite a lot. Now don't stop crying but listen to me if you can. Daniel can't tell them because Daniel can't speak so's you'd notice. And it doesn't matter anyway because no one's going to blame him. You heard what Mrs Whatever-her-name-is said about no one blaming him, the little innocent, how was he to know? Children aren't supposed to know what they're doing before they're seven, before the age of reason. Everyone is well aware of what Daniel gets up to in cars, everyone knows he did it before.'

'But he didn't do it this time.'

'Never say that again. Don't even think it. Everyone will assume it was Daniel and you will only have to confirm it.'

'I don't think I can, Ivan. I don't think I can face it.'

'You know what will happen to me if you can't face it, don't you?'

The police came before Nell had time to answer.

It was something of a dilemma for them because Daniel was so young, but he helped them by coming into the room where they were interviewing his father and confirming, so to speak, what Ivan had told them.

'Daniel drive.'

They exchanged glances with Ivan and Nell and one of them wrote Daniel's words down. It was as if, Nell thought, they were taking down what he said to use it in evidence at his trial, only Daniel, naturally, wouldn't have a trial. He sat on her lap, holding one of his cars in his hand, but in silence. Nell said afterwards to Ivan that from that day forwards he never said 'Brrm, brrm' again but neither of them could be sure of this. When it was time for the police to go they took Nell with them to the hospital where at last she had her hand cleaned and the wound stitched. The sister in the Out-patients, who didn't know the circumstances, said it was a pity she hadn't come as soon as it had happened, for now she would probably be scarred for life.

'I expect I shall,' said Nell.

'There's always plastic surgery,' the sister said in a cheerful way.

By the time the inquest took place, the car had been fitted with a new windscreen and was scheduled for a re-spray, the garage had been measured for a new door and Daniel had learnt to utter several more sentences. But those who had power in these matters, a doctor or two and the coroner and the coroner's officer, all agreed that it would be unwise from a psychological point of view to mention again in his hearing the events of that Saturday morning. Not, at least, until he was quite a lot older. It would be better not to attempt any questioning of him and admonition at this stage seemed useless. The wisest course, the coroner said when the inquest was almost over, was for his father to ensure that Daniel never again sat in the back of a car on his own unless he were strapped in or closely supervised.

Nell gave her evidence in a low subdued voice. Several times she had to be asked to speak more loudly. She described how she had sat in the car, feeling faint, her eyes closed. There was no one in the driver's seat, Charlotte had gone to close the garage door, when suddenly Daniel, shouting 'Brrm, brrm,' had precipitated himself forwards and seizing the controls, switched on the lights, flashed up the full beam, pushed the transmission into 'drive' set the water jets spraying across the windscreen, taken off the handbrake. No, it wasn't the first time he had done it, he had done it once before, only that time his mother wasn't in the path of the car, bending down to close the garage door.

The coroner asked if she had attempted to stop the child but Nell burst into tears at this and, in a gesture that seemed dramatic but was in fact involuntary, held out, palm-upwards, her wounded hand, at that time still thickly bandaged. She often found herself staring at that hand in the weeks, the months, the years to come, at the white scar which bisected it from the first joint of the forefinger to the fleshy pad which cushioned out at the point where hand met wrist. She looked at it when she held her third finger up for Ivan to put the wedding ring on.

'Death by misadventure' the verdict had been, 'misadventure', Ivan said, meaning 'accident'. She had cut her finger by misadventure and she sometimes wondered if any of this would have happened if she hadn't cut it. If, in point of fact, Daniel hadn't run up behind her and thrown his arms round her legs. So perhaps, in a curious way, it really was his fault after all. She said something of this to Ivan who agreed but he never mentioned anything about any of it again. Nell never mentioned it either. The event, which he had certainly witnessed, had no apparent ill effects on Daniel. He was four when they got married and talking like any other normal four-year-old. He didn't appear to miss his mother, but then, as Ivan said, he had always preferred Nell.

When Nell's daughter was born after they had been married five years and she was giving up hope of ever having a child, Daniel, eyeing the baby Emma, surprised her by asking about his mother. He asked her how Charlotte had died. In a car crash, Nell said, which was the answer she and Ivan had agreed on.

'One day you're going to have to tell him more,' said Nell. 'What are you going to tell him?'

4

Ivan didn't say anything. His expression was guarded yet calculating. As he got older the ruthlessness which had helped to give him his dashing piratical appearance now made him look wolfish. Nell repeated her question.

'What are you going to tell Daniel when he asks you how Charlotte died?'

'I shall say in a car crash.'

'Well, he's not going to be satisfied with that, is he? He'll want to know details. He'll want to know who was driving and was anyone else involved and all that.'

'I shall tell him the truth,' said Ivan.

'You can't tell him the truth! How can you possibly? What's he going to think of you if you tell him that? He'll hate your guts. I mean, he may even go and tell people that his father – well, you know. I can't, frankly, bring myself to put it into words.'

'I am delighted to hear there is something you can't bring yourself to put into words. It makes a pleasant change.' When something riled him Ivan had got into the habit of curling back his upper lip to expose his teeth and his red gums.

'What precisely do you intend to tell Daniel, Ivan?'

'When the occasion arises, I shall tell him the truth about Charlotte's death. I shall tell him that though he was technically responsible for it, he couldn't at his age be blamed. I shall tell him as honestly as I can that he got hold of the controls of the car and drove it into Charlotte.'

'And that's the truth?'

'You should know,' said Ivan, wolf-faced, his upper lip curling. 'That's what you told the inquest.'

Daniel had only asked about his mother, Nell thought, because he was jealous. He was jealous of Emma. Until then he had had all Nell's attention, or all the attention she could spare from Ivan. Seeing Nell with this newcomer, understanding perhaps that she would no longer be exclusively his, recalled to him that he had once had a real mother of his own.

There were many things to recall her to Nell. Each time – which was every day – she saw those Little Pet roses she thought of Charlotte. Ivan had planted them himself, the day after Charlotte's funeral. They never used the car again, that went in part-exchange for a new one. When Emma was a year old they moved out of the house and into a larger, older one. Nell was happy to be rid of those roses but she couldn't get rid of her own hand with the white scar across it that followed in that sinister way the path of the life line. And she couldn't avoid occasionally seeing a map of Scotland.

At the new house they lost their baby-sitter. The woman next door had sat for them but wasn't prepared to travel ten miles. Ivan had several times suggested they engage a mother's help but Nell was against this. She remembered the way Daniel had always seemed to prefer her to his own mother. Besides, since they married she had never been in what Ivan called gainful employment. She had worked, of course, but this had been at the tiring and time-consuming task of looking after Daniel and then Emma too. And she had kept the house very clean and beautiful, and learned to drive.

A girl who was employed by Ivan at the gallery lived no more than a couple of streets away. She said she loved children and offered to baby-sit for them once a week. Ivan told Nell she was called Denise and was twenty-three but nothing else, and it came as something of a shock to discover that she was also very pretty and with long wavy chestnut hair. In fact, they needed her less frequently than once a week, for Ivan so often worked late that on the evenings he did come home in time for dinner he didn't feel like going out again.

'Emma will grow up hardly knowing her father,' said Nell.

'Go and be a mother's help then,' said Ivan. 'If you can earn what I do I'll be happy to retire and look after the kids.'

Denise sat for them on the evening of their sixth wedding anniversary and on Nell's birthday. Emma, whom Nell suspected of being hyperactive, stayed awake most of the time Denise was there, sitting on Denise's lap, playing with the contents of Denise's handbag and screaming when attempts were made to put her back to bed. Denise said she didn't mind, she loved children. Emma clung to her and hit out at Nell with her fists when Nell tried to take her out of the girl's arms.

'I'll drive you home,' said Nell.

'You don't need to do that,' said Ivan. 'I'll do that. You stay here with Emma.'

Denise had a boyfriend she was always talking about. When she couldn't baby-sit it was because she was going out somewhere with her boyfriend. Ivan said he had seen him come for Denise at the gallery but when Nell asked what he was like the best Ivan could do in the way of a description was to say he was just ordinary and nothing in particular. Nell didn't know where they would find another baby-sitter but sometimes she hoped Denise was serious about her boyfriend because if this were so she might get married and move away.

It was preposterous of Ivan to suggest, even in a satirical way, that she might get a job herself. She had her hands full with Emma who had an abnormal amount of energy for a child of eighteen months. Emma had walked when she was ten months old and never slept for more than six hours a night, though sometimes during the day she would collapse and fall asleep through sheer exhaustion. It wasn't surprising that she hadn't yet uttered a word, she was younger than all that activity made her seem, and as Nell remarked to Daniel, she hadn't got time to talk.

'You didn't talk till you were nearly three,' said Nell, and mistakenly as she quickly realised, 'There must be something about your father's children . . .'

'Yes,' said Daniel, 'there must be. It can't be you or my mother. I'd like to know what happened to my mother.'

'It was a car crash.'

'Yes, I know. I mean I'd like to know details, I'd like to know exactly what happened.'

'Your father will tell you when you're older.'

Nell had made a mystery of it and this she knew was an error. She intended to warn Ivan but for days on end she hardly saw him. They had made an arrangement to go out on Friday evening but Ivan phoned to say he was working late and that he would get in touch with Denise and put her off. He got home at midnight and nearly as late on Saturday. Daniel managed to catch him on Sunday morning.

'In some ways the sooner Daniel goes away to school the better,' Ivan said to Nell.

'That won't be for a year.'

'It might be a good idea for him to go as a boarder somewhere for that year.'

'I don't want him to go away, I want him to stay here. And it's no good you saying he's not my child, it's nothing to do with me, because he's more mine than yours. You've never liked him.'

Ivan's hair, once the black of a raven's wing, had begun to go grey early. It was the colour of a wolf's pelt now and the moustache he had grown was iron grey. Perhaps it was the contrast this provided which made the inside of his mouth look so red and his teeth so white when he indulged in that ugly mannerism of curling back his upper lip. If he were an animal, Nell's mother said, you would call it a snarl, but men don't snarl.

'Are you saying I don't like my own child?'

'Yes, I am. I am saying that. We don't like the people we've injured, it's a well-known fact.'

'What utter nonsense. How am I supposed to have injured Daniel?'

Nell looked down at her left hand. This had become an almost involuntary gesture with her, like a tic. She turned it palm-downwards and put her thumb across the base of her forefinger to hide the scar.

'I suppose he asked you about Charlotte?' she said.

'I told him you were the only person who could tell him. You were there and I wasn't. Of course, if you weren't prepared to tell him, I said, that was your decision. I wish you'd have something done about your hand. It doesn't get less unsightly as you get older. They can do marvels with scars these days and it isn't as if I'd grudge the expense.'

It was six months since Denise had baby-sat for them. They didn't need her because they never went out. Or they never went out together. Ivan always went out. Nell stayed at home and looked after Daniel and Emma and kept the house very clean. She had become obsessive about it, her mother said, it wasn't healthy.

One afternoon she was putting the vacuum cleaner away when Emma who had been running in and out, shut her in the broom cupboard. The cupboard door, which was heavy and solid in that old house, had a handle on the outside but not the inside. Nell, determined not to panic, began cajoling Emma to open the door and release her, please Emma, there's a good girl, open the door Emma, let Mummy out . . .

5

For a little while Emma stood outside the door. Nell could hear her giggling.

'Let Mummy out, Emma. Emma's such a clever girl she can open the door but Mummy can't. Mummy's not clever enough to open the door.'

Nell thought this flattery and self-abasement might have some effect on Emma. The giggling stopped. Nell waited in the dark. It was pitch dark in the cupboard and there wasn't even a line of light round the edge of the door. It fitted into its frame too well for that. The cupboard was in the middle of the house, between an interior wall and the solid brick of the chimney bay. The air there was thick and black and it smelt of dust and soot. Emma gave another very light soft giggle. Nell knew why it sounded so soft. Emma was moving away from the door.

'Emma, come back. Come back and let Mummy out. Just turn the handle and the door will open and Mummy can get out.'

The little footsteps sounded very light as they retreated. They sounded too as if the feet that made them moved not with their customary swiftness but sluggishly. With a sinking of the heart, Nell realised what had happened. This was what often happened to Emma after a long frenzied spell of hyperactivity. She had tired herself out.

Seizing her opportunity, Nell would lay Emma down in her cot and cover her up, but what would Emma do in Nell's absence?

Injure herself? Go outside and shut herself out? This was an additional worry. Nell began to hammer on the door with her fists. She began to kick at the door. Not only was she shut up in this cupboard but her child, her less than two-year-old baby, was wandering alone about this big old house of many steps and corners and traps for little children. Emma was tired, Emma was exhausted. Suppose she got the cellar door open and fell down the cellar steps? Suppose she put her fingers into the electricity sockets? Or found matches or knives? Nell couldn't see her hand in the dark but she could feel with the fingers of her other hand the ridge of scar tissue that scored her palm. She hammered on the door and shouted, 'Emma, Emma, come back and let Mummy out!'

As well as being black-dark in the cupboard, it was airless. Or Nell imagined it would soon be airless. No air could get in and once she had used up what oxygen there was – she would die, wouldn't she? She would suffocate. Daniel wouldn't be home for hours, Ivan, to judge by his recent performance, not before midnight. The more she shouted, the more energy she used in beating at the door, the more oxygen her lungs needed.

It was Daniel who rescued her. About an hour after Emma shut Nell in the cupboard Daniel came home from school. He let himself in and found the house empty which was most unusual. By that time Nell had stopped shouting and beating on the door. She was sitting on the stone floor with her arms clasped round her knees, keeping very still so as not to exhaust the oxygen in the dusty sooty air. Daniel wasn't expected home for another hour at least. He should have gone straight to his violin lesson from school but he had forgotten his music and come home to fetch it.

Although it was almost unknown for Nell to be out when he came home, he knew he wasn't expected home yet. Perhaps she always went out while he was at his violin lesson. With very little time to spare, he would have gone straight up to his bedroom, fetched his music and gone out again, but as he passed the living-room door he caught a glimpse of pink where no pink should be. This was his sister's pink jumpsuit. Emma was asleep on the rug in the living room, her thumb in her mouth, the small brush attachment from the vacuum cleaner lying by her side. The brush provided him with a clue and as he approached the broom cupboard, Nell heard his footsteps and shouted to him: 'Daniel, Daniel, I'm in here, I'm in the cupboard!'

He released her. Nell staggered out of the cupboard with cobwebs in her hair and blinking her eyes at the light. Daniel seemed rather pleased to see Emma get into trouble, for even after nearly two years he hadn't quite got over his jealousy. He scolded Emma himself and for once Nell didn't stop him.

It was the first evening for weeks that Ivan had come home at a reasonable hour. He brought Denise with him. They had some unfinished work to get through and Ivan thought they might as well do it at home. Nell told them of the events of the afternoon and Denise said how clever and enterprising Daniel had been. If he had been less observant he would have left the house again immediately and where would poor Nell be now?

'It's hard to see what else he could have done,' said Ivan. 'You might say with more justice that this is the reverse of virtue rewarded. If Daniel hadn't be so careless as to leave his music behind he would never have come home when he did. How can you praise someone for that?'

He scowled unpleasantly, but not at Denise. He and Denise would get to work on the new catalogue until eight and then he would take her out to eat somewhere. They had to have dinner but there was no need for Nell to cook for them, he said more graciously, especially after her ordeal. Denise said she was terribly pleased Nell was all right. She couldn't wait to see her boyfriend's reaction when she told him the story.

Ivan came in very late. His brown wolf's eyes had a glazed look, sleepy and entranced, a look which Nell had once known very well. Next day she said to him, apropos of nothing in particular, that she thought the day was coming when she would feel obliged to tell Daniel the truth about what had happened to his mother. It might also mean having to tell others and therefore acknowledging that she had committed perjury at the inquest, but she couldn't help that, she would have to face that. Ivan said, didn't she mean *he* would have to face that? And then he said no one would believe her.

'If we split up,' Nell said, 'I should get custody of these children. Daniel not being my own wouldn't make any difference, I should get custody. But you wouldn't mind that, would you? You don't like children.'

'What nonsense. Of course I like children.'

'And you'd lose your house and half your income.'

'Two-thirds,' said Ivan.

'I think you'd like to see the back of Daniel. You can't stand him.

And the reason you can't stand him is because one day you know you're either going to have to tell him the truth which will be the end of you or tell him a lie that will blight the rest of his life.'

'How melodramatic you are,' said Ivan, 'and how wrong. Anyway, we aren't going to split up, are we?'

'I don't know. I can't go on living like this.'

He took Emma on his knee and explained to her how extremely naughty she had been to shut Nell up in the broom cupboard. It was a very dangerous thing to do because there was no air in the cupboard and people need air in order to stay alive. Emma squirmed and fidgeted and struggled to get down. When Ivan held her firmly so that she couldn't get away, she bounced up and down on his lap. Suppose Emma herself had come to some harm, asked Ivan who, judging others by himself, hadn't much faith in an appeal to altruism. Suppose she had fallen down the steps and hurt herself?

When Emma had gone to bed Ivan suggested he and Nell made a fresh start. He would make an effort, he promised, to be home at a reasonable time in the evenings. Dismissing Densie would be tricky but he thought she would leave of her own accord. And he wouldn't embark on these projects that necessitated working long hours.

'How about Daniel?' said Nell.

Ivan smiled slightly. It was a sad smile, Nell thought. 'I'm working out something to tell Daniel.' She thought he was looking at the scar on her hand and she turned it palm-downwards. 'I shall tell him how it was you sitting in the passenger seat and he was in the back, playing with his cars, and the engine was running. I shall make it plain that he was in no way to blame. Of course I'll explain to him that you were feeling too ill to know what you were doing.'

'You needn't make it sound as if I cut myself on purpose. I'm not going to die, you know. I'll be around to answer for myself.'

Ivan didn't reply. He said it would be a nice idea to have a party for their seventh wedding anniversary.

The people Ivan had known during his first marriage he knew no longer, they had been left behind when he and Nell came to this house. But they invited Nell's mother and Nell's sister and brother-in-law and their doctor and his wife and the neighbours and the woman at the gallery with her husband and the girl who had taken over from Denise. It was a fine moonlit evening for a barbecue and Emma was up and still rushing about the garden at nine, at ten. She was naughty and uncontrollable, Ivan told the doctor, brimming with energy, it was impossible to cope with her.

'Hyperactive, I suppose,' said the doctor.

'Exactly,' said Ivan. 'For example, only a few weeks ago she shut Nell up in a cupboard, closed the door, and just ran off and left her there. If my son hadn't happened to forget something and come back for it I don't know what would have happened. There's no air in that cupboard.' Everyone had stopped talking and was listening to Ivan. Nell, handing round little cheese biscuits, stopped and listened to Ivan. 'I gave her a talking-to, you can imagine the kind of thing, but she's only two. Precocious of course but basically a baby.' Ivan's smile was so wolfish, he looked as if he was about to lift his head and bay at the moon. 'I don't know why it is,' he said, 'but neither of my children ever do what they're told, they don't listen to a word I say.'

Nell dropped the plate and screamed. She stood there screaming until the woman from the gallery went up to her and slapped her face.

# Long Live the Queen

It was over in an instant. A flash of orange out of the green hedge, a streak across the road, a thud. The impact was felt as a surprisingly heavy jarring. There was no cry. Anna had braked but too late and the car had been going fast. She pulled in to the side of the road, got out, walked back.

An effort was needed before she could look. The cat had been flung against the grass verge which separated road from narrow walkway. It was dead. She knew before she knelt down and felt its side that it was dead. A little blood came from its mouth. Its eyes were already glazing. It had been a fine cat of the kind called marmalade because the colour is two-tone, the stripes like dark slices of peel among the clear orange. Paws, chest and part of its face were white, the eyes gooseberry green.

It was an unfamiliar road, one she had only taken to avoid roadworks on the bridge. Anna thought, I was going too fast. There is no speed limit here but it's a country road with cottages and I shouldn't have been going so fast. The poor cat. Now she must go and admit what she had done, confront an angry or distressed owner, an owner who presumably lived in the house behind that hedge.

She opened the gate and went up the path. It was a cottage but not a pretty one: of red brick with a low slate roof, bay windows downstairs with a green front door between them. In each bay window sat a cat, one black, one orange and white like the cat which had run in front of her car. They stared at her, unblinking, inscrutable, as if they did not see her, as if she was not there. She could still see the black one when she was at the front door. When she put her finger to the bell and rang it the cat did not move, nor even blink its eyes.

No one came to the door. She rang the bell again. It occurred to her that the owner might be in the back garden and she walked round the side of the house. It was not really a garden but a wilderness of long grass and tall weeds and wild trees. There was no one. She looked through a window into a kitchen where a tortoiseshell cat sat on top of the fridge in the sphynx position and on the floor, on a strip of matting, a brown tabby rolled sensuously, its striped paws stroking the air.

There were no cats outside as far as she could see, not living ones at least. In the left-hand corner, past a kind of lean-to coalshed and a clump of bushes, three small wooden crosses were just visible among the long grass. Anna had no doubt they were cat graves.

She looked in her bag and finding a hairdresser's appointment card, wrote on the blank back of it her name, her parents' address and their phone number, added, *Your cat ran out in front of my car. I'm sorry, I'm sure death was instantaneous.* Back at the front door, the black cat and the orange and white cat still staring out, she put the card through the letter box.

It was then that she looked in the window where the black cat was sitting. Inside was a small overfurnished living room which looked as if it smelt. Two cats lay on the hearthrug, two more were curled up together in an armchair. At either end of the mantelpiece sat a china cat, white and red with gilt whiskers. Anna thought there ought to have been another one between them, in the centre of the shelf, because this was the only clear space in the room, every other corner and surface being crowded with objects, many of which had some association with the feline: cat ashtrays, cat vases, photographs of cats in silver frames, postcards of cats, mugs with cat faces on them and ceramic, brass, silver and glass kittens. Above the fireplace was a portrait of a marmalade and white cat done in oils and on the wall to the left hung a cat calendar.

Anna had an uneasy feeling that the cat in the portrait was the one that lay dead in the road. At any rate, it was very like. She could not leave the dead cat where it was. In the boot of her car were two plastic carrier bags, some sheets of newspaper and a blanket she sometimes used for padding things she did not want to strike against each other while she was driving. As wrapping for the cat's body the plastic bags would look callous, the newspapers worse. She would sacrifice the blanket. It was a clean dark blue blanket, single size, quite decent and decorous.

The cat's body wrapped in this blanket, she carried it up the path. The black cat had moved from the left-hand bay and had taken up a similar position in one of the upstairs windows. Anna took another look into the living room. A second examination of the portrait confirmed her guess that its subject was the one she was carrying. She backed away. The black cat stared down at her, turned its head and yawned hugely. Of course it did not know she carried one of its companions, dead and now cold, wrapped in an old car blanket, having met a violent death. She had an uncomfortable feeling, a ridiculous feeling, that it would have behaved in precisely the same way if it had known.

She laid the cat's body on the roof of the coalshed. As she came back round the house she saw a woman in the garden next door. This was a neat and tidy garden with flowers and a lawn. The woman was in her fifties, white-haired, slim, wearing a twinset.

'One of the cats ran out in front of my car,' Anna said. 'I'm afraid it's dead.'

'Oh, dear.'

'I've put the – body, the body on the coalshed. Do you know when they'll be back?'

'It's just her,' the woman said. 'It's just her on her own.'

'Oh, well. I've written a note for her. With my name and address.'

The woman was giving her an odd look. 'You're very honest. Most would have just driven on. You don't have to report running over a cat, you know. It's not the same as a dog.'

'I couldn't have just gone on.'

'If I were you I'd tear that note up. You can leave it to me, I'll tell her I saw you.'

'I've already put it through the door,' said Anna.

She said goodbye to the woman and got back into her car. She was on her way to her parents' house where she would be staying for the next two weeks. Anna had a flat on the other side of the town but she had promised to look after her parents' house while they were away on holiday, and – it now seemed a curious irony – her parents' cat.

If her journey had gone according to plan, if she had not been delayed for half an hour by the accident and the cat's death, she would have been in time to see her mother and father before they left for the airport. But when she got there they had gone. On the hall table was a note for her in her mother's hand to say that they had had to leave, the cat had been fed and there was a cold roast chicken in the fridge for Anna's supper. The cat would probably like some too, to comfort it for missing them.

Anna did not think her mother's cat, a huge fluffy creature of a ghostly whitish-grey tabbyness, named Griselda, was capable of missing anyone. She could not believe it had affections. It seemed to her without personality or charm, to lack endearing ways. To her knowledge, it had never uttered beyond giving an occasional thin squeak that signified hunger. It had never been known to rub its body against human legs, or even against the legs of the furniture. Anna knew that it was absurd to call an animal selfish, an animal naturally put its survival first, self-preservation being its prime instinct, yet she thought of Griselda as deeply, intensely, callously selfish. When it was not eating it slept, and it slept in those most comfortable places where the people that owned it would have liked to sit but from which they could not bring themselves to dislodge it. At night it lay on their bed and if they moved, dug its long sharp claws through the bedclothes into their legs.

Anna's mother did not like hearing Griselda referred to as 'it'. She corrected Anna and stroked Griselda's head. Griselda, who purred a lot when recently fed and ensconced among cushions, always stopped purring at the touch of a human hand. This would have amused Anna if she had not seen that her mother seemed hurt by it, withdrew her hand and gave an unhappy little laugh.

When she had unpacked the case she brought with her, had prepared and eaten her meal and given Griselda a chicken leg, she began to wonder if the owner of the cat she had run over would phone. The owner might feel, as people bereaved in great or small ways sometimes did feel, that nothing could bring back the dead. Discussion was useless and so, certainly, was recrimination. It had not in fact been her fault. She had been driving fast, but not *illegally* fast, and even if she had been driving at thirty miles an hour she doubted if she could have avoided the cat which streaked so swiftly out of the hedge.

It would be better to stop thinking about it. A night's sleep, a day at work, and the memory of it would recede. She had done all she could. She was very glad she had not just driven on as the next-door neighbour had seemed to advocate. It had been some consolation to know that the woman had many cats, not just the one, so that perhaps losing one would be less of a blow.

When she had washed the dishes and phoned her friend Kate, and wondered if Richard, the man who had taken her out three times and to whom she had given this number, would phone and had decided he would not, she sat down beside Griselda, not *with* Griselda but on the same sofa as she was on, and watched television. It got to ten and she thought it unlikely the cat woman – she had begun thinking of her as that – would phone now.

There was a phone extension in her parents' room but not in the spare room where she would be sleeping. It was nearly eleven-thirty and she was getting into bed when the phone rang. The chance of its being Richard, who was capable of phoning late, especially if he thought she was alone, made her go into her parents' bedroom and answer it.

A voice that sounded strange, thin and cracked, said what sounded like, 'Maria Yackle.'

'Yes?' Anna said.

'This is Maria Yackle. It was my cat that you killed.'

Anna swallowed. 'Yes. I'm glad you found my note. I'm very sorry, I'm very sorry. It was an accident. The cat ran out in front of my car.'

'You were going too fast.'

It was a blunt statement, harshly made. Anna could not refute it. She said, 'I'm very sorry about your cat.'

'They don't go out much, they're happier indoors. It was a chance in a million. I should like to see you. I think you should make amends. It wouldn't be right for you just to get away with it.'

Anna was very taken aback. Up till then the woman's remarks had seemed reasonable. She did not know what to say.

'I think you should compensate me, don't you? I loved her, I love all my cats. I expect you thought that because I had so many cats it wouldn't hurt me so much to lose one.'

That was so near what Anna had thought that she felt a kind of shock as if this Maria Yackle or whatever she was called had read her mind. 'I've told you I'm sorry. I am sorry, I was very upset, I *hated* it happening. I don't know what more I can say.'

'We must meet.'

'What would be the use of that?' Anna knew she sounded rude but she was shaken by the woman's tone, her blunt, direct sentences.

There was a break in the voice, something very like a sob. 'It would be of use to me.'

The phone went down. Anna could hardly believe it. She had heard it go down but still she said several times over, 'Hallo? Hallo?' and 'Are you still there?'

She went downstairs and found the telephone directory for the area and looked up Yackle. It wasn't there. She sat down and worked her way through all the 'Y's. There were not many pages of 'Y's, apart from Youngs, but there was no one with a name beginning with Y at that address on the rustic road among the cottages.

She could not get to sleep. She expected the phone to ring again, Maria Yackle to ring back. After a while she put the bedlamp on and lay there in the light. It must have been three, and still she had not slept, when Griselda came in, got on the bed and stretched her length along Anna's legs. She put out the light, deciding not to answer the phone if it did ring, to relax, forget the run-over cat, concentrate on nice things. As she turned face-downwards and stretched her body straight, she felt Griselda's claws prickle her calves. As she shrank away from contact, curled up her legs and left Griselda a good half of the bed, a thick rough purring began.

The first thing she thought of when she woke up was how upset that poor cat woman had been. She expected her to phone back at breakfast time but nothing happened. Anna fed Griselda, left her to her house, her cat flap, her garden and wider territory, and drove to work. Richard phoned as soon as she got in. Could they meet the following evening? She agreed, obscurely wishing he had said that night, suggesting that evening herself only to be told he had to work late, had a dinner with a client.

She had been home for ten minutes when a car drew up outside. It was an old car, at least ten years old, and not only dented and scratched but with some of the worst scars painted or sprayed over in a different shade of red. Anna, who saw it arrive from a front window, watched the woman get out of it and approach the house. She was old or at least elderly – is elderly older than old or old older than elderly? – but dressed like a teenager. Anna got a closer look at her clothes, her hair, and her face when she opened the front door.

It was a wrinkled face, the colour and texture of a chicken's wattles. Small blue eyes were buried somewhere in the strawberry redness. The bright white hair next to it was as much of a contrast as snow against scarlet cloth. She wore tight jeans with socks pulled over the bottoms of them, dirty white trainers, and a big loose sweatshirt with a cat's face on it, a painted smiling bewhiskered mask, orange and white and green-eyed.

Anna had read somewhere the comment made by a young girl on an older woman's boast that she could wear a miniskirt because she had good legs: It's not your legs, it's your face. She thought of this as she looked at Maria Yackle but that was the last time for a long while she thought of anything like that.

'I've come early because we shall have a lot to talk about,' Maria Yackle said and walked in. She did this in such a way as to compel Anna to open the door further and stand aside. 'This is *your* house?'

She might have meant because Anna was so young or perhaps there was some more offensive reason for asking.

'My parents. I'm just staying here.'

'Is it this room?' She was already on the threshold of Anna's mother's living room.

Anna nodded. She had been taken aback but only for a moment. It was best to get this over. But she did not care to be dictated to.

'You could have let me know. I might not have been here.'

There was no reply because Maria Yackle had seen Griselda. The cat had been sitting on the back of a wing chair between the wings, an apparently uncomfortable place though a favourite, but at sight of the newcomer had stretched, got down and was walking towards her. Maria Yackle put out her hand. It was a horrible hand, large and red with rope-like blue veins standing out above the bones, the palm calloused, the nails black and broken and the sides of the forefingers and thumbs ingrained with brownish dirt. Griselda approached and put her smoky whitish muzzle and pink nose into this hand.

'I shouldn't,' Anna said rather sharply, for Maria Yackle was bending over to pick the cat up. 'She isn't very nice. She doesn't like people.'

'She'll like me.'

And the amazing thing was that Griselda did. Maria Yackle sat down and Griselda sat on her lap. Griselda the unfriendly, the cold-hearted, the cat who purred when alone and who ceased to purr when touched, the ice-eyed, the standoffish walker-by-herself, settled down on this unknown untried lap, having first climbed up Maria Yackle's chest and on to her shoulders and rubbed her ears and plump furry cheeks against the sweatshirt with the painted cat face.

'You seem surprised.'

Anna said, 'You could say that.'

'There's no mystery. The explanation's simple.' It was a shrill harsh voice, cracked by the onset of old age, articulate, the usage grammatical, but the accent raw cockney. 'You and your mum and dad too, no doubt, you all think you smell very nice and pretty. You have your bath every morning with bath essence and scented soap. You put talcum powder on and spray stuff in your armpits, you rub cream on your bodies and squirt on perfume. Maybe you've washed your hair too with shampoo and conditioner and what-do-they-call-it? – mousse. You clean your teeth and wash your mouth, put a drop more perfume behind your ears, paint your faces – well, I daresay your dad doesn't paint his face, but he shaves, doesn't he? More mousse and then after-shave.

'You put on your clothes. All of them clean, spotless. They've either just come back from the dry-cleaners or else out of the washing machine with biological soap and spring-fresh fabric softener. Oh, I know, I may not do it myself but I see it on the TV.

'It all smells very fine to you but it doesn't to her. Oh, no. To her it's just chemicals, like gas might be to you or paraffin. A nasty strong

174

chemical smell that puts her right off and makes her shrink up in her furry skin. What's her name?'

This question was uttered on a sharp bark. 'Griselda,' said Anna, and, 'How did you know it's a she?'

'Face, look,' said Maria Yackle. 'See her little nose. See her smily mouth and her little nose and her fat cheeks? Tom cat's got a big nose, got a long muzzle. Never mind if he's been neutered, still got a big nose.'

'What did you come here to say to me?' said Anna.

Griselda had curled up on the cat woman's lap, burying her head, slightly upward turned, in the crease between stomach and thigh. 'I don't go in for all that stuff, you see.' The big red hand stroked Griselda's head, the stripy bit between her ears. 'Cat likes the smell of me because I haven't got my clothes in soapy water every day, I have a bath once a week, always have and always shall, and I don't waste my money on odorisers and deodorisers. I wash my hands when I get up in the morning and that's enough for me.'

At the mention of the weekly bath, Anna had reacted instinctively and edged her chair a little further away. Maria Yackle saw, Anna was sure she saw, but her response to this recoil was to begin on what she had in fact come about: her compensation.

'The cat you killed, she was five years old and the queen of the cats, her name was Melusina. I always have a queen. The one before was Juliana and she lived to be twelve. I wept, I mourned her, but life has to go on. The queen is dead, I said, long live the queen! I never promote one, I always get a new kitten. Some cats are queens, you see, and some are not. Melusina was eight weeks old when I got her from the Animal Rescue people, and I gave them a donation of twenty pounds. The vet charged me twenty-seven pounds fifty for her injections, all my cats are immunised against feline enteritis and leptospirosis, so that makes forty-seven pounds fifty. And she had her booster at age two which was another twenty-seven fifty, I can show you the receipted bills, I always keep everything, and that makes seventy-five pounds. Then there was my petrol getting her to the vet, we'll say a straight five pounds though it was more, and then we come to the crunch, her food. She was a good little trencherwoman.'

Anna would have been inclined to laugh at this ridiculous word but she saw to her horror that the tears were running down Maria Yackle's cheeks. They were running unchecked out of her eyes, over the rough red wrinkled skin, and one dripped unheeded on to Griselda's silvery fur.

Take no notice. I do cry whenever I have to talk about her. I loved that cat. She was the queen of the cats. She had her own place, her throne, she used to sit in the middle of the mantelpiece with her two china ladies-in-waiting on each side of her. You'll see one day, when you come to my house.

'But we were talking about her food. She ate a large can a day, it was too much, more than she should have had, but she loved her food, she was a good little eater. Well, cat food's gone up over the years of course, what hasn't, and I'm paying fifty pee a can now, but I reckon it'd be fair to average it out at forty pee. She was eight weeks old when I got her, so we can't say five times three hundred and sixty-five. We'll say five times three fifty-five and that's doing you a favour. I've already worked it out at home, I'm not that much of a wizard at mental arithmetic. Five three hundred and fifty-fives are one thousand, seven hundred and seventy-five, which multiplied by forty makes fifty-three thousand pee or five hundred and thirty pounds. Add to that the seventy-four plus the vet's bill of fourteen pounds when she had a tapeworm and we get a final figure of seven hundred and ninety-nine pounds.'

Anna stared at her. 'You're asking me to give you nearly eight hundred pounds.'

'That's right. Of course we'll write it down and do it properly.'

'Because your cat ran under the wheels of my car?'

'You murdered her,' said Maria Yackle.

'That's absurd. Of course I didn't murder her.' On shaky ground, she said, 'You can't murder an animal.'

'You did. You said you were going too fast.'

Had she? She had been but had she said so?

Maria Yackle got up, still holding Griselda, cuddling Griselda, who nestled purring in her arms. Anna watched with distaste. You thought of cats as fastidious creatures but they were not. Only something insensitive and undiscerning would put its face against that face, nuzzle those rough grimy hands. The black fingernails brought to mind a phrase, now unpleasantly appropriate, that her grandmother had used to children with dirty hands: in mourning for the cat.

'I don't expect you to give me a cheque now. Is that what you thought I meant? I don't suppose you have that amount in your current account. I'll come back tomorrow or the next day.'

'I am not going to give you eight hundred pounds,' said Anna.

She might as well not have spoken.

'I won't come back tomorrow, I'll come back on Wednesday.'

Griselda was tenderly placed on the seat of an armchair. The tears had dried on Maria Yackle's face, leaving salt trails. She took herself out into the hall and to the front door. 'You'll have thought about it by then. Anyway, I hope you'll come to the funeral. I hope there won't be any hard feelings.'

That was when Anna decided Maria Yackle was mad. In one way this was disquieting, in another a comfort. It meant she was not serious about the compensation, the seven hundred and ninety-nine pounds. Sane people do not invite you to their cat's funeral. Mad people do not sue you for compensation.

'No, I shouldn't think she'd do that,' said Richard when they were having dinner together. He was not a lawyer but had studied law. 'You didn't admit you were exceeding the speed limit, did you?'

'I don't remember.'

'At any rate you didn't admit it in front of witnesses. You say she didn't threaten you?'

'Oh, no. She wasn't unpleasant. She cried, poor thing.'

'Well, let's forget her, shall we, and have a nice time?'

Although no note awaited her on the doorstep, no letter came and there were no phone calls, Anna knew the cat woman would come back on the following evening. Richard had advised her to go to the police if any threats were made. There would be no need to tell them she had been driving very fast. Anna thought the whole idea of going to the police bizarre. She rang up her friend Kate and told her all about it and Kate agreed that telling the police would be going too far.

The battered red car arrived at seven. Maria Yackle was dressed as she had been for her previous visit but because it was rather cold, wore a jacket made of synthetic fur as well. From its harsh too-shiny texure there was no doubt it was synthetic but from a distance it looked like a black cat's pelt.

She had brought an album of photographs of her cats for Anna to see. Anna looked through it – what else could she do? Some were recognisably of those she had seen through the windows. Those that were not she supposed might be of animals now at rest under the wooden crosses in Maria Yackle's back garden. While she was looking at the pictures, Griselda came in and jumped on to the cat woman's lap.

'They're very nice, very interesting,' Anna said. 'I can see you're devoted to your cats.'

'They're my life.'

A little humouring might be in order. 'When is the funeral to be?'

'I thought on Friday. Two o'clock on Friday. My sister will be there with her two. Cats don't usually take to car travel, that's why I don't often take any of mine with me, and shutting them up in cages goes against the grain, but my sister's two Burmese love the car, they'll go and sit in the car when it's parked. My friend from the Animal Rescue will come if she can get away and I've asked our vet but I don't hold out much hope there. He has his goat clinic on Fridays. I hope you'll come along.'

'I'm afraid I'll be at work.'

'It's no flowers by request. Donations to the Cats' Protection League instead. Any sum, no matter how small, gratefully received. Which brings me to money. You've got a cheque for me.'

'No, I haven't, Mrs Yackle.'

'Miss. And it's Yakop. J,A,K,O,B. You've got a cheque for me for eight hundred pounds.'

'I am not giving you any money, Miss Jakob. I'm very very sorry about your cat, about Melusina, I know how fond you were of her. But giving you compensation is out of the question. I'm sorry.'

The tears had come once more into Maria Jakob's eyes, had spilled over. Her face contorted with misery. It was the mention of the wretched thing's name, Anna thought. That was the trigger that started the weeping. A tear splashed on to one of the coarse red hands. Griselda opened her eyes and licked up the tear.

Maria Jakob pushed her other hand across her eyes. She blinked. 'We'll have to think of something else then,' she said.

'I beg your pardon?' Anna wondered if she had really heard. Things couldn't be solved so simply.

'We shall have to think of something else. A way for you to make up to me for murder.'

'Look, I will give a donation to the Cats' Protection League. I'm quite prepared to give them – say, twenty pounds.' Richard would be furious but perhaps she would not tell Richard. 'I'll give it to you, shall I, and then you can pass it on to them?'

'I certainly hope you will. Especially if you can't come to the funeral.'

That was the end of it then. Anna felt a great sense of relief. It was only now that it was over that she realised quite how it had got to her. It had actually kept her from sleeping properly. She phoned Kate and told her about the funeral and the goat clinic and Kate laughed and said, poor old thing. Anna slept so well that night that she did not notice the arrival of Griselda who, when she woke, was asleep on the pillow next to her face but out of touching distance.

Richard phoned and she told him about it, omitting the part about her offer of a donation. He told her that being firm, sticking to one's guns in situations of this kind, always paid off. In the evening she wrote a cheque for twenty pounds but instead of the Cats' Protection League, made it out to Maria Jakob. If the cat woman quietly held on to it, no harm would be done. Anna went down the road to post her letter, for she had written a letter to accompany the cheque, in which she reiterated her sorrow about the death of the cat and added that if there was anything she could do, Miss Jakob had only to let her know. Richard would have been furious.

Unlike the Jakob cats, Griselda spent a good deal of time out of doors. She was often out all evening and did not reappear until the small hours, so that it was not until the next day, not until the next evening, that Anna began to be alarmed at her absence. As far as she knew, Griselda had never been away so long before. For herself she was unconcerned, she had never liked the cat, did not particularly like any cats, and found this one obnoxiously self-centred and cold. It was for her mother, who unaccountably loved the creature, that she was worried. She walked up and down the street, calling Griselda, though the cat had never been known to come when it was called.

It did not come now. Anna walked up and down the next street, calling, and around the block and further afield. She half-expected to find Griselda's body, guessing that it might have met the same fate as Melusina. Hadn't she read somewhere that nearly forty thousand cats are killed on British roads annually? On Saturday morning she wrote one of those melancholy lost cat notices and attached it to a lamp standard, wishing she had a photograph. But her mother had taken no photographs of Griselda.

Richard took her to a friend's party and afterwards, when they were driving home, he said, 'You know what's happened, don't you? It's been killed by that old mad woman. An eye for an eye, a cat for a cat.'

'Oh, no, she wouldn't do that. She loves cats.'

'Murderers love people. They just don't love the people they murder.'

'I'm sure you're wrong,' said Anna, but she remembered how Maria Jakob had said that if the money was not forthcoming she must think of something else, a way to make up to her for Melusina's death, and she had not meant a donation to the Cats' Protection League.

'What shall I do?'

'I don't see that you can do anything. It's most unlikely you could prove it, she'll have seen to that. You can look at it this way, she's had her pound of flesh . . . '

'Fifteen pounds of flesh,' said Anna. Griselda had been a large heavy cat.

'OK, fifteen pounds. She's had that, she's had her revenge, it hasn't actually caused you any grief, you'll just have to make up some story for your mother.'

Anna's mother was upset but nowhere near as upset as Maria Jakob had been over the death of Melusina. To avoid too much fuss, Anna had gone further than she intended, told her mother that she had seen Griselda's corpse and talked to the offending motorist who had been very distressed. A month or so later Anna's mother got a kitten, a grey tabby tom kitten, who was very affectionate from the start, sat on her lap, purred loudly when stroked and snuggled up in her arms, though Anna was sure her mother had not stopped having baths or using perfume. So much for the Jakob theories.

Nearly a year had gone by before she again drove down the road where Maria Jakob's house was. She had not intended to go that way. Directions had been given her to a smallholding where they sold early strawberries on a roadside stall but she must have missed her way, taken a wrong turning and come out here.

If Maria Jakob's car had been parked in the front she would not have stopped. There was no garage for it to be in, it was not outside, therefore the cat woman must be out. Anna thought of the funeral she had not been to, she had often thought about it, the strange people and strange cats who had attended it.

In each of the bay windows sat a cat, a tortoiseshell and a brown tabby. The black cat was eyeing her from upstairs. Anna did not go to the front door but round the back. There, among the long grass, as she had expected, were four graves instead of three, four wooden crosses and on the fourth was printed in black gloss paint: *Melusina, the Queen of the Cats, murdered in her sixth year. RIP.*

That 'murdered' did not please Anna. It brought back all the resentment at unjust accusations of eleven months before. She felt much older, she felt wiser. One thing was certain, ethics or no ethics, if she ever ran over a cat again she'd drive on, the last thing she'd do was go and confess.

She came round the side of the house and looked in at the bay window. If the tortoiseshell had still been on the windowsill she probably would not have looked in, but the tortoiseshell had removed itself to the hearthrug.

A white cat and the marmalade and white lay curled up side by side in an armchair. The portrait of Melusina hung above the fireplace and this year's cat calendar was up on the left-hand wall. Light gleamed on the china cats' gilt whiskers and between them, in the empty space that was no longer vacant, sat Griselda.

Griselda was sitting in the queen's place in the middle of the mantelpiece. She sat in the sphynx position with her eyes closed. Anna tapped on the glass and Griselda opened her eyes, stared with cold indifference and closed them again.

The queen is dead, long live the queen!

# Dying Happy

I was sitting by his bedside. He had a pure white room all to himself.

'This place reminds me of something that happened to a friend of mine.'

'What friend?' I said.

'You didn't know him. He's dead now anyway. Or dead to all intents and purposes.' He gave me a sly sideways look. It was a look that dared me to ask what the last remark meant. I didn't ask and he said, 'I'll tell you about him.' He put his head back on the pillow and looked at the white ceiling. 'A long time ago, twenty years at least, he had a relationship with this woman.'

I had to interrupt. 'Oh, come on,' I said. 'I have a relationship with you. Come to that, I have a relationship with the milkman.'

'Well, an affair then. I hate the word too. I picked it up from Miriam.' Miriam was his wife. 'An affair,' he said. 'A love passage. He was married of course. But he was in love with this woman, about as much in love as anyone can be, I gather. Fathoms deep. He was a very romantic man. He didn't tell his wife but of course she found out and put a stop to it.'

'What was her name?' I said.

'The girlfriend? Susanna. Her name was Susanna. She wasn't any younger than his wife or better-looking or cleverer or anything. And none of them were young, you know. Even then, at the time, they weren't young. I said he put a stop to it but that was only for a while. They started up again in secret and this time when the wife found out Susanna herself stopped it. She said it wasn't fair to any of them and she didn't answer his phone calls or his letters or anything and after a while it sort of petered out as these things do. Anyway, this was all of twenty years ago, as I said.

'His wife would bring up Susanna's name every time they disagreed. You can imagine. And he wasn't above comparing his wife unfavourably with Susanna if she annoyed him. But after a time they stopped mentioning her, though my friend never stopped thinking about her. He said that never a day passed without him thinking of her. And she came into his dreams. He got to look forward to those dreams because he said at least that way he got to see her sometimes.'

'The poor devil,' I said.

'Yes, well, he was romantic.'

It was nearly as white outside as in. There was snow on the ground and lumps of snow on the tree branches. He turned his face to the dazzling snow, screwing up his eyes. 'He got some awful thing the matter with him. I'm speaking about the present day now more or less. They gave him a limited time to live, a matter of months, you know how they won't commit themselves. He got it into his head he had to see Susanna before he died. He had to see her, he could die happy or at least contented if he could see her.'

'Did he know where she was?' I said.

'Oh, yes, he knew. You have to understand that though they never spoke of her, he and his wife, he knew all about her, everything that had happened to her. He knew she had moved and that she had married. It was an agony to him when she married. He knew the day and the hour and he sat watching the clock. Her husband died and he tried not to rejoice. He sent anonymous flowers, not for her dead husband but to her. That was the only contact, if contact it can be called, between them in all those years. Now to see her again was an obsession with him. He dreamed of it, he thought of nothing else.

'His wife had said she'd do anything for him, anything he wanted she'd try to get him. Get me Susanna, he said. I want to see Susanna before I die. Well, that wasn't at all what she'd meant by anything he wanted. You can imagine. She shouted and wept and said if Susanna came there – he was at home then, he went into hospital later – if Susanna came, she'd kill her. Oh, grow up, he said. The way you dramatise everything. We're all old now, we can't do anything. Look at me, be reasonable, why d'you grudge me a bit of happiness? I won't trouble you for long.

'You're my husband, she said, you're mine. It's me you ought to want to see. God knows I see you every minute of every day, he said. I'll pull the phone wires out of the wall, she said. If you write to her I won't post the letter, I'll burn any letter you write to her. And if you get her here, I'll kill her. I'll hit her over the head like I would a burglar if I caught him in my house.'

He was staring hard at me now and breathing rather quickly. The white glare on his face made him look like death.

'Take it easy,' I said.

'I will. I am.' He managed a grin. 'It wasn't only his wife he saw. The neighbours used to come in. And his friends from the old days. He got one of them to post the letter. And Susanna answered by return of post. There was no question of his wife keeping the letter from him, she couldn't tell who his letters were from. That letter made him so happy, he had waited twenty years for it, he felt he could have died he was so happy. And maybe it would have been for the best if he had. Maybe it would.

'He phoned her, he spoke to her, they fixed a time for Susanna to come. Hearing her voice was another kind of ecstasy. He told his wife when she was coming and said the best thing would be for her to go out. I'll kill her before she walks through that door, his wife said. I don't think I said they'd never met, did I, Susanna and his wife? Well, they never had, never even heard each other's voice on the phone. Of course he didn't believe his wife would kill her. I mean, would you? No one would. He didn't even believe she'd do Susanna an injury.'

'What happened when Susanna came?' I said.

The hospice was set in parkland. Cedar trees stood very black and ragged against the snow. You could see visitors' cars approach from the time they entered the distant gate. He was watching a car worm its way along the road between the snow banks.

'He heard her come to the door and he waited. It was ages before she came up. And when she did his wife was with her. Susanna was changed but he didn't mind about that and they were all changed. How could it be otherwise? She didn't touch him, she didn't even touch his hand. She and his wife sat there talking across him. They talked about the books they read and knitting and painting in water colours and golf – he'd never realised they had so much in common. They even looked alike. After a while they went downstairs. Susanna came again next day but she only looked in on him for two minutes. She and his wife had dinner together downstairs and watched the gardening programme on television. The day after that he had to go into hospital.'

'This friend,' I said, 'it was you, wasn't it?'

'How did you know?'

'It always is,' I said. 'And I suppose I posted that letter for you.'

He nodded, looking very tired now. The door opened and two women came in, big florid Miriam with a fur hat on her red hair and a fur coat that made her look like a marmalade cat and big zip-up boots, and another one like a tortoiseshell cat, as furry and booted but a fraction taller. Miriam introduced me.

'We mustn't stay long, darling. We're learning Italian and we've got our lesson at two. We're planning on Rome together for Easter so there's no time to waste. Give him the chocolates, Susanna, and then we must rush. If the snow clears tomorrow we'll be on the golf course all weekend, so I don't suppose we'll see you again till Monday.'

# The Copper Peacock

Peter Seeburg lived in a flat without a kitchen.

'Kitchens make you fat,' he said.

Bernard asked if that was one of the principles of the Seeburg Diet which Peter was going to the United States to promote. Peter smiled.

'All one needs', he said, 'is an electric kettle in the bathroom and a fridge somewhere else.' He added rather obscurely, 'Eating out keeps you thin because it is so expensive.'

He was lending the flat to Bernard while he was in America. They walked around it and Peter explained how things worked. The place was very clean. 'A woman comes in three times a week. Her name's Judy. She won't get in your way.'

'Do I have to have her?'

'Oh dear yes, you do. If I get rid of her for three months I'll never get her back again and I can't do with that.'

He would have to put up with it, Bernard supposed. Peter's kindness in lending him the flat, rent-free, to write his new biography in was something he still found overwhelming. It was quiet here – was this the only street in West London not being renovated, not a noisy jumble of scaffolding and skips? No sounds of music penetrated the ceilings. The other tenants in the block did not, apparently, spend their mornings doing homework for their carpentry courses. The windows gave on to plane trees and Regency façades.

'She's very efficient. She'll probably wash your clothes if you leave them lying about. But you won't be sleeping here, will you?'

'Absolutely not,' said Bernard.

As it was he felt guilty about leaving Ann alone all day with the children. But it was useless to attempt working at home with a two-year-old and a three-year-old under the same roof with him. Memories were vivid of Jonathan climbing on his shoulders and Jeremy trying out felt-tipped pens on his notes while he was last correcting page proofs. Still, he would be back with them in the evenings. He would have to make up for everything to Ann in the evenings.

'There's no question of my sleeping here,' he said to Peter as if he hadn't heard him the first time.

Peter gave him the keys. On Monday morning he was flying to Los Angeles, the first leg of his tour. Bernard arrived in a taxi two hours after he left, bringing with him two very large bags full of books. The biography he was embarking on was the life of a rather obscure Edwardian poet. His last book had been the life of a rather obscure Victorian diarist and some critic had said of it that the excellence of the writing and the pace of the narrative transcended the fact that few had heard of its subject. Bernard had a gift for writing with elegance and panache about fairly undistinguished literary figures and for writing books that sold surprisingly well.

It was his habit to spread his works of reference out on the floor. He would create little islands of books and notebooks, a group here that dealt with his subject's childhood, a cluster there of criticism of his works, an archipelago of the views of his peers. Two or three rooms ideally should be reserved for this purpose. Some of the books lay open, others with slips of paper inserted between their pages. The notes were in piles that might seem haphazard to others but to Bernard were arranged in a complex but precise order.

As soon as he was inside Peter's flat and the front door closed behind him, Bernard began spreading his books out after this fashion. Already he felt a deep contentment that one particular notebook, containing new material he had assembled on his subject's ancestry, would lie undisturbed surrounded by its minor islets, instead of being seized upon by Jonathan, as had happened to one of its predecessors, and given a new function as a kneading board for play dough, Bernard created a further island in the bedroom. He wouldn't otherwise be using the bedroom and the books could just lie there for weeks, gathering dust. This was another image which afforded him an intense intellectual pleasure. His typewriter set up on the dining-table in the absence of a desk, he found himself making an enthusiastic start, something by no means usual with him.

On the following morning, though, he recalled that the books couldn't just lie there. No dust would gather because Judy would be coming in to see it did not. Resenting her presence in advance of her arrival, he picked up all the books, slipping bits of paper in at significant pages and sealing the bedroom pile by laying on top of it, open and face-downwards, the earliest published biography of his poet. Beginning as he meant to go on, he was at the typewriter, busily working away, rather more busily and noisily in fact than the prose he was committing to paper warranted, when just after ten-thirty he heard the front door open and close.

Some few minutes had passed before she came into the dining room. She knocked first. Bernard was surprised by her youth. She looked no more than twenty-seven. He had expected a stout aproned motherly creature in her fifties. What clichés we make of life! She was slim, pretty, dark-haired, wearing jeans and a blouse. But the prettiness was worn and the hair was rough and dry. She was too thin for the tight jeans to be tight on her and her hip bones stuck out like the sharp curved frame of a lyre.

'Could you do with a coffee?' she said. No introduction, no greeting. Her smile was friendly and cheerful. 'I get Peter his coffee about now.'

Bernard castigated himself for a snob. Why on earth should she call Peter Mr Seeburg anyway? 'Thank you. That's very kind of you.' He put out his hand. 'I'm Bernard Hope.'

'Pleased to meet you, Bernard. Peter's told me all about you.' For all the readily used Christian names, her manner was a little shy, her handshake tentative. 'Do you mind if I come in here for the milk?' she said. 'I have to make the coffee in the bathroom but he keeps his fridge in here.'

'No, please, go ahead.'

'Peter said you'd want all your books left just as they were but you're very tidy, aren't you? She didn't wait for an answer but said confidingly, with a slight giggle, 'I'll never get over him not having a kitchen. You have to laugh. I get a laugh out of it every time I come here.'

All this seemed ominous to Bernard. Fearing a prolonged disturbance of his peace, he set himself to typing furiously when she returned with the coffee. Perhaps this was effective as a deterrent or else she genuinely wanted to get on with her work, for she spoke no further word to him until the time came for her departure at half-past twelve. Appearing at the dining-room door in a padded jacket, she mimed – to his astonishment – the action of pounding a keyboard.

'Keep on with the good work. See you Wednesday.'

Bernard couldn't resist getting up to review the flat after she had gone. He was pleasantly surprised. Surfaces had been polished and there was a fresh flowery scent in the air. His books lay as he had left them, the slips of paper in place, the important notebook still face-downwards and guarding the stack beneath it. He re-created his islands. The coffee cups had disappeared, been washed and restored to their home in a china cabinet. On one of the tables in the living room was a tray covered with a cloth and on the tray was a plate of the kind of sandwiches that are called 'dainty', with a glass of orange juice, a polished red apple and a piece of cheese.

His lunch. Bernard felt quite touched, although he quickly realised that she must do this for Peter and no doubt regarded it as part of the duties for which she was paid. Since Jeremy was born Ann had never got lunch for him, he had always got his own. Not that he expected his wife to wait on him, of course not, she had the children and the house, more than enough to do. Two of the sandwiches were smoked salmon and two egg and cress. Judy must have brought their ingredients with her and assembled them in the bathroom. Next day he was preparing to say something gracious but he took a look at her and there was only one thing anyone could say.

'What have you done to yourself?'

She put her hand up to her face. She had a black eye. The cheekbone was dark red and shiny with bruising and the corner of her lip was cut. Her finger touched the bruise. 'Fell against the door, didn't I?' she said. It was a curious usage of language, that interrogatory. He wasn't sure if he had ever heard it before. 'Kitchen door with a handle sticking out.' She giggled. 'That's what comes of having kitchens. Maybe Peter's got the right idea.'

He asked her if she had seen a doctor. And when she said she hadn't, she hadn't the patience to sit waiting about for an hour or more just to get a prescription she'd have to pay for anyway, he thanked her for getting his lunch. 'You're welcome, love,' she said, and 'It's all in the day's work.' He watched her test the tenderness of her cut lip with a questing tongue. 'Ready for your coffee, are you, or d'you want to wait a bit?'

He had it later in the living room, perusing his notebook, while she cleaned the dining room. Things were just as he had left them when he went back except that she had closed the work of reference he had left open by the typewriter and had marked his place with a sheet torn from a scribbling block. Lunch that day was pâté sandwiches and there was a pear on the tray and a piece of walnut cake. Next time he got Gruyère cheese, mandarin yogurt and a bunch of red grapes. It was something of a chore going out to buy pizza on the intervening days. The awful things that had happened to Judy's face made him think she might be accident-prone and at first he waited to hear her drop things, but she moved almost soundlessly about the flat, putting her head round the door to tell him when she was going to use the vacuum cleaner, apologising in advance, and in the event getting it over as fast as possible. She made less noise about the place than Ann did, Ann who was exasperated by sweeping and dusting and who loudly cursed both tools and furniture. As soon as this thought came to him he felt guilty, so that night he took home a bottle of champagne and a begonia in a pot.

Peter phoned one afternoon during Bernard's third week there. It was early morning in Denver, Colorado, where he had arrived to spread the gospel of the Seeburg Diet. He wanted a book sent out to him. It was a book on calories and food-combining that Bernard would find on one of the shelves in the bedroom up on the right-hand side.

'Everything OK?' he said. 'How's the poet? How are you getting on with Judy?'

Bernard said the biography was progressing quite satisfactorily, thank you very much. Judy was fine, marvellous, very efficient. There seemed no point in adding that this morning, though her face had healed and the discoloration around her eye faded, he had noticed bruises on her left arm and a strip of plaster on her left hand. That was hardly the kind of thing to talk about with Peter.

'She's what my poet's contemporaries would have called a treasure.' His poet had in fact been attracted by servants, had a long-standing clandestine affair with his sister's nursery maid.

'Mind you say hello to her from me next time she comes.'

Her hand was still plastered and her face looked as if bruised anew. Only it couldn't be, he must be imagining this, or she was tired or one of those people whose skin marks at a touch. It couldn't really be that the damaged eye had been injured again.

'Peter said to say hello.'

The handy Americanism was evidently new to her but she worked it out. 'Sent his love, did he? You pass mine on next time he gives you a phone. I've got caviar for your sandwiches today, that lumpfish really, but I reckon it tastes the same.' She showed him the jar. 'Lovely colour, isn't it? More like strawberry jam.'

'You're good to me, Judy,' he said.

'Get off. Good to you! You appreciate it, that's what I like, not like Peter, cottage cheese and bean sprouts day after day for him. Still, what can you expect if you don't have a kitchen?'

He re-made his book islands once the front door had closed after her. The fate of his books, or rather the precariousness of the position of his bookmarks, no longer worried him. They were safe with Judy. Even if he failed to stack them before she came, they remained inviolate.

And a strange thing had happened. He no longer wanted total silence and unobtrusiveness from her. He had arranged with her to bring his coffee at eleven when he would break off for ten or even fifteen minutes for a chat. Mostly he talked to her and she listened while he spoke about his biography and his aims and his past career, necessarily simplifying things for this untutored audience. A look of wonder, or simple lack of comprehension, came into her thin hungry face. She admired him, he was sure of it, and he was curiously touched by her admiration. He told himself it made him feel humble.

And he had hardly realised before how much he liked gracious living. The turmoil of home, the chaos, he had accepted as an inevitable corollary of modern life. Peter's flat was as he remembered his mother's home, clean, orderly, the woodwork shining, the upholstery not stained with spilt milk and chocolate smears. In the bathroom it was not necessary to pick one's way between the hazards of potty, disposable napkin packets, drying dungarees and a menagerie of plastic amphibians in order to reach the lavatory. It was peaceful and silent and it smelt, not of urine, milk and disinfectant, but of floor wax and the civilised dry bitter-sweetness of the chrysanthemums Judy had bought at the same time as the caviar.

'You're quite in love with her,' said Ann.

'Get off,' said Bernard before he realised who he was quoting. 'I only said she was a good housewife.' She would hardly understand if he said he looked forward to ten-thirty, then to coffee time, to his conversation with this naive listener. It was more than he could understand himself, how an interruption had become a pleasure.

Peter phoned from Chicago. It was just before seven in the morning there, so not yet one in London and Judy was still in the flat. Bernard thought Peter must be phoning so early to wish him a happy birthday and he felt quite touched. Ann hadn't exactly forgotten what this day was, she had only forgotten to get him a present. But the reason for Peter's call was to say the food-combining book had arrived and would Bernard send him the phial of homoeopathic pills from the bathroom cabinet.

'I'm halfway through my life today,' said Bernard.

'Many happy returns. If I'd known I'd have sent you a card. Say hello to Judy for me.'

'You don't look forty,' she said to him, standing in the doorway in her padded jacket.

For a moment he didn't know what she meant. When he did, he was mildly affronted, then amused. 'Thirty-five,' he said. 'Halfway through man's allotted span. You think I'll make it to eighty, do you?'

'I didn't ought to have listened,' she said. 'Sorry. It was a bit of a cheek.'

He had a curious impulse to put his arm round her thin shoulders and press her quickly close to him. But of course he couldn't do that. 'Get off,' he said. 'Why shouldn't you listen? It wasn't private.'

She said goodbye and left and he put his books back on the floor. Rather reluctantly he returned to work. His subject had been acquainted with the great literary figures of his day and Bernard was about to write of his first meeting, while at university in Dublin, with James Joyce. Joyce, he reflected, had lived with and later married a servant – a chambermaid, wasn't she? It had been a happy partnership between the giant of letters and his Nora, the nearly illiterate woman.

Ham sandwiches and thinly sliced avocado, sesame seed biscuits, a glass of apple juice. For once he wasn't hungry for it. What he would have liked – he suddenly saw the rightness of it – was to have taken Judy out to lunch. Why hadn't he thought of it while she was still there? Why hadn't he thought of it as a way of celebrating his birthday? Although she had been gone twenty minutes he went to the window and looked out to see if, by remote chance, she might still be waiting at the bus stop. There was no one in the bus shelter but an old man reading the timetable.

They could have gone to the Italian restaurant round the corner. She was so thin, he wondered if she ever got a decent meal. He would have enjoyed choosing the dishes for her and selecting the wine. A light sparkling Lambrusco would have been just the thing to please her, and he would have put up with it even though it might be rather showy and obvious for him. But she had gone and it was too late. In her absence he felt restless, unable to concentrate. He had no phone number for her, no address, he didn't even know her surname. If she didn't come on Tuesday, if she never came again, he wouldn't know how to find her, he would have lost her for ever.

This anxiety was absurd, for of course she did come. His weekend had been unpleasant, with Jonathan developing a virus infection and Ann announcing that she meant to go back to work in the spring. He had to stay at home on Monday to look after the sick child while Ann took the other for a dental appointment. The quietness and order of Peter's flat received him, seemed to welcome him with a beckoning and a smile. Only another month and Peter would be home but he didn't want to think of that.

At ten-thirty Judy let herself in. She was always punctual. The bruises faded, the scars healed, she looked very pretty. He thought what an exceedingly good-looking woman she was with that flush on her cheeks and her eyes bright. Instead of going to his work table and his typewriter, he had waited for her in the living room, and when she came in he did something he normally did for women but had never done for her. He laid his book aside and stood up. It seemed almost to alarm her.

'Are you OK, Bernard?'

He smiled, nodded. He had never actually witnessed her arrival before and now he watched her remove her jacket, take indoor shoes out of her bag and put them on, remarking as she did so, reverting to the aspect of the place that endlessly amused her, that if Peter had had a kitchen she would have been able to change there. The scuffed boots she wore outdoors tucked inside the bag, she took from it a small package, a box it looked like, wrapped in silver-spotted pink paper. Her manner becoming awkward, she said to Bernard, thrusting the package into his hands, 'Here, this is for you. Happy birthday.'

She was blushing. She had gone a fiery red. Bernard untied the ribbon and took off the paper. Inside the box, on a piece of cotton wool, lay a metal object about six inches long and an inch wide. Its shaft was flat like the blade of a knife and attached to a hook on the top which curved backwards in a U-shape was a facsimile of a peacock with tail spread fan-wise, the whole executed in beaten copper and a mosaic of blue, green and purple glass chips. To Bernard it looked at first like some piece of cheap jewellery, a woman's hair ornament or clip. He registered its tawdry ugliness, felt at a loss for words. What was it? He looked up at her.

'It's a bookmark, isn't?' She spoke with intense earnestness. 'You put it in your book to show where you've got to.'

He was still mystified.

'Look, I'll show you.' She picked up the book he had been reading, a memoir of the Stephen family who had also been acquainted with his poet. At the place he had reached, she inserted the copper knife blade and, closing the book on it, hooked the peacock over the top of the spine. 'She how it works?'

'Yes, thanks. Thank you very much.'

Confidingly, she said, 'I couldn't help seeing, while I've been working about, the way you'd always leave one of your books open and face-down. Well, you don't like to turn down the corner of the page, do you, not when it's a library book? It doesn't seem right. So I thought, it's his birthday, I know what I'll do, I'll get him one of these. I'd seen them in this shop, hadn't I? One of those'd be just the thing for him and his books, I thought.'

It was a curious kind of a shock. The thing was hideous. It seemed more of an affront because it was books it must inevitably be associated with, books which he had such a special dedicated feeling about. If it didn't sound too silly and pretentious, he could almost have said books were sacred. The peacock's tail, curved breast and stupid face glittered against the dull brown of the binding. The manufacturer had even managed to get red into it. The bird's eyes were twin points of ruby red. Bernard took the book and his new bookmark into the dining room. He found himself closing the door for the first time in weeks. Of course he would have to use the bloody thing. She would look for it, expect to see it every time she came. If he left one of his books face-downwards she would want to know why he wasn't using his new bookmark.

'You do like it, don't you, Bernard?' she said when she brought his coffee.

'Of course I like it.' What else could he say?

'I thought you'd like it. When I saw it I thought that's just the thing for Bernard.'

Why did they always have to say everything twice, these people? She had seated herself as usual opposite him to wait for him to begin their conversation. But this morning he didn't want to talk, he had nothing to say. It even seemed to him that she had somehow betrayed him. She had shown him how little his words meant to her, if in spite of everything he had said and shown himself to be, she could still have bought him this tasteless vulgar object. He knew he was being ridiculous but he couldn't help feeling it. He took the coffee from her, feigning an absent manner, and returned to his typewriter.

Honest with himself – he tried to be that – he admitted what had been in his mind. He had meant to make love to her. To what end? Was she to have been his Nora? He had never progressed so far, even in his thoughts. Simply he had thought of love and pleasure, of taking her about and giving her a good time. Was he mad? They were poles apart, a great gulf fixed between them, as she had proved by her gross misunderstanding of everything he was and stood for. Serve him right for having such aims and intents. It must be his subject who was taking him over, his poet who at sixteen boasted to Frank Harris of getting his mother's kitchen maid pregnant.

He nodded absently to her when, ready to leave, she put her head round the door. Peter phoned from Philadelphia not long after she had gone, and after he had talked to him Bernard felt better about things. He was able to make quite an amusing story out of the presenting of the peacock bookmark. And Peter commiserated with him, agreeing that there was no doubt about it, he would have to use the thing, and prominently, for the duration of his stay. Naturally, Bernard said nothing about his now vanished desire for Judy, any more than he did when he repeated the tale to Ann that night. Ann had the advantage over Peter in that she could actually be shown the object.

'It's copper,' she said, 'and it doesn't look mass-produced. It was probably quite expensive. You can't actually use it, it's dreadful.'

'I don't want to hurt her feelings.'

'What about your feelings? Aren't they important? If you don't want to say straight out you can't bear the thing, tell her you've left it at home or you've lost it. Let me have it and I'll lose it for you.'

Next day he followed her advice and left the bookmark at home. Judy didn't say anything about it, though it was her day for dusting the bedroom and he had left his notebook in the bedroom, lying face-downwards on the stack of other books. She watered Peter's plants and cleaned the windows. He didn't take a break from work when she brought his coffee, only looked up and thanked her. But he could see she had her eye on the books which covered half the dining-table. He was sure she was looking for the peacock. He repeated his thanks in as dismissive a tone as he could manage and she turned at once and left the room. The sandwiches she left him for lunch were tinned salmon and cucumber with a strawberry yogurt and a chocolate bar. Bernard fancied the standard was less high than it had been.

It was a relief to be without her as he always was on Thursdays. On Friday her face was once more the way it had been that first week, one eye black and swollen, her cheek bruised, her mouth cut. But he said nothing about it. He could see her gazing at all the books on the table and after she had left the room he went quietly to the door and through the crack watched her slowly move the stacked volumes to dust the surface of a cabinet. By now it must have registered with her that he disliked the bookmark and had no intention of using it.

It was of course a mistake to be too friendly with these people, to put them on a level with oneself. He wasn't used to servants and that was the trouble. Who was, these days? Returning to work, he felt a flash of envy for his poet who, though comparatively poor, had nevertheless kept a man and two maids to look after him.

She spoke to him, as in the old days, when she brought his coffee.

Tentatively, as if she thought him in a bad mood and she was placating him, she said, 'I've been in the wars a bit.'

He glanced up, took in once again that awful damaged eye. How could he once have thought her pretty? The notion came to him that she was trying to tell him something, appeal to him. Was she perhaps going to ask yet again if he liked the bookmark? He put up his eyebrows, made a rueful face. 'Close the door after you, will you, Judy?'

Still, he had been wrong about the standard of lunch, having no fault to find with pastrami sandwiches, watercress salad and a slice of pineapple. Ann's advice was sound. By not yielding he had shown the woman that imposing her atrocious taste on him wasn't on. But he hadn't bargained for what happened on the Tuesday. She didn't come.

For a little while, when eleven was past and he was sure she wasn't coming, he felt awe at himself, at the stand he had taken. He had been strong and he had driven her away. Then he was pleased, he was relieved. Wasn't it absurd, a woman coming in three times a week to clean up after someone who didn't even sleep there, who scarcely ate there? Of course she would probably come back when Peter returned in three weeks' time. It was him she was ostracising. She had taken offence because he wouldn't give in to her and use her hideous gift.

He had worked himself up a bit over her defection by the time he got home. 'She could at least have phoned and made some excuse.'

'They don't,' said Ann. 'Those people don't.'

Any qualms he might have had about Judy's turning up later were soon allayed. It was clear she wasn't coming back. Bernard got into the way of buying himself something for his lunch on his way to the flat. He went without coffee. It wasn't as if he was used to it, as if Ann had ever made it for him. He left his books lying about all over the floors, face-downwards or with pieces of paper inserted between the pages. Of course he hadn't finished the life of his poet by the time Peter was due back, he wasn't even a quarter of his way through, but he had made such a good start he felt he could continue at home in spite of Jonathan and Jeremy, in spite of chaos and noise. He had broken the back of it.

Peter phoned the morning before he was due to leave New York. They talked about the weather, the heavy snowstorms which had been sweeping the east coast of America. Then Peter said, 'That was terrible about Judy.'

A strong word to use but Peter was inclined to be intense.

'How did you know?' Bernard said.

'I saw it in the paper, of course. I do make a point of seeing English newspapers while I'm here.'

They were at cross-purposes. 'What did you see in the paper?'

Peter sounded astonished. 'That he killed her, of course. I shouldn't have been surprised, I used to tell her he'd do it one day. I told her to leave him but she wouldn't. She must have talked to you about him surely? I can't believe she came in all that time without a mark on her from what he was doing to her. They've charged him with murdering her. Don't you read your newspaper?'

He hadn't known her name, he said, he hadn't known where she lived or anything about her.

'What did you talk about? Didn't you ask?'

Bernard said goodbye and slowly let the receiver slide into its rest. What had they talked about, he and Judy? His work, English literature, books, his past career. He had talked and she had listened. Raptly, he thought now, her battered face lifted, her damaged eyes watching him. Why hadn't she said what happened to her at home? Why, instead of giving him that ridiculous tasteless thing, hadn't she thrown herself on his mercy, confided in him, offered herself to him?

He didn't say a word about it to Ann. 'What happened to the peacock bookmark?'

'The children were playing with it and Jeremy kept putting it in his mouth, so I threw it out.'

He wanted to hit her, he wanted to strike her in the face, and he clasped his hands together to keep himself from that.

# Weeds

'I am not at all sure', said Jeremy Flintwine, 'that I would know a weed from whatever the opposite of a weed is.'

The girl looked at him warily. 'A plant.'

'But surely weeds *are* plants.'

Emily Hithe was not prepared to enter into an argument. 'Let me try and explain the game to you again,' she said. 'You have to see if you can find a weed. In the herbaceous borders, in the rosebeds, anywhere. If you find one all you have to do is show it to my father and he will give you a pound for it. Do you understand now?'

'I thought this was in aid of cancer research. There's not much money to be made that way.'

She smiled rather unpleasantly. 'You won't find any weeds.'

It cost two pounds each to visit the garden. Jeremy, a publisher who lived in Islington, had been brought by the Wragleys with whom he was staying. They had walked here from their house in the village, a very long walk for a Sunday afternoon in summer after a heavy lunch. Nothing had been said about fund-raising or playing games. Jeremy was already wondering how he was going to get back. He very much hoped to catch the twelve minutes past seven train from Diss to London.

The Wragleys and their daughter Penelope, aged eight, had disappeared down one of the paths that led through a shrubbery. People stood about on the lawn drinking tea and eating digestive biscuits which they had had to pay for. Jeremy always found country life amazing. The way everyone knew everyone else, for instance. The extreme eccentricity of almost everybody, so that you suspected people, wrongly, of putting it on. The clothes. Garments he had supposed obsolete, cotton frocks and sports jackets, were everywhere in evidence. He had thought himself suitably dressed but now he wondered. Jeans were not apparently correct wear except on the under-twelves and he was wearing jeans, an old, very clean, pair, selected after long deliberation, with an open-necked shirt and an elegantly shabby Italian silk cardigan. He was also wearing, in the top buttonhole of the cardigan, a scarlet poppy tugged up by its roots from the grass verge by Penelope Wragley.

The gift of this flower had been occasioned by one of George Wragley's literacy anecdotes. George, who wrote biographies of poets, was not one of Jeremy's authors but his wife Louise, who produced best-sellers for children and adored her husband, was. Therefore Jeremy found it expedient to listen more or less politely to George going on and on about Francis Thompson and the Meynells. It was during the two-mile-long trudge to the Hithes' garden that George related how one of the Meynell children, with appropriate symbolism, had presented the opium-addicted Thompson with a poppy in a Suffolk field, bidding him, 'Keep this for ever!' Penelope had promptly given Jeremy his buttonhole, which her parents thought a very sweet gesture, though he was neither a poet nor an opium addict.

They had arrived at the gates and paid their entry fee. A lot of people were on the terrace and the lawns. The neatness of the gardens was almost oppressive, some of the flowers looking as if they had been washed and ironed and others as if made of wax. The grass was the green of a billiard table and nearly as smooth. Jeremy asked an elderly woman, one of the tea drinkers, if Rodney Hithe did it all himself.

'He has a man, of course,' she said.

The coolness of her tone was not encouraging but Jeremy tried. 'It must be a lot of work.'

'Oh, old Rod's got that under control,' said the girl with her, a granddaughter perhaps. 'He knows how to crack the whip.'

This Jeremy found easy to believe. Rodney Hithe was a loud man. His voice was loud and he wore a jacket of loud blue and red checked tweed. Though seeming affable enough, calling the women 'darling' and the men 'old boy', Jeremy suspected he was the kind of person it would be troublesome to get on the wrong side of. His raucous voice could be heard from end to end of the garden, and his braying unamused laugh.

'I wouldn't want to find a weed,' said the granddaughter, voicing Jeremy's own feelings. 'Not for a pound. Not at the risk of confronting Rod with it.'

Following the path the Wragleys had taken earlier, Jeremy saw people on their hands and knees, here lifting a blossoming frond, there an umbelliferous stalk, in the forlorn hope of finding treasure underneath. The Wragleys were nowhere to be seen. In a far corner of the garden, where geometric rosebeds were bounded on two sides by flint walls, stood a stone seat. Jeremy thought he would sit down on this seat and have a cigarette. Surely no one could object to his smoking in this remote and secluded spot. There was in any case no one to see him.

He was taking his lighter from his jeans pocket when he heard a sound from the other side of the wall. He listened. It came again, an indrawing of breath and a heavy sigh. Jeremy wondered afterwards why he had not immediately understood what kind of activity would prompt the utterance of these sighs and half-sobs, why he had at first supposed it was pain and not pleasure that gave rise to them. In any case, he was rather an inquisitive man. Not hesitating for long, he hoisted himself up so that he could look over the wall. His experience of the countryside had not prepared him for this. Behind the wall was a smallish enclosed area or farmyard, bounded by buildings of the sty and byre type. Within an aperture in one of these buildings, on a heap of hay, a naked girl could be seen lying in the arms of a man who was not himself naked but dressed in a shirt and a pair of trainers.

'Lying in the arms of' did not accurately express what the girl was doing but it was a euphemism Jeremy much preferred to 'sleeping with' or anything franker. He dropped down off the wall but not before he had noticed that the man was very deeply tanned and had a black beard and that the girl's resemblance to Emily Hithe made it likely this was her sister.

This was no place for a quiet smoke. He walked back through the shrubbery, lighting a cigarette as he went. Weed-hunting was still in progress under the bushes and among the alpines in the rock garden, this latter necessarily being carried out with extreme care, using the fingertips to avoid bruising a petal. He noticed none of the women wore high heels. Rodney Hithe was telling a woman who had brought a Pekinese that the dog must be carried. The Wragleys were on the lawn with a middle-aged couple who both wore straw hats and George Wragley was telling them an anecdote about an old lady who had sat next to P. G. Wodehouse at a dinner party and enthused about his work throughout the meal under the impression he was Edgar Wallace. There was some polite laughter. Jeremy asked Louise what time she thought of leaving.

'Don't you worry, we shan't be late. We'll get you to the station all right. There's always the last train, you know, the eight forty-four.' She went on confidingly, 'I wouldn't want to upset poor old Rod by leaving the minute we arrive. Just between you and me, his marriage hasn't been all it should be of late and I'd hate to add to his troubles.'

This sample of Louise's arrogance rather took Jeremy's breath away. No doubt the woman meant that the presence of anyone as famous as herself in his garden conferred an honour on Rodney Hithe which was ample compensation for his disintegrating home life. He was reflecting on vanity and authors and self-delusion when the subject of Louise's remark came up to them and told Jeremy to put his cigarette out. He spoke in the tone of a prison officer addressing a habitual offender in the area of violent crime. Jeremy, who was not without spirit, decided not to let Hithe cow him.

'It's harmless enough out here surely.'

'I'd rather you smoked your filthy fags in my wife's drawing room than in my garden.'

Grinding it into the lawn would be an obvious solecism. 'Here,' Jeremy said, 'you can put it out yourself,' and he did his best to meet Hithe's eyes with an equally steady stare. Louise gave a nervous giggle. Holding the cigarette end at arm's length, Hithe went off to find some more suitable extinguishing ground, disappeared in the direction of the house and came back with a gun.

Jeremy was terribly shocked. He was horrified. He retreated a step or two. Although he quickly understood that Hithe had not returned to wreak vengeance but only to show off his new twelve-bore to the man in the straw hat, he still felt shaken. The ceremony of breaking the gun he thought it was called was gone through. The straw-hatted man squinted down the barrel. Jeremy tried to remember if he had ever actually seen a real gun before. This was an aspect of country life he found he disliked rather more than all the other things.

Tea was still being served from a trestle table outside the French windows. He bought himself a cup of tea and several of the more nourishing biscuits. It seemed unlikely that any train passing through north Suffolk on Sunday evening would have a restaurant or even a buffet car. The time was coming up to six. It was at this point that he noticed the girl he had last seen lying in the arms of the bearded man. She was no longer naked but wearing a T-shirt and a pair of shorts. In spite of these clothes, or perhaps because of them, she looked rather older than when he had previously seen her. Jeremy heard her say to the woman holding the dog, 'He ought to be called a Beijinese, you know,' and give a peal of laughter.

He asked the dog's owner, a woman with a practical air, how far it was to Diss.

'Not far,' she said. 'Two or three miles. Would you say two miles, Deborah, or nearer three?'

Deborah Hithe's opinion on this distance Jeremy was never to learn, for as she opened her mouth to speak, a bellow from Rodney silenced all conversation.

'You didn't find that in this garden!'

He stood in the middle of the lawn, the gun no longer in his hands but passed on for the scrutiny of a girl in riding breeches. Facing him was the young man with the tan and the beard, whom Jeremy knew beyond a doubt to be Deborah's lover. He held up, in teasing fashion for the provocation of Hithe, a small plant with a red flower. For a moment the only sound was Louise's giggle, a noise that prior to this weekend he would never have suspected her of so frequently making. A crowd had assembled quite suddenly, surely the whole population of the village, it seemed to Jeremy, which Louise had told him was something over three hundred.

The man with the beard said, 'Certainly I did. You want me to show you where?'

'He should never have pulled it out, of course,' Emily whispered. 'I'm afraid we forgot to put that in the rules, that you're not supposed to pull them out.'

'He's your sister's boyfriend, isn't he?' Jeremy hazarded.

The look he received was one of indignant rage. 'My *sister*? I haven't got a sister.'

Deborah was watching the pair on the lawn. He saw a single tremor shake her. The man who had found the weed made a beckoning gesture to Hithe to follow him along the shrubbery path. George Wragley lifted his shoulders in an exaggerated shrug and began telling the girl in riding breeches a long pointless story about Virginia Woolf. Suddenly Jeremy noticed it had got much colder. It had been a cool, pale grey, still day, a usual English summer day, and now it was growing chilly. He did not know what made him remember the gun, notice its absence.

Penelope Wragley, having ingratiated herself with the woman dispensing tea, was eating up the last of the biscuits. She seemed the best person to ask who Deborah was, the least likely to take immediate inexplicable offence, though he had noticed her looking at him and particularly at his cardigan in a very affronted way. He decided to risk it.

Still staring, she said as if he ought to know, 'Deborah is Mrs Hithe, of course.'

The implications of this would have been enough to occupy Jeremy's thoughts for the duration of his stay in the garden and beyond, if there had not come at this moment a loud report. It was, in his ears, a shattering explosion and it came from the far side of the shrubbery. People began running in the direction of the noise before its reverberations had died away. The lawn emptied. Jeremy was aware that he had begun to shake. He said to the child, who took no notice, 'Don't go!' and then set off himself in pursuit of her.

The man with the beard lay on his back in the rose garden and there was blood on the grass. Deborah knelt beside him, making a loud keening wailing noise, and Hithe stood between two of the geometric rosebeds, holding the gun in his hands. The gun was not exactly smoking but there was a strong smell of gunpowder. A tremendous hubbub arose from the party of weed-hunters, the whole scene observed with a kind of gloating horrified fascination by Penelope Wragley, who had reverted to infantilism and watched with her thumb in her mouth. The weed was nowhere to be seen.

Someone said superfluously, or perhaps not superfluously, 'Of course it was a particularly tragic kind of accident.'

'In the circumstances.'

The whisper might have come from Louise. Jeremy decided not to stay to confirm this. There was nothing he could do. All he wanted was to get out of this dreadful place as quickly as possible and make his way to Diss and catch a train, any train, possibly the last train. The Wragleys could send his things on.

He retreated the way he had come, surprised to find himself tiptoeing which was surely unnecessary. Emily went past him, running towards the house and the phone. The Pekinese or Beijinese dog had set up a wild yapping. Jeremy walked quietly around the house, past the drawing-room windows, through the open gates and into the lane.

The sound of that shot still rang horribly in his ears, the sight of red blood on the grass was still before his eyes. The unaccustomed walk might be therapeutic. It was a comfort, since a thin rain had begun to fall, to come upon a signpost which told him he was going in the right direction for Diss and it was only a mile and a half away. There was no doubt the country seemed to show people as well as nature in the raw. What a nightmare that whole afternoon had been, culminating in outrageous violence! How horrible, after all, the Wragleys and Penelope were and in a way he had never before suspected! Why were one's authors so awful? Why did they have such appalling spouses and ill-behaved children? Penelope had stared at him when he asked her about Deborah Hithe as disgustedly as if, like that poor man, he had been covered in blood.

And then Jeremy put his hand to his cardigan and felt the front of it, patted it with both hands like a man feeling for his wallet, looked down, saw that the scarlet poppy she had given him was gone. Her indignation was explained. The poppy must have fallen out when he hoisted himself up and looked over the wall.

It was a moment or two before he understood the cause of his sudden fearful dismay.

# The Fish-Sitter

Next door to the Empress Court Disco Roller Rink in Seoul
Road, Southend, was the South-east Essex branch of Daleth
Foods and next to that the Aquarium. It was a parade of
interesting and even exotic emporia as are often found in the hinterland
of seaside resorts. Goods were sold, services offered and entertainment
provided.

For instance, in a flatlet above Magda's Sports Equipment Ruta
Yglesias the clairvoyante told fortunes, next door was a beauty clinic
entirely devoted to eyes, the painting of their lids and lashes and the
enhancement of their sparkle, and at the photographer's, last in the
parade, little girls might dress up in tutus with ribbon laces cross-
gartered to their knees, and dream as they posed that they were
Veronica Spencer dancing *Giselle*.

The Aquarium's real name was Malvina's Marine Museum, a grand
title for what was quite a modest affair. On a sunny afternoon, when
the beaches and the shops were crowded, the amusement arcades busy
and the streets empty, Mrs Trevor was showing her fish-sitter round
the tank room. It was lit, even on a day like this, for each tank had
its own strip light as well as its own aeration pump. These were
necessarily at floor level, set to illuminate the green ever-moving, ever-
bubbling water below, and sending up into the tank room a glaucous,
rather misty, glow. In the room below, visitors to the aquarium could
be seen only occasionally and then dimly through glass and water as
they moved, mostly in silence, between the Sarcopterygii, the Selachii
and the Decapoda. Some paused to read the printed and illustrated
labels attached to the wall by each tank. Others pressed their faces
against the cool glass and the marine creatures swam close to inspect
them.

'Do you know, Cyril, this will be the first holiday I've had since I
started this place,' Mrs Trevor was saying. 'Well, come to that, the
first since I stopped working for you-know-who.'

Cyril Biggs knew very well who and was no more anxious to speak the name of the famous romantic novelist than was her erstwhile home help. This attitude, on both their parts, brought him a pang of guilt, for would he have ever known Mrs Trevor but for Louise Mitchell? This job, this temporary roof over his head, would certainly not have come about without her. Gazing down at the decapod among the weeds and branched coral below, he subtly changed the subject.

'I wonder that you chose to go on a Caribbean cruise, though. Won't it be rather a case of coals to Newcastle?'

'What very unfortunate and hackneyed metaphors you do pick on, Cyril,' said Mrs Trevor sharply. 'You always have. What do you know about cruises, anyway?'

A meek man, or one who had that reputation, Cyril only smiled. He could have said something about the days of his employment on a cruise ship but he did not, though as he watched the crab's sideways progress among darting jewel-bright chimaera he remembered the flying fish which had pursued the ship and his friend who supervised the ladies' cloakroom next door with her collection of newts she called salamanders. He also recalled the food on the *Calypso Queen*, the leavings of which had come his way and hers.

'The green-carapaced crab,' he said dreamily, 'whose meat is sweet to eat.'

'None of that, please. Part of my pleasure in running this place is in knowing these innocent creatures are safe from the fisherman's net and the treacherous lobster pot. You don't eat fish, do you, Cyril?'

'Not this sort at any rate,' said Cyril, his eyes now on some variety of many-tentacled octopus or squid. 'Why does nothing live in the biggest tank?'

'I'm hoping to acquire a shark,' said Mrs Trevor. 'Possibly even *Carcharhinus milberti*. Now you know what you have to do, don't you, Cyril? You close at five and then you come up here and feed the innocent creatures. Specific feeding instructions are all in the book. You turn off the lights but *not* the aeration and in certain cases cover the tanks with their lids. Is that understood?'

Cyril said it was and what about cleaning out the tanks? Some, he had noticed, were much overgrown with green algae which had even covered the back of the stone crab.

'Carlos will come in and do that. It's a specialist job. You're the kind of person who would use Persil Automatic.'

He knew she was angry with him for what he had said about crabmeat and not for the first time castigated himself for his tactless ways. They went downstairs and Mrs Trevor resumed her seat behind the ticket window so that Shana from the rink could get back to her duties. Cyril, in the cosy sitting room at the rear of the aquarium, found his instruction book *The Care of Cold-Blooded Aquatic Vertebrates and Crustaceae* on a shelf between *Story and Structure* and Louise's novel *Open Windows*. But he did not read it, he looked unseeing at the pages.

As usual in one of his reveries, he trudged across familiar ground. Biggs was not such a bad name. It was an improvement on Smalls, for instance, with its connotations of underclothes. Several saints had been called Cyril. He had looked them up in encyclopaedias. There were Saint Cyril of Jerusalem and Saint Cyril of Alexandria, both Doctors of the Church. There was that Saint Cyril who was responsible for Christianising the Danubian Slavs, and who invented the Cyrillic writing system. It is not everyone who can boast of sharing his name with an alphabet.

Was it his name which had doomed him to obscurity, and worse, to mockery? People laughed when they heard he was an insurance claims inspector, as if someone called that could hardly be anything else. But his venture at changing his name and adopting another profession had met with disaster. 'Maxwell Lawrie' sounded distinguished. For a time his books featuring Vladimir Klein, international espionage agent, had brought him success and promised fame. *Glasnost* had put an end to all hope there, for who cares for spies when there may soon be nothing and no one left to spy on?

You cannot get back into insurance when you have been absent from it for so long, but Cyril had not even tried. Before he came back to Southend and Malvina's Marine Museum, he had been living on alms given him by the Espionage Authors' Benevolent Association in a hotel room in Madagascar Road, NW2, paid for by Brent Council. There he had often sat and wondered what might be the destiny of one called Cyril Biggs. Surely there must be more than to be the prototype of the dull little man in the novel, the one with thinning hair and the ugly wife, the one with shoes always dull with the dust of mean streets. He sensed sometimes that he had never had his full potential realised, though he did know what that potential might be.

Malvina Trevor left for Southampton as soon as the Aquarium closed. She had dressed herself in a grey-green suit with a frilly blouse. Once her taxi had disappeared round the corner of Seoul Road, Cyril went up to the tank room and carefully scattered fish food into the tanks. He switched off the lights, but not the aeration and heating plant, and where instructed closed the lids. It was a complex routine which, once learned, became simple. Day after day it was repeated. From ten till five Cyril sat at the ticket window. At five-thirty he fed the fish and closed up the tank room. On two days a week Shana came in to relieve him and several times Ruta Yglesias asked him in to supper.

Louise Mitchell was there on one occasion, for the sisters had always been close, and their mother with them. On another Ruta had invited some people called Ann and Roger, whose surname Cyril no more learned than he did the Christian name of another guest, Mrs Greenaway. But it was quite a party and, to his surprise, Cyril enjoyed himself. He was not really gloomy by nature, only shy and lacking confidence. Before Malvina returned, and she would be back in less than a week, Cyril made up his mind to return Ruta's hospitality.

Giving dinner parties was not something he was accustomed to. For days he agonised over what he should give Ruta, Mrs Church and Mavis Ormitage to eat. With Shana ensconced behind the ticket window, he roved the front at Southend, eyeing the fish stalls, and in equal doubt and confusion paced between the freezers in the Presto supermarket. Food was expensive, or that kind was. The price of crabs and lobsters horrified him. He informed the stone crab in the Aquarium of the amount asked for its fellows when 'dressed' and offered for sale on the stalls. The crab's reply was to scamper sideways across its weedy coralline floor. I wonder if it is really green-carapaced, thought Cyril, or if its back is the reddy-pink colour of those I saw this afternoon. It is hard to tell because of the algae which covers it.

The main course was to be pasta, the kind the Italians call *alle vongole* because it has small clams mixed up in it. Cyril bought the pasta at Daleth Foods but naturally the Orthodox Jews who ran it would have nothing to do with seafood. The shellfish came from his favourite stall on the front – it was the cheapest – where he also bought a large dressed crab. Cyril mixed its sweet meat with Hellmann's mayonnaise to make it go further and everyone pronounced it delicious. But when Mavis made a remark about it being rather strange to eat shellfish with 'all that lot swimming about in there', he felt uncomfortable. Had he been wrong to choose this menu? Had he made himself look a fool?

'Does that mean zoo keepers must be vegetarians then, Mavis?' asked Mrs Church.

Mavis giggled. 'You know what I mean. If you had supper with a zoo keeper you wouldn't imagine you were eating lion chops but here – well, you know what I mean.'

They all did and Cyril could not help noticing that Ruta left a great many of her *vongole* on the side of her plate. What had induced him to made a lime mousse in a fish shape for pudding? It must have been seeing the copper mould in the window of the shop at the end of the parade where Mr Cybele sold antique scoops. Mr Cybele had lent him the fish mould and the pale green shape looked pretty. Unfortunately no one wanted to eat it after what Mavis Ormitage had said.

Cyril felt that his party had been a failure. That, of course, was nothing new. Most of his ventures, large and small, were failures. The arrival in the morning of Carlos with his tank-cleaning equipment distracted his mind from unhappy reminiscing. Cyril hung a notice on the Aquarium door, announcing that it would be closed till after lunch. He inspected the tanks before re-opening. The improvement in their appearance was quite wonderful. Everything sparkled, fresh and gleaming. Every aquatic invertebrate was rejuvenated – except the stone crab whose carapace was still overgrown with dense green fur.

Its appearance troubled him. When he went about his feeding routine he put one finger into the water, touched the shell and found he could easily scrape some of the crust of algae off with his fingernail. Carlos had cleaned the biggest tank in the middle of the rooms as well and Cyril, closing the lid on the crab, wondered when the new shark would arrive. Before Malvina's return or after? She was coming back in two days' time. Ruta and Mrs Church were driving to Southampton in Mrs Church's new Audi to fetch her.

Cyril slept badly that night. He saw himself as a social misfit. He wondered about his future, which seemed to have no existence beyond Malvina's return. A great crowd came to the Aquarium in the morning and entrance had to be restricted. Visitors had heard about the cleaning operation and for the first time Cyril saw a queue at the front door. When the last visitor had left at five he paced up and down the sitting room, uncertain what to do, torn by conflicting demands. Then, impulsively, he rushed upstairs. He lifted the large, algae-coated decapod out of its tank, took it to the bathroom and washed it under the running tap. It was the work of a moment. The crab's carapace was indeed green, a pure soft emerald green with a curious design like an ideograph in a dark purplish shade on its back.

Tenderly, Cyril restored it to its home. The crab scuttled through its woodland of weed across its coral floor, attended by a little shoal of fish coloured like jewels. If Malvina enquired, he decided, he would tell her it had somehow happened during Carlos's operations. But surely she would be delighted? Cyril suddenly found himself hyperanxious to please Malvina, to confront her with perfection, to have attained, so to speak, supererogatory heights of achievement. Merely to have done the appointed job was not enough. He spent most of Saturday night sweeping and vacuum-cleaning the Aquarium, tank room and the rest of the house, and on Sunday morning wrote in his best lettering a label for the biggest tank: *Carcharhinus milberti*, the Sandbar shark, which he followed by a careful description of its habitat and habits.

Mrs Trevor came back at seven in the evening, dressed exactly as she had been when she left. She entered the Aquarium alone and trembling with anger. Cyril had expected Ruta and Mrs Church to be with her but evidently they had thought it wisest to make themselves scarce. Malvina gave each tank a rapid penetrating glance, the stone crab a longer look. She went upstairs and Cyril followed. So far she had not uttered a word and Cyril had received no reply to his enquiries as to her health and enjoyment of her trip. In the tank room she stood looking down at the stone crab, turned to face Cyril and said in shrill tones,

'How dare you?'

Putting the blame on Carlos forgotten, Cyril stammered that the crab was not harmed, indeed seemed happier for the cleansing operation.

'Don't give me that. Don't even think of trying it. I know what you have done. Ruta and her mother told me all about the seafood extravaganza you served up to them – and the ingredients used. This particular decapod, I have no doubt, was purchased or stolen from the tank of one of the fish restaurants on the front. Monterroso's, most probably.'

'It isn't true, Malvina. They're lying. I wouldn't do that.'

'I'm not a fool, you know. It isn't even the same variety. Look at the colour! You're too ignorant to know that there are no less than 4,500 species of crab, aren't you? You thought, when you slaughtered that innocent creature to make mayonnaise, that one crab was very like another. Well, I shall expose you. I shall publish the whole story in the *Southend Times*. Needless to say, I shan't pay you. I shall not take you on as my permanent assistant, as was in my mind.'

Cyril did not think. He did not hesitate. He gave her a shove and she fell into the biggest tank with a scream and a loud splash. If he saw her floundering there, he might soften, he thought, for he had never been hard-hearted, so he put the lid on, went downstairs and out to the beach. In all his life he had never felt so happy, so free and so fulfilled. As he walked along the mudflats with the sea breezes in his hair, he understood his destiny and the meaning of his name.

He was not a novelist's character, no figment of fiction, but one to inspire literature in his own right. One day books would be written about him, his past, his history, his obscurity, his striving for an identity, and his name: Cyril Biggs, the Marine Museum Murderer. Newspapers would give him headlines and television a favoured position in the six o'clock news. At Madame Tussaud's, in the Chamber of Horrors, he would be placed by a water tank while a plastic facsimile of his victim floated within. He had found his vocation.

That night Cyril slept better than he had done for years. It was Shana's day to sit at the receipt of custom. Such news travels fast and, looking out of an upstairs window, Cyril was not surprised to see a queue winding its way from the front door the length of the parade. Presently he crept down to the tank room.

He did not lift the lid from the biggest tank but edged discreetly along the wall and peered into the stone crab's home, peered through sparkling, ever-bubbling jade-coloured water and gleaming spotless glass to the crowds beneath. There, pressed closely around the biggest tank were Louise Mitchell, Ruta Yglesias, Fenella, Mrs Church and Mrs Greenaway, Henry Bennett with the Ruler and his painted queen, the three Jewish grocers, Veronica Spencer and her husband Tim, Margaret Cavendish, Jane, several Italian boys in T-shirts and a host of others not recognisable to Cyril. Some were reading the label he had made for the Sandbar shark but those who could get close had their faces pressed against the glass, contemplating what was within.

They were polite middle-class people and as each had seen her or his fill, there was a stepping back and a parting to allow those behind to look. In one of these reshuffles, the tank was briefly revealed to Cyril's view and he saw floating inside it, flippers gently pulsating with the movement of the water, a vast grey-green shape with a frill about its neck like the ruff of a salamander.

# An Unwanted Woman

'It's not a matter for the police.'

He had said it before, to his wife, if not to this woman. The affair of Sophie Grant, bizarre, nearly incomprehensible, was outside the range of his experience. Deeply conservative, convinced of the superiority of past ways to those of the present, he was inclined to blame events on the decadence of the times he lived in. He repeated what he had said, adding, 'There's nothing we can do.'

Jenny's friend, who was not crying yet, who seemed on the verge of crying or even screaming, a desperate woman, said in the voice she could only just control, 'Then who am I to turn to? What can I do?'

'I've already suggested the Social Services,' said Jenny, 'but it's true what Hilary says, all they can do is take her into care, apply for a care order.'

'She's not in need of care,' Hilary said with bitterness, with venom. 'She doesn't need protecting. It's me, I'm the one who's suffering. I ought to be taken into care and looked after.' She had her voice and herself under control again. Her wineglass was empty. She took hold of it and after a small hesitation, held it up. 'I'm sorry, Jenny. I *need* it. It's not as if it was the hard stuff.'

Jenny refilled the glass with Frascati. Hilary had got through half the bottle. They were sitting in the living room of the Burdens' house in Glenwood Road, Kingsmarkham. It was just after nine on a winter's evening, Christmas not far off as evinced by the first few cards, greetings from the superpunctual, on the mantelpiece. A wooden engine, gaily painted, a worn rabbit and a Russian doll, its interlocking pieces separated, lay on the carpet, and these several objects Jenny now began picking up and dropping into a toy chest. Hilary watched her with increasing misery.

'I know I'm a nuisance. I know I'm disturbing you when you'd like a quiet evening on your own. I'm sorry, but you – well, Jenny – you're all I've got. I don't know who else to talk to. Except to Martin and he – sometimes I think he's *glad*. Well, he's not, I shouldn't say that, but when she was there she was so hateful to him, it must be a relief. You see –' She looked away from them, '– I'm so *ashamed*. That's why I can't tell other people, because of being ashamed.'

Burden thought he would have a drink, if only to make Hilary feel better. He fetched himself a beer from the fridge. When he came back Jenny had her arm round Hilary and Hilary had tears on her face.

'What is there to be ashamed of?'

'A woman whose child doesn't want to live with her? What sort of a mother can she be? What sort of a home has she got? Of course I'm ashamed. People look at me and they think, what was going on in that house? They must have been abusing her, they must have ill-treated her.'

'People don't *know*, Hilary. Hardly anyone actually knows. You're imagining all this.'

'I can see it in their eyes.'

Buoyed up by his drink, resigned to the ruin of his evening, Burden thought he might as well go the whole hog. Get it first-hand, though he could do nothing. Nothing could come of it but the slight relief to Hilary Stacey of relating it once again.

Jenny said suddenly, 'Does her father know?'

'Her father wouldn't care. It's once in a blue moon he writes to her, she hasn't heard from him for months.'

'Tell me exactly what happened, would you, Hilary? Jenny's told me but I'd like you to.' He was painfully aware of sounding like a policeman. On the other hand, she had *wanted* a policeman. 'Tell me from the beginning.'

'I thought you were going to say "in your own words", Mike.'

He inclined his head a little, not smiling.

'Sorry. Being so miserable makes me bitchy. What is this, therapy?'

'It might be that as well,' said Burden. He was foraging in his knowledge of the law, thinking of such vague and insubstantial offences as enticement and corruption of a minor. 'Let me have the facts. I'm not saying we can do anything, I'm sure we can't, but just tell me what happened, will you?'

She looked him in the eye. Her own eyes were a startling turquoise blue, large and prominent. It was easy to see why she never wore make-up, she was colourful enough without it, that white and rosy skin, those eyes, flaxen hair straight and shining. A woman with those attributes should have been good-looking but Hilary missed beauty by the length of her face that gave her a horsy look. She was very thin, thinner since this trouble started.

'It really began long before I married Martin,' she said, 'perhaps even when Peter and I were divorced five years ago. I didn't *want* a divorce, you know, I wanted to stay married for life. I know it sounds self-pitying but it was not my fault, it really wasn't, I was hard done-by. Peter's girlfriend was pregnant. I still didn't want a divorce, but how long can you keep on fighting? I knew he'd never come back.

'Sophie was nine. She made a big thing about saying she hated Peter. She told people he'd left "us", not that he'd left me. She knew about the girlfriend Monica and she used to say her father preferred Monica to us. Well, she wouldn't see Peter for months but gradually she came round. It was the baby, I think. He was her half-brother and she liked the idea of a brother. She started to enjoy spending weekends with Peter and Monica and the baby. I will say for Monica that she was very nice to her and of course it wasn't the usual situation where a child is jealous of a new sibling.

'I honestly think none of this would have happened if Peter and Monica were still here. I'm sure it's much more due to their going to America than to me marrying Martin. Peter had this job and no doubt it was the only course for him to take. He was always more or less indifferent to Sophie anyway, Monica was much nicer to her than her father was, and I don't think it bothered him that he wouldn't see his daughter for years. He could have afforded to pay her air fare to Washington but he wouldn't.

'It was a blow to her. It was a second blow. OK, I suppose you'll say my remarrying was the third. But what's a woman to do, Mike? I was on my own with Sophie, I had a full-time job and the school holidays were a nightmare. So I got a part-time job and even that was too much for me, and then when things were about as grim as they'd ever been I fell in love with Martin and he fell in love with me. I mean, it was like a dream, it was like something that you daren't dream about because it just won't happen, things as good as that don't happen. But it did. A nice kind clever successful good-looking man was in love with me and wanted to marry me and liked my daughter and thought she could be his daughter, and everything was wonderful.

'And she thought so too, Sophie thought so. She was happy, she was excited. I think she saw Martin as a wonderful new friend, hers as much as mine. Of course we were very careful in front of her, she was thirteen and that's a very difficult age. For ages I never let Martin even kiss me in her presence and then when he did he'd always kiss her too.

'We got married and she was at the wedding and she loved every minute of it. Next day she started to hate him. She loathed him. She did everything to try to split us up, she told lies to us about the other one, she'd seen Martin out with a woman, she'd heard me call a man "darling" on the phone, she'd heard me telling Jenny I married him for his money. Yes, *truly*. You wouldn't credit it, would you? When she saw she couldn't separate us, she did what she's done, walked out and went to live with Ann Waterton. That's where she is and where she intends to stay, she says.

'I've pleaded with her, I've begged her, I've even tried to bribe her to come back. I've pleaded with Ann Waterton, I've been there, I've even set it all down in writing, in letters to her. To do Ann justice, she hasn't enticed her or anything like that, she's lonely, she likes Sophie's company, but she's told her she ought to go home. Anyway, she says she has. Sophie won't. She's got a key to Ann's house, she comes and goes as she pleases, and she's very good to Ann, she looks after her. She likes cooking which Ann doesn't and she cooks special meals for them. She takes Ann her breakfast in bed before she goes to school.

'I've asked Ann to change the locks on the door but she won't, she says Sophie would stay out in the street all night, and I think she's right, Sophie would do that. She'd wrap herself in blankets and sit on the garden wall or sleep in Ann's garage.'

Burden said, 'Have you asked her what it is she wants?'

'Oh, yes.' Hilary Stacey gave a short bitter laugh. 'I've asked her. "Get rid of Martin," she says, "and then I'll come home."'

'What's the bugger done to her?' said Chief Inspector Wexford.

It was the following day and he and Burden were on their way to London. Donaldson was driving and Wexford and Burden sat in the back of the car. Their mission was to interview two men suspected of being concerned in a break-in at Barclay's Bank in Kingsmarkham High Street a week before. One lived in Hackney, the other was usually to be found around midday at a pub in Hanwell. Burden had been relating the story of Sophie Grant.

'Nothing,' he said. 'I'm sure of it. Oh, I know you can't tell. It's no good saying, I know the guy, I've had a meal in his house, I know he's not like that. The most unexpected men are like that. But I'd say he just didn't have time. He didn't have the time or the opportunity. He and Hilary Grant, as she was, were newly married, sharing a bedroom – that was partly the trouble. Sophie stayed around for three weeks and then she left.'

'But you say she seemed to like the chap before he married her mum?'

'I suppose she just didn't know, she didn't realise. She was nearly fourteen but she didn't realise her mother would be sharing a bed with Martin Stacey. And I expect there was some kissing and cuddling and touching in her presence – well, there was bound to be.'

'She thought it was a marriage for companionship, is that what you're saying? Yes, I can imagine. The mother was very careful, no doubt, *before* she was married, no physical contact when the girl was there, definitely no bed-sharing, no goodnight kisses. And then, after the wedding, a kind of explosion of sensuality, mother and stepfather having no need to curb their ardour. Because it would be OK, wouldn't it, they were *married*, it was respectable, nothing to object to. A shock to the girl, wouldn't you say?'

'According to Hilary it was pretty much like that.' Burden began assembling in his mind the facts and details as Hilary Stacey had told them. 'Sophie seems to have given him hell. Screamed at him, insulted him, then refused to speak to him at all. That went on for a week and one evening she just didn't come home from school. Hilary Stacey didn't have time to get worried. Sophie phoned her and said she was with Mrs Waterton and there she intended to stay.'

'Why Mrs Waterton?' Wexford asked.

'That's rather interesting in itself. Sophie is a very bright child, good at her school work, always in the top three. And does a lot of community service, visiting the elderly and the bereaved, that sort of thing. She does their shopping and sits with them. There's a blind woman she calls on and reads the newspaper to. As well as this she does baby-sitting – she baby-sits for us – and she used to do a paper round, only her mother stopped that, quite rightly in my view, it's dangerous even in a place like this.

'Ann Waterton's in her sixties. She lost her husband in the spring and apparently it hit her very hard. There were no children. Sophie used to go to her house after school, just to talk really. They seem to have got on very well.'

'A girl of that age,' Wexford said, 'will often get on a great deal better with an older woman than with her own mother. I take it this Ann Waterton's no slouch – I mean, she's got something to give a lively intelligent fourteen-year-old?'

'According to Hilary, she's a retired teacher. In his last years she and her husband were both studying for Open University degrees but she gave that up when he died. At one time she used to write the nature column for the *Kingsmarkham Courier*.'

Wexford looked dubious. The car had joined the queue of vehicles lining up for the toll at the Dartford Tunnel. They were in for a long wait. Burden looked at his watch, a fairly useless exercise.

'One evening about a month after George Waterton died Sophie called round there. It was about nine but light still. She was on her bicycle. Hilary Stacey and Ann Waterton live about a mile apart, Hilary in Glendale Road – you know, the next street to me – and Mrs Waterton in Coulson Gardens. Sophie couldn't make Mrs Waterton hear but the back door was unlocked and she went in, thinking she would find her fallen asleep over a book or the television.

'She did find her, in an armchair in the living room, and she appeared to be asleep. There was an empty pill bottle on the table beside her and a tumbler which seemed to have contained brandy. Sophie acted with great presence of mind. She phoned for an ambulance and she phoned her mother. Of course Hilary hadn't yet married Martin Stacey, though she was planning to marry him, the wedding being fixed for August.

'Hilary got there first. She and Sophie managed to get Ann Waterton on to her feet and were walking or dragging her up and down when the ambulance came. As we know, they were in time and Ann Waterton recovered.'

Wexford said unexpectedly, 'Was there a suicide note?'

'I don't know. Hilary didn't say. Apparently, not. She and Sophie had been very anxious it shouldn't appear as a suicide attempt but as an accidental taking of an overdose.'

'Bit indiscreet telling you then, wasn't it?' said Wexford derisively. 'Why did she tell you?'

'I don't know, Reg. It was all part of the background, I suppose. She knew I wouldn't broadcast it around.'

'You've told *me*. And Donaldson's not deaf.'

'That's all right, sir,' said Donaldson, no doubt indicating his willingness to be the soul of discretion.

'I imagine everybody knew about it,' said Wexford. 'Or guessed. And after that she and this Mrs Waterton became fast friends, is that it? The house in Coulson Gardens was the natural place for the girl to decamp to.' He pondered for a moment or two as the car moved sluggishly towards one of the toll booths. 'The mother might be able to get a care order made or a supervision order,' he said. 'She could try to get her made a Ward of Court. It's hardly a case for *Habeas Corpus*.'

'She doesn't want to do that and who can blame her? She wants the girl back living with her. Sophie is out of control, it's true, that is her mother can't control her to the extent of making her come home, but she hasn't done anything wrong, she's broken no law.'

'The danger', said Wexford, 'with getting a care order for someone who's out of control might be that it contained a requirement for the subject, that is, Sophie Grant, to reside with a named individual – and suppose that named individual was Ann Waterton?'

The car began to head for London up the motorway.

From the tall rather forbidding curtain wall of stone blocks rose thirteen towers. The arc lamps flooded them with white light and showed up the cloudy smoky texture of the sky behind, purplish, very dark, starless. In the great hall, which had lost its roof some six centuries before, which was open to this heavy rain-threatening sky, a performance of Elizabethan music was under way, was drawing to its close just in time, thought Burden, before the heavens opened. He was there, sitting in the second row, because Jenny was singing in the choir.

This was the first time he had been to Myland Castle, a type of fortification (according to the programme) innovative in Europe in the twelfth century. It was a huge fortress containing the remains of gateways and garderobes and kitchens and tunnel-vaulted rooms and features called rere-arches. Burden was more interested in the castle than the concert. It was too late in the year, in his opinion, for outdoor performances of anything. The evening was damp and raw rather than really cold but it was cold enough. The audience huddled inside sheepskin and anoraks.

It was a mystery why the organisers had picked on this place. Size alone must account for it, for the acoustics were so bad that the harpsichord was nearly inaudible and the sweet melodious voices seemed carried up into the sky where no doubt they could be clearly heard some two hundred feet in the air. As a soloist began on the final song, 'Though Amaryllis Dance in Green', Burden let his eyes rove along the tops of the walls and the catwalk between the towers. From the other side of the curtain wall, where the great buttresses fell steeply away to green slopes and a dry moat, the view across country must be very fine. Perhaps he would come back in the spring and bring Mark. If he didn't care for the view he would enjoy rolling down the green slopes, kids always did.

The applause was enthusiastic. Relief, they're glad it's all over, thought Burden the Philistine. Jenny, coming up to him, laying an icy hand on his, said, 'You couldn't hear, could you?'

Burden grinned. 'We couldn't hear as much as we were meant to.'

He was astonished and pleased to see it was not yet nine. Time had passed slowly. He took his wife's arm and they ran for it to the car as the rain began.

The extreme youth of their baby-sitter had worried him the first time she came. That Sophie Grant would phone her mother in the next street if there was any cause for alarm, did a lot to calm his fears. By the time she had sat for them three times he trusted her as entirely as he would have trusted someone three times her age. She might be fourteen but she looked seventeen. It was absurd, he reflected as he walked into his living room, to think of her in the context of care orders, of being in need of supervision or protection.

She was sitting on the sofa, with her books beside her, writing an essay on unlined paper attached to a clipboard. Her handwriting was strong, clearly legible, slightly forward-sloping. She looked up and said, 'I haven't heard a sound from him. I went up three times and he was fast asleep.' She smiled. 'With his rabbit. He's inseparable from that rabbit.'

'D'you want a drink, Sophie?' Jenny remembered she was a child. It was easy to forget. 'I mean, hot chocolate or a cup of tea or something?'

'No, thanks, I'd better get off.'

'What do we owe you?'

'Nine pounds, please, Jenny, three hours at three pounds an hour. I started at six-thirty, I think. 'Sophie spoke in a crisp and business-like way, without a hint of diffidence. She took the note and gave Jenny a pound coin.

Burden fetched her coat. It was a navy blue duffle and in it she immediately shed a few years. She was a schoolgirl again, tall, rather gawky, olive-skinned and dark-haired, the hair long and straight, pushed behind her ears. The shape of her face and the blue eyes were her mother's, but she was prettier. She packed books and clipboard into a rather battered briefcase.

'I'll walk you home,' said Burden. It was only round the corner, but these days you never knew. He had forgotten for the moment where home was for her now. She said, 'Coulson Gardens. It's a long walk.'

Should he dispute it? Argue? 'I'll drive you.'

They were uncomfortable together in the car. Or Burden was uncomfortable. The girl seemed tranquil enough. It was cowardice, he thought, that kept him from speaking. Was he afraid of a fourteen-year-old?

'How long are you going to keep this up, Sophie?' he said.

'Keep what up?' She wasn't going to help him.

'This business of living with Mrs Waterton, of refusing to go home to your mother.'

For a moment he thought she was going to tell him to mind his own business. She didn't. 'I haven't refused to go home,' she said. 'I've said I'll go home when he's not there. When she gets rid of him I'll go home.'

'Come on, he's her husband.'

'And I'm her daughter. You're going past it, Mike, it's the house with the red gate. She loves him, she doesn't love me. Why should I go to live with someone who doesn't care for me?'

She jumped out of the car before he could open the door for her. A small slim woman with short grey hair was looking out of a front window, the curtain caught on her shoulder. She smiled, gave a little wave, a flutter of fingers. Burden thought, I can't just leave it, I can't miss this opportunity.

'What's Martin Stacey done, Sophie? Why don't you like him? He's a nice enough chap, he's all right.'

'He made her deceive me. They pretended things. They both pretended he was going to look after us and earn money for us and *like* us both, not just her, not just want to be with her. And she pretended I was the most important person in the world to her. It was all false, all lies. I was nothing. He made me nothing and she *liked* it.' She spoke in a low intense voice that was almost a growl. A pause in which she drew a long breath, then, 'Thanks for the lift, Mike. Good night.'

She ran up the path and the door opened for her, but the figure of Mrs Waterton was not visible.

On the way home he thought, it's as much that woman's doing as the girl's. Why does she give her a room? Why does she feed her? She ought to go away for a bit, shut up the house. She would if she had any sense of responsibility. He said something of this to his wife.

'Oh, think, Mike, how Ann Waterton must love it. She was all alone, a widow, no children, probably not many friends. People don't want to know widows, or so they say. And then suddenly along comes a ready-made granddaughter, someone who actually *prefers* her over her own mother and her own home. I'm not saying she deliberately encouraged Sophie but I bet you she didn't make any positive moves to send her home. It must have brought her a new lease of life. Did she look happy?'

'I suppose she did,' said Burden.

'Well, then. And less than six months ago she was suicidal.'

It was a fortnight before he saw Sophie's mother again. Once more she was spending the evening with Jenny, Martin Stacey being away on a protracted business trip abroad.

'He's glad to get away from me, I expect. It's been nothing but trouble ever since we got married. Of course he's been angelic but how long can that go on? I'm always miserable, I cry every day, I'm always in a state, he can't put up with that for ever. So I've decided what to do. You tell him, Jenny. Tell him what I'm doing.'

Jenny said dryly, 'It's a case of if you can't beat 'em, join 'em. Hilary's idea is that the best thing for her to do is make friends with Ann Waterton.'

'I've stopped arguing about it, I've stopped telling her she has to send Sophie home and I've stopped threatening her.'

'Threatening her?' said Burden, on the alert.

'I only mean telling her I'd get an injunction to stop her seeing Sophie. I don't suppose I ever would have. But now I've decided to *like* her. The way I see it, I don't have a choice. And if it works – well, oh, it's all in the air as yet, but I thought maybe we could all live together. If Sophie's that crazy about old Ann the answer might be for us all to be together. Sell our houses and buy a big house for the lot of us.'

Burden thought, but surely it's not that Sophie is specially 'crazy' about Mrs Waterton but that she is specially un-crazy about her stepfather. He did not care to say this aloud. It occurred to him that Hilary Stacey, if not exactly unhinged by all this, was becoming rather strange.

'So what's happening?' said Jenny. 'You're inviting her to tea, are you? Taking her out for drives?'

'She can drive herself,' Hilary said shortly. 'This is deadly serious, Jenny, this is my life, my whole future existence we're talking about. You could say I've lost my only child.'

Jenny poured her another glass of wine.

'I reason', said Hilary, 'that if my daughter likes someone that much I could like her too. After all, we used to be very close, Sophie and I, we used to like the same things, the same people, we had the same taste in clothes, we liked the same food. There's got to be something about old Ann that I can like. And there is, there is. I can see there's a lot more to her than I thought at first. I thought Sophie was flattered – you know, a sort of granny-substitute buttering her up and telling her how pretty and clever and mature she was, all that, but Ann's a very bright woman, she's very well-read. It's just a matter of my meeting her more than half way.'

'I wonder what that poor devil of a husband's going to say,' was

Wexford's comment when Burden retailed all this to him, 'having a supererogatory mother-in-law shacking up with him.'

'Hardly "shacking up",' Burden protested, 'and it hasn't come to that yet. Personally, I don't think it ever will.'

'Does her mother make her an allowance? Give her pocket money?'

'I don't know. I never asked.'

'I was thinking of a scene from *The Last Chronicle of Barset*,' said Wexford, who was rereading his Trollope. 'The Archdeacon wants to know how to deal with a recalcitrant son. His daughter asks him if he allows her brother an income and when he replies, yes, says, "I should tell him that must depend upon his conduct."'

'Does it work?' said Burden, interested in spite of himself.

'No,' said Wexford rather sadly. 'No, it doesn't. I shouldn't expect it to, not with anyone of spirit, would you?'

An enquiry about an attack on a cyclist took Wexford and Sergeant Martin to Myland Castle. It was the fourth in a series of such assaults, each apparently motiveless, for the amount of money the cyclists carried was negligible. Three were men, one a woman. Two of the attacks happened by day, two after dark. The only pattern discernible seemed to be that the attacks increased in severity, the first, on the woman, consisting of not much more than pushing her off her bicycle and damaging the machine to make it temporarily unusable, but the fourth had put the victim into intensive care with broken bones and a ruptured spleen.

All these seemingly pointless acts of violence had taken place in the Myfleet–Myland neighbourhood, this last on the cycle path which led from the Myfleet Road to Myland village and passed on the outer side of the castle moat. Wexford had already questioned staff at the castle. The purpose of this return visit was to re-examine one of the guides. Two members of staff, those manning the south gate and the turnstile, claimed to have seen the victim, a frequent cyclist on the path, but only the guide admitted to the possibility of having seen the perpetrator. Just before the castle closed to the public at four, he had been standing in the gathering dusk on the curtain wall between the two south towers.

It was a fine day, a sunny island of a day in a week of fog and rain, and the number of visitors to Myland Castle was nearer a midsummer than a December average. While Martin talked to the woman at the turnstile, Wexford went across the great hall in search of the guide. The two o'clock tour had five more minutes to run. Wexford could see the group of about ten people standing on the battlements, the guide pointing across the meadows towards Myland church where the tombs of the castle builders were.

While he waited Wexford made his way to the remains of a chapel and hall, embedded in the inner court. This had been a town rather than a dwelling house, with gatehouses and barracks, almshouses and courts. From the passage along which he was walking, a flight of stone stairs led up on to the curtain wall and these he took, emerging into the fresh air but also to deep shadow. It was possible to walk round the battlements on this walkway, occasionally passing up and down steps inside the turrets. The wall on the inner side was high enough, it came up to his waist, but rather lower on the outer, and crenellated. However, the path was wide, the wall was more than small-child height, and even a venturesome older person would have had to lean over and lose balance in order to fall.

Falling would be an atrocious thing, Wexford thought. The battlements here were like cliffs but with no merciful sea at their base. Their height was increased by the moat, a fifteen-foot deep ditch, whose northern side at this point continued downwards the sheer slope of the castle wall. He walked along slowly, keeping in sight the guide, Peter Ratcliffe, and his group, now standing under the great bulwark of the gatehouse flanking tower.

He was not alone on the walkway. He could hear a party with children mounting the staircase behind him and in front, some twenty or thirty feet ahead, saw two women appear from the steps inside the first of the south turrets. It was probably his fancy that when she saw him – and saw also those behind him – the younger of the women whispered something to her companion and they turned back the way they had come. Most likely they had meant to turn back anyway and retrace their steps along the sunny side. An area of deep cold shade lay between them and Wexford.

He walked along and through it more quickly. Beyond the turret the sun began, and it was warm and benign on his face. The two women were still ahead of him and as he observed them, talking together, sometimes pointing across the fields or studying the guide book the older one carried, he knew who they were. That was putting it rather too strongly perhaps. He guessed who they might be, he *thought* he knew. The bright fair hair of one of them told him and her rather protuberant blue eyes, extraordinarily blue and clear just as Burden had described them. As if she sensed his watchfulness, she turned round and those eyes cast their blue beam on him.

The other woman was small and slight, very upright, perhaps sixty-five, with short grey hair. Hilary Stacey and Ann Waterton. He was so sure that he wouldn't have hesitated to address them by their names. Inside the gatehouse tower the main exit staircase went down. He saw them enter the arch to the tower and by the time he had reached it they had begun the descent. Ratcliffe's party immediately appeared, heading in their turn for the exit staircase. Wexford pressed himself against the wall to allow their passage and when the last of them was through, Ratcliffe came sauntering up, all smiles and helpfulness.

'Brain-picking time?' he said. 'They tell me I'm needed to help you with your enquiries.'

It was uttered in a facetious way, quotation marks very evident round the last words. Wexford said quietly, 'Perhaps we can go a few yards along the walkway, Mr Ratcliffe, to the place from which you saw the attacker.'

A neighbour called the police. It was nine o'clock on a Friday. He went out into his front garden and heard a car engine running. The only car nearby was shut up in Ann Waterton's garage. He opened the garage doors and the first thing he saw was the length of hose to the exhaust, passing through the driver's window.

He switched off the engine and pulled Ann Waterton out. Giving the kiss of life, what he, an elderly man, called 'artificial respiration', had no effect. She was dead. When the police came they found the house unlocked but empty. On the table in the dining room, in a sealed envelope marked 'To the Coroner', was what they concluded was a suicide note.

'Where was the girl?' Wexford asked when told about it the next day.

'Gone on a school trip to London,' said Burden. 'A theatre visit apparently. Shakespeare, something they were studying. They went in a coach, which didn't get back to Kingsmarkham until eleven-thirty.'

'And Sophie, finding what had happened, at last went home to mother?'

'It would seem so.'

At the inquest a verdict was returned on Ann Waterton of suicide while the balance of her mind was disturbed. The suicide note, written in the firm round characterless hand of the primary school teacher, was read aloud. *I cannot go on. Life has become a meaningless farce. I am totally alone now with no prospect of things ever changing. I am unwanted, an unnecessary woman, a useless drag on society. It is better for everyone this way, and much better for myself. Ann Waterton.*

'Totally alone?' Burden said to Jenny. 'She had Sophie, didn't she?'

'Sophie was going home.'

'What, you mean, before all this happened, Sophie meant to leave her? To go home? She'd given in at last?'

'Hilary said so in evidence at the inquest. The coroner asked her about her daughter living with Ann and she told him how Sophie was returning home. She told me privately, between outselves, that she and Sophie had had some talks. They had a talk with Ann there and some talks on their own and the upshot was that Sophie said, all right, she'd come home by Christmas and she made a few conditions, but the crux of it was she'd come home.'

'Conditions?' Burden took his little boy on his knee. He was wondering, not for the first time, how he would feel in ten years' time if this child, this apple of his eye, upped and packed his bags and went to live in someone else's house. 'What conditions?'

'Oh, they were to turn the attics into a sort of flat for her. It's quite a big house. She was to have her own kitchen and bathroom, live separately. Hilary must have agreed. She'd have agreed to almost anything to get Sophie back.'

'And Ann Waterton knew this?' Mark was thrusting a book under his father's nose, demanding to be read to. 'Yes, just a minute, I will, I promise I will.' He said to his wife, 'She knew it and that's what she meant by being "totally alone", and being "an unnecessary woman"?'

'I suppose so. It's rather awful, but it's nobody's fault. You have to think of it that if the girl hadn't gone there in the first place Ann Waterton would be dead anyway. She'd just have died six months sooner. She was determined to kill herself.'

Burden nodded. Mark had opened the book and was pointing rather sternly at the first word of the first line. His father began reading the latest adventure of *Postman Pat*.


'Anthony Trollope', said Wexford, 'wrote about fifty books. It's a lot, isn't it? One of them, a not very well-known one, is called *Cousin Henry*. I've just finished reading it.' He took note of the expression on Burden's face. 'I know this bores you. I wouldn't be telling you about it if I didn't think it was important.'

'Important?'

'Well, perhaps not important. Interesting. Significant. It gave me something to think about. Trollope wasn't what one would normally think of as a psychologist.'

'Too long ago for that, wasn't it?' Burden said vaguely. 'I mean, surely psychology wasn't invented till this century.'

'I wouldn't say that. Psychology is one of those things that was always with us, before anyone gave it a name, that is. Like, well, linguistics, for instance. And "invented" isn't quite the word. Discovered.'

It was the end of the day. They were at a table in the saloon bar of the Olive and Dove. Earlier, Wexford had made an arrest, that of Peter Ratcliffe, the Myland Castle guide. His attacks on the cyclists he was unable adequately to account for, though he had fully confessed to all of them. The explanation he gave Wexford was a strange one, it almost pointed to a disturbance of the man's mind. His daily presence in the castle, year after year, day after day, had brought him to a curious identification with its former defenders. It impelled him to attack those he saw as intruders. Perhaps it would only have been a matter of time before the paying visitors appeared to him in the same light and he injured one of them.

Wexford didn't know whether he believed this or not. No court would. Burden had stared in incredulous disgust when Wexford repeated Ratcliffe's words. That was why – partly why – he had changed the subject to *Cousin Henry*.

'Bear with me,' he said, 'while I give you a brief outline of the plot.' Burden didn't exactly demur, not quite. His face was a sigh incarnate. Wexford said, 'I promise you it's relevant.' He added, 'It even gets exciting.'

Burden nodded. He looked reflectively into his beer.

'The old squire dies', Wexford began, 'and leaves all his property to his nephew Henry. Or that's how it appears, that's what everyone thinks, and Henry comes into his inheritance. Then he finds a later will which leaves everything to his cousin Isabel. Henry's best bet is to destroy this will but he doesn't. He daren't. He hides it in a place where he thinks it will never be found, in fact in a book in the library, a book that is so boring no one would ever want to take it down and open it. Why doesn't he destroy it? He's afraid. It's an official document, an almost sacred thing, it exercises an awesome power over him, it's almost as if he's afraid of some unnamed retribution. Yet if he destroys it – a simple thing to do, though Henry, in his mind, discovers terrible difficulties in the way of doing this – if he does, all will be secure for ever and he the undisputed man in possession. But he can't destroy it, he daren't. Good psychology, don't you think? People behave like that, inexplicably, absurdly, but that's how they behave.'

'I suppose so. Thousands would. Have destroyed it, I mean. Most would.'

'Not the law-abiding. Not the conventional. Someone like you wouldn't.'

'I wouldn't have nicked it in the first place. What's the point of all this? You said there was a point.'

'Oh, yes. The Stacey-Grant-Waterton affair, that's the point.'

'Burden looked up at him, surprised. 'No wills involved in that, so far as I know.'

'No wills,' said Wexford, 'but another sort of document, a sacred sort of document. A suicide note.'

Wexford was silent for a moment, enjoying the look on Burden's face that was a mixture of incredulity and sheer alarm. 'Let me give you a scenario,' he said. 'Let me give you an alternative to what actually happened, a lonely unhappy woman at last succeeding at taking her own life.'

'Why have an alternative to the facts?'

'Just listen to a theory then. Ann Waterton didn't commit suicide. She had no reason to commit suicide. She was happy, she was happier than she had been since her husband died. She had found an affectionate, charming granddaughter, who *wanted* more than anything in the world to live with her.'

'Wait a minute,' said Burden. 'Sophie may have been living with her, but she wasn't going to go on doing that. She was going home. She was going back to her mother and her stepfather.'

'Was she? Do we have anyone's word for that but Hilary Stacey's?'

'She told the coroner under oath.'

'Hmm,' said Wexford. 'D'you want another drink?'

'I don't think I do. I want to hear the rest of what you've got to say.'

'All right. The fact is that we have no evidence that Sophie intended to go home but Hilary Stacey's word.'

'Sophie herself. Sophie could presumably confirm it?'

Wexford smiled rather enigmatically. 'Hilary Stacey's her mother. She may have been at odds with her but I don't think she'd shop her own mother.'

'Shop her?'

'Suppose Hilary Stacey murdered Ann Waterton? I saw them at Myland Castle about ten days ago. I recognised them from your description. If I hadn't been there, if so many visitors hadn't been there, an exceptional number for December but it was an exceptionally nice day, I think Hilary – Oh, yes, it's hindsight – was going to push Ann off that wall. It would have been, would have looked, like an accident. It was made impossible by the circumstances.

'Three days afterwards Sophie went on a school trip to a London theatre. Hilary was often at the house in Coulson Gardens, it would have been nothing out of the way for her to drop in during the evening. The next step was to give Ann a heavy dose of sleeping pills. She would have made them both a drink, given her the pills in that. Ann was a small slight woman, it looked to me as if she weighed no more than seven stone. Hilary Stacey, on the other hand, is tall and strong and no more than – what? Thirty-seven? Thirty-eight? She carried Ann out to the garage, by way of the communicating door from the house, sat her in the driving seat and fixed up that business with the hosepipe and the exhaust.

'No doubt she supposed Sophie would find the body. An unpleasant thought. No mother would do that to her child? Perhaps not. Perhaps Hilary intended to come back later and find the body herself. In the event the next-door neighbour found Ann Waterton.'

Burden said, 'It doesn't work, Reg. You're forgetting the suicide note. Ann left a note for the coroner.'

'I'm not forgetting it. The suicide note is at the heart of all this. We have to go back to last May or June, whenever it was. Ann Waterton attempted to kill herself but the attempt was frustrated by Sophie Grant and her mother. There was no suicide note – or was there? Has anyone heard of the existence of a suicide note? On the other hand, has the existence of such a note been denied? Let us postulate that there was such a note. On the mantelpiece or in a pocket of Ann's dress or by her bed. Remember that suicides, especially "home" suicides almost always leave a note.'

'Yes, but we've discussed this. That first time Hilary and Sophie wanted to keep it dark that there'd been a suicide attempt. For Ann's sake.'

'What are you saying, Inspector Burden? And you a policeman! Are you saying they *destroyed a suicide note* for no more reason than to protect the reputation of a woman who was then no more than an acquaintance? No, of course you aren't and of course they didn't. It's quite possible indeed that Sophie knew nothing about it but that Hilary, spotting what it was, picked it up and took it away with her.'

'But didn't destroy it?'

'No, no. Remember Cousin Henry. She took it. She had no prevision of any future need for it, Ann at that time had done her no harm and there was no hint that she would. She took it, as I say, and read it, as

Cousin Henry read his uncle's will, and decided to tell no one about it. Ann had been found in time, Ann would survive. And, by the way, I'd suggest at that time the note was in its envelope but *unsealed*. Hilary later did the sealing.

'She preserved it. Not for any nefarious purpose then but simply because it had become an official document, a document of great weight and significance, fraught almost with magic. Perhaps she thought she would give it back to Ann one day. Ann would be happy again and they would – dare she expect it? – laugh about it together. But I think the real reason for preserving it was Cousin Henry's, she was *afraid* to destroy it. And why do so anyway? Easier than destroying it was to slip it inside a book in the way Cousin Henry concealed the will, a book no one in the household was ever likely to want to read or even take down and look at.

'In Cousin Henry's case it was Jeremy Taylor's sermons. What book Hilary Stacey used we shall never know and it doesn't matter. Perhaps, anyway, she kept it in a drawer with her underclothes.

'But possession of the suicide note gave her the idea for Ann Waterton's murder. After she had put Ann into the car she had only to place the note on the table and, making sure she had left no fingerprints, return home and leave the body to be discovered.'

Burden, who had listened to the last part of this in silence and with his head bowed, now looked up. He shook his head a little, but rather as if in wonder at human depravity than in any particular doubt at what Wexford had told him. It might be true, Hilary Stacey had been angry enough, desperate enough. He realised he had never really liked her.

'You'll never prove it,' he said, and as he spoke he was confident Wexford would agree with him. Wexford would give him a rueful smile, accept the inevitable. His chief often, still, surprised him.

'I shall have a damn good try,' said Wexford.

Staying out drinking wasn't Burden's way. It never had been. He was an uxorious man, a home-loving man. Anyway, he liked to be with his little boy before Mark went to bed, liked if possible to put him to bed himself. If the licensing hours hadn't changed from a cast-iron regularity to depend instead upon the whim of the landlord, he wouldn't have been able to have a beer with Wexford at ten to five. As it was he was still early, though the evening was as dark as midnight. He walked home, thinking about Hilary Stacey. It seemed to him unfortunate she had been Jenny's friend. How much, he wondered, did Jenny care for her? And should he tell Jenny something of all this?

It might be best to wait a while, see what unfolded, see how Wexford progressed. There would be a point at which he would know the time had come to divulge horrors, undreamt-of intrigue. He found Jenny in an armchair by the fire, the child on her knee. Mark was in pyjamas and a blue dressing gown of classic cut, piped in navy and tied with a silk cord. Jenny was reading to him, Beatrix Potter this time, the one about the kitten who traps a mouse in her pocket handkerchief, but the mouse escapes through a hole. Mark was mad about literature, he would soon be able to read himself. Rather gloomily, Burden saw a future with a son always talking about books.

Mark got down from Jenny's lap and came over to his father. Another adventure of some thwarted predator or enterprising rodent was demanded. While Burden was looking through the collection on the bookshelf, the doorbell rang.

After dark he answered the door himself to unexpected visitors. You never could tell. He went out into the hall, Jenny behind him with the boy, holding his hand because he was nearly too heavy to carry. Burden opened the door and the girl came in. She stepped in quickly and stood for a moment in the hall, a suitcase in each hand.

'I've come,' Sophie said, smiling. 'I'll cook for you, I'll look after Mark, I won't be any trouble. Don't bother to come with me, Mike, I'll just take these straight up to the spare room.'

# Blood Lines

*For Don*

# Blood Lines

'I think you know who killed your stepfather,' said Wexford. It was a throwaway line, uttered on parting and over his shoulder as he reached the door. A swift exit was, however, impossible. The moment he got up he had not to duck his head merely but bend himself almost double. The girl he spoke to was a small woman, the boyfriend she lived with no more than five feet six. Life in the caravan, he thought, would otherwise have been insupportable.

Stuck in the doorway, he said when she made no reply, 'You won't mind if I come back in a day or two and we'll have another talk.'

'All the same if I do, isn't it?'

'You don't have to talk to me, Miss Heddon. It's open to you to say no.' It would all have been more dignified if he could have stood up and faced her, but Wexford wasn't much concerned with dignity. He spoke rather gravely but with gentleness. 'But if you've no objection we'll continue this conversation on Monday. I've a feeling you know a lot more than you've told me.'

She said it, one of those phrases that invariably means its opposite. 'I don't know what you're talking about.'

'That's unworthy of someone of your intelligence,' he said and he had meant it.

He opened the door and climbed out. Climbing, half-crouched, was the only way. It was with relief that he put his feet on the ground, got his head clear, and straightened himself up to his full height. She had followed him and stood there, holding the door, a pretty young woman of twenty who looked even younger than her age because her blonde hair was waist-length and her white blouse schoolgirlish.

'Monday, then,' Wexford said. 'Shall we say three-ish?'

'Suit yourself.' With one of her flashes of humour, she said, 'You must feel like a Rottweiler in a rabbit hutch in here.'

He smiled. 'You may be right. It's true my bite is worse than my bark.'

Possibly digesting this, she closed the door without another word.

He picked his way back to the car where Donaldson waited at the wheel. A path of cinders made a just usable track across the corner of a muddy field. In the cold haze the shape of a cottage converted from a railway carriage could just be seen against a grey tangle of wilderness. Two inches of rain had fallen in the week since Tom Peterlee's death and the sky of massive grey cumulus was loaded with more.

'We live in a caravan culture, Steve,' he said to Donaldson. 'As homes, I mean, not mobile tents. You can see two more over there – travelling farm workers, I imagine. The one on the corner patch up here has been there at least two years and to my knowledge is home to four people, a dog and a hamster.'

'It wouldn't suit me, sir. Though, mind you, I'd have gone down on my bended knees in gratitude for a caravan when the wife and me were first married and living with her mum.'

Wexford nodded, invisibly, from the back. 'Go by way of Feverel's, will you? I don't want to stop, just take a look.'

The Kenhurst road headed from the south for Edenwick and Kingsmarkham. Rain began to spit against the windscreen as they came to the outskirts of Edenwick and its half-mile-long village street. After the houses ended, Feverel's buildings appeared as the car rounded a loop-like bend in the road.

The farm shop remained closed, though a wooden board offering for sale apples, pears, plums and walnuts for pickling still stood by the gate. Wexford told Donaldson to stop the car and park for a few moments. Let Heather Peterlee see him. That sort of thing did no harm. He looked, for the dozenth time, at the shack that had been a shop, the huddle of wooden buildings, the house itself and the inevitable caravan.

'She'll have a job selling it, sir,' said Donaldson as if reading his mind. 'People won't much fancy the idea.'

'The murder took place in the kitchen,' Wexford said rather sharply, 'not in that thing.'

'It's all one to some,' Donaldson said cryptically.

The house was a Victorian building, rendered in a pale stone colour that the rain had turned to khaki, an uncompromising cheerless place with a window on either side of the front door that was plumb in the centre, and three windows above. No porch, balcony or even trellis broke the monotony of its façade. The shallow roof was of dull grey slate. Some ten yards of bleak ground, part gravel and part scrubby grass, separated the house from the shop. In between and a little distance behind, the caravan stood on a concrete slab, and beyond it stretched away the market gardens, looking from here no more than acres of cabbages. The only trees were the walnuts, still in leaf but the leaves tired and brown.

The shop, its double doors closed and padlocked, its windows boarded up, the display stalls which stood outside it gone, seemed a dilapidated hut. A sheet of the corrugated iron that roofed it had come loose and clanged up and down rhythmically in the increasing wind. It was a dreary place. No visitor would have difficulty in believing a man had been clubbed to death there. Wexford remembered, with distaste, the little crowd which had gathered outside this gate during the previous week, standing and watching, or sitting in the line of cars, some of them waiting for hours, staring at the house, hoping for happenings. Some of them recalling, no doubt, how a matter of days ago they had driven in for half a hundredweight of Maris Bards, a couple of pounds of Coxes and one of Heather Peterlee's apple pies from the freezer.

As Donaldson started the engine a dog came out from the back of the house and began barking inside the gate. It was a black spaniel, but not of so mild a nature as is usually found in the breed. Wexford had felt its teeth through his jacket sleeve, though blood had not been drawn.

'That the dog, is it, sir?'

They all knew the story, even those only remotely involved. Wexford confirmed that this indeed was the dog, this was Scamp. The poor creature had recovered the voice it lost, giving continual tongue at the voyeurs until strain on its vocal cords struck it dumb.

Wexford spared a glance for the neighbours, if a house fifty yards of field and copse away can be called neighbouring. Joseph Peterlee had a plant hire business and a customer was in the act of returning a mechanical digger with what looked like half a ton of the local chalky loam adhering to its giant wheels. In conversation with her husband and the digger driver on the concrete entrance, an area much cracked, pitted and now puddled, was Mrs Monica Peterlee in her unvarying uniform of rubber boots and floral crossover overall, holding over herself a green umbrella. And those are the characters in this drama, he thought, with the exception of one who (to paraphrase Kipling) has gone to the husband of her bosom the same as she ought to go, and one who has gone heaven only knows where.

Why was he so sure Arlene Heddon had the answer? Mike Burden, his second-in-command at Kingsmarkham CID, said with contempt that at any rate she was more attractive than the sister-in-law and the widow. With his usual distaste for those whose lives failed to approximate fairly closely to his own, he spoke scathingly of 'the Peterlee girl' as if having no job and no proper roof over one's head directly conduced to homicide.

'Her name', Wexford said rather dourly, 'is Heddon. It was her father's name. Heather Peterlee, if you remember, was a Mrs Heddon before she re-married.' He added, wondering as he did so why he bothered to indulge Burden's absurd prejudices. 'A widow, incidentally.'

Quick as a flash, Burden came back with, 'What did her first husband die of?'

'Oh God, Mike, some bone disease. We went into all that. But back to Arlene Heddon; she's a very intelligent young woman, you know.'

'No, I don't know. You must be joking. Intelligent girls don't live on benefit in caravans with unemployed welders.'

'What a snob you are.'

'*Married* welders. I'm not just a snob, I'm a moralist. Intelligent girls do well at school, go on to further education, get suitable well-paid jobs and buy themselves homes on mortgages.'

'Somehow and somewhere along the line Arlene Heddon missed out on that. In any case, I didn't say she was academically inclined. She's sharp, she's clever, she's got a good brain.'

'And her mother, the two-times widow, is she the genius Arlene inherited her IQ from?'

This was neither the time nor the place to be discussing the murder, Wexford's house on a Saturday evening, but Burden had come round for a drink, and whatever the topic of conversation, things had a way of coming back to the Peterlees. They came back to the extent of Wexford's suggesting they go over the sequence of events again. Dora, his wife, was present, but sitting on the window seat, reading tranquilly. For once, she didn't suggest he and Burden go somewhere private.

'You can set me right on the details,' Wexford began, 'but I think you'll agree it was broadly like this. On Thursday October 10 Heather Peterlee opened the farm shop at Feverel's as usual at nine a.m. They had on sale their own produce and other more exotic vegetables and fruit they bought in. Heather had her sister-in-law Mrs Monica Peterlee to help her, again as usual. Heather's husband, Tom, was working outside, and at lunchtime he brought up to the shop by tractor the vegetables he had lifted and picked during the morning.

'They ate their midday meal in the shop, keeping it open, and at three or thereabouts Joseph Peterlee arrived in his car to fetch his wife and take her shopping in Kingsmarkham. Tom and Heather served in the shop until closing time at five when they returned to the house and Heather began preparing a meal. Tom had brought in the shop's takings with him which he intended to put in the safe, but in the meantime he left the notes on the kitchen dresser that faces the outside door. The sum was about three hundred and sixty pounds. He put the money on the dresser shelf and placed on top of it his camera in its case, presumably to stop it blowing about when the door was opened. He then went to the caravan to discuss some matter of business with Carol Fox who had been living there since the summer. In fact, the matter of business was the question of raising the rent she paid.'

'Tom Peterlee wasn't killed for three hundred and sixty pounds,' said Burden.

'No, but various people would like us to think he was. It's a problem even guessing why he was killed. Everyone seems to have liked him. We have had . . .' Wexford hesitated, ' "golden opinions from all sorts of people". He was something of a paragon by all accounts, an ideal husband, good, kind, undeniably handsome. He was even handsome on the mortuary slab – forgive me, Dora.

'But I'll go on. They ate their meal at five-thirty. During the course of it, according to her statement, Tom said to his wife that they had fixed up the matter of the rent amicably. Carol wanted to stay on and understood the rent she was paying was inadequate . . .'

Dora interrupted him. 'Is that the woman who'd left her husband and Heather Peterlee said she could have their caravan because she'd nowhere to live?'

'A friend of Heather's from way back, apparently. According to Heather, she told Tom she'd be round in an hour to accompany her on a dog walk. Heather always took the dog out after supper and Carol had got into the habit of going with her. Heather washed up their dishes and Tom dried. As I've said, he was an ideal husband. At some point he went out to the woodshed and fetched in a basket of logs to feed the wood-burning stoves, of which there was one in the kitchen and another in the living room.

'Carol knocked on the door and came into the kitchen at twenty past six. It wasn't raining but it looked like rain and Carol was wearing only a cardigan. Heather suggested she put on one of the rainproof jackets of which there were several hanging behind the back door, and Carol took a fawn-coloured one.'

'Strange, wasn't it,' Burden put in, 'that she didn't fetch a coat of her own from the caravan? Especially a woman like that. Very conscious of her appearance, I'd say. But perhaps she wouldn't care, out on her own with another woman. It was a dull evening and they weren't likely to meet anyone.'

Dora gave him a look, enigmatic, half-smiling, but said nothing.

Her husband went on, 'If you remember, when the caravan was searched as the house was, the fact was remarked on that Carol Fox had no raincoat among her clothes. She has said and Heather has confirmed it that she always used one of Heather's. They took the dog and went for a walk through the Feverel's land, across the meadows by the public footpath and down to the river. It was sometime between six-twenty and six-thirty that they left. It was still light and would be for another half-hour. What Tom did in their absence we don't know and probably never shall know, except that putting that money into the safe wasn't among his activities.

'At about ten to seven Arlene Heddon arrived at Feverel's, brought in her boyfriend's van.' Wexford raised an eyebrow at Burden. 'The unemployed, married welder, Gary Wyatt.

'Arlene and Gary have no phone and Arlene got the message from Grandma on whose land she lives. She's not really her grandmother, of course, but she calls her Grandma.'

'The old witch,' said Dora. 'That's what people call her. She's well known.'

'I don't think she's as old as she looks and she's definitely not a witch, though she cultivates that appearance. To be the mother of Joseph and Tom she need be no more than sixty-five and I daresay she's not. The message Arlene got from Mrs Peterlee Senior was that Mum had finished her jumper and if she wanted it for the Friday, could she come and pick it up? The time suggested was about eight. Grandma said she'd drive Arlene herself on account of she was going to her Conservative Association meeting in Kingsmarkham – I kid you not, Dora – but she said, no, Gary and she would still be eating their tea. Gary would take her in the van a bit later on.

'In fact, Gary wanted to go out at half past six. He dropped her off at Feverel's, thus getting her there more than an hour earlier than her mother had suggested, and went on to have a drink with his pals in the Red Rose at Edenwick. Not that anyone has confirmed this. Neither the licensee nor the girl behind the bar remember him being there. Which is in direct contrast to the evidence of the old witch's witnesses. Strange as her presence there might seem, every Tory in Kingsmarkham seems to remember her in the Seminar Room of the Olive and Dove Hotel that night. Not until seven-thirty, however, when the meeting started. Where had she been in that lost hour and a half?

'Gary promised to come back for Arlene in an hour. Arlene went round the back of the house and entered by the kitchen door, which was unlocked. As a daughter of the house, she didn't knock or call out, but walked straight in.

'There, in the kitchen, on the floor, she found the body of her stepfather, Tom Peterlee, lying face-downwards, with a wound in the back of the head. She knelt down and touched his face. It was still faintly warm. She knew there was a phone in the sitting room but, fearing whoever had done this might still be in the house, she didn't go in there but ran back outside in the hope Gary had not yet gone. When she saw that he had she ran the hundred yards or so to Mr and Mrs Joe Peterlee's where she used their phone and dialled 999.

'Joe Peterlee was out, according to his wife. Arlene – all this is Arlene's evidence, partly confirmed by Monica Peterlee – Arlene asked her to come back with her and wait for the police but she said she was too frightened to do that, so Arlene went back alone. Within a very few minutes – it was now five past seven – her mother and Carol Fox returned from their walk with the dog. She was waiting for them outside the back door.

'She prepared them for what they would see and Heather cried out, pushed open the door and rushed into the kitchen. She threw herself on the body and when Arlene and Carol pulled her off and lifted her up, she began banging her head and face against the kitchen wall.'

Burden nodded. 'These two – what do we call them? Hysterical acts? Manifestations of grief? – account for the blood on the front of her jacket and the extensive bruising to her face. Or at least are possible explanations for them.'

'The police came and everyone was questioned on the spot. Of course no one had seen any suspicious characters hanging about Feverel's. No one ever has. Joe Peterlee has never been able to give a satisfactory account of his movements between six-twenty and six-fifty. Nor have Gary Wyatt and Grandma Peterlee.

'The money was gone. There was no weapon. No prints, other than those of Tom, Heather, Carol Fox and Arlene were found in the house. The pathologist says Tom died between six-fifteen and seven-fifteen, a time which can be much narrowed down if Arlene is to be believed. Remember, she says he felt warm when she touched him at six-fifty.

'I think she's lying. I think she's lying all along the line, she's protecting someone, and that's why I'm going to keep on talking to her until I find out who. Grandma or her boyfriend or her uncle Joe – or her mother.'

Dora wrinkled up her nose. 'Isn't it a bit distasteful, Reg, getting a girl to betray her own mother? It's like the KGB.'

'And we know what happened to them,' said Burden.

Wexford smiled. 'I may only be getting her to betray her step-aunt by marriage, or isn't that allowed either?'

Burden left them at about ten to ten. He was on foot, for he and Wexford lived less than a mile apart and walking was a preferable exercise to the kinds his wife suggested, riding a stationary bike or stomping up and down on a treadmill. His route home was to take him past the big new shopping mall, the York Crest Centre. He deplored the name and the place, all a far cry from what Kingsmarkham had been when first he came there.

Then there was life in the town at night, people entering or emerging from pubs and restaurants, cinema visitors, walkers strolling, in those days before the ubiquitous car. Television, the effects of recession and the fear of street violence had all combined to keep the townsfolk indoors and the place was deserted. It was silent, empty but brightly lit, and therefore slightly uncanny.

His footfalls made a faint hollow echo, he saw his solitary figure reflected in gleaming shop windows. Not a soul passed him as he entered York Street, not a single being waited on a corner or at the bus stop. He turned into the alley that ran along the side of the York Crest Centre, to cut a furlong or so off his journey. Does anyone know what a furlong is these days, thought old-fashioned nostalgic Burden.

Into his silent speculation burst the raiders.

It took him about thirty seconds to realise what this was. He had seen it on television but thought it confined to the north. A ram raid. That was what someone had named this kind of heist. The Land Rover first, turning on the paved court, reversing at the highest speed it could make into the huge glass double doors that shut off the centre by night. The noise of crashing glass was enormous, like a bomb.

It vanished inside, followed by two cars, a Volvo and a Volvo Estate, rattling over the broken glass, the wreckage of the doors. He didn't wait to see what happened. He had his cell-phone in his hand and switched on before the second car's tail lights had disappeared. 'No Service' came up on its screen and 'No Service' when he shook it and pulled the aerial out. It had gone wrong. Never before had that happened but it had to happen tonight when he was in the right place at the right time.

Burden raced down the alley to the phones on the post office wall, four of them under plastic hoods. The first he tried had been vandalised, the second worked. If he could get them there within five minutes, within ten even . . . He pounded back, remembered it would be advisable not to be heard, and crept the rest of the way. They were leaving, the Land Rover – stolen of course – with all its glass shattered, the two Volvos hard on its rear, and were gone God knew where by the time the Mid-Sussex Constabulary cars arrived.

The purpose of the raid had been to remove as much electronic equipment as the thieves could shift in five minutes from Nixon's in the Centre. It had been a tremendous haul and had probably taken twelve men to accomplish it.

The phone on the post office wall was repaired and on the following day vandalised again along with all the others in the row. That was on a Monday, the date of Wexford's second conversation with Arlene Heddon. He went along to the caravan on old Mrs Peterlee's land in the late afternoon. Arlene sometimes had a cleaning job but she was always in during the afternoons. He tapped on the door and she called out to him to come in.

The television was on and she was watching, lounging on the seat that ran the length of the opposite wall. She looked so relaxed, even somnolent, that Wexford thought she would switch off by means of the channel changer which lay on top of the partition that divided living/bedroom from kitchen, but she got up and pressed the switch. They faced each other, and this time she seemed anxious to talk. He began to take her through a series of new enquiries and all the old ones.

He noticed, then, that what she said differed very slightly from what she had said the first time, if in minor details. Her mother had not thrown herself on the body but knelt down and cradled the dead man's head in her arms. It was on one of the counters, not against the wall, that she had beaten her head.

The dog had howled at the sight of its dead master. The first time she said she thought she had heard a noise upstairs when first she arrived. This time she denied it, and said all had been silent. She had not noticed if the money was there or not when she first arrived. Now she said the money was there with the camera on top of the notes. When she came back from making her phone call she had not gone back into the house but had waited outside for her mother to return.

That was what she said the first time. Now she said she had gone briefly into the kitchen once more. The camera was there but the money gone.

Wexford pointed out these discrepancies in a casual way. She made no comment.

He asked, with apparent indifference, 'Just as a matter of interest, how did you know your mother was out with the dog?'

'The dog wasn't there and she wasn't.'

'You were afraid to use the phone in the house in case your stepfather's killer might still be there. You never considered the possibility that your mother might have been dead in some other part of the house? That Carol Fox might have taken the dog out on her own, as perhaps she sometimes did?'

'I didn't know Carol very well,' said Arlene Heddon.

It was hardly an answer. 'But she was a close friend of your mother's, an old friend, wasn't she? You might say your mother offered her sanctuary when she left her husband. That's the action of a close friend, isn't it?'

'I haven't lived at home since I was seventeen. I don't know all the friends my mother's got. I didn't know whether Carol took the dog out or what. Tom sometimes took him out and my mother did. I never heard of Carol going with my mother, but I wouldn't. I wasn't interested in Carol.'

'Yet you waited for them both to come back from their walk, Miss Heddon.'

'I waited for my mother,' she said.

Wexford left her, promising to come back for another talk on Thursday. Grandma was nowhere to be seen but as he approached his car hers swept in, bumping over the rough ground, lurching through a trough or two, skidding with a scream of brakes on the ice and, describing a swift half-circle round the railway carriage, juddering to a stop.

Florrie Peterlee, getting on for seventy and looking eighty, drove like an eighteen-year-old madbrain at the wheel of his first jalopy.

She gave the impression of clawing her way out. Her white hair was as long and straight as Arlene's and she was always dressed in trailing black that sometimes had a curiously fashionable look. On a teenager it would have been trendy. She had a hooky nose and prominent chin, bright black eyes. But Wexford couldn't offhand think of anyone he knew who so intensely seemed to enjoy herself as Mrs Peterlee Senior. Some of her pleasure derived from her indifference to what people thought of her, apart of course from her need to make them see her as a witch; some from her enduring good health and zest for life. So far she had shown no grief whatever at the death of her son.

'You're too old for her,' said the old witch.

'Too old for what?' said Wexford, refusing to be out-faced.

'Ooh, hark at him! That's a nice question to ask a senior citizen. Mind I don't put a spell on you. Why don't you leave her alone, poor lamb.'

'She's going to tell me who killed your son Tom.'

'Get away. She don't know. Maybe I did.' She stared at him with bold defiance. 'I all but killed his dad once. I said, you've knocked me about once too often, Arthur Peterlee, and I picked up the kitchen knife and come at him with it. I won't say he never touched me again, human nature never worked that way, but he dropped dead with his heart soon after, poor old sod. I was so glad to see the back of him I danced on his grave. People say that, I know, it's just a way of talking, but me, I really did it. Went up the cemetery with a half-bottle of gin and danced on the bugger's grave.'

Wexford could see her, hair flying, black draperies blowing, the bottle in one hand, her wrinkled face dabbled with gin, dancing under the rugged ilexes and the yew tree's shade. He raised his eyebrows. Before she had more chances to shock him, or try to, he asked her if she had thought any more about telling him where she had been in that lost hour on the evening of her son's death.

'You'd be surprised.'

She said it, not as a figure of speech, but as a genuine undertaking she could astonish him. He had no doubt she could. She grinned, showing even white teeth, not dentures. The sudden thought came to him that if she had a good bath, put her copious hair up and dressed in something more appropriate for a rural matriarch, she might look rather wonderful. He wasn't too worried about her alibi or lack of one, for he doubted if she had the strength to wield the 'blunt instrument' that had killed Tom Peterlee.

He was very certain he knew what that instrument was and what had become of it. Arriving at Feverel's within the hour, he had seen the wood splinters in Tom Peterlee's head wound before the pathologist arrived. With a sinking heart he had taken in the implications of a basket full of logs just inside the back door and the big wood-burning enclosed stove in an embrasure of the wall facing the door into the house. They would never find the weapon. Without being able to prove it, he knew from the first that it had been an iron-hard log of oak, maybe a foot long and three or four inches in diameter, a log used to strike again and again, then pushed in among the blazing embers in that stove.

He had even looked. The stove had been allowed to go out. Could you imagine anyone making up the fire at a time like that? A pale grey powdery dust glowed red still in one patch at the heart of it and as he watched, died. Later on, he had those ashes analysed. All the time he was up there the dog howled. Someone shut it up in a distant room but its long-drawn-out cries pursued him up the road on his way to see Joseph and Monica Peterlee.

He remembered wondering, not relevantly, if she dressed like that to sit down at table, to watch television. At nine o'clock at night she was still in her crossover overall, her black wellies. Her husband was a bigger and heavier version of his brother, three or four years older, his hair iron-grey where Tom's had been brown, his belly fat and slack where Tom's had been flat. They alibi'd each other, uselessly, and Joe had no alibi for the relevant time. He had been out shooting rabbits, he said, produced his shotgun and shotgun licence.

'They done Tom in for the money,' he told Wexford sagely. He spoke as if, without his proffered information, such a solution would never have occurred to the police. 'I told him. I said to him time and again I said, you don't want to leave that laying about, not even for an hour, not even in daylight. What you got a safe for if you don't use it? I said that, didn't I, girl?'

His wife confirmed that he had indeed said it. Over and over. Wexford had the impression she would have confirmed anything he said. For peace, for a quiet life. It was two days later that, interviewing them again, he asked about the relationship between Tom and Heather Peterlee.

'They was a very happy couple,' Joe said. 'Never a cross word in all the ten years they was married.'

Wexford, later, wondered what Dora would have said if he had made such a remark about relatives of his. Or Burden's wife Jenny if he had. Something dry, surely. There would have been some quick intervention, some 'Oh, come on, how would you know?' or, 'You weren't a fly on the wall.' But Monica said nothing. She smiled nervously. Her husband looked at her and she stopped smiling.

The ram raiders were expected to have another go the following

Saturday night. Instead they came on Friday, late shopping night at Stowerton Brook Buyers' Heaven, less than an hour after the shops closed. Another stolen Land Rover burst through the entrance doors, followed by a stolen Range Rover and a BMW. This time the haul was from Electronic World, but it was similar to that taken the previous time.

The men in those three vehicles got away with an astonishing thirty-five thousand pounds' worth of equipment.

This time Burden had not been nearby, on his way home. No one had, since the Stowerton Brook industrial site where Buyers' Heaven was lay totally deserted by night, emptier by far than Kingsmarkham town centre. The two guard dogs that kept watch over the neighbouring builders' supplies yard had been destroyed a month before in the purge on dangerous breeds.

Burden had been five miles away, talking to Carol Fox and her husband Raymond. To Burden, who never much noticed any woman's appearance but his wife's, she was simply rather above average good-looking. In her mid-thirties, ten years younger than Heather, she was brightly dressed and vivacious. It was Wexford who described her as one of that group or category that seems to have more natural colour than most women, with her pure red hair, glowing luminous skin, ivory and pink, and her eyes of gentian blue. He said nothing about the unnatural colour that decorated Mrs Fox's lips, nails and eyelids to excess. Burden assessed her as 'just a cockney with an awful voice'. Privately, he thought of her as common. She was loud and coarse, a strange friend for the quiet, reserved and mousy Heather.

The husband she had returned to after a six months' separation was thin and toothy with hag-ridden eyes, some sort of salesman. He seemed proud of her and exaggeratedly pleased to have her back. On that particular evening, the case not much more than a week old, he was anxious to assure Burden and anyone else who would listen that his and his wife's parting had been no more than a 'trial', an experimental living-apart to refresh their relationship. They were together again now for good. Their separation hadn't been a success but a source of misery to both of them.

Carol said nothing. Asked by Burden to go over with him once more the events of October 10, she reaffirmed six-twenty as the time she and Heather had gone out. Yes, there had been a basket of logs just inside the back door. She hadn't seen any money on the counter or the dresser. Tom had been drying dishes when she came in. He was alive and well when they left, putting the dishes away in the cupboard.

'I should be so lucky,' said Carol Fox with a not very affectionate glance at her husband.

'Did you like Tom Peterlee, Mrs Fox?'

Was it his imagination or had Raymond Fox's expression changed minutely? It would be too much to say that he had winced. Burden repeated his question.

'He was always pleasant,' she said. 'I never saw much of him.'

The results came from the lab, disclosing that a piece of animal bone had been among the stove ashes. Burden had found out, that first evening, what the Peterlees had had for their evening meal: lamb chops, with potatoes and cabbage Tom had grown himself. The remains were put into the bin for the compost heap, never into the stove. Bones, cooked or otherwise, the Peterlees weren't particular, were put on the back doorstep for the dog.

What had become of the missing money? It wasn't a large enough sum for the spending of it by any particular individual to be noticeable. They searched the house a second time, observing the empty safe, the absence of any jewellery, even of a modest kind, in Heather's possession, the absence of books, any kind of reading matter or any sign of the generally accepted contributions to gracious living.

Heather Peterlee shut herself up in the house and when approached, said nothing. Questioned, she stared dumbly and remained dumb. Everyone explained her silence as due to her grief. Wexford, without much hope of anything coming of it, asked to remove the film from the camera that had weighted down the missing notes. She shrugged, muttered that he could have it, he was welcome, and turned her face to the wall. But when he came to look, he found no film in the camera.

Burden said Wexford's continued visits to Arlene Heddon were an obsession, the Chief Constable that they were a waste of time. Since his second visit she had given precisely the same answers to all the questions he asked – the same, that is, as on that second occasion. He wondered how she did it. Either it was the transparent truth or she had total recall. In that case, why did it differ from what she had said the first time he questioned her? Now all was perfect consistency.

If she made a personal comment there might be something new, but she rarely did. Every time he referred to Tom Peterlee as her stepfather she corrected him by saying, 'I called him Tom,' and if he spoke of Joseph and Monica as her uncle and aunt she told him they weren't her uncle and aunt. Carol Fox was her mother's great friend, she had known her for years, but she, Arlene, knew Carol scarcely at all.

'I never heard of Carol walking the dog with my mother but I wouldn't. I wasn't interested in Carol.'

Sometimes Gary Wyatt was there. When Wexford came he always left. He always had a muttered excuse about having to see someone about something and being late already. One Monday – it was usually Mondays and Thursdays that Wexford went to the caravan – he asked Gary to wait a moment. Had he thought any more about giving details of where he was between six-forty-five and seven-thirty that evening? Gary hadn't. He had been in the pub, the Red Rose at Edenwick.

'No one remembers seeing you.'

'That's their problem.'

'It may become yours, Gary. You didn't like Tom Peterlee, did you? Isn't it a fact that Tom refused to let you and Arlene have the caravan Mrs Fox lived in because you'd left your wife and children?'

'That was the pot calling the kettle,' said Gary.

'And what does that mean?'

Nothing, they said. It meant nothing. He hadn't been referring to Tom. A small smile crossed Arlene's face and was gone. Gary went out to see someone about something, an appointment for which he was already late, and Wexford began asking about Heather's behaviour when she came home after her walk.

'She didn't throw herself on him,' Arlene said glibly, without, it seemed, a vestige of feeling. 'She knelt down and sort of held his head and cuddled it. She got his blood on her. Carol and me, we made her get up and then she started banging her face on that counter.'

It was the same as last time, always the same.

There had been no appeals to the public for witnesses to come forward. Witnesses to what? Heather Peterlee's alibi was supplied by Carol Fox and Wexford couldn't see why she should have lied or the two of them have been in cahoots. Friend she might be, but not such a friend as to perjure herself to save a woman who had motivelessly murdered an ideal husband.

He wondered about the bone fragment. But they had a dog. It was hardly too far-fetched to imagine a dog's bone getting in among the logs for the stove. Awkward, yes, but awkward inexplicable things do happen. It was still hard for him to accept that Arlene had simply taken it for granted her mother was out walking the dog with Carol Fox when she scarcely seemed to know that Carol lived there. And he had never really been able to swallow that business about Heather banging her face against the counter. Carol had only said, 'Oh, yes, she did,' and Heather herself put her hands over her mouth and turned her face to the wall.

Then a curious thing happened that began to change everything.

An elderly man who had been a regular customer at the farm shop asked to speak to Wexford. He was a widower who shopped and cooked for himself, living on the state pension and a pension from the Mid-Sussex Water Authority.

Frank Waterton began by apologising, he was sure it was nothing, he shouldn't really be troubling Wexford, but this was a matter which had haunted him. He had always meant to do something about it, though he was never sure what. That was why he had, in the event, done nothing.

'What is it, Mr Waterton? Why not tell me and I'll decide if it's nothing.' The old man looked at him almost wistfully. 'No one will blame you if it's nothing. You'll still have been public-spirited and have done your duty.'

Wexford didn't even know then that it was connected with the Peterlee case. Because he was due to pay one of his twice-weekly calls on Arlene Heddon, he was impatient and did his best not to let his impatience show.

'It's to do with what I noticed once or twice when I went shopping for my bits and pieces at Feverel's,' he said and then Wexford ceased to feel exasperated or to worry about getting to Arlene on time. 'It must have been back in June the first time, I know it was June on account of the strawberries were in. I can see her now looking through the strawberries to get me a nice punnet and when she lifted her face up – well, I was shocked. I was really shocked. She was bruised like someone had been knocking her about. She'd a black eye and a cut on her cheek. I said, you've been in the wars, Mrs Peterlee, and she said she'd had a fall and hit herself on the sink.'

'You say that was the first time?'

'That's right. I sort of half-believed her when she said that but not the next time. Not when I went in there again when the Coxes apples first came in – must have been late September – and her face was black and blue all over again. And she'd got her wrist strapped up – well, bandaged. I didn't comment, not that time. I reckoned it wouldn't be – well, tactful.

'I just thought I ought to come and tell someone. It's been preying on my mind ever since I heard about Tom Peterlee getting done in. I sort of hesitated and hummed and ha'ed. If it had been *her* found killed I'd have been in like a shot, I can tell you.'

He made it to Arlene's only a quarter of an hour late. Because it fascinated him, hearing her give all those same answers, parrot-like, except that the voice this parrot mimicked was her own, he asked her all the same things over again. The question about her mother's bruised face he left till last, to have the effect of a bombshell.

First of all, he got the same stuff. 'She knelt down and took hold of his head and sort of cuddled it. That's how she got his blood on her. Me and Carol pulled her off him and lifted her up and she started banging her face on the counter.'

'Was she banging her face on the counter in June, Miss Heddon? Was she doing the same thing in September? And how about her bandaged wrist?'

Arlene Heddon didn't know. She looked him straight in the eye, both her eyes into both his, and said she didn't know.

'I never saw her wrist bandaged.'

He turned deliberately from her hypnotic gaze and looked round the caravan. They had acquired a microwave since he was last there. An electric jug kettle had replaced the old chrome one. Presents from Grandma? The old witch was reputed to be well-off. It was said that none of the money she had made from selling off acres of her land in building lots had found its way into her sons' pockets. He had noticed a new car parked outside the railway carriage cottage and wouldn't have been surprised to learn that she replaced hers every couple of years.

'It'll be Tuesday next week, not Monday, Miss Heddon,' he said as he left.

'Suit yourself.'

'Gary found himself a job yet?'

'What job? You must be joking.'

'Perhaps I am. Perhaps there's something hilarious in the idea of either of you working. I mean, have you ever given it a thought? Earning your living is what I'm talking about.'

She shut the door hard between them.

After that, enquiries among the people who had known them elicited plenty of descriptions of Mrs Peterlee's visible injuries. Regular customers at the farm shop remembered her bandaged arm. One spoke of a black eye so bad that it had closed up and on the following day Heather Peterlee had covered it with a shade. She explained a scab on her upper lip as a cold sore but the customer to whom she had told this story hadn't believed her.

The myth of the ideal husband was beginning to fade. Only the

Peterlees themselves continued to support it and Monica Peterlee, when Burden asked her about it, seemed stricken dumb with fear. It was as if he had put his finger on the sorest part of a trauma and reawakened everything that caused the wound.

'I don't want to talk about it. You can't make me. I don't want to know.'

Joseph treated the suggestion as a monstrous calumny on his dead brother. He blustered. 'You want to be very careful what you're insinuating. Tom's dead and he can't defend himself, so you lot think you can say anything. The police aren't gods any more, you want to remember that. There's not an evening goes by when you don't see it on the telly, another lot of coppers up in court for making things up they'd writ down and saying things what never happened.'

His wife was looking at him the way a mouse in a corner looks at a cat that has temporarily mislaid it. Burden wasn't going to question Heather. They left her severely alone as they began to build up a case against her.

'What would you do if your husband knocked you about?' Wexford asked his wife.

'Are you talking about you or just any old husband?'

He grinned. 'Not me. One of those you didn't marry but might have.'

'Well, I know it's the conventional thing to say one wouldn't put up with it. You know, "He wouldn't do it a second time", that kind of thing, but that may be a bit shallow. If he was filled with remorse afterwards, for instance, or seemed to be. If one had no other means of support and nowhere else to go. If there were children. And, well, if it doesn't sound too silly, if one loved him.'

'Could you? Go on loving him?'

'Heaven knows. I won't say, women are strange. *People* are strange.'

'You said, "He wouldn't do it a second time." I wonder if there comes the final straw to break her back and he doesn't do it a *twenty-second time.'*

Jenny Burden said only that she wouldn't get herself into that position. She'd know before she married him.

'One way she might know,' Wexford said when this was passed on to him, 'was from what she heard of her future father-in-law's behaviour. There's a lot in what the psychologists say about the chain of family brutality. The child who is abused abuses his own children. Is it also true that the sons who see their mother battered by their father batter their own wives? They accept this behaviour as the marital norm?'

'Didn't you tell me old Mrs Peterlee said her husband knocked her about until she took a knife to him?'

Wexford nodded. 'That was her last straw and she retaliated. She danced on his grave, Mike. I wonder if Heather has it in mind to dance on Tom's?'

The day after the third ram raid – this time on the Kingsbrook Centre itself in the middle of Kingsmarkham – Wexford was back in Arlene Heddon's caravan and Arlene was saying, 'I never saw her wrist bandaged.'

'Miss Heddon, you know your stepfather repeatedly assaulted your mother. He knocked her about, gave her black eyes, cut her cheek. His brother Joseph doubtless hands out the same treatment to his wife. What have you got to gain by pretending you knew nothing about it?'

'She knelt on the floor and lifted up his head and sort of cuddled it. That's how she got blood on her. Me and Carol sort of pulled her off him and then she started banging—'

Wexford stopped her. 'No. She got those bruises because Tom hit her in the face. I don't know why. Do you know why? Maybe it was over money, the shop takings he left on the dresser. Or maybe she'd protested about him asking for more rent from her friend Carol Fox. If your mother argued with him he reacted by hitting her. That was his way.'

'If you say so.'

'No, Miss Heddon. It's not what I say, it's what you say.'

He waited for her to rejoin with, 'I never saw her wrist bandaged', but she lifted her eyes and he could have sworn there was amusement in them, a flash of it that came and went. She astounded him by what she said. It was the last thing he expected. She fidgeted for a moment or two with the channel changer on the divider between them, lifted her eyes and said slowly,

'Carol Fox was Tom's girlfriend.'

He digested this, saw fleetingly a host of possible implications, said, 'What, precisely, do you mean by that term?'

She was almost contemptuous. 'What everyone means. His girlfriend. His lover. What me and Gary are.'


'Not much point in denying it, is there?' said Carol Fox.

'I'm surprised you didn't give us this piece of information, Mr Fox,' Wexford said.

When her husband said nothing, Carol broke in impatiently, 'Oh, he's ashamed. Thinks it's a reflection on his manhood or whatever. I told him, you can't keep a thing like that dark, so why bother?'

'You kept it dark from us deliberately for a month.'

She shrugged, unrepentant. 'I felt a bit bad about Heather, to be honest with you. It was like Tom said I could live in this caravan on his land. He never said it was right next door. Still, there was another girl he'd had four or five years back he actually brought to live in the house. He called her the au pair, as if those Peterlees weren't one generation from gipsies when all's said and done.'

'Then I take it his visit to you that evening had nothing to do with raising the rent?'

The husband got up and left the room. Wexford didn't try to stop him. His presence hadn't much inhibited his wife but his absence freed her further. She smiled just a little. 'It's not what you're thinking. We had a drink.'

'A bit odd, wasn't it, you going out for a walk with his wife? Or didn't she know? That's pretty hard to believe, Mrs Fox.'

'Of course she knew. She hated me. And I can't say I was too keen on her. That wasn't true about us often going out together. That walk, that night, I fixed it up because I wanted to talk to her. I wanted to tell her I was leaving, it was all over between me and Tom, and I was going back to Ray.' She drew in a long breath. 'I'll be honest with you, it was a physical thing. The way he looked – well, between you and I, I couldn't get enough of it. Maybe it's all worked out for the best. But the fact is, it'd have been different if Tom'd have said he'd leave her, but he wouldn't and I'd had it.'

Wexford said, when he and Burden were out in the car, 'I was beginning to see Heather's alibi going down the drain. Her best friend lying for her. Not now. I can't see Tom's girlfriend alibi-ing the wife she wanted out of the way.'

'Well, no. Especially not alibi-ing the woman who'd killed the man she loved or once had loved. It looks as if we start again.'

'Does anyone but Heather have a motive? What was in it for Arlene and Gary Wyatt? The man's own mother's capable of anything her strength allows her but I don't think her strength would have allowed her this. Joseph had nothing to gain by Tom's death – the farm becomes Heather's – and it's evident all Monica wants is a quiet life. So we're left with the marauder who goes about the countryside murdering smallholders for three hundred and sixty quid.'

Next morning an envelope arrived addressed to him. It contained nothing but a photographic film processor's chit which was also a receipt for one pound. The receipt was on paper headed with the name of a pharmacist in the York Crest Centre. Wexford guessed the origin of the film before he had Sergeant Martin collect the processed shots. Arlene, at home to him on Tuesday, was back at her parrot game.

'I haven't lived at home since I was seventeen. I don't know all the friends my mother's got. I didn't know whether Carol took the dog out or what. Tom sometimes took him out and my mother did. I never heard of Carol going with my mother, but I wouldn't. I wasn't interested in Carol.'

'This is reaching the proportions of a psychosis, Miss Heddon.'

She knew what he meant. He didn't have to explain. He could see comprehension in her eyes and her small satisfied smile. Others would have asked when all this was going to stop, when would he leave it alone. Not she. She would give all the same answers to his questions infinitely, and every few weeks throw in a bombshell, as she had when she told him of Carol Fox's place in the Peterlees' lives. Always supposing, of course, that she had more bombshells to throw.

He knocked on the old witch's door. After rather a long time she came. Wexford wasn't invited in and he could see she already had company. An elderly man with a white beard, but wearing jeans and red leather cowboy boots, was standing by the fireplace pouring wine from a half-empty bottle into two glasses.

She gave him the grin that cracked her face into a thousand wrinkles and showed her remarkable teeth.

'I had half an hour going spare, Mrs Peterlee, so I thought I'd use it asking you where you were between six and seven-thirty on the evening your son was killed.'

She put her head on one side. 'I reckoned I'd keep you all guessing.'

'And now you're going to tell me,' he said patiently.

'Why not?' She turned and shouted over her shoulder at a pitch absurdly loud for the distance, 'If that one's finished, Eric, you can go and open another. It's on the kitchen table.' Wexford was favoured with a wink. 'I was with my boyfriend. *Him*. At his place. I always drop in for a quick one before the meeting.' She very nearly made him blush. 'A quick *drink*,' she said. 'You can ask him when he comes back. Rude bunch of buggers you cops are. It's written all over your face what you're thinking. Well, he'd marry me tomorrow if I said the word, but I'm shy, I've been bitten once. He may be nice as pie now and all lovey-dovey but it's another story when they've got the ring on your finger. Don't want another one knocking me to kingdom come when his tea's five minutes late on the table.'

'Is that why Tom beat up Heather, because his meal was late?'

If she was taken aback she didn't show it. 'Come on, they don't need a reason, not when the drink's in them. It's just you being there and not as strong as them and scared too, that's enough for them. You needn't look like that. I don't suppose you do like the sound of it. You want to've been on the receiving end. OK, Eric, I'm coming.'

Now that he no longer suspected her, after he had left her alone for a month, he went to Feverel's and saw Heather Peterlee. It was the night of the third ram raid and they knew it was coming when a Volvo Estate and a Land Rover were reported stolen during the day. But that was still three or four hours off.

Abused women have a look in common. Wexford castigated himself for not having seen it when he first came to the house. It had nothing to do with bruises and not much to do with a cowed, beaten way of holding themselves. That washed-out, tired, drained appearance told it all, if you knew what you were looking for.

She was very thin but not with the young vigorous slimness of her daughter or the wiriness of her mother-in-law. Her leanness showed slack muscles in her arms and stringy tendons at her wrists. There were hollows under her cheekbones and her mouth was already sunken. The benefits of weeks without Tom had not yet begun to show. Heather Peterlee had neglected herself and her home, had perhaps spent her time of widowhood in silent brooding here in this ugly dark house with only the spaniel for company.

The dog barked and snarled when Wexford came. To silence it she struck it too brutally across the muzzle. Violence begets violence, he thought. You receive it and store it up and then you transmit it – to whoever or whatever is feebler than you.

But even now she denied it. Sitting opposite him in a drab cotton dress with a thick knitted cardigan dragged shawl-like around her, she repudiated any suggestion that Tom had been less than good and gentle. As for Carol, yes it was true Tom had offered her the caravan and not she. Tom had been told by a friend she wanted a place to live. What friend? She didn't know the name. And the 'au pair'?

'You've been talking to my daughter.'

Wexford admitted that this was indeed the case, though not to what weary extent it was true.

'Arlene imagines things. She's got too much imagination.' A spark of vitality made a small change in her when she spoke of her daughter. Her voice became a fraction more animated. 'She's brainy, is Arlene, she's a bright one. Wanted to go in for the police, you know.'

'I'm sorry?'

'Get to be a policewoman or whatever they call them now.'

'A police officer,' said Wexford. 'Did she really? What stopped that, then?'

'Took up with that Gary, didn't she?'

It was hardly an answer but Wexford didn't pursue it. He didn't ask about her husband's involvement with Carol Fox either. He had proof of that, not only in Carol's own admission but in the film from Tom Peterlee's camera. All the shots were of Carol, three nudes taken with a flash inside the Feverel's caravan. They were decorous enough, not the kind of thing to raise a protest from any pharmacist Tom might have taken them to, for Carol had been coy in her posing, even skilled, in turning her body and smiling over her shoulder.

He studied the three photographs again that evening. Their setting, not their voluptuous subject, made them pathetic. Sordidness of background, a window with a sagging net curtain, a coat hanging up, a glimpse of an encrusted pot on a hotplate, gave an air of attempts at creating pornography in some makeshift studio. Erotica, for Wexford, required a total absence of ugliness, and Carol Fox had succeeded in that not uncommon achievement of sexiness without beauty.

Not that a hope of titillation was his motive for looking at the pictures. He looked rather coldly and even sadly. The identity of the sender of the processor's chit wasn't a problem. He had known that, if not from the moment he took it from its envelope, at least long before forensics matched with an existing set the fingerprints on the paper. He knew who had handed over the counter the film and the pound deposit. It was not even the subject of the shots that predominantly concerned him now. His slight depression vanished and he was immediately alert. From those pictures he suddenly knew who had killed Tom Peterlee and why.


The police were waiting, virtually encircling the Kingsbrook Centre, when the ram raiders arrived. This time there were only four of them, all inside the stolen Land Rover. If others were following through the narrow streets of the town centre, some prior warning turned them back. The same warning perhaps, maybe no more than feeling or intuition, which halted the Land Rover on the big paved forecourt from which the centre's entrance doors opened.

At first the watchers thought only that the Land Rover was reversing, prior to performing its backwards ramming of the doors. It was a few seconds before it became clear that this was a three-point turn, forwards up to the fifteen-foot-high brick wall, reverse towards the doors, then, while they braced themselves for the crash of the doors going down and the Land Rover backing through, it shot forward again and was away through the alley into the High Street.

But it never entered the wider road. Its occupants left it to block the exit, flung all four doors open, leapt out and dispersed. The police, there in thirty seconds, found an empty vehicle, with no trace of any occupancy but its owner's and not a print to be found.


He said to Burden, before they made the arrest, 'You see, she told us she didn't possess a raincoat and we didn't find one, but in this photo a raincoat is hanging up inside the caravan.'

Burden took the magnifying lens from him and looked. 'Bright emerald green and the buttons that sort of bone that is part white, part brown.'

'She came into the kitchen when she said she did or maybe five minutes earlier. I think it was true she'd finished with Tom, but that she meant to go for a long walk with Heather in order to tell her so, that was a fiction. She wore the raincoat because it was already drizzling and maybe because she knew she looked nice in it. She came to tell Heather she'd be leaving and no doubt that Heather could have him and welcome.

'Did she know Tom beat his wife? Maybe and maybe not. No doubt, she thought that if Tom and she had ever got together permanently he wouldn't beat *her*. But that's by the way. She came into the kitchen and saw Heather crouched against the counter and Tom hitting her in the face.

'It's said that a woman can't really defend herself against a brutal man, but another woman can defend her. What happened to Carol Fox, Mike? Pure anger? Total disillusionment with Tom Peterlee? Some pull of the great sisterhood of women? Perhaps we shall find out. She snatched up a log out of that basket, a strong oak log, and struck him over the back of the head with it. And again and again. Once she'd started she went on in a frenzy – until he was dead.'

'One of them,' said Burden, ' – and I'd say Carol, wouldn't you? – acted with great presence of mind then, organising what they must do. Carol took off the raincoat that was covered with blood and thrust it along with the weapon into the stove. In the hour or so before we got there everything was consumed but part of one of the buttons.'

'Carol washed her hands, put on one of Heather's jackets, they took the dog and went out down to the river. It was never, as we thought, Carol providing an alibi for Heather. It was Heather alibi-ing Carol. They would stay out for three-quarters of an hour, come back and "find" the body, or even try to get rid of the body, clean up the kitchen, pretend that Tom had gone away. What they didn't foresee was Arlene's arrival.'

'But Arlene came an hour early,' Burden said.

'Arlene assumed that her mother had done it and she would think she knew why. The mouse in the corner attacked when the cat's attention was diverted. The worm turned as Grandma turned when her husband struck her once too often.'

He said much the same to Arlene Heddon next day after Carol Fox had been charged with murder. 'You only told me she was Tom's girlfriend when you thought things were looking bad for your mother. You reasoned that if a man's mistress gave a man's wife an alibi it was bound to seem genuine. In case I didn't believe you and she denied it, you sent me the receipt they gave you when you took the film you'd removed from Tom Peterlee's camera along to the York Crest Centre to be processed. I suppose your mother told you the kind of pictures he took.'

She shrugged, said rather spitefully, 'You weren't so clever. All that about me knowing who'd killed Tom. I didn't know, I thought it was my mother.'

He glanced round the caravan, took in the radio and tape player, microwave oven, video, and his eye fell on the small black rectangle he had in the past, without a closer look, taken for a remote control channel changer. Now he thought how lazy you would have to be, how incapacitated almost, to need to change channels by this means. Almost anywhere in here you were within an arm's length of the television set. He picked it up.

It was a tape recorder, five inches long, two inches wide, flat, black. The end with the red 'on' light was and always had been turned towards the kitchen area.

So confident had she been in her control of things and perhaps in her superior intelligence that she had not even stripped the tiny label off its underside. Nixon's, York Crest, £54.99 – he was certain Arlene hadn't paid fifty-five pounds for it.

'You can't have that!' She was no longer cool.

'I'll give you a receipt for it,' he said, and then, 'Gary, no doubt, was with his pals that evening planning the first ram raid. I don't know where but I know it wasn't the Red Rose at Edenwick.'

She was quite silent, staring at him. He fancied she would have liked to snatch the recorder from him but did not quite dare. Serendipity or a long experience in reading faces and drawing conclusions made him say, 'Let's hear what you've been taping on here, Miss Heddon.'

He heard his own voice, then hers. As clear as a phone conversation. It was a good tape recorder. He thought, yes, Gary Wyatt was involved in the first ram raid, the one that took place after the murder and after the first time I came here to talk to her. From then on, from the second time . . .

'I didn't know Carol very well.'

'But she was a close friend of your mother's . . .' His voice tailed away into cracklings.

'I haven't lived at home since I was seventeen. I don't know all the friends my mother's got . . .'

'So that was how you did it,' he said. 'You recorded our conversations and learnt your replies off by heart. That was a way to guarantee your answers would never vary.'

In a stiff wooden voice she said, 'If you say so.'

He got up. 'I don't think Gary's going to be with you much longer, Miss Heddon. You'll be visiting him once a month, if you're so inclined. Some say there's a very thin line dividing the cop from the criminal, they've the same kind of intelligence. Your mother tells me you once had ambitions to be a police officer. You've got off to a bad start but maybe it's not too late.'

With the recorder in his pocket, stooping as he made his way out of the caravan, he turned back and said, 'If you like the idea, give me a ring.'

He closed the door behind him and descended the steps on to the muddy field and the cinder path.

# Lizzie's Lover

'The rain set early in tonight,' she said.

She came into the house and he shut the door behind her. Her head had been uncovered and her long fair hair was wet. He smiled at her. 'D'you know what you said?'

'I'm sorry?'

'The rain set early in tonight. That's the first line of "Porphyria's Lover".' He looked into her face for comprehension, saw none. 'Browning. It's a poem, Lizzie. Did you never do it at school?'

He took her coat which was very wet and, having thought better of his first idea, the hooks on the hall wall, draped it over the back of a chair. The house was small and low-ceilinged, a little brick house in a terrace in the far reaches of a South London suburb, unheard-of, far away from Underground stations and bus stops.

'Did you say Porphyria?' she said.

'That's right.'

'Porphyria's a disease, Michael. I don't know why it's called that but it is. Your urine goes purple.'

'Browning called the girl in his poem Porphyria before they named the disease. There's a sort of marble, too, called porphyry. It means purple. *Porphyra*, Greek, purple.'

'The things you know,' she said. 'You've got a hair drier, haven't you? I'd like to dry my hair.'

Michael couldn't bear the noise. 'The drier broke and I threw it out,' he lied. 'I've lit a fire. We'll have some wine and you can dry your hair by the fire.'

She was wearing a long skirt of a bluish-mauve colour with a dark purple top of velvet and a fine violet chiffon scarf. The hem of the skirt was wet. He thought how absurd it was that women who had emancipated themselves into trousers should revert back to what their great-grandmothers wore – and from choice. The fire was half-dead, a smouldering, flameless mass. While he opened the wine, she knelt down and worked at the fire with the fancy brass bellows he had bought in a junk shop.

He recited softly, '"She shut the cold out and the storm, And kneeled and made the cheerless grate Blaze up, and all the cottage warm."'

'Hardly that,' she said and she laughed. 'Is that more of "Porphyria"?'

'I was doing it with the kids in class today and now you seem to be acting it out. Here's your wine. She'd come to his house out of the rain, she had wet hair too, yellow hair, Browning says, which yours is, I suppose.'

'Yellow? I don't like the sound of that. What's your poem about? I know you're dying to tell me.'

He watched her dip her head down and spread out the hair in a wide golden fan. The firelight made the separate strands sparkle.

'I don't know the whole thing by heart,' he said, 'only bits. There's a feast in it, which reminds me I should start getting us some food. Or do you want to go out to eat?'

'I'm not hungry.' She began passing a comb through her hair. It made an electric crackling. 'Don't let's eat yet.'

'All right then,' he said. 'Come and sit here beside me.'

The little room had a sofa in it, covered with a piece of red and purple tapestry. Two table lamps had dark red shades and these he left on while turning out the central light. The room became cosy and at the same time seemed smaller. Michael sat on the sofa and patted the cushion next to him. When she was sitting beside him he lifted one of her hands and laid his in it.

'"She put my arm about her waist,"' he said. 'That's right, put my arm round your waist. "And made her smooth white shoulder bare."' Gently he drew the purple velvet neckline down, exposing her upper arm. 'Yours is more tanned than white. Victorian girls avoided the sun.'

'A lot of people would say that was wise. Go on with the poem.'

'I told you I can't remember it all. She makes him rest his cheek on her bare shoulder and then she spreads her hair "o'er all", meaning his face, one supposes.'

'Like this?'

Lizzie laid her hair across his face and her shoulder like a veil. He shook himself and sat up because he disliked getting hairs in his mouth. 'More wine?'

'Yes, please.'

He refilled her glass and brought it back to her. When she made a move to pick it up he took hold of her hand, held it, and bringing his mouth to hers, kissed her lingeringly. He smoothed the long hair away from her face, undid the knot in the purple scarf and kissed the hollow in her throat.

'Is that what the lover did with Porphyria?' she asked him softly.

'No, I don't believe he did. He didn't kiss her – not then. He was pleased because she'd come through wind and rain and not so pleased because she wouldn't give herself to him for ever.'

'If that means sleep with him, Victorians didn't, did they?'

'I expect some did,' said Michael. 'Anyway, he says that "passion sometimes would prevail" and in fact it was passion which had driven her to him that night.'

'Must have been the same thing with me,' said Lizzie. 'It took me nearly two hours to get here, what with the Victoria Line down and the buses all coming at once and then none for half an hour. Only passion kept me going.'

'"Be sure I looked up at her eyes,"' said Michael. '"Happy and proud; at last I knew Porphyria worshipped me."'

'Was she married? Like me?'

'Browning doesn't say. But he describes her as "perfectly pure and good", so one would suppose not. Unfaithful wives were criminals in his day.'

Lizzie looked away and drank some of her wine. Then she held Michael's wrist and lightly stroked the palm of his hand. She said dreamily, 'What happened next?'

'He strangled her.'

She dropped his hand as if it burnt her and retreated into the corner of the sofa. '*What?*'

'He strangled her with her own hair. To keep her for himself. For ever. "I found", he says, "A thing to do, and all her hair In one long yellow string I wound Three times her little throat around . . ."'

'And you do this poem with the kids at school?'

'They're sixteen, Lizzie. They're not babies.'

She edged back nearer to him. 'It wouldn't work. You couldn't strangle someone with her own hair.'

'Why not, if it was long enough?'

For answer she took hold of her own hair in one thick hank, golden and smooth, and held it out to him on her hand like someone offering an object for sale. He took the hair in both hands and twisted it once, drew it down past her right ear and across her throat. At first he wound it loosely then, pulling it tighter, succeeded in making almost two circuits of her smooth brown neck.

'"Her cheek once more",' he said, '"Blushed bright beneath my burning kiss."'

'He kissed her on the *cheek*?' said Lizzie.

'With the Victorians I sometimes think that was a euphemism for mouth.' Michael brought his to hers but, as he touched her skin, deflected his lips to where corner of mouth and cheek met. As he pressed his lips on the warm soft skin he took a firmer hold of her hair and gave a sharp tug.

'Michael!' It was almost a scream.

He was pulling on the skein of hair as hard as he could. Suddenly he released her. She pulled down her hair with both hands. 'For God's sake!'

'You were right. It can't be done. Your hair's not long enough.'

'Just as well. You frightened me for a moment.'

'Did I?' he said. 'Surely not.'

With both hands he smoothed her hair back over her shoulders. He put his hand under her chin and lifted it. Her eyes were doubtful. He looked deep into them.

'It was a way of keeping her for ever, wasn't it? No going back to the husband when the evening was over, no more pride or "vainer ties" to dissever. I can understand that.'

His hands were on her shoulders now and the eyes were mesmerising. Hers glazed over and her mouth trembled. He took hold of the two ends of the purple chiffon scarf, crossed them and, in a hard swift movement, pulled them tight. She screamed but no sound came. Porphyria hadn't fought at all but Lizzie fought, thrashing and kicking and flailing with her hands, choking and gasping. But when the struggles were over she too lay still, her head fallen into his lap.

He stroked the hair that hadn't been quite long enough. He quoted softly, '"And thus we sit together now, And all night long we have not stirred, And yet God has not said a word!"'

# Shreds and Slivers

I love my love with a ps because she is psychic; I hate her with a
ps because she is psilotic. I feed her on psalliota and psilotaceae;
her name is Psammis and she lives in a psalterium.

Forgive me. I am carried away by words sometimes, especially those
of Greek etymology that begin with a combination of unlikely
consonants. I love my love with a cn because she is cnidarian . . . But,
no. Let us return to psalliota. If you want to know what all those
other words mean you must look them up in a good dictionary.
Psalliota is nothing more nor less than the common mushroom:
psalliota campestris, to be precise.

I became interested in fungi only recently. Since being made
redundant I have, of course, had time on my hands, leisure to notice
things. I try not to brood. That this year was exceptional for an
abundance of fungi first struck me while taking a train to see my wife.
I can no longer afford to run a car. From the economy-class window
I observed meadows covered with whitish protrusions among the
grass. It took me only a little while to realise that these were mushrooms,
though I had never seen such a sight before.

Back at home after my day out, I explored my garden. Largely
untended (I sometimes mow the lawn) since my wife was stolen from
me ten years ago, it has gone back to nature in rather a pleasing way.
For instance, shrubs which she planted have transformed themselves
into trees. Under them, and in mossy corners against the walls, I came
upon a variety of fungi: agarics, lepiotas, horns-of-plenty and, of
course, the puffball. These names were unfamiliar to me then. Two
books and a video started me on what may become a lifelong obsession.

I am not a mushroom eater myself. My wife was particularly fond
of them. But in those days – I won't say when I last saw her, for I
make a point of *seeing* her, but when I last spoke to her – the only
mushrooms obtainable in the shops were the common kind, and the
only differentiation that between 'large' and 'button'. Things have
changed. To the uninitiated these supermarket cartons, wrapped in

clingfilm, may appear to contain only 'mixed mushrooms'; I, however, can name them as shitaki, canterelles, boletus and morels, pale slivers resembling slices of blood-drained flesh, lemony fibrous strips, plump glutinous gobbets, chocolate-brown elastic lumps. Well, there is no accounting for tastes.

The day I came upon amanita phalloides in my garden, under the sessile oak, was the day I saw my wife for the first time for some weeks. You understand that though I think about her every day, go to the town where she lives, keep an eye on her house and spend some time in her local shopping centre, I do not always see her. Needless to say, she *never* sees me. But on this occasion, invisible among the racks of shellsuits, I spotted her in the distance approaching the vegetable counters. I am not exaggerating when I say my heart quaked. It is always a shock, even after so long.

I watched from my sartorial hideaway. Too far away to see what she bought, I followed her with my eyes from vegetables to pizzas, from pasta to mineral waters, and thence to the check-out. That night I ran the video through once again. Yellow and white, with pallid gills and raggedy hat, phalloides blossomed on the screen in all its deadly glory. The death cap, as the voice-over called it, adding cheerfully that very small quantities cause intense suffering, then death.

If I were to grow cannabis sativa I would be breaking the law. The police would come, root up and destroy the plants. But it is no offence to grow phalloides, most deadly of all indigenous fungi. With impunity, I might if I wished turn my shady half-acre into a death cap plantation. If only I could! But fungi are capricious, inconstant, fungi are fitful and vicissitudinous. Who has not heard of those would-be mushroom farmers who have the kit and precisely obey the instructions only to find their growing barns empty and psalliota flourishing in the fields outside their property?

I have had to be content with what nature has supplied, and for my part can provide only encouragement in the form of shade, moisture and protection. It was in October that the young fruit first broke through and the stipe pushed above the ground, its snowy veil bursting to reveal the olive-yellow cap. The flesh, my book says, is white and smells of raw potatoes. How gratifying to discover that this was indeed so and I had not confused phalloides with, for instance, xerula. (I love my love with an x because she is xanthic, I hate her with an x because she is xylophagous.)

Careful not to touch the fruit bodies, using a knife and fork, I sliced into thin strips the cap and stipe of three specimens. They filled a large yogurt pot. With closed eyes, I stood there remembering my wife's ways, her fashion of cooking, her pleasure in eating, her smile. I remembered her slicing raw potatoes and I could smell the smell in my mind.

I took the yogurt pot with me next day and went straight from the station to the supermarket. There was no question of my wife's arriving for at least two hours; I have my memories, all too many of them, and I know her timetable, the order and regularity of her life. But for a while I waited, pacing, deep in thought, between bedlinen reductions and kitchenware. You must appreciate that until then, apart from the audio-tapes and the carefully chosen articles sent her, and the enlightening letters posted to her relatives, I had taken no positive steps against my wife. The time had come for action. I hesitated no longer.

With a little practice, it takes only seconds to detach the clingfilm from the base of a mixed mushroom carton, slip in a slice or two of phalloides and re-adhere the film. Among the fronds and filaments, the shreds and slivers, my delicate cilia passed unnoticed or passed for wisps of shitaki. I operated on some ten cartons, about half the stock, in this way. The place was not frequented at lunchtime. No one saw me, or if they did, they approved the prudence of what they took for close examination prior to purchase. I have noticed how, for example, in these hard times, it is not uncommon for shoppers to taste the grapes before they buy.

I waited long enough to see my wife come in. My heart began to jog. One day, if this does not stop, it will kill itself and me with it. Of course I realised that there was only a fifty per cent chance of my wife consuming one of the fatal batch. But in this game of culinary Russian Roulette, these are very favourable odds. Still, on my next visit with fresh supplies I operated on fifteen cartons. After all, she is not the only one to consider but also her live-in paramour and her extended family who all live nearby and whose sheepish faces and obese forms I often see in the aisles between the sauces and the frozen desserts.

At last, having heard and seen nothing of the consequence of my actions, I was obliged to sacrifice the last of phalloides, stripping the leafmould under the sessile oak bare of its potato-scented crop. This time – I was a little late – only fourteen cartons of mixed mushrooms remained and in less than two minutes the contents of the yogurt pot were nestling among the sinuate gills and elliptoid membranes. In fact, I had barely finished when I spotted her entering by way of exotic fruits and, my heart on its treadmill, I slipped away.

Three days later a small paragraph in the newspaper told me that the supermarket had withdrawn all 'mixed mushrooms' due to two unexplained deaths and several cases of severe illness. But the deaths, alas, were not hers nor his nor theirs. When it has blown over and 'mixed mushrooms' are back on the counter, I shall have to begin all over again next year.

At present the ground under the sessile oak is covered with snow. All fungi have succumbed to frost. I shall mark the spot where the spores of phalloides lie deep in the earth, for there must be no trampling or digging. And some mnemonic must be contrived to help me remember the precise location. Oh, I love my love with a mn because she is mnemic, I hate her with a mn because she is mnemonical, her name is Mnemosyne and she is the goddess of remembrance . . .

# Burning End

After she had been doing it for a year, it occurred to Linda that looking after Betty fell to her lot because she was a woman. Betty was Brian's mother, not hers, and Betty had two other children, both sons, both unmarried men. No one had ever suggested that either of them should take a hand in looking after their mother. Betty had never much liked Linda, had sometimes hinted that Brian had married beneath him, and once, in the heat of temper, said that Linda was 'not good enough' for her son, but still it was Linda who cared for her now. Linda felt a fool, for not having thought of it in these terms before.

She knew she would not get very far talking about it to Brian. Brian would say – and did say – that this was women's work. A man couldn't perform intimate tasks for an old woman, it wasn't fitting. When Linda asked why not, he told her not to be silly, everyone knew why not.

'Suppose it had been your dad that was left, suppose he'd been bedridden, would I have looked after him?'

Brian looked over the top of his evening paper. He was holding the remote in his hand but he didn't turn down the sound. 'He wasn't left, was he?'

'No, but if he had been?'

'I reckon you would have. There isn't anyone else, is there? It's not as if the boys were married.'

Every morning after Brian had gone out into the farmyard and before she went to work, Linda drove down the road, turned left at the church into the lane, and after a mile came to the small cottage on the large piece of land where Betty had lived since the death of her husband twelve years before. Betty slept downstairs in the room at the back. She was always awake when Linda got there, although that was invariably before seven-thirty, and she always said she had been awake since five.

Linda got her up and changed the incontinence pad. Most mornings she had to change the sheets as well. She washed Betty, put her into a clean nightgown and clean bedjacket, socks and slippers, and while Betty shouted and moaned, lifted and shoved her as best she could into the armchair she would remain in all day. Then it was breakfast. Sweet milky tea and bread and butter and jam. Betty wouldn't use the feeding cup with the spout. What did Linda think she was, a baby? She drank from a cup and unless Linda had remembered to cover her up with the muslin squares that had indeed once had their use for babies, the tea would go all down the clean nightgown and Betty have to be changed again.

After Linda had left her the district nurse would come, though not every day. The meals-on-wheels lady would come and give Betty her midday dinner, bits and pieces in foil containers, all labelled with the names of their contents. At some point Brian would come. Brian would 'look in'. Not to *do* anything, not to clear anything away or make his mother a cup of tea or run the vacuum cleaner around, but to sit in Betty's bedroom for ten minutes, smoking a cigarette and watching television. Perhaps once a month, the brother who lived two miles away would come for ten minutes and watch television with Brian. The other brother, the one who lived ten miles away, never came at all except at Christmas.

Linda knew if Brian had been there by the smell of smoke and the cigarette end stubbed out in the ashtray. But even if there had been no smell and no stub she would have known because Betty always told her. Betty thought Brian was a saint to spare a moment away from the farm to visit his old mother. She could no longer speak distinctly but she was articulate on the subject of Brian, the most perfect son any woman ever had.

It was about five when Linda got back there. Usually the incontinence pad needed changing again and often the nightdress too. Considering how ill she was, and partially paralysed, Betty ate a great deal. Linda made her scrambled egg or sardines on toast. She brought pastries with her from the cakeshop or, in the summer, strawberries and cream. She made more tea for Betty and when the meal was over, somehow heaved Betty back into that bed.

The bedroom window was never opened. Betty wouldn't have it. The room smelt of urine and lavender, camphor and meals-on-wheels, so every day on her way to work Linda opened the window in the front room and left the doors open. It didn't make much difference but she went on doing it. When she had got Betty to bed she washed the dishes and teacups and put all the soiled linen into a plastic bag to take home. The question she asked Betty before she left had become meaningless because Betty always said no, and she hadn't asked it once since talking to Brian about whose job it was to look after his mother, but she asked it now.

'Wouldn't it be better if we moved you in with us, Mum?'

Betty's hearing was erratic. This was one of her deaf days. 'What?'

'Wouldn't you be better off coming to live with us?'

'I'm not leaving my home till they carry me out feet first. How many times do I have to tell you?'

Linda said she would see her in the morning. Looking rather pleased at the prospect, Betty said she would be dead by the morning.

'Not you,' said Linda, which was what she always said, and so far she had always been right.

She went into the front room and closed the window. The room was furnished in a way which must have been old-fashioned even when Betty was young. In the centre of it was a square dining table, around which stood six chairs with seats of faded green silk. There was a large sideboard but no armchairs, no small tables, no books and no lamps but the central light which, enveloped in a shade of parchment panels stitched together with leather thongs, was suspended directly over the glass vase that stood on a lace mat in the absolute centre of the table.

For some reason, ever since the second stroke had incapacitated Betty, all the post, all the junk mail and every freebee news-sheet that was delivered to the cottage ended up on this table. Every few months it was cleared away but this hadn't been done for some time, and Linda noticed that only about four inches of the glass vase now showed above the sea of paper. The lace mat was not visible at all. She noticed something else as well.

It had been a warm sunny day, very warm for April. The cottage faced south and all afternoon the sunshine had poured through the window, was still pouring through the window, striking the neck of the vase so that the glass was too bright to look at. Where the sun-struck glass touched a sheet of paper a burning had begun. The burning glass was making a dark charred channel through the sheet of thin printed paper.

Linda screwed up her eyes. They had not deceived her. That was smoke she could see. And now she could smell burning paper. For a moment she stood there, marvelling at this phenomenon which she had heard of but had never believed in. A magnifying glass used to make Boy Scouts' fires, she thought, and somewhere she had read of a forest burnt down through a piece of glass left in a sunlit glade.

There was nowhere to put the pile of paper, so she found another plastic bag and filled that. Betty called out something but it was only to know why she was still there. Linda dusted the table, replaced the lace mat and the glass vase and, with a bag of soiled linen in one hand and a bag of waste paper in the other, went home to do the washing and get an evening meal for Brian and herself and the children.

The incident of the glass vase, the sun and the burning paper had been so interesting that Linda had meant to tell Brian and Andrew and Gemma all about it while they were eating. But they were also watching the finals of a quiz game on television and hushed her when she started to speak. The opportunity went by and somehow there was no other until the next day. But by that time the sun and the glass setting the paper on fire no longer seemed so remarkable and Linda decided not to mention it.

Several times in the weeks that followed Brian asked his mother to come and live with them at the farm. Betty responded very differently from when Linda asked her. Brian and his children, Betty said, shouldn't have to have a useless old woman under their roof, age and youth were not meant to live together, though nobody appreciated her son's generosity in asking her more than she did. Meanwhile Linda went on going to the cottage and looking after Betty and cleaning the place on Saturdays and doing Betty's washing.

One afternoon while Brian was sitting with his mother smoking a cigarette, the doctor dropped in to pay his twice-yearly visit. He beamed at Betty, said how nice it was for her to have her family around her and on his way out told Brian it was best for the old folks to end their days at home whenever possible. He made no comment on the cigarette. Brian must have picked up a pile of junk mail from the doormat and the new phone book from outside the door, for all this was lying on the table in the front room when Linda arrived at ten to five. The paper had accumulated during the past weeks but when she went to look for a plastic bag she saw that the stock had been used up. She made a mental note to buy some more and in the meantime had to put the soiled sheets and Betty's two wet nightdresses into a pillowcase to take home. The sun wasn't shining, it had been a dull day and the forecast was for rain, so there was no danger from the conjunction of glass vase with the piles of paper. It could safely remain as it was.

On her way home it occurred to Linda that the simplest solution was to remove, not the paper but the vase. Yet, when she went back next day, she didn't remove the vase. It was a strange feeling she had, that if she moved the vase on to the mantelpiece, say, or the sideboard, she would somehow have closed a door or missed a chance. Once she had moved it she would never be able to move it back again, for though she could easily have explained to anyone why she had moved it from the table, she would never be able to say why she had put it back. These thoughts made her feel uneasy and she put them from her mind.

Linda bought a pack of fifty black plastic sacks. Betty said it was a wicked waste of money. In the days when she had been up and about she had been in the habit of burning waste paper. All leftover food and cans and bottles got mixed up together and went out for the dustman. Betty had never heard of the environment. When Linda insisted, one hot day in July, on opening the bedroom windows, Betty said she was freezing and Linda was trying to kill her. Linda took the curtains home and washed them but she didn't open the bedroom window again, it wasn't worth it, it caused too much trouble.

But when Brian's brother Michael got engaged she did ask if Suzanne would take her turn looking after Betty once they were back from their honeymoon.

'You couldn't expect it of a young girl like her,' Brian said.

'She's twenty-eight,' said Linda.

'She doesn't look it.' Brian switched on the television. 'Did I tell you Geoff's been made redundant?'

'Then maybe he could help out with Betty if he hasn't got a job to go to.'

Brian looked at her and shook his head gently. 'He's feeling low enough as it is. It's a blow to a man's pride, that is, going on the dole. I couldn't ask him.'

Why does he have to be asked, Linda thought. It's his mother. The sun was already high in the sky when she got to the cottage at seven-thirty next morning, already edging round the house to penetrate the front room window by ten. Linda put the junk mail on the table and took the letter and the postcard into the bedroom. Betty wouldn't look at them. She was wet through and the bed was wet. Linda got her up and stripped off the wet clothes, wrapping Betty in a clean blanket because she said she was freezing. When she was washed and in her clean nightdress she wanted to talk about Michael's fiancée. It was one of her articulate days.

'Dirty little trollop,' said Betty. 'I remember her when she was fifteen.

Go with anyone, she would. There's no knowing how many abortions she's had, messed all her insides up, I shouldn't wonder.'

'She's very pretty in my opinion,' said Linda, 'and a nice nature.'

'Handsome is as handsome does. It's all that make-up and hair dye as has entrapped my poor boy. One thing, she won't set foot in this house while I'm alive.'

Linda opened the window in the front room. It was going to be a hot day, but breezy. The house could do with a good draught of air blowing through to freshen it. She thought, I wonder why no one ever put flowers in that vase, there's no point in a vase without flowers. The letters and envelopes and newsprint surrounded it so that it no longer looked like a vase but like a glass tube inexplicably poking out between a stack of paper and a telephone directory.

Brian didn't visit that day. He had started harvesting. When Linda came back at five Betty told her Michael had been in. She showed Linda the gift of chocolates that were his way of 'softsoaping' her, Betty said. Not that a few violet creams had stopped her speaking her mind on the subject of that trollop.

The chocolates had gone soft and sticky in the heat. Linda said she would put them in the fridge but Betty clutched the box to her chest, saying she knew Linda, she knew her sweet tooth, if she let that box out of her sight she'd never see it again. Linda washed Betty and changed her. While she was doing Betty's feet, rubbing cream round her toes and powdering them, Betty struck her on the head with the bedside clock, the only weapon she had to hand.

'You hurt me,' said Betty. 'You hurt me on purpose.'

'No, I didn't, Mum. I think you've broken that clock.'

'You hurt me on purpose because I wouldn't give you my chocolates my son brought me.'

Brian said he was going to cut the field behind the cottage next day. Fifty acres of barley and he'd be done by mid-afternoon if the heat didn't kill him. He could have seen to his mother's needs, he'd be practically on the spot, but he didn't offer. Linda wouldn't have believed her ears if she'd heard him offer.

It was hotter than ever. It was even hot at seven-thirty in the morning. Linda washed Betty and changed the sheets. She gave her cereal for breakfast and a boiled egg and toast. From her bed Betty could see Brian going round the barley field on the combine and this seemed to bring her enormous pleasure, though her enjoyment was tempered with pity.

'He knows what hard work is,' Betty said, 'he doesn't spare himself when there's a job to be done,' as if Brian was cutting the fifty acres with a scythe instead of sitting up there in a cabin with twenty kingsize and a can of Coke and the Walkman on his head playing Beatles' songs from his youth.

Linda opened the window in the front room very wide. The sun would be round in a couple of hours to stream through that window. She adjusted an envelope on the top of the pile, moving the torn edge of its flap to brush against the glass vase. Then she moved it away again. She stood, looking at the table and the papers and the vase. A brisk draught of air made the thinner sheets of paper flutter a little. From the bedroom she heard Betty call out, through closed windows to a man on a combine a quarter of a mile away, 'Hallo, Brian, you all right then, are you? You keep at it, son, that's right, you got the weather on your side.'

One finger stretched out, Linda lightly poked at the torn edge of the envelope flap. She didn't really move it at all. She turned her back quickly. She marched out of the room, out of the house, to the car.


The fire must have started somewhere around four in the afternoon, the hottest part of that hot day. Brian had been in to see his mother when he had finished cutting the field at two. He had watched television with her and then she said she wanted to have a sleep. Those who know about these things said she had very likely died from suffocation without ever waking. That was why she hadn't phoned for help, though the phone was by her bed.

A farmworker driving down the lane called the fire brigade. They were volunteers whose headquarters was five miles away and they took twenty minutes to get to the fire. By then Betty was dead and half the cottage destroyed. Nobody told Linda, there was hardly time; when she got to Betty's at five it was all over and Brian and the firemen were standing about, poking at the wet black ashes with sticks.

The will was a surprise. Betty had lived in that cottage for years without a washing machine or a freezer and her television set was rented by Brian. The bed she slept in was her marriage bed, new in 1947, the cottage hadn't been painted since she moved there and the kitchen had last been refitted just after the war. But she left what seemed an enormous sum of money. Linda could hardly believe it. A third was for Geoff, a third for Michael and the remaining third as well as the cottage or what was left of it, for Brian.

The insurance company paid up. It was impossible to discover the cause of the fire. Something to do with the great heat, no doubt, and the thatched roof and the ancient electrical wiring. Linda, of course, knew better but she said nothing. She kept what she knew and let it fester inside her, giving her sleepless nights and taking away her appetite.

Brian cried noisily at the funeral. All the brothers showed excessive grief and no one told Brian to pull himself together or be a man, but put their arms round his shoulders and said what a marvellous son he'd been and how he'd nothing to reproach himself with. Linda didn't cry but soon after went into a depression from which nothing could rouse her, not the doctor's tranquillizers, nor Brian's promise of a slap-up holiday somewhere, even abroad if she liked, nor people telling her Betty hadn't felt any pain but had just slipped away in her smoky sleep.

An application to build a new house on the sight of the cottage was favourably received by the planning authority and permission was granted. Why shouldn't they live in it, Brian said, he and Linda and the children? The farmhouse was ancient and awkward, difficult to keep clean, just the sort of place Londoners would like for a second home. How about a modern house, he said, with everything you want, two bathrooms, say, and a laundry room and a sun lounge? Design it yourself and don't worry about the cost, he said, for he was concerned for his wife who had always been so practical and efficient as well as easy-going and persuadable but was now a miserable, silent woman.

Linda refused to move. She didn't want a new house, especially a new house on the site of that cottage. She didn't want a holiday or money to buy clothes. She refused to touch Betty's money. Depression had forced her to give up her job but, although she was at home all day and there was no old woman to look after every morning and every evening, she did nothing in the house and Brian was obliged to get a woman in to clean.

'She must have been a lot fonder of Mum than I thought,' Brian said to his brother Michael. 'She's always been one to keep her feelings bottled up, but that's the only explanation. Mum must have meant a lot more to her than I ever knew.'

'Or else it's guilt,' said Michael, whose fiancée's sister was married to a man whose brother was a psychotherapist.

'Guilt? You have to be joking. What's she got to be guilty about? She couldn't have done more if she'd been Mum's own daughter.'

'Yeah, but folks feel guilt over nothing when someone dies, it's a well-known fact.'

'It is, is it? Is that what it is, doctor? Well, let me tell you something. If anyone ought to feel guilt it's me. I've never said a word about this to a soul. Well, I couldn't, could I, not if I wanted to collect the insurance, but the fact is it was me set that place on fire.'

'You what?' said Michael.

'I don't mean on purpose. Come on, what do you take me for, my own brother? And I don't feel guilty, I can tell you, I don't feel a scrap of guilt, accidents will happen and there's not a thing you can do about it. But when I went in to see Mum that afternoon I left my cigarette burning on the side of the chest of drawers. You know how you put them down, with the burning end stuck out. Linda'd taken away the damned ashtray and washed it or something. When I saw Mum was asleep I just crept out and left that fag end burning. Without a backward glance.'

Awed, Michael asked in a small voice, 'When did you realise?'

'Soon as I saw the smoke, soon as I saw the fire brigade. Too late then, wasn't it? I'd crept out of there without a backward glance.'

# The Man Who
# Was the God of Love

'Have you got *The Times* there?' Henry would say, usually at about eight, when she had cleared the dinner table and put the things in the dishwasher.

*The Times* was on the coffee table with the two other dailies they took, but it was part of the ritual to ask her. Fiona liked to be asked. She liked to watch Henry do the crossword puzzle, the *real* one of course, not the quick crossword, and watch him frown a little, then his handsome brow clear as the answer to a clue came to him. She could not have done a crossword puzzle to save her life (as she was fond of saying), she could not even have done the simple ones in the tabloids.

While she watched him, before he carried the newspaper off into his study as he often did, Fiona told herself how lucky she was to be married to Henry. Her luck had been almost miraculous. There she was, a temp who had come into his office to work for him while his secretary had a baby, an ordinary, not particularly good-looking girl who had no credentials but a tidy mind and a proficient way with a word processor. She had nothing but her admiration for him, which she had felt from the first and was quite unable to hide.

He was not appreciated in that company as he should have been. It had often seemed to her that only she saw him for what he was. After she had been there a week she told him he had a first-class mind.

Henry had said modestly, 'As a matter of fact, I have got rather a high IQ, but it doesn't exactly get stretched round here.'

'I suppose they haven't the brains to recognise it,' she said. 'It must be marvellous to be really intelligent. Did you win scholarships and get a double first and all that?'

He only smiled. Instead of answering he asked her to have dinner with him. One afternoon, half an hour before they were due to pack up and go, she came upon him doing *The Times* crossword.

'In the firm's time, I'm afraid, Fiona,' he said with one of his wonderful, half-rueful smiles.

He hadn't finished the puzzle but at least half of it was already filled in and when she asked him he said he had started it ten minutes before. She was lost in admiration. Henry said he would finish the puzzle later and in the meantime would she have a drink with him on the way home?

That was three years ago. The firm, which deserved bankruptcy it was so mismanaged, got into difficulties and Henry was among those made redundant. Of course he soon got another job, though the salary was pitiful for someone of his intellectual grasp. He was earning very little more than she was, as she told him indignantly. Soon afterwards he asked her to marry him. Fiona was overcome. She told him humbly that she would have gladly lived with him without marriage, there was no one else she had ever known to compare with him in intellectual terms, it would have been enough to be allowed to share his life. But he said no, marriage or nothing, it would be unfair on her not to marry her.

She kept on with her temping job, making sure she stopped in time to be home before Henry and get his dinner. It was ridiculous to waste money on a cleaner, so she cleaned the house on Sundays. Henry played golf on Saturday mornings and he liked her to go with him, though she was hopeless when she tried to learn. He said it was an inspiration to have her there to praise his swing. On Saturday afternoons they went out in the car and Henry had begun teaching her to drive.

They had quite a big garden – they had bought the house on an enormous mortgage – and she did her best to keep it trim because Henry obviously didn't have the time. He was engaged on a big project for his new company which he worked on in his study for most of the evenings. Fiona did the shopping in her lunchtime, she did all the cooking and all the washing and ironing. It was her privilege to care for someone as brilliant as Henry. Besides, his job was so much more demanding than hers, it took more out of him and by bedtime he was sometimes white with exhaustion.

But Henry was first up in the mornings. He was an early riser, getting up at six-thirty, and he always brought her a cup of tea and the morning papers in bed. Fiona had nothing to do before she went off to take first a bus and then the tube but put the breakfast things in the dishwasher and stack yesterday's newspapers in the cupboard outside the front door for recycling.

*The Times* would usually be on top, folded with the lower left-hand quarter of the back page uppermost. Fiona soon came to understand it was no accident that the section of the paper where the crossword was, the *completed* crossword, should be exposed in this way. It was deliberate, it was evidence of Henry's pride in his achievement, and she was deeply moved that he should want her to see it. She was touched by his need for her admiration. A sign of weakness on his part it might be, but she loved him all the more for that.

A smile, half-admiring, half-tender, came to her lips, as she looked at the neatly-printed answers to all those incomprehensible clues. She could have counted on the fingers of one hand the number of times he had failed to finish the crossword. The evening before his father died, for instance. Then it was anxiety which must have been the cause. They had sent for him at four in the morning and when she looked at the paper before putting it outside with the others, she saw that poor Henry had only been able to fill in the answers to four clues. Another time he had flu and had been unable to get out of bed in the morning. It must have been coming on the night before to judge by his attempt at the crossword, abandoned after two answers feebly pencilled in.

His father left him a house that was worth a lot of money. Henry had always said that when he got promotion, she would be able to give up work and have a baby. Promotion seemed less and less likely in view of recession and the fact that the new company appreciated Henry no more than had his previous employers. The proceeds of the sale of Henry's father's house would compensate for that and Fiona was imagining paying off the mortgage and perhaps handing in her notice when Henry said he was going to spend it on having a swimming pool built. All his life he had wanted a swimming pool of his own, it had been a childhood dream and a teenage ideal and now he was going to realise it.

Fiona came nearer than she ever had to seeing a flaw in her husband's perfection.

'You only want a baby because you think he might be a genius,' he teased her.

'*She* might be,' said Fiona, greatly daring.

'He, she, it's just a manner of speaking. Suppose he had my beauty and your brains. That would be a fine turn-up for the books.'

Fiona was not hurt because she had never had any illusions about being brighter than she was. In any case, he was implying, wasn't he, that she was good-looking? She managed to laugh. She understood that Henry could not always help being rather difficult. It was the penalty someone like him paid for his gifts of brilliance. In some ways intellectual prowess was a burden to carry through life.

'We'll have a heated pool, a decent-size one with a deep end,' Henry said, 'and I'll teach you to swim.'

The driving lessons had ended in failure. If it had been anyone else but Henry instructing her, Fiona would have said he was a harsh and intolerant teacher. Of course she knew how inept she was. She could not learn how to manage the gears and she was afraid of the traffic.

'I'm afraid of the water,' she confessed.

'It's a disgrace,' he said as if she had not spoken, 'a woman of thirty being unable to swim.' And then, when she only nodded doubtfully, 'Have you got *The Times* there?'


Building the pool took all the money the sale of Henry's father's house realised. It took rather more and Henry had to borrow from the bank. The pool had a roof over it and walls round, which were what cost the money. That and the sophisticated purifying system. It was eight feet deep at the deep end with a diving board and a chute.

Happily for Fiona, her swimming lessons were indefinitely postponed. Henry enjoyed his new pool so much that he would very much have grudged taking time off from swimming his lengths or practising his dives in order to teach his wife the basics.

Fiona guessed that Henry would be a brilliant swimmer. He was the perfect all-rounder. There was an expression in Latin which he had uttered and then translated for her which might have been, she thought, a description of himself: *mens sana in corpore sano*. Only for 'sana' or 'healthy' she substituted 'wonderful'. She would have liked to sit by the pool and watch him and she was rather sorry that his preferred swimming time was six-thirty in the morning, long before she was up.

One evening, while doing the crossword puzzle, he consulted her about a clue, as he sometimes did. 'Consulted' was not perhaps the word. It was more a matter of expressing his thoughts aloud and waiting for her comment. Fiona found these remarks, full of references to unknown classical or literary personages, nearly incomprehensible. She had heard, for instance, of Psyche but only in connection with 'psychological', 'psychiatric' and so on. Cupid to her was a fat baby with wings and she did not know this was another name for Eros, which to her was the statue.

'I'm afraid I don't understand at all,' she said humbly.

Henry loved elucidating. With a rare gesture of affection, he reached out and squeezed her hand. 'Psyche was married to Cupid who was, of course, a god, the god of love. He always came to her by night and she never saw his face. Suppose her husband was a terrible monster of ugliness and deformity? Against his express wishes –' here Henry fixed a look of some severity on his wife '– she rose up one night in the dark and, taking a lighted candle, approached the bed where Cupid lay. Scarcely had she caught a glimpse of his peerless beauty, when a drop of hot wax fell from the candle on to the god's naked skin. With a cry he sprang up and fled from the house. She never saw him again.

'Yes, well, she shouldn't have disobeyed him. Still, I don't see how that quite fits in here – wait a minute, yes, I do. Of course, that second syllable is an anagram on Eros . . .'

Henry inserted the letters in his net print. A covert glance told her he had completed nearly half the puzzle. She did her best to suppress a yawn. By this time of the evening she was always so tired she could scarcely keep awake while Henry could stay up for hours yet. People like him needed no more than four or five hours' sleep.

'I think I'll go up,' she said.

'Good night.' He added a kindly, 'darling.'

For some reason, Henry never did the crossword puzzle on a Saturday. Fiona thought this a pity because, as she said, that was the day they gave prizes for the first correct entries received. But Henry only smiled and said he did the puzzle for the pure intellectual pleasure of it, not for gain. Of course you might not know your entry was correct because the solution to Saturday's puzzle did not appear next day but not until a week later. Her saying this, perhaps naively, made Henry unexpectedly angry. Everyone knew that with this kind of puzzle, he said, there could only be one correct solution, even people who never did crosswords knew that.

It was still dark when Henry got up in the mornings. Sometimes she was aware of his departure and his empty half of the bed. Occasionally, half an hour later, she heard the boy come with the papers, the tap-tap of the letterbox and even the soft thump of *The Times* falling on to the mat. But most days she was aware of nothing until Henry reappeared with her tea and the papers.

Henry did nothing to make her feel guilty about lying in, yet she was ashamed of her inability to get up. It was somehow unlike him, it was out of character, this waiting on her. He never did anything of the kind at any other time of the day and it sometimes seemed to her that the unselfish effort he made must be almost intolerable to someone with his needle-sharp mind and – yes, it must be admitted – his undoubted lack of patience. That he never complained or even teased her about over-sleeping only added to her guilt.

Shopping in her lunch hour, she bought an alarm clock. They had never possessed such a thing, had never needed to, for Henry, as he often said, could direct himself to wake up at any hour he chose. Fiona put the alarm clock inside her bedside cabinet where it was invisible. It occurred to her, although she had as yet done nothing, she had not set the clock, that in failing to tell Henry about her purchase of the alarm she was deceiving him. This was the first time she had ever deceived him in anything and perhaps, as she reflected on this, it was inevitable that her thoughts should revert to Cupid and Psyche and the outcome of Psyche's equally innocent stratagem.

The alarm remained inside the cabinet. Every evening she thought of setting it, though she never did so. But the effect on her of this daily speculation and doubt was to wake her without benefit of mechanical aid. Thinking about it did the trick and Henry, in swimming trunks and towelling robe, had no sooner left their bedroom than she was wide awake. On the third morning this happened, instead of dozing off again until seven-thirty, she lay there for ten minutes and then got up.

Henry would be swimming his lengths. She heard the paper boy come, the letterbox make its double tap-tap and the newspapers fall on to the mat with a soft thump. Should she put on her own swimming costume or go down fully dressed? Finally, she compromised and got into the tracksuit that had never seen a track and scarcely the light of day before.

This morning it would be she who made Henry tea and took *him* the papers. However, when she reached the foot of the stairs there was no paper on the mat, only a brown envelope with a bill in it. She must have been mistaken and it was the postman she had heard. The time was just on seven, rather too soon perhaps for the papers to have arrived.

Fiona made her way to the swimming pool. When she saw Henry she would just wave airily to him. She might call out in a cheerful way, 'Carry on swimming!' or make some other humorous remark.

The glass door to the pool was slightly ajar. Fiona was barefoot. She pushed the door and entered silently. The cold chemical smell of chlorine irritated her nostrils. It was still dark outside, though dawn was coming, and the dark purplish-blue of a pre-sunrise sky shimmered through the glass panel in the ceiling. Henry was not in the pool but sitting in one of the cane chairs at the glass-topped table not two yards from her. Light from a ceiling spotlight fell directly on to the two newspapers in front of him, both folded with their back pages uppermost.

Fiona saw at once what he was doing. That was not the difficulty. From today's *Times* he was copying into yesterday's *Times* the answers to the crossword puzzle. She could see quite clearly that he was doing this but she could not for a moment believe it. It must be a joke or there must be some other purpose behind it.

When he turned round, swiftly covering both the newspapers with the *Radio Times*, she knew from his face that it was neither a joke nor the consequence of some mysterious purpose. He had turned quite white. He seemed unable to speak and she flinched from the panic that leapt in his eyes.

'I'll make us a cup of tea,' she said.

The wisest and kindest thing would be to forget what she had seen. She could not. In that split second when she had stood in the doorway of the pool watching him he had been changed for ever in her eyes. She thought about it on and off all day. It was impossible for her to concentrate on her work.

She never once thought that he had deceived her, only that she had caught him out. Like Psyche, she had held the candle over him and seen his true face. His was not the brilliant intellect she had thought. He could not even finish *The Times* crossword. Now she understood why he never attempted it on a Saturday, knowing there would be no opportunity next morning or on the Monday morning to fill in the answers from that day's paper. There were a lot of other truths that she saw about Henry. No one recognised his mind as first class because it wasn't first class. He had lost that excellent well-paid job because he was not intellectually up to it.

She knew all that and she loved him the more for it. Just as she had felt an almost maternal tenderness for him when he left the newspaper with its completed puzzle exposed for her to see, now she was overwhelmed with compassion for his weakness and his childlike vulnerability. She loved him more deeply than ever, and if admiration and respect had gone, what did those things matter, after all, in the tender intimacy of a good marriage?

That evening he did not touch the crossword puzzle. She had known he wouldn't and, of course, she said nothing. Neither of them had said a word about what she had seen that morning and neither of them ever would. Her feelings for him were completely changed, yet she believed her attitude could remain unaltered. But when, a few days later, he said something more about it being disgraceful that a woman of her age was unable to swim, instead of agreeing ruefully, she laughed and said, really, he shouldn't be so intolerant and censorious, no one was perfect.

He gave her a complicated explanation of some monetary question that was raised on the television news. It sounded wrong, he was confusing dollars with pounds, and she said so.

'Since when have you been an expert on the stock market?' he said.

Once she would have apologised. 'I'm no more an expert than you are, Henry,' she said, 'but I can use my eyes and that was plain to see. Don't you think we should both admit we don't know a thing about it?'

She no longer believed in the accuracy of his translations from the Latin nor the authenticity of his tales from the classics. When some friends who came for dinner were regaled with his favourite story about how she had been unable to learn to drive, she jumped up laughing and put her arm round his shoulder.

'Poor Henry gets into a rage so easily I was afraid he'd give himself a heart attack, so I stopped our lessons,' she said.

He never told that story again.

'Isn't it funny?' she said one Saturday on the golf course. 'I used to think it was wonderful you having a handicap of twenty-five. I didn't know any better.'

He made no answer.

'It's not really the best thing in a marriage for one partner to look up to the other too much, is it? Equality is best. I suppose it's natural to idolise the other one when you're first married. It just went on rather a long time for me, that's all.'

She was no longer in the least nervous about learning to swim. If he bullied her she would laugh at him. As a matter of fact, he wasn't all that good a swimmer himself. He couldn't do the crawl at all and a good many of his dives turned into belly-flops. She lay on the side of the pool, leaning on her elbows, watching him as he climbed out of the deep end up the steps.

'D'you know, Henry,' she said, 'you'll lose your marvellous figure if you aren't careful. You've got quite a spare tyre round your waist.'

His face was such a mask of tragedy, there was so much naked misery there, the eyes full of pain, that she checked the laughter that was bubbling up in her and said quickly, 'Oh, don't look so sad, poor darling. I'd still love you if you were as fat as a pudding and weighed twenty stone.'

He took two steps backwards down the steps, put up his hands and pulled her down into the pool. It happened so quickly and unexpectedly that she didn't resist. She gasped when the water hit her. It was eight feet deep here, she couldn't swim more than two or three strokes, and she made a grab for him, clutching at his upper arms.

He prised her fingers open and pushed her under the water. She tried to scream but the water came in and filled her throat. Desperately she thrashed about in the blue-greenness, the sickeningly chlorinated water, fighting, sinking, feeling for something to catch hold of, the bar round the pool rim, his arms, his feet on the steps. A foot kicked out at her, a foot stamped on her head. She stopped holding her breath, she had to, and the water poured into her lungs until the light behind her eyes turned red and her head was black inside. A great drum beat, boom, boom, boom, in the blackness, and then it stopped.

Henry waited to see if the body would float to the surface. He waited a long time but she remained, starfish-like, face-downwards, on the blue tiles eight feet down, so he left her and, wrapping himself in his towelling robe, went into the house. Whatever happened, whatever steps if any he decided to take next, he would do *The Times* crossword that evening. Or as much of it as he could ever do.

# The Carer

The house and the people were new to her. They had given her a key, as most did. Angela had a cat to feed and a rubber plant to water. These tasks done, she went upstairs, feeling excited, and into the bedroom where she supposed they slept.

They had left it very tidy, the bed made with the covers drawn tight, everything on the dressing table neatly arranged. She opened the cupboards and had a look at their clothes. Then she examined the contents of the dressing-table drawers. A box of jewellery, scarves, handkerchiefs that no one used any more. Another drawer was full of face creams and cosmetics. In the last one was a bundle of letters, tied up with pink ribbon. Angela untied the ribbon and read the letters which were from Nigel to Maria, the people who lived here, love letters written before they were married and full of endearments, pet names and promises of what he would do to her next time they met and how he expected she would respond.

She read them again before tying the ribbon round them and putting them back. Letters were a treat, she rarely came upon any in her explorations of other people's houses. Letters, like so many other things, had gone out of fashion. She went downstairs again, repeating under her breath some of the phrases Nigel had written and savouring them.

In the street where she lived Angela was much in demand as baby-sitter, dog-walker cat-feeder and general carer. Her clients, as she called them, thought her absolutely reliable and trustworthy. No one had ever suspected that she explored their houses while alone in them. After all, it had never occurred to Peter and Louise to place hairs across drawer handles; Elizabeth would hardly have known how to examine objects for fingerprints; Miriam and George were not observant people. Besides, they trusted her.

Angela lived alone in the house that had been her parents' and spent one weekend a month staying with her aunt in the Cotswolds, and while there she went to the Methodist church on Sunday. She had a job in the bank half a mile away. Once a year she and another single woman she had met at work went to Torquay or Bournemouth for a fortnight's holiday. She had never been out with a man, she never met any men except the ones in the street, who were married or living with a partner. She had no real friends. She knitted, she read a lot, she slept ten hours a night.

Sometimes she asked herself how she had come to this way of living, why her life had not followed the pattern of other women's, why it had been without adventure or even event, but she could only answer that this was the way it had happened. Gradually it had happened without her seeing an alternative or knowing how to stop its inexorable progress to what it had become. Until, that is, Humphrey asked her to feed the cat while he was away and from that beginning she built up her business.

She had keys to eleven houses. Caring for them, their owners' children, elderly parents, pets and plants, had become her only paid employment for, thankful to do so at last, she had given up her job. At first, performing these tasks punctually and efficiently had been enough; the gratitude she received and the payment. She liked her neighbours' dependence on her. She had become indispensable and that gave her pleasure. But after a time she had grown restless, sitting in John and Julia's living room with a sleeping baby upstairs; she had felt frustrated as she locked Humphrey's door and went home after feeding the cat. There should be something more, though more what? One night, when Diana's baby cried and she had been in to quieten it, her footsteps, as if independently of her will, took her along the passage into its parents' bedroom. And so it began.

The contents of cupboards and drawers, the bank statements and bills, Louise's diary that was her most prized find, Ken's certificates, Miriam's diplomas, Peter's prospectuses, Diana's holiday snapshots, all this showed her what life was. That it was the life of other people and not hers did not much trouble her. It educated her. Searching for it, finding new aspects of it, additions to what had been examined and learned before, was something to look forward to. There had not been much looking forward in her existence, or much looking back, come to that.

The neighbour who had written the love letters had recently moved into the house four doors down. She was recommended to him and his wife by Rose and Ken next door.

'If you'd like to let me have a key,' Angela had said. 'It will be quite safe with me.' She made the little joke she always made. 'I keep all the keys under lock and key.'

'We're away quite a lot,' said Maria, and Nigel said, 'It would be a load off our minds if we could rely on you to feed Absalom.'

When her business first started Angela conducted her investigations of someone else's property only when legitimately there with a duty to perform. But after a while she became bolder and entered a house whenever the fancy took her. She would watch to see when her neighbours went out. Most of them were out at work all day anyway. It was true that all the keys were kept locked up. They were in a strongbox, each one labelled. Angela always asked for the back door key. She said it was more convenient if there was a pet to be fed and perhaps exercised. What she didn't say was that you were less likely to be seen entering a house by the back door than the front.

The principal bedroom at Nigel and Maria's had been thoroughly explored on her first visit. But only that one bedroom. Once, greedy for sensation, during a single two-hour duty at John and Julia's she had searched every room, but since then she had learned restraint. It was something to dread, that the treasures in all the houses she had keys to might become exhausted, every secret laid bare, her goldmines overworked and left barren. So she had left the desk in Maria's living room for another time, though it had been almost more than she could bear, seeing it there, virgin so to speak, inviolate. She had left the desk untouched and all the cupboards and filing cabinets unplundered in the study they had made out of the third bedroom.

Maria went away one evening. Nigel told Angela she had gone and he would be joining her in a day or two. She noticed he stayed away from work and she waited for him to call and ask her to feed Absalom in his absence. He never came. Angela was much occupied with child-sitting for Peter and Louise, driving Elizabeth's mother to the hospital, letting in the meter man and the plumber for Miriam and George and taking Humphrey's cat to the vet, but she had time to wonder why he hadn't asked.

Returning home from watering Julia's peperomias, she met Nigel unlocking his car. He had Absalom with him in a wicker basket.

'Going away tonight?' Angela said hopefully.

'I shall be joining Maria. We thought we'd try taking Absalom with us this time, so we shan't require your kind services. But I expect you've plenty to do, haven't you?' Thinking of the evening ahead, Angela said she had. She was almost as excited as on the day she began reading Louise's diary.

Angela gave it an hour after Nigel's car had gone. She took the key out of the strongbox and let herself into the house. A happy two hours were spent in a search of the desk, and although it uncovered no more love letters, it did disclose several final demands for payment of bills, an angry note from George complaining about Absalom's behaviour in his garden and, best of all, an anonymous letter.

This letter was printed in ink and suggested that Maria had been having an affair with someone called William. Angela thought about this and wondered what it would be like, having an affair when you were married that is, and she wondered what being married was like anyway, and whether it was William's wife or girlfriend who had written the letter. She put everything back in the desk just as she had found it, being careful not to tidy up.

The rooms upstairs she left for the next day. It was a Friday and she was due to drive to Auntie Joan's for the weekend that evening, but first she had Elizabeth's dog to walk morning and afternoon and Elizabeth's mother to fetch from the hospital, the electrician to let in for Rose and Ken and Louise's little girl to meet from school. There were two hours to spare between coming back from the hospital and fetching Alexandra. Taking care not to be seen by the electrician, putting in a new point next door in the back room, Angela let herself into Nigel and Maria's house.

Overnight, she had felt rather nervous about that desk and the first thing she did was check that everything was back in place. An examination quickly reassured her that she had accurately replicated their untidiness. Then she went upstairs and along the passage to the study. Louise's diary notwithstanding, Maria and Nigel's house promised to afford her the richest seam of treasure she had yet encountered. And who knew what would be behind this door in the cupboards and the filing cabinets? More love letters, perhaps, hers to him this time, more insinuations of Maria's infidelity, more unpaid bills, even something pointing to illegality or crime.

Angela opened the door. She took a step into the room, then a step backwards, uttering a small scream she would have suppressed if she could. Maria lay on the floor, wearing a nightdress, her long hair loose and spread out. There was a large brown stain that must be blood on the front of her nightdress and unmistakable blood on the floor around her. Angela stood still for what seemed a very long time, holding her hand over her mouth. She forced herself to advance upon Maria and touch her. It was her forehead she touched, white as marble. Her fingertip encountered icy coldness and she pulled it away with a shudder. Maria's dead eyes looked at her, round and blue like marbles.

Angela went quickly downstairs. She was trembling all over. She let herself out of the back door, locked the door and put the key through the letterbox at the front. It somehow seemed essential to her not to have that key in her possession.

She went home and packed a bag, found her car keys. Fetching Alexandra was forgotten and so were Elixabeth's dogs. Angela got into her car and drove off northwards, exceeding the speed limit within the first five minutes. She thought she would stay at least a fortnight with Auntie Joan. Perhaps she would never come back at all. If this was life they could keep it. It was death too.

# Expectations

No varnish can hide the grain of the wood, as my cousin Matthew once said of my late husband, adding that no man who was not a true gentleman at heart ever was a true gentleman in manner. George, however, succeeded in passing himself off as well-born and well-educated and in his last years only his wife and daughter knew the real man behind the smile and the black clothes and those snow-white pocket handkerchiefs. I and Estella alone knew the criminality hidden under the mellifluous speech-making and verse-quoting and his handsome looks.

But a gentleman who is upright and admirable is not found stabbed to death on Epsom Racecourse as George was three weeks ago. A man as virtuous as some of his acquaintance believed him to be does not leave on his death a contented widow and a joyful daughter. The truth is that, shocked as I was when the news of his murder was brought to me, I was also relieved. These twenty years gone by have sometimes been almost intolerable – though what course is there for a woman but to tolerate? – and George's death, horrible though the circumstances of it were, lifted the load from my shoulders in the twinkling of an eye.

His grave is in our village churchyard. Living in London, I missed the countryside and longed to go back. The brewery and all the property of course became George's on our marriage. I only deceive myself if I deny that it was to possess them that George married me but I am glad he kept Satis House, in spite of disliking it so thoroughly. I have returned to it and am about to take my place in county society with my daughter who comes out in a year's time. By then my mourning will be over and I shall give a ball for her. There will be some hearts broken when the young blades thereabouts set eyes on Estella. Her very name means a star. I always vowed that if I had a girl she should be called Estella, and George for once put up no opposition. He, of course, wanted a son.

She is far more beautiful than I ever was. She is tall like her father and has his dark curly hair. It is extraordinary to me now the effect he had upon me when Arthur brought him home to meet me all those years ago. I fell in love with him that first evening. But even then, blind as I was to everything but George's beauty and George's grace, I retained sense enough to wonder why my half-sibling – I will not dignify Arthur with the name of brother – was so desirous that his friend should like me and I return that particular regard.

Arthur was envious because our father left the greater part of his property to me, his elder child. Perhaps I should have reminded him more often that his riotous and undutiful behaviour almost secured his disinheritance. It was only on his death bed that Papa relented and left him a share in the brewery. But that and the income which come with it was insufficient for Arthur, as I soon understood, though it was not until just before my marriage that I knew of the conspiracy got up between him and George.

Should I have refused George money? Would a prudent young woman have refused? I was so afraid to lose him. Of course I had suitors enough, but I wanted none of them. I wanted George. And the truth of what he said to me was undeniable.

'Why not a thousand pounds now, my dearest, bearing in mind that it will all be mine once we are married? Mine to husband for you and watch over diligently when you are my wife?'

So I agreed. Then, and again and again.

Three weeks before our wedding George was staying in the house and one night, unable to sleep, I came downstairs to find myself a book from the library. They were inside, Arthur and George, sitting over the dying fire with, no doubt, the brandy bottle. The door was a little ajar and I heard their voices.

I had been so certain they would have retired by now that I had come down in my nightgown with only a shawl thrown about me. So I paused at the door, uncertain of what to do next.

Then I heard Arthur say, 'She shall have my share of the brewery, my boy, but I'll want a great sum for it, so mind you tell her not to jib at the price.'

George laughed. 'I'm likely to do that, am I? What, when you and I are dividing the sum between us?'

The man I had been used to call my brother said, 'You'll be off then, Compeyson, will you?'

'Don't speak so loud.' George's voice was almost too low for me to hear. 'The long and the short of it is that I'll only marry her if she won't buy you out. But she will, she will. Why, she's so much in love she'd follow me to the ends of the earth in her petticoat.'

It was true. But I trembled as I stood there, drawing the ends of the shawl about me, returning to bed slowly, moving like a sleepwalker. There was no sleep for me that night. I had no one to advise me, though I knew, ignorant as I was, what advice the wise would give. But I loved him. In spite of his treachery, I love him. I saw the grain through the varnish but still I loved him.

Next day and the next and the next George pleaded with me. When he was my husband, he said, it was only fitting that he should hold the brewery and manage it all. For a while I played the same game as he played. I asked Arthur's price and pretended to be appalled at the sum. I counted the days to our wedding day, nineteen days, then eighteen days. My clothes were bought, I had had three fittings for my wedding gown. George said all that would be needful was for me to sign a paper he would bring me.

Over the first paper I succeeded in spilling ink. Fifteen days, fourteen. I sent to the town for an attorney. He came and looked at the paper, he took it away with him and the days passed, thirteen, twelve, eleven, but he returned with the paper and pronounced it a legal document. There was no obstacle to my signing it. Except myself. I took my courage in my hands and told George I would be happiest to have *him* buy Arthur out, that I was a mere woman and unfit for business. Once we were married he would have an ample sum with which to purchase Arthur's share.

That was six days before the wedding. George was gone and I saw and heard nothing of him. I had no sleep, I could scarcely rest. But the wedding dress was finished and the bride-cake made and at last the day of my marriage came. Arthur was to give me away but I heard nothing of Arthur. George was to be my husband and I had received no sign from him for a week.

It was twenty minutes to nine in the morning and I was seated at my dressing table in front of a gilded looking glass. My maid had dressed me in satin and lace, all white, and put bridal flowers in my hair and Mama's diamonds about my neck. Half-packed trunks stood about the room. I remember the moment when the note came. My veil was but half arranged, and I had but one shoe on, the other being on the table near my hand with trinkets and gloves and a Prayer Book and some flowers, all confusedly heaped about the looking glass.

My maid came in and put the note into my hand. Time and the whole world seemed to stop and I thought, if this letter tells me he is gone time shall indeed stop and I will remain for ever in this moment.

I will wear this dress for the rest of my life, with one shoe off and one on, until my hair is white and my skin is yellow. The feast shall remain spread until dust covers it and the bride-cake be a nest for spiders to veil with their webs.

I opened George's letter. 'My dearest,' he wrote, and he went on to say he loved me, he had been unavoidably absent these past days but he would be awaiting me in the church. I let my maid arrange my veil, I put on my shoe, the rings on my fingers and then the gloves. I took up the flowers and the Prayer Book and descended the stairs to meet Arthur at the foot and have him take me to be married.

Love was faded within the year. The varnish was striped away and I saw only the grain, but yet I was married, I was Mrs George Compeyson with the dignity of a wife. I had my child to watch grow in health and beauty. Satis House, the name that means a sufficiency, awaited me for my widowhood, and they used to say, when the name was given, that whoever had that house could want nothing else. Enough of my fortune remains after George's depredations for me to live in comfort and give Estella twenty thousand pounds on her marriage.

If I sometimes feel a little low and see myself growing old, my life wasted, I go into that room that was once my bedchamber and sit at the dressing table. There, staring into the looking glass, I tell myself to be thankful for what I did and what I did not do, for a year of love and a lovely child, and that I am not still in that white dress and veil, one shoe off and one shoe on, doomed to be for ever Miss Havisham.

# Clothes

'I'd like this, please.'

She had put the dress down on the counter. The look the assistant gave her was slightly apprehensive. Alison had sounded breathless, she had sounded elated. Now that it was too late she restrained herself.

'How would you like to pay?'

Instead of answering, she laid the credit card on the counter where the dress was now being folded, amid layers of tissue paper. The bill came waving out of the machine and she signed in the too-small space on the right-hand side. At this point, and it was always the same, she couldn't wait to get away. Lingering, chatting to the assistant – 'You'll get a lot of wear out of this one', 'Enjoy wearing it'– embarrassed her. She felt as if she was there on false pretences or as if her secret self must inevitably be revealed. She walked off quickly and she was happy, she felt the familiar buzz, the swing of light-headedness, the rush of adrenalin. She had made her day, she had bought something.

Once outside, she took the dress out of the bag and put it into her briefcase, along with the outline plans for the Grimwood project. That way the people in the office would not know what she had been doing. The carrier went into a litter bin and the bill with it. A taxi came and she got into it. Already the level of excitement had begun to flag. By the time she walked into the PR consultancy of which she was chief executive none of it was left. She smiled and told her assistant lunch had gone on longer than expected.

On the way home she bought something else. She didn't mean to. But that went without saying, for she scarcely ever did mean to. It was where she lived, she sometimes thought, the dangerous place she lived in, Knightsbridge, shopping country. If she and Gil moved, out into the sticks, some distant suburb . . . She knew they wouldn't.

She should have had a taxi to her doorstep, not used the tube. Some of it was the fault of the dress, for now she knew she disliked the dress, the colour, the cut, she would never wear it, and the amount she had spent on it printed itself on her mind in black letters. The elation it had brought her had turned to panic. Absurdly, she had taken the tube to save money, because it cost ninety pence and a taxi would have been five pounds. But it gave her a half-mile walk down Sloane Street. At six, on late-closing night.

Sometimes Alison thought of the things she might have done at leisure in London. Gone to the National Gallery, the Wallace Collection, walked in the parks, joined the London Library. She had heard the Museum of the Moving Image was wonderful. Instead she went shopping. She bought things. Well, she bought clothes. Halfway down the long street of shops, her eye was caught by a sweater in a window. The feeling was familiar, the faint breathlessness, the drying mouth, the words repeated in her head – she must have it, she must have it. On these occasions she seemed to see the future so clearly. She seemed to live in advance the regret she would feel if she didn't have the thing, whatever it was. The remorse experienced when she *did* have it was forgotten.

The knob on the shop door was a heavy glass ball, set in brass. She closed her hand over the knob. She paused. But that was not unusual. Hesitating on the doorstep, she told herself she was buying this sweater because she had made a mistake with the dress. She didn't like the dress but the sweater would make up for that. She turned the knob and the door came open. Inside, a woman sat at a gilded table with a marble top. She lifted her head, smiled at Alison and said, 'Hi.' Alison knew the woman wouldn't get up and come over and start showing her things, it wasn't that kind of shop, and Alison knew about shops. She went to the rail where the sweater and its fellows hung. The fever was already upon her and reason gone. This feeling was like a combination of sexual excitement and the effect of one strong drink. When it had her in its clutch she stopped thinking, or rather, she thought only of the garment before her; how it would look on her, where she would wear it and when, how possessing it would change her life for the better.

Shopping had to be done in a rush. That was part of the whole character of it. Do it fast and do it impulsively. The blood beat in her head. She took the sweater off its hanger, held it up against herself.

The woman said, 'Would you like to try it on?'

'I'll have it,' Alison said. She took an identical sweater off the rail, but in a darker shade. 'In fact, I'll have both.' She responded to the assistant's smile with a radiant smile of her own.

When she had paid and was outside the shop once more, she looked at her watch and saw that the whole transaction had taken seven minutes. The two sweaters were too bulky to go in the briefcase, so she took out the dress and put it in the black shiny white-lettered bag with her new purchases. She began to think of how she was going to get into the flat without Gil seeing she had been shopping.

He might not be home yet. Sometimes he came in first, sometimes she did. If he was home she might be able to get into the bedroom and hide the bag before he saw. If the worst came to the worst and he saw the bag he would suppose there was only one garment inside it, not three. The buzz was easing up, the adrenalin was being absorbed, and she understood something else; that this was the first time she had bought something without trying it on first.

The glass doors opened for her and she walked in. She went up in the lift. Her key slipped into the lock and turned and the front door opened. It was impossible to tell if he was there or not. She called out, 'Gil?' and his voice answering from the kitchen, 'I'm in here,' made her jump. She ran into the bedroom and thrust the bag into the back of the clothes cupboard.

It was his evening to cook. She had forgotten. When she was shopping she forgot everything else. She went into the kitchen and put her arms round him and kissed him. He was wearing an apron and holding a wooden spoon.

'Tell me,' he said. 'Do you actually like dried tomatoes?'

'Dried tomatoes? I've never thought about it. Well, no, I don't suppose I do really.'

'No one does. That's my great culinary discovery of the week. No one does but they pretend to, like they do about green peppers.'

He enlarged on this. Gil produced a cookery programme for television and he began telling her about a soufflé that kept going wrong. At the fourth attempt the star of the programme, a temperamental man, had picked up and upended the spoiled soufflé over the head of one of the camera crew. Alison listened and laughed in the right places and told him about the latest developments in the Grimwood account. He said he'd give her a shout when the food was ready and she went away into the bedroom to change.

Every evening, if they weren't going out, she changed into jeans or tracksuit pants and a sweatshirt. The irony was that these were old, she had had them for years, while the cupboard groaned under the weight of new clothes. There was barely room for the new dress and the sweaters to squeeze in. When would she wear any of them? Perhaps never. Perhaps, unworn, they would join the stack that must soon be packed into her largest suitcase and be taken to the hospice shop.

They loved her in the hospice shop. They called her Alison, they knew her so well. 'What lovely clothes you always bring us, Alison,' and 'You have quite a turnover in clothes, Alison – well, you must have in your job.' They could probably run the hospice for a week on what they raised by the sale of her clothes.

It was an addiction, it was like alcoholism or drugs or gambling, and more expensive than drinking or the fruit machines. Last week, when she was coming in with a bright yellow bag and an olive-green bag, Gil had caught her in the hall. Caught her. She had used the words inadvertently, without thinking, and inaccurately. For Gil was the kindest and best of men, he would never never reproach her. The worst thing was that he would *praise* her. He would tell her it was her money, she earned more than he did anyway, she could do what she liked with it. Why shouldn't she buy herself some new clothes?

She had imagined telling him then, when they came face to face and she had those bags in her hands. She imagined confessing, saying to him, I've something to tell you. His face would change, he would think what everyone thought when they heard those words from their partner. She would sit on the floor at his feet – all this she imagined, building an absurd scenario – and hold his hand and tell him, I do this, I am mad, it's driving me mad, and I can't stop. I keep buying clothes. Not jewellery or ornaments or furniture or pictures, not stuff to put on my face or my hair, not even shoes or hats or gloves. I buy clothes. A dress shop is a wine bar to me. It is my casino. I can't pass it. If I go into a department store to buy a box of tissues or a bathmat, I go upstairs, I buy clothes.

He would laugh. He would be happy and relieved because she was telling him she liked buying things to wear, not that she'd met someone else and was leaving him. Kisses then and reassurances and a heartening, why shouldn't you spend your own money? He, who was so understanding, wouldn't understand this.

His voice called out, 'Alison! It's ready.'

They were to have a glass of wine first. This wine had been much praised on the programme and he wanted her to try it. He raised his glass to her. 'Do you know what today is?'

Some anniversary. It was women who were supposed to remember these things, not men. 'Should I? Oh, dear.'

'Not the first time we met,' he said. 'Not even the first time you took me out to dinner. The first time I took you out. Three years ago today.'

She put into the words all the emotion with which her thoughts had charged her. 'I love you.'

Gil scarcely knew what clothes she possessed. He never looked in her cupboard. Sometimes, when she wore one of the new dresses or suits or shirts, he would say, 'I like that. It's new, isn't it?'

'I've had it for ages. You must have seen it before.'

And he accepted that. He didn't notice clothes much, he wasn't interested. But when he asked, she should have told him. Or when the credit card statements came in. Instead of paying the huge sums secretly, she should have said, 'Look at this. This is what I do with my money. This is my madness and you must stop me.'

She couldn't. She was too ashamed. She even wondered what the credit card people must think of her when month after month they assessed her expenditure and found another thousand pounds gone on clothes. The shop assistants wrote 'clothes' in the space on the chit and she had once thought, stupidly, of asking them to put 'goods' instead. It was because of what she was that the humiliation was so intense, because she was clever and accomplished with a good degree and a dazzling CV, at the top of her profession, sought-after, able to ask fees that raised eyebrows but seldom deterred. And her addiction was the kind that afflicted the football pools winners or sixteen-year-old school-leavers.

They were better than she. At least they were honest and open about it. Some could be frank and admit it, even make a joke of it. A few months back she had travelled to Edinburgh with a client to make a product presentation. They had stayed overnight. Edinburgh is not a place that immediately comes to mind as a shopping centre, while there are many other interesting things to do there, but the client announced as soon as they got into the station taxi that she would like to spend the two hours they had to spare at the shops.

'I'm a compulsive shopper, you know. It's what gives me a buzz.'

Alison had said restrainedly, 'What did you want to buy?'

'Buy? Oh, I don't know. I'll know when I see it.'

So Alison had gone shopping with her and seen all the signs and symptoms that she saw in herself, but with one exception. This woman was not ashamed, she was not deceitful.

'I'm crazy, really,' she said when she had bought a suit she confessed she 'didn't like all that much'. 'I've got wardrobes full of stuff I never wear.' And she laughed merrily. 'I suppose you plan everything you buy terribly carefully, don't you?'

And Alison, who had stood by while the suit was bought, sick with desire to buy herself, controlling herself with all her might, wearing what she now feared had been a supercilious half-smile, agreed that this was so. She smiled like a superior being, one who bought clothes when the old ones wore out.

On that trip she had managed to avoid buying anything. The energy expended in denial had left her exhausted. In London afterwards she went on a dreadful splurge, like the bulimic's binge. It was that day, or the day after, she had read the piece in the paper about compulsive behaviour. Eating disorders, for instance, indicated some deep-seated emotional disturbance. It was the same with gambling, even with shopping. The compulsive shopper buys as a way of masking a need for love and to cover up inadequacy.

It wasn't true. She loved Gil. She had everything she wanted. Her life was good and satisfying. The compulsion to buy had only begun when she realised she was rich, she had more than enough, she could afford it now. Only she couldn't, hardly anyone could. Hardly anyone's income could stand this drain on it.

Compulsive shopping was a cry for help. That was what the psychologists said. But help for what? To stop compulsive shopping?


Passing the shop where she had bought the sweaters – in a taxi, for safety's sake – she reflected on something she had thought of only momentarily at the time. She had bought the sweaters without trying them on. It was as if she was saying, I don't care if they fit or not, that is not why I am buying them, I want to *buy*, not to have.

The office was in the City, in a part where there were few shops. This, of course, was a blessing, yet she had recognised lately her dissatisfaction with the absence of clothes shops, the peculiar kind of *hunger* this lack brought her. Once she was outside in the street, an almost overwhelming impulse came to get in a taxi and be taken to where the shops were. She managed to resist. She had work to do, she had to be at her desk, near those phones, beside that fax machine. But as the days passed, the shop-less days, she began to think, it will be all right for me to go shopping next time I have the opportunity, it won't be sick, it won't be neurotic, because it has been so long, it has been a whole week . . .

There was an evening when it rained and she couldn't find a taxi. Again she took the tube and at Knightsbridge looked for a taxi to take her that half-mile. It was quite possible to walk home by residential streets, there were many options, and it was one of the most charming parts of London. Even in the rain. But compulsive shopping began before she came to the shops, she had learnt that now, it was what led her steps to Sloane Street when she might so easily have taken Seville Street and Lowndes Square.

Her thoughts were strange. She recognised them as strange. Mad, perhaps. She was thinking that if she controlled herself this evening, she would not have to do so on the following day. Next day, after the client conference, she would find herself in Piccadilly, at the bottom of Bond Street, and if she walked up towards the tube station, her route would take her along Brook Street and into South Molton Street, into one of the Meccas of shopping, into heaven, buying country, shopland.

She passed the shop with the globular glass door knob and as she came to the next, already able to see ahead of her the gleam of a single shimmering garment isolated in its window, footsteps came running behind her and Gil's arm was round her, his umbrella held high over her head.

'You ought to buy that,' he said. 'You'd look good in that.'

She shuddered. He felt the shudder and looked at her in concern.

'A designer walked over my grave,' she said.

It was the time to say she wouldn't buy the dress and tell him why not. She couldn't do it. All she felt was resentment that he had caught up with her and, by his presence and his kind, innocent suggestion, stopped her buying it. He was like the well-intentioned friend who offers the secret drinker a double scotch.

In the morning she went in late, walking up Sloane Street. There was nothing to do before the conference. She went into the shop and bought the dress Gil had said would look good on her. She didn't try it on but told the surprised assistant it was her size, she knew it would fit. High on adrenalin, she told herself this purchase need not stop her buying later in the day. The day was gone anyway, she thought, it was spoiled by buying the dress and there was no point in taking a stand today, a preliminary shot of the drug had gone in. If control was possible it could start tomorrow. In the office she took the dress out of her briefcase and stuffed it in a desk drawer.

The conference was over by three. For the past hour or more she had scarcely been attending. Once her own talk was over she lost interest and let her thoughts run in the direction they always did these days. Even during the talk she once or twice lost the thread of what she was saying, needed to refer to her notes, seemed to fumble with words. The company chairman asked her if she was feeling unwell.

Sitting down again, taking a drink of water, she looked ahead of her to the great thoroughfare of shops waiting for her, full of things waiting to be bought, sitting there and waiting, and a huge longing took hold of her. She almost ran out of that building, she was breathless and she was thirsty, as if she had never taken a drink of that water.

On her way up Bond Street she bought a suit and a jacket. She tried both on but it was only for form's sake and because she cringed under the shop assistant's surprised look.

A taxi came as if to rescue her while she walked onwards and upwards, carrying her bags, but she let it pass by and turned into Brook Street. By this time, at this *stage* of her indulgence, her feet seemed to lose contact with the ground. She floated or skimmed the surface of the pavement. In the road she was always in danger of being run over. If she had met someone she knew she would have passed him by unseeing. Her body had undergone chemical changes which had a profound effect on recognition, on logical thought, on rational behaviour. They negated reason. She was unable to control the urge to buy because for these moments, this hour perhaps, she rejected a 'cure', she wanted her compulsion, she loved it, she was drunk on it.

Thoughts she had, words in her head, but they were always simple and direct. Why shouldn't I have these things? I can afford them. Why shouldn't I be well-dressed? I mustn't be guilty about this simple, enjoyable, *happy* pastime . . . They repeated themselves in her mind as she floated along, aware too of her steadily beating heart.

In South Molton Street she bought a shirt and in the shop next door a skirt with a sweater that matched it. She tried neither on and when she was outside something made her look at the label on the skirt and sweater, which showed her she had bought them two sizes too big. She stood there, in the street, feeling elation drop, knowing she couldn't go back in there.

She was ashamed. The fall was very swift from reckless excitement to a kind of visionary horror, it slid off her like oversize clothes slipping from her shoulders to the floor, and there came a sudden flash of appalled insight. She began to walk mechanically. Nearly at Oxford Street, she put the new clothes bags into the first rubbish bin she came to. Then she put the suit and the jacket in too. She turned her back and ran.

In the taxi she was crying. The taxi driver said, 'Are you OK, love?' She said she wasn't well, she would be all right in a minute. The waste, the wickedness of such waste, were what she thought of. There were thousands, millions, who never had new clothes, who wore hand-me-

301

downs or rags or just managed to buy secondhand. She had thrown away new clothes.

For some reason she thought of Gil, who trusted and loved her. She couldn't face him again, she would have to go to some hotel for the night. By a tortuous route the taxi was winding through streets behind Broadcasting House, behind Langham Place. It came down into Regent Street and she told the driver to let her off. He didn't like that and she gave him a five-pound note. What was five pounds? She had just thrown away two hundred times that.

Carrying only her briefcase, she went into a department store. She caught sight of herself in a mirror, her wild hair, her staring eyes, the whiteness of her face: a madwoman. Something else struck her, as she paused there briefly. She wasn't well-dressed, almost any woman she passed was better-dressed than she was. Every week, nearly every day, she bought clothes, mountains of clothes, cupboards-full, clothes to be unloaded on charities or thrown away unworn, but she was dressed less well than a woman who bought what she wore out of the money a husband gave her for housekeeping.

She hated clothes. Understanding came in migraine-like flashes of light and darkness. Why had she never realised how she hated clothes? They made her feel sick, the new, slightly bitter smell of them, their sinuous slithering pressures on her, surrounding her as they now did, rails of coats and jackets, suits and dresses. She was in designer country and she could smell and feel, but she saw very little. Her eyes were affected by her mental state and a mist hung in front of them.

Fumbling, she began to slide clothes off the rail, a shirt here, a sweater there. She opened her briefcase and stuffed the things inside. A label hung out and part of a sleeve when she closed the case. She snatched a knitted garment, long and sleeveless and buttoned, and a blouse of stiff organza, another sweater, another shirt. No one saw her, or if they did they made no attempt to intervene.

She pulled a scarf from a shelf and wound it round her neck. Pulling at the ends, she thought how good it would be to lose consciousness, for the scarf quietly to strangle her. With her overflowing briefcase, too full to close, she began to walk down the stairs. No one came after her. No one had seen. On her way through leather goods she picked up a handbag, though it was unusual for her to be attracted by such things, then a wallet and a pair of gloves. She held them in one hand, while the other held the briefcase, the bigger garments over her arm.

Between the inner glass doors and the entrance doors a bell began ringing urgently. The security officer approached. She sat down on the floor with all the stolen things around her and when he came up to her, she said quite sanely, though with a break in her voice, 'Help me, someone help me.'

# Unacceptable Levels

'Y ou shouldn't scratch it. You've made it bleed.'
'It itches. It's giving me hell. You don't react to mosquito bites the way I do.'

'It's just where the belt on your jeans rubs. I think I'd better put a plaster on it.'

'They're in the bathroom cabinet,' he said.

'I know where they are.'

She removed the plaster from its plastic packing and applied it to the small of his back. He reached for his cigarettes, put one in his mouth and lit it.

'I wonder if you're allergic to mosquito bites,' she said. 'I mean, I wonder if you should be taking anti-histamine when you get bitten. You know, you should try one of those sprays that ease the itching.'

'They don't do any good.'

'How do you know, if you don't try? I don't suppose smoking helps. Oh, yes, I know that sounds ridiculous to you, but smoking does affect your general health. I bet you didn't tell the doctor you had all these allergies when you were examined for that life insurance you took out.'

'What do you mean, "all these allergies"? I don't have allergies. I have rather a strong reaction to mosquito bites.'

'I bet you didn't tell them you smoked,' she said.

'Of course I told them. You don't mess about when you're taking out a hundred thousand pounds' worth of insurance on your life.' He lit a cigarette from the stub of the last one. 'Why d'you think I pay such high premiums?'

'I bet you didn't tell them you smoked forty a day.'

'I said I was afraid I was a heavy smoker.'

'You ought to give it up,' she said. 'Mind you, I'd like a thousand pounds for every time I've said that. I'd like a *pound*. You smokers don't know what it's like living with it. You don't know how you smell, your clothes, your hands, the lot. It gets in the curtains. You may laugh but it's no joke.'

'I'm going to bed,' he said.

In the morning she had a shower and washed her hair. She made a cup of tea and brought it up to him. He stayed in bed smoking while he drank his tea. Then he had a shower.

'And wash your hair,' she said. 'It stinks of smoke.'

He came back into the bedroom with a towel round him. 'The plaster came off.'

'I expect it did. I'll put another one on.'

She took another plaster out of its pack.

'Did I make it bleed?'

'Of course you make it bleed when you scratch it. Here, keep still.'

'You'd think it would stop itching after a couple of days, wouldn't you?'

'I told you, you should have used an anti-allergenic spray. You should have taken anti-histamine. You've got a very nasty sore place there and you're going to have to keep it covered for at least another forty-eight hours.'

'Anything you say.'

He lit a cigarette.

In the evening they ate their meal outdoors. It was very warm. He smoked to keep the mosquitos away.

'Any excuse,' she said.

'One of those little buggers has just bitten me in the armpit.'

'Oh, for God's sake. Just don't scratch this one.'

'Do you really think I should have told the insurance people I'm allergic to mosquito bites?'

'I don't suppose it matters,' she said. 'I mean, how could anyone tell after you were dead?'

'Thanks very much,' he said.

'Oh, don't be silly. You're much more likely to die of smoking than of a mosquito bite.'

Before they went to bed she renewed the plaster on his back and, because he had scratched the new bite, gave him another. He could put that one on himself. He had to get up in the night, the bites drove him mad and he couldn't just lie there. He walked about the house, smoking. In the morning he told her he didn't feel well.

'I don't suppose you do if you didn't get any sleep.'

'I found a packet of nicotine patches in the kitchen,' he said. 'Nicorella or something. I suppose that's your latest ploy to stop me smoking.'

She said nothing for a moment. Then, 'Are you going to give it a go, then?'

'No, thanks very much. You've wasted your money. D'you know what it says in the instructions? "While using the patches it is highly dangerous to smoke." How about that?'

'Well, of course it is.'

'Why is it?'

'You could have a heart attack. It would put unacceptable levels of nicotine into your blood.'

'"Unacceptable levels" – you sound like a health minister on telly.'

'The idea,' she said, 'is to stop smoking while using the patch. That's the point. The patch gives you enough nicotine to satisfy the craving *without* smoking.'

'It wouldn't give me enough.'

'No, I bet it wouldn't,' she said, and she smiled.

He lit a cigarette. 'I'm going to have my shower and then perhaps you'll re-do those plasters for me.'

'Of course I will,' she said.

# In all Honesty

Ever since Beatrix Cooper-Gibson had had her teeth capped she
had been afraid of one or more of the crowns coming adrift
while she was asleep, sticking in her throat and choking her to
death. It was in vain that her dentist told her this could never happen.
Caps did loosen, it was a well-known fact, so why not hers? And why
not in the night?

The result was that she became a bad sleeper. Always supposing
she could get to sleep, she woke up after an hour or so and felt about
in her mouth to make sure the caps were all still there. It took a while
to get to sleep again and then she was bound to wake up after another
hour and begin the exploratory process once more.

As she grew older so her fears increased, for there were others. If
she sat close to a wall she was afraid a picture might fall on her, even
if she sat inches away, a foot away, for there was no guarantee it
would not fly outwards in its descent. Gradually she had all the
furniture moved into the centre of the rooms. Flies were anathema
to her and since spiders catch flies, she allowed no spiders' webs to
be removed. She was more frightened of electricity than almost
anything, expected every plug to be pulled out of every socket before
the household retired for the night and pulled out the plug on her
bedlamp herself. This meant that if she wanted light in the night she
would have to get up first to replace the plug in the socket, so she
kept a torch on the bedside cabinet and a candle in a candlestick in
case the torch battery failed.

Unsympathetic companions might have made her life very difficult
or unhappy (or cured her of these neurotic compulsions) but Gwenda
and Clive thought these anxieties only reasonable. Or Gwenda did,
and Clive went along with what Gwenda thought, as she went along
with what he thought, for their marriage was exceptionally harmonious.
Gwenda thought Beatrix Cooper-Gibson a sensible prudent woman.

'The house hasn't burnt down, has it?' Gwenda said. 'And in all
honesty –' she used this expression a lot, often when neither truth nor

probity were in question '– no one's ever been hit on the head by a picture.'

'And say what you like,' said loyal Clive, 'food poisoning has never been an issue.'

These arguments had been occasioned by Beatrix Cooper-Gibson's son Alexander protesting about what he called his mother's 'barminess'. She was getting worse, he said. She was seventy-five, would probably live another ten years, and what further eccentricities would she develop before that?

It was in Gwenda and Clive's interest to keep Beatrix alive as long as possible. Eighty-five was nothing. Why not ninety-five when they would be eligible for their own retirement pensions? The job was a sinecure, lovely flat, colour TV and video, bathroom with jacuzzi, personal microwave, and if Beatrix insisted that they too moved the furniture into the middle of each room, that was no hardship. It signified her care and affection for them, a tenderness both returned. She didn't need much looking after, bless her, fit as a fiddle she was, wonderful for her age.

'In all honesty,' Gwenda said, 'it's like having one's own dear mother in one's home.'

If Alexander minded that – after all, they were in Beatrix's house, not she in theirs – he gave no sign of it. He pointed out that the place had been completely re-wired two years before and that his mother's dentist had assured him the cement he used to fix her caps in place would take a pulling power of five hundred h.p. to shift it.

'Accidents do happen,' said Clive, a remark which earned him an encouraging smile from his wife.

Alexander cast up his eyes. His mother's latest whim was to have the whole house re-fitted with a deep shag pile carpet in various pale shades. She had read somewhere or heard (or invented, Alexander thought) that whereas close carpet in a dark colour absorbs heat and even a certain amount of light, pale shag with inch-long fibres traps warmth and then reflects it back. It was dreadful to think, she said, of all that expensive heat being sucked up by the thin dark surface, leaving the rooms cold and probably even damp, encouraging colds, flu, bronchitis, allergies, pneumonia, catarrh, pleurisy and hypothermia. She painted a grim picture of a dark greenish-brown tight-woven mass, fungoid or swamp-like, drawing into itself, as might a carnivorous plant draw in insects, all the health-giving warmth from the central heating and radiant light from the sun.

'It will cost a bomb,' said Alexander.

'So what? I'm not asking you to pay for it.'

He would scarcely have minded if she had. Money was not at issue. He had as much of it as she had, and if he had made his while his father had left her hers, it was all money to be spent as money should be on an enhancement of the quality of life. But to blue it on hideous anaemic floor covering, having ripped up acres of prime Wilton . . .!

'I'm going to have it done, Alexander. I can't sleep at night for worrying about it. I lie awake thinking about all that heat draining through the floors.'

'Better take the doctor's sleeping pills,' said Alexander.

'Oh, yes, definitely,' said his mother with heavy sarcasm, 'and get such a good night's sleep I choke to death on my own teeth.'

The carpet fitters came in a month later and removed the chocolate and olive-green and crimson Wilton from the floors. Beatrix told them it had absorbed not only ten years of heat but also billions upon billions of microbes, and to take it away and dispose of it. The foreman took it home, had it cleaned and re-laid it all over his housing association duplex.

The shrimp pink and albino and mouse and meal-coloured shag was unrolled. Beatrix measured the strands in the pile with a ruler and found them an acceptable inch-and-a-half long. The foreman called it four centimetres but she wasn't having any truck with that. It took days to lay the carpet in every room of the house, Beatrix often hindering operations by reminding the workmen not to move the furniture too close to the walls and not to touch the spiders' webs.

'Oh, isn't it beautiful!' said Gwenda, clapping her hands. 'Don't you love those delicate pastel shades?'

Alexander said it wasn't exactly to his taste and his sister Julia said it would be a lot harder to keep clean.

'In all honesty,' said Gwenda, 'and if you don't mind me saying so, that's my problem. To be frank, I encouraged Mrs C-G to have this lovely wall-to-wall and I'm not a bit sorry I did. Light and bright is what you need when you're young in heart if not in years.'

Alexander might have said no more, for the deed was done now, and if the new carpet was more suited to high-tech or Bauhaus furniture, to walls of glass and ceilings of marble, than to his mother's early Victorian *chaises-longues*, family portraits and watercolours, it was her house and her choice. But Julia was less able to contain her feelings. It was because of this failure of self-control that she came to see Beatrix less often than he did.

'I'm sorry, but I think it's totally ghastly and utterly unsuitable.' Julia was a bit of a snob. 'It's actually the kind of thing the working classes have in council flats.' The foreman had, and had rectified this as soon as something superior was available. 'I'm sorry, but it's simply not fair on this lovely old house.'

Gwenda had not liked that reference to the working class, to which she belonged. She 'had no time', in her own phrase, expressed only to Clive, for 'Little Miss Clever'. But she stood, as she always did when 'the family' were all together, in a submissive and perfect servant-like fashion, with her hands clasped and her head bowed. A small gentle and resigned smile tip-tilted her lips and her eyes roved appreciatively across the shag pile carpet, which in this room was the colour of frosted cornflakes. She did not look at Beatrix. There was no need to. She knew Beatrix was not a woman to receive criticism meekly or reproaches with a shrug.

'What did you say?' was how Beatrix began her counter-attack.

'Oh, Mamma, you heard me. You know what I said.'

'I know you were setting yourself up as an arbiter of taste and an expert on social distinctions.' Beatrix smiled, showing off the well-anchored caps. She was not one to pull her punches. 'Considering that suburban eyesore you live in with that bank clerk, I'm sure you're qualified to judge.'

'Bertie is not a bank clerk, he is a departmental manager,' said Julia.

'Who cares? The only thing about him that interests me is why such a boring and conventional man can't bring himself to do the traditional thing and marry you.'

'You shut up, you evil-tongued old bat!'

'Excuse me,' said Gwenda. 'I'm intruding. I'll go, I have things to see to.'

'Stay exactly where you are, Gwenda. A witness to this behaviour is required. Are you going to stand there, Alexander, and let your sister speak to me like that?'

'If you don't like the way I am,' said Julia, 'you've only yourself to blame. You're my mother.'

'Yes, indeed, and giving birth to you was the biggest mistake I ever made. The most miserable day of my life! Now you can apologise. I never want to hear language like that again in my own drawing room. I wonder how you'll feel after I'm gone and you find I've left this "lovely old house" to somebody else.'

This was standard. Beatrix threatened to change her will every time Julia paid a visit. So far she had not done so and Julia had never apologised or changed her habit of speaking, but simply walked out of the house muttering, to return two or three months later as if nothing had happened. This time was no different and perhaps would have had no different results if Julia had not come back with Alexander after a week had gone by.

Gwenda admitted them to the house. Letting her son have a key was not the kind of thing that suited Beatrix. The expression on Gwenda's face betrayed her feelings, astonishment at 'Miss Clever's' swift return and perhaps a happy anticipation of renewed strife. Beatrix ignored her daughter. She addressed herself to Alexander, telling him of a new danger. This was from toxic rays emanating from the video recorder if tapes were re-used more than ten times. Ten was the crucial number. At this point chemical changes took place not in the tape itself but in the black plastic cassette which contained it and an invisible but noxious ray, or rather gas, was emitted via the medium of the television screen. She had sent Clive out to replace all the video cassettes and burn the old ones.

Alexander said it seemed very far-fetched. His sister curled back her upper lip the way people do when they smell something nasty. She said, though not referring to the poisonous videotapes, that she had been speaking about Beatrix's neuroses (her word) to a friend of hers who was a distinguished physicist. This woman had told her it was all nonsense about dark carpets absorbing heat, a complete myth.

'Women shouldn't be physicists,' said Beatrix. 'They should stay at home and look after the children. I blame the mess the world is in on women working.'

'She hasn't got any children.'

'I'm not surprised. Her reproductive processes have been poisoned by the work she does. Or pretends to do.'

'To hear you talk,' said Julia, 'anyone would think you'd had a dozen children instead of stopping at just the two. What happened to your reproductive processes? Or were you too selfish to have any more?'

'I'll just pop out into the kitchen and see to my casserole,' said Gwenda, though making no move to go.

'Stay right where you are, please,' said Beatrix. 'This is it. She has done it this time. Have you ever in all your experience, Gwenda, heard a young woman utter such words to her mother?'

'Oh, leave me out of it, Mrs C-G. I'm only a servant. I wouldn't wish to pass judgment.'

'Your very tone gives you away, Gwenda. I can hear your loyalty in it. I can hear your natural deep disapproval.' Beatrix had an extraordinarily loud voice for a woman of seventy-five. She raised it to its maximum decibels. 'Get out of my house!'

'If I go,' said Julia, 'I won't come back.'

'I sincerely hope not. It would give me a little holiday in my heart to have seen the last of you. I'll see *you* on Tuesday, Alexander.'

And she did. But by that time she had changed her will. Gwenda brought her the mobile phone, she called Mr Webley and asked him to lunch. He came on the Monday. Clive, who did the cooking when there was company, made *mozzarella tricolore*, chicken a là king and charlotte russe, for both Beatrix and her solicitor were fond of their food. While they were drinking their coffee and Beatrix, but not Mr Webley for he had to drive, was having a Drambuie with it, he took his pad out of his briefcase and noted down his client's wishes: not a sausage (her words) to Julia, a token sum to Alexander and everything else to Clive and Gwenda.

Mr Webley remonstrated gently.

'When you've quite finished,' said Beatrix, 'perhaps you'll remember it's my money.'

The will was drawn up and sent to Beatrix for her approval. This was not the first time this had happened, though in the past there had been different sets of beneficiaries and always the new will had been torn up or, at any rate, not returned to Mr Webley. The old one, the one that left everything to Alexander and Julia, remained valid. But this time Beatrix had meant what she said.

She read the will carefully and when Gwenda came into the room told her she wanted two witnesses.

'Clive and me will be happy to do that for you,' said Gwenda untruthfully. She was on tenterhooks.

Beatrix gave her a long meaningful look. 'That wouldn't do at all,' she said. 'Perhaps you'll just step across the road and ask Lady Huntly if she would be so kind as to come over for a glass of sherry. Oh, and Gwenda, if Brian is still doing the yew hedge he might come in too. Make sure he washes his hands first.'

Lady Huntly was the widow of a county councillor and Lord Lieutenant who had been knighted for giving large sums of money to the Conservative party. She was a sprightly little old lady with bright red lips and a wig of blue curls. Sizable sums of money remained, enabling her to live in the big Edwardian turreted house opposite, keep up the BMW and spend part of every winter in Fort Lauderdale. Her principal recreation was ballroom dancing which she indulged in three times a week at teatime, partnered by an old man who had been her boyfriend before she met the county councillor. Beatrix liked her because she listened sympathetically to her anxieties and to some extent shared her fears about toxic video tapes and swallowing one's teeth, in Lady Huntly's case a plate.

The gardener, Brian Gospel, was a singer with a country and western band, his real name being Gobbett. He mowed Beatrix's lawn and trimmed her hedges between gigs. Julia said her mother should be careful and she hoped she was insured to cover all eventualities because Brian had chorea, you only had to see his tics, and was certainly unsafe around the electric trimmer. She refused to believe Beatrix when she said he was only miming an armpit guitar. He was twenty-three years old, tall, dark and ugly in a sexy sort of way.

These were the two people Gwenda brought in to witness Beatrix's will.

'In the presence of the testatrix and of each other,' said Gwenda, who had read these instructions in a pamphlet from the Citizen's Advice Bureau.

She still thought Beatrix might change her mind. She stood there with her arms folded and her head bowed, holding her breath. Beatrix signed. Lady Huntly signed, using her own Mont Blanc fountain pen. Brian signed and said he didn't suppose the ladies would fancy coming along to an evening of nostalgia and sing along with Merle Haggard's greatest hits. Fluttering her extended eyelashes, Lady Huntly said she would think about it and after Brian had gone back to his hedge, she and Beatrix settled down to schooners of oleroso.

Jubilant in the kitchen, Gwenda said to Clive that they had done it this time. She would take the will to the post and catch the five-thirty collection.

'Or I could drive into town and drop it through Webley's letterbox.'

'We don't want to do anything to draw attention to ourselves,' said Gwenda. She put her arms round him, gave him a passionate kiss, and then she took the will down the road, dropping it in the letterbox at ten past five.

But the next morning she wished she had let Clive do as he suggested. She had never felt so nervous. Suppose there had been a mail robbery? Such things happened. Or a wicked postman, with no idea of his duty to the Post Office and the public, had stolen a selection of the contents of the box in the hope of discovering five-pound notes slipped into letters? She resisted for two hours and then she phoned Mr Webley. Mrs Cooper-Gibson, she said, was very anxious to know if the will had arrived. Oh, yes, certainly, he had it in his hand at that moment, said Mr Webley, sounding none too pleased and rather suspicious.

Gwenda wished she hadn't done it. What would happen if he told Beatrix? A new will? Oh, the shame and the pain! Alexander came in the afternoon and talked for a long time in a maudlin way about how much he wished his mother and sister got on better. He implied that it was largely his mother's fault. Had she thought of seeing a psychotherapist or perhaps a counsellor? Beatrix told him to go, she was tired, she disliked being lectured in her own house. Coming back from virtually pushing him out of the front door, she leaned back against the wall and stamped her foot. She stamped one heavily shod solid foot and then the other and a large oil painting in a gilt frame fell off the wall and struck her on the neck and back.

Her worst misgivings were realised. Beatrix yelled for Gwenda. She wasn't much hurt but she was frightened. Her fears had been real and yet they had not been real, they were of the kind that wake the sufferer with vague apprehensions during the night but are not much more than an eccentricity by day, superstitious injunctions that if not obeyed may result in disaster, so why not obey them? But this had proved them right, proved *her* right. Gwenda offered to call the doctor.

'I don't want him,' said Beatrix. At their last encounter she had overheard him telling Gwenda her troubles were 'in the old soul's imagination'.

'Well, shall I have a look at your back, Mrs C-G?'

'No, leave me alone. Now this has happened I shan't sleep a wink. Or if I do I shall re-live the nightmare of that picture falling on me.'

The picture, a portrait of Beatrix's grandfather in a morning coat with some sort of chain of office hanging round his neck, was examined by Clive who found its cord badly frayed. There must have been thirty or forty pictures of equal size and weight – if not all of such unattractive subjects – in the house, and Beatrix said she would be unable to sleep ever again until she knew all the cords had been replaced. Clive set about it straight away, although it was half-past nine in the evening.

Beatrix said, 'I may be doing a very imprudent thing, Gwenda, but I am going to take a sleeping pill.'

'Quite right,' said Gwenda. 'After all, the odds against your caps coming off and sticking in your throat must be about ten thousand to one.'

'I wouldn't know about that. I'm not a bookmaker. As a matter of fact I would normally consider the chances quite high, as you know, only not now the picture has fallen on me.'

'Pardon?'

'Lightning isn't going to strike twice, is it? It's not in the nature of things for a picture to fall on me and then for my teeth to get stuck in my throat. You might as well say that tonight I'm just as much in danger as ever of being burnt to death by faulty electricity when obviously I'm not.'

'If you say so,' said Gwenda doubtfully and she found the sleeping pills and brought one to Beatrix with her hot drink.

By eleven-fifteen Clive had renewed the cords on twenty-two pictures. 'I shall call it a day,' he said to his wife. 'Enough is enough.'

'You'll check up on the electric plugs, won't you?'

Clive did. He went into his own flat and to bed just before midnight. Gwenda put her arms round him in her sleep. On the floor below, at the front of the house, in the big master bedroom newly fitted in shell-pink shag, Beatrix lay perilously near the edge of the bed. The drug had a powerful effect on her because in all her life she had only taken a soporific twice before. Still and totally relaxed, she lay as one dead. But some imperceptible movements must have occurred in her deep sleep, for an acute observer, if there had been one, who had watched her for the past hour, would have noticed that from the centre of the four-poster she had shifted in that time some six inches towards the edge. By half-past midnight her gradual forward progress had increased the distance to nine inches. At one-fifteen she was poised on the very edge.

The bedclothes were not tucked in. They never were. Beatrix had another phobia about that. She insisted that an inevitable result of tucking in the bedclothes was a nightmare in which she was sewn up in a sack with a snake and a monkey and thrown in the Bosphorus. So the sheet and blanket hung loose, while the quilt had slithered back to the far side of the bed. Beatrix's left arm hung over the edge. Her left leg dipped over the edge and slowly her right leg joined it. Although she was fast asleep, she waved her right arm to save herself, but nevertheless slipped forward and tumbled on to the floor.

Beatrix lay prone with her face buried in the soft long-haired pink carpet. If her progress across the bed had been backwards she would have fallen into a supine position and very likely have recovered. But, still deeply asleep, she lay face-down with thick fluff pressing into her nose and mouth and it suffocated her. Within half an hour she was dead. The time was just before two.

Entering the bedroom at nine, Gwenda called out her usual merry 'good morning, Mrs C-G', a cry which turned to a shriek of terror. Her first thought was that the most-feared had happened and Beatrix had swallowed the caps off her teeth. She told the doctor that and he reacted to what she said with suspicion, not to say indignation. By then he had seen the bruise on the back of Beatrix's neck.

The pathologist the police called in found more bruises on Beatrix's back. Gwenda was questioned. She told the detective inspector about the picture falling on Beatrix, adding that the cord holding it in place had become frayed. When no signs of fraying could be seen Clive described how he had renewed the cord not only on the portrait of Beatrix's grandfather but on twenty-one other paintings in the house. The inspector seemed to find this very odd especially as Alexander told him he knew nothing about a picture falling on his mother. The fear of such a thing happening was a factor in her neurosis, bearing no relation to reality.

Suspicion increased when the contents of the will were made known. The will itself was dated only two days before. Its provisions were that everything Beatrix had to leave, her house, her investments, as well as a huge capital sum, went to Clive and Gwenda. The inquest on Beatrix was adjourned while the police continued to make enquiries.

Lady Huntly told the inspector that she had been greatly surprised to be called as a witness to the will. Gwenda had rushed across the road with unseemly haste as if it were a matter of life or death. No doubt it was. Of course she had been able to see which way the wind was blowing as soon as she understood neither Clive nor Gwenda was to be the other witness. The inspector talked to Brian and Brian told him he had never been inside the house before and would have refused to have anything to do with this will business had not Gwenda implored him to 'do this one little thing for her before the old trout changed her mind'.

Mr Webley described how astonished he had been to receive a phone call from Gwenda not five minutes after the will had come in the post. He had scarcely taken it out of its envelope. Mrs Cooper-Gibson had often in the past talked of changing her will and the process had frequently gone as far as a draft will being drawn up or even a will itself sent to her for signature, but in these cases things had gone no further.

Julia intended to contest the will. Or she said she did. That shag carpet had been fitted on Gwenda's advice, she told the inspector. Her mother would never have got rid of her Wilton but for Gwenda and Clive who had gained an unhealthy hold over Beatrix. It was easy to imagine those two persuading Beatrix to break the rule of a lifetime, take a sleeping pill, and while she was unconscious roll her off the bed on to the floor and suffocate her by pressing her face into the carpet. The bruises were evidence of manhandling – what more did the police want?

Day after day Gwenda and Clive were questioned, sometimes at home, more often at the police station. They remained in Beatrix's house, *their* house now. Their flat was repeatedly searched and scrutinised, their possessions tested and photographed and surface-scraped, examined for pink fibres that might have found their way from the floor of Beatrix's bedroom into theirs. No one ever told them whether or not such fibres had been found. They had begun to be uneasy with each other, more polite and considerate than usual but with less to say.

Julia phoned or wrote letters to the police every day, quoting remarks Gwenda was alleged to have made on the state of Beatrix's health, the extent of her income and the likelihood of her accidental death. After she had written thirty-five such letters she had a nervous breakdown, retired to a psychiatric hospital and gave up contesting the will.

Alexander got married. He had never fancied the idea of his mother and any wife of his in conjunction.

Sometimes Clive spent the night in a cell at the police station, they were getting used to him there, put a drop of whisky in his night-time cocoa and gave him an extra blanket, but the law restrained them from holding him for more than twenty-four hours. Gwenda they often reduced to tears by asking her why she didn't confess and so save them all a lot of time and expense.

'We shall never give this up,' said the detective inspector, 'not if it takes us twenty years.'

Lady Huntly refused to speak to Gwenda and Clive. She and her dancing partner ignored them pointedly, walking past with their noses in the air. All the neighbours followed suit. Mr Webley dined out on the tale of how he had been served *mozzarella tricolore*, chicken a là king and charlotte russe by the notorious carpet murderers.

This went on for about a year. Gwenda and Clive gave up sharing a bed. Gwenda said she couldn't sleep when the person beside her had such awful dreams, waking up with a yell two or three times in the night. Your own dreams aren't in the best of taste, Clive said, moving into the spare room.

Brian went to Nashville with the band. It was a package tour and included Graceland and Disneyworld but of course they hoped to be talent-spotted. While in the United States he read a piece in a newspaper that he thought worth bringing home for the police. It told of a wealthy Texan widow from Beach City who had died through suffocation. She too had fallen out of bed and smothered in the shag pile carpeting. 'After a ten-month investigation,' said the newspaper, 'her death has been ruled due to a freak accident.'

The inquest on Beatrix was reopened and a verdict of accidental death returned.

The neighbours continued to ignore Gwenda and Clive. Alexander's wife had a baby. Julia came out of hospital and wrote a long letter to Gwenda, apologising for her insinuations and suggesting she take on, at a peppercorn rent, the flat which used to be theirs. Bertie the bank departmental manager had left her and gone to Hong Kong. Mr Webley's partner warned him that the stories he was spreading of poisoned charlotte russe and stomach upsets after every visit he had paid to Beatrix's house might well constitute slander.

Clive and Gwenda sold the house and moved away. They also sold most of the furniture but Clive held on to the portrait of Beatrix's grandfather in morning coat and chain of office as a keepsake. Gwenda kept the video recorder to remind her of happier days when they had been a couple, sharing their home with a woman who had been as good as a mother to them. For they were no longer together. Their marriage, for a quarter of a century so happy, had broken up.

'In all honesty,' said Gwenda, for once using the phrase correctly, 'did you kill her?'

'You know I didn't,' said Clive. 'I was asleep in bed with you. You were asleep in bed with me.' He thought about that one. 'Or were you?'

'You know I was, Clive.'

'You were just as capable of killing her as me.'

'But I didn't.'

'You would say that,' said Clive.

'So would you.'

Clive bought a seven-roomed bungalow on the Isle of Wight, Gwenda a seventeenth-century farmhouse in Shropshire. Their notoriety travelled before them and they were rejected by the local inhabitants. Still, as Gwenda wrote, replying to Julia's Christmas card, there was something to be said, in all honesty, for being unhappy in luxury.

# The Strawberry Tree

## I

The hotel where we are staying was built by my father. Everyone assures me it is the best in Llosar and it is certainly the biggest and ugliest. From a distance it looks as if made of white cartridge paper or from hundreds of envelopes with their flaps open. Inside it is luxurious in the accepted way with sheets of bronze-coloured mirrors and tiles of copper-coloured marble and in the foyer, in stone vessels of vaguely Roman appearance, stands an army of hibiscus with trumpet flowers the red of soldiers' coats.

There is a pool and a room full of machines for exercise, three restaurants and two bars. A machine polishes your shoes and another makes ice. In the old days we used to watch the young men drink *palo* out of long thin bow-shaped vessels from which the liquor spouted in a curving stream. Now the hotel barman makes cocktails called *Mañanas* that are said to be famous. We tried them yesterday, sitting on the terrace at the back of the hotel. From there, if you are not gazing at the swimming pool as most people do, you can rest your eyes, in both senses, on the garden. There the arbutus has been planted and flourishes, its white flowers blooming and strawberry fruits ripening at the same time, something I have heard about but never seen before, for it is October and I was last here all those years ago in summer.

We have rooms with envelope balconies and a view of the bay. There are no fishing boats any more, the pier of the old hotel with its vine canopy is gone and the old hotel itself has become a casino. But the harbour is still there with the statue of the Virgin, *Nuestra Doña de los Marineros*, where, swimming in the deep green water, Piers and Rosario and I first saw Will sitting on the sturdy stone wall.

All along the 'front', as I suppose I must call it, are hotels and restaurants, souvenir shops and tourist agencies, cafés and drinking places, where once stood a string of cottages. The church with its brown campanile and shallow pantiled roof that used to dominate this shore has been almost lost among the new buildings, dwarfed by the gigantic Thomson Holiday hotel. I asked the chambermaid if they had had jellyfish at Llosar lately but she only shook her head and muttered about *contaminación*.

The house we were lent by José-Carlos and Micaela is still there but much 'improved' and extended, painted sugar-pink and surrounded by a fence of the most elaborate wrought ironwork I have ever seen, iron lace for a giant's tablecloth around a giant's child's iced cake. I would be surprised if Rosario recognised it. Inland, things are much the same, as far as I can tell. Up to now I have not ventured there, even though we have a most efficient rented car. I climb up a little way out of the village and stare at the yellow hills, at the olive trees and junipers, and the straight wide roads which now make seams across them, but I cannot see the little haunted house, the *Casita de Golondro*. It was never possible to see it from here. A fold in the hills, crowned with woods of pine and carob, hides it. The manager of our hotel told me this morning it is now a *parador*, the first on Majorca.

When I have performed the task I came here to do I shall go and have a look at it. These state-run hotels, of which there are many on the mainland, are said to be very comfortable. We might have dinner there one evening. I shall propose it to the others. But as for removing from here to there, if any of them suggest it, I shall make up my mind to turn it down. For one thing, if I were staying there I should sooner or later have to rediscover *that* room or deliberately avoid it. The truth is I no longer want an explanation. I want to be quiet, I want, if this does not sound too ludicrous, to be happy.

My appointment in Muralla is for ten o'clock tomorrow morning with an officer of the *Guardia Civil* whose rank, I think, would correspond to our detective superintendent. He will conduct me to see what is to be seen and I shall look at the things and try to remember and give him my answer. I haven't yet made up my mind whether to let the others come with me, nor am I sure they would want to come. Probably it will be best if I do this, as I have done so much in the past, alone.

2

Nearly forty years have passed since first we went to Majorca, Piers and I and our parents, to the house our Spanish cousin lent us because my mother had been ill. Her illness was depression and a general feeling of lowness and lethargy, but the cause of it was a lost child, a miscarriage. Even then, before there was real need, my parents were trying to have more children, had been trying to have more, although I was unaware of this, since soon after my own birth thirteen years before. It was as if they knew, by some sad superstitious prevision, that they would not always have their pigeon pair.

I remember the letter to my father from José-Carlos. They had fought side by side in the Spanish Civil War and been fast friends and sporadic correspondents ever since, although he was my mother's cousin, not my father's. My mother's aunt had married a Spaniard from Santander and José-Carlos was their son. Thus we all knew where Santander was but had scarcely heard of Majorca. At any rate, we had to search for it on the map. With the exception of Piers, that is. Piers would have known, Piers could have told us it was the largest of the Balearic Islands, Baleares Province in the western Mediterranean, and probably too that it covered something over fourteen hundred square miles. But one of the many many nice things about my clever brother, child of good fortune, was his modesty. Handing out pieces of gratuitous information was never his way. He too stood and looked over our father's shoulder at Goodall and Darby's *University Atlas*, a pre-war edition giving pride of place to the British Empire and in which the Mediterranean was an unimportant inland sea. He looked, as we did, in silence.

The tiny Balearics floated green and gold on pale blue, held in the arms of Barcelona and Valencia. Majorca (Mallorca in brackets) was a planet with attendant moons: Formentera, Cabrera, but Minorca too and Ibiza. How strange it now seems that we had never heard of Ibiza, had no idea of how to pronounce it, while Minorca was just the place a chicken was named after.

José-Carlos's house was at a place called Llosar. He described it and its setting deprecatingly, making little of the beauty, stressing rustic awkwardnesses. It was on the north-west coast, overlooking the sea, within a stone's throw of the village, but there was not much to the village, only a few little shops and the hotel. His English was so good it put us to shame, my father said. They would have to brush up their Spanish, my mother and he.

The house was ours for the months of July and August, or for us children's school holidays. We would find it very quiet, there was nothing to do but swim and lie in the sun, eat fish and drink in the local tavern, if my parents had a mind to that. In the south-east of the island were limestone caves and subterranean lakes, worth a visit if we would entrust ourselves to the kind of car we would find for hire. Tourists had begun to come, but there could not be many of these as there was only one hotel.

Llosar was marked on our map, on a northern cape of the island. The capital, Palma, looked quite big until you saw its letters were in the same size print as Alicante on the mainland. We had never been abroad, Piers and I. We were the children of war, born before it, confined by it to our own beleaguered island. And since the end of war we had been fated to wait patiently for something like this that would not cost much or demand a long-term plan.

I longed for this holiday. I had never been ill but now I dreaded some unspecified illness swooping down on me as the school term drew to its close. It was possible. Everyone, sooner or later, in those days before general immunisation, had measles. I had never had it. Piers had been in hospital for an operation the previous year but I had never so much as had my tonsils out. Anything could happen. I felt vulnerable. I lived in daily terror of the inexplicable gut pain, the rash appearing, the cough. I even began taking my temperature first thing in the morning, as my poor mother took hers, although for a different reason. They would go without me. Why not? It would be unfair to keep four people at home for the sake of one. I would be sent, after I came out of hospital, to stay with my Aunt Sheila.

What happened was rather different. We were not to be a member of the party fewer but to be joined by one more. José-Carlos's second letter was even more apologetic and this time, in my view at least, with justice. He had a request. We must of course say no at once if what he asked was unacceptable. Rosario would very much like to be at the house while we were there. Rosario loved the place so much and always stayed there in the summer holidays.

'Who is he?' I said.

'He's a girl,' my mother said. 'José-Carlos's daughter. I should think she must be fifteen or sixteen by now.'

'It's one of those Spanish names,' said my father, 'short for Maria of the something-or-other, Maria del Pilar, Maria del Consuelo, in this case Maria of the rosary.'

I was very taken aback. I didn't want her. The idea of a Spanish girl joining us filled me with dismay. I could imagine her, big and dark, with black flowing hair and tiers of skirts that would swing as she danced, a comb and mantilla, although I stopped at the rose between her teeth.

'We can write to José-Carlos and say it's not acceptable.' This seemed perfectly reasonable to me. 'He says we are to, so we can. We can do it at once and she'll know in plenty of time not to be there.'

My mother laughed. My father did not. No, so long afterwards, I can look back and believe he already understood the way I was and it worried him. He said gently but not smiling, 'He doesn't mean it. He's being polite. It would be impossible for us to say no.'

'Besides,' said Piers, 'she may be very nice.' That was something I could never consider as possible. I was wary of almost everyone then and I have changed very little. I still prepare myself to dislike people and be disliked by them. Their uncharitableness I anticipate, their meanness and envy. When someone invites me to dinner and tells me that such-and-such an acquaintance of theirs will be there, a man or a woman I shall love to meet, I invariably refuse. I dread such encounters. The new person, in my advance estimation, will be cold, self-absorbed, malicious, determined to slight or hurt me, will be handsome or beautiful, well-dressed and brilliant, will find me unattractive or stupid, will either not want to talk to me or will want to talk with the object of causing humiliation.

I am unable to help this. I have tried. Psychotherapists have tried. It is one of the reasons why, although rich beyond most people's dreams and good-looking enough, intelligent enough and able to talk, I have led until recently a lonely life, isolated, not so much neglected as the object of remarks such as:

'Petra won't come, so there is really no point in asking her,' and 'You have to phone Petra or write to her so far in advance and make so many arrangements before you drop in for a cup of tea, it hardly seems worth it.'

It is not so much that I am shy as that, cold myself, I understand the contempt and indifference of the cold-hearted. I do not want to be its victim. I do not want to be reduced by a glance, a laugh, a wounding comment, so that I shrivel and grow small. That is what the expression means: to make someone feel small. But another phrase, when someone says he wants the earth to open and swallow him up, that I understand, that is not something I long for but something which happens to me daily. It is only in this past year that the thaw has begun, the slow delayed opening of my heart.

So the prospect of the company of Rosario spoiled for me those last days before we left for Spain. She would be nicer to look at than I was. She would be taller. Later on in life the seniority of a friend is to one's advantage but not at thirteen. Rosario was older and therefore more sophisticated, more knowledgeable, superior and aware of it. The horrible thought had also struck me that she might not speak English. She would be a grown-up speaking Spanish with my parents and leagued with them in the great adult conspiracy against those who were still children.

So happy anticipation was spoiled by dread, as all my life it has been until now.


If you go to Majorca today special flights speed you there direct from Heathrow and Gatwick and, for all I know, Stansted too. It may well be true that more people go to Majorca for their holidays than anywhere else. When we went we had to take the train to Paris and there change on to another which carried us through France and the night, passing the walls of Carcassonne at sunrise, crossing the frontier into Spain in the morning. A small, light and probably ill-maintained aircraft took us from Barcelona to Palma and one of the hired cars, the untrustworthy rackety kind mentioned by José-Carlos, from Palma to the north.

I slept in the car, my head on my mother's shoulder, so I absorbed nothing of that countryside that was to grow so familiar to us, that was to ravish us with its beauty and in the end betray us. The sea was the first thing I saw when I woke up, of a deep, silken, peacock blue, a mirror of the bright cloudless sky. And the heat wrapped me like a shawl when I got out and stood there on dry pale stones, striped with the thin shadows of juniper trees.

I had never seen anywhere so beautiful. The shore which enclosed the bay was thickly wooded, a dark massy green, but the sand was silver. There was a skein of houses trailed along the shore, white cottages with flat pantiled roofs, the church with its clean square companile and the hotel whose terrace, hung with vines and standing in the sea, was a combination of pier and tree house. Behind all this and beyond it, behind *us* the way we had come, a countryside of yellow hills scattered with grey trees and grey stones, stretched itself out and rolled up into the mountains. And everywhere stood the cypresses like no trees I had ever seen before, blacker than holly, thin as stems, clustered like groups of pillars or isolated like single obelisks, with shadows which by evening would pattern the turf with an endlessly repeated tracery of lines. Upon all this the sun shed a dry, white, relentless heat.

Children look at things. They have nothing else to do. Later on, it is not just a matter of this life being full of care and therefore worthless if we have no time to stand and stare. We have no time, we cannot change back, that is the way it is. When we are young, before the time of study, before love, before work and a place of our own to live in, everything is done for us. If we have happy childhoods, that is, and good parents. Our meals will be made and our beds, our clothes washed and new ones bought, the means to buy earned for us, transport provided and a roof over our heads. We need not think of these things or fret about them. Time does not press its hot breath on us, saying to us, go, go, hurry, you have things to do, you will be late, come, come, hurry.

So we can stand and stare. Or lean on a wall, chin in hands, elbows on the warm rough stone, and look at what lies down there, the blue silk sea unfolding in a splash of lace on the sand, the rocks like uncut agate set in a strip of silver. We can lie in a field, without thought, only with dreams, gazing through a thousand stems of grasses at the tiny life which moves among them as between the tree trunks of a wood. In a few years' time, a very few, it will be possible no more, as all the cares of life intrude, distract the mind and spoil the day, introducing those enemies of contemplation, boredom and cold and stiffness and anxiety.

At thirteen I was at the crossing point between then and now. I could still stand and stare, dawdle and dream, time being still my toy and not yet my master, but adult worries had begun. People were real, were already the only real threat. If I wanted to stay there, leaning on my wall, from which hung like an unrolled bolt of purple velvet the climber I learned to call the bougainvillea, it was as much from dread of meeting José-Carlos and his wife Micaela and Rosario, their daughter, as from any longing for the prolongation of my beautiful view. In my mind, as I gazed at it, I was rehearsing their remarks, designed to diminish me.

'Petra!'

My father was calling me, standing outside a white house with a balcony running all the way around it at first floor level. Cypresses banded its walls and filled the garden behind it, like spikes of dark stalagmites. There was a girl with him, smaller than me, I could tell even from that distance, small and thin and with a tiny face that looked out between great dark doors of hair, as through the opening in a gateway. Instead of guessing she was Rosario, I thought she must be the child of a caretaker or cleaner. Introductions would not be made. I scarcely glanced at her. I was already bracing myself for the coming meeting, hardening myself, emptying my mind. Up through the white sunlight to the house I went and was on the step, had pushed open the front door, when he said her name to me.

'Come and meet your cousin.'

I had to turn and look then. She was not at all what I expected. People never are and I know that – I think I even knew it then – but this was a knowledge which made no difference. I have never been able to say, wait and see, make no advance judgements, reserve your defence. I managed to lift my eyes to hers. We did not shake hands but looked at each other and said hallo. She had difficulty with the H, making it too breathy. I noticed, close up beside her, that I was an inch taller. Her skin was pale with a glow behind it, her body as thin as an elf's. About the hair only I had been right and that not entirely. Rosario's hair was the colour of polished wood, of old furniture, as smooth and shining, and about ten times as long as mine. Later she showed me how she could sit on it, wrap herself in it. My mother told her, but kindly, meaning it as a compliment, that she could be Lady Godiva in a pageant. And then, of course, Piers, who knew the story properly, had to explain who Lady Godiva was.

Then, when we first met, we did not say much. I was too surprised. I must say also that I was gratified, for I had expected a young lady, an amalgam of Carmen and a nun, and found instead a child with Alice in Wonderland hair and ankle socks. She wore a little short dress and on a chain around her neck a seed-pearl locket with a picture of her mother. She preceded me into the house, smiling over her shoulder in a way unmistakably intended to make me feel at home. I began to thaw and to tremble a little, as I always do. Her parents were inside with my mother and Piers, but not to stay long. Once we had been shown where to find things and where to seek help if help were needed, they were to be off to Barcelona.

We had been travelling for a day and a night and half a day. My mother went upstairs to rest in the big bed under a mosquito net. My father took a shower in the bathroom which had no bath and where the water was not quite cold but of a delectable cool freshness.

Piers said, 'Can we go in the sea?'

'If you like to.' Rosario spoke the very correct, oddly-accented English of one who had been taught the language with care but seldom heard it spoken by an English person. 'There is no tide here. You can swim whenever you want. Shall we go now and I can show you?'

'In a place like this,' said my brother, 'I should like to go in the sea every day and all day. I'd never get tired of it.'

'Perhaps not.' She had her head on one side. 'We shall see.'

We did grow tired of it eventually. Or, rather, the sea was not always the sweet buoyant blessing it appeared to be that first afternoon. A plague of jellyfish came and on another day someone thought he saw a basking shark. Fishermen complained that swimmers frightened off their catch. And, as a day-long occupation we grew tired of it. But that first time and for many subsequent times when we floated in its warm blue embrace and looked through depths of jade and green at the abounding marine life, at fishes and shells and the gleaming tendrils of subaqueous plants, all was perfect, all exceeded our dreams.

Our bodies and legs were white as fishes. Only our arms had a pale tan from the English summer. Piers had not been swimming since his illness but his trunks came up just high enough to hide the scar. Rosario's southern skin was that olive colour that changes only a little with the seasons but her limbs looked brown compared to ours. We sat on the rocks in the sun and she told us we must not leave the beach without covering ourselves or walk in the village in shorts or attempt to go in the church – this one was for me – with head and arms uncovered.

'I don't suppose I shall want to go in the church,' I said.

She looked at me curiously. She wasn't at all shy of us and what we said made her laugh. 'Oh, you will want to go everywhere. You will want to see everything.'

'Is there much to see?' Piers was already into the way of referring back to the textual evidence. 'Your father said there would only be swimming and a visit to the caves.'

'The caves, yes. We must take you to the caves. There are lots and lots of things to do here, Piers.'

It was the first time she had spoken his name. She pronounced it like the surname 'Pearce'. I saw him look at her with more friendliness, with more warmth, than before. And it is true that we are *warmed* by being called by our names. We all know people who hardly ever do it, who only do it when they absolutely must. They manage to steer conversations along, ask questions, respond, without ever using a first name. And they chill others with their apparent detachment, those others who can never understand that it is diffidence which keeps them from committing themselves to the use of names. They might get the names wrong, or use them too often, be claiming an intimacy to which they have no right, be forward, pushy, presumptuous. I know all about it for I am one of them.

Rosario called me Petra soon after that and Piers called her Rosario. I remained, of course, on the other side of that bridge which I was not to cross for several days. We went up to the house and Rosario said,

'I'm so happy you have come.'

It was not said as a matter of politeness but rapturously. I could not imagine myself uttering those words even to people I had known all my life. How could I be so forward, lay myself open to their ridicule and their sneers, *expose* myself to their scorn? Yet when they were spoken to me I felt no scorn and no desire to ridicule. Her words pleased me, they made me feel needed and liked. But that was far from understanding how to do myself what Rosario did, and forty years later I am only just learning.

'I'm so happy you have come.'

She said it again, this time in the hearing of my parents.

Piers said, 'We're happy to be here, Rosario.'

It struck me then, as I saw him smile at her, that until then he had not really known any girls but me.

3

My brother had all the gifts, looks, intellect, charm, simple niceness and, added to these, the generosity of spirit that should come from being favoured by the gods but often does not. My mother and father doted on him. They were like parents in a fairy story, poor peasants who know themselves unworthy to bring up the changeling prince some witch has put into their own child's cradle.

Not that he was unlike them, having taken for himself the best of their looks, the best features of each of them, the best of their talents, my father's mathematical bent, my mother's love of literature, the gentleness and humour of both. But these gifts were enhanced in him, he bettered them. The genes of outward appearance that met in him made for greater beauty than my mother and father had.

He was tall, taller at sixteen than my father. His hair was a very dark brown, almost black, that silky fine dark hair that goes grey sooner than any other. My father, who was not yet forty, was already grey. Piers's eyes were blue, as are all the eyes in our family except my Aunt Sheila's which are turquoise with a dark rim around the pupils. His face was not a film star's nor that of a model posing in smart clothes in an advertisement, but a Pre-Raphaelite's meticulous portrait. Have you seen Holman Hunt's strange painting of Valentine rescuing

Sylvia, and the armed man's thoughtful, sensitive, gentle looks?

At school he had always been top of his class. Examinations he was allowed to take in advance of his contemporaries he always passed and passed well. He was destined to go up to Oxford at seventeen instead of eighteen. It was hard to say whether he was better at the sciences than the arts, and if it was philosophy he was to read at university, it might equally have been classical languages or physics.

Modern languages were the only subjects at which he failed to excel, at which he did no better and often less well than his contemporaries, and he was quick to point this out. That first evening at Llosar, for instance, he complimented Rosario on her English.

'How do you come to speak English so well, Rosario, when you've never been out of Spain?'

'I learn at school and I have a private teacher too.'

'We learn languages at school and some of us have private teachers, but it doesn't seem to work for us.'

'Perhaps they are not good teachers.'

'That's our excuse, but I wonder if it's true.'

He hastened to say what a dunce he was at French, what a waste of time his two years of Spanish. Why, he would barely know how to ask her the time or the way to the village shops. She looked at him in that way she had, her head a little on one side, and said she would teach him Spanish if he liked, she would be a good teacher. No English girl ever looked at a boy like that, in a way that was frank and shrewd, yet curiously maternal, always practical, assessing the future. Her brown river of hair flowed down over her shoulders, rippled down her back, and one long tress of it lay across her throat like a trailing frond of willow.

I have spoken of my brother in the past – 'Piers was' and 'Piers did' – as if those qualities he once had he no longer has, or as if he were dead. It is not my intention to give a false impression, but how otherwise can I recount these events? Things may be less obscure if I talk of loss rather than death, irremediable loss in spite of what has happened since, and of Piers's character only as it was at sixteen, making clear that I am aware of how vastly the personality changes in forty years, how speech patterns alter, specific learning is lost and huge accumulations of knowledge gained. Of Piers I felt no jealousy but I think this was a question of sex. If I may be allowed to evolve such an impossible thesis I would say that jealousy might have existed if he had been my sister. It is always possible for the sibling, the less favoured, to say to herself, ah, this is the way members of the opposite sex are treated, it is different for them, it is not that I am inferior or less loved, only different. Did I say that? Perhaps, in a deeply internal way. Certain it is that the next step was never taken; I never asked, where then are the privileges that should be accorded to my difference? Where are the special favours that come the way of daughters which their brothers miss? I accepted and I was not jealous.

At first I felt no resentment that it was Piers Rosario chose for her friend and companion, not me. I observed it and told myself it was a question of age. She was nearer in age to Piers than to me. And a question too perhaps, although I had no words for it then, of precocious sex. Piers had never had a girlfriend and she, I am sure, had never had a boyfriend. I was too young to place them in a Romeo and Juliet situation but I could see that they liked each other in the way boys and girls do when they begin to be aware of gender and the future. It did not matter because I was not excluded, I was always with them, and they were both too kind to isolate me. Besides, after a few days we found someone to make a fourth.


At this time we were still enchanted, Piers and I, by the beach and all that the beach offered: miles of shore whose surface was a combination of earth and sand and from which the brown rocks sprang like living plants, a strand encroached upon by pine trees with flat umbrella-like tops and purplish trunks. The sea was almost tideless but clean still, so that where it lapped the sand there was no scum or detritus of flotsam but a thin bubbly foam that dissolved at a touch into clear blue water. And under the water lay the undisturbed marine life, the bladder weed, the green sea grass and the weed-like trees of pleated brown silk, between whose branches swam small black and silver fish, sea anemones with pulsating whiskered mouths, creatures sheathed in pink shells moving slowly across the frondy seabed.

We walked in the water, picking up treasures too numerous to carry home. With Rosario we rounded the cape to discover the other hitherto invisible side, and in places where the sand ceased, we swam. The yellow turf and the myrtle bushes and the thyme and rosemary ran right down to the sand, but where the land met the sea it erupted into dramatic rocks, the colour of a snail's shell and fantastically shaped. We scaled them and penetrated the caves that pocked the cliffs, finding nothing inside but dry dust and a salty smell and, in the largest, the skull of a goat.

After three days spent like this, unwilling as yet to explore further, we made our way in the opposite direction, towards the harbour and the village where the little fishing fleet was beached. The harbour was enclosed with walls of limestone built in a horseshoe shape, and at the end of the right arm stood the statue of the Virgin, looking out to sea, her own arms held out, as if to embrace the world.

The harbour's arms rose some eight feet out of the sea, and on the left one, opposite *Nuestra Doña*, sat a boy, his legs dangling over the wall. We were swimming, obliged to swim for the water was very deep here, the clear but marbled dark green of malachite. Above us the sky was a hot shimmering silvery-blue and the sun seemed to have a palpable touch. We swam in a wide slow circle and the boy watched us.

You could see he was not Mallorquin. He had a pale freckled face and red hair. Today, I think, I would say Will has the look of a Scotsman, the bony, earnest, clever face, the pale blue staring eyes, although in fact he was born in Bedford of London-born parents. I know him still. That is a great understatement. I should have said that he is still my friend, although the truth is I have never entirely liked him, I have always suspected him of things I find hard to put into words. Of some kind of trickery perhaps, of having deep-laid plans, of using me. Ten years ago when he caused me one of the greatest surprises of my life by asking me to marry him, I knew as soon as I had recovered it was not love that had made him ask.

In those days, in Majorca, Will was just a boy on the watch for companions of his own age. An only child, he was on holiday with his parents and he was lonely. It was Piers who spoke to him. This was typical of Piers, always friendly, warm-hearted, with no shyness in him. We girls, if we had been alone, would probably have made no approaches, would have reacted to the watchful gaze of this boy on the wall by cavorting in the water, turning somersaults, perfecting our butterfly stroke and other hydrobatics. We would have *performed* for him, like young female animals under the male eye, and when the display was over have swum away.

Contingency has been called the central principle of all history. One thing leads to another. Or one thing does not lead to another because something else happens to prevent it. Perhaps, in the light of what was to come, it would have been better for all if Piers had not spoken. We would never have come to the *Casita de Golondro*, so the things which happened there would not have happened, and when we left the island to go home we would all have left. If Piers had been less than he was, a little colder, a little more reserved, more like me. If we had all been careful not to look in the boy's direction but had swum within the harbour enclosure with eyes averted, talking perhaps more loudly to each other and laughing more freely in the way people do when they want to make it plain they need no one else, another will not be welcome. Certain it is that the lives of all of us were utterly changed, then and now, because Piers, swimming close up to the wall, holding up his arm in a salute, called out,

'Hallo. You're English, aren't you? Are you staying at the hotel?'

The boy nodded but said nothing. He took off his shirt and his canvas shoes. He stood up and removed his long trousers, folded up his clothes and laid them in a pile on the wall with his shoes on top of them. His body was thin and white as a peeled twig. He wore black swimming trunks. We were all swimming around watching him. We knew he was coming in but I think we expected him to hold his nose and jump in with the maximum of splashing. Instead, he executed a perfect dive, his body passing into the water as cleanly as a knife plunged into a pool.

Of course it was done to impress us, it was 'showing off'. But we didn't mind. We *were* impressed and we congratulated him. Rosario, treading water, clapped her hands. Will had broken the ice as skilfully as his dive had split the surface of the water.

He would swim back with us, he liked 'that end' of the beach.

'What about your clothes?' said Piers.

'My mother will find them and take them in.' He spoke indifferently, in the tone of the spoiled only child whose parents wait on him like servants. 'She makes me wear a shirt and long trousers all the time,' he said, 'because I burn. I turn red like a lobster. I haven't got as many skins as other people.'

I was taken aback until Piers told me later that everyone has the same number of layers of skin. It is a question not of density but of pigment. Later on, when we were less devoted to the beach and began investigating the hinterland, Will often wore a hat, a big wide-brimmed affair of woven grass. He enjoyed wrapping up, the look it gave him of an old-fashioned adult. He was tall for his age which was the same as mine, very thin and bony and long-necked.

We swam back to our beach and sat on the rocks, in the shade of a pine tree for Will's sake. He was careful, fussy even, to see that no dappling of light reached him. This, he told us, was his second visit to Llosar. His parents and he had come the previous year and he remembered seeing Rosario before. It seemed to me that when he said this he gave her a strange look, sidelong, rather intimate, mysterious, as if he knew things about her we did not. All is discovered, it implied, and retribution may or may not come. There was no foundation for this, none at all. Rosario had done nothing to feel guilty about, had no secret to be unearthed. I noticed later he did it to a lot of people and it disconcerted them. Now, after so long, I see it as a blackmailer's look, although Will as far as I know has never demanded money with menaces from anyone.

'What else do you do?' he said. 'Apart from swimming?'

Nothing, we said, not yet anyway. Rosario looked defensive. After all, she almost lived here and Will's assumed sophistication was an affront to her. Had she not only three days before told us of the hundred things there were to do?

'They have bullfights sometimes,' Will said. 'They're in Palma on Sunday evenings. My parents went last year but I didn't. I faint at the sight of blood. Then there are the Dragon Caves.'

'*Las Cuevas del Drac*,' said Rosario.

'That's what I said, the Dragon Caves. And there are lots of other caves in the west.' Will hesitated. Brooding on what possibly was forbidden or frowned on, he looked up and said in the way that even then I thought of as sly, 'We could go to the haunted house.'

'The haunted house?' said Piers, sounding amused. 'Where's that?'

Rosario said without smiling, 'He means the *Casita de Golondro*.'

'I don't know what it's called. It's on the road to Pollença – well, in the country near that road. The village people say it's haunted.'

Rosario was getting cross. She was always blunt, plain-spoken. It was not her way to hide even for a moment what she felt. 'How do you know what they say? Do you speak Spanish? No, I thought not. You mean it is the man who has the hotel that told you. He will say anything. He told my mother he has seen a whale up close near Cabo de Pinar.'

'Is it supposed to be haunted, Rosario?' said my brother.

She shrugged. 'Ghosts,' she said, 'are not true. They don't happen. Catholics don't believe in ghosts, they're not supposed to. Father Xaviere would be very angry with me if he knew I talked about ghosts.' It was unusual for Rosario to mention her religion. I saw the look of surprise on Piers's face. 'Do you know it's one-thirty?' she said to Will, who had of course left his watch behind with his clothes. 'You will be late for your lunch and so will we.' Rosario and my brother had already begun to enjoy their particular rapport. They communicated even at this early stage of their relationship by a glance, a movement of the hand. Some sign he made, perhaps involuntary and certainly unnoticed by me, seemed to check her. She lifted her shoulders again, said, 'Later on, we shall go to the village, to the lace shop. Do you like to come too?' She added, with a spark of irony, her head tilted to one side, 'The sun will be going down, not to burn your poor skin that is so thin.'

The lace-makers were producing an elaborate counterpane for Rosario's mother. It had occurred to her that we might like to spend half an hour watching these women at work. We walked down there at about five, calling for Will at the hotel on the way. He was sitting by himself on the terrace, under its roof of woven vine branches. Four women, one of whom we later learned was his mother, sat at the only other occupied table, playing bridge. Will was wearing a clean shirt, clean long trousers and his grass hat, and as he came to join us he called out to his mother in a way that seemed strange to me because we had only just met, strange but oddly endearing,

'My friends are here. See you later'

Will is not like me, crippled by fear of a snub, by fear of being thought forward or pushy, but he lives in the same dread of rejection. He longs to 'belong'. His dream is to be a member of some inner circle, honoured and loved by his fellows, privileged to share knowledge of a secret password. He once told me, in an unusual burst of confidence, that when he heard someone he knew refer to him in conversation as 'my friend', tears of happiness came into his eyes.

While we were at the lace-makers' and afterwards on the beach at sunset he said no more about the *Casita de Golondro*, but that night, sitting on the terrace at the back of the house, Rosario told us its story. The nights at Llosar were warm and the air was velvety. Mosquitos there must have been, for we all had nets over our beds, but I only remember seeing one or two. I remember the quietness, the dark blue clear sky and the brilliance of the stars. The landscape could not be seen, only an outline of dark hills with here and there a tiny light glittering. The moon, that night, was increasing towards the full, was melon-shaped and melon-coloured.

The others sat in deckchairs, almost the only kind of 'garden furniture' anyone had in those days and which, today, you never see. I was in the hammock, a length of faded canvas suspended between one of the veranda pillars and a cypress tree. My brother was looking at Rosario in a peculiarly intense way. I think I remember such a lot about that evening because that look of his so impressed me. If was as if he had never seen a girl before. Or so I think now. I doubt if I thought about it in that way when I was thirteen. It embarrassed me

334

then, the way he stared. She was talking about the *Casita* and he was watching her, but when she looked at him, he smiled and turned his eyes away.

Her unwillingness to talk of ghosts on religious grounds seemed to be gone. It was hard not to make the connection and conclude it had disappeared with Will's return to the hotel. 'You could see the trees around the house from here,' she said, 'if it wasn't night,' and she pointed through the darkness to the south-west where the mountains began. '*Casita* means "little house" but it is quite big and it is very old. At the front is a big door and at the back, I don't know what you call them, arches and pillars.'

'A cloister?' said Piers.

'Yes, perhaps. Thank you. And there is a big garden with a wall around it and gates made of iron. The garden is all trees and bushes, grown over with them, and the wall is broken, so this is how I have seen the back with the word you said, the cloisters.'

'But no one lives there?'

'No one has ever lived there that I know. But someone owns it, it is someone's house, though they never come. It is all locked up. Now Will is saying what the village people say but Will *does not know* what they say. There are not ghosts, I mean there are not dead people who come back, just a bad room in the house you must not go in.'

Of course we were both excited, Piers and I, by that last phrase, made all the more enticing by being couched in English that was not quite idiomatic. But what returns to me most powerfully now are Rosario's preceding words about dead people who come back. It is a line from the past, long-forgotten, which itself 'came back' when some string in my memory was painfully plucked. I find my self repeating it silently, like a mantra, or like one of the prayers from that rosary for which she was named. Dead people who come back, lost people who are raised from the dead, the dead who return at last.

On that evening, as I have said, the words which followed that prophetic phrase affected us most. Piers at once asked about the 'bad' room but Rosario, in the finest tradition of tellers of ghost stories, did not admit to knowing precisely which room it was. People who talked about it said the visitor knows. The room would declare itself.

'They say that those who go into the room never come out again.'

We were suitably impressed. 'Do you mean they disappear, Rosario?' asked my brother.

'I don't know. I cannot tell you. People don't see them again – that is what they say.'

'But it's a big house, you said. There must be a lot of rooms. If you knew which was the haunted room you could simply avoid it, couldn't you?'

Rosario laughed. I don't think she ever believed any of it or was ever afraid. 'Perhaps you don't know until you are in this room and then it is too late. How do you like that?'

'Very much,' said Piers. 'It's wonderfully sinister. Has anyone ever disappeared?'

'The cousin of Carmela Valdez disappeared. They say he broke a window and got in because there were things to steal, he was very bad, he did no work.' She sought for a suitable phrase and brought it out slightly wrong. 'The black goat of the family.' Rosario was justly proud of her English and only looked smug when we laughed at her. Perhaps she could already hear the admiration in Piers's laughter. 'He disappeared, it is true, but only to a prison in Barcelona, I think.'

The meaning of *golondro* she refused to tell Piers. He must look it up. That way he would be more likely to remember it. Piers went to find the dictionary he and Rosario would use and there it was: a whim, a desire.

'The little house of desire,' said Piers. 'You can't imagine an English house called that, can you?'

My mother came out then with supper for us and cold drinks on a tray. No more was said about the *Casita* that night and the subject was not raised again for a while. Next day Piers began his Spanish lessons with Rosario. We always stayed indoors for a few hours after lunch, siesta time, the heat being too fierce for comfort between two and four. But adolescents can't sleep in the daytime. I would wander about, fretting for the magic hour of four to come round. I read or wrote in the diary I was keeping or gazed from my bedroom window across the yellow hills with their crowns of grey olives and their embroidery of bay and juniper, like dark upright stitches on a tapestry, and now I knew of its existence, speculated about the location of the house with the sinister room in it.

Piers and Rosario took over the cool white dining room with its furnishings of dark carved wood for their daily lesson. They had imposed no embargo on others entering. Humbly, they perhaps felt that what they were doing was hardly important enough for that, and my mother would go in to sit at the desk and write a letter while Concepçion, who cleaned and cooked for us, would put silver away in one of the drawers of the press or cover the table with a clean lace cloth. I wandered in and out, listening not to Rosario's words but to her patient tone and scholarly manner. Once I saw her correct Piers's pronunciation by placing a finger on his lips. She laid on his lips the finger on which she wore a ring with two tiny turquoises in a gold setting, holding it there as if to model his mouth round the soft guttural. And I saw them close together, side by side, my brother's smooth dark head, so elegantly shaped, Rosario's crown of red-brown hair, flowing over her shoulders, a cloak of it, that always seemed to me like a cape of polished wood, with the depth and grain and gleam of wood, as if she were a nymph carved from the trunk of a tree.

So they were together every afternoon, growing closer, and when the lesson was over and we emerged all three of us into the afternoon sunshine, the beach or the village or to find Will by the hotel, they spoke to each other in Spanish, a communication from which we were excluded. She must have been a good teacher and my brother an enthusiastic pupil, for he who confessed himself bad at languages learned fast. Within a week he was chattering Spanish, although how idiomatically I never knew. He and Rosario talked and laughed in their own world, a world that was all the more delightful to my brother because he had not thought he would ever be admitted to it.

I have made it sound bad for me, but it was not so bad as that. Piers was not selfish, he was never cruel. Of all those close to me only he ever understood my shyness and my fears, the door slammed in my face, the code into whose secrets, as in a bad dream, my companions have been initiated but I have not. Half an hour of Spanish conversation and he and Rosario remembered their manners, their duty to Will and me, and we were back to the language we all had in common. Only once did Will have occasion to say,

'We all speak English, don't we?'

It was clear, though, that Piers and Rosario had begun to see Will as there for me and themselves as there for each other. They passionately wanted to see things in this way, so very soon they did. All they wanted was to be alone together. I did not know this then, I would have hated to know it. I simply could not have understood, though now I do. My brother, falling in love, into first love, behaved heroically in including myself and Will, in being polite to us and kind and thoughtful. Between thirteen and sixteen a great gulf is fixed. I knew nothing of this but Piers did. He knew there was no bridge of understanding from the lower level to the upper, and accordingly he made his concessions.

On the day after the jellyfish came and the beach ceased to be inviting, we found ourselves deprived, if only temporarily, of the principal source of our enjoyment of Llosar. On the wall of a bridge over a dried-up river we sat and contemplated the arid but beautiful interior, the ribbon of road that traversed the island to Palma and the side-track which led away from it to the northern cape.

'We could go and look at the little haunted house,' said Will.

He said it mischievously to 'get at' Rosario, whom he liked no more than she liked him. But instead of reacting with anger or with prohibition, she only smiled and said something in Spanish to my brother.

Piers said, 'Why not?'

4

They were very beautiful, those jellyfish. Piers kept saying they were. I found them repulsive. Once, much later, when I saw one of the same species in a marine museum, I felt sick. My throat closed up and seemed to stifle me, so that I had to leave. *Phylum cnidaria*, the medusa, the jellyfish. They are named for the Gorgon with her writhing snakes for hair, a glance at whose face turned men to stone.

Those which were washed up in their thousands on the shore at Llosar were of a glassy transparency the colour of an aquamarine, and from their umbrella-like bodies hung crystalline feelers or stems like tassels. Or so they appeared when floating below the surface of the blue water. Cast adrift on the sand and rocks, they slumped into flat gelatinous plates, like collapsed blancmanges. My kind brother, helped by Will, tried to return them to the water, to save them from the sun, but the creeping sea, although nearly tideless, kept washing them back. It was beyond my understanding that they could bear to touch that quivering clammy jelly. Rosario too held herself aloof, watching their efforts with a puzzled amusement.

By the following day a great stench rose from the beach where the sun had cooked the medusas and was now hastening the process of rot and destruction. We kept away. We walked to the village and from there took the road to Pollença which passed through apricot orchards and groves of almond trees. The apricots were drying on trays in the sun, in the heat which was heavy and unvarying from day to day. We had been in Llosar for two weeks and all that time we had never seen a cloud in the sky. Its blueness glowed with the hot light of an invisible sun. We only saw the sun when it set and dropped into the sea with a fizzle like red-hot iron plunged into water.

The road was shaded by the fruit trees and the bridge over the bed of the dried-up river, by the dense branches of pines. Here, where we rested and sat and surveyed the yellow hillsides and the olive groves, Will suggested we go to look at 'the little haunted house' and my brother said, 'Why not?' Rosario was smiling a small secret smile and as we began to walk on, Will and I went first and she and Piers followed behind.

It was not far to the *Casita de Golondro*. If it had been more than two kilometres, say, I doubt if even 'mad tourists', as the village people called us, would have considered walking it in that heat. There was a bus which went to Palma but it had left long before we started out. Not a car passed us and no car overtook us. It is hard to believe that in Majorca today. Of course there were cars on the island. My parents had several times rented a car and a driver and two days afterwards we were all to be driven to the Dragon Caves. But motor transport was unusual, something to be stared at and commented upon. As we came to the side road which would lead to the *Casita*, an unmetalled track, a car did pass us, an aged Citroën, its black bodywork much scarred and splintered by rocks, but that was the only one we saw that day.

The little haunted house, the little house of a whim, of desire, was scarcely visible from this road. A dense concentrated growth of trees concealed it. This wood, composed of trees unknown to us, carob and holm oak and witches' pines, could be seen from Llosar, a dark opaque blot on the bleached yellows and greys, while the house could not. Even here the house could only be glimpsed between tree trunks, a segment of wall in faded ochreish plaster, a shallow roof of pantiles. The plastered wall which surrounded the land which Piers called the 'demesne' was too high for any of us to see over, and our first sight of the *Casita* was through the broken bars and loops and curlicues of a pair of padlocked wrought-iron gates.

We began to follow the wall along its course which soon left the road and climbed down the hillside among rocky outcroppings and stunted olive trees, herb bushes and myrtles, and in many places split open by a juniper pushing aside in its vigorous growth stones and mortar. If we had noticed the biggest of these fissures from the road we might have saved ourselves half a kilometre's walking. Only Rosario objected as Will began to climb through. She said something about our all being too old for this sort of thing but my brother's smile – she saw it too – told us how much this amused him. It was outside my understanding then but not now. You see, it was very unlike Piers to enter into an adventure of this kind. He really would have considered himself too old and too responsible as well. He would have said a gentle 'no' and firmly refused to discuss the venture again. But he had agreed and he had said, 'Why not?' I believe it was because he saw the *Casita* as a place where he could be alone with Rosario.

Oh, not for a sexual purpose, for making love, that is not what I mean. He would not, surely, at that time, at that stage of their relationship, have thought in those terms. But only think, as things were, what few opportunities he had even to talk to her without others being there. Even their afternoon Spanish lessons were subject to constant interruption. Wherever they went I, or Will and I went with them. On the veranda, in the evenings, I was with them. It would not have occurred to me not to be with them and would have caused me bitter hurt, as my brother knew, if the most tactful hint was dropped that I might leave them on their own. I think it must be faced too that my parents would not at all have liked the idea of their being left alone together, would have resisted this vigorously even perhaps to the point of taking us home to England.

Had he talked about this with Rosario? I don't know. The fact is that she was no longer opposed to taking a look at the 'little haunted house' while formerly she had been very positively against it. If Piers was in love with her she was at least as much in love with him. From a distance of forty years I am interpreting words and exchanged glances, eyes meeting and rapturous looks, for what they were, the signs of first love. To me then they meant nothing unless it was that Piers and Rosario shared some specific knowledge connected with the Spanish language which gave them a bond from which I was shut out.

The garden was no longer much more than a walled-off area of the hillside. It was irredeemably overgrown. Inside the wall a few trees grew of a kind not to be seen outside. Broken stonework lay about among the myrtles and arbutus, the remains of a fountain and moss-grown statuary. The air was scented with bay which did not grow very profusely elsewhere and there were rosy pink heathers in flower as tall as small trees. Paths there had once been but these were almost lost under the carpet of small tough evergreens. In places it was a battle to get through, to push a passage between thorns and bay and laurels, but our persistence brought us through the last thicket of juniper into a clearing paved in broken stone. From there the house could suddenly be seen, alarmingly close to us, its cloisters only yards away. It was like being in a dream where distance means very little and miles

340

are crossed in an instant. The house appeared, became visible, as if it had stepped out to meet us.

It was not a 'little' house. This is a relative term and the people who named it may have owned a palace somewhere else. To me it seemed a mansion, bigger than any house I had ever been in. José-Carlos's villa in Llosar and our house in London could have both been put inside the *Casita* and lost somewhere among its rooms.

Its surface was plastered and the plaster in many places had fallen away, exposing pale brickwork beneath. The cloisters were composed of eight arches supported on pillars Will said were 'Moorish', though without, I am sure, quite knowing what this meant. Above was a row of windows, all with their shutters open, all with stone balconies, a pantiled over-hang, another strip of plaster, carved or parged in panels, and above that the nearly flat roof of pink tiles.

Within the cloister, on the left-hand side of a central door, was (presumably) the window that Carmela Valdez's cousin had broken. Someone had covered it with a piece of canvas nailed to the frame, plastic not being in plentiful supply in those days. Will was the first of us to approach nearer to the house. He was wearing his grass hat and a long-sleeved shirt and trousers. He picked at the canvas around the broken window until a corner came away, and peered in.

'There's nothing inside,' he said. 'Just an old empty room. Perhaps it's *the* room.'

'It's not.' Rosario offered no explanation as to how she knew this.

'I could go in and open the door for you.'

'If it's *the* room you won't come out again,' I said.

'There's table in there with a candle on it.' Will had his head inside the window frame. 'Someone's been eating and they've left some bread and stuff behind. What a stink, d'you reckon it's rats?'

'I think we should go home now.' Rosario looked up into Piers's face and Piers said very quickly,

'We won't go in now, not this time. Perhaps we won't ever go in.'

Will withdrew his head and his hat fell off. 'I'm jolly well going in sometime. I'm not going home without getting in there. We go back home next week. If we go now I vote we all come back tomorrow and go in there and explore it and then we'll *know*.'

He did not specify exactly what it was we should know but we understood him. The house was a challenge to be accepted. Besides we had come too far to be daunted now. And yet it remains a mystery to me today that we, who had the beaches and the sea, the countryside, the village, the boats which would take us to Pinar or Formentor whenever we wished to go, were so attracted by that deserted house and its empty rooms. For Piers and Rosario perhaps it was a trysting place but what was there about it so inviting, so enticing, to Will and me?

Will himself expressed it, in words used by many an explorer and mountaineer. 'It's *there*.'

On the following day we all went to the *Cuevas del Drac*. Will's parents, whom our parents had got to know, came too and we went in two cars. Along the roadside between C'an Picafort and Arta grew the arbutus that Will's mother said would bear white flowers and red fruit simultaneously in a month or two. I wanted to see that, I wondered if I ever would. She said the fruit was like strawberries growing on branches.

'They look like strawberries but they have no taste.'

That is one of the few remarks of Iris Harvey's I can remember. Remember word for word, that is. It seemed sad to me then but now I see it as an aphorism. The fruit of the arbutus is beautiful, red and shiny, it looks like strawberries but it has no taste.

The arbutus grew only in this part of the island, she said. She seemed to know all about it. What she did not know was that these same bushes grew in profusion around the little haunted house. I identified them from those on the road to C'an Picafort, from the smooth glossy leaves that were like the foliage of garden shrubs, not wild ones. Among the broken stones, between the junipers and myrtle, where all seemed dust-dry, I had seen their leaves, growing as green as if watered daily.

On our return we inspected the beach and found the jellyfish almost gone, all that remained of them gleaming patches on the rocks like snails' trails. Piers and Rosario sat on the veranda doing their Spanish and Will went back to the hotel, his shirt cuffs buttoned, his hat pulled well down.

'Tomorrow then,' Piers had said to him as he left and Will nodded.

That was all that was necessary. We did not discuss it among ourselves. A decision had been reached, by each of us separately and perhaps simultaneously, in the cars or the caves or by the waters of the subterranean lake. Tomorrow we should go into the little haunted house, to see what it was like, because it was *there*. But a terrible or wonderful thing happened first. It was terrible or wonderful, depending on how you looked at it, how *I* looked at it, and I was never quite sure how that was. It filled my mind, I could scarcely think of anything else.

My parents had gone to bed. I was in the bedroom I shared with

Rosario, not in bed but occupied with arranging my mosquito net. This hotel where we now are is air-conditioned, you never open the windows. You move and dress and sleep in a coolness which would not be tolerated in England, a breezy chill that is very much at odds with what you can see beyond the glass, cloudless skies and a desiccated hillside. I liked things better when the shutters could be folded back against the walls, the casements opened wide, and the net in place so that you were protected from insects, yet in an airy room. The net hung rather like curtains do from a tester on an English four-poster and that morning, in a hurry to be off to the *Cuevas*, I had forgotten to close them.

Having made sure there were no mosquitos inside the curtains, I drew them and switched off the light so that no more should be attracted into the room. Sentimentally, rather than kill it, I carried a spider in my handkerchief to the window to release it into the night. The moon was waxing, a pearl drop, and the stars were brilliant. While dark, with a rich clear somehow shining darkness, everything in the little walled garden could clearly be seen. All that was missing was not clarity but colour. It was a monochrome world out there, black and silver and pewter and pearl and lead-colour and the opaque velvety greyness of stone. The moon glowed opal-white and the stars were not worlds but light-filled holes in the heavens.

I did not see them at first. I was looking past the garden at the spread of hills and the mountains beyond, serrated ranges of darkness against the pale shining sky, when a faint sound or tiny movement nearer at hand drew my eyes downwards. They had been sitting together on the stone seat in the deep shade by the wall. Piers got up and then Rosario did. He was much taller than she, he was looking down at her and she up at him, eye to eye. He put his arms round her and his mouth on hers and for a moment, before they stepped back into the secretive shadow, they seemed to me so close that they were one person, they were like two cypresses intertwined and growing as a single trunk. And the shadow they cast was the long spear shape of a single cypress on moon-whitened stone.

I was very frightened. I was shocked. My world had changed in a moment. Somewhere, I was left behind. I turned away with the shocked rejecting movement of someone who has seen a violent act. Once inside my mosquito net, I drew its folds about me and lay hidden in there in the dark. I lay there rigid, holding my hands clasped, then turned on to my face with my eyes crushed into the pillow.

Rosario came upstairs and into our room and spoke softly to me

343

but I made her no answer. She closed the door and I knew she was undressing in the dark. In all my life I had never felt so lonely. I would never have anyone, I would always be alone. Desertion presented itself to me as a terrible reality to be confronted, not to be avoided, and the last image that was before me when sleep came was of getting up in the morning and finding them all gone, my parents and Piers and Rosario, the hotel empty, the village abandoned, Majorca a desert island and I its only wild, lost, crazed inhabitant. Not quite the last image. That was of the twin-trunked cypress tree in the garden, its branches interwoven and its shadow a single shaft.

5

We entered the little house of desire, the little haunted house (*la casita que tiene fantasmas*) by the front door, Rosario going first. Will had climbed in through the broken window and opened the door inside the cloisters. It had the usual sort of lock which can be opened by turning a knob on the inside but from the outside only with a key. Piers followed her and I followed him, feeling myself to be last, the least there, the unwanted.

This, of course, was not true. The change was in my mind, not in outward reality. When I got up that morning it was not to find myself deserted, abandoned in an alien place by all those close to me, but treated exactly as usual. Piers was as warm to me as ever, as *brotherly*, my parents as affectionate, Rosario the same kind and interested companion. I was different. I had seen and I was changed.

As I have said, I could think of nothing else. What I had seen did not excite or intrigue me, nor did I wish not to have seen it, but rather that it had never happened. I might have been embarrassed in their company but I was not. All I felt, without reason, was that they liked each other better than they liked me, that they expressed this in a way neither of them could ever have expressed it to me, and that, obscurely but because of it, *because of something he did not and could not know*, Will too must now prefer each of them to me.

On the way to the *Casita* I had said very little. Of course I expected Piers to ask me what was the matter. I would have told him a lie. That was not the point. The point was that I was unable to understand. Why, why? What made them do that, behave in the way I had seen them in the garden? Why had they spoiled things? For me, they had become different people. They were strangers. I saw them as mysterious beings. It was my first glimpse of the degree to which human beings are unknowable, my first intimation of what it is that makes for loneliness. But what I realised at the time was that we who had been a cohesive group were now divided into two parts: Piers and Rosario, Will and me.

Yet I had not chosen Will. We *choose* very few of the people we know and call our friends. In various ways they have been thrust upon us. We never have the chance to review a hundred paraded before us and out of them choose one or two. I knew nothing of this then and I resented Will for being Will, cocky, intrusive, with his red hair and his thin vulnerable skin, his silly hat, and for being so much less nice to know than either my brother or Rosario. But he was for me and they were not, not any more. I sensed that he felt much the same way about me. I was the third best but all he could get, his companion by default. This was to be my future lot in life – and perhaps his, but I cared very little about that. It was because of this, all this, that as we entered the *Casita*, Piers and Rosario going off into one of the rooms, Will making for the half at the front of the house, I left them and went up the staircase on my own.

I was not afraid of the house, at least not then. I was too sore for that. All my misery and fear derived from human agency, not the supernatural. If I thought of the 'bad room' at all, it was with that recklessness, that fatalism, which comes with certain kinds of unhappiness: things are so bad that *anything* which happens will be a relief – disaster, loss death. So I climbed the stairs and explored the house, looking into all the rooms, without trepidation and without much interest.

It was three storeys high. With the exception of a few objects difficult to move or detach, heavy mirrors on the walls in gilded frames, an enormous bed with black oak headboard and bedposts, a painted wooden press, it was not furnished. I heard my brother's and Rosario's voices on the staircase below and I knew somehow that Piers would not have remained in the house and would not have let us remain if there had been furniture and carpets and pictures there. He was law-abiding and responsible. He would not have trespassed in a place he saw as someone's home.

But this house had been deserted for years. Or so it seemed to me. The mirrors were clouded and blue with dust. The sun bore down unchecked by shutters or curtains and its beams were layers of sluggishly moving dust that stretched though spaces of nearly intolerable heat.

I suppose it was because I was a child from a northern country that I associated hauntings with cold. Although everything I had experienced since coming to Llosar taught otherwise, I had expected the *Casita de Golondro* to be cold inside and dark.

The heat was stifling and the air was like a gas. What you breathed was a suspension of warm dust. The windows were large and hazy dusty sunshine filled the house, it was nearly as light as outside. I went to the window in one of the rooms on the first floor, meaning to throw it open, but it was bolted and the fastenings too stiff for me to move. It was there, while I was struggling with the catch, that Will crept up behind me and when he was only a foot away made that noise children particularly associate with ghosts, a kind of warbling crescendo, a howling siren-sound.

'Oh, shut up,' I said. 'Did you think I couldn't hear you? You made more noise than a herd of elephants.'

He was undaunted. He was never daunted. 'Do you know the shortest ghost story in the world? There was this man reached out in the dark for a box of matches but before he found them they were stuck into his hand.'

I pushed past him and went up the last flight of stairs. Piers and Rosario were nowhere to be seen or heard. I saw the double cypress tree again and its shadow and felt sick. Somewhere they were perhaps doing that again now, head close together, looking into each other's eyes. I stood in the topmost hallway of the house, a voice inside me telling me what it has often told me since, when human relations are in question: don't think of them, forget them, stand alone, you are safer alone. But my brother . . .? It was different with my brother.

The rooms on the top floor had lower ceilings, were smaller than those below and even hotter. It sounds incomprehensible if I say that these attics were like cellars, but so it was. They were high up in the house, high under the roof, but they induced the claustrophobia of basements, and there seemed to be weighing on them a great pressure of tiers of bricks and mortar and tiles.

What happened to me next I feel strange about writing down. This is not because I ever doubted the reality of the experience or that time has dimmed it but really because, of course, people don't believe me. Those I have told – a very few – suggest that I was afraid, expectant of horrors, and that my mind did the rest. But I was *not* afraid. I was so unafraid that even Will's creeping up on me had not made me jump. I was expectant of nothing. My mind was full of dread but it was dread of rejection, of loneliness, of others one by one discovering the secret of life and I being left in ignorance. It was fear of losing Piers.

All the doors to all the rooms had been open. In these circumstances, if you then come upon a closed door, however miserable you may be, however distracted, natural human curiosity will impel you to open it. The closed door was at the end of the passage on the left. I walked down the passage, through the stuffiness, the air so palpable you almost had to push it aside, tried the handle, opened the door. I walked into a rather small oblong room with, on its left-hand wall, one of those mirrors, only this one was not large or gilt-framed or fly-spotted, but rather like a window with a plain wooden frame and a kind of shelf at the bottom of it. I saw that it was a mirror but I did not look into it. Some inner voice was warning me not to look into it.

The room was dark. No, not dark, but darker than the other rooms. Here, although apparently nowhere else, the shutters were closed. I took a few steps into the warm gloom and the door closed behind me. Hindsight tells me that there was nothing supernatural or even odd about this. It had been closed while all the others in the house were open which indicates that it was a 'slamming' door or one which would only remain open when held by a doorstop. I did not think of this then. I thought of nothing reasonable or practical, for I was beginning to be frightened. My fear would have been less if I could have let light in but the shutters, of course, were on the outside of the window. I have said it was like a cellar up there. I felt as if I was in a vault.

Something held me there as securely as if I were chained. It was as if I had been tied up preparatory to being carried away. And I was aware that behind me, or rather to the left of me, was that mirror into which I must not look. Whatever happened I must not look into it and yet something impelled me to do so, I *longed* to do so.

How long did I stand there, gasping for breath, in that hot timeless silence? Probably for no more than a minute or two. I was not quite still, for I found myself very gradually rotating, like a spinning top that is slowing before it dips and falls on its side. Because of the mirror I closed my eyes. As I have said, it was silent, with the deepest silence I have ever known, but the silence was broken. From somewhere, or inside me, I heard my brother's voice.

I heard Piers say, 'Where's Petra?'

When I asked him about this later he denied having called me. He was adamant that he had not called. Did I imagine his voice just as I then imagined what I saw? Very clearly I heard his voice call me, the tone casual. But concerned, for all that, caring.

'Where's Petra?'

It broke the invisible chains. My eyes opened on to the hot, dusty, empty room. I spun round with one hand out, reaching for the door. In doing so I faced the mirror, I moved through an arc in front of the mirror, and saw, not myself, *but what was inside it.*

Remember that it was dark. I was looking into a kind of swimming gloom and in it the room was reflected but in a changed state, with two windows where no windows were, and instead of myself the figure of a man in the farthest corner pressed up against the wall. I stared at him, the shape or shade of a bearded ragged man, not clearly visible but clouded by the dark mist which hung between him and me. I had seen that bearded face somewhere before – or only in a bad dream? He looked back at me, a look of great anger and malevolence. We stared at each other and as he moved away from the wall in my direction, I had a momentary terror he would somehow break through the mirror and be upon me. But, as I flinched away, holding up my hands, he opened the reflected door and disappeared.

I cried out then. No one had opened the door on my side of the mirror. It was still shut. I opened it, came out and stood there, my back to the door, leaning against it. The main passage was empty and so was the side passage leading away to the right. I ran along the passage, feeling I must not look back, but once round the corner at the head of the stairs I slowed and began walking. I walked down, breathing deeply, turned at the foot of the first flight and began to descend the second. There I met Piers coming up.

What I would best have liked was to throw myself into his arms. Instead, I stopped and stood above him, looking at him.

'Did you call me?' I said.

'No. When do you mean? Just now?'

'A minute ago.'

He shook his head. 'You look as if you've seen a ghost.'

'Do I?' Why didn't I tell him? Why did I keep silent? Oh, I have asked myself enough times. I have asked myself why that warning inner voice did not urge me to tell and so, perhaps, save him. No doubt I was afraid of ridicule, for even then I never trusted to kindness, not even to his. 'I went into a room,' I said, 'and the door closed on me. I was a bit scared, I suppose. Where are the others?'

'Will found the haunted room. Well, he says it's the haunted room. He pretended he couldn't get out.'

How like Will that was! There was no chance for me now, even if I could have brought myself to describe what had happened. My eyes met Piers's eyes and he smiled at me reassuringly. Never since in all my life have I so longed to take someone's hand and hold it as I longed then to take my brother's. But all that was possible for me was to grip my own left hand in my right and so hold everything inside me.

We went down and found the others and left the house. Will pinned the canvas back over the broken window and we made our way home in the heat of the day. The others noticed I was unusually quiet and they said so. There was my chance to tell them but of course I could not. Will had stolen a march on me. But there was one curious benefit deriving from what had happened to me in the room with the closed shutters and the slamming door. My jealousy, resentment, insecurity I suppose we would call it now, over Piers and Rosario had quite gone. The new anxiety had cast the other out.

Nothing would have got me back to the *Casita*. As we walked across the hillside, among the prickly juniper and the yellow broom, the green-leaved arbutus and the sage, I was cold in the hot sun, I was staring ahead of me, afraid to look back. I did not look back once. And later that day, gazing across the countryside from my bedroom window, although the *Casita* was not visible from there, I would not even look in its direction, I would not even look at the ridge of hillside which hid it.

That evening Piers and Rosario went out alone together for the first time. There was no intention to deceive, I am sure, but my parents thought they had gone with me and Will and Will's mother to see the country dancing at Muro. It was said the *ximbombes* would be played and we wanted to hear them. Piers and Rosario had also shown some interest in these Mallorquin drums but they had not come with us. Will thought they had gone with my parents to see the Roman theatre, newly excavated at Puerto de Belver, although by then it was too dark to see anything.

When we got home they were already back. They were out on the veranda, sitting at the table. The moon was bright and the cicadas very noisy and of course it was warm, the air soft and scented. I had not been alone at all since my experience of the morning and I did not want to be alone then, shrouded by my mosquito net and with the moonlight making strange patterns on the walls. But almost as soon as I arrived home Rosario got up and came upstairs to bed. We hardly spoke, we had nothing to say to each other any more.

Next evening they went out together again. My father said to Piers,

'Where are you going?'

'For a walk.'

I thought he would say, 'Take Petra', because that was what he was almost certain to say, but he did not. His eyes met my mother's. Did they? Can I remember that? I am sure their eyes must have met and their lips twitched in small indulgent smiles.

It was moonlight. I went upstairs and looked out of the window of my parents' room. The village was a string of lights stretched along the shore, a necklace in which, here and there, beads were missing. The moon did not penetrate these dark spaces. A thin phosphorescence lay on the calm sea. There was no one to be seen. Piers and Rosario must have gone the other way, into the country behind. I thought, suppose I turn round and there, in the corner of this room, in the shadows, that man is.

I turned quickly and of course there was nothing. I ran downstairs and to while away the evening, my parents and I, we played a lonely game of beggar-my-neighbour. Piers and Rosario walked in at nine. On the following day we were on the beach where Will, for whom every day was April Fool's Day, struck dismay into our hearts with a tale of a new invasion of jellyfish. He had seen them heading this way from the hotel pier.

This was soon disproved. Will was forgiven because it was his next but last day. He boasted a lot about what he called his experiences in the 'haunted room' of the *Casita* two days before, claiming that he had had to fight with the spirits who tried to drag him through the wall. I said nothing, I could not have talked about it. When siesta time came I lay down on my bed and I must have slept, for Rosario had been on the other bed but was gone when I awoke, although I had not heard or seen her leave.

They were gone, she and my brother, when I came downstairs and the rest of us were preparing to go with Will and his parents in a hired car to see the gardens of a Moorish estate.

'Piers and Rosario won't be coming with us,' my mother said, looking none too pleased, and feeling perhaps that politeness to the Harveys demanded more explanation. 'They've found some local fisherboy to take them out in his boat. They said, would you please excuse them.'

Whether this fisherboy story was true or not, I don't know. I suspect my mother invented it. She could scarcely say – well, not in those days – 'My son wants to be alone with his girlfriend.' Perhaps there was a boy and a boat and perhaps this boy was questioned when the time came. I expect everyone who might have seen or spoken to Piers and Rosario was questioned, everyone who might have an idea of their whereabouts, because they never came back.

6

In those days there were few eating places on the island, just the dining rooms of the big hotels or small local *tabernas*. On our way back from the Moorish gardens we found a restaurant, newly opened with the increase of tourism, at a place called Petra. Of course this occasioned many kindly jokes on my name and the proprietor of the *Restorán del Toro* was all smiles and welcome.

Piers and Rosario's evening meal was to have been prepared by Concepçion. She was gone when we returned and they were still out. My parents were cross. They were abstracted and unwilling to say much in front of me, although I did catch one sentence, an odd one and at the time incomprehensible.

'Their combined ages only add up to thirty-one!'

It is not unusual to see displeasure succeeded by anxiety. It happens all the time. *They're late, it's inexcusable, where are they, they're not coming, something's happened.* At about half-past nine this change-over began. I was questioned. Did I have any idea where they might be going? Had they said anything to me?

We had no telephone. That was far from unusual in a place like that forty years ago. But what use could we have put it to if we had had one? My father went out of the house and I followed him. He stood there looking up and down the long shoreline. We do this when we are anxious about people who have not come, whose return is delayed, even though if they are there, hastening towards us, we only shorten our anxiety by a moment or two. They were not there. No one was there. Lights were on in the houses and the strings of coloured lamps interwoven with the vine above the hotel pier, but no people were to be seen. The waning moon shone on an empty beach where the tide crawled up a little way and trickled back.

Apart from Concepçion, the only people we really knew were Will's parents and when another hour had gone by and Piers and Rosario were not back my father said he would walk down to the hotel, there to consult with the Harveys. Besides, the hotel had a phone. It no longer seemed absurd to talk of phoning the police. But my father

351

was making a determined effort to stay cheerful. As he left, he said he was sure he would meet Piers and Rosario on his way.

No one suggested I should go to bed. My father came back, not with Will's parents who were phoning the police 'to be on the safe side', but with Concepçion at whose cottage in the village he had called. Only my mother could speak to her but even she could scarcely cope with the Mallorquin dialect. But we soon all understood, for in times of trouble language is transcended. Concepçion had not seen my brother and cousin that evening and they had not come for the meal she prepared for them. They had been missing since five.

That night remains very clearly in my memory, every hour distinguished by some event. The arrival of the police, the searching of the beach, the assemblage in the hotel foyer, the phone calls that were made from the hotel to other hotels, notably the one at Formentor, and the incredible inefficiency of the telephone system. The moon was only just past the full and shining it seemed to me for longer than usual, bathing the village and shoreline with a searching whiteness, a providential floodlighting. I must have slept at some point, we all must have, but I remember the night as white and wakeful. I remember the dawn coming with tuneless birdsong and a cool pearly light.

The worst fears of the night gave place in the warm morning to what seemed like more realistic theories. At midnight they had been dead, drowned, but by noon theirs had become a voluntary flight. Questioned, I said nothing about the cypress tree, entwined in the garden, but Will was not so reticent. His last day on the island had become the most exciting of all. He had seen Piers and Rosario kissing, he said, he had seen them holding hands. Rolling his eyes, making a face, he said they were 'in lo-ove'. It only took a little persuasion to extract from him an account of our visit to the *Casita* and a quotation from Piers, probably Will's own invention, to the effect that he and Rosario would go there to be alone.

The *Casita* was searched. There was no sign that Piers and Rosario had been there. No fisherman of Llosar had taken them out in his boat, or no one admitted to doing so. The last person to see them, at five o'clock, was the priest who knew Rosario and who had spoken to her as they passed. For all that, there was for a time a firm belief that my brother and Rosario had run away together. Briefly, my parents ceased to be afraid and their anger returned. For a day or two they were angry, and with a son whose behaviour had scarcely ever before inspired anger. He who was perfect had done this most imperfect thing.

Ronald and Iris Harvey postponed their departure. I think Iris liked my mother constantly telling her what a rock she was and how we could not have done without her. José-Carlos and Micaela were sent for. As far as I know they uttered no word of reproach to my parents. Of course, as far as I know is not very far. And I had my own grief – no, not that yet. My wonder, my disbelief, my panic.

Piers's passport was not missing. Rosario was in her own country and needed no passport. They had only the clothes they were wearing. Piers had no money, although Rosario did. They could have gone to the mainland of Spain. Before the hunt was up they had plenty of time to get to Palma and there take a boat for Barcelona. But the police found no evidence to show that they had been on the bus that left Llosar at six in the evening, and no absolute evidence that they had not. Apart from the bus the only transport available to them was a hired car. No one had driven them to Palma or anywhere else.

The difficulty with the running away theory was that it did not at all accord with their characters. Why would Piers have run away? He was happy. He loved school, he had been looking forward to this sixth form year, then to Oxford. My mother said, when Will's mother presented to her yet again the 'Romeo and Juliet' theory,

'But we wouldn't have stopped him seeing his cousin. We'd have invited her to stay. They could have seen each other every holiday. We're not strict with our children, Iris. If they were really that fond of each other, they could have been engaged in a few years. But they're so young!'

At the end of the week a body was washed up on the beach at Alcudia. It was male and young, had a knife wound in the chest, and for a few hours was believed to be that of Piers. Later that same day a woman from Muralla identified it as a man from Barcelona who had come at the beginning of the summer and been living rough on the beach. But that stab wound was very ominous. It alerted us all to terrible ideas.

The *Casita* was searched again and its garden. A rumour had it that part of the garden was dug up. People began remembering tragedies from the distant past, a suicide pact in some remote inland village, a murder in Palma, a fishing boat disaster, a mysterious unexplained death in a hotel room. We sat at home and waited, and the time our departure from the island was due came and went. We waited for news, we three with José-Carlos and Micaela, all of us but my mother expecting to be told of death. My mother, then and in the future, never wavered in her belief that Piers was alive and soon to get in touch with her.

After a week the Harveys went home, but not to disappear from our lives. Iris Harvey had become my mother's friend, they were to remain friends until my mother's death, and because of this I continued to know Will. He was never very congenial to me, I remember to this day the *enjoyment* he took in my brother's disappearance, his unholy glee and excitement when the police came, when he was permitted to be with the police on one of their searches. But he was in my life, fixed there, and I could not shed him. I never have been able to do so.

One day, about three weeks after Piers and Rosario were lost, my father said,

'I am going to make arrangements for us to go home on Friday.'

'Piers will expect us to be here,' said my mother. 'Piers will write to us here.'

My father took her hand. 'He knows where we live.'

'I shall never see my daughter again,' Micaela said. 'We shall never see them again, you know that, we all know it, they're dead and gone.' And she began crying for the first time, the unpractised sobs of the grown-up who has been tearless for years of happy life.

My father returned to Majorca after two weeks at home. He stayed in Palma and wrote to us every day, the telephone being so unreliable. When he wasn't with the police he was travelling about the island in a rented car with an interpreter he had found, making enquiries in all the villages. My mother expected a letter by every post, not from him but from Piers. I have since learned that it is very common for the mothers of men who have disappeared to refuse to accept that they are dead. It happens all the time in war when death is almost certain but cannot be proved. My mother always insisted Piers was alive somewhere and prevented by circumstances from coming back or from writing. What circumstances these could possibly have been she never said and arguing with her was useless.

The stranger thing was that my father, who in those first days seemed to accept Piers's death, later came part of the way round to her opinion. At least, he said it would be wrong to talk of Piers as dead, it would be wrong to give up hope and the search. That was why, during the years ahead, he spent so much time, sometimes alone and sometimes with my mother, in the Balearics and on the mainland of Spain.

Most tragically, in spite of their brave belief that Piers would return or the belief that they *voiced*, they persisted in their determination to have more children, to compensate presumably for their loss. At first my mother said nothing of this to me and it came as a shock when I overheard her talking about it to Iris harvey. When I was fifteen she had a miscarriage and later that year, another. Soon after that she began to pour out to me her hopes and fears. I cannot have known then that my parents were doomed to failure but I seemed to know, I seemed to sense in my gloomy way perhaps, that something so much wished-for would never happen. It would not be allowed by the fates who rule us.

'I shouldn't be talking like this to you,' she said, and perhaps she was right. But she went on talking like that. 'They say that longing and longing for a baby prevents you having one. The more you want it the less likely it is.'

This sounded reasonable to me. It accorded with what I knew of life.

'But no one tells you how to stop longing for something you long for,' she said.

When they went to Spain I remained behind. I stayed with my Aunt Sheila who told me again and again she thought it a shame my parents could not be satisfied with the child they had. I should have felt happier in her house if she had not asked quite so often why my mother and father did not take me with them.

'I don't want to go back there,' I said. 'I'll never go back.'

7

The loss of his son made my father rich. His wealth was the direct result of Piers's disappearance. If Piers had come back that night we should have continued as we were, an ordinary middle-class family living in a semi-detached suburban house, the breadwinner a surveyor with the local authority. But Piers's disappearance made us rich and at the same time did much to spoil Spain's Mediterranean coast and the resorts of Majorca.

He became a property developer. José-Carlos, already in the building business, went into partnership with him, raised the original capital, and as the demands of tourism increased, they began to build. They built hotels: towers and skyscrapers, shoebox shapes and horseshoe shapes, hotels like ziggurats and hotels like Piranesi palaces. They built holiday flats and plazas and shopping precincts. My father's reason for going to Spain was to find his son, his reason for staying was this new enormously successful building enterprise.

He built a house for himself and my mother on the north-west coast at Puerto de Soller. True to my resolve I never went there with them and eventually my father bought me a house in Hampstead. He and my mother passed most of their time at Puerto de Soller, still apparently trying to increase their family, even though my mother was in her mid-forties, still advertising regularly for Piers to come back to them, wherever he might be. They advertised, as they had done for years, in the *Majorca Daily Bulletin* as well as Spanish national newspapers and *The Times*. José-Carlos and Micaela, on the other hand, had from the first given Rosario up as dead. My mother told me they never spoke of her. Once, when a new acquaintance asked Micaela if she had any children, she had replied with a simple no.

If they had explanations for the disappearance of Piers and Rosario, I never heard them. Nor was I ever told what view was taken by the National Guard, severe brisk-spoken men in berets and brown uniforms. I evolved theories of my own. They *had* been taken out in a boat, had both drowned and the boatman been too afraid later to admit his part in the affair. The man whose body was found had killed them, hidden the bodies and then killed himself. My parents were right up to a point and they had run away together, being afraid of even a temporary enforced separation, but before they could get in touch had been killed in a road accident.

'That's exactly when you would know,' Will said. 'If they'd died in an accident that's when it would have come out.'

He was on a visit to us with his mother during the school summer holidays, a time when my parents were always in England. The mystery of my brother's disappearance was a subject of unending interest to him. He never understood, and perhaps that kind of understanding was foreign to his nature, that speculating about Piers brought me pain. I remember to this day the insensitive terms he used. 'Of course they've been bumped off,' was a favourite with him, and 'They'll never be found now, they'll just be bones by now.'

But equally he would advance fantastic theories of their continued existence. 'Rosario had a lot of money. They could have gone to Spain and stopped in a hotel and stolen two passports. They could have stolen passports from the other guests. I expect they earned money singing and dancing in cafés. Spanish people like that sort of thing. Or she could have been someone's maid. Or an artist's model. You can make a lot of money at that. You sit in a room with all your clothes off and people who're learning to be artists sit round and draw you.'

Tricks and practical jokes still made a great appeal to him. To stop him making a phone call to my mother and claiming to be, with the appropriate accent, a Frenchman who knew Piers's whereabouts, I had to enlist the help of his own mother. Then, for quite a long time, we saw nothing of Ronald and Iris Harvey or Will in London, although I believe they all went out to Puerto de Soller for a holiday. Will's reappearance in my life was heralded by the letter of condolence he wrote to me seven years later when my mother died.

He insisted then on visiting me, on taking me about, and paying a curious kind of court to me. Of my father he said, with his amazing insensitivity,

'I don't suppose he'll last long. They were very wrapped up in each other, weren't they? He'd be all right if he married again.'

My father never married again and, fulfilling Will's prediction, lived only another five years. Will did not marry either and I always supposed him homosexual. My own marriage to the English partner in the international corporation begun by my father and José-Carlos, took place three years after my mother's death. Roger was very nearly a millionaire by then, two-and-a-half times my age. We led the life of rich people who have too little to do with their time, who have no particular interests and hardly know what to do with their money.

It was not a happy marriage. At least I think not, I have no idea what other marriages are like. We were bored by each other and frightened of other people but we seldom expressed our feelings and spent our time travelling between our three homes and collecting seventeenth-century furniture. Apart from platitudes, I remember particularly one thing Roger said to me:

'I can't be a father to you, Petra, or a brother.'

By then my father was dead. As a direct result of Piers's death I inherited everything. If he had lived or there had been others, things would have been different. Once I said to Roger,

'I'd give it all to have Piers back.'

As soon as I had spoken I was aghast at having expressed my feelings so freely, at such a profligate flood of emotion. It was so unlike me. I blushed deeply, looking fearfully at Roger for signs of dismay, but he only shrugged and turned away. It made things worse between us. From that time I began talking compulsively about how my life would have been changed if my brother had lived.

'You would have been poor,' Roger said. 'You'd never have met me. But I suppose that might have been preferable.'

That sort of remark I made often enough myself. I took no notice of it. It means nothing but that the speaker has a low self-image and no one's could be lower than mine, not even Roger's.

'If Piers had lived my parents wouldn't have rejected me. They wouldn't have made me feel that the wrong one of us died, that if I'd died they'd have been quite satisfied with the one that was left. They wouldn't have wanted more children.'

'Conjecture,' said Roger. 'You can't know.'

'With Piers behind me I'd have found out how to make friends.'

'He wouldn't have been behind you. He'd have been off. Men don't spend their lives looking after their sisters.'

When Piers and Rosario's disappearance was twenty years in the past a man was arrested in the South of France and charged with the murder, in the countryside between Bedarieux and Lodeve, of two tourists on a camping holiday. In court it was suggested that he was a serial killer and over the past two decades had possibly killed as many as ten people, some of them in Spain, one in Ibiza. An insane bias against tourists was the motive. According to the English papers, he had a violent xenophobia directed against a certain kind of foreign visitor.

This brought to mind the young man's body with the stab wound that had been washed up on the beach at Alcudia. And yet I refused to admit to myself that this might be the explanation for the disappearance of Piers and Rosario. Like my parents, Roger said, I clung to a belief, half fantasy, half hope, that somewhere they were still alive. It was a change of heart for me, this belief, it came with my father's death, as if I inherited it from him along with all his property.

And what of the haunted house, the *Casita de Golondro*? What of my strange experience there? I never forgot it, I even told Roger about it once, to have my story received with incomprehension and the remark that I must have been eating some indigestible Spanish food. But in the last year of his life we were looking for a house to buy, the doctors having told him he should not pass another winter in a cold climate. Roger hated 'abroad', so it had to be in England, Cornwall or the Channel Islands. In fact no house was ever bought, for he died that September, but in the meantime I had been viewing many possibilities and one of these was in the south of Cornwall, near Falmouth.

It was a Victorian house and big, nearly as big as the *Casita*, ugly Gothic but with wonderful views. An estate agent took me over it and, as it turned out, I was glad of his company. I had never seen such a thing before, or thought I had not, an internal room without windows.

Not uncommon, the young man said, in houses of this age, and he hinted at bad design.

This room was on the first floor. It had no windows but the room adjoining it had, and in the wall which separated the two was a large window with a fanlight in it which could be opened. Thus light would be assured in the windowless room if not much air. The Victorians distrusted air, the young man explained.

I looked at this dividing window and twenty-eight years fell away. I was thirteen again and in the only darkened room of a haunted house, looking into a mirror. But now I understood. It was not a mirror. It had not been reflecting the room in which I stood but affording me a sight of a room beyond, a room with windows and another door, and of its occupant. For a moment, standing there, remembering that door being opened, not a reflected but a real door, I made the identification between the man I had seen, the man at the wheel of the battered Citroën and the serial killer of Bedarieux. But it was too much for me to take, I was unable to handle something so monstrous and so ugly. I shuddered, suddenly seeing impenetrable darkness before me, and the young man asked me if I was cold.

'It's the house,' I said. 'I wouldn't dream of buying a house like this.'

Will was staying with us at the time of Roger's death. He often was. In a curious way, when he first met Roger, before we were married, he managed to present himself in the guise of my rejected lover, the devoted admirer who knows it is all hopeless but who cannot keep away, so humble and selfless is his passion. Remarks such as 'may the best man win' and 'some men have all the luck' were sometimes uttered by him, and this from someone who had never so much as touched my hand or spoken to me a word of affection. I explained to Roger but he thought I was being modest. What other explanation could there be for Will's devotion? Why else but from long-standing love of me would he phone two or three times a week, bombard me with letters, angle for invitations? Poor Roger had made his fortune too late in life to understand that the motive for pursuing me might be money.

Roger died of a heart attack sitting at his desk in the study. And there Will found him when he went in with an obsequious cup of tea on a tray, even though we had a housekeeper to do all that. He broke the news to me with the same glitter-eyed relish as when I remembered him recounting to the police tales of the little haunted house. His voice was lugubrious but his eyes full of pleasure.

Three months later he asked me to marry him. Without hesitating for a moment, I refused.

'You're going to be very lonely in the years to come.'

'I know,' I said.

8

Never once did I seriously think of throwing in my lot with Will. But that was a different matter from telling him I had no wish to see him again. He was distasteful to me with his pink face, the colour of raw veal, the ginger hair that clashed with it, and the pale blue bird's-egg eyes. His heart was as cold as mine but hard in a way mine never was. I disliked everything about him, his insensitivity, the pleasure he took in cruel words. But for all that, he was my friend, he was my only friend. He was a man to be taken about by. If he hinted to other people that we were lovers, I neither confirmed nor denied it. I was indifferent. Will pleaded poverty so often since he had been made redundant by his company that I began allowing him an income but instead of turning him into a remittance man, this only drew him closer to me.

I never confided in him, I never told him anything. Our conversation was of the most banal. When he phoned – I *never* phoned him – the usual platitudes would be exchanged and then, desperate, I would find myself falling back on that well-used silence-filler and ask him.

'What have you been doing since we last spoke?'

When I was out of London, at the house in Somerset or the 'castle', a castellated shooting lodge Roger had bought on a whim in Scotland, Will would still phone me but would reverse the charges. Sometimes I said no when the operator asked me if I would pay for the call, but Will – thick-skinned mentally, whatever his physical state might be – simply made another attempt half an hour later.

It was seldom that more than three days passed without our speaking. He would tell me about the shopping he had done, for he enjoys buying things, troubles with his car, the failure of the electrician to come, the cold he had had, but never of what he might understand love to be of his dreams or his hopes, his fear of growing old and of death, not even what he had been reading or listening to or looking at. And I was glad of it, for I was not interested and I told him none of these things either. We were best friends with no more intimacy than acquaintances.

The income I allowed him was adequate, no more, and he was always complaining about the state of his finances. If I had to name one topic

360

we could be sure of discussing whenever we met or talked it would be money. Will grumbled about the cost of living, services bills, fares, the small amount of tax he had to pay on his pension and what he got from me, the price of food and drink and the cost of the upkeep of his house. Although he did nothing for me, a fiction was maintained that he was my personal assistant, 'secretary' having been rejected by him as beneath the dignity of someone with his status and curriculum vitae. Will knew very well that he had no claim at all to payment for services rendered but for all that he talked about his 'salary', usually to complain that it was pitifully small. Having arrived – without notice – to spend two weeks with me in Somerset, he announced that it was time he had a company car.

'You've got a car,' I said.

'Yes,' he said, 'a rich man's car.'

What was that supposed to mean?

'You need to be rich to keep the old banger on the road,' he said, as usual doubling up with mirth at his own wit.

But he nagged me about that car in the days to come. What was I going to do with my money? What was I saving it for, I who had no child? If he were in my place it would give him immense pleasure to see the happiness he could bring to others without even noticing the loss himself. In the end I told him he could have my car. Instead of my giving it in part exchange for a new one, he could have it. It was a rather marvellous car, only two years old and its sole driver had been a prudent middle-aged woman, that favourite of insurers, but it was not good enough for Will. He took it but he complained and we quarrelled. I told him to get out and he left for London in my car.

Because of this I said nothing to him when the lawyer's letter came. We seldom spoke of personal things but I would have told him about the letter if we had been on our normal terms. I had no one else to tell and he, anyway, was the obvious person. But for once, for the first time in all those years, we were out of touch. He had not even phoned. The last words he had spoken to me in hangdog fashion, sidling out of the front door, were a truculent muttered plea that in spite of everything I would not stop his allowance.

So the letter was for my eyes only, its contents for my heart only. It was from a firm of solicitors in the City and was couched in gentle terms. Nothing, of course, could have lessened the shock of it, but I was grateful for the gradual lead-up, and for such words as 'claim', 'suggest', 'allege' and 'possibility'. There was a softness, like a tender touch, in being requested to prepare myself and told that at this stage there was no need at all for me to rush to certain conclusions.

I could not rest but paced up and down, the letter in my hand. Then, after some time had passed, I began to think of hoaxes, I remembered how Will had wanted to phone my mother and give her that message of hope in a Frenchman's voice. Was this Will again? It was the solicitors I phoned, not Will, and they told me, yes, it was true that a man and a woman had presented themselves at their offices, claiming to be Mr and Mrs Piers Sunderton.

9

I am not a gullible person. I am cautious, unfriendly, morose and anti-social. Long before I became rich I was suspicious. I distrusted people and questioned their motives, for nothing had ever happened to me to make me believe in disinterested love. All my life I had never been loved but the effect of this was not to harden me but to keep me in a state of dreaming of a love I had no idea how to look for. My years alone have been dogged by a morbid fear that everyone who seems to want to know me is after my money.

There were in my London house a good many photographs of Piers. My mother had cherished them religiously, although I had hardly looked at them since her death. I spread them out and studied them; Piers as a baby in my mother's arms, Piers as a small child, a schoolboy, with me, with our parents and me. Rosario's colouring I could remember, her sallow skin and long hair, the rich brown colour of it, her smallness of stature and slightness, but not what she looked like. That is, I had forgotten her features, their shape, arrangement and juxtaposition. Of her I had no photograph.

From the first, even though I had the strongest doubts about this couple's identity as my brother and his wife, I never doubted that any wife he might have had would be Rosario. Illogical? Absurd? Of course. Those convictions we have in the land of emotion we can neither help nor escape from. But I told myself as I prepared for my taxi ride to London Wall that if it was Piers that I was about to see, the woman with him would be Rosario.

I was afraid. Nothing like this had happened before. Nothing had *got this far* before. Not one of the innumerable 'sightings' in those first months, in Rome, in Naples, Madrid, London, the Tyrol, Malta, had resulted in more than the occasional deprecating phone call to my father from whatever police force it might happen to be. Later on there had been claimants, poor things who presented themselves at my door and who lacked the nous even to learn the most elementary facts of Piers's childhood, fair-haired men, fat men, short men, men too young or too old. There were probably ten of them. Not one got further than the hall. But this time I was afraid, this time my intuition spoke to me, saying, 'He has come back from the dead,' and I tried to silence it, I cited reason and caution, but again the voice whispered, and this time more insistently.

They could be changed out of all knowledge. What was the use of looking at photographs? What use are photographs of a boy of sixteen in recognising a man of fifty-six? I waited in an ante-room for three minutes. I counted those minutes. No I counted the seconds which composed them. When the girl came back and led me in, I was trembling.

The solicitor sat behind a desk and on a chair to his left and a chair to his right sat a tall thin grey man and a small plump woman, very Spanish-looking, her face brown and still smooth, her dark hair sprinkled with white pulled severely back. They looked at me and the two men got up. I had nothing to say but the tears came into my eyes. Not from love or recognition or happiness or pain but for time which does such things to golden lads and girls, which spoils their bodies and ruins their faces and lays dust on their hair.

My brother said, 'Petra,' and my sister-in-law, in that voice I now remembered so precisely, in that identical heavily-accented English, 'Please forgive us, we are so sorry.'

I wanted to kiss my brother but I could hardly go up to a strange man and kiss him. My tongue was paralysed. The lawyer began to talk to us but of what he said I have no recollection, I took in none of it. There were papers for me to see, so-called 'proofs', but although I glanced at them, the print was invisible. Speech was impossible but I could think. I was thinking, I will go to my house in the country, I will take them with me to the country.

Piers had begun explaining. I heard something about Madrid and the South of France, I heard the word 'ashamed' and the words 'too late', which someone has said are the saddest in the English language, and then I found a voice in which to say,

'I don't need to hear that now, I understand, you can tell me all that later, much later.'

The lawyer, looking embarrassed, muttered about the 'inevitable ensuing legal proceedings'.

'What legal proceedings?' I said.

'When Mr Sunderton has satisfied the court as to his identity, he will naturally have claim on your late father's property.'

I turned my back on him. For I knew Piers's identity. Proofs would not be necessary. Piers was looking down, a tired, worn-out man a man who looked unwell. He said, 'Rosario and I will go back to our hotel now. It's best for us to leave it to Petra to say when she wants another meeting.'

'It's best,' I said, 'for us to get to know each other again. I want you both to come to the country with me.'

We went, or rather Rosario and I went, to my house near Wincanton. Piers was rushed to hospital almost before he set foot over my threshold. He had been ill for weeks, had appendicitis which became peritonitis, and they operated on him just in time.

Rosario and I went to visit him every day. We sat by his bedside and we talked, we all had so much to say. And I was fascinated by them, by this middle-aged couple who had once like all of us been young but who nevertheless seemed to have passed from adolescence into their fifties without the intervention of youth and middle years. They had great tenderness for each other. They were perfectly suited. Rosario seemed to know exactly what Piers would want, that he only liked grapes which were seedless, that although a reader he would only read magazines in hospital, that the slippers he required to go to the day room must be of the felt not the leather kind. He disliked chocolates, it was useless bringing any.

'He used to love them,' I said.

'People change, Petra.'

'In many ways they don't change at all.'

I questioned her. Now the first shock and joy were passed I could not help assuming the role of interrogator, I could not help putting their claim to the test, even though I knew the truth so well. She came through my examination very well. Her memory of Majorca in those distant days was even better than mine. I had forgotten – although I recalled it when she reminded me – our visit to the monastery at Lluc and the sweet voices of the boy choristers. Our parents' insistence that while in Palma we all visited the *Mansion de Arte*, this I now remembered, and the Goya etchings which bored us but which my mother made us all look at.

José-Carlos and Micaela had both been dead for several years. I could tell she was unhappy speaking of them, she seemed ashamed. This brought us to the stumbling block, the difficulty which reared up every time we spoke of their disappearance. Why had they never got in touch? Why had they allowed us all, in such grief, to believe them dead?

She – and later Piers – could give me no reason except their shame. They could not face my parents and hers, it was better for us all to accept that they were dead. To explain why they had run away in the first place was much easier.

'We pictured what they would all say if we said we were in love. Imagine it! We were sixteen and fifteen, Petra. But we were right, weren't we? You could say we're still in love, so we were right.'

'They wouldn't have believed you,' I said.

'They would have separated us. Perhaps they would have let us meet in our school holidays. It would have killed us, we were dying for each other. We couldn't live out of sight of the other. That feeling has changed now, of course it has. I am not dying, am I, though Piers is in the hospital and I am here? It wasn't just me, Petra, it was Piers too. It was Piers's idea for us to – go.'

'Did he think of his education? He was so brilliant, he had everything before him. To throw it up for – well, he couldn't tell it would last, could he?'

'I must tell you something, Petra. Piers was not so brilliant as you thought. Your father had to see Piers's headmaster just before you came on that holiday. He was told Piers wasn't keeping up with his early promise, he wouldn't get that place at Oxford, the way he was doing he would be lucky to get to a university at all. They kept it a secret, you weren't told, even your mother wasn't, but Piers knew. What had he to lose by running away with me?'

'Well, comfort,' I said, 'and his home and security and me and his parents.'

'He said – forgive me – that I made up for all that.'

She was sweet to me. Nothing was too much trouble for her. I, who had spent so much time alone that my tongue was stiff from disuse, my manners reclusive, now found myself caught up in her gaiety and her charm. She was the first person I have ever known to announce in the morning *ideas* for how to spend the day, even if those notions were often only that I should stay in bed while she brought me my breakfast and then that we should walk in the garden and have a picnic lunch there. When there was a need for silence, she was silent, and when I longed to talk but scarcely knew how to begin she would talk to me, soon involving us in a conversation of deep interest and a slow realisation of the tastes we had in common. Soon we were companions and by the time Piers came home, friends.

Until we were all together again I had put off the discussion of what happened on the day they ran away. Each time Rosario had tried to tell me I silenced her and asked for more about how they had lived when first they came to the Spanish mainland. Their life at that time had been a series of adventures, some terrible, some hilarious. Rosario had a gift for story-telling and entertained me with her tales while we sat in the firelight. Sometimes it was like one of those old Spanish picaresque novels, full of event, anecdote, strange characters and hairsbreadth escapes, not all of it I am afraid strictly honest and above-board. Piers had changed very quickly or she had changed him.

They had worked in hotels, their English being useful. Rosario had even been a chambermaid. Later they had been guides, and at one time, in a career curiously resembling Will's scenario, had sung in cafés to Piers's hastily improvised guitar-playing. In her capacity as a hotel servant – they were in Madrid by this time – Rosario had stolen two passports from guests and with these they had left Spain and travelled about the South of France. The names of the passport holders became their names and in them they were married at Nice when he was eighteen and she seventeen.

'We had a little boy,' she said. 'He died of meningitis when he was three and after that no more came.'

I thought of my mother and put my arms around her. I, who have led a frozen life, have no difficulty in showing my feelings to Rosario. I, in whom emotion has been something to shrink from, can allow it to flow freely in her company and now in my brother's. When he was home again, well now and showing in his face some vestiges of the Piers I had known so long ago, I found it came quite naturally to go up to him, take his hand and kiss his cheek. In the past I had noticed, while staying in other people's houses, the charming habit some have of kissing their guests good night before everyone retires to their rooms. For some reason, a front of coldness perhaps, I had never been the recipient of such kisses myself. But now – and amazing though it was, I made the first move myself – I was kissing both of them good night and we exchanged morning kisses when we met next day.

One evening, quite late, I asked them to tell me about the day itself, the day which ended so terribly in fear and bright empty moonlight. They looked away from me and at each other, exchanging a rueful nostalgic glance. It was Rosario who began the account of it.

It was true that they had met several times since that first time in the little haunted house. They could be alone there without fear of interruption and there they had planned, always fearfully and daringly, their escape. I mentioned the man I had seen, for now I was sure it had been a man seen through glass and no ghost in a mirror, but it meant nothing to them. At the *Casita* they had always found absolute solitude. They chose that particular day because we were all away at the gardens but made no other special preparations, merely boarding the afternoon bus for Palma a little way outside the village. Rosario, as we had always known, had money. She had enough to buy tickets for them on the boat from Palma to Barcelona.

'If we had told them or left a note they would have found us and brought us back,' Rosario said simply.

She had had a gold chain around her neck with a cameo that they could sell, and a gold ring on her finger.

'The ring with the two little turquoises,' I said.

'That was the one. I had it from my grandmother when I was small.'

They had sold everything of value they had, Piers's watch and his fountain pen and his camera. The ring saved their lives, Piers said, when they were without work and starving. Later on they became quite rich, for Piers, like my father, used tourism to help him, went into partnership with a man they met in a café in Marseille, and for years they had their own hotel.

There was only one question left to ask. Why did they ever come back?

They had sold the business. They had read in the deaths column of a Spanish newspaper they sometimes saw that Micaela, the last of our parents, was dead. Apparently, the degree of shame they felt was less in respect to me. I could understand that, I was only a sister. Now I think I understood everything. Now when I looked at them both, with a regard that increased every day, I wondered how I could ever have doubted their identities, how I could have seen them as old, as unutterably changed.

The time had come to tell Will. We were on speaking terms again. I had mended the rift myself, phoning him for the first time ever. It was because I was happy and happiness made me kind. During the months Piers and Rosario had been with me he had phoned as he always did, once or twice we had met away from home, but I had not mentioned them. I did not now, I simply invited him to stay.

To me they were my brother and sister-in-law, familiar loved figures with faces already inexpressibly dear, but he I knew would not know them. I was not subjecting them to a test, I needed no test, but the idea of their confronting each other without preparation amused me.

A small deception had to be practised and I made them reluctantly agree to my introducing them as 'my friends Mr and Mrs Page'.

For a few minutes he seemed to accept it. I watched him, I noticed his hands were trembling. He could bear his suspicion no longer and burst out:

'It's Piers and Rosario, I know it is!'

The years could not disguise them for him, although they each separately confessed to me afterwards that if they had not been told they would never have recognised him. The red-headed boy with 'one skin too few' was not just subsumed in the fat red-faced bald man but utterly lost.

Whether their thoughts often returned to those remarks the solicitor had made on the subject of legal proceedings I cannot say. When mine did for the second time I spoke out. We were too close already for litigation to be conceivable. I told Piers that I would simply divide all my property in two, half for them and half for me. They were shocked, they refused, of course they did. But eventually I persuaded them. What was harder for me to voice was my wish that the property itself should be divided in two, the London house, the Somerset farm, my New York apartment, literally split down the middle. Few people had ever wanted much of my company in the past and I was afraid they would see this as a bribe or as taking advantage of my position of power. But all Rosario said was,

'Not too strictly down the middle, Petra, I hope. It would be nicer to *share*.'

All I stipulated was that in my altered will I should leave all I possessed to my godchild and cousin, Aunt Sheila's daughter, and Piers readily agreed, for he intended to leave everything he had to the daughter of his old partner in the hotel business.

So we lived. So we have lived for rather more than a year now. I have never been so happy. Usually it is not easy to make a third with a married couple. Either they are so close that you are made to feel an intruder or else the wife will see you as an ally to side with her against her husband. And when you are young the danger is that you and the husband will grow closer than you should. With Piers and Rosario things were different. I truly believe that each wanted my company as much as they wanted each other's. In those few months they came to love me and I, who have loved no one since Piers went away, reciprocated. They have shown me that it is possible to grow warm and kind, to learn laughter and pleasure, after a lifetime of coldness. They have unlocked something in me and liberated a lively spirit that must always have been there but which languished for long years, chained in a darkened room.

It is two weeks now since the Majorcan police got in touch with me and told me what the archaeologists had found. It would be helpful to them and surely of some satisfaction to myself to go to Majorca and see what identification I could make, not of remains, it was too late for that, but of certain artefacts found in the caves.

We were in Somerset and once more Will was staying with us. I suggested we might all go. All those years I had avoided revisiting the island but things were different now. Nothing I could see there could cause me pain. While I had Piers and Rosario I was beyond pain, it was as if I was protected inside the warm shell of their affection.

'In that case,' Will said, 'I don't see the point of going. You know the truth. These bits of jewellery, clothes, whatever they are, can't be Piers's and Rosario's because they sold theirs, so why try to identify what in fact you can't identify?'

'I want to see the place again,' I said. 'I want to see how it's changed. This police thing, that's just an excuse for going there.'

'I suppose there will be bones too,' he said, 'and maybe more than bones even after so long.' He has always had a fondness for the macabre. 'Did the police tell you how it all got into the caves?'

'Through a kind of pothole from above, they think, a fissure in the cliff top that was covered by a stone.'

'How will you feel about going back, Piers?' asked Rosario.

'I shan't know till I get there,' he said, 'but if Petra goes we go too. Isn't that the way it's always going to be?'

10

When I woke up this morning it was with no sense of impending doom. I was neither afraid nor hopeful. I was indifferent. This was no more than a chore I must perform for the satisfaction of officials, as a 'good citizen'. For all that, I found my room confining in spite of the wide-open windows, the balcony and view of the sea, and cancelling my room service order, I went down to breakfast.

To my surprise I found the others already there in the terrace dining room. It was not quite warm enough to sit outside so early. They were all unaware of my approach, were talking with heads bent and close together above the table. I was tempted to come up to them in silence and lay a light loving hand on Rosario's shoulder but somehow I knew that this would make her start. Instead I called out a 'good morning' that sounded carefree because it was.

Three worried faces were turned to me, although their frowns cleared to be replaced in an instant by determined smiles on the part of my brother and his wife and a wary look on Will's. They were concerned, it appeared, about *me*. The effect on me of what they called the 'ordeal' ahead had been the subject of that heads-together discussion. Horrible sights were what they were afraid of, glimpses of the charnel house. One or all of them should go with me. They seemed to believe my life had been sheltered and perhaps it had been, compared to theirs.

'I shan't be going into the caves,' I said as I ordered my breakfast. 'It will be some impersonal office with everything spread out and labelled, I expect, like in a museum.'

'But you'll be alone.'

'Not really. I shall know you're only a few miles away, waiting for me.'

The table was bare except for their coffee cups. None of them had eaten a thing. My rolls arrived and butter and jam, my fruit and fruit juice. I suddenly felt unusually hungry.

'Let's see,' I said, 'what shall we do for the rest of the day? We could take the boat to Formentor for lunch or drive to Lluc. This evening, don't forget, we're having dinner at the Parador de Golondro. Have we booked a table?'

'I'm sorry, Petra, I'm afraid I forgot to do that,' Piers said.

'Could you do it while I'm out?' A little fear struck me. I was going to say I don't know why it did, but I do know. 'You *will* all be here when I get back, won't you?'

Rosario's voice sounded unlike her. I had never heard bitterness in it before. 'Where should we go?'

The car came for me promptly at ten. The driver turned immediately inland and from the road, just before he took the turn for Muralla, I had a sudden bold sight of the *Casita*, glimpsed as it can be between the parting of the hills. It seemed a deeper, brighter colour, an ochreish gold, an effect either of new paint or of the sun. But when does the sun not shine? The yellow hills, with their tapestry stitches of grey and dark green, slipped closed again like sliding panels and the house withdrew behind them.

I was right about what awaited me in Muralla, a new office building made of that whitish grainy concrete which has defaced the Mediterranean and is like nothing so much as blocks of cheap ice-cream. Inside, in what I am sure they call the 'atrium', was a forest of plastic greenery. There was even a small collection, in styrofoam amphorae, of plastic strawberry trees. I was led via jungle paths to a room marked *privado* and then and only then, hesitating as two more policemen joined us and a key to the room was produced, did my heart misgive me and a tiny bubble of panic run up to my throat so that I caught my breath.

They were very kind to me. They were big strong macho men enjoyably occupied in doing what nature had made them for, protecting a woman from the uglinesses of life. One of them spoke tolerable English. If I would just look at the things, look at them very carefully, think about what I had seen and then they would take me away and ask me one or two simple questions. There would be nothing unpleasant. The bones found in the cave – he apologised for their very existence. There was no need for me to see them.

'I would like to see them,' I said.

'They cannot be identified after so long.'

'I would like to see them.'

'Just as you wish,' he said with a shrug and then the door was opened.

An empty room. A place of drawers and bench tops, like a dissecting room except that all the surfaces were of light polished wood and at the windows hung blinds of pale grey vertical strips. Drawers were opened, trays lifted out and placed on the long central table. I approached it slowly, holding one of my hands clasped in the other and feeling my cold fingertips against my cold damp palm.

Spread before me were two pairs of shoes, the woman's dark blue leather with sling backs and wedge heels, the man's what we call trainers now but 'plimsolls' then or 'gym shoes'; rags, gnawed by vermin, might once have been a pair of flannel trousers, a shirt, a dress with a tiny pearl button still attached to its collar; a gold chain with pendent cross, a gold watch with bracelet and safety chain, a heavier watch with its leather strap rotted, a child's ring for a little finger, two pinhead turquoises on a gold band thin as wire.

I looked at it all. I looked with indifference but a pretence of care for the sake of those onlookers. The collection of bones was too pitiful to be obscene. Surely this was not all? Perhaps a few specimens only had found their way to this room. I put out my hand and lifted up one of the long bones. The man who had brought me there made a movement towards me but was checked by his superior, who stood there watching me intently. I held the bone in both my hands, feeling its dry worn deadness, grey and grainy, its long-lifeless age, and then I put it down gently.

I turned my back on the things and never looked at them again.

'I have never seen any of this before,' I said. 'It means nothing to me.'

'Are you quite sure? Would you like some time to think about it?'

'No, I am quite sure? I remember very well what my brother and my cousin were wearing.'

They listened while I described clothes that Piers and Rosario had had. I enumerated items of jewellery. There was a locket I remembered her wearing the first time we met, a picture of her mother in a gold circlet under a seed pearl lid.

'Thank you very much. You have been most helpful.'

'At least I have eliminated a possibility,' I said, knowing they would not understand.

They drove me back to Llosar. The fruit on the strawberry trees takes a year to ripen. This year's flowers, blooming now, will become the fruit of twelve months' time. And immediately it ripens they pick it for making fruit pies. I had this sudden absurd yearning to see those strawberries in the hotel garden again, to see them before the bushes were stripped. I opened the car door myself, got out and walked up to the hotel without looking back. But instead of going up the steps, I turned aside into the shady garden, the pretty garden of geometric paths and small square pools with yellow fish, the cypresses and junipers gathered in groups as if they had met and stopped to gossip. To the left of me, up in the sun, rose the terrace and beyond it was the swimming pool, but down here grew the arbutus, its white blossom gleaming and its red fruits alight, as shiny as decorations on some northern Christmas tree.

Piers and Rosario were up on the terrace. I am not sure how I knew this for I was not aware of having looked. I felt their anguished eyes on me, their dread communicated itself to me on the warm, still, expectant air. I knew everything about them, I knew how they felt now. They saw me and read into my action in coming here, in coming immediately to this garden, anger and misery and knowledge of betrayal. Of course I understood I must put an end to their anguish at once, I must go to them and leave adoration of these sweet-scented snowy flowers and strawberry fruits until another day.

But first I picked one of the fruits and put it in my mouth. Iris Harvey had been wrong. It was not tasteless, it tasted like some fresh crisp vegetable, sharp and strange. It was different, different from any other fruit I had tasted, but not unpleasant. I thought it had the kind of flavour that would grow on me. I walked up the steps to the terrace. Will was nowhere to be seen. With the courage I knew they had, their unconquered brave hearts, they were waiting for me. Decorously, even formally, dressed for that place where the other guests were in swimming costumes, they were nevertheless naked to me, their eyes full of the tragedy of long, wretched, misspent lives. They were holding hands.

'Petra,' Piers said. Just my name.

To have kept them longer in suspense would have been the cruellest act of my life. In the time they had been with me I had learned to speak like a human being, like someone who understands love and knows warmth.

'My dears,' I said. 'How sad you look. There's nothing wrong, is there? I've had such a stupid morning. It was a waste of time going over there. They had nothing to show me but a bundle of rags I've never seen before and some rubbishy jewellery. I don't know what they expected – that all that was something to do with you two?'

They remained there, quite still. I know about the effects of shock. But slowly the joined hands slackened and Rosario withdrew hers. I went up to each of them and kissed them gently. I sat down on the third chair at the table and smiled at them. Then I began to laugh.

'I'm sorry,' I said. 'I'm only laughing because I'm happy. Children laugh from happiness, so why not us?'

'Why not?' said Piers as if it was a new thought, as if a new world opened before him. 'Why not?'

I was remembering how long long ago I had heared my brother ask that same rhetorical question, give that odd form of assent when Will proposed going into the *Casita* and Rosario had demurred. For a moment I saw us all as we had been, Will in his grass hat, long-legged Rosario with her polished hair, my brother eager with love. I sighed and turned the sigh to a smile.

'Now that's behind me,' I said, 'we can stay on here and have a holiday. Shall we do that?'

'Why not?' said Piers again, and this time the repetition of those words struck Rosario and me as inordinately funny and we both began to laugh as at some exquisite joke, some example of marvellous wit.

It was thus, convulsed with laughter, that we were found by Will when, having no doubt been watching from some window up above for signs of good or ill, he judged the time right and safe to come out and join us.

'Did you book that table at Golondro?' I said, hoarse with laughter, weak with it.

Will shook his head. I knew he would not have, that none of them would have. 'I'll do it this minute,' he said.

'Don't be long,' I called after him. 'We're going to celebrate. I'm going to order a bottle of champagne.'

'What are we celebrating, Petra?' said Rosario.

'Oh, just that we're here together again,' I said.

They smiled at me for I was bestowing on them, on both of them, the tender look I had never given to any lover. And the feeling which inspired it was better than a lover's glance, being without self-deception, without illusion. Of course I had never been deceived. I had known, if not quite from the first, from the third day of their appearance, that they were not my brother and his wife. For one thing, a man is not operated on twice in his life for appendicitis. But even without that I would have known. My blood told me and my bones, my thirteen years with a brother I was closer to than to parents or any friend. I knew – always – they were a pair of imposters Will had found and instructed. I knew, almost from the beginning, it was a trick played on me for their gain and Will's.

But there is another way of looking at it. I have bought them and they are mine now. They have to stay, they have nowhere else to go. Isn't that what Piers meant when he said being together was the way it always would be? They are my close companions. We have nothing more to gain from each other, we have made our wills, and the death of one of us will not profit the others.

They have made me happier than I have ever been. I know what people are. I have observed them. I have proved the truth of the recluse's motto, that the onlooker sees most of the game. And I know that Piers and Rosario love me now as I love them, and dislike Will as I dislike him. Not doubt they have recompensed him, I don't want to know how, and I foresee a gradual loosening of whatever bond it is that links him to us. It began when I sent him back into the hotel to make that phone call, when Rosario's eyes met mine and Piers pursed his lips in a little *moue* of doubt.

Am I to end all this with a confrontation, an accusation, casting them out of my life? Am I to retreat – and this time, at my age, finally, for good – into that loneliness that would be even less acceptable than before because now I have seen what else is possible?

I have held my dear brother's bone in my hands. I have seen his clothes that time and decay have turned to rags and touched the ruin of a shoe that once encased his strong slender foot. Now I shall begin the process of forgetting him. I have a new brother and sister to be happy with for the rest of my life.

Will has come back, looking sheepish, not understanding at all what has happened, to tell us we are dining at the Parador de Golondro, the little house of desire, at nine tonight. This is the cue, of course, for some characteristic British complaining about the late hour at which the Spanish dine. Only Rosario has nothing to say, but then she is Spanish herself – or is she?

I resolve never to try to discover this, never to tease, to lay traps, attempt a catching-out. After all, I have no wish to understand the details of the conspiracy. And when the time comes I will neither listen to nor make deathbed confessions.

For I saw in their eyes just now, as I came to their table to reassure them, that they are no more deceived in me than I am in them. They know that I know and that we all, in our mutual love, can accept.

# Piranha to Scurfy

# Piranha to Scurfy

It was the first time he had been away on holiday without Mummy. The first time in his life. They had always gone to the Isle of Wight, to Ventnor or Totland Bay, so, going alone, he had chosen Cornwall for the change that people say is as good as a rest. Not that Ribbon's week in Cornwall had been entirely leisure. He had taken four books with him, read them carefully in the B and B's lounge, in his bedroom, on the beach and sitting on the clifftop, and made meticulous notes in the loose-leaf notebook he had bought in a shop in Newquay. The results had been satisfactory, more than satisfactory. Allowing for the anger and disgust-making these discoveries invariably aroused, he felt he could say he had had a relaxing time. To use a horrible phrase much favoured by Eric Owlberg in his literary output, he had recharged his batteries.

Coming home to an empty house would be an ordeal. He had known it would be and it was. Instead of going out into the garden, he gave it careful scrutiny from the dining-room window. Everything outside and indoors was as he had left it. In the house, all the books in their places. Every room contained books. Ribbon was not one to make jokes but he considered it witty to remark that while other people's walls were papered his were booked. No one knew what he meant for hardly anyone except himself ever entered 21 Grove Green Avenue, Leytonstone, and those to whom he uttered his little joke smiled uneasily. He had put up the shelves himself, buying them from IKEA. As they filled he bought more, until the shelves extended from floor to ceiling. A strange appearance was given to the house by this superfluity of books as the shelves necessarily reduced the size of the rooms, so that the living room, originally fifteen feet by twelve, shrank to thirteen feet by ten. The hall and landing were 'booked' as densely as the rooms. The place looked like a library, but one mysteriously divided into small sections. His windows appeared as alcoves set deep in the walls, affording a view at the front of the house of a rather gloomy suburban street, thickly treed. The back gave on to the yellow-brick rears of other houses and, in the foreground, his garden which was mostly lawn, dotted about with various drab shrubs. At the far end was a wide flowerbed the sun never reached and in which grew creeping ivies and dark-leaved flowerless plants which like the shade.

He had got over expecting Mummy to come downstairs or walk into a room. She had been gone five months now. He sighed, for he was a long way from recovering from his loss and his regrets. Work was in some ways easier without her and in others immeasurably harder. She had reassured him, sometimes she had made him strong. But he had to press on, there was really no choice. Tomorrow things would be back to normal.

He began by ranging before him on the desk in the study – though was not the whole house a study? – the book review pages from the newspapers which had arrived while he was away. As he had expected, Owlberg's latest novel, *Paving Hell*, appeared this very day in paperback, one year after hardcover publication. It was priced at £6.99 and by now would be in all the shops. Ribbon made a memo about it on one of the plain cards he kept for this purpose. But before continuing he let his eyes rest on the portrait of Mummy in the plain silver frame that stood on the table where used, read and dissected books had their temporary home. It was Mummy who had first drawn his attention to Owlberg. She had borrowed one of his books from the public library and pointed out to Ribbon with indignation the mass of errors, solecisms and abuse of the English language to be found in its pages. How he missed her! Wasn't it principally to her that he owed his choice of career as well as the acumen and confidence to pursue it?

He sighed anew. Then he returned to his newspapers and noted down the titles of four more novels currently published in paperback as well as the new Kingston Marle, *Demogorgon*, due to appear this coming Thursday in hardcover with the maximum hype and fanfares of metaphorical trumpets, but almost certainly already in the shops. A sign of the degeneracy of the times, Mummy had said, that a book whose publication was scheduled for May appeared on sale at the end of April. No one could wait these days, everyone was in a hurry. It certainly made his work harder. It increased the chances of his missing a vitally important novel which might have sold out before he knew it was in print.

Ribbon switched on his computer and checked that the printer was linked to it. It was only nine in the morning. He had at least an hour before he need make his trip to the bookshop. Where should it be today? Perhaps the City or the West End of London. It would be unwise to go back to his local shop so soon and attract too much attention to himself. Hatchards, perhaps then, or Books Etc or Dillons, or even all three. He opened the notebook he had bought in Cornwall, reread what he had written and with the paperback open on the desk, reached for the *Shorter Oxford Dictionary*, Brewer's *Dictionary of Phrase and Fable* and *Whittaker's Almanack*. Referring to the first two and noting down his finds, he began his letter.

> *21 Grove Green Avenue,*
> *London E11 4ZH*

*Dear Joy Anne Fortune,*

*I have read your new novel* Dreadful Night *with very little pleasure and great disappointment. Your previous work has seemed to me, while being without any literary merit whatsoever, at least to be fresh, occasionally original and largely free from those errors of fact and slips in grammar which, I may say, characterise* Dreadful Night.

*Look first at page 24. Do you really believe 'desiccated' has two 's's and one 'c'? And if you do, have your publishers no copy editor whose job it is to recognise and correct these errors? On page 82 you refer to the republic of Guinea as being in East Africa and as a former British possession, instead of being in West Africa and formerly French, and on page 103 to the late General Sikorski as a one-time prime minister of Czechoslovakia rather than of Poland. You describe, on page 139, 'hadith' as being the Jewish prayers for the dead instead of what it correctly means, the body of tradition and legend surrounding the Prophet Mohammed and his followers, and on the following page 'tabernacle' as an entrance to a temple. Its true meaning is a portable sanctuary in which the Ark of the Covenant was carried.*

*Need I go on? I am weary of underlining the multifarious mistakes in your book. Needless to say, I shall buy no more of your work, and shall advise my highly literate and discerning friends to boycott it.*

*Yours sincerely,*
*Ambrose Ribbon*

The threat in the last paragraph was an empty one. Ribbon had no friends and could hardly say he missed having any. He was on excellent, at least speaking, terms with his neighbours and various managers of bookshops. There was a cousin in Gloucestershire he saw occasionally. Mummy had been his friend. There was no one he had ever met who could approach replacing her. He wished, as he did every day, she were back there beside him and able to read and appreciate his letter.

He addressed an envelope to Joy Anne Fortune care of her publishers – she was not one of 'his' authors unwise enough to reply to him on headed writing paper – put the letter inside it and sealed it up. Two more must be written before he left the house, one to Graham Prink pointing out mistakes in *Dancing Partners,* 'lay' for 'lie' in two instances and 'may' for 'might' in three, and the other to Jeanne Pettle to tell her that the plot and much of the dialogue in *Southern Discomfort* had been blatantly lifted from *Gone With the Wind*. He considered it the most flagrant plagiarism he had seen for a long while. In both he indicated how distasteful he found the authors' frequent use of obscenities, notably those words beginning with an 'f' and a 'c' and the taking of the Deity's name in vain.

At five to ten Ribbon took his letters, switched off the computer and closed the door behind him. Before going downstairs, he paid his second visit of the day to Mummy's room. He had been there for the first time since his return from Cornwall at seven the previous evening, again before he went to bed and once more at seven this morning. While he was away his second greatest worry had been that something would be disturbed in there, an object removed or its position changed, for, though he did his own housework, Glenys Next-door had a key and often in his absence, in her own words, 'popped in to see that everything was OK'.

But nothing was changed. Mummy's dressing table was exactly as she had left it, the two cut-glass scent bottles with silver stoppers set one on each side of the lace-edged mat, the silver-backed hairbrush on its glass tray alongside the hair tidy and the pink pincushion. The wardrobe door he always left ajar so that her clothes could be seen inside, those dear garments, the afternoon dresses, the coats and skirts – Mummy had never possessed a pair of trousers – the warm winter coat, the neatly placed pairs of court shoes. Over the door, because he had seen this in an interiors magazine, he had hung, folded in two, the beautiful white and cream tapestry bedspread he had once given her but which she said was too good for daily use. On the bed lay the dear old one her own mother had worked, and on its spotless if worn bands of lace, her pink silk nightdress. He lingered, looking at it.

After a moment or two he opened the window two inches at the top. It was a good idea to allow a little fresh air to circulate. He closed Mummy's door behind him and, carrying his letters, went downstairs. A busy day lay ahead. His tie straightened, one button only out of the three on his linen jacket done up, he set the burglar alarm. Eighteen fifty-two was the code, one-eight, five-two, the date of the first edition of *Roget's Thesaurus*, a compendium Ribbon had found useful in his work. He opened the front door and closed it just as the alarm started braying. While he was waiting on the doorstep, his ear to the keyhole, for the alarm to cease until or unless an intruder set it off again, Glenys Next-door called out a cheery 'Hiya!'

Ribbon hated this mode of address, but there was nothing he could do to stop it, any more than he could stop her calling him Amby. He smiled austerely and said good morning. Glenys Next-door – this was her own description of herself, first used when she moved into 23 Grove Green Avenue fifteen years before, 'Hiya, I'm Glenys Next-door' – said it was the window cleaner's day and should she let him in?

'Why does he have to come in?' Ribbon said rather testily.

'It's his fortnight for doing the back, Amby. You know how he does the front on a Monday and the back on the Monday fortnight and inside and out on the last Monday in the month.'

Like any professional with much on his mind, Ribbon found these domestic details almost unbearably irritating. Nor did he like the idea of a strange man left free to wander about his back garden. 'Well, yes, I suppose so.' He had never called Glenys Next-door by her given name and did not intend to begin. 'You know the code, Mrs Judd.' It was appalling that she had to know the code but since Mummy passed on and no one was in the house it was inevitable. 'You do know the code, don't you?'

'Eight one five two.'

'No, no, no.' He must not lose his temper. Glancing up and down the street to make sure there was no one within earshot, he whispered, 'One eight five two. You can remember that, can't you? I really don't want to write it down. You never know what happens to something once it has been put in writing.'

Glenys Next-door had started to laugh. 'You're a funny old fusspot you are, Amby. D'you know what I saw in your garden last night? A fox. How about that? In *Leytonstone*.'

'Really?' Foxes dig, he thought.

'They're taking refuse, you see. Escaping the hunters. Cruel, isn't it? Are you off to work?'

'Yes and I'm late,' Ribbon said, hurrying off. 'Old fusspot' indeed. He was a good ten years younger than she.

Glenys Next-door had no idea what he did for a living and he intended to keep her in ignorance. 'Something in the media, is it?' she had once said to Mummy. Of course, 'for a living' was not strictly true, implying as it did that he was paid for his work. That he was not was hardly for want of trying. He had written to twenty major publishing houses, pointing out to them that what he did, by uncovering errors in their authors' works and showing them to be unworthy of publication, was potentially saving the publishers hundreds of thousands of pounds a year. The least they could do was offer him some emolument. He wrote to four national newspapers as well, asking for his work to receive publicity in their pages, and to the Department of Culture, Media and Sport, in the hope of recognition of the service he performed. A change in the law was what he wanted, providing something for him in the nature of the Public Lending Right (he was vague about this) or the Value Added Tax. None of them replied, with the exception of the Department, who sent a card saying that his communication had been noted, not signed by the Secretary of State, though, but by some underling with an indecipherable signature.

It was the principle of the thing, not that he was in need of money. Thanks to Daddy, who, dying young had left all the income from his royalties to Mummy and thus, of course, to him. No great sum but enough to live on if one was frugal and managing as he was. Daddy had written three textbooks before death came for him at the heart-breaking age of forty-one, and all were still in demand for use in business schools. Ribbon, because he could not help himself, in great secrecy and far from Mummy's sight, had gone through those books after his usual fashion, looking for errors. The compulsion to do this was irresistible, though he had tried to resist it, fighting against the need, conscious of the disloyalty, but finally succumbing, as another man might ultimately yield to some ludicrous autoeroticism. Alone, in the night, his bedroom door locked, he had perused Daddy's books and found – nothing.

The search was the most shameful thing he had ever done. And this not only on account of the distrust in Daddy's expertise and acumen that it implied, but also because he had to confess to himself that he did not understand what he read and would not have known a mistake if he had seen one. He put Daddy's books away in a cupboard after that and, strangely enough, Mummy had never commented on their absence. Perhaps, her eyesight failing, she hadn't noticed.

Ribbon walked to Leytonstone tube station and sat on the seat to wait for a train. He had decided to change at Holborn and take the Piccadilly Line to Piccadilly Circus. From there it was only a short walk to Dillons and a further few steps to Hatchards. He acknowledged that Hatchards was the better shop but Dillons guaranteed a greater anonymity to its patrons. Its assistants seemed indifferent to the activities of customers, ignoring their presence most of the time and not apparently noticing whether they stayed five minutes or half and hour. Ribbon liked that. He liked to describe himself as reserved, a private man, one who minded his own business and lived quietly. Others, in his view, would do well to be the same. As far as he was concerned, a shop assistant was there to take your money, give you your change and say thank you. The displacement of the high street or corner shop by vast impersonal supermarkets was one of few modern innovations he could heartily approve.

The train came. It was three-quarters empty, as was usually so at this hour. He had read in the paper that London Transport was thinking of introducing Ladies Only carriages in the tube. Why not Men Only carriages as well? Preferably, when you considered what some young men were like, Middle-aged Scholarly Gentlemen Only carriages. The train stopped for a long time in the tunnel between Mile End and Bethnal Green. Naturally, passengers were offered no explanation for the delay. He waited a long time for the Piccadilly Line train, due apparently to some signalling failure outside Cockfosters, but eventually arrived at his destination just before eleven thirty.

The sun had come out and it was very hot. The air smelt of diesel and cooking and beer, very different from Leytonstone on the verges of Epping Forest. Ribbon went into Dillons, where no one showed the slightest interest in his arrival, and the first thing to assault his senses was an enormous pyramidal display of Kingston Marle's *Demogorgon*. Each copy was as big as the average-sized dictionary and encased in a jacket printed in silver and two shades of red. A hole in the shape of a pentagram in the front cover revealed beneath it the bandaged face of some mummified corpse. The novel had already been reviewed and the poster on the wall above the display quoted the *Sunday Express*'s encomium in exaggeratedly large type: '*Readers will have fainted with fear before page 10.*'

The price, at £18.99, was a disgrace but there was no help for it. A legitimate outlay, if ever there was one. Ribbon took a copy and, from what a shop assistant had once told him were called 'dump bins', helped himself to two paperbacks of books he had already examined and commented on in hardcover. There was no sign in the whole shop of Eric Owlberg's *Paving Hell*. Ribbon's dilemma was to ask or not to ask. The young woman behind the counter put his purchases in a bag and he handed her Mummy's direct debit Visa card. Lightly, as if it were an afterthought, the most casual thing in the world, he asked about the new Owlberg. 'Already sold out, has it?' he said with a little laugh.

Her face was impassive. 'We're expecting them in tomorrow.'

He signed the receipt B. J. Ribbon and passed it to the girl without a smile. She need not think he was going to make this trip all over again tomorrow. He made his way to Hatchards, on the way depositing the Dillons bag in a litter bin and transferring the books into the plain plastic holdall he carried rolled up in his pocket. If the staff at Hatchards had seen Dillons' name on the bag he would have felt rather awkward. Now they would think he was carrying his purchases from a chemist or a photographic store.

One of them came up to him the minute he entered Hatchards. He recognised her as the marketing manager, a tall, good-looking dark woman. She recognised him too and to his astonishment and displeasure addressed him by his name. 'Good morning, Mr Ribbon.'

Inwardly he groaned, for he remembered having had forebodings about this at the time. On one occasion he had ordered a book, he was desperate to see an early copy, and had been obliged to say who he was and give them his phone number. He said good morning in a frosty sort of voice.

'How nice to see you,' she said. 'I rather think you may be in search of the new Kingston Marle, am I right? *Demogorgon*? Copies came in today.'

Ribbon felt terrible. The plastic of his carrier was translucent rather than transparent but he was sure she must be able to see the silver and the two shades of red glowing through the cloudy film that covered it. He held it behind his back in a manner he hoped looked natural. 'It was *Paving Hell* I actually wanted,' he muttered, wondering what rule of life or social usage made it necessary for him to explain his wishes to marketing managers.

'We have it, of course,' she said with a radiant smile and picked the paperback off a shelf. He was sure she was going to point out to him in schoolmistressy fashion that he had already had it in hardcover, she quite distinctly remembered, and why on earth did he want another copy. Instead she said, 'Mr Owlberg is here at this moment, signing

386

stock for us. It's not a public signing but I'm sure he'd love to meet such a constant reader as yourself. And be happy to sign a copy of his book for you.'

Ribbon hoped his shudder hadn't been visible. No, no, he was in a hurry, he had a pressing engagement at 12.30 on the other side of town, he couldn't wait, he'd pay for his book . . . Thoughts raced through his mind of the things he had written to Owlberg about his work, all of it perfectly justified, of course, but galling to the author. His name would have lodged in Owlberg's mind as firmly as Owlberg's had in his. Imagining the reaction of *Paving Hell*'s author when he looked up from his signing, saw the face and heard the name of his stern judge made him shudder again. He almost ran out of the shop. How fraught with dangers visits to the West End of London were! Next time he came up he'd stick to the City or Bloomsbury. There was a very good Waterstone's in the Gray's Inn Road. Deciding to walk up to Oxford Circus tube staion and thus obviate a train change, he stopped on the way to draw money out from a cash dispenser. He punched in Mummy's pin number, her birth date, 1-5-27, and drew from the slot one hundred pounds in crisp new notes.


Most authors to whom Ribbon wrote his letters of complaint either did not reply at all or wrote back in a conciliatory way to admit their mistakes and promise these would be rectified for the paperback edition. Only one, out of all the hundreds, if not thousands, who had had a letter from him, reacted violently and with threats. This was a woman called Selma Gunn. He had written to her, care of her publishers, criticising, but quite mildly, her novel *A Dish of Snakes,* remarking how irritating it was to read so many verbless sentences and pointing out the absurdity of her premiss that Shakespeare, far from being a sixteenth-century English poet and dramatist, was in fact an Italian astrologer born in Verona and a close friend of Leonardo da Vinci. Her reply came within four days, a vituperative response in which she several times used the 'f' word, called him an ignorant swollen-headed nonentity and threatened legal action. Sure enough, on the following day a letter arrived from Ms Gunn's solicitors, suggesting that many of his remarks were actionable, all were indefensible and they awaited his reply with interest.

Ribbon had been terrified. He was unable to work, incapable of thinking of anything but Ms Gunn's letter and the one from Evans Richler Sabatini. At first he said nothing to Mummy, though she, of course, with her customary sensitive acuity, could tell something was wrong. Two days later he received another letter from Selma Gunn. This time she drew his attention to certain astrological predictions in her book, told him that he was one of those Nostradamus had predicted would be destroyed when the world came to an end next year and that she herself had occult powers. She ended by demanding an apology.

Ribbon did not, of course, believe in the supernatural but, like most of us, was made to feel deeply uneasy when cursed or menaced by something in the nature of necromancy. He sat down at his computer and composed an abject apology. He was sorry, he wrote, he had intended no harm, Ms Gunn was entitled to express her beliefs; her theory as to Shakespeare's origins was just as valid as identifying him with Bacon or Ben Jonson. It took it out of him, writing that letter, and when Mummy, observing his pallor and trembling hands, finally asked him what was wrong, he told her everything. He showed her the letter of apology.

Masterful as ever, she took it from him and tore it up. 'Absolute nonsense,' she said. He could tell she was furious. 'On what grounds can the stupid woman bring an action, I should like to know? Take no notice. Ignore it. It will soon stop, you mark my words.'

'But what harm can it do, Mummy?'

'You coward,' Mummy said witheringly. 'Are you a man or a mouse?'

Ribbon asked her, politely but as manfully as he could, not to talk to him like that. It was almost their first quarrel – but not their last.

He had bowed to her edict and stuck it out in accordance with her instructions, as he did in most cases. And she had been right, for he heard not another word from Selma Gunn or from Evans Richler Sabatini. The whole awful business was over and Ribbon felt he had learned something from it – to be brave, to be resolute, to soldier on. But this did not include confronting Owlberg in the flesh, even though the author of *Paving Hell* had promised him in a letter responding to Ribbon's criticism of the hardcover edition of his book that the errors of fact he had pointed out would all be rectified in the paperback. His publishers, he wrote, had also received Ribbon's letter of complaint and were as pleased as he to have had such informed critical comment. Pleased, my foot! What piffle! Ribbon had snorted over this letter, which was a lie from start to finish. The man wasn't pleased, he was aghast and humiliated, as he should be.

Ribbon sat down in his living room to check in the paperback edition for the corrections so glibly promised. He read down here and wrote upstairs. The room was almost as Mummy had left it. The changes were only in that more books and bookshelves had been added and in the photographs in the silver frames. He had taken out the picture of himself as a baby and himself as a schoolboy and replaced them with one of his parents' wedding, Daddy in Air Force uniform, Mummy in cream costume and small cream hat, and one of Daddy in his academic gown and mortarboard. There had never been one of Ribbon himself in similar garments. Mummy, for his own good, had decided he would be better off at home with her, leading a quiet sheltered life, than at a university. Had he regrets? A degree would have been useless to a man with a private income, as Mummy had pointed out, a man who had all the resources of an excellent public library system to educate him.

He opened *Paving Hell*. He had a foreboding, before he had even turned to the middle of chapter one where the first mistake occurred, that nothing would have been put right. All the errors would be still there, for Owlberg's promises meant nothing, he had probably never passed Ribbon's comments on to the publishers; and they, if they had received the letter he wrote them, had never answered it. For all that, he was still enraged when he found he was right. Didn't the man care? Was money and a kind of low notoriety, for you couldn't call it fame, all he was interested in? None of the errors had been corrected. No, that wasn't quite true; one had. On page 99 Owlberg's ridiculous statement that the One World Trade Center tower in New York was the world's tallest building had been altered. Ribbon noted down the remaining mistakes, ready to write to Owlberg next day. A vituperative letter it would be, spitting venom, catechising illiteracy, carelessness and a general disregard (contempt?) for the sensibilities of readers. And Owlberg would reply to it in his previous pusillanimous way, making empty promises, for he was no Selma Gunn.

Ribbon fetched himself a small whisky and water. It was six o'clock. A cushion behind his head, his feet up on the footstool Mummy had embroidered, but covered now with a plastic sheet, he opened *Demogorgon*. This was the first book by Kingston Marle he had ever read but he had some idea of what Marle wrote about. Murder, violence, crime, but instead of a detective detecting and reaching a solution, supernatural interventions, demonic possession, ghosts, as well as a great deal of unnatural or perverted sex, cannibalism and torture. Occult manifestations occurred side by side with rational, if unedifying, events. Innocent people were caught up in the magical dabblings, frequently going wrong, of so-called adepts. Ribbon had learned this from the reviews he had read of Marle's books, most of which, surprisingly to him, received good notices in periodicals of repute. That is, the serious and reputable critics engaged by literary editors to comment on his work praised the quality of the prose as vastly superior to the general run of thriller writing. His characters, they said, convinced and he induced in the reader a very real sense of terror, while a deep vein of moral theology underlay his plot. They also said that his serious approach to mumbo-jumbo and such nonsense as evil spirits and necromancy was ridiculous, but they said it *en passant* and without much enthusiasm. Ribbon read the blurb inside the front cover and turned to chapter one.

Almost the first thing he spotted was an error on page 2. He made a note of it. Another occurred on page 7. Whether Marle's prose was beautiful or not he scarcely noticed, he was too incensed by errors of fact, spelling mistakes and grammatical howlers. For a while, that is. The first part of the novel concerned a man living alone in London, a man in his own situation whose mother had died not long before. There was another parallel: the man's name was Charles Ambrose. Well, it was common enough as surname, much less so as baptismal name, and only a paranoid person would think any connection was intended.

Charles Ambrose was rich and powerful, with a house in London, a mansion in the country and a flat in Paris. All these places seemed to be haunted in various ways by something or other but the odd thing was that Ribbon could see what that reviewer meant by readers fainting with terror before page 10. He wasn't going to faint but he could feel himself growing increasingly alarmed. 'Frightened' would be too strong a word. Every few minutes he found himself glancing up towards the closed door or looking into the dim and shadowy corners of the room. He was such a reader, so exceptionally well read, that he had thought himself proof against this sort of thing. Why, he had read hundreds of ghost stories in his time. As a boy he had inured himself by reading first Dennis Wheatley, then Stephen King, not to mention M. R. James. And this *Demogorgon* was so absurd, the supernatural activity the reader was supposed to accept so pathetic, that he wouldn't have gone on with it but for the mistakes he kept finding on almost every page.

After a while he got up, opened the door and put the hall light on. He had never been even mildly alarmed by Selma Gunn's *A Dish of Snakes,* nor touched with disquiet by any effusions of Joy Anne Fortune's. What was the matter with him? He came back into the living room, put on the central light and an extra table lamp, the one with the shade Mummy had decorated with pressed flowers. That was better. Anyone passing could see in now, something he usually disliked, but for some reason he didn't feel like drawing the curtains. Before sitting down again he fetched himself some more whisky.

This passage about the mummy Charles Ambrose brought back with him after the excavations he had carried out in Egypt was very unpleasant. Why had he never noticed before that the diminutive by which he had always addressed his mother was the same word as that applied to embalmed bodies? Especially nasty was the paragraph where Ambrose's girlfriend Kaysa reaches in semi-darkness for a garment in her wardrobe and her wrist is grasped by a scaly paw. This was so upsetting that Ribbon almost missed noticing that Marle spelt the adjective 'scaley'. He had a sense of the room being less light than a few moments before, as if the bulbs in the lamps were weakening before entirely failing. One of them did indeed fail while his eyes were on it, flickered, buzzed and went out. Of course, Ribbon knew perfectly well this was not a supernatural phenomenon but simply the result of the bulb coming to the end of its life after a thousand hours or whatever it was. He switched off the lamp, extracted the bulb when it was cool, shook it to hear the rattle that told him its usefulness was over, and took it outside to the waste bin. The kitchen was in darkness. He put on the light and the outside light which illuminated part of the garden. That was better. A siren wailing on a police car going down Grove Green Road made him jump. He helped himself to more whisky, a rare indulgence for him. He was no drinker.

Supper now. It was almost eight. Ribbon always set the table for himself, either here or in the dining room, put out a linen table napkin in its silver ring, a jug of water and a glass, and the silver pepper pot and salt cellar. This was Mummy's standard and if he had deviated from it he would have felt he was letting her down. But this evening, as he made toast and scrambled two large free-range eggs in a buttered pan, filled a small bowl with mandarin oranges from a can and poured evaporated milk over them, he found himself most unwilling to venture into the dining room. It was at the best of times a gloomy chamber, its rather small window set deep in bookshelves, its furnishing largely a reptilian shade of brownish-green Mummy always called 'crocodile'. Poor Mummy only kept the room like that because the crocodile-green had been Daddy's choice when they were first married. There was only a central light, a bulb in a parchment shade, suspended above the middle of the mahogany table. Books covered as yet only two sides of the room, but new shelves had been bought and were waiting for him to put them up. One of the pictures on the wall facing the window had been most distasteful to Ribbon when he was a small boy, a lithograph of some Old Testament scene and entitled *Saul Encounters the Witch of Endor*. Mummy, saying he should not fear painted devils, refused to take it down. He was in no mood tonight to have that lowering over him while he ate his scrambled eggs.

Nor did he much fancy the kitchen. Once or twice, while he was sitting there, Glenys Next-door's cat had looked through the window at him. It was a black cat, totally black all over, its eyes large and of a very pale crystalline yellow. Of course he knew what it was and had never in the past been alarmed by it but somehow he sensed it would be different tonight. If Tinks Next-door pushed its black face and yellow eyes against the glass it might give him a serious shock. He put the plates on a tray and carried it back into the living room with the replenished whisky glass.

It was both his job and his duty to continue reading *Demogorgon* but there was more to it than that, Ribbon admitted to himself in a rare burst of honesty. He *wanted* to go on, he wanted to know what happened to Charles Ambrose and Kaysa de Floris, whose the embalmed corpse was and how it had been liberated from its arcane and archaic (writers always muddled up those adjectives) sarcophagus, and whether the mysterious and saintly rescuer was in fact the reincarnated Joseph of Arimathea and the vessel he carried the Holy Grail. By the time Mummy's grandmother clock in the hall struck eleven, half an hour past his bedtime, he had read half the book and would no longer have described himself as merely alarmed. He was frightened. So frightened that he had to stop reading.

Twice during the course of the past hour he had refilled his whisky glass, half in the hope that strong drink would induce sleep when, finally at a quarter past eleven, he went to bed. He passed a miserable night, worse even than those he experienced in the weeks after Mummy's death. It was, for instance, a mistake to take *Demogorgon* upstairs with him. He hardly knew why he had done so, for he certainly had no intention of reading any more of it that night, if ever. The final chapter he had read – well, he could scarcely say what had upset him most, the orgy in the middle of the Arabian desert in which Charles and Kaysa had both enthusiastically taken part, wallowing in perverted practices, or the intervention, disguised as a Bedouin tribesman, of the demon Kabadeus, later revealing in his nakedness his hermaphrodite body with huge female breasts and trifurcated member.

As always, Ribbon placed his slippers by the bed. He pushed the book a little under the bed but he couldn't forget that it was there. In the darkness he seemed to hear sounds he had never heard, or never noticed, before: a creaking as if a foot trod first on one stair, then the next; a rattling of the windowpane, though it was a windless night; a faint rustling on the bedroom door as if a thing in grave clothes had scrabbled with its decaying hand against the panelling. He put on the bed lamp. Its light was faint, showing him deep wells of darkness in the corners of the room. He told himself not to be a fool. Demons, ghosts, evil spirits had no existence. If only he hadn't brought the wretched book up with him! He would be better, he would be able to sleep, he was sure, if the book weren't there, exerting a malign influence. Then something dreadful occurred to him. He couldn't take the book outside, downstairs, away. He hadn't the nerve. It would not be possible for him to open the door, go down the stairs, carrying that book.

The whisky, asserting itself in the mysterious way it had, began a banging in his head. A flicker of pain ran from his eyebrow down his temple to his ear. He climbed out of bed, crept across the floor, his heart pounding, and put on the central light. That was a little better. He drew back the bedroom curtains and screamed. He actually screamed aloud, frightening himself even more with the noise he made. Tinks Next-door was sitting on the windowsill, staring impassively at curtain linings, now into Ribbon's face. It took no notice of the scream but lifted a paw, licked it and began washing its face.

Ribbon pulled the curtains back. He sat down on the end of the bed, breathing deeply. It was two in the morning, a pitch-black night, ill-lit by widely spaced yellow chemical lamps. What he would really have liked to do was rush across the passage – do it quickly, don't think about it – into Mummy's room, burrow down into Mummy's bed and spend the night there. If he could only do that he would be safe, would sleep, be comforted. It would be like creeping back into Mummy's arms. But he couldn't do it, it was impossible. For one thing it would be a violation of the sacred room, the sacrosanct bed, never to be disturbed since Mummy spent her last night in it. And for another, he dared not venture out on to the landing.

Trying to court sleep by thinking of himself and Mummy in her last years helped a little. The two of them sitting down to an evening meal in the dining room, a white candle alight on the table, its soft light dispelling much of the gloom and ugliness. Mummy had enjoyed television when a really good programme was on, *Brideshead Revisited*, for instance, or something from Jane Austen. She had always liked the curtains drawn, even before it was dark, and it was his job to do it, then fetch each of them a dry sherry. Sometimes they read aloud to each other in the gentle lamplight, Mummy choosing to read her favourite Victorian writers to him, he picking a book from his work, correcting the grammar as he read. Or she would talk about Daddy and her first meeting with him in a library, she searching the shelves for a novel whose author's name she had forgotten, he offering to help her and finding – triumphantly – Mrs Henry Wood's *East Lynne*.

But all these memories of books and reading pulled Ribbon brutally back to *Demogorgon*. The scaly hand was the worst thing and, second to that, the cloud or ball of visible darkness that arose in the lighted room when Charles Ambrose cast salt and asafoetida into the pentagram. He reached down to find the lead on the bed lamp where the switch was and encountered something cold and leathery. It was only the tops of his slippers, which he always left just beside his bed, but he had once again screamed before he remembered. The lamp on, he lay still, breathing deeply. Only when the first light of morning, a grey trickle of dawn, came creeping under and between the curtains at about six did he fall into a troubled doze.

Morning makes an enormous difference to fear and to depression. It wasn't long before Ribbon was castigating himself for a fool and blaming the whisky and the scrambled eggs for his disturbed night rather than Kingston Marle. However, he would read no more of *Demogorgon*. No matter how much he might wish to know the fate of Charles and Kaysa or the identity of the bandaged reeking thing, he preferred not to expose himself any longer to this distasteful rubbish or Marle's grammatical lapses.

A hot shower, followed by a cold one, did a lot to restore him. He breakfasted, but in the kitchen. When he had finished he went into the dining room and had a look at *Saul Encounters the Witch of Endor*. It was years since he had even glanced at it, which was no doubt why he had never noticed how much like Mummy the witch looked. Of course, Mummy would never have worn diaphanous grey draperies and she had all her own teeth, but there was something about the nose and mouth, the burning eyes and the pointing finger, this last particularly characteristic of Mummy, that reminded him of her. He dismissed the disloyal thought but, on an impulse, took the picture down and put it on the floor, its back towards him, to lean against the wall. It left behind it a paler rectangle on the ochre-coloured wallpaper but the new bookshelves would cover that.

Ribbon went upstairs to his study and his daily labours. First, the letter to Owlberg.

21 Grove Green Avenue,
London E11 4ZH

Dear Sir,

In spite of your solemn promise to me as to the correction of errors in your new paperback publication, I find you have fulfilled this undertaking only to the extent of making **one single amendment.**

This, of course, in anyone's estimation, is a gross insult to your readers, displaying as it does your contempt for them and for the TRUTH. I am sending a copy of this letter to your publishers and await an explanation both from you and them.

Yours faithfully,
Ambrose Ribbon

Letting off steam always put him in a good mood. He felt a joyful adrenalin rush and inspired to write a congratulatory letter for a change. This one was addressed to: The Manager, Dillons Bookshop, Piccadilly, London W1.

21 Grove Green Avenue,
London E11 4ZH

Dear Sir or Madam [there were a lot of women taking men's jobs these days, poking their noses in where they weren't needed].

I write to congratulate you on your excellent organisation, management and the, alas, now old-fashioned attitude you have to your book buyers. I refer, of course, to the respectful distance and detachment maintained between you and them. It makes a refreshing change from the over-familiarity displayed by many of your competitors.

Yours faithfully,
Ambrose Ribbon

Before writing to the author of the novel which had been directly responsible for his loss of sleep, Ribbon needed to look something up. A king of Egypt of the seventh century BC called Psamtik I he had come across before in someone else's book. Marle referred to him as Psammetichus I and Ribbon was nearly sure this was wrong. He would have to look it up and the obvious place to do this was the *Encyclopaedia Britannica*.

Others might have recourse to the Internet. Because Mummy had despised such electronic devices, Ribbon did so too. He wasn't even on the Net and never would be. The present difficulty was that Psamtik I would be found in volume VIII of the Micropaedia, the one that covered subjects from *Piranha to Scurfy*. This volume he had had no occasion to use since Mummy's death, though his eyes sometimes strayed fearfully in its direction. There it was placed, in the bookshelves to the left of where he sat facing the window, bound in its black, blue and gold, its position between *Montpel to Piranesi* and *Scurlock to Tirah*. He was very reluctant to touch it but he *had to*. Mummy might be dead but her injunctions and instructions lived on. Don't be deterred, she had often said, don't be deflected by anything from what you know to be right, not by weariness, nor indifference nor doubt. Press on, tell the truth, shame these people.

There would not be a mark on *Piranha to Scurfy*, he knew that, nothing but his fingerprints and they, of course, were invisible. It had been used and put back, and was unchanged. Cautiously he advanced upon the shelf where the ten volumes of the Micropaedia and the nineteen of the Macropaedia were arranged and put out his hand to volume VIII. As he lifted it down he noticed something different about it, different, that is, from the others. Not a mark, not a stain or scar, but a slight loosening of the 1002 pages as if at some time it had been mistreated, violently shaken or in some similar way abused. It had. He shivered a little but he opened the book and turned the pages to the 'P's. It was somewhat disappointing to find that Marle had been right. Psamtik was right and so was the Greek form, Psammetichus I, it was optional. Still, there were enough errors in the book, a plethora of them, without that. Ribbon wrote as follows, saying nothing about his fear, his bad night and his interest in *Demogorgon* characters:

*Sir,*

*Your new farrago of nonsense (I will not dignify it with the name of 'novel' or even 'thriller') is a disgrace to you, your publishers and those reviewers corrupt enough to praise your writing. As to the market you serve, once it has sampled this revolting affront to English literary tradition and our noble language, I can hardly imagine its members will remain your readers for long. The greatest benefit to the fiction scene conceivable would be for you to retire, disappear, and take your appalling effusions with you into outer darkness.*

*The errors you have made in the text are numerous. On page 30 alone there are three. You cannot say 'less people'. 'Fewer people' is correct. Only the illiterate would write: 'He gave it to Charles and I.' By 'mitigate against' I suppose you mean 'militate against'. More howlers occur on pages 34, 67 and 103. It is unnecessary to write 'meet with'. 'Meet' alone will do. 'A copy' of something is sufficient. 'A copying' is a nonsense.*

*Have you any education at all? Or were you one of these children who somehow missed schooling because their parents were neglectful or itinerant? You barely seem able to understand the correct location of an apostrophe, still less the proper usage of a colon. Your book has wearied me too much to allow me to write more. Indeed, I have not finished it and shall not. I am too fearful of its corrupting my own prose.*

He wrote 'Sir' without the customary endearment so that he could justifiably sign himself 'yours truly'. He reread his letters and paused a while over the third one. It was very strong and uncompromising. But there was not a phrase in it he didn't sincerely mean (for all his refusing to end with that word) and he told himself that he who hesitates is lost. Often when he wrote a really vituperative letter he allowed himself to sleep on it, not posting it till the following day and occasionally, though seldom, not sending it at all. But he quickly put all three into envelopes and addressed them, Kingston Marle's care of his publishers. He would take them to the box at once.

While he was upstairs his own post had come. Two envelopes lay on the mat. The direction on one was typed, on the other he recognised the handwriting of his cousin Frank's wife Susan. He opened that one first. Susan wrote to remind him that he was spending the following weekend with herself and her husband at their home in the Cotswolds, as he did at roughly this time every year. Frank or she herself would be at Kingham station to pick him up. She supposed he would be taking the one-fifty train from Paddington to Hereford which reached Kingham at twenty minutes past three. If he had other plans perhaps he would let her know.

Ribbon snorted quietly. He didn't want to go, he never did, but they so loved having him he could hardly refuse after so many years. This would be his first visit without Mummy or Auntie Bee as they called her. No doubt they too desperately missed her. He opened the other letter and had a pleasant surprise. It was from Joy Anne Fortune and she gave her own address, a street in Bournemouth, not her publishers' or agents'. She must have written by return of post.

Her tone was humble and apologetic. She began by thanking him for pointing out the errors in her novel *Dreadful Night*. Some of them were due to her own carelessness but others she blamed on the printer. Ribbon had heard that one before and didn't think much of it. Ms Fortune assured him that all the mistakes would be corrected if the book ever went into paperback, though she thought it unlikely that this would happen. Here Ribbon agreed with her. However, this kind of letter – though rare – was always gratifying. It made all his hard work worthwhile.

He put stamps on the letters to Eric Owlberg, Kingston Marle and Dillons, and took them to the postbox. Again he experienced a quiver of dread in the pit of his stomach when he looked at the envelope addressed to Marle and recalled the words and terms he had used. But he drew strength from remembering how stalwartly he had withstood Selma Gunn's threats and defied her. There was no point in being in his job if he was unable to face resentful opposition. Mummy was gone but he must soldier on alone and he repeated to himself Paul's words about fighting the good fight, running a straight race and keeping the faith. He held the envelope in his hand for a moment or two after the Owlberg and Dillons letters had fallen down inside the box. How much easier it would be, what a lightening of his spirits would take place, if he simply dropped that envelope into a litter bin rather than this postbox! On the other hand, he hadn't built up his reputation for uncompromising criticism and stern incorruptible judgement by being cowardly. In fact, he hardly knew why he was hesitating now. His usual behaviour was far from this. What was wrong with him? There in the sunny street, a sudden awful dread took hold of him that when he put his hand to that aperture in the postbox and inserted the letter a scaly paw would reach out of it and seize hold of his wrist. How stupid could he be? How irrational? He reminded himself of his final quarrel with Mummy, those awful words she had spoken, and quickly, without more thought, he dropped the letter into the box and walked away.

At least they hadn't to put up with that ghastly old woman, Susan Ribbon remarked to her husband as she prepared to drive to Kingham station. Old Ambrose was a pussy cat compared to Auntie Bee.

'You say that,' said Frank. 'You haven't got to take him down the pub.'

'I've got to listen to him moaning about being too hot or too cold or the bread being wrong or the tea or the birds singing too early or us going to bed too late.'

'It's only two days,' said Frank. 'I suppose I do it for my Uncle Charlie's sake. He was a lovely man.'

'Considering you were only four when he died I don't see how you know.'

Susan got to Kingham at twenty-two minutes past three and found Ambrose standing in the station approach, swivelling his head from left to right, up the road and down, a peevish look on his face. 'I was beginning to wonder where you were,' he said. 'Punctuality is the politeness of princes, you know. I expect you heard my mother say that. It was a favourite dictum of hers.'

In her opinion Ambrose appeared far from well. His face, usually rather full and flabby, had a pasty, sunken look. 'I haven't been sleeping,' he said as they drove through Moreton-in-Marsh. 'I've had some rather unpleasant dreams.'

'It's all those highbrow books you read. You've been overtaxing your brain.' Susan didn't exactly know what it was Ambrose did for a living. Some sort of freelance editing, Frank thought. The kind of thing you could do from home. It wouldn't bring in much, but Ambrose didn't need much, Auntie Bee being in possession of Uncle Charlie's royalties. 'And you've suffered a terrible loss. It's only a few months since your mother died. But you'll soon feel better down here. Good fresh country air, peace and quiet, it's a far cry from London.'

They would go into Oxford tomorrow, she said, do some shopping, visit Blackwell's, perhaps do a tour of the colleges and then have lunch at the Randolph. She had asked some of her neighbours in for drinks at six, then they would have a quiet supper and watch a video.

Ambrose nodded, not showing much interest. Susan told herself to be thankful for small mercies. At least there was no Auntie Bee. On that old witch's last visit with Ambrose, the year before she died, she had told Susan's friend from Stow that her skirt was too short for someone with middle-aged knees, and at ten thirty informed the people who had come to dinner that it was time they went home.

When he had said hallo to Frank she showed Ambrose up to his room. It was the one he always had but he seemed unable to remember the way to it from one year to the next. She had made a few alterations. For one thing, it had been redecorated and for another, she had changed the books in the shelf by the bed. A great reader herself, she thought it rather dreary always to have the same selection of reading matter in the guest bedroom.

Ambrose came down to tea, looking grim. 'Are you a fan of Mr Kingston Marle, Susan?'

'He's my favourite author,' she said, surprised.

'I see. Then there's no more to be said, is there?' Ambrose proceeded to say more. 'I rather dislike having a whole shelfful of his works by my bed. I've put them out on the landing.' As an afterthought, he added, 'I hope you don't mind.'

After that, Susan decided against telling her husband's cousin the prime purpose of their planned visit to Oxford next day. She poured him a cup of tea and handed him a slice of Madeira cake. Manfully, Frank said he would take Ambrose to see the horses and then they might stroll down to the Cross Keys for a nourishing glass of something.

'Not whisky, I hope,' said Ambrose.

'Lemonade, if you like,' said Frank in an out-of-character sarcastic voice.

When they had gone Susan went upstairs and retrieved the seven novels of Kingston Marle which Ambrose had stacked on the floor outside his bedroom door. She was particularly fond of *Evil Incarnate* and noticed that its dust jacket had a tear in the front on the bottom right-hand side. That tear had certainly not been there when she put the books on the shelf two days before. It looked, too, as if the jacket of *Wickedness in High Places* had been removed, screwed up in an angry fist and later replaced. Why on earth would Ambrose do such a thing?

She returned the books to her own bedroom. Of course, Ambrose was a strange creature. You could expect nothing else with that monstrous old woman for a mother, his sequestered life and, whatever Frank might say about his being a freelance editor, the probability that he subsisted on a small private income and had never actually worked for his living. He had never married nor even had a girlfriend, as far as Susan could make out. What did he do all day? These weekends, though only occurring annually, were terribly tedious and trying. Last year he had awakened her and Frank by knocking on their bedroom door at three in the morning to complain about a ticking clock in his room. Then there had been the business of the dry-cleaning spray. A splash of olive oil had left a pinpoint spot on the (already not very clean) jacket of Ambrose's navy-blue suit. He had averred that the stain remover Susan had in the cupboard left it untouched, though Susan and Frank could see no mark at all after it had been applied, and insisted on their driving him into Cheltenham for a can of a particular kind of dry-cleaning spray. By then it was after five and by the time they got there all possible purveyors of the spray were closed till Monday. Ambrose had gone on and on about that stain on his jacket right up to the moment Frank dropped him at Kingham station on Sunday afternoon.

The evening passed uneventfully and without any real problems. It was true that Ambrose remarked on the silk trousers she had changed into, saying on a slightly acrimonious note that reminded Susan of Auntie Bee what a pity it was that skirts would soon go entirely out of fashion. He left most of his pheasant *en casserole*, though without comment. Susan and Frank lay awake a long while, occasionally giggling and expecting a knock at their door. None came. The silence of the night was broken only by the melancholy hooting of owls.


It was a fine morning, though not hot, and Oxford looked particularly beautiful in the sunshine. When they had parked the car they strolled up the High and had coffee in a small select café outside which tables and chairs stood on the wide pavement. The Ribbons, however, went inside where it was rather gloomy and dim. Ambrose deplored the adoption by English restaurants of Continental habits totally unsuited to what he called 'our island climate'. He talked about his mother and the gap in the company her absence caused, interrupting his own monologue to ask in a querulous tone why Susan kept looking at her watch. 'We have no particular engagement, do we? We are, as might be said, free as air?'

'Oh, quite,' Susan said. 'That's exactly right.'

But it wasn't *exactly* right. She resisted glancing at her watch again.

There was, after all, a clock on the café wall. So long as they were out of there by ten to eleven they would be in plenty of time. She didn't want to spend half the morning standing in a queue. Ambrose went on talking about Auntie Bee, how she lived in a slower-paced and more gracious past, how, much as he missed her, he was glad for her sake she hadn't survived to see the dawn of a new, and doubtless worse, millennium.

They left at eight minutes to eleven and walked to Blackwell's. Ambrose was in his element in bookshops, which was partly, though only partly, why they had come. The signing was advertised in the window and inside, though there was no voice on a public address system urging customers to buy and get the author's signature. And there he was, sitting at the end of a table loaded with copies of his new book. A queue there was but only a short one. Susan calculated that by the time she had selected her copy of *Demogorgon* and paid for it she would be no further back than eighth in line, a matter of waiting ten minutes.

She hadn't counted on Ambrose's extraordinary reaction. Of course, she was well aware – he had seen to that – of his antipathy to the works of Kingston Marle, but not that it should take such a violent form. At first, the author and perhaps also the author's name, had been hidden from Ambrose's view by her own back and Frank's, and the press of people around him. But as that crowd for some reason melted away, Frank turned round to say a word to his cousin and she went to collect the book she had reserved, Kingston Marle lifted his head and seemed to look straight at Frank and Ambrose.

He was a curious-looking man, tall and with a lantern-shaped but not unattractive face, his chin deep and his forehead high. A mass of long, dark, womanish hair sprang from the top of that arched brow, flowed straight back and descended to his collar in full, rather untidy curves. His mouth was wide and with the sensitive look lips shaped like this usually give to a face. Dark eyes skimmed over Frank, then Ambrose, and came to rest on her. He smiled. Whether it was this smile or the expression in Marle's eyes that had the effect on Ambrose it apparently did Susan never knew. Ambrose let out a little sound, not quite a cry, more a grunt of protest. She heard him say to Frank, 'Excuse me – must go – stuffy in here – can't breathe – just pop out for some fresh air,' and he was gone, running faster than she would have believed him capable of.

When she was younger she would have thought it right to go after him, ask what was wrong, could she help and so on. She would have left her book, given up the chance of getting it signed and given all her attention to Ambrose. But she was older now and no longer believed it was necessary inevitably to put others first. As it was, Ambrose's hasty departure had lost her a place in the queue and she found herself at number ten. Frank joined her.

'What was all that about?'

'Some nonsense about not being able to breathe. The old boy gets funny ideas in his head, just like his old mum. You don't think she's been reincarnated in him, do you?'

Susan laughed. 'He'd have to be a baby for that to have happened, wouldn't he?'

She asked Kingston Marle to inscribe the book on the title page: *For Susan Ribbon*. While he was doing so and adding, *with best wishes from the author, Kingston Marle*, he told her hers was a very unusual name. Had she ever met anyone else called Ribbon?

'No, I haven't. I believe we're the only ones in this country.'

'And there aren't many of us,' said Frank. 'Our son is the last of the Ribbons but he's only sixteen.'

'Interesting,' said Marle politely.

Susan wondered if she dared. She took a deep breath. 'I admire your work very much. If I sent you some of my books – I mean, your books – and if I put in the postage, would you – would you sign those for me too?'

'Of course. It would be a pleasure.'

Marle gave her a radiant smile. He rather wished he could have asked her to have lunch with him at the Lemon Tree instead of having to go to the Randolph with this earnest bookseller. Susan, of course, had no inkling of this and, clutching her signed book in its Blackwell's bag, she went in search of Ambrose. He was standing outside on the pavement, staring at the roadway, his hands clasped behind his back. She touched his arm and he flinched.

'Are you all right?'

He spun round, nearly cannoning into her. 'Of course I'm all right. It was very hot and stuffy in there, that's all. What have you got in there? Not his latest?'

Susan was getting cross. She asked herself why she was obliged to put up with this year after year, perhaps until they all died. In silence, she took *Demogorgon* out of the bag and handed it to him. Ambrose took it in his fingers as someone might pick up a package of decaying refuse prior to dropping it in an incinerator, his nostrils wrinkling and his eyebrows raised. He opened it. As he looked at the title page his expression and his whole demeanour underwent a violent change. His face had gone a deep mottled red and a muscle under one eye began to twitch. Susan thought he was going to hurl the book in among the passing traffic. Instead he thrust it back at her and said in a very curt, abrupt voice, 'I'd like to go home now. I'm not well.'

Frank said, 'Why don't we all go into the Randolph – we're lunching there anyway – have a quiet drink and a rest, and I'm sure you'll soon feel better, Ambrose. It is a warm day and there was a quite a crowd in there. I don't care for crowds myself, I know how you feel.'

'You don't know how I feel at all. You've just made that very plain. I don't want to go to the Randolph, I want to go home.'

There was little they could do about it. Susan, who seldom lunched out and sometimes grew very tired of cooking, was disappointed. But you can't force an obstinate man to go into an hotel and drink sherry if he is unwilling to do so. They went back to the car park and Frank drove home. When she and Frank had a single guest, it was usually Susan's courteous habit to sit in the back of the car and offer the visitor the passenger seat. She had done this on the way to Oxford but this time she sat next to Frank and left the back to Ambrose. He sat in the middle of the seat, obstructing Frank's view in the rear mirror. Once, when Frank stopped at a red light, she thought she felt Ambrose trembling, but it might only have been the engine which was inclined to judder.

On their return he went straight up to his room without explanation and remained there, drinkless, lunchless and, later on, tealess. Susan read her new book and was soon totally absorbed in it. She could well understand what the reviewer had meant when he wrote about readers fainting with fear, though in fact she herself had not fainted but only felt pleasurably terrified. Just the same, she was glad Frank was there, a large, comforting presence, intermittently reading *The Times* and watching the golf on television. Susan wondered why archaeologists went on excavating tombs in Egypt when they knew the risk of being laid under a curse or bringing home a demon. Much wiser to dig up a bit of Oxfordshire as a party of archaeology students were doing down the road. But Charles Ambrose – how funny he should share a name with such a very different man! – was nothing if not brave and Susan felt total empathy with Kaysa de Floris when she told him one midnight, smoking *kif* on Mount Ararat, '*I could never put my body and soul into the keeping of a coward.*'

The bit about the cupboard was almost too much for her. She decided to shine a torch into her wardrobe that night before she hung up her dress. And make sure Frank was in the room. Frank's roaring with laughter at her she wouldn't mind at all. It was terrible, that chapter where Charles first sees the small dark *curled-up* shape in the corner of the room. Susan had no difficulty in imagining her hero's feelings. The trouble (or the wonderful thing) was that Kingston Marle wrote so well. Whatever people might say about only the plot and the action and suspense being of importance in this sort of book, there was no doubt that good literary writing made threats, danger, terror, fear and a dark nameless dread immeasurably more real. Susan had to lay the book down at six; their friends were coming in for a drink at half past.

She put on a long skirt and silk sweater, having first made Frank come upstairs with her, open the wardrobe door and demonstrate, while shaking with mirth, that there was no scaly paw inside. Then she knocked on Ambrose's door. He came at once, his sports jacket changed for a dark-grey, almost black suit, which he had perhaps bought new for Auntie Bee's funeral. That was an occasion she and Frank had not been asked to. Probably Ambrose had attended it alone.

'I hadn't forgotten about your party,' he said in a mournful tone.

'Are you feeling better?'

'A little.' Downstairs, his eye fell at once on *Demogorgon*. 'Susan, I wonder if you would oblige me and put that book away. I hope I'm not asking too much. It is simply that I would find it extremely distasteful if there were to be any discussion of that book in my presence among your friends this evening.'

Susan took the book upstairs and put it on her bedside cabinet. 'We are only expecting four people, Ambrose,' she said. 'It's hardly a party.'

'A gathering,' he said. 'Seven is a gathering.'

For years she had been trying to identify the character in fiction of whom Ambrose Ribbon reminded her. A children's book, she thought it was. *Alice in Wonderland? The Wind in the Willows?* Suddenly she knew. It was Eeyore, the lugubrious donkey in *Winnie the Pooh*. He even looked rather like Eeyore, with his melancholy grey face and stooping shoulders. For the first time, perhaps the first time ever, she felt sorry for him. Poor Ambrose, prisoner of a selfish mother. Presumably, when she died, she had left those royalties to him, after all. Susan distinctly remembered one unpleasant occasion when the two of them had been staying and Auntie Bee had suddenly announced her intention of leaving everything she had to the Royal National Lifeboat Institute. She must have changed her mind.

\* \* \*

405

Susan voiced these feelings to her husband in bed that night, their pillow talk consisting of a review of the 'gathering', the low-key, rather depressing supper they had eaten afterwards and the video they had watched failing to come up to expectations. Unfortunately, in spite of the novel's absence from the living room, Bill and Irene had begun to talk about *Demogorgon* almost as soon as they arrived. Apparently, this was the first day of its serialisation in a national newspaper. They had read the instalment with avidity, as had James and Rosie. Knowing Susan's positive addiction to Kingston Marle, Rosie wondered if she happened to have a copy to lend to them. When Susan had finished reading it, of course.

Susan was afraid to look at Ambrose. Hastily she promised a loan of the novel and changed the subject to the less dangerous one of the archaeologists' excavations in Haybury Meadow and the protests it occasioned from local environmentalists. But the damage was done. Ambrose spoke scarcely a word all evening. It was as if he felt Kingston Marle and his book underlying everything that was said and threatening always to break through the surface of the conversation, as in a later chapter in *Demogorgon* the monstrous Dragosoma, with the head and breasts of a woman and the body of a manatee, rises slowly out of the Sea of Azov. At one point a silvery sheen of sweat covered the pallid skin of Ambrose's face.

'Poor devil,' said Frank. 'I suppose he was very cut up about his old mum.'

'There's no accounting for people, is there?'

They were especially gentle to him next day, without knowing exactly why gentleness was needed. Ambrose refused to go to church, treating them to a lecture on the death of God and atheism as the only course for enlightened mankind. They listened indulgently. Susan cooked a particularly nice lunch, consisting of Ambrose's favourite foods, chicken, sausages, roast potatoes and peas. It had been practically the only dish on Auntie Bee's culinary repertoire, Ambrose having been brought up on sardines on toast and tinned spaghetti, the chicken being served on Sundays. He drank more wine than was usual with him and had a brandy afterwards.

They put him on an early afternoon train for London. Though she had never done so before, Susan kissed him. His reaction was very marked. Seeing what was about to happen, he turned his head abruptly as her mouth approached and the kiss landed on the bristles above his right ear. They stood on the platform and waved to him.

'That was a disaster,' said Frank in the car. 'Do we have to do it again?'

Susan surprised herself. 'We have to do it again.' She sighed. 'Now I can go back and have a nice afternoon reading my book.'


A letter from Kingston Marle, acknowledging the errors in *Demogorgon* and perhaps offering some explanation of how they came to be there, with a promise of amendment in the paperback edition, would have set everything to rights. The disastrous weekend would fade into oblivion and those stupid guests of Frank's with it. Frank's idiot wife, good-looking, they said, though he had never been able to see it, but a woman of neither education nor discernment, would dwindle away into the mists of the past. Above all, that lantern-shaped face, that monstrous jaw and vaulted forehead, looming so shockingly above its owner's blood-coloured works, would lose its menace and assume a merely arrogant cast. But before he reached home, while he was still in the train, Ambrose, thinking about it – he could think of nothing else – knew with a kind of sorrowful resignation that no such letter would be waiting for him. No such letter would come next day or the next. By his own foolhardy move, his misplaced *courage*, by doing his duty, he had seen to that.

And yet it had scarcely been all his own doing. If that retarded woman, his cousin's doll-faced wife, had only had the sense to ask Marle to inscribe the book 'to Susan', rather than 'to Susan Ribbon', little harm would have been done. Ribbon could hardly understand why she had done so, unless from malice, for these days it was the custom, and one he constantly deplored, to call everyone from the moment you met them, or even if you only talked to them on the phone, by their first names. Previously, Marle would have known his address but not his appearance, not seen his face, not established him as a real and therefore vulnerable person.

No letter had come. There were no letters at all on the doormat, only a flyer from a pizza takeaway company and two hire car cards. It was still quite early, only about six. Ribbon made himself a pot of real tea – that woman used *teabags* – and decided to break with tradition and do some work. He never worked on a Sunday evening but he was in need of something positive to distract his mind from Kingston Marle. Taking his tea into the front room, he saw Marle's book lying on the coffee table. It was the first thing his eye lighted on. The Book. The awful book that had been the ruin of his weekend. He must have left

*Demogorgon* on the table when he abandoned it in a kind of queasy disgust halfway through. Yet he had no memory of leaving it there. He could have sworn he had put it away, tucked it into a drawer to be out of sight and therefore of mind. The dreadful face, fish-belly white between the bandages, leered at him out of the star-shaped hole in the red and silver jacket. He opened the drawer in the cabinet where he thought he had put it. There was nothing there but what had been there before, a few sheets of writing paper and an old diary of Mummy's. Of course there was nothing there, he didn't possess two copies of the horrible thing, but it was going in there now . . .

The phone rang. This frequent event in other people's homes happened seldom in Ribbon's. He ran out into the hall where the phone was and stood looking at it while it rang. Suppose it should be Kingston Marle? Gingerly he lifted the receiver. If it was Marle he would slam it down fast. That woman's voice said, 'Ambrose? Are you all right?'

'Of course I'm all right. I've just got home.'

'It was only that we've been rather worried about you. Now I know you're safely home that's fine.'

Ribbon remembered his manners and recited Mummy's rubric. 'Thank you very much for having me, Susan. I had a lovely time.'

He would write to her, of course. That was the proper thing. Upstairs in the office he composed three letters. The first was to Susan.

*21 Grove Green Avenue,*
*London E11 4ZH*

*Dear Susan,*

*I very much enjoyed my weekend with you and Frank. It was very enjoyable to take a stroll with Frank and take in 'the pub' on the way. The ample food provided was tip-top. Your friends seemed charming people, though I cannot commend their choice of reading matter!*

*All is well here. It looks as if we may be in for another spell of hot weather.*

*With kind regards to you both,*
*Yours affectionately,*
*Ambrose*

Ribbon wasn't altogether pleased with this. He took out 'very much' and put in 'enormously' and for 'very enjoyable' substituted 'delightful'. That was better. It would have to do. He was rather pleased with that acid comment about those ridiculous people's reading matter and hoped it would get back to them.

During the weekend, particularly during those hours in his room on Saturday afternoon, he had gone carefully through the two paperbacks he had bought at Dillons. Lucy Grieves, author of *Cottoning On*, had meticulously passed on to her publishers all the errors he had pointed out to her when the novel appeared in hardcover down to 'on to' instead of 'onto'. Ribbon felt satisfied. He was pleased with Lucy Grieves, though not to the extent of writing to congratulate her. The second letter he wrote was to Channon Scott Smith, the paperback version of whose novel *Carol Conway* contained precisely the same mistakes and literary howlers as it had in hardcover. That completed, a scathing paean of contempt if ever there was one, Ribbon sat back in his chair and thought long and hard.

Was there some way he could write to Kingston Marle and *make things all right* without grovelling, without apologising? God forbid that he should apologise for boldly telling truths that needed to be told. But could he compose something, without saying he was sorry, that would mollify Marle, better still that would make him understand? He had a notion that he would feel easier in his mind if he wrote to Marle, would sleep better at night. The two nights he had passed at Frank's had been very wretched, the second one almost sleepless.

What was he afraid of? Afraid of writing and afraid of not writing? Just afraid? Marle couldn't do anything to him. Ribbon acknowledged to himself that he had no absurd fears of Marle's setting some hit man on to him or stalking him or even atempting to sue him for libel. It wasn't that. What was it then? The cliché came into his head unbidden, the definition of what he felt: a nameless dread. If only Mummy were here to advise him! Suddenly he longed for her and tears pricked the backs of his eyes. Yet he knew what she would have said. She would have said what she had that last time.

That *Encyclopaedia Britannica* Volume VIII had been lying on the table. He had just shown Mummy the letter he had written to Desmond Erb, apologising for correcting him when he wrote about 'the quinone structure'. Of course he should have looked the word up but he hadn't. He had been so sure it should have been 'quinine'. Erb had been justifiably indignant, as writers tended to be, when he corrected an error in their work that was in fact not an error at all. He would never forget Mummy's anger, nor anything of that quarrel, come to that;

how, almost of their own volition, his hands had crept across the desk towards the black, blue and gold volume . . .

She was not here now to stop him and after a while he wrote this:

*Dear Mr Marle,*

*With reference to my letter of June 4th, in which I pointed out certain errors of fact and of grammar and spelling in your recent novel, I fear I may inadvertently have caused you pain. This was far from my intention. If I have hurt your feelings I must tell you that I very much regret this. I hope you will overlook it and forgive me.*

*Yours sincerely,*

Reading this over, Ribbon found he very much disliked the bit about overlooking and forgiving. 'Regret' wasn't right either. Also he hadn't actually named the book. He ought to have put in its title but, strangely, he found himself reluctant to type the word *Demogorgon*. It was as if, by putting it into cold print, he would set something in train, spark off some reaction. Of course, this was mad. He must be getting tired. Nevertheless, he composed a second letter.

*Dear Mr Marle,*

*With reference to my letter to yourself of June 4th, in which I pointed out certain errors in your recent and highly acclaimed novel, I fear I may inadvertently have hurt your feelings. It was not my intention to cause you pain. I am well aware – who is not? – of the high position you enjoy in the ranks of literature. The amendments I suggested you make to the novel when it appears in paperback – in many hundreds of thousand copies, no doubt – were meant in a spirit of assistance, not criticism, simply so that a good book might be made better.*

*Yours sincerely,*

Sycophantic. But what could be more mollifying than flattery? Ribbon endured half an hour's agony and self-doubt, self-recrimination and self-justification too, before writing a third and final letter.

*Dear Mr Marle,*

*With reference to my letter to your good self, dated June 4th, in which I presumed to criticise your recent novel, I fear I may inadvertently have been wanting in respect. I hope you will believe me when I say it was not my intention to offend you. You enjoy a high and well-deserved position in the ranks of literature. It was gauche and clumsy of me to write to you as I did.*

*With best wishes,*

*Yours sincerely,*

To grovel in this way made Ribbon feel actually sick. And it was all lies too. Of course it had been his intention to offend the man, to cause him pain and to make him angry. He would have given a great deal to recall that earlier letter but this – he quoted silently to himself those hackneyed but apt words about the moving finger that writes and having writ moves on – neither he nor anyone else could do. What did it matter if he suffered half an hour's humiliation when by sending this apology he would end his sufferings? Thank heavens only that Mummy wasn't here to see it.

Those letters had taken him hours and it had grown quite dark. Unexpectedly dark, he thought, for nine in the evening in the middle of June with the longest day not much more than a week away. But still he sat there, in the dusk, looking at the backs of houses, yellow brick punctured by the bright rectangles of windows, at the big shaggy trees, his own garden, the square of grass dotted with dark shrubs, big and small. He had never previously noticed how unpleasant ordinary privets and cypresses can look in deep twilight when they are not clustered together in a shrubbery or copse; when they stand individually on an otherwise open space, strange shapes, tall and slender or round and squat, or with a branch here and there protruding like a limb, and casting elongated shadows.

He got up abruptly and put on the light. The garden and its gathering of bushes disappeared. The window became dark, shiny, opaque. He switched off the light almost immediately and went downstairs. Seeing *Demogorgon* on the coffee table made him jump. What was it doing there? How did it get there? He had put it in the drawer. And there was the drawer standing open to prove it.

It couldn't have got out of the drawer and returned to the table on its own. Could it? *Of course not.* Ribbon put on every light in the room. He left the curtains open so that he could see the street lights as well. He must have left the book on the table himself. He must have intended to put it into the drawer and for some reason not done so. Possibly he had been interrupted. But nothing ever interrupted what he was doing, did it? He couldn't remember. A cold teapot and a cup of cold tea stood on the tray on the coffee table beside the book. He couldn't remember making tea.

After he had taken the tray and the cold teapot away and poured the cold tea down the sink, he sat down in an armchair with Chambers dictionary. He realised that he had never found out what the word Demogorgon meant. Here was the definition: *A mysterious infernal deity first mentioned about* AD *450. [Appar Gr* daimon *deity, and* gorgo *Gorgon, from* gorgos *terrible.]* He shuddered, closed the dictionary and opened the second Channon Scott Smith paperback he had bought. This novel had been published four years before but Ribbon had never read it, nor indeed any of the works of Mr Scott Smith before the recently published one, but he thought this fat volume might yield a rich harvest, if *Carol Conway* were anything to go by. But instead of opening *Destiny's Suzerain,* he found that the book in his hands was *Demogorgon*, open one page past where he had stopped a few days before.

In a kind of horrified wonder he began to read. It was curious how he was compelled to go on reading, considering how every line was like a faint pinprick in his equilibrium, a tiny physical tremor through his body, reminding him of those things he had written to Kingston Marle and the look Marle had given him in Oxford on Saturday. Later he was to ask himself why he had read any more of it at all, why he hadn't just stopped, why indeed he hadn't put the book in the rubbish for the refuse collectors to take away in the morning.

The dark shape in the corner of Charles Ambrose's tent was appearing for the first time: in his tent, then his hotel bedroom, his mansion in Shropshire, his flat in Mayfair. A small curled-up shape like a tiny huddled person or small monkey. It sat or simply *was*, amorphous but for faintly visible hands or paws and uniformly dark but for pinpoint malevolent eyes that stared and glinted. Ribbon looked up from the page for a moment. The lights were very bright. Out in the street a couple went by, hand in hand, talking and laughing. Usually, the noise they made would have angered him but tonight he felt curiously comforted. They made him feel he wasn't alone. They drew him, briefly, into reality. He would post the letter in the morning and once it had gone all would be well.

He read two more pages. The unravelling of the mystery began on page 423. The demogorgon was Charles Ambrose's own mother who had been murdered and whom he had buried in the grounds of his Shropshire house. Finally, she came back to tell him the truth, came in the guise of a cypress tree which walked out of the pinetum. Ribbon gasped out loud. It was his own story. How had Marle known? What was Marle – some kind of god or magus that he knew such things? The dreadful notion came to him that *Demogorgon* had not always been like this, that the ending had originally been different, but that Marle, seeing him in Oxford and immediately identifying him with the writer of that defamatory letter, *had by some remote control or sorcery altered the end of the copy that was in his, Ribbon's, possession.*

He went upstairs and rewrote his letter, adding to the existing text: *Please forgive me. I meant you no harm. Don't torment me like this. I can't stand any more.* It was a long time before he went to bed. Why go to bed when you know you won't sleep? With the light on – and all the lights in the house were on now – he couldn't see the garden, the shrubs on the lawn, the flowerbed, but he drew the curtains just the same. At last he fell uneasily asleep in his chair, waking four or five hours later to the horrid thought that his original letter to Marle was the first really vituperative criticism he had sent to anyone since Mummy's death. Was there some significance in this? Did it mean he couldn't get along without Mummy? Or, worse, that he had killed all the power and confidence in himself he had once felt?

He got up, had a rejuvenating shower but was unable to face breakfast. The three letters he had written the night before were in the postbox by nine and Ribbon on the way to the tube station. Waterstone's in Leadenhall Market was his destination. He bought Clara Jenkins's *Tales My Lover Told Me* in hardcover as well as Raymond Kobbo's *The Nomad's Smile* and Natalya Dreadnought's *Tick* in paperback. Copies of *Demogorgon* were everywhere, stacked in piles or displayed in fanciful arrangements. Ribbon forced himself to touch one of them, to pick it up. He looked over his shoulder to see if any of the assistants was watching him and, having established that they were not, opened it at page 423. It was as he had thought, as he had hardly dared put into words. Charles Ambrose's mother made no appearance, there was nothing about a burial in the grounds of Montpellier Hall or a cypress tree walking. The end was quite different. Charles Ambrose, married to Kaysa in a ceremony conducted in a balloon above the Himalayas, awakens on his wedding night and sees in the corner of the honeymoon bedroom the demon curled up, hunched and small, staring at him with gloating eyes. It had followed him from Egypt to Shropshire, from London to Russia, from Russia to New Orleans and from New Orleans to Nepal. It would never leave him, it was his for life and perhaps beyond.

Ribbon replaced the book, took up another copy. The same thing, no murder, no burial, no tree walking, only the horror of the demon in the bedroom. So he had been right. Marle had infused this alternative ending into *his* copy alone. It was part of the torment, part of the revenge for the insults Ribbon had heaped on him. On the way back to Liverpool Street Station a shout and a thump made him look over his shoulder – a taxi had clipped the rear wheel of a motorbike – and he saw, a long way behind, Kingston Marle following him.

Ribbon thought he would faint. A great flood of heat washed over him, to be succeeded by shivering. Panic held him still for a moment. Then he dived into a shop, a sweetshop it was, and it was like entering a giant chocolate box. The scent of chocolate swamped him. Trembling, he stared at the street through a window draped with pink frills. Ages passed before Kingston Marle went by. He paused, turned his head to look at the chocolates and Ribbon, again almost fainting, saw an unknown man, lantern-jawed but not monstrously so, long-haired but the hair sparse and brown, the blue eyes mild and wistful. Ribbon's heartbeat slowed, the blood withdrew from the surface of his skin. He muttered, 'No, no thank you,' to the woman behind the counter and went back into the street. What a wretched state his nerves were in! He'd be encountering a scaly paw in the wardrobe next. Clasping his bag of books, he got thoughtfully into the train.


What he really should have done was add a PS to the effect that he would appreciate a prompt acknowledgement of his letter. Just a line saying something like *Please be kind enough to acknowledge receipt.* However, it was too late now. Kingston Marle's publishers would get his letter tomorrow and send it straight on. Ribbon knew publishers did not always do this but surely in the case of so eminent an author and one of the most profitable on their list . . .

Sending the letter should have allayed his fears but they seemed to crowd in upon him more urgently, jostling each other for pre-eminence in his mind. The man who had followed him along Bishopsgate, for instance. Of course, he knew it had not been Kingston Marle, yet the similarity of build, of feature, of height, between the two men was too great for coincidence. The most likely explanation was that his stalker was Marle's younger brother, and now, as he reached this reasonable conclusion, Ribbon no longer saw the man's eyes as mild but sly and crafty. When his letter came Marle would call his brother off but, in the nature of things, the letter could not arrive at Marle's home before Wednesday at the earliest. Then there was the matter of The Book itself. The drawer in which it lay failed to hide it adequately. It was part of a mahogany cabinet (one of Mummy's wedding presents, Ribbon believed), well polished but of course opaque. Yet sometimes the wood seemed to become transparent and the harsh reds and glaring silver of *Demogorgon* shone through it as he understood a block of radium would appear as a glowing cuboid behind a wall of solid matter. Approaching closely, creeping up on it, he would see the bright colours fade and the woodwork reappear, smooth, shiny and *ordinary* once more.

In the study upstairs on Monday evening he tried to do some work but his eye was constantly drawn to the window and what lay beyond. He became convinced that the bushes on the lawn had moved. That small thin one had surely stood next to the pair of tall fat ones, not several yards away. Since the night before it had shifted its position, taking a step nearer to the house. Drawing the curtains helped but after a while he got up and pulled them apart a little to check on the big round bush, to see if it had taken a step further or had returned to its previous position. It was where it had been ten minutes before. All should have been well but it was not. The room itself had become uncomfortable and he resolved not to go back there, to move the computer downstairs, until he had heard from Kingston Marle.

The doorbell ringing made him jump so violently he felt pain travel through his body and reverberate. Immediately he thought of Marle's brother. Suppose Marle's brother, a strong young man, was outside the door and, when it was opened, would force his way in? Or, worse, was merely checking that Ribbon was at home and when footsteps sounded inside, intended to disappear? Ribbon went down. He took a deep breath and threw the door open. His caller was Glenys Next-door.

Marching in without being invited, she said 'Hiya, Amby' and that Tinks Next-door was missing. The cat had not been home since the morning when he was last seen by Sandra On-the-other-side, sitting in Ribbon's front garden eating a bird.

'I'm out of my mind with worry, as you can imagine, Amby.'

As a matter of fact, he couldn't. Ribbon cared very little for songbirds but he cared for feline predators even less. 'I'll let you know if I come across him. However –' he laughed lightly '– he knows he's not popular with me so he makes himself scarce.'

This was the wrong thing to say. In the works of his less literate authors Ribbon sometimes came upon the expression 'to bridle' – 'she bridled' or even 'the young woman bridled'. At last he understood what it meant.

Glenys Next-door tossed her head, raised her eyebrows and looked down her nose at him. 'I'm sorry for you, Amby, I really am. You must find that attitude problem of yours a real hang-up. I mean socially. I've tried to ignore it all these years but there comes a time when one has to speak one's mind. No, don't bother, please, I can see myself out.'

This was not going to be a *good* night. He knew that before he switched the bedside light off. For one thing, he always read in bed before going to sleep. Always had and always would. But for some reason he had forgotten to take *Destiny's Suzerain* upstairs with him and though his bedroom was full of reading matter, shelves and shelves of it, he had read all the books before. Of course, he could have gone downstairs and fetched himself a book, or even just gone into the study which was lined with books. Booked, not papered, indeed. He *could* have done so, in theory he could have, but on coming into his bedroom he had locked the door. Why? He was unable to answer that question, though he put it to himself several times. It was a small house, potentially brightly lit, in a street of a hundred and fifty such houses, all populated. A dreadful feeling descended upon him as he lay in bed that if he unlocked that door, if he turned the key and opened it, something would come in. Was it the small thin bush that would come in? These thoughts, ridiculous, unworthy of him, puerile, frightened him so much that he put the bedside lamp on and left it on till morning.

Tuesday's post brought two letters. Eric Owlberg called Ribbon 'a little harsh' and informed him that printers do not always do as they are told. Jeanne Pettle's letter was from a secretary who wrote that Ms Pettle was away on an extended publicity tour but would certainly attend to his 'interesting communication' when she returned. There was nothing from Dillons. It was a bright, sunny day. Ribbon went into the study and contemplated the garden. The shrubs were, of course, where they had always been. Or where they had been before the large round bush stepped back into its original position?

'Pull yourself together,' Ribbon said aloud.

Housework day. He started, as he always did, in Mummy's room, dusting the picture rail and the central lamp with a bunch of pink and blue feathers attached to a rod, and the ornaments with a clean fluffy yellow duster. The numerous books he took out and dusted on alternate weeks but this was not one of those. He vacuumed the carpet, opened the window wide and replaced the pink silk nightdress with a pale-blue one. He always washed Mummy's nightdresses by hand once a fortnight. Next his own room and the study, then downstairs to the dining and front rooms. Marle's publishers would have received his letter by the first post this morning and the department which looked after this kind of thing would, even at this moment probably, be readdressing the envelope and sending it on. Ribbon had no idea where the man lived. London? Devonshire? Most of those people seemed to live in the Cotswolds, its green hills and lush valleys must be chock-full of them. But perhaps Shropshire was more likely. He had written about Montpellier Hall as if he really knew such a house.

Ribbon dusted the mahogany cabinet and passed on to Mummy's little sewing table, but he couldn't quite leave things there and he returned to the cabinet; to stand, duster in hand, staring at that drawer. It was not transparent on this sunny morning and nothing could be seen glowing in its depths. He pulled it open suddenly and snatched up The Book. He looked at its double redness and at the pentagram. After his experiences of the past days he wouldn't have been surprised if the bandaged face inside had changed its position, closed its mouth or moved its eyes. Well, he would have been surprised, he'd have been horrified, aghast. But the demon was the same as ever, The Book was just the same, an ordinary, rather tastelessly jacketed, cheap thriller.

'What on earth is the matter with me?' Ribbon said to The Book.

He went out shopping for food. Sandra On-the-other-side appeared behind him in the queue at the check-out. 'You've really upset Glenys,' she said. 'You know me, I believe in plain speaking, and in all honesty I think you ought to apologise.'

'When I want your opinion I'll ask for it, Mrs Wilson,' said Ribbon.

Marle's brother got on the bus and sat behind him. It wasn't actually Marle's brother, he only thought it was, just for a single frightening moment. It was amazing, really, what a lot of people there were about who looked like Kingston Marle, men and women too. He had never noticed it before, had never had an inkling of it until he came face to face with Marle in that bookshop. If only it were possible to go back. For the moving finger, having writ, not to move on but to retreat, retrace its strokes, white them out with correction fluid and begin writing again. He would have guessed why that silly woman, his cousin's wife, was so anxious to get to Blackwell's, her fondness for

Marle's works – distributed so tastelessly all over his bedroom – would have told him, and he would have cried off the Oxford trip, first warning her on no account to let Marle know her surname. Yet – and this was undeniable – Marle had Ribbon's home address, the address was on the letter. The moving finger would have to go back a week and erase *21 Grove Green Avenue, London E11 4ZH* from the top right-hand corner of his letter. Then, and only then, would he have been safe . . .

Sometimes a second post arrived on a weekday but none came that day. Ribbon took his shopping bags into the kitchen, unpacked them, went into the front room to open the window – and saw *Demogorgon* lying on the coffee table. A violent trembling convulsed him. He sat down, closed his eyes. He *knew* he hadn't taken it out of the drawer. Why on earth would he? He hated it. He wouldn't touch it unless he had to. There was not much doubt now that it had a life of its own. Some kind of kinetic energy lived inside its covers, the same sort of thing as moved the small thin bush across the lawn at night. Kingston Marle put that energy into objects, he infused them with it, he was a sorcerer whose powers extended far beyond his writings and his fame. Surely that was the only explanation why a writer of such appallingly bad books, misspelt, the grammar non-existent, facts awry, should enjoy such a phenomenal success, not only with an ignorant illiterate public but among the cognoscenti. He practised sorcery or was himself one of the demons he wrote about, an evil spirit living inside that hideous lantern-jawed exterior.

Ribbon reached out a slow, wavering hand for The Book and found that, surely by chance, he had opened it at page 423. Shrinking while he did so, holding The Book almost too far away from his eyes to see the words, he read of Charles Ambrose's wedding night, of his waking in the half-dark with Kaysa sleeping beside him and seeing the curled-up shape of the demon in the corner of the room . . . So Marle had called off his necromancer's power, had he? He had restored the ending to what it originally was. Nothing about Mummy's death and burial, nothing about the walking tree. Did that mean he had already received Ribbon's apology? It might mean that. His publishers had hardly had time to send the letter on, but suppose Marle, for some reason – and the reason would be his current publicity tour – had been in his publishers' office and the letter had been handed to him. It was the only explanation, it fitted the facts. Marle had read his letter, accepted his apology and, perhaps with a smile of triumph, whistled back whatever dogs of the occult carried his messages.

Ribbon held The Book in his hands. Everything might be over now but he still didn't want it in the house. Carefully, he wrapped it up in newspaper, slipped the resulting parcel into a plastic carrier, tied the handles together and dropped it in the waste bin. 'Let it get itself out of that,' he said aloud. 'Just let it try.' Was he imagining that a fetid smell came from it, swathed in plastic though it was? He splashed disinfectant into the waste bin, opened the kitchen window.

He sat down in the front room and opened *Tales My Lover Told Me* but he couldn't concentrate. The afternoon grew dark, there was going to be a storm. For a moment he stood at the window, watching the clouds gather, black and swollen. When he was a little boy Mummy had told him a storm was the clouds fighting. It was years since he had thought of that and now, remembering, for perhaps the first time in his life he questioned Mummy's judgement. Was it quite right so to mislead a child?

The rain came, sheets of it blown by the huge gale which arose. Ribbon wondered if Marle, among his many accomplishments, could raise a wind, strike lightning from some diabolical tinderbox and, like Jove himself, beat the drum of thunder. Perhaps. He would believe anything of that man now. He went around the house closing all the windows. The one in the study he closed and fastened the catches. From his own bedroom window he looked at the lawn, where the bushes stood as they had always stood, unmoved, immovable, lashed by rain, whipping and twisting in the wind. Downstairs, in the kitchen, the window was wide open, flapping back and forth, and the waste bin had fallen on its side. The parcel lay beside it, the plastic bag that covered it, the newspaper inside, torn as if a scaly paw had ripped it. Other rubbish, food scraps, a sardine can, were scattered across the floor.

Ribbon stood transfixed. He could see the red and silver jacket of The Book gleaming, almost glowing under its torn wrappings. What had come through the window? Was it possible the demon, unleashed by Marle, was now beyond his control? He asked the question aloud, he asked Mummy, though she was long gone. The sound of his own voice, shrill and horror-stricken, frightened him. Had whatever it was come in to retrieve the – he could hardly put it even into silent words – the *chronicle of its exploits*? Nonsense, nonsense. It was Mummy speaking, Mummy telling him to be strong, not to be a fool. He shook himself, gritted his teeth. He picked up the parcel, dropped it into a black rubbish bag and took it into the garden, getting very wet in the process. In the wind the biggest bush of all reached out a needly arm and lashed him across the face.

He left the black bag there. He locked all the doors and even when the storm had subsided and the sky cleared he kept all the windows closed. Late that night, in his bedroom, he stared down at the lawn, The Book in its bag was where he had left it but the small thin bush had moved, in a different direction this time, stepping to one side so that the two fat bushes, the one that had lashed him and its twin, stood close together and side by side like tall heavily built men gazing up at his window. Ribbon had saved half a bottle of Mummy's sleeping pills. For an emergency, for a rainy day. All the lights blazing, he went into Mummy's room, found the bottle and swallowed two pills. They took effect rapidly. Fully clothed, he fell on to his bed and into something more like a deep trance than sleep. It was the first time in his life he had ever taken a soporific.

In the morning he looked through the Yellow Pages and found a firm of tree fellers, operating locally. Would they send someone to cut down all the shrubs in his garden? They would, but not before Monday. On Monday morning they would be with him by nine. In the broad daylight he asked himself again what had come through the kitchen window, come in and taken That Book out of the waste bin and, sane again, wondered if it might have been Glenys Next-door's fox. The sun was shining, the grass gleaming wet after the rain. He fetched a spade from the shed and advanced upon the wide flowerbed. Not the right-hand side, not there, avoid that at all costs. He selected a spot on the extreme left, close by the fence dividing his garden from that of Sandra On-the-other-side. While he dug he wondered if it was a commonplace with people, this burying of unwanted or hated or threatening objects in their back gardens. Maybe all the gardens in Leytonstone, in London suburbs, in the United Kingdom, in the world, were full of such concealed things, hidden in the earth, waiting . . .

He laid *Demogorgon* inside. The wet earth went back over the top of it, covering it, and Ribbon stamped the surface down viciously. If whatever it was came back and dug The Book out he thought he would die.


Things were better now *Demogorgon* was gone. He wrote to Clara Jenkins at her home address – for some unaccountable reason she was in *Who's Who* – pointing out that in chapter one of *Tales My Lover Told Me* Humphry Nemo had blue eyes and in chapter twenty-one brown eyes, Thekla Pattison wore a wedding ring on page 20 but denied, on page 201, that she had ever possessed one, and on page 245 Justin Armstrong was taking part in an athletics contest, in spite of having broken his leg on page 223, a mere five days before. But Ribbon wrote with a new gentleness, as if she had caused him pain rather than rage.

Nothing had come from Dillons. He wondered bitterly why he had troubled to congratulate them on their service if his accolade was to go unappreciated. And more to the point, nothing had come from Kingston Marle by Friday. He had the letter of apology, he must have, otherwise he wouldn't have altered the ending of *Demogorgon* back to the original plot line. But that hardly meant he had recovered from all his anger. He might still have other revenges in store. And, moreover, he might intend never to answer Ribbon at all.

The shrubs seemed to be back in their normal places. It would be a good idea to have a plan of the garden with the bushes all accurately positioned so that he could tell if they moved. He decided to make one. The evening was mild and sunny, though damp and, of course, at not long past midsummer, still broad daylight at eight. A deckchair was called for, a sheet of paper and, better than a pen, a soft lead pencil. The deckchairs might be up in the loft or down here, he couldn't remember, though he had been in the shed on Wednesday evening to find a spade. He looked through the shed window. In the far corner, curled up, was a small dark shape.

Ribbon was too frightened to cry out. A pain seized him in the chest, ran up his left arm, held him in its grip before it slackened and released him. The black shape opened its eyes and looked at him, just as the demon in The Book looked at Charles Ambrose. Ribbon hunched his back and closed his eyes. When he opened them and looked again he saw Tinks Next-door get up, stretch, arch its back and begin to walk in leisurely fashion towards the door. Ribbon flung it open. 'Scat! Get out! Go home!' he screamed.

Tinks fled. Had the wretched thing slunk in there when he opened the door to get the spade? Probably. He took out a deckchair and sat on it, but all heart had gone out of him for drawing a plan of the garden. In more ways than one, he thought, the pain receding and leaving only a dull ache. You could have mild heart attacks from which you recovered and were none the worse. Mummy said she had had several, some of them brought on – he sadly recalled – by his own defections from her standards. It could be hereditary. He must take things easy for the next few days, not *worry*, try to put stress behind him.

\* \* \*

Kingston Marle had signed all the books she sent him and returned them with a covering letter. Of course she had sent postage and packing as well, and had put in a very polite little note, repeating how much she loved his work and what a great pleasure meeting him in Blackwell's had been. But still she had hardly expected such a lovely long letter from him, nor one of quite that nature. Marle wrote how very different she was from the common run of fans, not only in intellect but in appearance too. He hoped she wouldn't take it amiss when he told her he had been struck by her beauty and elegance among that dowdy crowd.

It was a long time since any man had paid Susan such a compliment. She read and reread the letter, sighed a little, laughed and showed it to Frank.

'I don't suppose he writes his own letters,' said Frank, put out. 'Some secretary will do it for him.'

'Well, hardly.'

'If you say so. When are you seeing him again?'

'Oh, don't be silly,' said Susan.

She covered each individual book Kingston Marle had signed for her with cling film and put them all away in a glass-fronted bookcase from which, to make room, she first removed Frank's *Complete Works of Shakespeare*, Tennyson's *Poems*, *The Poems of Robert Browning* and Kobbé's *Complete Opera Book*. Frank appeared not to notice. Admiring through the glass, indeed gloating over, her wonderful collection of Marle's works with the secret inscriptions hidden from all eyes, Susan wondered if she should respond to the author. On the one hand a letter would keep her in the forefront of his mind but on the other it would be in direct contravention of the playing-hard-to-get principle. Not that Susan had any intention of being 'got', of course not, but she was not averse to inspiring thoughts about her in Kingston Marle's mind or even a measure of regret that he was unable to know her better.

Several times in the next few days she surreptitiously took one of the books out and looked at the inscription. Each had something different in it. In *Wickedness in High Places* Marle had written, 'To Susan, met on a fine morning in Oxford' and in *The Necromancer's Bride,* 'To Susan, with kindest of regards', but on the title page of *Evil Incarnate* appeared the inscription Susan liked best. 'She was a lady sweet and kind, ne'er a face so pleased my mind – ever yours, Kingston Marle.'

Perhaps he would write again, even if she didn't reply. Perhaps he would be *more likely* to write if she didn't reply.

\* \* \*

On Monday morning the post came early, soon after eight, delivering just one item. The computer-generated address on the envelope made Ribbon think for one wild moment that it might be from Kingston Marle. But it was from Clara Jenkins, and it was an angry, indignant letter, though containing no threats. Didn't he understand her novel was fiction? You couldn't say things were true or false in fiction, for things were as the author, who was all-powerful, wanted them to be. In a magic realism novel, such as *Tales My Lover Told Me*, only an ignorant fool would expect facts (and these included spelling, punctuation and grammar) to be as they were in the dreary reality he inhabited. Ribbon took it into the kitchen, screwed it up and dropped it in the waste bin.

He was waiting for the tree fellers who were due at nine. Half past nine went by, ten went by. At ten past the front doorbell rang. It was Glenys Next-door.

'Tinks turned up,' she said. 'I was so pleased to see him I gave him a whole can of red sockeye salmon. She appeared to have forgiven Ribbon for his 'attitude'. 'Now don't say what a wicked waste, I can see you were going to. I've got to go and see my mother, she's fallen over, broken her arm and bashed her face, so would you be an angel and let the washing machine man in?'

'I suppose so.' The woman had a mother! She must be getting on for seventy herself.

'You're a star. Here's the key and you can leave it on the hall table when he's been. Just tell him it's full of pillowcases and water, and the door won't open.'

The tree fellers came at eleven thirty. The older one, a joker, said, 'I'm a funny feller and he's a nice feller, right?'

'Come this way,' Ribbon said frostily.

'What d'you want them lovely Leylandiis down for then? Not to menton that lovely flowering currant?'

'Them currants smell of cat's pee, Damian,' said the young one. 'Whether there's been cats peeing on them or not.'

'Is that right? The things he knows, guv. He's wasted in this job, ought to be fiddling with computers.'

Ribbon went indoors. The computer and printer were downstairs now, in the dining room. He wrote first to Natalya Dreadnought, author of *Tick*, pointing out in a mild way that 'eponymous' applies to a character or object which gives a work its name, not to the name derived from the character. Therefore it was the large blood-sucking mite of the Acarina order which was eponymous, not her title. The letter he wrote to Raymond Kobbo would correct just two mistakes in *The Nomad's Smile*, but for both Ribbon needed to consult *Piranha to Scurfy*. He was pretty sure the Libyan caravan centre should be spelt 'Sabha', not 'Sebha', and he was even more certain that 'qalam', meaning a reed pen used in Arabic calligraphy, should start with a K. He went upstairs and lifted the heavy tome off the shelf. Finding that Kobbo had been right in both instances – 'Sabha' and 'Sebha' were optional spellings and 'qalam' perfectly correct – unsettled him. Mummy would have known, Mummy would have set him right in her positive, no-nonsense way, before he had set foot on the bottom stair. He asked himself if he could live without her and could have sworn he heard her sharp voice say, 'You should have thought of that before.'

Before what? That day in February when she had come up here to – well, oversee him, supervise him. She frequently did so and in later years he hadn't been as grateful to her as he should have been. By the desk here she had stood and told him it was time he earned some money by his work, by a man's fifty-second year it was time. She had made up her mind to leave Daddy's royalties to the lifeboat people. But it wasn't this which finished things for him, or triggered things off, however you liked to put it. It was the sneering tone in which she told him, her right index finger pointing at his chest, that he was no good, he had failed. She had kept him in comfort and luxury for decade after decade, she had instructed him, taught him everything he knew, yet in spite of this, his literary criticism had not had the slightest effect on authors' standards or effected the least improvement in English fiction. He had wasted his time and his life through cowardice and pusillanimity, through mousiness instead of manliness.

It was that word 'mousiness' which did it. His hands moved across the table to rest on *Piranha to Scurfy*, he lifted it in both hands and brought it down as hard as he could on her head. Once, twice, again and again. The first time she screamed but not again after that. She staggered and sank to her knees and he beat her to the ground with Volume VIII of the *Encyclopaedia Britannica*. She was an old woman, she put up no struggle, she died quickly. He very much wanted not to get blood on the book – she had taught him books were sacred – but there was no blood. What was shed was shed inside her.

Regret came immediately. Remorse followed. But she was dead. He buried her in the wide flowerbed at the end of the garden that night, in the dark without a torch. The widows on either side slept soundly, no one saw a thing. The ivies grew back and the flowerless plants that liked shade. All summer he had watched them slowly growing. He told only two people she was dead, Glenys Next-door and his cousin Frank. Neither showed any inclination to come to the 'funeral', so when the day he had appointed came he left the house at ten in the morning, wearing the new dark suit he had bought, a black tie that had been Daddy's and carrying a bunch of spring flowers. Sandra On-the-other-side spotted him from her front room window and, approving, nodded sombrely while giving him a sad smile. Ribbon smiled sadly back. He put the flowers on someone else's grave and strolled round the cemetery for half an hour.

From a material point of view, living was easy. He had more money now than Mummy had ever let him have. Daddy's royalties were paid into her bank account twice a year and would continue to be paid in. Ribbon drew out what he wanted on her direct debit card, his handwriting being so like hers that no one could tell the difference. He had been collecting her retirement pension for years, and he went on doing so. It occurred to him that the Department of Social Security might expect her to die some time and the bank might expect it too, but she had been very young when he was born and might in any case have been expected to outlive him. He could go on doing this until what would have been her hundredth birthday and even beyond. But could he live without her? He had 'made it up to her' by keeping her bedroom as a shrine, keeping her clothes as if one day she would come back and wear them again. Still he was a lost soul, only half a man, a prey to doubts and fears and self-questioning and a nervous restlessness.

Looking down at the floor, he half expected to see some mark where her small, slight body had lain. There was nothing, any more than there was a mark on Volume VIII of *Britannica*. He went downstairs and stared out into the garden. The cypress he had associated with her, had been near to seeing as containing her spirit, was down, was lying on the grass, its frondy branches already wilting in the heat. One of the two fat shrubs was down too. Damian and the young one were sitting *on Mummy's grave*, drinking something out of a vacuum flask and smoking cigarettes. Mummy would have had something to say about that, but he lacked the heart. He thought again how strange it was, how horrible and somehow wrong, that the small child's name for its mother was the same as that for an embalmed Egyptian corpse.

In the afternoon, after the washing machine man had come and been let into Glenys Next-door's, Ribbon plucked up the courage to phone Kingston Marle's publishers. After various people's voice mail, instructions to press this button and that and requests to leave messages, he was put through to the department which sent on authors' letters. A rather indignant young woman assured him that all mail was sent on within a week of the publishers receiving it. Recovering a little of Mummy's spirit, he said in the strongest tone he could muster that a week was far too long. What about readers who were waiting anxiously for a reply? The young woman told him she had said 'within a week' and it might be much sooner. With that he had to be content. It was eleven days now since he had apologised to Kingston Marle, ten since his publishers had received the letter. He asked tentatively if they ever handed a letter to an author in person. For a while she hardly seemed to understand what he was talking about, then she gave him a defiant 'no', such a thing could never happen.

So Marle had not called off his dogs because he had received the apology. Perhaps it was only that the spell, or whatever it was, lasted no more than, say, twenty-four hours. It seemed, sadly, a more likely explanation. The tree fellers finished at five, leaving the wilted shrubs stacked on the flowerbed, not on Mummy's grave but on the place where The Book was buried. Ribbon took two of Mummy's sleeping pills and passed a good night. No letter came in the morning, there was no post at all. Without any evidence as to the truth of this, he became suddenly sure that no letter would come from Marle now, it would never come.

He had nothing to do, he had written to everyone who needed reproving, he had supplied himself with no more new books and had no inclination to go out and buy more. Perhaps he would never write to anyone again. He unplugged the link between computer and printer and closed the computer's lid. The new shelving he had bought from IKEA to put up in the dining room would never be used now. In the middle of the morning he went into Mummy's bedroom, tucked the nightdress under the pillow and quilt, removed the bedspread from the wardrobe door and closed the door. He couldn't have explained why he did these things, it simply seemed time to do them. From the window he saw a taxi draw up and Glenys Next-door get out of it. There was someone else inside the taxi she was helping out but Ribbon didn't stay to see who it was.

He contemplated the back garden from the dining room. Somehow he would have to dispose of all those logs, the remains of the cypresses, the flowering currant, the holly and the lilac bush. For a ten-pound note the men would doubtless have taken them away but Ribbon hadn't thought of this at the time. The place looked bleak and characterless now, an empty expanse of grass with a stark ivy-clad flowerbed at the end of it. He noticed, for the first time, over the wire dividing fence, the profusion of flowers in Glenys Next-door's, the bird table, the little fishpond (both hunting grounds for Tinks), the red-leaved Japanese maple. He would burn that wood, he would have a fire.

Of course he wasn't supposed to do this. In a small way it was against the law, for this was a smokeless zone and had been for nearly as long as he could remember. By the time anyone complained – and Glenys Next-door and Sandra On-the-other-side would both complain – the deed would have been done and the logs consumed. But he postponed it for a while and went back into the house. He felt reasonably well, if a little weak and dizzy. Going upstairs made him breathless in a way he never had been before, so he postponed that for a while too and had a cup of tea, sitting in the front room with his feet up. What would Marle do next? There was no knowing. Ribbon thought that when he was better he would find out where Marle lived, go to him and apologise in person. He would ask what he could do to make it up to Marle and whatever the answer was he would do it. If Marle wanted him to be his servant he would do that, or kneel at his feet and kiss the ground or allow Marle to flog him with a whip. Anything Marle wanted he would do, whatever it was.

Of course, he should't have buried the book. That did no good. It would be ruined now and the best thing, the *cleanest* thing, would be to cremate it. After he was rested he made his way upstairs, crawled really, his hands on the stairs ahead of him, took *Piranha to Scurfy* off the shelf and brought it down. He'd burn that too. Back in the garden he arranged the logs on a bed of screwed-up newspaper, rested Volume VIII of *Britannica* on top of them and, fetching the spade, unearthed *Demogorgon*. Its plastic covering had been inadequate to protect it and it was sodden as well as very dirty. Ribbon felt guilty for treating it as he had. The fire would purify it. There was paraffin in a can somewhere, Mummy had used it for the little stove that heated her bedroom. He went back into the house, found the can and sprinkled paraffin on newspaper, logs and books, and applied a lighted match.

The flames roared up immediately, slowed once the oil had done its work. He poked at his fire with a long stick. A voice started shouting at him but he took no notice, it was only Glenys Next-door complaining. The smoke from the fire thickened, grew dense and grey. Its flames had reached The Book's wet pages, the great thick wad of 427 of them, and as the smoke billowed in a tall whirling cloud an acrid smell poured from it. Ribbon stared at the smoke for, in it now, or behind it, something was taking shape, a small, thin and very old woman swathed in a mummy's bandages, her head and arm bound in white bands, the skin between fish-belly white. He gave a small choking cry and fell, clutching the place where his heart was, holding on to the overpowering pain.


'The pathologist seems to think he died of fright,' the policeman said to Frank. 'A bit fanciful, that, if you ask me. Anyone can have a heart attack. You have to ask yourself what he could have been frightened *of*. Nothing, unless it was of catching fire. Of course, strictly speaking, the poor chap had no business to be having a fire. Mrs Judd and her mother saw it all. It was a bit of a shock for the old lady, she's over ninety and not well herself, she's staying with her daughter while recovering from a bad fall.'

Frank was uninterested in Glenys Judd's mother and her problems. He had a severe summer cold, could have done without any of this and doubted if he would be well enough to attend Ambrose Ribbon's funeral. In the event, Susan went to it alone. Someone had to. It would be too terrible if no one was there.

She expected to find herself the only mourner and she was very surprised to find she was not alone. On the other side of the aisle from her in the crematorium chapel sat Kingston Marle. At first she could hardly believe her eyes, then he turned his head, smiled and came to sit next to her. Afterwards, as they stood admiring the two wreaths, his, and hers and Frank's, he said that he supposed some sort of explanation would be in order.

'Not really,' Susan said. 'I just think it's wonderful of you to come.'

'I saw the announcement of his death in the paper with the date and place of the funeral,' Marle said, turning his wonderful deep eyes from the flowers to her. 'A rather odd thing had happened. I had a letter from your cousin – well, your husband's cousin. It was a few days after we met in Oxford. His letter was an apology, quite an abject apology, saying he was sorry for having written to me before, asking me to forgive him for criticising me for something or other.'

'What sort of something or other?'

'That I don't know. I never received his previous letter. But what he said reminded me that I *had* received a letter intended for Dillons bookshop in Piccadilly and signed by him. Of course I sent it on to them and thought no more about it. But now I'm wondering if he put the Dillons letter into the envelope intended for me and mine into the one for Dillons. It's easily done. That's why I prefer e-mail myself.'

Susan laughed. 'It can't have had anything to do with his death, anyway.'

'No, certainly not. I didn't really come here because of the letter, that's not important, I came because I hoped I might see you again.'

'Oh.'

'Will you have lunch with me?'

Susan looked around her, as if spies might be about. But they were alone. 'I don't see why not,' she said.

# Computer Seance

Sophia de Vasco (Sheila Vosper on her birth certificate) was waiting at the bus stop when she saw her brother coming out of a side turning. Her brother looked a lot younger than he had before he died seven years before, but any doubts she might have had as to his identity were dispelled when he came up to her and asked her for money. 'Price of a cup of tea, missus?'

'You haven't changed, Jimmy,' said Sophia with a little laugh.

He didn't reply but continued to hold out his hand.

Sophia said roguishly, 'Now how would I know the price of a cup of tea, eh?'

'Fifty pee,' said Jimmy's ghost. 'A couple of quid for a cuppa and a butty.'

'I think you've been following my career from the Other Side, Jimmy. You know I've done rather well for myself since you passed over. You've seen how I've been responsible for London's spiritualist renaissance, haven't you? But you have to realise that I am no more made of money than I have ever been. If you're thinking Mother and Father left me anything you're quite wrong.'

'You some sort of loony tune?' He was looking at her fake fur, her high-heeled boots, the two large carriers and small leather case she carried. 'What's in the bag?'

'That is my computer. An indispensable tool of my trade, Jimmy. You could call it a symbol of the electronic advances spiritualism has made in recent years. My bus is coming now so I'll say goodbye.'

She went upstairs. She thought he might follow her but when she was sitting down she looked behind her and he was nowhere to be seen. Encounters with her dead relatives were not unusual events in Sophia's life. Only last week her aunt Lily had walked into her bedroom at midnight – she had always been a nocturnal type – and brought her a lot of messages from her mother, mostly warnings to Sophia to be on her guard in matters of men and money. Then, two evenings ago, an old woman came through the wall while Sophia was eating her supper. They manifested themselves so confidently, Sophia thought, because she never showed fear, she absolutely wasn't frightened. The old woman didn't stay long but flitted about the flat, peering at everything, and disappeared after telling Sophia that she was her maternal grandmother who had died in the Spanish flu epidemic of 1919.

So it was no great surprise to have seen Jimmy. In life he had always been feckless, unable to hold down a job, chronically short of money, with a talent for nothing but sponging off his relations. Few tears had been shed when his body was found floating in the Grand Union Canal, into which he had fallen after two or three too many in the Hero of Maida. Sophia devoutly hoped he wouldn't embarrass her by manifesting himself at the seance she was about to hold in half an hour's time at Mrs Paget-Brown's.

But, in fact, he was to make a more positive, almost concrete, appearance before that. As she descended the stairs from the top of the bus she saw him waiting for her at the stop. A less sensitive woman than Sophia might have assumed that he too had come on the bus and had sat downstairs, but she knew better. Why go on a bus when, in the manner of spirits, he could travel through space in no time and be wherever he wished in the twinkling of an eye?

Sophia decided that the only wise course was to ignore him. She shook her head in his direction and set off at a brisk pace along Kendal Street. Outside the butcher's she looked round and saw him following her. There was nothing to be done about it, she could only hope he wasn't going to attach himself to her, even take up residence in her flat, for that might mean all the trouble and expense of an exorcism.

Mrs Paget-Brown lived in Hyde Park Square. Before she rang the bell Sophia looked behind her once more. It was growing dark and she could no longer see Jimmy, but it might only be that he was already inside, in the drawing room, waiting for her. It couldn't be helped. Mrs Paget-Brown opened the door promptly. She had everything prepared, the long rectangular table covered by a dark-brown chenille cloth, Sophia's chair, the semicircle of chairs behind it. Five guests were expected, of whom two had already arrived. They were in the dining room, having a cup of herb tea, for Sophia discouraged the consumption of alcohol before encounters with denizens of the Other Side.

When Mrs Paget-Brown had gone back to her guests, Sophia took her laptop out of its case and set it on the table. She raised its lid so that the keyboard and screen could be seen. Then she took a large screen out of one of her carriers and plugged its cable into one of the computer ports. Glancing over her shoulder to check that Mrs Paget-Brown was really gone and the door shut, she took a big keyboard out of the other carrier and plugged its cable into a second port.

The doorbell rang, and rang again five minutes afterwards. That probably meant everyone had arrived, for two of the expected guests were a husband and wife, a Mr and Mrs Jameson, hoping for an encounter with their dead daughter. Mrs Paget-Brown had told her a lot about this daughter, how she had been called Deirdre, had had a husband and two small children and had been a harpist. Sophia sometimes felt a warm glow of happiness when she reflected how often she was able to bring relief and hope to such people as the Jamesons by putting them in touch with those who had gone before.

The computer was switched on, the small screen dark, the big screen alight but blank. She had settled herself into the big chair with the keyboard on her lap and it and her hands covered by the overhang of the chenille cloth, when someone tapped on the door and asked if she was ready. In a fluting voice Sophia asked them to come in.

She wouldn't have been at all surprised if Jimmy had been among them. They wouldn't have been able to see him, of course, but she would. Still, only six people entered the room, including Mrs Paget-Brown herself, the couple called Jameson who had the dead daughter, a very fat man who wheezed and two elderly women, one very smartly dressed in a turquoise suit, the other dowdy with untidy hair.

Sophia said a gracious, 'Good evening' and then, 'Please take a seat behind me where you can see the screen. In a moment we shall turn out the lights but before that I want to explain what will happen. What *may* happen. Of course, I can guarantee nothing if the spirits are unwilling.'

They sat down. The asthmatic man breathed noisily. Turquoise suit took off her hat. Sophia could see their faces reflected in the screen, Mrs Jameson's eyes bright with hope and yearning. The dowdy woman said could she ask a question and when Sophia said, certainly, my pleasure, asked if they would see anything or would it only be a matter of table raps and ectoplasm.

Sophia couldn't help laughing at the idea of ectoplasm. These people were so incredibly behind the times. But her laughter was kindly and she explained that there would be no table-rapping. The spirits, who were very advanced about such things, made their feelings and their messages known through the computer. Those seekers after truth who sat behind her would see answers appear on the screen.

Of course, everyone's eyes went to the laptop's small integral keyboard. And when the lights were lowered it was possible to imagine those keys moving. Sophia kept her hands under the cloth, her fingers on the big keyboard. She was ceaselessly thankful that she had taken that touch-typing course all those years ago when she was a girl.

The asthmatic man's wife was the first spirit to present herself. Her husband asked her if she was happy and YES appeared in green letters on the screen. He asked her if she missed him and WAITING FOR YOU TO FOLLOW DEAR appeared. Very much impressed, Mrs Paget-Brown summoned up her father. She said in an awed voice that she could see the keys very faintly moving on the integral keyboard as his spirit fingers touched thim. Her father answered YES when she asked if he was with her mother and NO when she enquired if death had been a painful experience. Sophia leaned back a little and closed her eyes. Communing with spirits took it out of her.

But she supplied the dowdy woman with a fairly satisfactory dead fiancé, her dead husband's predecessor. In answer to a rather timid question he replied that he had always regretted not marrying her and his life had been a failure. When the dowdy woman reminded him that he had fathered five children, owned three houses, been a junior minister in Margaret Thatcher's administration and later on chairman of a multinational company, Sophia told herself to be more careful.

She was more successful with Deirdre Jameson. The Jamesons were transfixed with joy when Deirdre declared her happiness on the screen and intimated that she watched over her husband and children from afar. Where she now was she had ample opportunity to play the harp and did so for all the company of heaven. For a moment Sophia wondered if she had gone too far but Mr and Mrs Jameson accepted everything and when the lights went on again, thanked her, as they put it, from the bottom of their hearts. 'Thank you, thank you, you have done a wonderful thing for us, you've transformed our lives.'

As she packed everything up again, Sophia reflected on something she had occasionally thought of in the past. It wasn't possible for her to go too far, it wasn't possible for her to deceive. Although she might conceal from these seekers after truth the hidden keyboard and the busy activity of her hands, the truth must be that these spirits were present and waiting to communicate. She was a true medium and her hands were the means they entered in order to transmit their messages. The world wasn't ready yet to have the keyboard and the moving fingers exposed, there was too much ignorance and prejudice, but one day . . .

One day, Sophia believed, everyone would be attuned to seeing and speaking to the dead, as she had seen and spoken to Jimmy. One day, when the earth was filled with the glory of the supernatural.

Carrying her bags and her laptop in its case, she tapped on the dining room door, was admitted and given a small glass of sherry. Discreetly, Mrs Paget-Brown slipped an envelope containing her cheque into her hand. Turquoise suit wanted to know if she would hold a seance for herself and some personal friends in Westbourne Terrace next week and the Jamesons asked for more revelations from Deirdre. Sophia graciously accepted both invitations.

She was always the first to leave. It was wiser not to engage in too much conversation with the guests but to preserve the vague air of mystery that surrounded her. By now it was very dark and there were so many trees in this neighbourhood that the street lights failed to make much of a show. But there was enough light for her to see her brother. He was waiting for her on the corner of Hyde Park Street and Connaught Street.

No one else was about, the Edgware Road wasn't a very pleasant area for a woman to be alone in at night, and Sophia thought that, nuisance though Jimmy was, she wouldn't be altogether averse to a man's escort until her bus came. Then, of course, she realised how absurd this was. Jimmy's presence at her side would be no deterrent to a mugger who would be unable to see him. 'It's time you went back to wherever you came from, Jimmy,' she said rather severely. 'I must say I doubt if it's the pleasantest of places but you should have thought of that while you were on earth.'

'Loony tune,' said Jimmy. 'I want the bag. I want all the bags. You give them to me and you'll be OK.'

'Give you my computer? What an idea. You couldn't even carry it. The handle would pass right through your hand.'

As if to demonstrate her error, Jimmy made a grab for the laptop in its case. Sophia snatched it back and held it above her head. She didn't cry out. It was all too absurd. She didn't see the knife either. In fact, she never saw it, only felt it like a blow that robbed her first of breath, then of life. She dropped the carriers. The secret keyboard made a little clatter when it struck the pavement.

Jimmy, or Darren Palmer, picked up the bags and retrieved the case. Next morning he sold the lot to a man he knew in Leather Lane market and spent the money on crack cocaine.

# Fair Exchange

'**Y**ou're looking for Tom Dorchester, aren't you?' Penelope said.
I nodded. 'How did you know?'

'I've been expecting you to ask. I mean, he's always been at this conference in the past. Quite a fixture. This must be the first he hasn't come to in – what? Fifteen years? Twenty?'

'He's not here, then?'

'He's dead.'

I wanted to say, 'He can't be!' But that's absurd. Anyone can be dead. Here today and gone tomorrow, as the saying goes. Still, the more full of vitality a person is the more you feel he has a firmer grasp on life than the rest of us. Only violence, some appalling accident, could prise him loose. And Tom was – had been, I should say – more vital, more enthusiastic and more interested in everything than most people. He seemed to love and hate more intensely, specially to love. I remember him once saying he needed no more than five hours' sleep a night, there was too much to do, to learn, to appreciate, to waste time sleeping. And then his wife had become ill, very ill. Much of his abundant energy he devoted to finding a cure for her particular kind of cancer. Or trying to find it.

I said, stupidly, I suppose, 'But it was Frances who was going to die.'

Penelope gave me a strange, indecipherable look. 'I'll tell you about it, if you like. It's an odd story. Of course, I don't know how much you know.'

'About what? I wouldn't have called Tom a close friend but I'd known him for years. I know he adored Frances. I mean, I adore Marian but – well, you know what I mean. He was like a young lover. To say he worshipped the ground she trod on wouldn't be an exaggeration.'

Penelope took her cigarettes out of her handbag and offered me one.

'I've given it up.'

'I wish I could but I know my limitations. Now, d'you want the story?' I nodded. 'You may not like it. It's pretty awful one way and another. He killed himself, you know.'

'He *what*? *Tom Dorchester*?'

'Did away with himself, committed suicide, whatever.'

There was only one possible event that could make this believable. 'Ah, you mean Frances did die?'

Penelope shook her head. She took a sip of her drink. 'It was June or July of last year, about a month after the conference. You'll remember Tom only came for two days because he felt he couldn't leave Frances any longer than that, though their younger daughter was with her. They had two daughters, both married, and the older one has three children. The eldest child was twelve at the time.'

'I had dinner with Tom,' I said. 'There were a couple of other people there but he mostly talked to me. He was telling me about some miracle cure they'd tried on Frances but it hadn't worked.'

'It was at a clinic in Switzerland. They dehydrate you and give you nothing but walnuts to eat, something like that. When she came back and she was worse than ever, Tom found a healer. I actually met her. Chris and I went round to Tom's one evening and this woman was there. Very weird she was, very weird indeed.'

'What do you mean, weird?'

'Well, you think of a healer as laying on hands, don't you? Or reciting mantras while using herbal remedies, something like that. This woman wasn't like that. She did it all by talk and the power of thought. That's what she said, the power of thought. Her name was Davina Tarsis and she was quite young. Late thirties, early forties, very strangely dressed. Not that sort of floaty hippy look, oriental garments and beads and whatever, not like that at all. She was very thin, only a very thin woman could have got away with wearing skin-tight white leggings and a white tunic with a great orange sun printed on the front of it. Her hair was long and dyed a deep purplish red. I don't know why I say "was". I expect she's still got purple hair. No make-up, of course, a scrubbed face and a ring in one nostril – not a stud, a ring.

'Tom thought she was wonderful. He claimed she'd cured a woman who had been having radiotherapy at the same time as Frances. Now the odd thing was that she didn't talk much to Frances at all – I had a feeling Frances didn't altogether care for her. She talked to Tom. Not while we were there, I don't mean that. I mean in private. Apparently they had long sessions, like a kind of mad form of psychotherapy. Chris said maybe she was making a play for Tom but

I don't think it was that. I think she really believed in what she was doing and so did he. So, my God, did he.

'She taught him to believe that anything you wished for hard enough you could have. He told me that – not at the time, when it was all over.'

'What do you mean,' I said, 'when it was all over?'

'When Tom had got what he wanted.'

'Presumably, that was for Frances to be cured.'

'That's right. He got very emotional with me one night – Chris was out somewhere – and he started crying and sobbing. I know men do cry these days but I've never known a man cry like Tom did that night. The tears poured out of his eyes. There was quite a long time when he couldn't speak, he choked on the words. It was dreadful, I didn't know what to do. I gave him some brandy but he'd only take a sip of it because he was driving and he had to go back to Frances before his daughter and *her* daughter had to go home. That's the nine-year-old, Emma she's called. Anyway, he calmed down after a bit and then he said he couldn't live without Frances, he couldn't imagine life without her, he'd kill himself . . .'

'Ah,' I said.

'Ah, nothing. That had nothing to do with it. Frances went back into hospital soon after that. They were trying some new kind of chemotherapy on her. Tom hadn't any faith in it. By then he only had faith in Tarsis. He was having daily talk sessions with her. He'd taken leave from his job and he'd spend an entire morning talking to Tarsis, mostly about his feelings for Frances, I gather, and how he felt about the rest of his family, and how he and Frances had met and so on. She'd make him go over and over it and the more he repeated himself the more approving she was.

'Frances came home and she was very ill, thin, with no appetite. Her hair began to fall out. She could barely walk. The side effects from the chemo were the usual ghastly thing, nausea and faintness and ringing in the ears and all that. Tarsis came round and took a look at her, said the chemo was a mistake but in spite of it, she thought she could heal Frances completely. Then came the crunch. I didn't know this at the time, Tom didn't tell me until – oh, I don't know, two or three months afterwards. But this is what Tarsis said to him.

'They talked while Frances was asleep. Tarsis said, "What would you give to make Frances live?" Well, of course, Tom asked what she meant and she said, "Whose life would you give in exchange for Frances's life?" Tom said that was nonsense, you couldn't trade one

437

person's life for another and Tarsis said, oh yes, you could. The power of thought could do that for you. She'd trained Tom in practising the power of thought and now all he had to do was wish for Frances to live. Only he had to offer someone else up in her place.

'That was when he started to see her for what she was. A charlatan. But he played along, he said. He wanted to see what she'd do. Called her bluff, was what he said, but he was deceiving himself in that. He still half believed. Who would he offer up, she asked him. "Oh, anyone you like," he said and he laughed. She was deadly serious. That day she'd met Tom's elder daughter and the granddaughter Emma. Tom said – he hated telling me this but on the other hand he was really past caring what he told anyone – he said Emma hadn't been very polite to Davina Tarsis. She'd sort of stared at her, at the tight leggings and the sun on her tunic and sneered a bit, I suppose, and then she'd said it wasn't Tarsis but the chemo that was doing her grandmother good, it stood to reason that was what it was.'

I interrupted her. 'What do you mean, he hated telling you?'

'Wait and see. He had good reason. It was after Emma and her mother had gone and Frances was resting that they had this talk. When Tom said it could be anyone she liked, Tarsis said it wasn't what she liked but what Tom wanted, and then she said, "How about that girl Emma?" Tom told her not to be ridiculous but she persisted and at last he said that, well, yes, he supposed so, he would give Emma, only the whole thing was absurd. The fact was that he'd give anyone to save Frances's life if it were possible to do that, so of course, yes, he'd give Emma.'

'It must have put him off this Davina Tarsis, surely?'

'You'd think so. I'm not sure. All this was about nine or ten months ago. Frances started to get better. Oh, yes, she did. You needn't look like that. It was just an amazing thing. The doctors were amazed. But it wasn't unheard-of, it wasn't a miracle, though people said it was. Presumably, the chemo worked. All the things that should get right got right. I mean, her blood count got to be normal, she put on weight, the pain went, the tumours shrivelled up. She simply got a bit better every day. It wasn't a remission, it was a recovery.'

'Tom must have been over the moon,' I said.

Penelope made a face. 'He was. For a while. And then Emma died.'

'*What?*'

'In a road crash. She died.'

'You're not saying this witch woman, this Davina Tarsis . . .?'

'No, I'm not. Of course I'm not. At the time of the crash Tarsis and

Tom were together in Tom's house with Frances. Besides, there was no mystery about the accident. It *was* indisputably an accident. Emma was on a school bus coming back from a visit with the rest of her class to some stately home. There was ice on the road, the bus skidded and overturned, and three of the pupils were killed, Emma among them. You must have read about it, if was all over the media.'

'I think I did,' I said. 'I can't remember.'

'It affected Tom – well, profoundly. I don't mean in the way the death of a grandchild would affect any grandparent. I mean he was racked with guilt. He had such faith in Tarsis that he really believed he'd done it. He believed he'd given Emma's life in exchange for Frances's. And another awful thing was that his love for Frances simply vanished, all that great love, that amazing devotion that was an example to us all, really, it disappeared. He came to dislike her. He told me it wasn't that he had no feeling for her any more, he actively disliked her.

'So there was nothing for him to live for. He believed he'd ruined his own life and ruined his daughter's and destroyed his love for Frances. One night after Frances was asleep he drank a whole bottle of liquid morphia she'd had prescribed but hadn't used and twenty paracetamol and a few brandies. He died quite quickly, I believe.'

'That's terrible,' I said. 'The most awful tragedy. I'd no idea. And poor Frances. One's heart goes out to Frances.'

Penelope looked at me and took another cigarette. 'Don't feel too sorry for her,' she said. 'She's as fit as a fiddle now and about to start a new life. Her GP lost his wife about the time he diagnosed her cancer and he and Frances are getting married next month. So you could say that all's well that ends well.'

'I wouldn't go as far as that,' I said.

# The Wink

The woman in reception gave her directions. Go through the day room, then the double doors at the back, turn left and Elsie's in the third room on the right. Unless she's in the day room.

Elsie wasn't but the Beast was. Jean always called him that, she had never known his name. He was sitting with the others watching television. A semicircle of chairs was arranged in front of the television, mostly armchairs but some wheelchairs, and some of the old people had fallen asleep. He was in a wheelchair and he was awake, staring at the screen where celebrities were taking part in a game show.

Ten years had passed since she had last seen him but she knew him, changed and aged though he was. He must be well over eighty. Seeing him was always a shock but seeing him in here was a surprise. A not unpleasant surprise. He must be in that chair because he couldn't walk. He had been brought low, his life was coming to an end.

She knew what he would do when he saw her. He always did. But possibly he wouldn't see her, he wouldn't turn round. The game show would continue to hold his attention. She walked as softly as she could, short of tiptoeing, round the edge of the semicircle. Her mistake was to look back just before she reached the double doors. His eyes were on her and he did what he always did. He winked.

Jean turned sharply away. She went down the corridor and found Elsie's room, the third on the right. Elsie too was asleep, sitting in an armchair by the window. Jean put the flowers she had brought on the bed and sat down on the only other chair, an upright one without arms. Then she got up again and drew the curtain a little way across to keep the sunshine off Elsie's face.

Elsie had been at Sweetling Manor for two weeks and Jean knew she would never come out again. She would die here – and why not? It was clean and comfortable, and everything was done for you and probably it was ridiculous to feel, as Jean did, that she would prefer anything to being here, including being helpless and old and starving and finally dying alone.

They were the same age, she and Elsie, but she felt younger and thought she looked it. They had always known each other, had been at school together, had been each other's bridesmaids. Well, Elsie had been her matron of honour, having been married a year by then. It was Elsie she had gone to the pictures with that evening, Elsie and another girl whose name she couldn't remember. She remembered the film, though. It had been Deanna Durbin in *Three Smart Girls*. Sixty years ago.

When Elsie woke up she would ask her what the other girl was called. Christine? Kathleen? Never mind. Did Elsie know the Beast was in here? Jean remembered then that Elsie didn't know the Beast, had never heard what happened that night, no one had, she had told no one. It was different in those days, you couldn't tell because you would get the blame. Somehow, ignorant though she was, she had known that even then.

Ignorant. They all were, she and Elsie and the girl called Christine or Kathleen. Or perhaps they were just afraid. Afraid of what people would say, would think of them. Those were the days of blame, of good behaviour expected from everyone, of taking responsibility, and often punishment, for one's own actions. You put up with things and you got on with things. Complaining got you nowhere.

Over the years there had been extraordinary changes. You were no longer blamed or punished, you got something called empathy. In the old days what the Beast did would have been her fault. She must have led him on, encouraged him. Now it was a crime, *his* crime. She read about it in the papers, saw about things called helplines on television, and counselling and specially trained women police officers. This was to avoid your being marked for life, traumatised, though you could never forget.

That was true, that last part, though she had forgotten for weeks on end, months. And then, always, she had seen him again. It came of living in the country, in a small town, it came of her living there and his going on living there. Once she saw him in a shop, once out in the street, another time he got on a bus as she was getting off it. He always winked. He didn't say anything, just looked at her and winked.

Elsie had looked like Deanna Durbin. The resemblance was quite marked. They were about the same age, born in the same year. Jean remembered how they had talked about it, she and Elsie and Christine/Kathleen, as they left the cinema and the others walked with her to the bus stop. Elsie wanted to know what you had to do to get a screen test and the other girl said it would help to be in Hollywood, not Yorkshire. Both of them lived in the town, five minutes' walk away, and Elsie said she could stay the night if she wanted. But there was no way of letting her parents know. Elsie's had a phone but hers didn't.

Deanna Durbin was still alive, Jean had read somewhere. She wondered if she still looked like Elsie or if she had had her face lifted and her hair dyed and gone on diets. Elsie's face was plump and soft, very wrinkled about the eyes, and her hair was white and thin. She smiled faintly in her sleep and gave a little snore. Jean moved her chair closer and took hold of Elsie's hand. That made the smile come back but Elsie didn't wake.

The Beast had come along in his car about ten minutes after the girls had gone and Jean was certain the bus wasn't coming. It was the last bus and she hadn't known what to do. This had happened before, the driver just hadn't turned up and had got the sack for it, but that hadn't made the bus come. On that occasion she had gone to Elsie's and Elsie's mother had phoned her parents' next-door neighbours. She thought that if she did that a second time and put Mr and Mrs Rawlings to all that trouble, her dad would probably stop her going to the pictures ever again.

It wasn't dark. At midsummer it wouldn't get dark till after ten. If it had been she mightn't have gone with the Beast. Of course, he didn't seem like a Beast then but young, a boy, really, and handsome and quite nice. And it was only five miles. Mr Rawlings was always saying five miles was nothing, he used to walk five miles to school every day and five miles back. But she couldn't face the walk and, besides, she wanted a ride in a car. It would only be the third time she had ever been in one. Still, she would have refused his offer if he hadn't said what he had when she told him where she lived.

'You'll know the Rawlings then. Mrs Rawlings is my sister.'

It wasn't true but it sounded true. She got in beside him. The car wasn't really his, it belonged to the man he worked for, he was a chauffeur, but she found that out a lot later.

'Lovely evening,' he said. 'You been gallivanting?'

'I've been to the pictures,' she said.

After a couple of miles he turned a little way down a lane and stopped the car outside a derelict cottage. It looked as if no one could possibly live there but he said he had to see someone, it would only take a minute and she could come too. By now it was dusk but there were no lights on in the cottage. She remembered he was Mrs Rawlings's brother. There must have been a good ten years between them but that hadn't bothered her. Her own sister was ten years older than she was.

She followed him up the path, which was overgrown with weeds and brambles. Instead of going to the front door, he led her round the back where old apple trees grew among waist-high grass. The back of the house was a ruin, half its rear wall tumbled down.

'There's no one here,' she said.

He didn't say anything. He took hold of her and pulled her down in the long grass, one hand pressed hard over her mouth. She hadn't known anyone could be so strong. He took his hand away to pull her clothes off and she screamed, but the screaming was just a reflex, a release of fear, and otherwise useless. There was no one to hear. What he did was rape. She knew that now – well, had known it soon after it happened, only no one called it that then. Nobody spoke of it. Nowadays the word was on everyone's lips. Nine out of ten television series were about it. Rape, the crime against women. Rape, that these days you went into court and talked about. You went to self-defence classes to stop it happening to you. You attended groups and shared your experience with other victims.

At first she had been most concerned to find out if he had injured her. Torn her, broken bones. But there was nothing like that. Because she was all right and he was gone, she stopped crying. She heard the car start up and then move away. Walking home wasn't exactly painful, more a stiff, achy business, rather the way she had felt the day after she and Elsie had been learning to do the splits. She had to walk anyway, she had no choice. As it was, her father was in a rage, wanting to know what time she thought this was.

'Anything could have happened to you,' her mother said.

Something had. She had been raped. She went up to bed so they wouldn't see she couldn't stop shivering. She didn't sleep at all that night. In the morning she told herself it could have been worse, at least she wasn't dead. It never crossed her mind to say anything to anyone about what had happened, she was too ashamed, too afraid of what they would think. It was past, she kept telling herself, it was all over.

One thing worried her most. A baby. Suppose she had a baby. Never in all her life was she so relieved about anything, so happy, as when she saw that first drop of blood run down the inside of her leg a day early. She shouted for joy. She was all right! The blood cleansed her and now no one need ever know.

Trauma? That was the word they used nowadays. It meant a scar. There was no scar that you could see and no scar she could feel in her body, but it was years before she would let a man come near her. Afterwards she was glad about that, glad she had waited, that she hadn't met someone else before Kenneth. But at the time she thought about what had happened every day, she relived what had happened, the shock and the pain and the dreadful fear, and in her mind she called the man who had done that to her the Beast.

Eight years went by and she saw him again. She was out with Kenneth, he had just been demobbed from the Air Force and they were walking down the High Street arm in arm. Kenneth had asked her to marry him and they were going to buy the engagement ring. It was a big jewellers they went to, with several aisles. The Beast was in a different aisle, quite a long way away, on some errand for his employer, she supposed, but she saw him and he saw her. He winked.

He winked, just as he had ten minutes ago in the day room. Jean shut her eyes. When she opened them again Elsie was awake.

'How long have you been there, dear?'

'Not long,' Jean said.

'Are those flowers for me? You know how I love freesias. We'll get someone to put them in water. I don't have to do a thing in here, don't lift a finger. I'm a lady of leisure.'

'Elsie,' said Jean, 'what was the name of that girl we went to the pictures with when we saw *Three Smart Girls*?'

'What?'

'It was nineteen thirty-eight. In the summer.'

'I don't know, I shall have to think. My memory's not what it was. Bob used to say I looked like Deanna Durbin.'

'We all said you did.'

'Constance, her name was. We called her Connie.'

'So we did,' said Jean.

Elsie began talking of the girls they had been at school with. She could remember all their Christian names and most of their surnames. Jean found a vase, filled it with water and put the freesias into it because they showed signs of wilting. Her engagement ring still fitted on her finger, though it was a shade tighter. How worried she had been that Kenneth would be able to tell she wasn't a virgin! They said men could always tell. But of course, when the time came, he couldn't. It was just another old wives' tale.

Elsie, who already had her first baby, had worn rose-coloured taffeta at their wedding. And her husband had been Kenneth's best man. John was born nine months later and the twins eighteen months after that. There was a longer gap before Anne arrived but still she had had her hands full. That was the time, when the children were little, that she thought less about the Beast and what had happened than at any other time in her life. She forgot him for months on end. Anne was just four when she saw him again.

She was meeting the other children from school. They hadn't got a car then, it was years before they got a car. On the way to the school they were going to the shop to buy Anne a new pair of shoes. The Red Lion was just closing for the afternoon. The Beast came out of the public bar, not too steady on his feet, and he almost bumped into her. She said, 'Do you mind?' before she saw who it was. He stepped back, looked into her face and winked. She was outraged. For two pins she'd have told Kenneth the whole tale that evening. But of course she couldn't. Not now.

'I don't know what you mean about your memory,' she said to Elsie. 'You've got a wonderful memory.'

Elsie smiled. It was the same pretty teenager's smile, only they didn't use that word teenager then. You were just a person between twelve and twenty. 'What do you think of this place, then?'

'It's lovely,' said Jean. 'I'm sure you've done the right thing.'

Elsie talked some more about the old days and the people they'd known and then Jean kissed her goodbye and said she'd come back next week.

'Use the short cut next time,' said Elsie. 'Through the garden and in by the french windows next door.'

'I'll remember.'

She wasn't going to leave that way, though. She went back down the corridor and hesitated outside the day room door. The last time she'd seen the Beast, before *this* time, they were both growing old. Kenneth was dead. John was a grandfather himself, though a young one, the twins were joint directors of a prosperous business in Australia and Anne was a surgeon in London. Jean had never learned to drive and the car was given up when Kenneth died. She was waiting at that very bus stop, the one where he had picked her up all those years before. The bus came and he got off it, an old man with white hair, his face yellowish and wrinkled. But she knew him, she would have known him anywhere. He gave her one of his rude stares and he winked. That time it was an exaggerated, calculated wink, the whole side of his face screwed up and his eye squeezed shut.

She pushed open the day room door. The television was still on but he wasn't there. His wheelchair was empty. Then she saw him. He was being brought back from the bathroom, she supposed. A nurse held him tightly by one arm. The other rested heavily on the padded top of a crutch. His legs, in pyjama trousers, were half buckled and on his face was an expression of agony as, wincing with pain, he took small tottering steps.

Jean looked at him. She stared into his tormented face and his eyes met hers. Then she winked. She winked at him as he had winked at her that last time, and she saw what she had never thought to see happen to an old person. A rich, dark blush spread across his withered face. He turned away his eyes. Jean tripped lightly across the room towards the exit, like a sixteen-year-old.

# Catamount

The sky was the biggest she had ever seen. They said the skies of Suffolk were big and the skies of Holland, but those were small, cosy, by comparison. It might belong on another planet, covering another world. Mostly a pale soft azure or a dark hard blue, it was sometimes overcast with huge rolling cumulus, swollen and edged with sharp white light, from which rain roared without warning.

Chuck's and Carrie's house was only the second built up there, under that sky. The other was what they called a modular home and Nora a prefab, a frame bungalow standing on a bluff between the dirt road and the ridge. The Johanssons who lived there kept a few cows and fattened white turkeys for Thanksgiving. It was – thank God, said Carrie – invisible from her handsome log house, built of yellow Montana pine. She and Chuck called it Elk Valley Ranch, a name Nora had thought pretentious when she read it on their headed notepaper but not when she saw it. The purpose of the letter was to ask her and Gordon to stay and she could hardly believe it, it seemed too glorious, the idea of a holiday in the Rocky Mountains, though she and Carrie had been best friends for years. That was before she married a captain in the US Air Force stationed at Bentwaters and went back home to Colorado with him.

It was August when they went the first time. The little plane from Denver took them to the airport at Hogan and Carrie met them in the Land Cruiser. The road ran straight and long, parallel with the Crystal river that was also straight, like a canal, with willows and cottonwood trees along its banks. Beyond the flat flowery fields the mountains rose, clothed in pine and scrub oak and aspen, mountains that were dark, almost black, but with green sunlit meadows bright between the trees. The sun shone and it was hot but the sky looked like a winter sky in England, the blue very pale and the clouds stretched across it like torn strips of chiffon.

There were a few small houses, many large barns and stables. Horses were in the fields, one chestnut mare with a new-born foal.

447

Carrie turned in towards the western mountains and through a gateway with Elk Valley Ranch carved on a board. It was still a long way to the house. The road wound through curves and hairpin bends, and as they went higher the mountain slopes and the green canyons opened out below them, mountain upon mountain and valley upon valley, a herd of deer in one deep hollow, a golden eagle perched on a spar. By the roadside grew yellow asters and blue Michaelmas daisies, wild delphiniums, pale-pink geraniums and the bright-red Indian paintbrush, and above the flowers brown and yellow butterflies hovered.

'There are snakes,' Carrie said. 'Rattlesnakes. You have to be a bit careful. One of them was on the road last night. We stopped to look at it and it lashed against our tyres.'

'I'd like to see a porcupine.' Gordon had his Rocky Mountains wildlife book with him, open on his knees. 'But I'd settle for a raccoon.'

'You'll very likely see both,' Carrie said. 'Look, there's the house.'

It stood on the crown of a wooded hill, its log walls a dark gamboge, its roof green. A sheepdog came down to the five-barred gate when it saw the Land Cruiser.

'You must have spectacular views,' Gordon said.

'We do. If you wake up early enough you see fabulous things from your window. Last week I saw the cougar.'

'What's a cougar?'

'Mountain lion. I'll just get out and open the gate.'

It wasn't until she was home again in England that Nora had looked up the cougar in a *Mammals of North America* book. That night and for the rest of the fortnight she had forgotten it. There were so many things to do and see. Walking and climbing in the mountains, fishing in the Crystal river, picking a single specimen of each flower and pressing it in the book she bought for the purpose, photographing hawks and eagles, watching the chipmunks run along the fences. Driving down to the little town of Hogan (where on their way to Telluride, Butch Cassidy and Sundance had stopped to rob the bank), visiting the hotel where the Clanton Gang had left bullets from their handguns in the bathroom wall, shopping, sitting in the hot springs and swimming in the cold pool. Eating in Hogan's restaurant where elk steaks and rattlesnake burgers were specialities, and drinking in the Last Frontier Bar.

Carrie and Chuck said to come back next year or come in the winter when the skiing began. That was at the time when Hogan Springs was emerging as a ski resort. Or come in the spring when the snows melted and the alpine meadows burst into bloom, miraculous with gentians and avalanche lilies. And they did go again, but in late summer, a little later than in the previous year. The aspen leaves were yellowing, the scrub oak turning bronze.

'We shall have snow in a month,' Carrie said.

A black bear had come with her cubs and eaten Lily Johansson's turkeys. 'Like a fox at home,' Gordon said. They went up to the top of Mount Opie in the new ski lift and walked down. It was five miles through fields of blue flax and orange gaillardias. The golden ridge and the pine-covered slopes looked serene in the early autumn sunshine, the skies were clear until late afternoon when the clouds gathered and the rain came. The rain was torrential for ten minutes and then it was hot and sunny again, the grass and wild flowers steaming. A herd of elk came close up to the house and one of them pressed its huge head and stubby horns against the window. They saw the black bear and her cubs through Chuck's binoculars, loping along down in the green canyon.

'One day I'll see the couger,' Nora said and Gordon asked if cougars were an endangered species.

'I wouldn't think so. There are supposed to be mountain lions in every state of the United States, but I guess most of them are here. You ought to talk to Lily Johansson, she's often seen them.'

'There was a boy got killed by one last fall,' Carrie said. 'He was cycling and the thing came out of the woods, pulled him off his bike and well – ate him, I suppose. Or started to eat him. It was scared off. They're protected, so there was nothing to be done.'

Cougar stories abounded. Everyone had one. Some of them sounded like urban – rural, rather – myths. There was the one about the woman out walking with her little boy in Winter Park and who came face to face with a cougar on the mountain. She put the child on her shoulders and told him to hold up his arms so that, combined, they made a creature eight feet tall, which was enough to frighten the animal off. The boy in the harness shop in Hogan had one about the man out with his dog. To save himself he had to let the cougar kill and eat his dog while he got away. In the town Nora bought a reproduction of Audubon's drawing of a cougar, graceful, powerful, tawny, with a cat's mysterious closed-in face.

'I thought they were small, like a lynx,' Gordon said.

'They're the size of an African lion – well, lioness. That's what they look like, a lioness.'

'I shall frame my picture,' Nora said, 'and one day I'll see the real thing.'

They came back to Hogan year after year. More houses were built but not enough to spoil the place. Once they came in winter but, at their age, it was too late to learn to ski. Seventeen feet of snow fell. The snowplough came out on to the roads on Christmas Eve and cleared a passage for cars, making ramparts of snow where the flowers had been. Nora wondered about the animals. What did they live on, these creatures? The deer ate the bark of trees. Chuck put cattle feed out for them and hay.

'The herds have been reduced enough by mountain lions,' he said. 'You once asked if they were endangered. There are tens of thousands of them now, more than there have ever been.'

Nora worried about the golden eagle. What could it find to feed on in this white world? The bears were hibernating. Were the cougars also? No one seemed to know. She would never come again in winter when everything was covered, sleeping, waiting, buried. It was one thing for the skiers, another for a woman, elderly now, afraid to go out lest she slip on the ice. The few small children they saw had coloured balloons tied to them on long strings so that their parents could see and rescue them if they sank too deep down in the snow. All Christmas Day the sun blazed, melting the snow on the roof, and by night frost held the place in its grip, so that the guttering round the house grew a fringe of icicles.

The following spring Gordon died. Lily Johansson wrote a letter of sympathy and when Jim Johansson died next Christmas Nora wrote one to her. She delayed going back to the mountains for a year, two years. Driving from the airport with Carrie, she noticed for the first time something strange. It was a beautiful landscape but not a comfortable one, not easeful, not conducive to peace and tranquillity. There was no lushness and, even in the heat, no warmth. Lying in bed at night or sitting in a chair at dawn, watching for elk or the cougar, she tried to discover what was not so much wrong, it was far from wrong, but what made this feeling. The answer came to her uncompromisingly. It was fear. The countryside was full of fear, and the fear, while it added to the grandeur and in a strange way to the beauty, denied peace to the observer. Danger informed it, it threatened while it smiled. Always something lay in wait for you round the corner, though it might be only a beautiful butterfly. It never slept, it never rested even under snow. It was alive.

Lily Johansson came round for coffee. She was a large, heavy woman with calloused hands who had had a hard life. Six children had been born to her, two husbands had died. She was alone, struggling to make a living from hiring out horses, from a dozen cows and turkeys. Every morning she got up at dawn, not because she had so much to do but because she couldn't sleep after dawn. The cougar, passing the night high up in the mountains, came down many mornings past Lily's fence to hunt along the green valley. It might be days before she came back to her mountain hideout but she would come back, and next morning lope down the rocky path between the asters and the Indian paintbrush past Lily's fence.

'Why do you call it "she"?' Nora asked. Was this an unlikely statement of feminist principles?

Lily smiled. 'I guess on account of knowing she's a mother. There was weeks went by when I never saw her, and then one morning she comes down the trail and she's two young ones with her. Real pretty kittens they was.'

'Do you ever speak to her?'

'Me? I'm scared of her. She'd kill me as soon as look at me. Sometimes I says to her, "Catamount, catamount", but she don't pay me no attention. You want to see her, you come down and stop over and maybe we'll see her in the morning.'

Nora went a week later. They sat together in the evening, the two old widows, drinking Lily's root beer, and talking of their dead husbands. Nora slept in a tiny bedroom, with linen sheets on the narrow bed and a picture on the wall of (appropriately) Daniel in the lion's den. At dawn Lily came in with a mug of tea and told her to get up, put on her 'robe' and they'd watch.

The eastern sky was black with stripes of red between the mountains. The hidden sun had coloured the snow on the peaks rosy pink. All the land lay still. Along the path where the cougar passed the flowers were still closed up for the night.

'What makes her come?' Nora whispered. 'Does she see the dawn or feel it? What makes her get up from her bed and stretch, and maybe wash her paws and her face, and set off?'

'Are you asking me? I don't know. Who does? It's a mystery.'

'I wish we knew.'

'Catamount, catamount,' said Lily. 'Come, come, catamount.'

But the cougar didn't come. The sun rose, a magnificent spectacle, almost enough to bring tears to your eyes, Nora thought, all that purple and rose and orange and gold, all those miles and miles of serene blue. She had coffee and bread and blueberry jam with Lily and then she went back to Elk Valley Ranch.

'One day I'll see her,' she said to herself as she stroked the sheepdog

451

and went to let herself in by the yard door.

But would she? She had almost made up her mind not to come back next year. This was young people's country and she was getting too old for it. It was for climbers and skiers and mountain bikers, it was for those who could withstand the cold and enjoy the heat. Sometimes when she stood in the sun, its power frightened her, it was too strong for human beings. When rain fell it was a wall of water, a cascade, a torrent, and it might drown her. Snakes lay curled up in the long grass and spiders were poisonous. If anything could be too beautiful for human beings to bear, this was. Looking at it for long made her heart ache, filled her with strange undefined longings. At home once more in the mild and gentle English countryside, she looked at her Audubon and thought how this drawing of the cougar symbolised for her all that landscape, all that vast green and gold space, yet she had never seen it in the flesh, the bones, the sleek tawny skin.

Two years passed before she went back. It would be the last time. Chuck was ill and Elk Valley was no place for an old, sick man. He and Carrie were moving to an apartment in Denver. They no longer walked in the hills or skied on the slopes or ate barbecue on the bluff behind the house. Chuck's heart was bad and Carrie had arthritis. Nora, who had always slept soundly at Elk Valley Ranch, now found that sleep eluded her; she lay awake for hours with the curtains drawn back, gazing at the black velvet starry sky and listening to the baying of the coyotes at the mountain's foot. Sleepless, she began getting up earlier and earlier, and on the second morning, tiptoeing to the kitchen, she found that Carrie got up early too. They sat together, drinking coffee and watching the dawn.

The night of the storm she slept and awoke, and slept till the thunder woke her at four. The storm was like nothing she had ever known and she, who had never been frightened by thunder and lightning, was afraid now. The lightning lit the room with searchlight brilliance and while it lingered, dimming and brightening, for a moment too bright to look at, the thunder rolled and cracked as if the mountains themselves moved and split. Into the ensuing silence the rain broke. If you were out in it, you couldn't defend yourself against it, it would beat you to the ground.

Carrie's calling fetched her out of her room. No lights were on. Carrie was feeling her way about in the dark.

'What is it?'

'Chuck's sick,' Carrie said. 'I mean, very sick. He's lying in bed on his back with his mouth all drawn down to one side and when he speaks his voice isn't like his voice, it's slurred; he can't form the words.'

'How do you phone the emergency services? I'll do it.'

'Nora, you can't. I've tried calling them. The phone's down. Why do you think I've no lights on? The power's gone.'

'What shall we do? I don't suppose you want to leave him but I could do something.'

'Not in this rain,' Carrie said. 'When it stops, could you take the Land Cruiser and drive into Hogan?'

Then Nora had to admit she had never learned to drive. They both went to look at Chuck. He seemed to be asleep, breathing noisily through his crooked mouth. A crash from somewhere overhead drove the women into each other's arms, to cling together.

'I'm going to make coffee,' Carrie said.

They drank it, sitting near the window, watching the lightning recede, leap into the mountains. Nora said, 'The rain's stopping. Look at the sky.'

The black clouds were streaming apart to show the dawn. A pale, tender sky, neither blue nor pink but halfway between, revealed itself as the banks of cumulus and the streaks of cirrus poured away over the mountain peak into the east. The rain lifted like a blind rolled up. One moment it was a cascade, the next it was gone, and the coming light showed gleaming pools of water and grass that glittered and sparkled.

'Try the phone again,' Nora said.

'It's dead,' said Carrie and, realising what she'd said, shivered.

'Do you think Lily's phone would be working? I could go down there and see. If her phone's down too, maybe she'd drive me into Hogan.'

'Please, Nora, would you? I can't leave him.'

The air was so fresh, it made her dizzy. It made her think how seldom most people ever breathe such air as this or know what it is, but that once the whole world's atmosphere was like this, as pure and as clean. The sun was rising, a red ball in a sea of pale lilac, and while on the jagged horizon black clouds still massed, the huge deep bowl of sky was scattered over with pink and golden cirrus feathers. Soon the sun would be hot and the land and air as dry as a desert.

She made her way down the hairpin bends of the mountain road, aware of how poor a walker she had become. An ache spread from her thighs into her hips, particularly on the right side, so that in order to make any progress she was forced to limp, shifting her weight on to the left. But she was near Lily Johansson's house now. Lily's two horses stood placidly by the gate into the field.

Then, suddenly, they wheeled round and cantered away down the meadow as if the sight of her had frightened them. She said aloud, 'What's wrong? What's happened?'

As if in answer, the animal came out of the flowery path on to the surface of the road. She was the size of an African lioness, so splendidly loose-limbed and in control of her long fluid body that she seemed to flow from the grass and the asters and the pink geraniums. On the road she stopped and turned her head. Nora could see her amber eyes and the faint quiver of her golden cheeks. She forgot about making herself tall, putting her hands high above her head, advancing menacingly. She was powerless, gripped by the beauty of this creature, this cougar she had longed for. And she was terribly afraid.

'Catamount, catamount,' she whispered, but no voice came.

The cougar dropped on to her belly, a quivering cat flexing her muscles, as she prepared to spring.

# Walter's Leg

While he was telling the story about his mother taking him to the barber's, the pain in Walter's leg started again. A shooting pain – appropriate, that – and he knew very well what caused it. He shifted Andrew on to his other knee.

The story was about how his mother and he, on the way to get his hair cut, stopped on the corner of the High Street and Green Lanes to talk to a friend who had just come out of the fishmonger's. His mother was a talkative lady who enjoyed a gossip. The friend was like-minded. They took very little notice of Walter. He disengaged his hand from his mother's, walked off on his own down Green Lanes and into Church Road, found the barber's, produced sixpence from his pocket and had his hair cut. After that he walked back the way he had come. His mother and the friend were still talking. The five-year-old Walter slipped his little hand into his mother's and she looked down and smiled at him. His absence had gone unnoticed.

Emma and Andrew marvelled at this story. They had heard it before but they still marvelled. The world had changed so much, even they knew that at six and four. They were not even allowed to stand outside on the pavement on their own for two minutes, let alone go anywhere unaccompanied.

'Tell another,' said Emma.

As she spoke a sharp twinge ran up Walter's calf to the knee and pinched his thigh muscle. He reached down and rubbed his bony old leg.

'Shall I tell you how Haultrey shot me?'

'Shot you?' said Andrew. 'With a gun?'

'With an airgun. It was a long time ago.'

'Everything that's happened to you, Grandad,' said Emma, 'was a long time ago.'

'Very true, my sweetheart. This was sixty-five years ago. I was seven.'

'So it wasn't as long ago as when you had your hair cut,' said Emma, who already showed promise as an arithmetician.

Walter laughed. 'Haultrey was a boy I knew. He lived down our road. We used to play down by the river, a whole bunch of us. There were fish in the river then but I don't think any of us were fishing that day. We'd been climbing trees. You could get across the river by climbing willow trees, the branches stretched right across.

'And then one of us saw a kingfisher, a little tiny bright-blue bird it was, the colour of a peacock, and Haultrey said he was going to shoot it. I knew that would be wrong, even then I knew. Maybe we all did except Haultrey. He had an airgun, he showed it to us. I clapped my hands and the kingfisher flew away. All the birds went, we'd frightened them away with all the racket we were making. I had a friend called William Robbins, we called him Bill, he was my best friend, and he said to Haultrey that he'd bet he couldn't shoot anything, not aim at it and shoot it. Well, Haultrey wasn't having that and he said, yes, he could. He pointed to a stone sticking up out of the water and said he'd hit that. He didn't, though. He shot me.'

'Wow,' said Andrew.

'But he didn't mean to, Grandad,' said Emma. 'He didn't do it on purpose.'

'No, I don't suppose he did but it hurt all the same. The shot went into my leg, into the calf, just below my right knee. Bill Robbins went off to my house, he ran as fast as he could, he was a very good runner, the best in the school, and he fetched my dad and my dad took me to the doctor.'

'And did the doctor dig the bullet out?'

'A pellet, not a bullet. No, he didn't dig it out.' Walter rubbed his leg, just below the right knee. 'As a matter of fact, it's still there.'

'It's still *there*?'

Emma got off the arm of the chair and Andrew got off Walter's lap, and both children stood contemplating his right leg in its grey flannel trouser leg and grey-and-white Argyll pattern sock. Walter pulled up the trouser leg to the knee. There was nothing to be seen.

'If you like,' said Walter, 'I'll show you a photograph of the inside of my leg next time you come to my house.'

The suggestion was greeted with rapture. They wanted 'next time' to be now but were told by their mother that they would have to wait till Thursday. Walter was glad he'd come in the car. He wouldn't have fancied walking home, not with this pain. Perhaps he'd better go back to his GP, get a second opinion, ask to be sent to a – what would it be called? – an orthopaedic surgeon, presumably. Andrew, surely, had had the right idea when he asked if the doctor had dug the pellet out of his leg. Out of the mouths of babes and sucklings, thought old-fashioned Walter, hast thou ordained strength. It was hard to understand why the doctor hadn't dug it out sixty-five years ago, but in those days, so long as something wasn't life-threatening, they tended to leave well – or ill – alone. Ten years ago the specialist merely said he doubted if it was the pellet causing the pain, it was more likely arthritis. Walter must accept that he wasn't as young as he used to be.

Back home, searching through his desk drawers for the X-rays, Walter thought about something else Andrew had said. No, not Andrew, Emma. She'd said Haultrey hadn't done it on purpose and he'd said he didn't suppose he had. Now he wasn't so sure. For the first time in sixty-five years he recreated in his mind the expresion on Haultrey's face that summer's evening when he boasted he could hit the stone.

Bill Robbins was sitting on the river bank, two other boys whose names he had forgotten were up the willow tree, while he, Walter, was down by the water's edge, looking up at the kingfisher, and Haultrey was higher up with his airgun. The sun had been low in a pale-blue July sky. Walter had clapped his hands then and when the kingfisher flew away, turned his head to look at Haultrey. And Haultrey's expression had been resentful and revengeful, too, because Walter had scared the bird away. That was when he started boasting about hitting the stone. So perhaps he had meant to shoot him, shot him in the leg because he'd been baulked of his desire. I didn't think of that at the time, though, Walter thought. I took it for an accident and so did everyone else.

'I'm imagining things,' he said aloud, and he laid the X-rays on top of the desk ready to show them to Emma and Andrew. Their mother brought the children along after school on Thursday. The pictures were admired and a repetition of the story demanded. In telling it, Walter said nothing about the look on Haultrey's face.

'You forgot the bit about Bill running to your house and being the best runner in the school,' said Emma.

'So I did but now you've put it in yourself.'

'What was his other name, Grandad? Haultrey what?'

'It must have been a case of what Haultrey,' said Walter and he thought, as he often did, of how times had changed. It would be incomprehensible to these children that one might have known someone only by his surname. 'I don't know what he was called. I can't remember.'

The children suggested names. In his childhood the ones they knew would have been unheard-of (Scott, Ross, Damian, Liam, Seth) or, strangely enough, too old-fashioned for popular use (Joshua, Simon, Jack, George). He put up some ideas himself, appropriate names for the time (Kenneth, Robert, Alan, Ronald) but none of them was right. He'd know Haultrey's name when he heard it.

His daughter Barbara was looking at the X-rays. 'You'll have to go back to the doctor with that leg, Dad.'

'It does give me jip.' Walter realised he'd used an expression that was out of date even when he was a boy. It was a favourite of his own father's. 'It does give me jip,' he said again.

'See if they can find you a different consultant. They must be able to do something.'

When Barbara and the children had gone he looked Haultrey up in the phone book. The chances were that Haultrey wouldn't be there, not in the same place after sixty-five years, and he wasn't. No Haultreys were in it. Walter's leg began to ache dreadfully. He tried massaging it with some stuff he'd bought when he'd pulled a muscle in his back. It heated the skin but did nothing for the pain. He tried to remember Haultrey's first name. It wasn't Henry, was it? No, Henry was old-fashioned in the twenties and not revived till the eighties. David? It was a possibility but Haultrey hadn't been called David.

Bill Robbins had known Haultrey a lot better than he had. The Haultreys and the Robbinses had lived next door but one to each other. Bill was dead, he'd died ten years before, but up until his death he and Walter had remained friends, played golf together, been fellow members of the Rotary Club, and Walter still kept in touch with Bill's son. He phoned John Robbins.

'How are you, Walter?'

'I'm fine but for a spot of arthritis in my leg.'

'We're none of us getting any younger.' This was generous from a man of forty-two.

'Tell me something. D'you remember those people called Haultrey who lived near your grandparents?'

'Vaguely. My gran would.'

'She's still alive?'

'She's only ninety-six, Walter. That's nothing in our family barring my poor dad.'

John Robbins said it would be nice to see him and to come over for a meal and Walter said thanks very much, he'd like to. Old Mrs Robbins was in the phone book, in the same house she'd lived in since she got married seventy-three years before. She answered the phone in a brisk, spry voice. Certainly she remembered the Haultreys, though they'd been gone since 1968, and she particularly remembered the boy with his airgun. He'd taken a pot-shot at her cat but he'd missed.

'Lucky for the cat.' Walter rubbed his leg.

'Lucky for Harold,' said Mrs Robbins grimly.

'That was his name, Harold,' said Walter.

'Of course it was. Harold Haultrey. He disappeared in the war.'

'Disappeared?'

'I mean he never came back here and I wasn't sorry. He was in the army, never saw active service, of course not. He was in a camp down in the West Country somewhere for the duration, took up with a farmer's daughter, married her and stopped there. I reckon he thought he'd come in for the farm and maybe he has. Why don't you ever come and see me, Walter? You come over for a meal and I'll cook you steak and chips, you were always partial to that.'

Walter said he would once he'd had his leg seen to. He got an appointment with an orthopaedic surgeon, a different one, who looked at the new X-rays and said Walter had arthritis. *Everyone* of Walter's age had arthritis somwhere. The children liked the new X-rays and Emma said they were an improvement on the old ones. Andrew asked for one of them to put on his bedroom wall along with a magazine cut-out of the Spice Girls and his *Lion King* poster.

'You ought to get a second opinion on that leg, Dad,' said Barbara.

'It would be a third opinion by now, wouldn't it?'

'Tell about Haultrey, Grandad,' said Andrew.

So Walter told it all over again, this time adding Haultrey's Christian name. 'Harold Haultrey pointed at a stone in the water and said he'd shoot that, but he shot me.'

'And Bill Robbins, who was the fastest runner in the whole school, ran to your house and fetched your dad,' said Emma. 'But Harold didn't mean to do it, he didn't mean to hurt you, did he?'

'Who knows?' said Walter. 'It was a long time ago.'

They were all going away on holiday together, Barbara and her husband Ian and the children and Walter. It was a custom they'd established after Walter's wife died five years before. If he'd been completely honest, he'd have preferred not to go. He didn't much like the seaside or the food in the hotel and he was embarrassed about exposing his skinny old body in the swimming pool. And he suspected that if they were completely honest – perhaps they were, secretly, when alone together – Barbara and Ian would have preferred not to have him with them. The children liked him there, he was

459

pretty sure of that, and that was why he went.

The night before they left he went round to old Mrs Robbins's. John was there and John's wife, and they all ate steak and chips and tiramisu, which Mrs Robbins had become addicted to in extreme old age. They all asked about Walter's leg and he had to tell them nothing could be done. A discussion followed on how different things would be these days if a child of seven had been shot in the leg by another child. It would have got into the papers and Walter would have had counselling. Haultrey would have had counselling too, probably.

Driving down to Sidmouth with Emma beside him, trying to keep in convoy with Ian and Barbara and Andrew in the car ahead, Walter asked himself if Haultrey had ever said he was sorry. He hadn't. There had been no opportunity, for Walter was sure he'd never seen Haultrey again. Suddenly he thought of something. Ever since the pain in his leg started he'd thought about Haultrey every single day. He was becoming obsessed with Haultrey.

'I'm bored, Grandad,' said Emma. 'Tell me a story.'

Not Haultrey. Not the visit to the barber, which for some reason reminded him of Haultrey. 'I'll tell you about our dog Pip who stole a string of sausages from the butcher's and once bit the postman's hand when he put it through the letter box.'

Another world, it was. Sausages no longer came in strings and supermarkets were more common than butchers. These days the postman would have had counselling and a tetanus injection, and Pip would have been threatened with destruction, only his parents would have fought the magistrates' decision and taken it to the High Court, and Pip's picture would have been in the papers. Walter was tired by the time they got to Sidmouth while Emma was as fresh as a daisy and raring to go. He had related the entire history of his childhood to her, or as much as he could recall, several times over.

His leg ached. He still thought exercise better for him than rest. While the others went down to the beach, he took a walk along the seafront and through streets of Georgian houses. He hardly knew what made him glance at the brass plate on one of the pillars flanking a front door, perhaps the brilliant polish on it caught the sun, but he did look and there he read: *Jenkins, Haultrey, Hall, Solicitors and Commissioners for Oaths*. It couldn't be his Haultrey, could it? Harold Haultrey as a solicitor was a laughable thought.

After dinner and a drink in the bar he went early to his room. Leave the young ones alone for a bit. He looked for a telephone directory and finally found one inside the wardrobe behind a spare blanket.

Jenkins, Haultrey, Hall were there and so was Haultrey, A. P. at an address in the town. Under this appeared: Haultrey, H., Mingle Valley Farm, Harcombe. That was him all right. That was Harold Haultrey. The solicitor with the initials A. P. would be his son. Why don't I phone him, thought Walter, lying in bed, conjuring up pictures in the dark, why don't I phone him in the morning and ask him over for a drink? Meeting him will take him off my mind. I bet if I had counselling I'd be told to meet him. Confront him, that would be the word.

An answering machine was what he got. Of course, the voice wasn't recognisable. Not after all these years. It didn't say it was Harold Haultrey but that this was the Haultrey Jersey Herd and to leave a message after the tone. Walter tried again at midday and again at two. After that they all went to Lyme Regis and he had to leave it.

When he got back he expected the message light on his phone to be on but there was nothing. And nothing next day. Haultrey had chosen not to get in touch. Briefly, Walter thought of phoning the son, the solicitor, but dismissed the idea. If Haultrey didn't want to see him he certainly didn't want to see Haultrey. That evening Walter sat with the children while Ian and Barbara went out to dinner and on the following afternoon, because it was raining, they all went to the cinema and saw *The Hunchback of Notre-Dame*.

On these holidays Walter always behaved as tactfully as he could, doing his share of looking after the children and sometimes more than his share, but also taking care not to be intrusive. So it was his policy, on at least one occasion, to take himself off for the day. This time he had arranged to visit a cousin who lived in Honiton. Hearing he was coming to Sidmouth, the cousin had invited him to lunch.

On the way back, approaching Sidbury, he noticed a sign to Harcombe. Why did that ring a bell? Of course. Harcombe was where Haultrey lived, he and his Jersey herd. Walter had taken the Harcombe turning almost before he knew what he was doing. In the circumstances it would be ridiculous to be so near and not go to Mingle Valley Farm, an omission he might regret for the rest of his life.

Beautiful countryside, green woods, dark-red earth where the harvested fields had already been ploughed, a sparkling river that splashed over stones. He saw the cattle before he saw the house, cream-coloured elegant beasts, bony and mournful-eyed, hock-deep in the lush grass. Hundreds of them – well, scores. If he said 'scores' to Emma and Andrew they wouldn't know what he was talking about. On a gatepost, lettered in black on a white board, he read: *Mingle Valley*

*Farm, the Haultrey Jersey Herd* and under that, *Trespassers Will Be Prosecuted.*

He left the car. Beyond the gate was only a path, winding away between flowery grass verges and tall trees. A pheasant made him jump, uttering its harsh, rattling cry and taking off on clumsy wings. The path took a turn to the left, the woodland ended abruptly and there ahead of him stretched lawns and beyond them, the house. It was a sprawling half-timbered place, very picturesque, with diamond-paned windows. On the lawn rabbits cropped the grass.

He had counted fifteen rabbits when a man came out from behind the house. Even from this distance Walter could tell he was an old man. He could see, too, that this old man was carrying a gun. Six decades fell away and instead of a green Devon lawn, Walter saw a sluggish river on the outskirts of London, willow trees, a kingfisher. He did as he had done then and clapped his hands.

The rabbits scattered. Walter heard the sharp crack of the shotgun, expected to see a rabbit fall but fell himself instead. Rolled over as pain stabbed his leg. It was his left leg this time but the pain was much the same as it had been when he was seven. He sat up, groaning, blood all over his trousers. A man was standing over him with a mobile phone in one hand and the gun bent over in the middle – broken, did they call it? – in the other. Walter would have known that resentful glare anywhere, even after sixty-five years.

In the hospital they took the shot out and for good measure – 'might as well while you're in here' – extracted the pellet from his right leg. With luck, the doctor said, he'd be as good as new.

'Remember we're none of us getting any younger.'

'Really?' said Walter. 'I thought I was.'

Haultrey didn't come to see him in hospital. He told Barbara her father was lucky not to have been prosecuted for trespass.

# The Professional

The girls had the best of it. Dressed in models from the Designer Room, they disposed themselves in one of the windows that fronted on to the High Street, one in a hammock from *House and Garden*, another in an armchair from *Beautiful Interiors*, holding best-sellers from the book department and pretending to read them. Small crowds gathered and stared at them, as if they were caged exotic animals.

The boys had seats inside, between Men's Leisurewear and Perfumery, facing the escalators. Anyone coming down the escalators was obliged to look straight at them. They sat surrounded by the materials of their craft, ten pairs of brushes each, thirty different kinds of polishes and creams and sprays, innumerable soft cloths, all of different colours, all used just the once, then discarded. Customers had comfortable leather chairs to sit in and padded leather footrests for their feet. A big notice said: *Let our professionals clean your shoes to an unrivalled high standard. £2.50.*

It was a lot harder work than what the girls did. Nigel resented the girls, lounging about doing bugger all, getting to wear the sort of kit they'd never afford in their wildest dreams. But Ross pointed out to him that the boys would do better out of it in the long run. After all, it was a load of rubbish Karen and Fiona thinking this was the first step to a modelling career. As if it was Paris (or even London), as if they were on the catwalk instead of in a department store window in a city that had one of the highest rates of unemployment in the country.

Besides, he and Nigel were trained. They'd both had two weeks' intensive training. When he had been at his pitch at the foot of the escalator a week, Ross's parents came in to see how he was getting on. Ross hadn't much liked that, it was embarrassing, especially as his father thought he could get his shoes cleaned for free. But his mother understood.

'Professional,' she said, nudging his father, 'you see that. That's what it says, "our professionals". You always wanted him to get some real training and now he's got it. For a profession.'

The W. S. Marsh Partnership got a subsidy for taking them on. Sixty pounds a week per head, someone had told him. And a lot of praise and a framed certificate from the Chamber of Commerce for their 'distinguished contribution to alleviating youth unemployment'. The certificate hung up on the wall at the entrance to Men's Leisurewear, which Ross privately thought rather too close for comfort. Still, it was a job and a job for which he was trained. He was twenty and it was the first employment he'd had since he left school four years before.

At school, when he was young and didn't know any better, he was ambitious. He thought he could be an airline pilot or something in the media.

'Yeah, or a brain surgeon,' said Nigel.

But of course it turned out that any one of those was as unlikely as the others. His aims were lower now, but at least he could have aims. The job with the W. S. Marsh Partnership had made that possible. He'd set his sights on the footwear trade. Manager of a shoe shop. How to get there he didn't know because he didn't know how managers of shoe shops got started but still he thought he had set his foot on to the lowest rung of the ladder. While he cleaned shoes he imagined himself fitting on shoes, or better still, calling to an assistant to serve this customer or that. In these daydreams of his the assistant was always Karen, obliged to do his bidding, no longer favouring him with disdainful glances as he walked by her window on his way to lunch. Karen, though, not Fiona. Fiona sometimes lifted her head and smiled.

The customers – Nigel called them 'punters' – mostly treated him as if he didn't exist. Once they'd paid, that is, and said what they wanted done. But no, that wasn't quite right. Not as if he didn't exist, more as if he was a machine. They sat down, put their feet on the footrest and nodded at him. They kept their shoes on. Women always took their shoes off, passed him the shoes and left their slender and delicate stockinged feet dangling. They talked to him, mostly about shoes, but they talked. The women were nicer than the men.

'Yeah, well, you know what they're after, don't you?' said Nigel.

It was a good idea, but Ross didn't think it was true. If he had asked any of those pretty women who showed off their legs in front of him what they were doing that evening or did they fancy a movie, he'd have expected to get his face smacked. Or be reported. Be reported and probably sacked. The floor manager disliked them anyway. He was known to disapprove of anything that seemed designed to waylay or entrap customers. No assistants stood about in Perfumery spraying passing customers with scent. Mr Costello wouldn't allow it. He even discouraged assistants from asking customers if they might help them. He believed in the total freedom of everyone who entered W. S. Marsh's doors. Short of shoplifting, that is.

Every morning, when Ross and Nigel took up their position facing the escalators ten minutes before the store opened at nine, Mr Costello arrived to move them back against the wall, to try to reduce their allotted space and to examine both of them closely, checking that they were properly dressed, that their hair was short enough and their hands clean. Mr Costello himself was a model of elegance, six feet tall, slender, strongly resembling Linford Christie, if you could imagine Linford Christie dressed in a black suit, ice-white shirt and satin tie. When he spoke he usually extended one long – preternaturally long – well-manicured sepia forefinger in either Nigel's direction or Ross's and wagged it as if beating time to music.

'You do not speak to the customers until they speak to you. You do not say "hi", you do not say "cheers".' Here the unsmiling glance was turned on Nigel and the finger wagged. ' "Cheers" is no substitute for "thank you". You do not attract attention to yourselves. Above all, you do not catch customers' eyes or seem to be trying to attact their attention. Customers of the W. S. Marsh Partnership must be free to pay *untrammelled* visits to this store.'

Mr Costello had a degree in business studies and 'untrammelled' was one of his favourite words. Neither Ross nor Nigel knew what it meant. But they both understood that Mr Costello would prefer them not to be there. He would have liked an excuse to be rid of them. Once or twice he had been heard to say that no one paid an employer to take him on when he was twenty, he had been obliged to take an evening job to make ends meet at college. Any little thing would be an excuse, Ross sometimes thought, any stepping out of line in the presence of a customer.

But they had few customers. After those early days when he and Nigel had been a novelty, business ceased to boom. Having your shoes cleaned at W. S. Marsh was expensive. Out in the High Street you could get it done for a pound and guests in the hotels used the electric shoe polisher for nothing. Mostly it was the regulars who came to them, businessmen from the big office blocks, women who had nothing to do but go shopping and had time on their hands. This worried Ross, especially as in Mr Costello's opinion, sixty pounds a week or no sixty pounds, no commercial concern was going to keep them on in idleness.

'It's not as if you are an ornament to the place,' he said with an unpleasant smile.

And they were often idle. After the half-dozen who came first thing in the morning would come a lull until, one by one and infrequently, the women appeared. It was typical of the women to stand and look at them, to consider, maybe discuss the matter with a companion, smile at them and pass on into Perfumery. Ross sat on his stool, gazing up the escalator. If you did what Nigel did and stared at the customers at ground level, if you happened to eye the girls' legs, you got a reprimand. Mr Costello walked round the ground floor all day, passing the foot of the escalators once an hour, observing everything with his Black and Decker drill eyes. When there was nothing to do Ross watched the people going up the escalator on the right-hand side and coming down the escalator on the left. And he watched them with his face fixed into a polite expression, careful to catch no eyes.

Karen and Fiona seldom came to get their shoes cleaned. After all, they only wore their own shoes to come in and go home in. But sometimes, on wet days, at lunchtime, one or other of them would present herself to Ross to have a pair of damp or muddy loafers polished. They didn't like the way Nigel looked at them and both preferred Ross.

Karen didn't open her mouth while he cleaned her suede boots. Her eyes roved round the store as if she was expecting to see someone she knew. Fiona talked, but still he couldn't believe his luck when, extending a slim foot and handing him a green leather brogue, she asked him if he'd like to go for a drink on the way home. He nodded, he couldn't speak, but looked deep into her large turquoise eyes. Then she went, her shoes sparkling, turning once to flash him a smile. Nigel pretended he hadn't heard but a flush turned his face a mottled red. Ross, his heart thudding, gazed away to where he always gazed, the ascending and descending escalators.

He was getting somewhere. He was trained, a professional. It could only lead onwards and to better things. Fiona, of the kingfisher eyes and the cobweb-fine feet, was going to have a drink with him. He gazed upwards, dreaming, seeing his future as the escalator that ceaselessly and endlessly climbed. Then he saw something else.

At the top of the escalator stood a woman. She was holding on to the rail and looking back over one shoulder towards the man who came up behind her. Ross recognised the man, he had once or twice cleaned his shoes and actually been talked to and smiled at and thanked. And once he had seen him outside, giving a passing glance at Fiona's and Karen's window. He was about forty but the woman was older, a thin, frail woman in a very short skirt that showed most of her long bony legs. She had bright hair, the colour of the yellow hammock Fiona reclined in. As she turned her head to look down the escalator, as she stepped on to it, Ross saw the man put out one hand and give her a hard push in the middle of her back.

Everything happened very fast. The woman fell with a loud protracted scream. She fell forward, just like someone diving into deep water, but it wasn't water, it was moving metal, and halfway down as her head caught against one of the steps she rolled over in a perfect somersault. All the time she was screaming.

The man behind her was shouting as he ran down. People at the top of the escalator shrank back from it as the man went down alone. Ross and Nigel had sprung to their feet. The screaming had fetched assistants and customers running from Perfumery and Men's Leisurewear but it had stopped. It had split the air as an earthquake splits rock but now it had stopped and for a moment there was utter silence.

In that moment Ross saw her, lying spread at the foot of the escalator. A funny thought came to him, that he'd never seen anyone look so relaxed. Then he understood she looked relaxed because she was dead. He made a sound, a kind of whimper. He could no longer see her, she was surrounded by people, but he could see the man who had pushed her, he was so tall, he towered above everyone, even above Mr Costello.

Nigel said, 'Did you see her shoes? Five-inch heels, at least five-inch. She must have caught her heel.'

'She didn't catch her heel,' Ross said.

A doctor had appeared. There was always a doctor out shopping, which was the reason the National Health Service was in such a mess, Ross's mother said. The main doors burst open and an ambulance crew came running in. Mr Costello cleared a path among the onlookers to let them through and then he tried to get people back to work or shopping or whatever they'd been doing. But before he had got very far a voice came over the public address system telling customers the south escalators would be out of service for the day and Perfumery and Men's Leisurewear closed.

'What d'you mean, she didn't catch her heel?' said Nigel.

Ross ought to have said then. This was his first chance to tell. He nearly did. He nearly told Nigel what he'd seen. But then he got separated from Nigel by the ambulance men carrying the woman out

467

on a stretcher, pushing Nigel to one side and him to the other, the tall man walking behind them, his face white, his head bowed.

Mr Costello came up to them. 'I suppose you thought you could skive off for the rest of the day,' he said. 'Sorry to disappoint you. We're making you a new pitch upstairs in Ladies' Shoes.'

This was his second chance. Mr Costello stood there while they packed their materials into the cases. Nigel carried the notice board that said *Let our professionals clean your shoes to an unrivalled high standard. £2.50.* The escalators had stopped running, so they followed Mr Costello to the lifts, and Ross pressed the button and they waited. Now was the time to tell Mr Costello what he had seen. He should tell Mr Costello and through Mr Costello the top management and through them, or maybe before they were brought into it, the police.

'I saw the man that was with her push her down the escalator.'

He didn't say it. The lift came and took them up to the second floor. The departmental manager, a woman, showed them their new pitch and they laid out their things. No one had their shoes cleaned but a girl Nigel knew who worked in the stockroom came over and told them that the woman who fell down the escalator was a Mrs Russell, the tall man with her was her husband and they had a big house up on The Mount, which was the best part where all the nobs lived. They were good customers of the Marsh Partnership, they were often in the store, Mrs Russell had an account there and a Marsh Partnership Customer Card. Ross went off for his lunch and when he returned Nigel went off for his, coming back to add more details that he had picked up in the cafeteria. Mr and Mrs Russell had only been married a year, they were devoted to each other.

'Mr Russell is devastated,' said Nigel. 'They're keeping him under sedation.'

When the departmental manager came along to see how they were getting on, Ross knew that this was his third chance and perhaps his last. She told them everything would be back to normal next day, they'd be back at the foot of the escalator between Perfumery and Men's Leisurewear, and now he should tell her what he had seen. But he didn't and he wouldn't. He knew that now because he saw very clearly what would happen if he told.

He would attract attention to himself. In fact, it was hard to think of any way to attract *more* attention to himself. He would have to describe what he had seen, identify Mr Russell – a customer, a good customer! – say he had seen Mr Russell put his hand in the middle of his wife's back and push her down the escalator. He alone had seen it. Not Nigel, not the other customers, but himself alone. They wouldn't believe him, he'd get the sack. He had had this job just six weeks and he would get the sack.

So he wouldn't tell. At least, he wouldn't tell Mr Costello. There was only one person he really wanted to tell and that was Fiona, but when they met and had their drink and talked and had another drink and she said she'd see him again the next night, he didn't say anything about Mr Russell. He didn't want to spoil things, have her think he was a nut or maybe a liar. Once he was at home he thought about telling his mother. Not his father, his father would just get on to the police, but his mother who sometimes had glimmerings of understanding. But she had gone to bed and next morning he wasn't in the mood for talking about it.

Something strange had happened in the night. He was no longer quite sure of his facts. He had begun to doubt. Had he really seen that rich and powerful man, that tall middle-aged man, one of the few men who had ever talked to him while he had his shoes cleaned, had he really seen that man push his wife down the escalator? Was it reasonable? Was it *possible*? What motive could he have had? He was rich, he had only recently married, he was known for being devoted to his wife.

Ross tried to re-create the sight in his mind, to rewind the film, so to speak, and run it through once more. To stop it at that point and freeze the frame. With his eyes closed he attempted it. He could get Mrs Russell to the top of the escalator, he could turn her head round to look back at her approaching husband, he could turn her head once more towards the escalator, but then came a moment of darkness, of a blank screen, as had happened once or twice to their TV set when there was a power cut. His power cut lasted only ten seconds but when the electricity came on again it was to show Mrs Russell plunging forward and to transmit the terrible sound of her scream. The bit where Mr Russell had put his hand on her back and pushed her had vanished.

They were back that morning at the foot of the escalator. Things were normal, as if it had never happened. Ross could hardly believe his ears when Mr Costello came by and said he wanted to congratulate them, him and Nigel, for keeping their heads the day before, behaving politely, not attracting unnecessary attention to themselves. Nigel blushed at that but Ross smiled with pleasure and thanked Mr Costello.

Business picked up wonderfully from that day onwards. One memorable Wednesday afternoon there was actually a queue of customers waiting to have their shoes cleaned. The accident had been in all the papers and someone had got a photograph. Just as there is always a doctor on hand, so is there always someone with a camera. People wanted to have their shoes cleaned by the two professionals who had seen Mrs Russell fall down the stairs, who had been there when it was all happening.

Fall down the stairs, not get pushed down. The more Ross heard the term 'fall down' the more 'pushed down' faded from his consciousness. He hadn't seen anything, of course he hadn't, it had been a dream, a fantasy, a craving for excitement. He was very polite to the customers, he called them sir and madam with every breath, but he never talked about the accident beyond saying how unfortunate it was and what a tragedy. When they asked him directly he always said, 'I'm afraid I wasn't looking, madam, I was attending to a customer.'

Mr Costello overheard approvingly. Three months later, when there was a vacancy in Men's Shoes, he offered Ross the job. By that time Ross and Fiona were going steady, she had given up all ideas of modelling for hairdresser training and they had moved together into a studio flatlet. Karen had disappeared. Fiona had never known her well, she was a deep one, never talked about her personal life, and now she was gone and the window where they had both sat and pretended to read best-sellers from the book department had been given over to Armani for Men.

While in Men's Shoes, Ross managed to get into a day release scheme and took a business studies course at the metropolitan college. His mother was disappointed because he wasn't a professional any more but everyone else saw all this as a great step forward. And so it was, for two weeks before he and Fiona got engaged he was taken on as assistant manager at a shop in the precinct called The Great Boot Sale at twice the salary he was getting from the Marsh Partnership.

In all that time he had heard very little of Mr Russell beyond that he had let the house on The Mount and moved away. It was his mother who told Ross he was back and having his house done up, before moving into it with his new wife. 'It's a funny thing,' she said, 'but I've noticed it time and time again. A man who's been married to a woman a lot older than him will always marry a woman a lot younger than him the second time round. Now why is that?'

No one knew. Ross thought very little of it. He had long ago convinced himself that the whole escalator incident had been in his imagination, a kind of daydream, probably the result of the kind of videos he had been watching. And when he encountered Mr Russell in the High Street he wasn't surprised the man didn't recognise him. After all, it was a year ago.

But to see Karen walk past with her nose in the air did surprise him. She tucked her hand into Mr Russell's arm – the hand with the diamond ring on it and the wedding ring – and turned him round to look where she was looking, into the jeweller's window. Ross looked at their reflections in the glass and shivered.

# The Beach Butler

The woman was thin and stringy, burnt dark brown, in a white bikini that was too brief. Her hair, which had stopped looking like hair long ago, was a pale dry fluff. She came out of the sea, out of the latest crashing breaker, waving her arms and crying, screaming of some kind of loss. Alison, in her solitary recliner, under her striped hood (hired at $6 a morning or $10 a whole day) watched her emerge, watched people crowd about her, heard complaints made in angry voices, but not what was said.

As always, the sky was a cloudless blue, the sea a deeper colour. The Pacific but not peaceable. It only looked calm. Not far from the shore a great swell would bulge out of the sea, rise to a crest and crash on whoever happened to be there at the time, in a cascade of overwhelming, stunning, irresistible water, so that you fell over before you knew what was happening. Just such a wave had crashed on the woman in the white bikini. When she had struggled to her feet she had found herself somehow damaged or bereft.

Alone, knowing nobody, Alison could see no one to ask. She put her head back on the pillow, adjusted her sunglasses, returned to her book. She had read no more than a paragraph when she heard his gentle voice asking her if there was anything she required. Could he get her anything?

When first she heard his – well, what? His title? – when first she heard he was called the beach butler it had made her laugh, she could hardly believe it. She thought of telling people at home and watching their faces. The beach butler. It conjured up a picture of an elderly man with a paunch wearing a white dinner jacket with striped trousers and pointed patent shoes like Hercule Poirot. Agustin wasn't like that. He was young, handsome, he was wary and polite, and he wore shorts and the white trainers. His T-shirts were always snow-white and immaculate, he must get through several a day. She wondered who washed them. A mother? A wife?

He stood there, smiling, holding the pad on which he wrote down orders. She couldn't really afford to order anything, she hadn't known the package didn't include drinks and midday meals and extras like this recliner and hood. On the other hand, she could hardly keep pretending she never wanted a drink. 'A Diet Coke then,' she said.

'Something to eat, ma'am?'

It must be close on lunchtime. 'Maybe some crisps.' She corrected herself. 'I mean, chips.'

Agustin wrote something on his pad. He spoke fairly good English but only, she suspected, when food was the subject. Still, she would try. 'What was wrong with the lady?'

'The lady?'

'The one who was screaming.'

'Ah. She lose her . . .' He resorted to miming, holding up his hands, making a ring with his fingers round his wrist. 'The ocean take her – these things.'

'Bracelet, do you mean? Rings?'

'All those. The ocean take. Bracelet, rings, these . . .' He put his hands to the lobes of his ears.

Alison shook her head, smiling. She had seen someone go into the sea wearing sunglasses and come out, having lost them to the tide. But jewellery . . .!

'One Diet Coke, one chips,' he said. 'Suite number, please?'

'Six-0-seven – I mean, six-zero-seven.'

She signed the chit. He passed on to the couple sitting in chairs under a striped umbrella. It was all couples here, couples or families. When they decided to come, she and Liz, they hadn't expected that. They'd expected young unattached people. Then Liz had got appendicitis and had to cancel and Alison had come alone, she'd paid, she couldn't afford not to come, and she'd even been excited at the prospect. Mostly Americans, the travel agent had said and she had imagined Tom Cruise lookalikes. American men were all tall and in the movies they were all handsome. On the long flight over she had speculated about meeting them. Well, about meeting one.

But there were no men. Or, rather, there were plenty of men of all ages, and they were tall enough and good-looking enough, but they were all married or with partners or girlfiends and most of them were fathers of families. Alison had never seen so many children all at once. The evenings were quiet, the place gradually becoming deserted, as all these parents disappeared into their suites – there were no rooms here, only suites – to be with their sleeping children. By ten the band stopped playing, for the children must be allowed to sleep, the restaurant staff brought the tables indoors, the bar closed.

She had walked down to the beach that first evening, expecting lights, people strolling, even a barbecue. It had been dark and silent, no one about but the beach butler, cleaning from the sand the day's litter, the drinks cans, the crisp bags and the cigarette butts.

He brought her Diet Coke and her crisps. He smiled at her, his teeth as white as his T-shirt. She had a sudden urge to engage him in conversation, to get him to sit in a chair beside her and talk to her, so as not to be alone. She thought of asking him if he had had his lunch, if he'd have a drink with her, but by the time the words were formulated he had passed on. He had gone up to the group where sat the woman who had screamed.

Alison had been taught by her mother and father and her swimming teacher at school that you must never go into sea or pool until two hours have elapsed after eating. But last week she had read in a magazine that this theory is now old hat, you may go swimming as soon as you like after eating. Besides, a packet of crisps was hardly a meal. She was very hot, it was the hottest time of the day.

Looking at herself in one of the many mirrors in her suite, she thought she looked as good in her black bikini as any woman there. Better than most. Certainly thinner, and she would get even thinner because she couldn't afford to eat much. It was just that so many on the beach were younger than she, even the ones with two or three children. Or they looked younger. When she thought like that panic rushed upon her, a seizure of panic that gripped her like physical pain. And the words which came with it were 'old' and 'poor'. She walked down to the water's edge. Showing herself off, hoping they were watching her. Then she walked quickly into the clear warm water.

The incoming wave broke at her feet. By the time the next one had swollen, reared up and collapsed in a roar of spray, she was out beyond its range. There were sharks but they didn't come within a thousand yards of the beach and she wasn't afraid. She swam, floated on the water, swam again. A man and a woman, both wearing sunglasses, swam out together, embraced, began a passionate kissing while they trod water. Alison looked away and up towards the hotel, anywhere but at them.

In the travel brochure the hotel had looked very different, more golden than red and the mountains behind it less stark. It hadn't looked like what it was, a brick-red building in a brick-red desert. The lawns around it weren't exactly artificial but they were composed of the kind of grass that never grew and so never had to be cut. Watering took

474

place at night. No one knew where the water came from because there were no rivers or reservoirs and it never rained. Brilliantly coloured flowers, red, pink, purple, orange hung from every balcony and the huge tubs were filled with hibiscus and bird of paradise. But outside the grounds the only thing that grew was cactus, some like swords and some like plates covered with prickles. And through the desert went the white road that came from the airport and must go on to somewhere else.

Alison let the swell carry her in, judged the pace of the waves, let one break ahead of her, then ran ahead through the shallows, just in time before the next one came. The couple who had been kissing had both lost their sunglasses. She saw them complaining and gesticulating to Agustin as if he were responsible for the strength of the sea.

The tide was going out. Four little boys and three girls began building a sandcastle where the sand was damp and firm. She didn't like them, they were a nuisance, the last thing she wanted was for them to talk to her or like her, but they made her think that if she didn't hurry up she would never have children. It would be too late, it was getting later every minute. She dried herself and took the used towel to drop it into the bin by the beach butler's pavilion. Agustin was handing out snorkelling equipment to the best-looking man on the beach and his beautiful girlfriend. Well, the best-looking man after Agustin.

He waved to her, said, 'Have a nice day, ma'am.'

The hours passed slowly. With Liz there it would have been very different, despite the lack of available men. When you have someone to talk to you can't think so much. Alison would have preferred not to keep thinking all the time but she couldn't help herself. She thought about being alone and about apparently being the only person in the hotel who was alone. She thought about what this holiday was costing, some of it already paid for, but not all.

When she had arrived they had asked for an imprint of her credit card and she had given it, she didn't know how to refuse. She imagined a picture of her pale-blue and grey credit card filling a computer screen and every drink she had and slice of pizza she ate and every towel she used and recliner she sat in and video she watched depositing a red spot on its pastel surface, until the whole card was filled up with scarlet. Until it burst or rang bells and the computer printed 'no, no, no' across the screen.

She lay down on the enormous bed and slept. The air-conditioning kept the temperature at the level of an average January day in England

and she had to cover herself up with the thick quilt they called a comforter. It wasn't much comfort but was slippery and cold to the touch. Outside the sun blazed on to the balcony and flamed on the glass so that looking at the windows was impossible. Sleeping like this kept Alison from sleeping at night but there was nothing else to do. She woke in time to see the sunset. The sun seemed to sink into the sea or be swallowed up by it, like a red-hot iron plunged in water. She could almost hear it fizz. A little wind swayed the thin palm trees.

After dinner, pasta and salad and fruit salad and a glass of house wine, the cheapest things on the menu, after sitting by the pool with the coffee that was free – they endlessly refilled one's cup – she went down to the beach. She hardly knew why. Perhaps it was because at this time of the day the hotel became unbearable with everyone departing to their rooms, carrying exhausted children or hand in hand or arms round each other's waists, so surely off to make love it was indecent.

She made her way along the pale paths, under the palms, between the tubs of ghost-pale flowers, now drained of colour. Down the steps to the newly cleaned sand, the newly swept red rocks. Recliners and chairs were all stacked away, umbrellas furled, hoods folded up. It was warm and still, the air smelling of nothing, not even of salt. Down at the water's edge, in the pale moonlight, the beach butler was walking slowly along, pushing ahead of him something that looked from where she stood like a small vacuum cleaner.

She walked towards him. Not a vacuum cleaner, a metal detector. 'You're looking for the jewellery people lose,' she said.

He looked at her, smiled. 'We never find.' He put his hand into the pocket of his shorts. 'Find this only.'

Small change, most of it American, a handful of sandy nickels, dimes and quarters.

'Do you get to keep it?'

'This money? Of course. Who can say who has lost this money?'

'But jewellery, if you found that, would it be yours?'

He twitched off the detector. 'I finish now.' He seemed to consider, began to laugh.

From that laughter she suddenly understood so much, she was amazed at her own intuitive powers. His laughter, the tone of it, the incredulous note in it, told her his whole life; his poverty, the wonder of having this job, the value to him of five dollars in small change, his greed, his fear, his continuing amazement at the attitudes of these rich people. A lot to read into a laugh but she knew she had got it

476

right. And at the same time she was overcome by a need for him that included pity and empathy and desire. She forgot about having to be careful, forgot that credit card. 'Is there any drink in the pavilion?'

The laughter had stopped. His head a little on one side, he was smiling at her. 'There is wine, yes. There is rum.'

'I'd like to buy you a drink. Can we do that?'

He nodded. She had supposed the pavilion was closed and he would have to unlock a door and roll up a shutter, but it was still open. It was open for the families who never came after six o'clock. He took two glasses down from a shelf.

'I don't want wine,' she said. 'I want a real drink.'

He poured tequila into their glasses and soda into hers. His he drank down at one gulp and poured himself a refill. 'Suite number, please,' he said.

It gave her a small unpleasant shock to be asked. 'Six-zero-seven,' she said, not daring to read what it cost, and signed the chit. He took it from her, touching her fingers with his fingers. She asked him where he lived.

'In the village. It is five minutes.'

'You have a car?'

He started laughing again. He came out of the pavilion carrying the tequila bottle. When he had pulled down the shutters and locked them and locked the door, he took her hand and said, 'Come.' She noticed he had stopped calling her ma'am. The hand that held hers went round her waist and pulled her closer to him. The path led up among the red rocks, under pine trees that looked black by night. Underfoot was pale dry sand. She had thought he would take her to the village but instead he pulled her down on to the sand in the deep shadows.

His kisses were perfunctory. He threw up her long skirt and pulled down her tights. It was all over in a few minutes. She put up her arms to hold him, expecting a real kiss now and perhaps a flattering word or two. He sat up and lit a cigarette. Although it was two years since she had smoked she would have liked one too, but she was afraid to ask him; he was so poor, he probably rationed his cigarettes.

'I go home now,' he said and he stubbed out the cigarette into the sand he had cleaned of other people's butts.

'Do you walk?'

He surprised her. 'I take the bus. In poor countries are always many buses.' He had learned that. She had a feeling he had said it many times before.

Why did she have to ask? She was half afraid of him now but his attraction for her was returning. 'Shall I see you again?'

'Of course. On the beach. Diet Coke and chips, right?' Again he began laughing. His sense of humour was not of a kind she had come across before. He turned to her and gave her a quick kiss on the cheek. 'Tomorrow night, sure. Here. Same time, same place.'

Not a very satisfactory encounter, she thought as she went back to the hotel. But it had been sex, the first for a long time, and he was handsome and sweet and funny. She was sure he would never do anything to hurt her and that night she slept better than she had since her arrival.

All mornings were the same here, all bright sunshine and mounting heat and cloudless sky. First she went to the pool. He shouldn't think she was running after him. But she had put on her new white swimming costume, the one that was no longer too tight, and after a while, with a towel tied round her sarong-fashion, she went down to the beach.

For a long time she didn't see him. The American girl and the Caribbean man were serving the food and drink. Alison was so late getting there that all the recliners and hoods had gone. She was provided with a chair and an umbrella, inadequate protection against the sun. Then she saw him, leaning out of the pavilion to hand someone a towel. He waved to her and smiled. At once she was elated and, leaving her towel on the chair, she ran down the beach and plunged into the sea.

Because she wasn't being careful, because she had forgotten everything but him and the hope that he would come and sit with her and have a drink with her, she came out without thinking of the mountain of water that pursued her, without any awareness that it was behind her. The great wave broke, felled her and roared on, knocking out her breath, drenching her hair. She tried to get a purchase with her hands, to dig into the sand and pull herself up before the next breaker came. Her eyes and mouth and ears were full of salt water. She pushed her fingers into the wet slippery sand and encountered something she thought at first was a shell. Clutching it, whatever it was, she managed to crawl out of the sea while the wave broke behind her and came rippling in, a harmless trickle.

By now she knew that what she held was no shell. Without looking at it she thrust it into the top of her swimming costume, between her breasts. She dried herself, dried her eyes that stung with salt, felt a raging thirst from the brine she had swallowed. No one had come to her aid, no one had walked down to the water's edge to ask if she was all right. Not even the beach butler. But he was here now beside her, smiling, carrying her Diet Coke and packet of crisps as if she had ordered  them.

'Ocean smack you down? Too bad. I don't think you lose no jewels?'

She shook her head, nearly said, 'No, but I found some.' But now wasn't the time, not until she had had a good look. She drank her Diet Coke, took the crisps upstairs with her. In her bathroom, under the cold tap, she washed her find. The sight came back to her of Agustin encircling his wrist with his fingers when he told her of the white bikini woman's loss. This was surely her bracelet or some other rich woman's bracelet.

It was a good two inches wide, gold set with broad bands of diamonds. They flashed blindingly when the sun struck them. Alison examined its underside, found the assay mark, the proof the gold was 18 carat. The sea, the sand, the rocks, the salt, had damaged it not at all. It sparkled and gleamed as it must have done when first it lay on blue velvet in some Madison Avenue or Beverly Hills jeweller's shop.

She took a shower, washed her hair and blew it dry, put on a sundress. The bracelet lay on the coffee table in the living area of the suite, its diamonds blazing in the sun. She had better take it downstairs and hand it over to the management. The white bikini woman would be glad to have it back. No doubt, though, it was insured. Her husband would already have driven her to the city where the airport was (Ciudad something) and bought her another.

What was it worth? If those diamonds were real, an enormous sum. And surely no jeweller would set any but real diamonds in 18-carat gold? Alison was afraid to leave it in her suite. A safe was inside one of the cupboards. But suppose she put the bracelet into the safe and couldn't open it again? She put it into her white shoulder bag. The time was only just after three. She looked at the list of available videos, then, feeling reckless, at the room service menu. Having the bracelet – though of course she meant to hand it in – made her feel differently about that credit card. She picked up the phone, ordered a pina colada, a half bottle of wine, seafood salad, a double burger and french fries, and a video of *Shine*.

Eating so much didn't keep her from a big dinner four hours later. She went to the most expensive of the hotel's three restaurants, drank more wine, ate smoked salmon, lobster thermidor, raspberry Pavlova. She wrote her suite number on the bill and signed it without even glancing at the amount. Under the tablecloth she opened her bag and looked at the gold and diamond bracelet. Taking it to the management now would be very awkward. They might be aware that she hadn't been to the beach since not long after lunchtime, they might want to know what she had been doing with the bracelet in the meantime. She made a decision. She wouldn't take it to the management, she would take it to Agustin.

The moon was bigger and brighter this evening, waxing from a sliver to a crescent. Not quite sober, for she had had a lot to drink, she walked down the winding path under the palms to the beach. This time he wasn't plying his metal detector but sitting on a pile of folded beach chairs, smoking a cigarette and staring at the sea. It was the first time she had seen the sea so calm, so flat and shining, without waves, without even the customary swell.

Agustin would know what to do. There might be a reward for the finder, almost sure to be. She would share it with him, she wouldn't mind that, so long as she had enough to pay for those extras. He turned round, smiled, extended one hand. She expected to be kissed but he didn't kiss her, only patted the seat beside him.

She opened her bag, said, 'Look.'

His face seemed to close up, grow tight, grow instantly older. 'Where you find this?'

'In the sea.'

'You tell?'

'You mean, have I told anyone? No, I haven't. I wanted to show it to you and ask your advice.'

'It is worth a lot. A lot. Look, this is gold. This is diamond. Worth maybe fifty thousand, hundred thousand dollar.'

'Oh, no, Agustin!'

'Oh, yes, yes.'

He began to laugh. He crowed with laughter. Then he took her in his arms, covered her face and neck with kisses. Things were quite different from the night before. In the shadows, under the pines, where the rocks were smooth and the sand soft, his lovemaking was slow and sweet. He held her close and kissed her gently, murmuring to her in his own language.

The sea made a soft lapping sound. A faint strain of music, the last of the evening, reached them from somewhere he was telling her he loved her. I love you, I love. He spoke with the accents of California and she knew he had learned it from films. I love you.

'Listen,' he said. 'Tomorrow we take the bus. We go to the city . . .' Ciudad Something was what he said but she didn't catch the name. '. . . We sell this jewel, I know where, and we are rich. We go to Mexico City, maybe Miami, maybe Rio. You like Rio?'

'I don't know. I've never been there.'

'Nor me. But we go. Kiss me. I love you.'

She kissed him. She put her clothes on, picked up her handbag. He watched her, said, 'What are you doing?' and when she began to walk down the beach, called after her, 'Where are you going?'

She stood at the water's edge. The sea was swelling into waves now, it hadn't stayed calm for long, its gleaming ruffled surface black and silver. She opened her bag, took out the bracelet and threw it as far as she could into the sea.

His yell was a thwarted child's. He plunged into the water. She turned and began to walk away up the beach towards the steps. When she was under the palm trees she turned to look back and saw him splashing wildly, on all fours scrabbling in the sand, seeking what could never be found. As she entered the hotel the thought came to her that she had never told him her name and he had never asked.

# The Astronomical Scarf

It was a very large square, silk in the shade of blue called midnight which is darker than royal and lighter than navy, and the design on it was a map of the heavens. The Milky Way was there and Charles's Wain, Orion, Cassiopeia and the Seven Daughters of Atlas. A young woman who was James Mullen's secretary saw it in a shop window in Bond Street, draped across the seat of a (reproduction) Louis Quinze chair with a silver chain necklace lying on it and a black picture hat with a dark-blue ribbon covering one of its corners.

Cressida Chilton had been working for James Mullen for just three months when he sent her out to buy a birthday present for his wife. Not jewellery, he had said. Use your own judgement, I can see you've got good taste, but not jewellery. Cressida could see which way the wind was blowing there.

'Not jewellery' were the fateful words. Elaine Mullen was his second wife and had held that position for five years. Office gossip had it that he was seeing one of the management trainees in Foreign Securities. I wish it were me, thought Cressida, and she went into the shop and bought the scarf – appropriately enough, for an astronomical price – and then, because no shops gift-wrapped in those days, into a stationer's round the corner for a sheet of pink and silver paper and a twist of silver string.

Elaine knew the meaning of the astronomical scarf. She knew who had wrapped it up too and it wasn't James. She had expected a gold bracelet and she could see the writing on the wall as clearly as if James had turned graffitist and chalked up something to the effect of all good things coming to an end. As for the scarf, didn't he know she never wore blue? Hadn't he noticed that her eyes were hazel and her hair light-brown? That secretary, the one who was in love with him, had probably bought it out of spite. Elaine gave it to her blue-eyed sister who happened to come round and saw it lying on the dressing table. It was the very day she was served with her divorce papers under the new law, Matrimonial Causes Act, 1973.

Elaine's sister wore the scarf to a lecture at the Royal Society of Lepidopterists, of which she was a fellow. Cloakroom arrangements in the premises of learned societies are often somewhat slapdash and here, in a Georgian house in Bloomsbury Square, fellows, members and their guests were expected to hang up their coats themselves on a row of hooks in a dark corner of the hall. When all the hooks were in use coats had either to be placed over those already there or laid on the floor. Elaine's sister, arriving rather late, took off her coat, threaded the astronomical scarf through one sleeve, in at the shoulder and out at the cuff, and draped the coat cover someone's very old ocelot.

Sadie Williamson was a world authority on the genus *Argynnis*, its global distribution and habitats. She was also a thief. She stole something nearly every day. The coat she was wearing she had stolen from Harrods and the shoes on her feet from a friend's clothes cupboard after a party. She was proud too (to herself) that she had never given anyone a present she had had to pay for. Now, in the dim and deserted hall, on the walls of which a few eighteenth-century prints of British butterflies were just visible, Sadie searched among the garments for some trifle worth picking up.

An unpleasant smell arose from the clothes, compounded of dirty cloth, old sweat, mothballs, cleaning fluid and something in the nature of wet sheep. Sadie curled up her nose distastefully. She would have liked to wash her hands but someone had hung an *Out of Order* sign on the washroom door. Not much worth bothering about here, she was thinking, when she saw the hand-rolled and hemstitched corner of a blue scarf protruding from a coat sleeve. She gave it a tug. Rather nice, she was thinking, and quickly tucked it into her coat pocket because she could hear footsteps coming from the lecture room.

Next day she took it round to the cleaners. Most things she stole she had dry-cleaned, even if they were fresh off a hanger in a shop. You never knew who might have tried them on.

'The Zodiac,' said the woman behind the counter. 'Which sign are you?'

'I don't believe in it but I'm Cancer.'

'Oh, dear,' said the woman, 'I never think that sounds very nice, do you?'

Sadie put the scarf into a box that had contained a pair of tights she had stolen from Selfridges, wrapped it up in a piece of paper that had wrapped a present given to *her* and sent it to her godchild for Christmas. The parcel never got there. It was one of those lost in the robbery of a mail train travelling between Norwich and London.

Of the two young men who snatched the mailbags, it was the elder who helped himself to the scarf. He thought it was new, it looked new. He gave it to his girlfriend. She took one look and asked him who he thought she was, her own mother? What was she supposed to do with it, tie it round her head when she went to the races?

She meant to give it to her mother but accidentally left it in the taxi in which she was travelling from Kilburn to Acton. It was found, along with a pack of two hundred cigarettes, two cans of Diet Coke and a copy of *Playboy*, the lot in a rather worn Harrods carrier, by the taxi driver's next fare. She happened to be Cressida Chilton, who was still James Mullen's secretary, but who failed to recognise the scarf because it was enclosed in the paper wrapped round it by Sadie Williamson. Besides, she was still in a state of shock from what she had read in the paper that morning, the announcement of James's imminent marriage, his third.

'This was on the floor,' she said, handing the bag over with the taxi driver's tip.

'They go about in a dream,' he said. 'You wouldn't believe the stuff they leave behind. I had a full set of Masonic regalia left in my cab last week and the week before that it was a baby's pot, no kidding, and a pair of wellies. How am I supposed to know who the stuff belongs to? They'd leave themselves behind only they have to get out when they pay, thank God. I mean, what is it this time? Packets of fags and a dirty book . . .'

'I hope you find the owner,' said Cressida, and she rushed off through the swing door and up in the lift to be sure of getting there before James did, to be ready with her congratulations, all smiles.

'Find the owner, my arse,' said the taxi driver to himself.

He drew up at the red light next to another taxi whose driver he knew and, having already seen this copy, passed him *Playboy* through their open windows. The cigarettes he smoked himself. He gave the Diet Coke and the scarf to his wife. She said it was the most beautiful scarf she had ever seen and she wore it every time she went anywhere that required dressing up.

Eleven years later her daughter Maureen borrowed it. Repeatedly the taxi driver's wife asked for it back and Maureen meant to give it back, but she always forgot. Until one day when she was about to go to her mother's and the scarf came into her head, a vision inspired by a picture in the *Radio Times* of the night sky in September. Her flat was always untidy, a welter of clothes and magazines and tape cassettes and full ashtrays. But once she had started looking she really wanted to find the scarf. She looked everywhere, grubbed about in cupboards and drawers, threw stuff on the floor and fumbled through half-unpacked suitcases. The result was that she was very late in getting to her mother's but she had not found the astronomical scarf.

This was because it had been taken the previous week – borrowed, she too would have said – by a boyfriend who was in love with her but whose love was unrequited. Or not as fully requited as he wished. The scarf was not merely intended as a sentimental keepsake but to be taken to a clairvoyant in Shepherd's Bush who had promised him dramatic results if she could only hold in her hands 'something of the beloved's'. In the event, the spell or charm failed to work, possibly because the scarf belonged not to Maureen but to her mother. Or did it? It would have been hard to say who its owner was by this time.

The clairvoyant meant to return the scarf to Maureen's boyfriend at his next visit but that was not due for two weeks. In the meantime she wore it herself. She was only the second person into whose possession it had come to look on it with love and admiration. Elaine Mullen's sister had worn it because it was obviously of good quality and because it was *there*; Sadie Williamson had recognised it as expensive; Maureen had borrowed it because the night had turned cold and she had a sore throat. But only her mother and now the clairvoyant had truly appreciated it.

This woman's real name was not known until after she was dead. She called herself Thalia Essene. The scarf delighted her, not because of the quality of the silk, not its hand-rolled hem, nor its colour, but because of the constellations scattered across its midnight-blue. Such a map was to her what a chart of the Atlantic Ocean might have been to some early navigator, essential, enrapturing, mysterious, indispensable, life-saving. Its stars were the encyclopaedia of her trade, the impenetrable spaces between them the source of her predictions. She sat for many hours in meditative contemplation of the scarf, which she spread on her lap, stroking it gently and sometimes murmuring incantations. When she went out she wore it along with her layers of trailing garments, black cloak and pomander of asafoetida grass.

Roderick Thomas had never been among her clients. He was a neighbour, having just moved into one of the rooms below her flat in the Uxbridge Road. Years had passed since he had done any work or anyone had shown the slightest interest in him, wished for his company or paid attention to what he said, let alone cared about him. Thalia Essene was one of the few people who actually spoke to him and all she said when she saw him was 'Hi', or 'Rain again'.

One day, though, she made the mistake of saying a little more. The sun was shining out of a cloudless sky. 'The goddess loves us this morning.'

Roderick Thomas looked at her with his mouth open. 'You what?'

'I said, the goddess loves us today. She's shedding her glorious sunshine on to the face of the earth.'

Thalia smiled at him and walked on. She was on her way to the shops in King Street. Roderick Thomas started shambling after her. For some years he had been on the lookout for the Antichrist, who he knew would come in female form. He followed Thalia into Marks and Spencer's and the cassette shop where she was in the habit of buying music as background for her fortune-telling sessions. She was well aware of his presence and, growing increasingly angry, then nervous, went home in a taxi.

Next day he hammered on her door. She told him to go away.

'Say that about the sunshine again,' he said.

'It's not sunny today.'

'You could pretend. Say about the goddess.'

'You're mad,' said Thalia.

A client who had been having his palm read and had heard it all, gave her a funny look. She told him his lifeline was the longest she had ever seen and he would probably make it to a hundred. When she went downstairs Roderick Thomas was waiting for her in the hall. He looked at the scarf.

'Clothed in the sun,' he said, 'and upon her head a crown of twelve stars.'

Thalia said something so alien to her philosophy of life, so contrary to all her principles, that she could hardly believe she'd uttered it. 'If you don't leave me alone I'll call the police.'

He followed her just the same. She walked up to Shepherd's Bush Green. Her threats gave her a dark aura and he saw the stars encircling her. She fascinated him, though he was beginning to see her as a source of danger. In Newcastle, where he had been living until two years before, he had killed a woman he had mistakenly thought was the Antichrist because she told him to go to hell when he spoke to her. For a long time he expected to be sent to hell and although the fear had somewhat abated, it came back when he was confronted by manifestly evil women.

A man was standing on one of the benches on the green, preaching to the multitude. Well, to four or five people. Roderick Thomas had followed Thalia to the tube station but there he had to abandon pursuit for lack of money to buy a ticket. He wandered on to the green. The man on the bench stared straight at him and said, 'Thou shalt have no other gods but me!'

Roderick took that for a sign, you'd have to be daft not to get the message, but he asked his question just the same. 'What about the goddess?'

'For Solomon went after Ashtaroth,' said the man on the bench, 'and after Milcom the abomination of the Ammonites. Wherefore the Lord said unto Solomon, I will surely rend the kingdom from thee and will give it to thy servant.'

That was fair enough. Roderick went home and bided his time, listening to the voice of the preacher which had taken over from the usual voice he heard during his waking hours. It told him of a woman in purple sitting on a scarlet-coloured beast, full of names of blasphemy, having seven heads and ten horns. He watched from his window until he saw Thalia Essene come in, carrying a large recycled paper bag in a dull purple with *Celestial Seconds* printed on its side.

Thalia was feeling happy because she hadn't seen Roderick for several hours and believed she had shaken him off. She was going out that evening to see a play at the Lyric, Hammersmith, in the company of a friend who was a famous water diviner. To this end she had bought herself a new dress or, rather, a 'nearly new' dress, purple Indian cotton with mirror work and black embroidery. The blue starry scarf, which she had taken to calling the *astrological* scarf, went well with it. She draped it round her neck, lamenting the coldness of the night. A shawl would be inadequate and all this would have to be covered by her old black coat.

A quick glance at her engagement book showed her that Maureen's boyfriend was due for a consultation next morning. The scarf must be returned to him. She would wear it for the last time. As it happened, Thalia was wearing all these clothes for the last time, doing everything she did for the last time but, clairvoyant though she was, of her imminent fate she had no prevision.

She walked along, looking for a taxi. None came. She had plenty of time and decided to walk to Hammersmith. Roderick Thomas was behind her but she had forgotten about him and she didn't look round. She was thinking about the water diviner whom she hadn't seen for eighteen months but who was reputed to have split up from his girlfriend.

Roderick Thomas caught up with her in one of the darker spots of Hammersmith Grove. It wasn't dark to him but illuminated by the seven times seventy stars on the clothing of her neck and the sea of glass like unto crystal on the hem of her garment. He spoke not a word but took the two ends of the starry cloth in his hands and strangled her.

After they had found the body her killer was not hard to find. There was little point in charging Roderick Thomas with anything or bringing him up in court but they did. The astronomical scarf was Exhibit A at the trial. Roderick Thomas was found guilty of the murder of Noreen Blake, for such was Thalia's real name, and committed to a prison for the criminally insane.

The exhibits would normally have ended up in the Black Museum but a young police officer called Karen Duncan, whose job it was to collect together such memorabilia, thought it all so sad and distasteful – the poor devil should never have been allowed out into the community in the first place – that she put Thalia's carrier bag and theatre ticket in the shredder and took the scarf home with her. Although it had been dry-cleaned, the scarf had never been washed. Karen washed it in cold water gel for delicates and ironed it with a cool iron. Nobody would have guessed it had been used for such a macabre purpose, there wasn't a mark on it.

But an unforeseen problem arose. Karen couldn't bring herself to wear it. It wasn't the scarf's history that stopped her so much as her fear other people might recognise it. There had been some publicity for the Crown Court proceedings and much had been made of the midnight-blue scarf patterned with stars. Cressida Chilton had read about it and wondered why it reminded her of James Mullen's second wife, the one before the one before his present one. She didn't think she could face a fourth divorce and fifth marriage, she'd have to change her job. Sadie Williamson read about the scarf and for some reason there came into her head a picture of butterflies and a dark house in Bloomsbury.

After some inner argument, reassurance countered by denial and self-rebuke, Karen Duncan took the scarf round to the charity shop where they let her exchange it for a black velvet hat. Three weeks later it was bought by a woman who didn't recognise it, though the man who ran the charity shop did and had been in a dilemma about it ever since Karen brought it in. Its new owner wore it for a couple of years. At the end of that time she got married to an astronomer. The scarf shocked and enraged him. He explained to her what an inaccurate representation of the heavens it was, how it was quite impossible for these constellations to be adjacent to each other or even visible at the same time, and if he didn't forbid her to wear it that was because he wasn't that kind of man.

The astronomer's wife gave the scarf to the woman who did the cleaning three times a week. Mrs Vernon never wore the scarf, she didn't like scarves, could never keep them from slipping off, but it wouldn't have occurred to her to say no to something that was offered to her. When she died, three years later, her daughter came upon it among her effects.

Bridget Vernon was a silversmith and member of a celebrated craft society. One of her fellow members made quilts and was always on the lookout for likely fabrics to use in patchwork. The quiltmaker, Fenella Carbury, needed samples of blue, cream and ivory silks for a quilt which had been commissioned by a millionaire businessman, well known for his patronage of arts and crafts, and for his charitable donations. No charity was involved here. Fenella worked hard and she worked long hours. The quilt would be worth every penny of the £2000 she would be asking for it.

For the second time in its life the scarf was washed. The silk was as good as new, its dark blue unfaded, its stars as bright as they had been twenty years before. From it Fenella was able to cut forty hexagons which, interspersed with forty ivory damask diamond shapes and forty sky-blue silk lozenge shapes from a fabric shop cut-off, formed the central motif of the quilt. When finished it was large enough to cover a king-size bed.

James Mullen allowed it to hang on exhibition in Chelsea at the Chenil Gallery for precisely two weeks. Then he collected it and gave it to his new bride for a wedding present along with a diamond bracelet, a cottage in Derbyshire and a Queen Anne four-poster to put the quilt on.

Cressida Chilton had waited through four marriages and twenty-one years. Men, as Oscar Wilde said, marry because they are tired. Men, as Cressida Mullen said, always marry their secretaries in the end. It's dogged as does it and she had been dogged, she had persevered and she had her reward.

Before getting into bed on her wedding night, she contemplated the £2000 quilt and told James it was the loveliest thing she had ever seen.

'The middle bit reminds me of you when you first came to work for me,' said James. 'I should have had the sense to marry you then. I can't think why it reminds me, can you?'

Cressida smiled. 'I suppose I had stars in my eyes.'

# High Mysterious Union

1

Before Ben, I'd never lent the house to anyone. No one had ever asked. By the time Ben asked I had doubts about it being the kind of place to inflict on a friend, but I said yes because if I'd said no I couldn't have explained why. I said nothing about the odd and disquieting things, only that I hadn't been there myself for months.

I'm not talking about the house. The house was all right. Or it would have been if it hadn't been where it was. A small grey Gothic house with a turret would have been fine by a Scottish loch or in some provincial town, only this one, mine, was in a forest. To put it precisely, on the edge of the great forest that lies on the western borders of – well, I won't say where. Somewhere in England, a long drive from London. It was for its position that I bought it. This beautiful place, the village, the woods, the wetlands, had changed very little while everything else all around was changing. My house was about a mile outside the village, at the head of a large man-made lake. And the western tip of the forest enclosed house and lake in a curved sweep with two embracing arms, the shape of a horseshoe.

It was the village that was wrong; right for the people and wrong for the others, a place to be born in, to live and die in, not for strangers.

Ben had been there once to stay with me. Just for the weekend. His wife was to have come too but cried off at the last moment. Ben said later she took her chance to spend a night with the man she's with now. It was July and very hot. We went for a walk but the heat was too much for us and we were glad to reach the shade of the trees on the lake's eastern side. Then we saw the bathers. They must have gone into the water after we'd started our walk, for they were up near the house, had gone in from the little strip of gravel I called 'my beach'.

The sky was cloudless and the sun hot in the way it only is in the east of England, brilliant white, dazzling, the clean hard light falling on a greenness that is so bright because it's well watered. The lake water, absolutely calm, looked phosphorescent, as if a white fire burned on the flat surface. And out of that blinding fiery water we saw the bathers rise and extend their arms, stand up and with uplifted faces, slowly rotate their bodies to and away from the sun.

It hurt the eyes but we could see. They wanted us to see, or one of them did.

'They're children,' I said.

'She's not a child.'

She wasn't, but I knew that. We're all inhibited about nudity, especially when we come upon it by chance and in company, when we're unprepared. It's all right if we can see it when alone and ourselves unseen. Ben wasn't especially prudish but he was rather shy and he looked away.

The girl in the burning water, entirely naked, became more and more clearly visible to us, for we continued to walk towards her, though rather slowly now. We could have stopped and at once become voyeurs. Or turned back and provoked – I knew – laughter from her and her companions. And from God knows who else hidden, for all I could tell, among the trees.

They were undoubtedly children, her companions, a boy and a girl. The three of them stretched upwards and gazed at the dazzling blueness while the sun struck their wet bodies. That was another thing that troubled me, *that* sun, inflicting surely a fierce burning on white skin. For they were all white, white as milk, as white lilies, and the girl's uplifted breasts, raised by her extended arms, were like plump white buds, tipped with rosy pink.

What Ben thought of it I didn't quite know. He said nothing about it till much later. But his face flushed darkly, reddening as if with the sun, as those bodies should have reddened but somehow, I knew, would not, would stay, by the not always happy magic of this place, inviolable and unstained. He had taken his hands from his eyes and was feeling with his fingertips the hot red of his cheeks.

He didn't look at the bathers again. He kept his head averted, staring into the wood as if spotting there an array of interesting wildlife. They waded out of the water as we approached, the children running off to the shelter of the trees. But the girl stood for a moment on the little beach, no longer exposing herself to us but rather as if – there is only one word I can use, only one that gives the real sense of how she was – as if *ashamed*. Her stance was that of Aphrodite on her shell in the painting, one hand covering the pale fleece of hair between her thighs, the other, and the white arm glittering with water drops, across her breasts. But Aphrodite gazes innocently at the onlooker. This girl stood with hanging head, her long white-blonde hair dripping, and though there was nothing to detain her there, remained in her attitude of shame as might a slave exhibited in a marketplace.

Yet she was enjoying herself. She was acting a part and enjoying what she acted. You could tell. I thought even then, before I knew much, that she might equally have chosen to be the bold visitor to the nude beach or the flaunting stripper or the shopper surprised in the changing room, but she had chosen the slave. It was a game, yet it was part of her nature.

When we were some twenty yards from her, she lifted her head and behaved as if she had only just seen us. We were to think, for it can't have been sincere, that until that moment she had been unconscious of our approach, of our being there at all. She gave a little artificial shriek, then a laugh of shocked merriment, waving her arms in a mime of someone grasping at clothes, seizing invisible garments out of the air and wrapping them round her, as she ran into the long grass, the low bushes and at last into the tall, concealing trees.

'I don't know who that was,' I said to him as we went into the house. 'One of the village people perhaps.'

'Why not a visitor?' he said.

'No, I'm sure. One of the village people.'

I was sure. There were ways of telling, though I hardly ever went near the village. Not by that time. Not to the church or the pub or the shop. And I didn't take Ben there. The place was gradually becoming less and less attractive to me, Gothic House somewhere I thought I ought occasionally to go to but put off visiting. You could only reach it with ease by driving through the village and I avoided that village as much as I could. By the time he asked me if he could borrow it I had already decided to sell the house.

His wife had left him. Or made it plain to him she expected him to leave *her*, leave her, that is, the house they lived in. He'd bought a flat in London but before he ever lived in it he'd had a kind of breakdown from an accumulation of causes but mainly Margaret's departure. He wanted to get away somewhere, to get away from everyone and every-thing he knew, the people and places and things that reminded him. And he wanted to be somewhere he could work in peace.

Ben is a translator. He translates from French and Italian, fiction and non-fiction, and was about to embark on the biggest and most complex work he'd ever undertaken, a book called *The Golden Apple* by a French psychoanalyst that examined from a Jungian viewpoint the myths attendant on the Trojan War, Helen of Troy and Paris, Priam and Hecabe and the human mind. He took his word processor with him, his Collins–Robert French dictionary and his Liddell and Scott Greek dictionary, and Graves's *The Greek Myths*.

I gave him a key to Gothic House. 'There are only two in existence. Sandy has the other.'

'Who's Sandy?'

'A sort of odd-job man. Someone has to be able to get in in case of fire or, more likely, flood.'

Perhaps I said it unhappily, for he gave me an enquiring look, but I didn't enlighten him. What was there to say without saying it all?


There was nothing sinister about the village and its surroundings. It is important that you understand that. It was the most beautiful place and in spite of all the trees, the crowding forest that stretched to the horizon, it wasn't dark. The light even seemed to have a special quality there, the sky to be larger and the sun out for longer than elsewhere. I am sure there were more unclouded skies than to the north and south of us. Mostly, if you saw clouds, you saw them rolling away towards that bluish wooded horizon. Sunsets were pink, the colour of a bullfinch's breast.

I don't know how it happened that the place was so unspoilt. Trunk roads passed within ten miles on either side but the two roads into the village and the three out were narrow and winding. New building had taken place but not much and what there was by some lucky chance was tasteful and plain. The old school still stood, no industry had come there and no row of pylons marched across the fields of wheat and the fields grazing beasts. Nothing interrupted the view everyone in the village had of the green forest of oak and ash, and the black forest of fire and pine. The church had a round tower like a castle, but its surface was of cut flints.

That is not to say there were no strangenesses. I am sure there was much that was unique in the village and much of what happened there happened nowhere else in England. Well, I know it now, of course, but even then, when I first came and in those first years . . .

I told Ben some of it before he left. I thought I owed him that.

'I shan't want to socialise with a lot of middle-class people,' he said.

'You won't be able to. There aren't any.'

His lack of surprise was due, I think, to his ignorance of country life. I had told him that the usual mix of the working people whose families had been there for generations with commuters, doctors, solicitors, retired bank managers, university and schoolteachers and businessmen wasn't to be found. A parson had once been in the rectory but for a couple of years the church had been served by the vicar of a parish some five miles away who held a service once a week.

'I'd never thought of you as a snob,' said Ben.

'It isn't snobbery,' I said, 'it's fact.'

There were no county people, no 'squire', no master of foxhounds or titled lady. No houses existed to put them in. A farmer from Lynn had bought the rectory. The hall, a pretty Georgian manor house of which a print hung in my house, had burned down in the fifties.

'It belongs to the people,' I said. 'You'll see.'

'A sort of ideal communism,' he said, 'the kind we're told never works.'

'It works. For them.'

Did it? I wondered after I'd said it, what I'd meant. Did it really belong to the people? How could it? The people there were as poor and hard-pressed as anywhere else, there was the same unemployment, the same number living on benefit, the same lack of work for the agricultural labourer, driven from the land by mechanisation. Yet another strange thing was that the young people didn't leave. There was no exodus of school leavers and the newly married. They stayed and somehow there were enough houses to accommodate them. The old people, when they became infirm, were received, apparently with joy, into the homes of their children.

Ben went down there one afternoon in May and he phoned that night to tell me he'd arrived and all was well. That was all he said, then. Nothing about Sandy and the girl. For all I knew he had simply let himself into the house without seeing a soul.

'I can hear birds singing,' he said. 'It's dark and I can hear birds. How can that be?'

'Nightingales,' I said.

'I didn't know there were such things any more.'

And though he didn't say, I had the impression he put the phone down quickly so that he could go outside and listen to the nightingales.

The front door was opened to him before he had a chance to use his key. They had heard the car or seen him coming from a window, having plenty of opportunity to do that, for he had stopped for a while at the point where the road comes closest to the lake. He wanted to look at the view.

He'd left London much later than I thought he would, not till after six, and the sun was setting. The lake was glazed with pink and purple, reflecting the sky, and it was perfectly calm, its smooth and glassy surface broken only by the dark-green pallets of water lily pads. Beyond the further shore the forest grew black and mysterious as the light withdrew into that darkening sky. He'd been depressed, 'feeling low', as he put it, and the sight of the lake and the woodland, the calmness and the colours, if they hardly made him happy, comforted him and steadied him into a kind of acceptance of things. He must have stood there gazing, watching the light fade, for some minutes, perhaps ten, and they must have watched him and wondered how long it would be before he got back into the car.

The front door came open as he was feeling in his pocket for the key. A girl stood there, holding the door, not saying anything, not smiling, just holding the door and stepping back to let him come in. The absurd idea came to him that this was the *same* girl, the one he had seen bathing, and for a few minutes he was sure it was, it didn't seem absurd to him.

He even gave some sort of utterance to that thought. 'You,' he said. 'What are you . . .?'

'Just here to see everything's all right, sir.' She spoke deferentially but in a practical way, a sensible way. 'Making sure you're comfortable.'

'But haven't I – no. No, I'm sorry.' He saw his mistake in the light of the hallway. 'I thought we'd –' 'met' was not quite the word he wanted '– seen each other before.'

'Oh, no.' She looked at him gravely. 'I'd remember if I'd seen you before.'

She spoke with the broad up-and-down intonation they have in this part of the country, a woodland sing-song burr. He saw now in the lamplight that she was much younger than the woman he had seen bathing, though as tall. Her height had deceived him, that and her fairness and her pallor. He thought then that he had never seen anyone who was not ill look so delicate and so fragile.

'Like a drawing of a fairy,' he said to me, 'in a children's book. Does that give you an idea? Like a mythological creature from this book I'm translating, Oenone, the fountain-nymph, perhaps. Tall but so slight and frail that you wonder she could have a physical existence.'

She offered to carry his luggage upstairs for him. It seemed to him the most preposterous suggestion he had ever heard, that this fey-like being, a flower on a stalk, should be able to lift even his laptop. He fetched the cases himself and she watched him, smiling. Her smile was intimate, almost conspiratorial, as if they shared some past unforgettable experience. He was halfway up the stairs when the man spoke. It froze him and he turned round.

'What were you thinking of, Lavinia, to let Mr Powell carry his own bags?'

Hearing his own name spoken like that, so casually, as if it was daily on the speaker's lips, gave him a shock. Come to that, to hear it at all . . . How did the man know? Already he knew there would be no explanation. He would never be able to fetch out an explanation, now or at any time – not, that is, a true one – a real, factual, honest account of why anything was or how. Somehow he knew that.

'Alexander Clements, Mr Powell. Commonly known as Sandy.'

The girl followed him upstairs and showed him his bedroom. I'd told him to sleep where he liked, he had the choice of four rooms, but the girl showed him to the big one in the front with the view of the lake. That was his room, she said. Would he like her to unpack for him? No one had ever asked him that before. He had never stayed in the kind of hotel where they did ask. He shook his head, bemused. She drew the curtains and turned down the bedcovers.

'It's a nice big bed, sir. I put the clean sheets on for you myself.'

The smile returned and then came a look of a kind he had never seen before – well, he had but in films, in comedy Westerns and a movie version of a Feydeau farce. At any rate, he recognised it for what it was. She looked over her shoulder at him. Her expression was one of sweet naughty coyness, her head dipped to one side. Her eyebrows went up and her eyes slanted towards him and away. 'You'll be lonely in that big bed, won't you?'

He wanted to laugh. He said in a stifled voice, 'I'll manage.'

'I'm sure you'll *manage*, sir. It's just Sandy I'm thinking of, I wouldn't want to get on the wrong side of Sandy.'

He had no idea what she meant but he got out of that bedroom quickly.

Sandy was waiting for him downstairs and the table was laid for one, cold food on it and a bottle of wine. 'I hope everything's to your liking, Mr Powell?'

He said it was, thank you, but he hadn't expected it, he hadn't expected anyone to be there.

'Arrangements were made, sir. It's my job to see things are done properly and I hope they have been. Lavinia will be in to keep things shipshape for you and see to any necessary cookery. I'll be on hand for the more masculine tasks, if you take my meaning, your motor and the electricals et cetera. Never underrate the importance of organisation.'

'What organisation?' I said when he told me. 'I didn't arrange anything. I knew Sandy Clements still had a key and I've been meaning to ask for it back. Still, as for asking him to organise anything, to make "arrangements". . .'

'I thought you'd got them in, Sandy and the girl. I thought she came in to clean for you and you'd arranged she'd do the same for me. I didn't want her but I hardly liked to interfere with your arrangement.'

'No,' I said, 'no, I see that.'

They stood there until he was seated at the table and unfolding the white napkin Lavinia had presumably provided. I don't know where it came from, I haven't any white table linen. Sandy opened the bottle of wine, which Ben saw to his dismay was a supermarket Riesling. The horror was compounded by Sandy's pouring an inch of it into Ben's wineglass and watching while Ben tasted it.

He said he was almost paralysed by this time, though seeing what he thought then was 'the funny side'. After a while he didn't find anything particularly funny but he did that evening. They had cheered him up. He saw the girl as a sort of stage parlourmaid. She was even dressed somewhat like that, a white apron with its sash tied tightly round her tiny waist, a white bow on her pale-blonde hair. He thought they were trying to please him. These unsophisticated rustics were doing their best, relying on an experience of magazines and television, to entertain the visitor from London in the style to which he was accustomed.

Once he'd started eating they left. It was quite strange, the manner in which they left. Lavinia opened the door and let Sandy pass through ahead of her, looking back to give him another of those conspiratorial naughty looks. She delayed for longer than was necessary, her eyes meeting his until his turned away. A fleeting smile and then she was gone, the door and the front door closing behind her.

Only a few seconds passed before he heard the engine of Sandy's van. He got up to draw the curtains and saw the van moving off down the road towards the village, its red tail lights growing small and dimmer until they were altogether swallowed up in the dark. A bronze-coloured light that seemed to be slowly ascending showed through the treetops. It took him a little while before he realised it was the moon he was looking at, the coppery golden disc of the moon.

He ate some of the ham and cheese they had left him and managed to drink a glass of the wine. The deep silence that prevailed after Sandy and the girl had gone was now broken by birdsong, unearthly trills of sound he could hardly at first believe in, and he went outside to try to confirm that he had really heard birds singing in the dark.

The rich yet cold singing came from the nearest trees of the wood, was clear and unmistakable, but it seemed unreal to him, on a par, somehow, with the behaviour he had just witnessed, with the use of his name, with the fountain-nymph's coy glances and come-hither smiles. Yet when he came inside and phoned me it was the nightingales' song he talked about. He said nothing of the man and the girl, the food, the bed, the 'arrangements'.

'Why didn't you?' I asked him when I came down for a weekend in June. 'Why didn't you say?'

'I don't know. I consciously made up my mind I wouldn't. You see, I thought they were ridiculous but at the same time I thought they were your – well, "help", your cleaner, your handyman. I felt I couldn't thank you for making the arrangement with Lavinia without laughing about the way she dressed and the way Sandy talked. Surely you can see that?'

'But you never mentioned it. Not ever till now.'

'I know,' he said. 'You can understand why, can't you?'


2


When I first came to Gothic House Sandy was about twenty-five, so by the time Ben went there he would have been seven years older than that, a tall fair man with very regular features who still escaped being quite handsome. His eyes were too pale and the white skin of his face had reddened, as it does with some of the locals after thirty.

He came to me soon after I bought Gothic House and offered his services. I told him I couldn't afford a gardener or a handyman and I didn't need anyone to wash my car. He held his head a little on one side. It's an attitude that implies total understanding of the other person's mind, indulgence, even patience. 'I wouldn't want paying.'

'And I wouldn't consider employing you without paying you.'

He nodded. 'We'll see how things go then, shall we? We'll leave things as they are for now.'

'For now' must have meant a couple of weeks. The next time I went to Gothic House for the weekend the lawn in front of the house that slopes down to the wall above the lake shore had been mown. A strip of blocked guttering on the back that I had planned to see to had been cleared. If Sandy had presented himself while I was there I would have repeated my refusal of his services, and done so in definite terms, for I was angry. But he didn't present himself and at that time I had no idea where he lived.

On my next visit I found part of the garden weeded. Next time the windows had been cleaned. But when I came down and found a window catch mended, a repair that could only have been done after entry to the house, I went down into the village to try to find Sandy.

That was my first real exploration of the village, the first time I noticed how beautiful it was and how unspoilt. Its centre, the green, was a triangle of lawn on which the trees were the kind generally seen on parkland, cedars and unusual oaks and a swamp cypress. The houses and cottages either had rendered walls or were faced with flints, roofs of slate or thatch. It was high summer and the gardens, the tubs, the window boxes were full of flowers. Fuchsia hedges had leaves of a deep soft green spangled with sharp red blossoms. The whole place smelt of roses. It was the sort of village television production companies dream of finding when they film Jane Austen serials. The cars would have to be hidden, but otherwise it looked unchanged from an earlier century.

A woman in the shop identified Sandy for me and told me where he lived. She smiled and spoke about him with a kind of affectionate admiration. Sandy, yes, of course, Sandy was much in demand. But he wouldn't be at home that morning, he'd be up at Marion Kirkman's. This was a cottage facing the pretty green and easily found. I recognised

Sandy's van parked outside, opened the gate and went into the garden.

By this time my anger had cooled – the shop woman's obvious liking for and trust of Sandy had cooled it – and I asked myself if I could legitimately go up to someone's front door, demand to see her gardener and harangue him in front of her. In the event I didn't have to do that. I walked round to the back, hoping to find him alone there and I found him – with her.

They had their backs to me, a tall fair man and a tall fair woman, his arm round her shoulders, hers round his waist. They were looking at something, a flower on a climber or an alighted butterfly perhaps, and then they turned to face each other and kissed. A light, gentle, loving kiss such as lovers give each other after desire has been satisfied, after desire has been satisfied many times over months or even years, a kiss of acceptance and trust, and deep mutual knowledge.

It was not so much the kiss as their reaction to my presence that decided me. They turned round. They were not in the least taken aback and they were quite without guilt. For a few moments they left their arms where they were while smiling at me in innocent friendliness. And I could see at once what I'd stumbled upon, a long-standing loving relationship and one that, in spite of Marion Kirkman's evident seniority, would likely result in marriage.

Two women, then, in the space of twenty minutes, had given their accolade to Sandy. I asked him only how he had got into my house.

'Oh, I've keys to a good many houses round here,' he said.

'Sandy makes it his business to have keys,' Marion Kirkman said. 'For the security, isn't it, Sandy?'

'Like a neighbourhood watch, you might say.'

I couldn't quite see where security came into it, understanding as I always had that the fewer keys around the safer. But the two of them, so relaxed, so smiling, so firm in their acceptance of Sandy's perfect right of access to anyone's house, seemed pillars of society, earnest upholders of social order. I accepted Marion's invitation to a cup of coffee. We sat in a bright kitchen, all its cupboards refitted by Sandy, I was told, the previous year. It was then that I said I supposed it would be all right, of course he must come and do these jobs for me.

'You'll be alone in this village otherwise,' said Marion, laughing, and Sandy gave her another kiss, this time planted in the centre of her smooth pink cheek.

'But I'm going to insist on paying you.'

'I won't say no,' said Sandy. 'I'm not an arguing man.'

And after that he performed all these necessary tasks for me, regularly, unobtrusively, efficiently, winning my trust, until one day things (as he might have put it) changed. Or they would have changed, had Sandy had his way. Of course, they changed anyway, life can never be the same between two people after such a happening, but though Sandy kept my key he was no longer my handyman and I ceased paying him. I believed that I was in control.

So why did I say nothing of this to Ben before he went to Gothic House? Because I was sure, for reasons obvious to me, that the same sort of thing couldn't happen to him.

The therapist Ben had been seeing since his divorce advised him to keep a diary. He was to set down his thoughts and feelings rather than the actual events of each day, his emotions and his dreams. Now Ben had never done this, he had never 'got around to it', until he came to Gothic House. There, perhaps because – at first – he had few distractions and there wasn't much to do once he'd worked on his translation and been out for a walk, he began a daily noting down of what passed through his mind.

This was the diary he later allowed me to see part of, other entries he read aloud to me and he had it by him to refer to when he recounted the events of that summer. It had its sensational parts but to me much of it was almost painfully familiar. At first, though, he confined himself to descriptions of his state of mind, his all-pervading sadness, a feeling that his life was over, the beauties of the place, the lake, the woodland, the sunshine, the huge blue cirrus-patterned sky, somehow remote from him, belonging to other people.

He walked daily: around the lake, along a footpath high above damp meadows crossed by ditches full of watercress; down the lane to a hamlet where there was a green and a crossroads and a pub, though he never at that time ventured into the forest. Once he went to the village and back, but saw no one. Though it was warm and dry, nobody was about. He knew he was watched, he saw eyes looking at him from windows, but that was natural and to be expected. Villagers were always inquisitive about and even antagonistic to newcomers, that was a cliché that even he, as a townee, had grown up with. Not that he met with antagonism. The postman, collecting from the pillar box, hailed him and wished him good morning. Anne Whiteson, the shop woman, was friendly and pleasant when he went into the shop for teabags and a loaf. He supposed he couldn't have a newspaper delivered? He could.

Indeed he could. He had only to say what he wanted and 'someone' would bring it up every morning.

The 'someone' turned out to be Sandy, arriving at eight thirty with his *Independent*. Lavinia Fowler had already been twice but this was the first time he had seen Sandy since that first evening. Though unasked, Lavinia brought tea for both of them, so Ben was obliged to put up with Sandy's company in the kitchen while he drank it. How was he getting on with Lavinia? Was she giving satisfaction?

Ben thought this a strange, almost archaic, term. Or should another construction be put on it? Apparently it should, for Sandy followed up his enquiry by asking if Ben didn't think Lavinia a most attractive girl. The last thing Ben intended to do, he said, was enter into this sort of conversation with the handyman. He was rather short with Sandy after that, saying he had work to do and to excuse him.

But he found it hard to settle to *The Golden Apple*. He had come to a description of the contest between the three goddesses when Paris asks Aphrodite to remove her clothes and let fall her magic girdle, but he could hear sounds from the kitchen, once or twice a giggle, the soft murmur of voices. Too soft, he said, too languorous and cajoling, so that, in spite of himself, he got up and went to listen at the door.

He heard no more and shortly afterwards saw Sandy's van departing along the lake shore. But, as a result of what Sandy had said, he found himself looking at Lavinia with new eyes. Principally, she had ceased to be a joke to him and when she came in with his mid-morning coffee he was powerfully aware of her femininity, that fragile quality of hers, her vulnerability. She was so slender, so pale and her white thin skin looked – these were his words, the words he put in his diary – as if waiting to be bruised.

Her fair hair was as fine and soft as a baby's but longer than any baby ever had, a gauzy veil, almost waist-length, very clean and smelling faintly of some herb. Thyme, perhaps, or oregano. As she bent over his desk to put the cup down her hair just brushed his cheek and he felt that touch with a kind of inner shiver just as he felt the touch of her finger. For he put out his hand to take the coffee mug while she still held it. Instead of immediately relinquishing her hold she left her forefinger where it was for a moment, perhaps thirty seconds, so that it lay alongside his own and skin delicately touched skin.

Again he thought, before he abruptly pulled his hand away, of skin waiting to be bruised, of how it would be if he took that white wrist, thin as a child's, blue-veined, in a harsh grip and squeezed, his fingers more than meeting, overlapping and crushing until she cried out. He had never had such thoughts before, never before about anyone, and they made him uncomfortable. Departing from the room, she again gave him one of those over-the-shoulder glances, but this time wistful – disappointed?

Yet she didn't attract him, he insisted on that. He was very honest with me about all of it. She didn't attract him except in a way he didn't wish to be attracted. Oenone, shepherdess and daughter of the river, was how he saw her. Her fragility, her look of utter weakness, as of a girl to be blown over by the wind or felled by a single touch, inspired in him only what he insisted it would inspire in all men, a desire to ravish, to crush, to injure and to conquer.

'Ravish' was his word, not 'rape'. 'You really felt all that?'

'I thought about it afterwards. I don't say I felt that at the time. I thought about it and that's how I felt about her. It didn't make me happy, you know, I wasn't proud of myself. I'm trying to tell you the honest truth.'

'She was –' I hesitated '– offering herself to you?'

'She had been from the first. Every time we encountered each other she was telling me by her looks and her gestures that she was available, that I could have her. And, you know, I'd never come across anything quite like that before.'

Since the separation from his wife he had been celibate. And he could see no end to his celibacy; he thought it would go on for the rest of his life, for the step that must be taken to end it seemed too great for him to consider, let alone take. Now someone else was taking that step for him. He had only to respond, only to return that glance, let his finger lie a little longer against that finger, close his fingers around that wrist.

Any of these responses was also too great to make. Besides, he was afraid. He was afraid of himself, of those horrors that presented themselves to him as his need. His active imagination showed him how it would be with him when he saw her damaged and at his hands, the bruised whiteness, the abraded skin. But her image came into his consciousness many times throughout that day and visited him in the night like a succubus. He stood at the open window listening to the nightingales and felt her come into the room behind him, could have sworn one of those transparent fingers of hers softly brushed his neck. When he spun round no one was there, nothing was there but the faint herby smell of her, left behind from that morning.

That night was the first time he dreamt of the lake and the tower. The lake was as it was in his conscious hours, a sheet of water that took twenty minutes to walk round, but the tower on Gothic House was immensely large, as high as a church spire. It had absorbed the house, there was no house, only this tall and broad tower with crenellated top and *oeil de boeuf* windows, as might be part of a battlemented castle. He had seen the tower and then he was on the tower, as is the way in dreams, and Lavinia the river god's daughter was walking out of the lake, water streaming from her body and her uplifted arms. She came to the tower and embraced it, pressing her wet body against the stone. But the curious thing, he said, was that by then *he* had become the tower, the tower was himself, stone still but about to be metamorphosed, he felt, into flesh that could respond and act. He woke up before that happened and he was soaking wet as if a real woman had come out from the lake and embraced him.

'Sweat,' he said, 'and – well, you can have wet dreams even at my age.'

'Why not?' I said, though at that time, in those early days, I was still surprised by his openness.

'Henry James uses that imagery, the tower for the man and the lake for the woman. *The Turn of the Screw*, isn't it? I haven't read it for a hundred years but I suppose my unconscious remembered.'

Lavinia didn't come next day. It wasn't one of her days. On the Friday he prepared himself for her coming, nervous, excited, afraid of himself and her, recalling always the dream and the feel against his body of her wet slippery skin, her small soft breasts. He put in the diary that he remembered water trickling down her breasts and spilling from the nipples.

She was due at eight thirty. By twenty to nine when she still hadn't come – she was never late – he knew he must have offended her. His lack of response she saw as rejection. He reminded himself that the woman in the dream was not she but an imagined figment. The real woman knew nothing of his dreams, his fears, his terrible self-reproach.

She didn't come. No one did. He was relieved but at the same time sorry for the hurt he must have done her. Apart from that, he was well content, he preferred his solitude, the silence of the house. Having to make his own mid-morning coffee wasn't a chore but a welcome interruption of the work to which he went back, refreshed. He was translating a passage from Eustathius on Homer that the author cited as early evidence of sexual deviation. Laodameia missed her husband so much when he set sail for the Trojan War that she made a wax statue of him and laid it in the bed beside her.

It was an irony, Ben thought, that the first time he'd been involved since the end of his marriage in any amorous temptation happened to coincide with his translating this disturbingly sexy book. Or did the book disturb him only because of the Lavinia episode? He knew he hadn't been tempted by Lavinia because of the book. And when he went out for his walk that afternoon he understood that he was no longer tempted; the memory of her, even the dream, had no power to stir him. All that was past.

But it – and perhaps the book – had awakened his long-dormant sexuality. He had lingered longer than he needed over the passage where Laodameia's husband, killed in the war, comes back as a ghost and inhabits as her lover the wax image. It had left him a prey to undefined, aimless, undirected desire.

That evening he wrote his diary. It was full of sexual imagery. And when he slept he dreamt flamboyantly, the dreams full of colour, teeming with luscious images, none approximating to anything he'd known in life. Throughout the day he was restless, working automatically, distracted by sounds from outside: birdsong, a car passing along the road, the arrival of Sandy, and then by the noise of the lawnmower. He couldn't bring himself to ask what had happened to Lavinia. He didn't speak to Sandy at all, disregarding the man's waves and smiles and other meaningless signals.

It occurred to him when he was getting up on the Wednesday that Lavinia might come. She might have been ill on Monday or otherwise prevented from coming. Perhaps those signs that Sandy had made to him had indicated a wish to impart some sort of information about Lavinia. It was an unpleasant thought. He dreaded the sight of her.

He had already begun work on the author's analysis of a suggestion that the real Helen fled to Egypt while it was only a simulacrum that Paris took to Troy, when distantly he heard the back door open and close, footsteps cross the tiles. It was not Lavinia's tread, these were not Lavinia's movements. For a moment he feared Sandy's entry into his room, Sandy with an explanation, or worse, Sandy *asking* for an explanation. Somehow he felt that was possible.

Instead, a girl came in, a different girl. She didn't knock. She walked into his room without the least diffidence, confidently, as if it were her right. 'I'm Susannah, I've taken over from Lavinia. You won't mind, will you? We didn't think you'd mind. It's not as if it will make a scrap of difference.'


I know the girl he meant, this Susannah. Or I think I do, though perhaps it's one of her sisters that I know, that I have seen in the village outside her parents' house. Her father was one of those rarities not native to the place, but a newcomer when he married her mother, a man for some reason acceptable and even welcomed. There were a few of such people, perhaps four. As for the girl . . .

'She was so beautiful,' he said.

'There are a lot of good-looking people in the village,' I said. 'In fact, there's no one you could even call ordinarily plain. They're a handsome lot.'

He went on as if I hadn't spoken. Her beauty struck him forcibly from that first moment. She had golden looks, film star looks. If that had a vulgar sound, I was to remember that this particular appearance was only associated with Hollywood *because* it was the archetype, because no greater beauty could be found than the tall blonde with the full lips, straight nose and large blue eyes, the plump breasts and narrow hips and long legs. Susannah had all that and a smile of infinite sweetness.

'And she didn't throw herself at me,' he said. 'She cleaned the house and made me coffee and she wasn't – well, servile, the way Lavinia was. She smiled. She talked to me when she brought the coffee and before she left, and she talked sensibly and simply, just about how she'd cycled to the house and the fine weather and her dad giving her a Walkman for her birthday. It was nice. It was *sweet*. Perhaps one of the best things was that she didn't mention Sandy. And there was something *curative* about her coming. I didn't dream the dreams again and as for Lavinia – Lavinia vanished. From my thoughts, I mean. That weekend I felt something quite new to me, contentment. I worked. I was satisfied with my rendering of *The Golden Apple*. I was going to be all right. I didn't even mind Sandy turning up on Sunday and cleaning all the windows inside and out.'

'Young Susannah must be a marvel if she could do all that,' I said.

He didn't exactly shiver but he hunched his shoulders as if he was cold. In a low voice he began to read from his diary entries.


3


She seemed very young to him. The next time she came and the next he wanted to ask her how old she was but he had a natural aversion from asking that question of anyone. He looked at her breasts, he couldn't help himself, they were so beautiful, so perfect. The shape of a young woman's breasts was like nothing else on earth, he said, there was nothing they could be compared to and all comparison was vulgar pornography.

At first he told himself he looked at them so because he was curious about her age – was she sixteen or seventeen or more? – but that wasn't the reason, that was self-deception. She dressed in modest clothes, or at least in clothes that covered most of her, a high-necked T-shirt, a long skirt, but he could tell she wore nothing underneath, nothing at all. Her navel showed as a shallow declivity in the clinging cotton of the skirt and the material was lifted by her mount of Venus (his words, not mine). When he thought of these things as well as when he looked the blood pumped loudly in his head and his throat constricted. She wore sandals that were no more than thongs which left her small high-instepped feet virtually bare.

It never occurred to him at that time that he was the object of some definite strategy. His mind was never crossed even by the suspicion that Susannah might have taken Lavinia's place because he'd made it plain he didn't find Lavinia desirable. That it would be most exceptional for two young girls, coming to work for him in succession, both – immediately – to make attempts to fascinate him, indeed to seduce him.

There should have been no doubt in his mind, after all, for all he had said about Susannah not throwing herself at him, that in the ordinary usages of society a girl doesn't come to work for and be alone with a man stark naked under her skirt and top unless she is extending an invitation. But he didn't see it. He saw the movement of her breasts under that thin stuff but he saw only innocence. He saw the cotton stretched across her belly, close as a second skin, and put down her choice of dressing like this to juvenile naivety. The blame for it was his – and Lavinia's. Lavinia, he told himself, had awakened an amorousness in him that he would have been happy never to feel again. Instead, he had lost all peace and contentment; with her stupid coyness, her posturing and her clothes, she had robbed him of that. And now he was in thrall to this beautiful, simple and innocent girl.

She was subtle. Not for her the blatant raising of her arms above her head to reach a high shelf, still less the climbing on to a chair or up a pair of steps, the stuff of soft pornography. He asked her to sit and have her coffee with him and she demurred but finally agreed, and she sat so modestly, taking extravagant care to cover not only her knees but her legs almost to those exquisite ankles. She even tucked her skirt round her legs and tucked it tightly, thus revealing – he was sure in utter innocence – as much as she concealed. While she talked about her family, her mother who had been a Kirkman, her father who came from a hundred miles away, from Yorkshire, her big sister and her little sister, she must have seen the direction his eyes took, for she folded her arms across her breasts.

It dismayed him. He wasn't that sort of man. Before his wife he had had girlfriends but there had been nothing casual, no pick-ups, no one-night stands. He might almost have said he had never made love to a woman without being, or in a fair way to being, in love with her. But this feeling he had was lust. He was sure that it had nothing to do with 'being in love', though it was as strong and as powerful as love. And it was her beauty alone that was to blame – he said 'to blame' – he couldn't have said if he liked her, liking didn't come into it. Her appearance, her presence, the aura of her, stunned him but at the same time had him desperately staring. It was an amazement to him that others didn't see that desperation.

Not that there were others, with the exception, of course, of Sandy.

While Ben was working, Sandy, if he was outside, would sometimes appear at the window to smile and point up his thumbs. Ben would be working on some abstruse lining up of Jungian archetypes with Helen and Achilles, and be confronted by Sandy's grinning face. If the weather was fine enough for the window to be open Sandy put his head inside and enquired if everything was all right. 'Things going OK, are they?'

Ben moved upstairs. He took his word processor and his dictionary into a back bedroom with an inaccessible window. And all this time he thought these people were my servants, 'help' paid by me to wait on him. He couldn't dismiss them, he felt, or even protest. I was charging him no rent, he paid only for his electricity and the telephone. It would have seemed to him the deepest ingratitude and impertinence to criticise my choice. Yet if he had been free to do so he would not only have got rid of Sandy but of Susannah also. He could scarcely bear her in his presence. Yet he wondered what greyness and emptiness would replace her.

I must not give the impression all this went on for long. No more than three weeks, perhaps, before the change came and his world was overturned. He thought afterwards that the change was helped along by his taking his work upstairs. She might not have done what she did if he had been in the room on the ground floor with its view of the lake – and affording a view to other people driving by the lake and to window-cleaning, lawn-mowing, flowerbed-weeding Sandy.

She always came into his room to tell him when she was leaving. He had reached a point when the sound of her footsteps ascending the stairs heated his body and set his blood pounding. The screen of the word processor clouded over and his hands shook above the keyboard. That's how bad it was.

One of the things which terrified him was that she might touch him. Playfully, or in simple friendliness, she might lay her hand on his arm or even, briefly, take his hand. She never had, she wasn't a 'toucher'. But if she did he didn't know what he would do, he felt he couldn't be responsible for his own actions, he might do something outrageous or his body, without his volition, something shameful. The strange thing was that in all this it never seems to have occurred to him that she might want *him*, or at least be acquiescent. She came into the room. His desire blazed out of him but he was long beyond controlling it.

'I'll be off then, sir.'

How he hated that 'sir'! It must be stopped and stopped now, whatever I might require from my 'help'.

'Please don't call me that. Call me Ben.'

It came from him like a piteous cry. He might have been crying to her that he had a mortal illness or someone close to him was dead.

'Ben,' she said, 'Ben.' She said it as if it was new to her or distantly exotic instead of, as he put it, the name of half the pet dogs in the district. 'I like it.' And then she said, 'Are you all right?'

'It doesn't matter,' he said. 'Ignore me.'

'Why would I want to do that, Ben?'

The burr in her voice was suddenly more pronounced. She spoke in a radio rustic's accent. Perhaps she had experience of men in Ben's condition, probably it was a common effect of her presence, for she knew exactly what was wrong with him. What was *right* with him?

She said, 'Come here.'

He got up, mesmerised, not yet believing, a long way still from believing. But she took his hands and laid them on her breasts. It was her way to do that, to take his hands to those soft hidden parts of her body where she most liked to feel his touch. She put her mouth up to his mouth, the tip of her tongue on his tongue, she stood on tiptoe, lifting her pelvis against him. Then, with a nod, with a smile, she took him by the hand and led him into his bedroom.

Before Ben went to Gothic House it had been arranged that I should go down myself for a weekend in June. I'd decided to put the house on the market as soon as Ben left and there were matters to see to, such as what I was going to do about the furniture, which of it I wanted to keep and which to sell. As the time grew near I felt less and less like going. To have his company would be good – perhaps rather more than that – but I could have his company in London. It was the place I didn't care to be in. In the time I'd been away from it my aversion had grown. If that was possible, I felt even worse about it than when I'd last been there.

At this time, of course, I knew almost nothing of what Ben was doing. We'd spoken on the phone just once after the nightingale conversation and he had said only that the change of air was doing him good and the translation was going well. The girls weren't mentioned and neither was Sandy, so I knew nothing of Susannah beyond what I'd seen of her some two or three years before.

That was when I had my encounters with her parents. Peddar, they were called, and they had three young daughters, Susannah, Carol and another one whose name I couldn't remember. I couldn't even remember which was the eldest and which the youngest. Of course, I have plenty of cause to do so now. I'd been to the village quite a lot by that time and even taken a small part in village life, attended a social in the village hall and gone to Marion Kirkman's daughter's wedding.

The villagers were guarded at first, then gradually friendlier. Just what one would expect. I went to the wedding and to the party afterwards. In spite of all that has happened since, I still think it was the nicest wedding I've ever been to, the best party, the handsomest guests, the best food, the greatest joy. Everyone was tremendously nice to me. If I had the feeling that I was closely watched, rather as if the other people there were studying me for a social survey, I put that down to imagination. They were curious, that was all. They were probably shy of my middle-classness, for I had noticed by that time that there were no professional people in the village: agricultural labourers, mechanics, shopworkers and cleaners – who went to their jobs elsewhere – plumbers, electricians, builders, thatchers and pargeters, a hairdresser and, because even there modern life intruded, a computer technician, but no one who worked otherwise than with his or her hands.

I think, now, I was a fool. I should have kept myself to myself. I should have resisted the seductions of friendliness and warmth. Instead, because I'd accepted hospitality, I decided to give a party. It would be a Sunday morning drinks party, after church. I invited everyone who had invited me and a good many who hadn't but whom I had met at other people's gatherings. Sandy offered to serve the drinks and in the event did so admirably.

They came and the party happened. Everyone was charming, everyone seemed to know that if you go to a party you should endeavour to be entertaining, to talk, to listen, to appear carefree. What was lacking was middle-class sophistication and it was a welcome omission. The party resulted in an invitation, just one, from the Peddars, who delivered it as they were leaving, a written invitation in an envelope, evidently prepared beforehand with great care. Would I come to supper the following Friday? And I need not bother to drive, John Peddar would collect me and take me home.

It must have been about that time that I noticed another oddity – if good manners and friendliness can be called that – about the village and its people. I'd already, of course, observed my own resemblance to the general appearance of them, a sort of look we had in common. I was tall and fair with blue eyes and so were they. Not that they were all the same, not clone-like, I don't mean that, some were shorter, some less slender, eyes varied from midnight-blue through turquoise to palest sky and hair from flaxen to light-brown, but they had a certain look of all belonging to the same tribe. Danes used to look like that, I was once told, before the influx of immigrants and visitors; if you sat outside a café on Strøget you saw all these blue-eyed blondes pass by, all looking like members of a family. Thus it was in the village, as if their gene pool was small and I might have been one of them.

So might Ben, though I didn't think of it then. Why should I?

I wrote a note to the Peddars, saying I'd be pleased to come on Friday.


It sounds very cowardly, what I'm about to say. Well, it will have to sound that way. Although I'd much have preferred to postpone going to Gothic House till the Saturday, I'd told Ben I'd come on the Friday and I kept to that. But I drove down in the evening so as to pass through the village in the dark and since, in June, it didn't start getting dark till after nine thirty, I was late arriving.

I braced myself, even took a deep breath, as I reached the corner where the first house was, some half-mile from the rest, Mark and Kathy Gresham's house. There were lights on but no windows open, though it was a warm night. I drove on quickly. A dozen or so teenagers had assembled with their bikes by the bus shelter, they were the only people about. The light from the single lamp in the village street shone on their fair hair. They turned as one as I passed, recognising the car, but not one of them waved.

An estate agent's 'For Sale' board was up outside the Old Rectory. So the farmer from Lynn hadn't been able to stand it either. Or they hadn't been able to stand him. I slowed and, certain no one was about, stopped. No lights were on in the big, handsome Georgian house. It was in darkness and it was deserted. You can always tell from the outside if a house is empty – no wonder burglars are so successful.

No doubt he spent as little time there as possible. He hadn't been there long, perhaps two years, and I'd known him only by sight, a big, dark man with a pretty blonde wife, much younger than he. As I started the car again I wondered what they had done to him and why.

The sky was clear but moonless. In the dark, glassy lake whole constellations were reflected and a single bright planet shining like a torch held under the water. A little wind had got up and the woodland trees rustled their heavy weight of leaves. In my headlights Gothic House had its fairy-tale castle look, grey but bright, its lighted windows orange oblongs with arched tops, the crenellated crown of the turret the only part of it reflected in the water.

Ben and I had never kissed. But now he took me in his arms and kissed me with great affection. 'Louise, how wonderful that you're here. Welcome to your own house!'

I thought him a changed man.


It was only half an hour since Susannah had left him and gone home to her father's house. He told me that while we sat drinking whisky at the window with its view of the lake. The moon had risen, a bright full moon whose radiance was nearly equal to winter sunshine. Its silver-green light painted the tree trunks like lichen.

'Susannah Peddar?' I was finding an awkwardness in saying it, already remembering.

'Why the surprise?' he said. 'You employ her. And, come to that, Sandy.'

I told him I used to employ Sandy but no longer. As for Susannah

. . . She wasn't quite the last person from that village I'd have wanted in my house but nearly. I didn't say that. I said I was glad he'd found someone to look after him. He went on talking about her, already caught up in the lover's need to utter repeatedly the beloved's name, but I didn't know that then. I only wondered why he dwelt so obsessively on the niceness, the cleverness and the beauty of someone I still thought of as a village teenager.

That night he said nothing of what had happened between them but went off to bed in pensive mood, still astonished that Susannah wasn't employed by me. I, who had been relaxed, moving into a quiet, sleepy frame of mind, was now unpleasantly wide awake and I lay sleepless for a long time, thinking of the Peddars and of other things.


The evening with John and Iris Peddar was very much what I'd expected it would be, or the early part was. They lived in one of the newer houses, originally a council house, but they had done a great deal of work on it, building an annexe and turning the two downstairs rooms into one.

I'd calculated, in my middle-class way, my deeply English class-conscious way, that they would dress up for me. He would wear a suit, she a dress with fussy jewellery and the three little girls frilly frocks. So I decided to dress up for them and did that rare thing, wore a dress and stockings and shoes with heels. When John Peddar arrived to collect me I was surprised to see him in jeans and an open-necked check shirt but supposed that he intended to change when we got to his house.

In my opinion, everyone looks better in informal clothes. Something of the absurd is inseparable from gowns and jewels and men's dark suits. But I didn't expect them to feel this. I was astonished when Iris came out to greet me in jeans and striped T-shirt. The children too wore what they'd worn at school that day, or even what they'd changed into after the greater formality of school.

Even now, knowing what I know, I marvel at the psychology of it, at their knowledge of people and taste. They *knew* I wouldn't necessarily be easier with them dressed like that, but that I would unquestionably find one or all of them more attractive. They were a good-looking family, John especially, tall, thin, fair with a fine-featured face and enquiring eyes, eyebrows that went up often, as if commenting with secret laughter on the outrageous. She was pretty with commonplace

Barbie doll looks, but the three little girls were all beauties, two of them golden blondes who favoured their father, the third unlike either parent, the image of a Millais child with nut-brown hair and soulful eyes.

We drank sherry before the meal. John drank as much as Iris and I did and as much wine. I think I must have known by that time that in the village you drank as much as you liked before driving. The police who drove their little car round the streets every so often would never stop a villager, still less breath-test him. Two PCs lived here, after all, and one was Jennifer Fowler's brother.

We had avocado with prawns, chicken casserole and chocolate mousse. That, at any rate, was what I'd expected. The children went to bed, the eldest one last as was fair. Iris called me upstairs to see Her bedroom that she and John had newly decorated, and I went – it was still light, though dusk, the soft violet dusk that comes to woodland places – and there, while I admired the wallpaper, she tucked her arm into mine and stood close up against me.

It was friendliness, the warm outgoing attitude of one woman to another whom she finds congenial. So I thought as she squeezed my arm and pressed her body against mine. She had had a great deal to drink. Her inhibitions had gone down. I still thought that when she moved her arm to my shoulders and slowly turning me to her, brought her lips to within an inch of mine. I stepped aside, I managed a small laugh. I was anxious, terribly anxious in that moment, to avoid her doing anything she might bitterly regret next morning. We all know the feeling of waking to horrified memory, to the what-have-I-done self-enquiry that sets the blood pounding.

About an hour later he drove me home. She was all pleasantness and charm, begging me to come again, it was delightful that we'd got to know each other at last. This time I had no choice but to allow the kiss, it was no more than a cool pecking of the air around my cheek. John showed no signs of the amount he'd drunk. But neither, then, had she, apart from that bedroom overture I was sure now came from nothing more than a sudden impulse of finding she liked me.

In the car, sitting beside me, he told me I was a beautiful woman. It made me feel uncomfortable. All possible rejoinders were either coy or vulgar, so I said nothing. He drove me home and said he'd come in with me, he wouldn't allow me to go alone into a dark empty house. It was late, I said, I was tired. All the more reason for him to come in with me. Once inside I put on a lot of lights; I offered him a drink. He had seated himself comfortably as if at home.

'Won't Iris wonder where you are?'

He looked at me and those eyebrows rose. 'I don't think she will.'

It was clear what he meant. I was revolted. His intrigues must be so habitual that his wife accepted with resignation that if he was late home he was with a woman. It explained her overture to me, a gesture born of loneliness and rejection.

He began talking about her, how he would never do anything to hurt her or imperil their marriage. Nothing *could* imperil it, he insisted. Most women have heard that sort of thing from men at some time or other, it is standard philander-speak. Yet if he hadn't said it, if he'd been a little different, less knowing, less confident, and yes, less rustic, I might have felt his attraction, at least the attraction of his looks. I'd have done nothing because of her, but I might have felt like doing something. As it was, I was simply contemptuous. But I didn't want trouble, I didn't want a scene. Was I afraid of him? Perhaps a little. He was a tall, strong man who had had a lot to drink and I was alone with him.

In the end, when he'd had a second whisky, I stood up, said I was desperately tired, I was going to have to turn him out. I know now that physical violence was quite foreign to his nature but I didn't then and I hated it when he put his hand under my chin, lifted my face and kissed me. You could just – only just – have called it a friendly social kiss.

Just as Ben was later to have those dreams, so did I. Something in the air? Or, more subtly, the atmosphere of the place? The first of my dreams was that night. John Peddar was different in the dream, looking the same but more my kind of man. 'Civilised' is the word that comes to mind, yet it's not quite the right one. Gentler, more sensitive, less crude in his approach. I suppose that the I who was dreaming arranged all that, but whatever it was I didn't repulse him, I began to make love with him, I began to enjoy him in a luxuriating way, but the dawn chorus of birds awoke me with their singing.

He came back in the morning, the real man, not the dream image.

It was a dull morning of heavy cloud. I've said the sky was always clear and the sun always shining but of course it wasn't. All that is fantasy, myth and magic. The house was quite dark inside. Before the dream came I had slept badly. That was the beginning of sleeping badly at Gothic House, of bad nights and later total insomnia. I came downstairs in my dressing gown, thinking it must be Sandy at the door. He came in and – I don't know how to put this – took the door

515

out of my hands, took my hands from it and closed it himself, shot the bolt across it.

I was taken aback by this appropriation of actions that should be exclusively mine. I stared. He took me in his arms in a curious caressing gesture, a sweeping of light gentle hands down my arms, my body, my thighs. He drew me close to him murmuring 'darling' and 'darling' again and 'sweetheart', his voice thick and breathless. Before his mouth could touch mine I pushed him away with a great shove and he staggered back against the wall.

'Please go,' I said. I can't stand this. Please go.'

I expected trouble, excuses that I'd invited him, defences that he could sense my desire, accusations finally of frigidity. But there was nothing. For a moment he looked at me enquiringly. Then he nodded as if something suspected had been confirmed. He even smiled. My front door, that he had previously taken possession of, he opened, let himself out, and closed it quietly and very carefully behind him.

Ben told me about Susannah. He told me all those things I have already told you and more than that. We sat out in the garden, there was a stone table, a bench and chairs, on the lawn in front of the house under a mulberry tree, and we sat there in the heat of the day. Its fallen fruit lay about on the grass like spoonfuls of crimson jam.

The tree gave enough shade to make sitting there pleasant. You could no more look at the lake than you could at a mirror with the full sun shining on it. A few cars passed along the road, village people off to shop in the town supermarkets, and the drivers waved. At Ben, of course, they wouldn't wave at me. He told me how his early love-making with Susannah had become a full-blown love affair.

No inhibition held him back from telling me about it. He had to tell someone. I'd never known him so open, so revelatory.

'I'm glad it's making you happy,' I said.

What lies we tell for the sake of social accord!

'It won't last, of course, I know that. It's entirely physical.' (I'm always sceptical when people say that. What do they mean? Do they know what they mean?) 'She's years younger than I am.'

'Yes.' Oh, yes, she was. 'How old *is* she?'

'Eighteen, I suppose.'

'And you wouldn't –' I tried to put it tactfully '– exactly call her an educated person, would you?'

'What does that matter? I'm not going to marry her, I'm not going to settle down with her for life. It's not as if I were in love with her. I'm having with her – oh, something I've never had with anyone in my life before, something I've only read about: pure, uncomplicated, beautiful sex. Sex without questions, without pain, without consequences. It's as if we're mythical beings at the beginning of the world, we're Paris and Helen, mutually exulting in the sweetest and most innocent pleasure known to mankind.'

'My goodness,' I said.

'I suppose you think that very high-flown, but it's an accurate expression of my feelings.'

Why didn't I warn him then? Why didn't I tell him about Susannah's father and Sandy and Roddy Fowler and meetings in the village hall? Or my suspicions about the farmer's wife from Lynn? Quite simply because I thought *the difference of gender made the difference.* He was a man. I thought men would be exempt. But later that day, after I'd made a rough inventory of the furniture I'd keep and noted the few small repairs the house needed before it could be put up for sale, I found myself looking at him, assessing things about him.

I was very fond of him, had started to grow fond after he separated from his wife, but it was very much for his mind and his manner. His gentleness pleased me and his thoughtfulness, his sensitivity and modesty. Pointless to pretend that he was much to look at, though I liked his looks, the intelligence in his face and the perceptiveness, his expressions of understanding and of pondering. But he was somewhat below medium height and very thin with an unfit slack-muscled thinness. He looked older than his age – thirty-seven? Thirty-eight? – his face was lined, as thin fair faces soon become with time, and his hair was fast receding.

I knew what I saw in him but not what Susannah did. The older man, perhaps, a father figure, though she had a perfectly adequate father of her own, very little older than Ben. They marry early in the village. But who can account for love? Even for attraction?

We went out for our dinner that evening to a restaurant ten miles away. During the meal he asked me if he should be paying Sandy. Wasn't there something wrong about Sandy working for him without payment?

'If you don't pay him,' I said, 'maybe he'll get the message and go away. He's a pest and a nuisance.' I said nothing about Sandy's attempts to make love to me after the John Peddar incident and my outrage. I would have if I'd thought it would make a difference.

'But for him,' he said, 'I suppose I'd never have met Susannah.'

He would have but I didn't know it then.

'When are you seeing her again?' I meant this joke question seriously and that was how he took it.

'On Monday morning. It's a bit awkward her going on cleaning the house and paying her is very awkward. I shall have to try and get someone else. Of course, we meet in the evenings – well, she comes here. I can't exactly go to her father's house.'

I had nothing to say to that. But from what I knew of her father's house, an orgy in the front room in broad daylight wouldn't have been unacceptable. I had revised my sympathy for Iris when at a village dance she tried to introduce me, with unmistakable motive, to her younger unattached brother, Roddy. For some reason the Peddar family had done their best to find me a sexual partner and apparently anyone would do, if not either of them or a relation of theirs, some other villager. Sandy, I supposed, had been put up to it by them. After all, I knew him already and in their eyes perhaps that was the only necessary prerequisite.

While showing me something he'd done in the garden he put his arm round me. I told him not to do that. He looked sideways at me and asked why not.

'Because,' I said. 'Because I don't want you to. Isn't that enough?'

'Come on, it's not natural, a nice-looking woman like yourself, never with a man.'

'None of this is any business of yours.' How ridiculous one sounds when offended!

'Is it women that you fancy? You can say, you needn't be shy. I know about those things, I've been around.'

'You needn't be around here any more, that's for sure,' I said. 'I don't want you working for me any longer. Please go and don't come back.'

Ben wouldn't have been interested in any of that, so I didn't tell him. We went home to Gothic House and next day I said I thought of putting it on the market at the end of August.

'You'll have finished your translation by then, won't you?'

'Yes, I'm sure I will.' He looked rather dismayed. 'I said three months, didn't I? It's so beautiful here and the situation on the house, this village – won't you regret getting rid of it?'

'I come here so seldom,' I said, 'it's really not worth keeping it up.'

## 5

It was strange how infrequently those people went out in the evenings. They visited each other, I know that now, but they hardly ever left the village after six. I spent two weeks there once, when I was trying to teach myself to like the place, and not a single car passed along the road by the lake in the evenings. I might not have seen cars if they had passed but I would have seen the beams from their headlights sweep across my ceilings. They stayed at home. They preferred their isolation.

I believe I was their principal concern at that time. No doubt they had a meeting in the village hall, called especially for the discussion of *me*. I blundered into one of those meetings once, having mistaken it for a teenage cancer fund-raising night. Utter silence prevailed as I walked in, they had heard or sensed my coming. Mark Gresham came down the hall to me, explained my mistake and escorted me out with such care and exquisite politeness that the thinnest-skinned couldn't have taken offence.

Sometimes, in those days, the last of those days, the watchers in the windows waved to me. There was never any question of concealing from me that they *were* watching. They waved or they smiled and nodded. And then, suddenly, all smiles and waving ceased, all friendliness came to an end. When Ben came down for that weekend and we saw the bathers they were still amiably inclined towards me. Next time I came everything had changed and the antagonism was almost palpable.


Ben fell in love with her.

Perhaps he'd really been in love from the first but refused to allow himself to admit it and all that insistence on matters between them being 'entirely physical' was self-deception. Whatever it was, by the middle of July he was in love, 'deeply in, in up to his neck', as he told me, utterly, obsessively, committed to love.

Not that he told me *then*. That came much later. At the time, though I heard from him it was not to mention Susannah. He wrote to ask if I was sincere about selling Gothic House and if I was, would I sell it to him. His former wife had found a buyer for the home they had shared and under the terms of the divorce settlement half the proceeds were to be his. Gothic House might even so be beyond his means and if this was the case he would look for some cottage in the village. In a mysterious oblique sentence he wrote that he thought 'living elsewhere might not be acceptable to everyone concerned'.

Why live there? He was a Londoner. He had lived abroad but never other than in a big city. The answer was that in the short time he'd been there he'd become very attached to the place. He loved it. How could he return to London and its painful memories? As a translator he could live anywhere. The village was a place in which he thought he could he happy as he had never been before.

Perhaps I was slow but I attached no particular significance to any of this. The truth was that I felt it awkward. It was a principle of mine, never before needing to be acted on, that one does not sell a house, a car or any large valuable item or object, maybe anything at all, to a friend. The passing of money will break the friendship, or that was the theory.

I waited a few days before replying. The seriousness of this, the projected sale or refusal to sell, caused me to write rather than phone. If I had phoned I might have learned more. But at last I wrote to say that as I'd told him I wasn't intending to sell yet. Let us wait till the end of August. Didn't he really need more time before committing himself? If by then he still wanted to live in the village and still wanted Gothic House, then we could talk about it.

No answer came to my letter. I found out later that Ben, exasperated by my delaying tactics, had gone next day to an estate agent to enquire about cottages. He didn't much care what he lived in, what roof was over his head, so long as he could live there with Susannah.

When it was all over and we were talking, when he poured out his heart to me, he told me that love had come to him in a moment, with an absolute suddenness. From being a contented man with a beautiful young lover whose body he enjoyed more than perhaps he'd ever enjoyed any woman's, he became lost, at once terrified and exalted, obsessed, alone and desperate. Yet it came to him when she was out of his sight, when she was at home in her father's house.

They had made love in his bed at Gothic House, had eaten a meal and drunk wine and gone back to bed to make love again. And then quite late, but not as late as midnight, he had done what he was now in the habit of doing, had driven her home, discreetly dropping her at the end of the street. Useless, all this secrecy, as I could have told him. Everyone would have known. They would have known from the first kiss that passed between those two. But to him the love affair was a secret that, almost as soon as he recognised his feelings for what they truly were, he wanted everything out in the open, he wanted the world to know.

He walked about the house, putting dishes in the sink, drinking the last of the wine and suddenly he found himself longing for her. A pain caught him in the chest and shoulders. Like a heart attack, he said, or what he imagined a heart attack would be. He hugged himself in his arms. He sat down and said aloud, 'I'm in love and I know I've never been in love before.'

The pain flowed out of him and left him tired and spent. He was filled with what he called 'a glory'. He saw her in his mind's eye, naked and smiling, coming to him so sweetly, so tenderly, to put her arms round him and touch him with her lips. The wrench of it was so bad that he said he didn't know how he continued to sit there, how he resisted jumping in the car and rushing back to her, beating on her father's door to demand her release into his arms. And he did get up but only to pace the room, the house, speaking her name, Susannah, and uttering into that silent place, 'I love you, oh, I love you.'

Next day he told her. She seemed surprised. 'I know,' she said.

'You know?' He gazed at her, holding her hands. 'How clever you are, my love, my sweetheart, to know what I didn't know. Do you love *me*? Can you love me?'

She said with the utmost tranquillity, 'I've always loved you. From the first. Of course I love you.'

'Do you, darling Susannah?'

'Did you think I'd have done those things we've done if I didn't love you?'

He was chastened. He should have known. She was no Lavinia. Yet I suppose some caution, some vestige of prudence or perhaps just his age and the remembrance of his marriage, prevented his asking her there and then to marry him. For that was what he had wanted from the first moment of his realisation, to marry her. It was what you did, he said to me, when you were in love like that, irrevocably, profoundly, you didn't want any trial time, you wanted commitment for life. Besides, she was half his age, she was very young, it wasn't as if he was a fellow teenager and the two of them experimenting with passion. Honourably, he must marry her.

'But you didn't ask her?' I said.

'Not then. I intended to wait a week. She was so sweet that week, Louise, so loving, I can't tell you how giving she was, how passionate. Of course I wouldn't tell you, it's not something I'd speak of. I wrote some of it down in my diary. You can see the diary. Why should I care now?'

She had shown him, when they made love, things he wouldn't have suspected she knew. Things he had hardly known himself. She was adventurous and entirely uninhibited. He was even, once, quite shocked.

'Oh, I wouldn't do it,' she said serenely, 'if I didn't love you so much.'

She still came to clean the house. His suggestion that it was no longer suitable, that he must find someone else, was met with incredulity, with laughter. Of course she would come to clean the house and she had done, regularly, without fail. Only sometimes she came to him away from her work to kiss him or hold her arms round his neck and lay her cheek sweetly against his.

It was a Saturday when she made that remark about loving him so much and he expected her on the Monday morning. No, that is to put it too tamely. He hadn't seen her for thirty hours and he yearned for her. Waiting for the appointed hour, eight thirty, he paced the house, watching for her from window after window.

She didn't come.

After a half-hour of hell in which he speculated every possible disaster, a road accident, her father's wrath, when he at last decided he must phone the Peddars' house, Lavinia came.

She had no explanation to offer him beyond saying Susannah couldn't be there and had sent her as a substitute. Susannah had come round to her mother's very early and asked if she, Lavinia, would do the Gothic House duty that day. Only today? he had asked, and she said as far as she knew. She, at any rate, doubted if she would be coming again herself. But when she said this she gave him one of her coy looks over her thin white shoulder, somehow making him understand that future visits could happen, might be contingent on his response. He was disgusted and angry. He did his best to ignore her, put her money downstairs on the kitchen table and fled to his room upstairs. Susannah would come that evening, they had an arrangement for her to come at seven, and then all would be well, all would be explained.

Soon after Lavinia left the estate agent phoned. A cottage had just been put on to the market. It was in the heart of the village. Would he be interested? If so, the estate agent would meet him outside the cottage at three and show him round. The owner was a Mrs Fowler, an old lady growing infirm who intended to move in with her son and his wife.

Ben walked to the village. It was a lovely day. The sun was brighter for him than for others, the lake bluer and its waters more sparkling, the flowers in the gardens more scented and more brilliant and the air sweeter – because he was in love. Sometimes 'the glory' came back to him and when that happened he wanted to leap and sing, he wanted to prostrate himself on the ground and cry aloud to whomever or whatever had given him the joy of love, had given him Susannah. All this was in his diary. A phrase from the Bible kept coming back to him: And sorrow and sighing shall flee away. He said it to himself as he walked along – there shall be no more pain, and sorrow and sighing shall flee away. He didn't think the word in the text was 'pain' but he couldn't really remember.

Mrs Fowler's was a tiny cottage, two up and two down, with a thatched roof. The frowsty little bedroom, low-ceilinged, the floor piled with layers of rugs, the bed with layers of dingy whitish covers, fringed or lacy and now inhabited by sleeping cats, he saw as it would be when transformed, when occupied by himself and Susannah. A four-poster they would have, he thought, and he imagined her kneeling up naked on the quilt, drawing back the curtains to disclose herself to him, the two of them sinking embraced into that silky, shadowy, scented warmth . . .

He looked out of the window and faces looked back at him, one in each of the windows opposite. A curtain dropped, another pair of eyes appeared.

Mrs Fowler said comfortably, 'Everyone likes to know your business down here.'

She was a tiny upright woman, still handsome in extreme age, hawk-faced and no doubt hawk-eyed, those eyes a sparkling pale turquoise.

'My granddaughter does for you,' she said.

He thought for some reason she meant Lavinia, but she didn't.

'Susannah Peddar.'

There was the suspicion of a smile at the corners of her mouth when she said the name. She looked conspiratorial. In that moment he longed to tell her. An overpowering desire to tell her seized him, to come out with it. He wanted to say that this was why he needed a house in the village, a home to which he could bring his bride, a bower for Susannah, among her own people, a stone's throw from her mother. How splendid it was, how serendipitous, that the very house in the whole village that might seem almost home to Susannah was the one he could buy.

He managed to suppress that desire, but all ideas of purchasing Gothic House vanished. This was the house for him, the only one. He would have offered her double what she was asking, anything to possess it and present it to Susannah. Probably it was as well he had been cautioned only to make his offer through the estate agents.

'At least I was saved from making a total fool of myself,' he wrote in his diary.

The agent, he discovered, had his own home in the village. He was a villager born and bred. Mrs Fowler would very likely take an offer, he said. Anyway, there would be no harm in trying.

'I wouldn't want to lose it,' Ben said.

The estate agent smiled. 'No fear of that. Think about it and come back to me.'

Rather late in the day Ben reflected that he should have asked Susannah first. She should have been asked if she wanted to live in a house that had belonged to her grandmother. He would ask her that night. He would propose marriage to her and he had no doubt she would accept, since she had told him she loved him. Then he'd tell her about the cottage. She was, he told himself, a simple country girl. Of course she was a goddess, his Helen and Oenone and Aphrodite, an ideal woman, a queen, the perfect paramour, but she was a country girl also, only eighteen, and one who would have no latter-day urban preferences for cohabitation over marriage or any nonsense of that sort.

At seven thirty she still hadn't come. He was mad with worry and terror. He didn't want to phone her father's house, he'd never done so, and he'd got it into his head – without any evidence for so doing – that the Peddars disapproved of him. Perhaps she was ill. He had a moment's comfort from thinking that. (Thus do lovers console themselves, deriving peace of mind from the beloved's incapacity.) He had forgotten for the moment that she had gone out 'very early' to Lavinia's house, hardly the behaviour of someone too ill to go to work. He would phone, he had to.

Her voice was magical to him, soft, sweet, with the lilting accent he had come to hear as pretty and, of course, seductive. He had never heard it on the phone, but somehow he knew that when he did hear it he would be silenced, for seconds he would be unable to reply, he would have to listen, be captured by her voice and feel it run into his blood, and take away his breath. He dialled the number and waited, waited for *her*. It was the first time in his life he had ever suffered the awfulness of hearing the ringing tone repeated and repeated while longing, praying, for an answer.

Someone answered at last. It was a young girl's voice, soft, sweet, with that same accent, but without the power to stir him, a voice immediately recognisable as not hers. One of the sisters, he supposed. She didn't say.

'Sue's gone round to Kim's.'

It sounded like a code to him, a spatter of phonemes. He had to ask her to repeat it.

'Sue', she said more slowly, 'has gone round to Kim's house, OK?'

'Thank you,' he said.

He realised he knew nothing of her friends, nothing of her life away from him. He had supposed her so young and artless as to be satisfied with the company of her parents and her sisters, remaining at home in the evenings until he rescued her from this rustic domesticity. But of course she had friends, girls she had been to school with, the daughters of neighbours. None of that accounted for her failure to come to him and he racked his mind for reasons. Had he inadvertently said something to hurt her feelings?

Could it be that, after taking thought, she found herself offended by his enquiry as to her sexual adventurousness? But she had replied that she would only do these things with someone she loved and she loved him so much. That had been almost the last thing she had said to him when they parted on the previous Friday a hundred yards from her father's house, that she loved him so much. He was driven to think – he *wanted* to think – that it was that father and that mother who, having discovered the truth from Susannah, her heart too full to keep love to herself, had taken a heavy line and sent her to spend the evening not at Gothic House but with a girlfriend.

Night is the enemy of the unhappy lover, for it's then that fearful thoughts come and horrible forebodings. It would have been better if the night had been dull and wet but it was warm, with a yellow moon rising, a moon fattening to the full. He walked out and down to the lake, expecting to hear the nightingales, not knowing that they cease to sing once early June is past. The moonlight was almost golden, laying a pale sheen on the water and on the lilies, closed into buds for the hours of darkness. He wrote about that in his diary, the things he observed and the sounds he heard, a single cry from the woods as of an animal attacked by a fox, a disturbance of lily pads as a roosting moorhen shifted and folded its wings. Above him the sky was a clear bright opal, the stars too weak to show in the light of that moon.

He thought about Susannah, perhaps lying in her bed wakeful and longing for him as he longed for her. He lay down on the dry turf of the shoreline, face downwards, his arms outstretched, and whispered her name into the sand, Susannah, Susannah.

\* \* \*

The following morning he tried to work. Over and over he read the last passage he had translated, of Hecabe's dream that she had given birth to a burning brand that split into coils of fiery serpents. The French text swam before his eyes like tadpoles, meaningless black squiggles. He spent the rest of the day trying to reach Susannah.

He phoned and no one answered. He tried again and still there was no reply. Her job at Gothic House wasn't the only one she had, he knew that. She cleaned for someone else somewhere, she minded the children of one of the schoolteachers, she washed hair and swept up for the hairdresser who operated from two rooms over the shop. The irony escaped him that in London, in his old life, he would never have considered taking a woman who earned her living by performing such menial tasks for a living out for a drink, still less been intent on marrying her.

He had very little idea when and where she went to these jobs. The hairdresser's perhaps, he could find that number and try that. Anne Whiteson at the shop gave him the number. It was his imagination, it must be, but he had an uncomfortable sense that she knew something he didn't know or was humouring him, was playing along with him in some indefinable way. A great deal to read into a woman's voice asking after his health and giving him a phone number, but, as he said, his imagination was very active, was pulsating with theories and suspicions and terrors.

Susannah wasn't at the hairdresser's. She wasn't expected there till Wednesday afternoon. He phoned her father's house again and again there was no reply. He imagined phones unplugged by determined parents. Nothing more was done on the translation that day and in the late afternoon he drove down to her home, anxious, very apprehensive, not in the least wanting to confront John Peddar or Iris but seeing no other way.

A little girl came to the door. That was how he described her, Julie, the youngest one, who must have been fourteen or fifteen but whom he saw as a child.

'They've all gone to the seaside. They won't be back till late.'

It wasn't the voice on the phone. He thought she was lying but could hardly tell her so. 'Why didn't you go, then?' This was the nearest to an accusation he could get.

'I was at school, wasn't I?'

By then he had noticed how seldom people left the village but to work or shop. The seaside story strained his credulity, he thought they must all be hidden in the house, Susannah perhaps a prisoner, and that evening, in his misery, he sat in the window watching for the Peddar van to pass along the lake road, that being the way the family would be obliged to return from the coast. But only two cars passed and they were both saloons.

He dreamt of Susannah, naked and chained like Andromeda, who appeared briefly in the preface to *The Golden Apple*, on her dragon-menaced rock. He struck off the chains and they fell from her at a single blow but when he took her into his arms and felt the smooth resilience of her breasts and thighs press against him, the flesh began to melt and pour through his hands in a scented sticky flood like cream or some cosmetic fluid. He woke up crying out, put his head in his hands, then saw the time and knew that Lavinia would soon come. Or would she? Hadn't she said she had no plans to come on Wednesday? Was it possible that after everything *Susannah* would come?

The girl who let herself into the house and came into the kitchen where he stood staring, his fists cleanched, his teeth set, was the one whose voice he had heard the only time one of his calls was answered.

'Sue won't be coming today.'

He said rudely, 'Who are you?'

'Carol,' she said. 'I'm the middle one.'

She opened the cupoard where the cleaning things were kept, pulled out the vacuum cleaner, inspected a not very clean duster and sniffed it. He could hardly believe what he was seeing. It was as if the whole family had united and conspired together to control him, keep an eye on him, *handle* him and keep him from Susannah. He was a man of thirty-seven, an intellectual, a highly respected linguist taken over by a bunch of peasants of whom this pert sixteen-year-old blonde was the representative. No doubt we say such things to ourselves when we are desperately unhappy and frightened. Ben wouldn't normally have talked about peasants nor about himself as belonging to an elite. Besides, his Susannah was one of them . . .

'I want an explanation,' he said.

She smiled, about to leave the room. 'Do you?'

He took her by the wrist. 'You have to tell me. I want you to tell me – now. What's going on. Why can't I see Susannah?'

She looked at his hand gripping her wrist. 'Let me go.'

'All right,' he said. 'But you can sit down, sit down here at the table, and tell me.'

'I came to tell you, as a matter of fact,' she said calmly. 'I thought I'd get your bits and pieces done and then I'd tell you over a coffee.'

'Tell me now.'

She smiled comfortably. It was the smile of a woman much older than she was, a middle-aged smile, as of a mother speaking of some gratifying event, a daughter's wedding, for instance. Yet she was a smooth-faced pink-cheeked adolescent, full-mouthed, her lips as red as lipstick but unpainted, not a line or mark on her velvety skin.

'You can see Sue again, of course you can. There's no question of anything else. But not all the time. You can't –' she brought the word out as if someone had taught it to her that morning '– monopolise her. You can't do that. Don't you see?'

'I don't see anything,' he said. 'I love Susannah and she loves me.' He might as well tell her. It must all come into the open now. 'I want to marry Susannah.'

She shrugged. She said the unbelievable thing. 'Sue's engaged to Kim Gresham.'

His voice almost went. He said hoarsely, 'I don't know what you mean.'

'Sue's been engaged to Kim for a year now. They'll be getting married in the spring.' She got up. 'There are plenty of other girls, you know.'

## 6

On a warm September evening I saw the bathers in the lake outside my house. Not the woman and the two children who appeared to us when Ben was staying with me for that weekend, but a whole group who arrived to swim from 'my' beach. This was after I'd repulsed John Peddar and after I'd dismissed Sandy but before the really alarming things happened.

They were all women and all good to look at. I suppose it was then that I realised there were no grossly fat women in the village, none who was misshapen, and even as they grew older their bodies seemed not pulled down by gravity or ridged with wrinkles or marked with distorted veins. These things are very much a matter of genes. I had plenty of chance to observe the results of a good gene pool when I watched the women from my front garden in that soft twilight.

It wasn't quite warm enough to bathe. Not strictly. If I'd gone closer I expect I should have seen gooseflesh on limbs but I didn't go closer, though they evidently wanted me to. They waved. Jennifer Fowler called out, 'It's lovely in the water!'

They swam among the lilies. Those lilies were like a Monet painting, red and pink and white cups floating among their flat duck-green leaves on the pale water. One of the women picked a red lily and tucked its brown snaky stem into the knot of yellow hair she had tied up on top of her head. The wife of the farmer from Lynn was there, floating on her back beside Jennifer on the calm gleaming surface, her outstretched hand clasping Jennifer's hand.

Have I said they were naked, every one of them? They swam but mostly they played in the shallow water by the shore, splashing each other, then lying down and submerging themselves but for uplifted laughing faces and long hair spread on rippling water. The farmer's wife, whose name I never knew, stood up and in a gesture at once erotic and innocent – didn't that sum them all up? – lifted her full breasts, one cupped in each hand, while Kathy Gresham splashed her with handfuls of water.

All the time they were glancing at me, smiling at me, giving me smiles of encouragement. It was plain they wanted me to come in too. I didn't disapprove, I didn't mind what they did, the lake was free and as much theirs as anyone's, but I did object to an attitude they all had, unmistakable though hard to define. It was as if they were laughing at me. It was as if they were saying, and probably were saying to each other, that I was a fool, inhibited, shy, perhaps ashamed of my own body. Go in there with them and all that would change. But I didn't want to go in there. It's not an excuse to say that it was really by this time quite cold. I got up and went into the house.

Later I saw them all emerge from the woods where their clothes were, fully dressed, still laughing, slowly dancing homewards along the lake shore, some of them holding hands. It was dusk by then and all I could see as they receded into the distance were shadowy forms, still dancing and no doubt still laughing, coming together and parting as if taking part in some elegant pavane.

If any bathers came to display themselves to Ben he didn't mention them in his diary. But there was a lot he left out. I suppose he couldn't bear to put it down or perhaps look at it on the page after he'd written it. Some of it he told me but there must have been a lot he didn't, a great deal I shall never know.

The actions of others he faithfully recorded. It was his own that he became, for a few days, reticent about. For example, he didn't seem to mind putting on paper that Carol Peddar had offered herself to him. After she said that about there being plenty of other girls, she looked into his eyes and, smiling, said there was herself. Didn't he like her? A lot of men thought she was prettier than her sister. 'Try me,' she said, and then, 'Touch me' and she reached for his hand.

He told her to go, to get out, and never to come back. He still believed, you see, that it was a family conspiracy that was trying to separate him from Susannah, a plot in which every Peddar was involved and Carol with them.

'I even believed the engagement was an arranged thing,' he told me. 'I thought they'd fixed it up. Perhaps that was the way marriages happened in that village. I knew something strange was going on and I thought there must be a tradition of arranged marriages. Susannah and this Kim Gresham had been destined for each other from babyhood, like something in India or among the Habsburgs. You see, I knew it was me she wanted, I knew it as I know you and I are sitting here together now.'

'You thought you did,' I said.

'Later on, when I really knew, I tried telling myself I'd only known her for a couple of months, it couldn't be real, it must be sex and infatuation, whatever that is. I told myself what you told me that weekend, that she wasn't an educated person and that she was too young for me.'

'Did I say that?'

'You meant it whether you said it or not,' he said. 'I told myself all that and I asked myself what we had in common. Would she even understand what I did for a living, for instance? That sort of thing ought to matter but it didn't. I was in love with her. I'd never felt for anyone what I felt for her, not even for Margaret when we were first married. I'd have given the whole world, I'd have given ten years of my life, for her to have walked in at that moment and said the engagement story was nonsense, made up by her family, and it was me she was going to marry.'

Ten years of his life, in those circumstances, was the last thing he should have thought of giving. Still, he wasn't called on to give anything. He went to the Peddars' house that evening, demanded admittance and got it. John and Iris were at home with Carol and Julie but there was no sign of Susannah. She was out, Iris said. No, she didn't know where, she didn't think a person of eighteen ought to have to account to her parents for everywhere she went.

'Especially in this village,' John said. 'This is a safe place. Horrible things don't happen here, never have and never will.'

He sounded absolutely sure of himself, Ben said. He was smiling. Had I ever noticed how much they smiled in that village? The men always had a grin on their faces and the women sunny smiles.

'Now you mention it,' I said, 'I suppose I have.' Until they changed towards me and all smiles stopped.

Ben was tremendously angry. He thought of himself – and others thought of him – as a quiet, reserved sort of man, but by then he was angry. How did he know she wasn't in the house, that they hadn't got her hidden somewhere?

'You're welcome to look,' Iris said and then, incredibly, the self-conscious housewife: 'It's not very tidy upstairs, I'm afraid.'

Of course he didn't look. They wouldn't have given him the chance if she'd been there. John was looking him up and down as if summing him up for some purpose. Then he asked him why he wanted Susannah. What did he want her *for*?

Carol, no doubt, had reported back their conversation of the morning, so they must know about himself and Susannah, that he wanted to marry her. He told them so then and there, he repeated what he'd said.

'It takes two to agree to that,' Iris said comfortably.

'We are two,' he said. 'She loves me, she's told me often enough. I don't know what you're doing, how you're controlling her or coercing her, but it won't work. She's eighteen, she doesn't need your consent, she can please herself.'

'She has pleased herself, Ben.' It was the first time anyone from the village but Susannah had called him by his given name. 'She's pleased herself and chosen Kim.'

'I don't believe it,' he said. 'I don't believe *you*.'

'That's up to you,' said John. 'You can believe what you like.'

He said it serenely, he was smiling. Ben said then what I'd often thought, that they were so happy in that village, as if they'd found the secret of life, always smiling, never ruffled, calm, forbearing. They were mostly quite poor, a lot of them were unemployed, a few were on the edge of being comfortably off, that was all, but they didn't need material things, they were happy without them.

'As if they were all in love,' Ben said bitterly. 'All in love all the time.'

'Perhaps,' I said, 'in a way they were.'

After he'd told Ben he could believe what he liked and added that that was his privilege, John said why be so set on marrying Susannah. Why not, for instance, Carol?

'This I don't believe,' Ben said.

'Ah, but you'll have to change your way of thinking. That's the point, don't you see? If you're going to live here, if you're going to take on my mother-in-law's place.'

'There are no secrets in this village,' said Iris, 'but you know that.'

John nodded. 'Carol's as lovely in her way as Susannah and she likes you. I wouldn't be saying any of this if she didn't like you. That's not our way. Stand up, Carol.'

The girl stood. She held her head high and slowly turned to show herself in profile, then fully frontal. Like a slave for sale, he thought, and he remembered the bather emerging from the lake. She put up her arms and untied the ribbon that confined her hair in a ponytail. It was thick, shiny hair, the colour of the corn they'd begun cutting that day.

'You could be engaged to Carol if you like,' said Iris.

He got up and walked out of the house, slamming the front door behind him.

At the house next door he rang the bell hard. He didn't know who lived there, that hardly mattered. The woman who answered the door he recognised at once. Later on he found out she was Gillian Atkins but all he knew then was that she was the bather he had seen when with me and had been thinking of only a moment before. It gave him, he said, a horrible feeling of having stumbled into another world, a place of dreams and magic and perhaps science fiction. Or into the French analyst's myths where goddesses appeared out of clouds and where gods, in order to seduce, disguised themselves as swans and bulls and showers of gold.

She was smiling, of course. He stared, then he asked her if she knew where Kim Gresham lived. That made her smile again. As if she wouldn't know that, as if anyone in this place wouldn't know a thing like that. She told him to go to the house on the outskirts of the village.

When he got there the house was shut up. He knew, as one does, that there was no one at home. It was a lovely place, like a cottage on an old-fashioned calendar or chocolate box lid, thatch coming down over eyelid dormers, a pheasant made of straw perched on the roof. Roses climbed over the half-timbering and a white-flowering climber with them that gave off a rich heavy scent. It made him feel sick.

The evening was warm, the sky lilac and pink. Birds flew homewards in flocks as dense as swarms of bees. He walked back to where he'd left his car, passing the cottage he meant to buy, he still at that time meant to buy. Old Mrs Fowler was taking the air, sitting on the wooden bench in the front garden beside an old man. They were holding hands and they waved to him and smiled. He said that though he was in a turmoil, he was profoundly aware of them and that he had never seen such a picture of tranquillity.

He knew where Susannah would be next day. On Wednesday afternoons she went to work for the hairdresser. He expected Lavinia to come in the morning – it surely wouldn't be Carol after what had happened – but instead a stranger arrived, brought to his door by Sandy.

'We didn't want to let you down,' Sandy said, 'did we, Teresa? This is Teresa, she's taking Susannah's place.'

'Teresa what?' he said.

'Gresham,' the woman said. 'Teresa Gresham. It's my husband's nephew that Susannah's engaged to.'

She was probably thirty-five, shorter and plumper than the girls, browner-skinned and with light-brown hair, an exquisitely pretty face, her eyes the bright dark-blue of delphiniums. The summer dress she wore he had learned to think of as an old-fashioned garment. This one was pink with white flowers on it. Her legs were bare and she had white sandals on her strong brown feet.

'They tried everything,' I said when he told me.

'I suppose they did. But she wasn't flirtatious like Lavinia or blatant like Carol. I suppose you could say she was – *maternal*. She talked to me in a soothing way, she was cheerful and comforting – or she thought she was being comforting. Of course, the whole village knew about Susannah and me by then, and they knew what had happened. Teresa made me coffee and brought it up. I was still working upstairs, still hiding from Sandy's grins and gestures, and she brought the coffee in and said not to be unhappy, life was too short for that. Smiling all the time, of course, need I say? She didn't tell me there were plenty more girls in the village, she said there were more fish in the sea than ever came out of it.'

Sandy knocked on the back door at one to take her home in his van. Ben had suspected there was something between those two, he sensed a close affectionate intimacy, but then Sandy announced he was getting married in ten days' time and would Ben like to come. The village church at twelve noon. He didn't say whom he was marrying but it couldn't be Teresa because she had talked of a husband and Marion Kirkman also was married. Almost anything could have been believed of the villagers by that time, he thought, but no doubt they drew the line at bigamy.

He said he didn't know if he could accept, he didn't know where he'd be on the Saturday week, he'd have to see.

'Oh, you'll come,' Sandy said airily. 'Things'll work out, you'll see. Everything'll be coming up roses by then.'

You had to pass through the shop to get to the hairdresser's, through the shop and up the stairs. Anne Whiteson, behind the counter, detained him too long, smiling, friendly, asking after his health, his work, his opinion of the enduring hot weather. He heard Susannah's voice while he was climbing the steep staircase and, much as he longed to see her, he stood for a moment experiencing the pleasure and the pain, not knowing which predominated, of those soft sweet tones, that rustic burr, the sunny warmth that informed everything she said. Not that she said anything particularly worth hearing, even he knew that, though it was poetry to him. It was something about a kind of shampoo she was discussing and whether it really made a perm last longer but it thrilled him so that he was both shivering and awestruck.

The door was open but as he came to it two hairdryers started up simultaneously. He walked in. All the women had their backs to him: Angela Burns the hairdresser and her assistant Debbie Kirkman – he learned their names later – two older women with their grey hair wound up on to pink plastic curlers, and Gillian Atkins whose long blonde curls were at that moment being liberated from a battery of rollers by Susannah herself. He was beginning to see Gillian Atkins as some kind of evil genius who dogged his steps and appeared at crucial moments of his life. Aphrodite or Hecate.

Although the windows were open the place was very hot and when Susannah turned round her cheeks were flushed and her hair curled into tendrils round her face like one of Botticelli's girls. He thought she had never looked more beautiful. In front of them all she came up to him, put her arms round his neck and kissed him. Over her shoulder he could see five pairs of eyes watching them, heads all turned round to see. In front of them he couldn't speak but she could. 'It's all right,' she said. 'It's going to be fine. Trust me. I'll come to you tomorrow evening.'

Someone laughed. The five women started clapping. They clapped as at a play or a show put on for their benefit. Horribly embarrassed, he muttered something and ran down the stairs and out through the shop. But she'd restored him, he was better now, she had told him to trust her. He could see it all, the arranged marriage, the established engagement, two sets of parents and a bunch of siblings all wanting the marriage, everyone set on it but the promised bride who was set on *him*.

That evening he managed to do some good work. The French was about sacrifice as propitiation of the gods. Agamemnon's killing of Iphigenia and the sacrifice of Polyxena on Achilles' tomb, and the subject demanded a similarly elegant grave prose. He worked upstairs in that room that had a view of the forest, not the lake, and when he reached Polyxena's burial, a wind sprang up like that which had risen while the Greeks waited to embark from Rhoetea. The forest trees bent and fluttered in this freakish wind that blew and howled and died after half an hour.

Once he had the Greeks embarked for Thrace, he abandoned the translation and turned to write in his diary instead, the diary that had been untouched for almost a week. He wrote about Susannah and how she had reassured him and about the dark forest too and the strange sounds he could hear as he sat there with the dark closing in. 'A yelping like a puppy,' he wrote, unaware that what he heard must have been the cry of the Little Owl out hunting.

He slept soundly that night and next day, at lunchtime, on a whim, he walked down to the pub. Have I mentioned there was a pub? I don't think I have but there was one and it was kept by Jean and David Stamford. It should have been called by some suitable name in that village, the Cupid's Bow perhaps or the Maiden's Prayer, Ben said, but it wasn't, it was called the Red Lion. Like almost every house along the village street and round the green, it was a pretty building, half-timbered, with flowers climbing over it and flowers in tubs outside. Ben went in there to lunch off a beer and a sandwich for no better reason than that he was happy.

You could always tell strangers from the village people. They looked different. Ben said brutally that strangers were fat or dark or ugly or all those things together. There were several couples like that in the bar. He had noticed their cars parked outside. They were passing through, all they would be permitted to do, he said, though in fact the Red Lion did have rooms available and visitors had been known to stay a few nights or even a week.

The farmer from Lynn was sitting by himself up at the bar. It's a measure of the way the village people regarded him and had for quite a long time regarded him that no one ever uttered his name or called him by it, which is why even now I don't know what it was. He sat in miserable solitude while the rest of the clientele enjoyed themselves, greeting Ben enthusiastically, the old man he had seen holding hands with Mrs Fowler actually slapping him on the back. No doubt the farmer had come in there out of defiance, refusing to be browbeaten.

He drank his beer and after sitting there a further five minutes, staring at the bottles behind the bar, got down from his stool and left.

To Ben's astonishment everyone laughed and clapped. It was like the scene in the hairdresser's all over again. When the applause died down Jean Stamford announced to the assembled company that a little bird had told her the Old Rectory was sold. Everyone seemed to know that the little bird was the village's resident agent and her brother-in-law. Mrs Fowler's friend asked how much the farmer had got for it and Jean Stamford named a sum so large that the customers could only shake their heads in silence.

'Who's bought it?' Ben asked.

They seemed to like his intervention. There was a kind of hum of approval. It was apparently the right enquiry put at the right time. But no one knew who had bought the Old Rectory, only that it was nobody from the village.

'More's the pity,' said the old man.

'And a pity for them,' David Stamford said strangely, 'if they don't suit.'

Ben walked home. All this talk of houses as well as the prospect of his reunion with Susannah prompted him to ring up the estate agent and make an offer for Mrs Fowler's house. The agent assured him it would be accepted, no doubt about it.

The combination of the beer, the walk and the sunshine sent him to sleep. It was gone five before he woke and he immediately set about putting wine in the fridge and preparing a meal for Susannah and himself, avocados and chicken salad and ice cream. He wrote all this down in his diary next morning while she still slept. It was the first time she had ever stayed a whole night with him.

From his bedroom window he'd watched for her to come. She hadn't said a time and he watched for her for an hour, quietly going mad, unable to remain still. When at last she arrived it was in her father's van which she was driving herself. The sight of it filled him with joy, with enormous exhilaration. All the suspense and terrors of the past hour were forgotten. If she could come in her father's own car this must mean that, miraculously, her parents had given their approval, minds had changed and he was to be received, the accredited lover.

She was wearing nothing underneath her thin silk almost transparent trousers and a loose top of lilac-coloured silk. He had never been so aware of the beauty of her young body, her long legs and very slightly rounded belly in which the navel was a shallow well. Her loose hair covered her breasts as if spread there from modesty. She lifted to him warm red lips and her tongue darted against the roof of his mouth.

'Susannah, I love you so. Tell me you love me.'

'I love you, dear Ben.'

He was utterly consoled. Those were the words he wrote down next morning. She shared the wine with him, she ate. She talked excitedly of Sandy Clements's wedding to Rosalind Wantage, the present her parents had bought, the dress she would wear to the ceremony. And Ben must come with her, they would go together. He would, wouldn't he? Ben laughed. He'd have gone to the ends of the earth with her, let alone to the village church.

His laughter died and he asked her about Kim Gresham. She was to tell him there was nothing in it or at least that it was over. He could bear an old love, a love from the past.

She said seriously, 'Let's not talk about other people', and, as if repeating a rule, 'We don't. Not here. You'll soon learn, darling Ben.'

They made love many times that night. Ben wrote that there had never been such a night in all his life. He didn't know it could be like that, he had read of such things and thought they existed only in the writer's imagination. And one of the strange things was that those actions of hers he had previously thought of as adventurous, even as shocking, weren't indulged in, or if they were they became *unmemorable*, for something else had happened. It was as if in the midst of this bodily rapture they had somehow become detached from their physical selves, it was sex made spirit and all the stuff of sex transcended. They were taken from themselves to be made angels or gods and everything they did took on the aspect of acts of grace or sacred rituals, yet at the same time made a continuum of pleasure.

He wrote that in his diary in the morning. He couldn't have brought himself to tell it to me in words.

She slept with her head on his pillow and her hair spread out, 'rayed' out, was how he put it, 'like the sun in splendour'. He watched her sleeping and he remembered her telling him to trust her. He couldn't therefore account for his terror, his awful fear. What was he afraid of?

Teresa Gresham came at eight thirty to clean the house and at nine Susannah woke up.

7

Dodging Teresa, avoiding knowing glances, he made coffee for

Susannah and set a tray with orange juice, toast and fruit. But when he took it up to her she was already dressed, sitting on the edge of the bed combing her hair. She smiled at him and held out her arms. They held each other and kissed and he asked her when they could be married.

She gave him a sidelong look. 'You've never asked me to marry you.'

'Haven't I?' he said. 'I've told almost everyone else it's what I want.'

'Anyway, darling Ben . . .' She always called him that, 'dear Ben' or 'darling Ben' and it sat oddly – charmingly to him – with her rustic accent. But what she had to say wasn't charming. 'Anyway, darling Ben, I can't because I'm going to marry Kim.'

He didn't believe he'd heard that, he literally didn't believe his ears. She must have asked if he'd thought she was marrying Kim.

He asked her what she'd said and she repeated it. She said, 'You know I'm engaged to Kim. Carol said she'd told you.'

'This is a joke, isn't it?' he said.

She took his hand, kissed it and held it between her breasts. 'It's nice that you want to marry me. Marriage is very important, you only do it once, so I think it's lovely that you want to be with me like that for ever and ever. But that's the way I'm going to be with Kim. Live in the same house and share the same bed and bring up children together. It can't be changed, darling Ben. But I can still see you, we can be like we were last night. No one will mind. Did you think they would mind?'

She was his dear love, his adored Susannah, but she was a madwoman too. Or a child who understood nothing of life. But he knew that wasn't so. She was eighteen but the depths of her eyes weren't, they were as old as her grandmother's, as knowledgeable, in her own way as sophisticated.

He took his hand away. It didn't belong there. She picked up her coffee cup and repeated what she'd said. She was patient with him but she didn't know what it was he failed to understand. It seemed as clear as glass to her. 'Look, I'm not good at this,' she said. 'Ask Teresa.'

The last person he wanted at that moment was Teresa Gresham but Susannah went to the door and called her, and Teresa came upstairs.

She looked quite unembarrassed, she wasn't even surprised. 'We all do as we please here,' she said. 'Marriage is for life, of course, just the once. But love-making, that's another matter. Men go with who they like and so do women. There's only been one divorce in this village in thirty years,' she said. 'And before that no one got divorced, anyway. No one outside here – in the world, that is.'

It made him shudder to hear the village talked of as if it were heaven or some utopian planet. 'In the world', out there, two miles away . . .

'I couldn't believe it,' he said to me. 'Human beings wouldn't stand for it, not as a theory of life. It may be all right in a commune, a temporary thing, but for everyone of all ages, a whole village community in *England*? I asked her about jealousy. Teresa, I mean. I asked her. She said they used to say jealousy wasn't in their blood but now they thought it was rather that a gene of jealousy had been left out of them. After all, they were all more or less the same stock, they came out of the same gene pool.' He asked me, 'Did you know about all this?'

'I? No, I didn't know.'

'Not the green-eyed monster,' he said, 'but the blue-eyed fairy. You didn't know when you came down for that weekend?'

'I knew there was something. I thought it was because I was a woman and it wouldn't happen to a man.'

'We sat in that bedroom, Susannah and Teresa and I, and Teresa told me all about it. She'd known it all her life, it was part of everyone's life, and as far as they knew it had always been so, perhaps for hundreds of years. When new people tried to live in the village they judged whether they'd be acceptable or not, did they have the right physical appearance, would they *join in*.'

'You mean take part in this sexual free-for-all?'

'They tested them. John Peddar passed the test. If they didn't pass they – got rid of them. Like they were getting rid of the man from Lynn. He wouldn't, Teresa said, but she would, and naturally the poor man didn't want her to.'

'And I wouldn't,' I said, 'and you wouldn't.'

'They knew enough to be aware that new genes ought to be introduced sometimes, though no defects ever appeared in the children. As to who their fathers were it just as often wasn't the mother's husband but he'd have children elsewhere so no one minded. If a man's children weren't his they were very likely a brother's or a cousin's.'

'How about accidental brother and sister incest?'

'Perhaps they didn't care,' he said, and then he added, 'I've told you all this as if I believed it when I was first told. But I didn't believe it. I thought Susannah had been brainwashed by her parents and Teresa roped in because she was articulate, a suitable spokeswoman. You see, it wasn't possible for me to take this in after – well, after the way Susannah had been with me and the things she'd said. Teresa hadn't been there, thank God – what did she know? I thought the Peddar family had instructed Susannah in what to say and they and Teresa concocted this tale to make me back off.'

'It was true, though, wasn't it?'

He said, 'Even the Olympian gods were jealous. Hera persecuted the lovers of Zeus. Persephone was jealous of the King of the Underworld.' Then he answered me. 'Oh, yes, it was true.'

After Susannah had gone and Teresa had followed her, for he had told Teresa to get out of the house and never to come back, he shifted the blame from the Peddar family on to her and on to Kim Gresham. Wasn't she, after all, Kim Gresham's aunt? (Or cousin or second cousin or even sister.) Kim Gresham was holding Susannah to her engagement even though she loved him, Ben. In the light of what he'd just heard this wasn't a logical assumption, but he was beyond logic.

He would go to the Greshams' house and see Kim, have it out with him, drive down to the village and find out where he worked. But something strange happened while he was locking up, getting the car out. It was another beautiful day, sunny and warm, the blue sky flecked with tiny clouds like down. A pair of swans had appeared on the lake to swim on the calm glassy water among the lily pads. The forest was a rich velvety green and for a moment he stood staring at the green reflected in the blue.

He found himself thinking that if, as he put it, 'all things had been equal', if he hadn't been in love with Susannah, how idyllic would be the life Teresa had presented to him: unlimited love and pleasure without jealousy or recrimination, without fear or risk, free love in all senses, something to look forward to all day and look back on every morning. Love of which one never wearied because if one did it could without pain or damage be changed. An endless series of love affairs in this beautiful place where everyone was kind and warm and liked you, where people clapped at the sight of kisses. He thought of his wife whom he hated because she had been unfaithful to him. Here he would have given her his blessing and they would still be together.

If he believed what Teresa said. But he didn't. The sun didn't always shine. Jealousy hadn't been left out of his genetic make-up nor, he was sure, out of Susannah's. It hadn't occurred to him before this that she might have slept with Kim Gresham but now it did and the green of the forest turned red, the sky blazed with a hard yellow light, passion roared inside his head, and he forgot about idylls and blessings and unlimited love.

He drove to the village, parked the car and went into the shop, source of all his supplies of food and information. Anne Whiteson was less friendly than usual and it occurred to him that Teresa might already have begun spreading the tale of her expulsion from Gothic House. She was less friendly but it was no worse than that and she was quite willing to tell him where Kim Gresham was to be found: at home with his parents in their house on the village outskirts. He had lost his job as a mechanic in a garage four miles away and was, until he found another, on the dole.

Scorn was now added to Ben's rage against Kim. Those Peddars were willing for their daughter to marry an unemployed man who couldn't support her. They preferred that man to him. He made his way to the Greshams' house, that pretty house a little way outside the village with the roses round the door. Kathy opened it and let him in, and he found Kim sprawled in the front room in front of the television. In his eyes that compounded the offence.

Kim got up when Ben came in and, all unsuspecting, smiling – how they all smiled and smiled! – held out his hand. He was a tall, well-built young man, very young, perhaps twenty, several inches taller than Ben and probably two stone heavier. Ben ignored the hand. It suddenly came to him that it wouldn't do to have a row in Kim's parents' house, he had no particular quarrel with the parents, and he told Kim to come outside.

Though obviously in the dark about all this, Kim followed Ben out into the front garden. I suppose he thought Ben wanted to show him something, possibly there was something wrong with his car. After all, he was a motor mechanic. Outside, among the flowers, standing on a lawn with a bird bath in the middle of it, Ben told him he was in love with Susannah and she with him, there was no room for Kim in that relationship, he'd been replaced, his time with Susannah was past. Did he understand?

Kim said he didn't know what Ben was talking about. 'I'm going to marry Susannah,' he said, and he said it with no show of emotion, in the tone he might have used to say he was going bowling or down to the pub. 'The wedding's been fixed for September. Second Saturday in September. You can come if you want. I know you like her, she's said, and that's OK with me. She's told me all about it, we don't have secrets.'

Ben hit him. He said it was the first time in his life he'd ever hit anyone and it wasn't a very successful blow. He had lashed out and struck Kim on the neck below the jawbone and he hit him again with the other fist, this time striking his head, but neither seemed to have

541

much effect. Unlike adversaries in films, Kim didn't reel back or fall over. He got hold of Ben round his neck, in that armlock the police are advised not to use on people they arrest, propelled him down the path and out of the gate, where Ben collapsed and sat down heavily on the ground. Ben told me all this quite openly. He said he was utterly humiliated.

Kim Gresham, who probably watched a lot of televison, said to Ben not to try anything further or he might 'be obliged to hurt him'. Then he asked him if he was all right and when Ben didn't answer, went back into the house and closed the front door quietly behind him.

Because the Gresham house stood alone with fields on either side of it – Greshams, someone had told me, always liked to live a little way away from the village – there were no witnesses. Ben got up and rubbed his neck and thought that, with luck, no one else would know of his defeat and humiliation. His ignorance of the village and its ways was still sublime. He still thought there were things he could do outside his own four walls and no one would know.

He walked back to the village to where he had parked. In his absence his car had received attention. Someone had printed on the windscreen in a shiny red substance, probably nail varnish: *Go away*. Even then he knew they didn't just mean go away for now, don't park here. The village street was empty. It often was but if people were about this was the time they would be, eleven in the morning. There was no one to be seen. Even the front gardens were empty and on this fine August day all the front doors and windows were closed. Eyes watched him. No one made any pretence that those eyes weren't watching.

Back at Gothic House he cleaned the printed letters off with nail varnish remover he found in the bathroom cabinet. Deterred by what had happened but willing himself to be strong, he phoned the Peddars. A woman answered, Iris, he supposed, for the voice didn't belong to Susannah or her sisters.

He said, 'This is Ben Powell.'

Without another word, she put the receiver down. In the afternoon he phoned the hairdresser. Before the horrible things began to happen, on the previous evening when he and Susannah had been so happy, she'd told him she worked for the hairdresser on Friday afternoons as well. He phoned at two. Angela Burns answered and, when he said who it was, she put the receiver down.

That shook him because it seemed to him to prove that Kim Gresham or his mother had talked of what had happened. Teresa had talked.

It was one thing telling the Peddars but the news had spread to the hairdresser's. His defeat of the morning made him feel he had to be brave. If he was to achieve anything, overcome these people and secure Susannah for himself exclusively, he had to have courage now. He drove back to the village but this time he parked the car directly outside the shop.

When Anne Whiteson saw him she said straight out she wasn't going to serve him. Then she walked into the room at the back and shut the door behind her. Ben went to the staircase but before he'd gone up half a dozen stairs Susannah appeared at the top. She came down and met him halfway. Or, rather, she stood two stairs above him. He put out his hand to her. She shook her head and said very softly so that no one else should hear, 'It's over, Ben.'

'What do you mean?' he said. 'What do you mean, over? Because of what these people say and do? The rest of the world isn't like this, Susannah. You don't know that but I do, I've seen, believe me.'

'It's over,' she said and now she was whispering. 'I thought it needn't be, I thought it could go on, because I do love you, but it has to be over because of what you've done and, Ben, because of what you *are*.'

'What I am?'

'You're not like my dad, not many are. You're like the man who lives in the rectory, you're like the lady Gothic House belongs to. I didn't think you were but you are.'

'This is all nonsense.' He wasn't going to whisper, no matter what she might do. 'It's rubbish, it's irrelevant. Listen, Susannah, I want us to go away. Come away with me.' He forgot about her grandmother's cottage. 'I've got a place in London, we can go there tonight, we can go there *now*.'

'You must go, Ben. I'm not going anywhere. This is where I live and I always will, you know. The people who live here never want to go away.' She reached down from her higher stair and touched him on the arm. It was electric, that touch, he felt the shock of it run up his arm and rattle his body. 'But you must go,' she said.

'Of course I'm not going,' he shouted. 'I'm staying here and I'm going to get you away from these people.'

He meant it. He thought he could. He ran back to his car and drove home to Gothic House where he began composing a letter to Susannah's parents and another, for good measure I suppose, to Susannah's grandmother. Perhaps he was thinking of her in the capacity of a village elder. Then, by one of those coincidences, just as he was writing 'Dear Mrs Fowler . . .' the phone rang and it was the estate agent to tell him Susannah's grandmother had received a better offer than his for her house.

'What is it?' he said. 'I'll match it.' Recklessness, that can be as much the effect of terror as of happiness, made him say, 'I'll top it.'

'Mrs Fowler has already accepted the offer.'

He tore up the letter he'd started writing. The one he'd written to the Peddars remained on his desk. But he intended to send it. He intended to fight. This time he refused to allow himself to become despondent. He pushed away the longings for her that came, the desire that was an inevitable concomitant of thinking of her. He would fight for her, he would think of that. What did the loss of the cottage matter? They couldn't live in this village anyway.

He refused to let her become part of what he saw as an exceptionally large commune, where wife-swapping was the norm and husbands couldn't tell which were their own offspring. For a moment he had seen it, very briefly he'd seen it, as the ideal that all men, and women too perhaps, would want. But that had been a moment of madness. These people had made a reality out of a common fantasy but he was not going to be drawn into it and nor was Susannah. Nor was he going to leave the village until it was to take her with him.

8

They got rid of me. I had no idea of the reason for my expulsion – no, that's not true, I did have ideas, they just weren't the right ones. I did have explanations of a kind. I was a 'foreigner', so to speak, born and bred a long way off with most of my life lived elsewhere. I'd sacked Sandy. When I asked myself if it also had something to do with my repudiation of John Peddar I was getting near the truth but I thought it too far-fetched. Aware that I had somehow offended, I could never believe that I had done anything reprehensible enough to deserve the treatment I got.

The day after the bathers had extended their invitation to me – the final overture, as it happened, from any of them – I went to church. I tried to go to church. It was St John's day and the church's dedication was to St John, and I had noticed that a special service was always held on that day, whether it fell during the week or on a Sunday. They had a wonderful organist at St John's, a Burns who came from a village some miles away but was, I suppose, a cousin of that Angela, the hairdresser. The visiting clergyman preached a good sermon and everyone sang the hymns lustily.

One of the sidesmen or wardens, I don't know what he was but he was a Stamford, I knew that, met me in the church porch. He was waiting for me. They knew I'd come and they despatched him to wait for me.

'The service is private this morning,' he said.

'What do you mean, private?'

'I'm not obliged to explain to you,' he said and he stood with his back against the heavy old door, barring my way.

There wasn't much I could do. There was nothing I could do. I couldn't get involved in a struggle with him. I went back to my car and drove home, indignant and humiliated. I wasn't frightened then, not yet, not by then.

A week later I came down again. I came on the Friday evening as I often did when I could make it. Of course, I'd thought a lot about what had happened when I tried to get into the church but the incident became less a cause for rage and indignation the more I considered it. Perhaps I'd asked my question aggressively and Stamford, also being inclined to belligerence, had answered in kind. Perhaps he was having a bad day, was already angry. It was nonsense, I decided, to suppose 'they' had sent him, it was paranoia. He happened to be there, was probably just arriving himself, when I arrived.

All this, somewhat recycled and much reviewed, was passing through my mind as I reached the village at dusk that Friday evening. They knew I would come, knew too approximately what time I'd come and besides that, I had to pass the Greshams' house two minutes before I entered the village proper. They used the phone and their own grapevine.

It was like pictures that one sees of streets that royalty or some other celebrity is about to pass through. They were all outside, standing in front of their houses. They stood in front gardens if they had them, on the road itself if they didn't. But those waiting to welcome someone famous are preparing to smile and wave, even to cheer. These people, these Kirkmans and Burnses, Stamfords and Wantages, Clementses and Atkinses and Fowlers, all of them, some with children in their arms, tall, fair, handsome people, stood and stared.

As I approached I saw their eyes all turned in my direction and as I passed I've no doubt their eyes followed, for in my driving mirror I could see them staring after me. All down that village street they were outside their houses, waiting for me. Not one of them smiled. Not one of them even moved beyond turning their eyes to follow me. Outside the last house three old people stood, a woman between two men, all holding hands. I don't know why this handholding particularly unnerved me. Perhaps it was the implication of total solidarity it conveyed. Now I think it symbolised what I had rejected, diffused love.

A little way down the road I slowed and saw in the mirror the three of them turn and go back into the house. I drove to Gothic House and when I got out of the car I found that I was trembling. They had done very little but they had frightened me. I hadn't much food in the house and I'd meant to go to the village shop in the morning, but now I wouldn't go, I'd take the road that didn't pass through the village to the town four miles away.

I've since wondered if they approached every newcomer to the village or if they applied some system of selection. Would they, for instance, tolerate someone for the sake of a spouse, as in the case of the farmer from Lynn? Would elderly retired people be welcome? I thought not, since their principal motivation was to draw in new genes to their pool and the old were past breeding.

I should therefore, I suppose, have been flattered, for I was getting on for forty. Did they hope I would settle there, would *live* there, *marry* some selected man? I shall never know. I shall never know why they wanted Ben, although it has occurred to me that it might have been for his intellect. He had a good mind and perhaps they thought that brains too might be passed on. Perhaps whoever decided these things – all of them in concert? Like a parliament? – discerned a falling intelligence quotient in the village.

He too tried to go to church. It was Sandy's wedding and Susannah had said they would go to it together. His mind had magnified her invitation to a firm promise and he still believed she'd honour it. He stuck for a long while to his belief that, having said many times that she loved him, she would come to him and stay with him.

He wasn't, then, frightened of the village the way I was. He walked there boldly and knocked on the Peddars' door. Carol opened it. When she saw who it was she tried to shut the door but he put his foot in the way. He pushed past her into the house and she came after him as he kicked the door open and burst into their living room. There was nobody there, all the Peddars but Carol had already gone to the wedding. He didn't believe her and he ran upstairs, going into all the rooms.

546

'Where's Susannah?'

'Gone,' she said. 'Gone to the church. You'll never get her, you might as well give up. Why don't you go away?'

Leave the house, was what he thought she meant. He didn't, then, take in the wider implication. Sandy was just arriving at the church when he got there, Sandy in a morning coat and carrying a topper, looking completely different from the handyman and window cleaner Ben knew. His best man was one of the Kirkmans, similarly dressed, red-faced, very blond, self-conscious. Ben stood by the gate and let them go in. Then he tried to get in himself and his way was barred by two tall men who came out of the porch and simply marched at him. Ben didn't recognise them, though they sounded from his description like George Whiteson and Roger Atkins. They marched at him and he stood his ground.

For a moment. It's hard to do that when you're being borne down upon but Ben did his best. He walked at them and there was an impasse as he struggled to break through the high wall their bodies made and they pushed at him with the flats of their hands. They were determined not to assault him directly, Ben was sure of that. He, however, was indifferent as to whether he assaulted them or not. He said he beat at them with his fists and that was when other men joined in, John Peddar who came out of the church, Philip Wantage who had just arrived with his daughter, the bride. They pinned Ben's arms behind him, lifted him up and dropped him on to the grass on the other side of the wall.

With these indignities heaped on him, he sat up in time to see Rosalind Wantage in white lace and streaming veil proceed up the path with a bevy of pink-clad Kirkman and Atkins and Clements girls behind her. He tried to go after them but was once more stopped at the porch. Another tall, straight-backed guardian gave him a heavy push, which sent him sprawling, and retreated into the church. Ben sprang at the door in time to hear a heavy bolt pushed across it on the inside.

The more of this they did the more he believed that they might be acting on Susannah's behalf but not with her consent. It was a conspiracy to keep her from him. He sat on the grass outside the church gate and waited for the wedding to be over. It was a fine, sunny day and such windows in the church as could be opened were open. Hymns, swelling from the throats of almost the entire village, floated out to him, 'Love divine, all loves excelling' and 'The voice that breathed o'er Eden'.

For dower of blessed children,
For love and faith's sweet sake,
For high mysterious union
Which nought on earth may break.

No one should break the union he had with Susannah and, sitting out there in the sunshine, perhaps he thought of the night they had spent, of transcendence and sex made spirit, that he had written of in his diary. It didn't occur to him then, though it did later, that a high mysterious union was what that village had, what those village people had.

They began coming out of the church, bride and bridegroom first, bridesmaids, parents. Susannah came out with her parents and Carol. He said that when he saw her he saw no one else. Everyone else became shadows, gradually became invisible, when she was there. She came down the path, let herself out of the gate. What the others did he said he didn't know, if they stared after her or made to follow her, he had no eyes for them.

Susannah was in a pale-blue dress. If she had stood against the sky, he said, it would have disappeared into the blueness, it was like a thin, scanty slip of sky. She pushed back her hair with long pale fingers. He wanted to fall at her feet, her beautiful white feet, and worship her.

'You must go away, Ben,' she said to him. 'I've told you that before but you didn't hear me.'

'They've put you up to this,' he said. 'You're wrong to listen. Why do you listen? You're old enough to make up your own mind. Don't you understand that away from here you can have a great life? You can do anything.'

'I don't want us to have to hurt you, Ben.' She didn't say 'them' she said 'us'. She said 'we'. 'We needn't do that if you go. You can have a day, you don't have to go till Monday, but you must go on Monday.'

'You and I will go on Monday.' But her use of that 'us' and that 'we' had shaken him. 'You're coming with me, Susannah,' he said, but his doubts had begun.

'No, Ben, you'll go. You'll have to.' She added, as if inconsequentially, but it was a consequence, it was an absolute corollary, 'Sandy's buying the cottage, grandma's cottage, for him and Roz to live in.'


I haven't said much about the forest.

The forest surrounded the lake in a horseshoe shape with a gap on the side where the road left its shores and turned towards the village. Behind the arms of the horseshoe it extended for many miles, dense and intersected only by rides or as a scattered sprinkling of trees with heathy clearings between them. It was protected and parts of it were a nature reserve, the habitat of the Little Owl and the Greater Spotted Woodpecker. If I haven't mentioned it much, if I've avoided referring to it, it's because of the experience I had within its depths, the event that drove me from the village and made me decide to sell Gothic House.

Already, by then, the place was losing its charms for me. I avoided it for a whole month after that Friday night drive through the village, confronted as I'd been by the silent staring inhabitants. But I still liked the house and its situation, I loved the lake and walking in the forest, the nightingales in spring and the owl calling in winter, the great skies and the swans and water lilies. Unwilling to face that silent hostility again, I drove down very late. I passed through half an hour before midnight.

No one was about but every light was on. They had turned on the lights in every room in the front of their houses, upstairs and down. The village was ablaze. And yet not a face showed at any of those bright windows. It was if they had turned on their lights and left, departed somewhere, perhaps to be swallowed up by the forest. I think those lights were more frightening than the hostile stares had been, and then and there I resolved not to pass through the village again, for, as I slowed and turned to look, the lights were one after another turned off, all died into darkness. No one had departed, they were there and they had done their work.

I wouldn't pass through the village again, not, at least, until they had got over whatever it was, had come to accept me once more. I really believed, then, that this would happen. But not passing through hardly meant I had to stay indoors. There is, after all, little point in a weekend retreat in the country if you never go out of it.

On Saturday afternoons I was in the habit of going for a walk in the forest. If I had a guest I asked that guest to go with me, if I was alone I went alone. They knew I was alone that weekend. If I hadn't seen them behind their lights they had seen me, alone at the wheel in an otherwise empty car.

At three in the afternoon I set out into the forest. It was May, just one year before Ben went there, not a glorious day but fine enough, the sun coming out for half an hour, then retreating behind white fluffy cloud. A little wind was blowing, not then much more than a breeze. Ten minutes in and I saw the first of them. I was walking on the wide path that ran for several miles into the forest's heart. He stood close to the silver-grey trunk of a beech tree; I recognised him as George Whiteson, but if he recognised me – and of course he did, I was why he was there – he gave no sign of it. He wasn't staring this time, but looking at the ground around his feet.

A hundred yards on three of them were sitting on a log, Kirkmans or Kirkmans and an Atkins, I forget and it doesn't matter, but I saw them and they affected not to see me, and almost immediately there were more, a man and a woman on the ground embraced – a demonstration for my benefit, I suppose – two children in the branches of a tree, a knot of women, those bathers, standing in a ring, holding hands.

The sun was shining on to a clearing and it was beautiful in there, all the tiny wild flowers in blossom in the close heathy turf, crabapple trees flowering and the sunlight flitting, as the wind drove clouds across it and bared it again. But it was terrible too, with those people, the whole village it seemed, there waiting for me but making no sign they'd seen me. They were everywhere, near at hand or in the depths of the forest, close to the path or just discernible at the distant end of a green ride, Burnses and Whitesons, Atkinses and Fowlers and Stamfords, men and women, young and old. And as I walked on, as I tried to stick it out and keep on, I became aware that they were following me. As I passed they fell into silent step behind, so that when I turned round – it was quite a long time before I turned round – I saw behind me this stream of people padding along quietly on the sandy path, on last year's dry fallen leaves.

It was as if I were the Pied Piper. But the children I led were not in happy thrall to me, not following me to some paradise, but dogging my steps with silent menace, driving me ahead of them. To what end? To what confrontation in the forest depths?

I was terribly afraid. It's not an exaggeration to say I feared for my life. The whole tribe of them, as one, had gone mad, had succumbed to spontaneous psychopathy, had conceived some fearful paranoiac hatred of me. They would surround me in some dark green grove and murder me. In their high mysterious union. In silence.

But I never quite came to believe that. If I wanted to crouch on the ground and cover my head and whimper to them to let me go, to leave me alone, I didn't do that either. By some sort of effort of will that I achieved, God knows how, I turned, clenched my fists, set one foot before the other and began walking back the way I'd come.

This brought me face to face with the vanguard of them, with John Peddar and one of his daughters, Susannah herself for all I know. They fell back out of my path. It was gracefully done, one by one they all yielded, half bowing, as if this were some complicated ritual dance and they were giving place to the principal dancer who must now pass with prescribed steps down the space between them. Only I had no partner in this minuet, I was alone.

No one spoke. I didn't speak. I wanted to, I wanted to challenge them, to ask why, but I couldn't. I suppose I knew I wouldn't get an answer or perhaps that no voice would come when I tried to speak. The speechlessness was one of the worst things, that and the closed faces and the silent movements. Another was the sound of the rising wind.

They followed me all the way back. While I was in the forest the wind could be heard but not much felt. It met me as I emerged on to the lake shore and even held me back for a moment as if pushing me with its hands. The surface of the lake was ruffled into waves and the tree branches were pulled and stretched and beaten. By the shore the people who followed me let me go and turned aside, two hundred of them I suppose, at least two hundred.

From having been perfectly silent, they broke into talk and laughter as soon as they were separated from me and, buffeted by the wind, made their way homewards. I ran into my house. I shut myself inside but I could still hear their voices, raised in conversation, in laughter, and at last in song. It would be something to chronicle, wouldn't it, if they'd sung an ancient ballad, a treasure for an anthropologist, something whose words had come down unbroken from the time of Langland or Chaucer? But they didn't. The tune I heard carried by the wind, receding, at last dying into silence, was 'Over the Rainbow'.

That evening the gale became a storm. Trees went down on the edge of the woodland and four tiles blew off the roof of Gothic House. The people of the village weren't to blame but that was not how it seemed to me at the time, as I cowered in my house, as I lay in bed listening to the storm, the crying of the wind and the crash of falling tree branches. It was just a lucky happening for them that this gale blew up immediately after their slow dramatic pursuit of me in the forest. But that night I could have believed them all witches and magicians, Wicca people who could control the elements and raise a wind.

9

They had something else in store for Ben.

'I was determined not to go,' he said. 'I would have gone immediately if Susannah had come too but without her I was going to stay put. On the Sunday I went back to the village to try to find her but no one would answer the door to me, not just the Peddars, no one.'

'It was brave of you to try,' I said and that was when I told him what had happened to me, the silent starers, the blazing lights, the pursuit through the forest.

'I'd stopped being a coward – well, I thought I had.'

Next morning someone was due to come and clean the house. Which girl would they send? Or was it possible Susannah might come? Of course, he hadn't slept much, he hadn't really slept for four nights and exhaustion was beginning to tell on him. If he managed to doze off it would be to plunge into dreams of Susannah, always erotic dreams, but deeply unsatisfying. In them she was always naked. She began making love with him, kissing him, placing his hands on her body as was her habit, kissing his fingers and taking them to the places she loved to be touched. Then, suddenly, she would spring out of his arms and run to whomsoever had come into the room, Kim Gresham or George Whiteson or Tom Kirkman, it could be any of them, and in a frenzy begin stripping off their clothes, nuzzling them, gasping with excitement. He'd reached a point where he didn't want to sleep for fear of those dreams.

By eight thirty next morning he'd been up for more than two hours. He'd made himself a pot of coffee and drunk it. His head was banging and he felt sick. The time went by, nine o'clock went by, and no one came. No one would come now, he knew that.

The weather had changed and become dull and cool. He went outside for a while and walked about, he couldn't say why. There wasn't anyone to be seen, there seldom was, but he had a feeling that he was being watched. He took his work into the ground-floor front room because he knew it would be impossible for him to stay upstairs in the back. If he did that, sat up there where he could only see the rear garden and the forest, something terrible might happen in the front, by the lake, some awful event take place that he ought to witness. It was an unreasonable feeling but he gave in to it and moved into the living room.

The author of *The Golden Apple* was analysing Helen, her narcissism, her choice of Menelaus declared by hanging a wreath round his neck, her elopement with Paris. Ben tried to concentrate on translating this, firstly to understand which events stemmed in the writer's estimation from destiny and which from character, but he couldn't stop himself constantly glancing up at the window. Half an hour had passed, and he had translated only two lines, when a car came along the road from the village. It parked by the lake in front of Gothic House.

I suppose there were about a hundred yards between the house and the little beach, and it was on the grass just above the beach. He watched and waited for the driver or the driver and passenger to get out of it and come up to the house. No one did. Nothing moved. Then, about ten minutes later, the car windows were wound down. He saw that the driver was Kim Gresham and his passenger an unknown woman.

He tried to work. He translated the lines about Helen taking one of her children on the elopement with her, read what he had written and saw that the prose was barely comprehensible and the sense lost. There was no point in working in these conditions. He wondered what would happen if he tried to go out and felt sure that if he attempted a walk to the village those two would stop him. They would seize hold of him and frogmarch him back to the house. 'I thought of calling the police,' he said.

'Why didn't you?'

'The man they'd have sent lived in the police house in the village. He's one of them, he's called Michael Wantage. If anyone else had come, what could I have said? That two people were sitting in a parked car admiring the view? I didn't call the police. I got my car out of the garage.'

He put his work aside and decided to drive to the town four miles away and do his weekly shopping. He watched them watching him as he backed the car out.

'I think they were hoping I'd fetch out suitcases and the word processor and my books. Then they'd know I was being obedient and leaving. They'd just have let me go, I'm sure of that. A sigh of relief would have been heaved and they'd have gone back to the village.'

As it was, they followed him. He saw the car behind him all the way. They made no attempt at secrecy. In the town he left his car and went to the supermarket but, as far as he knew, they remained in theirs. When he got back they were still sitting in their car and when he drove home they were behind him.

In the early afternoon a second car arrived and the first one left. They were operating a shift system. From Ben's description it seemed as if Marion Kirkman was driving the second car. He had no doubt as to the identity of her passenger. It was Iris Peddar. Later on another car replaced it and was still there when darkness came.

Perhaps a car was there all night. He didn't know. By then he didn't want to know, he just desperately hoped this surveillance would have ceased by morning. Just after sunrise he pulled back the curtains and looked out. A car was there. He couldn't see who was inside it. It was then that he told himself he could be as strong and as resolute as they. He could stick it out. He simply wouldn't look, he'd do what seemed impossible the day before, work in the back, not look, ignore them. They meant him no harm, they only mounted this guard to stop him going to the village to find Susannah. But there must be other ways of reaching Susannah. He could do a huge circular detour via the town and come into the village from the other direction. He could park *his* car outside her father's house. But if he did that, all that, any of that, they would follow him . . .

All that day he stayed indoors. He couldn't work, he couldn't read, he didn't want to eat. At one point he lay down and slept, only to dream of Susannah. This time he was in a tower, tall and narrow with a winding stair inside like a windmill, and he was watching her from above, through a hole in the floor. He heard her footsteps climbing the stairs, hers and another's, and when she came into the room below she was with Sandy Clements. Sandy began to undress her, taking the bracelet from her arm and the necklace from her neck, and held one finger of her right hand as she stepped naked out of the blue dress. She looked up to the ceiling and smiled, stretching out her hands, one to him, one to Sandy, turning her body languorously for them to gaze at and worship. He awoke with a cry and, forgetting his resolve, stumbled into the front room to look for the car. A red one this time, Teresa Gresham's. She was alone in it.

At about seven in the evening, long before dark, she got out of the car and came up to the house. He'd forgotten he'd left the back door unlocked. She walked in. He asked her what the hell she thought she was doing.

'You asked me to come up and do your ironing,' she said.

'That's rubbish,' he said. 'I asked you nothing. Now get out.'

She had apparently been gone five minutes when he saw, in the far distance, a bicycle approaching. The very first time she came Susannah had been on a bicycle and that was who he thought it was. The surveillance was over, she had persuaded them to end it, and she was coming to him. She had told them they couldn't prevent her being with him, she was over age, she loved him. He opened the front door and stood on the doorstep waiting for her.

It wasn't Susannah. It was the younger of her two sisters, the fourteen-year-old Julie. Disappointment turned inside his body as love does, with a wrench, an apparent lurching of the heart. But he called out a greeting to her. She rested her bicycle against the garden wall, fastened chain and padlock to its front wheel, the good girl, the responsible teenager. Who did she think would steal it out here? He let her into the house, certain she must have a message for him, perhaps a message from Susannah who was allowed to reach him in no other way.

She was a pretty little girl – his words – who was much shorter than her sisters, who clearly would never reach Susannah's height, with a very slight childish figure. She wore a short skirt and a white sweatshirt, ankle socks and white trainers. Her straw-coloured hair was shoulder-length and she had a fringe.

'She looked exactly like the girl in the Millais painting, the one who's sitting up in bed and looking surprised but not unhappy.'

'I know the one,' I said. 'It's called *Just Awake*.'

'Is it?' he said. 'I wonder what Millais meant by "awake". D'you think a double meaning was intended?'

Julie sat down sedately in my living room. He asked her if she had a message for him from Susannah and she shook her head. 'You asked me to come,' she said. 'You phoned up an hour ago and said if I'd come over you'd let me have those books you told Susannah I could have.'

'What books?' He had no idea what she meant.

'For my schoolwork. For my English homework.'

It was at this point that he had the dreadful feeling they had sent her as the next in progression. They'd decided it was still worth trying to keep him and make him one of them. He didn't want Lavinia or Carol, stubbornly he still wanted monogamy with Susannah, but since he'd rejected the more mature Teresa, wasn't it possible he'd be attracted by her antithesis, by this child?

Of course, he was wrong there. They weren't perverse. In their peculiar way they were innocent. But by this time he'd have believed anything of them and he did, for a few minutes, believe they'd sent her to tempt him. He'd been sitting down but he jumped up and she too got up.

'Why are you really here?'

She forgot about the books. 'I'm to tell you to go away,' she said. 'I'm to say it's your last chance.'

'This is ridiculous,' he said. 'I'm not listening to this.'

'You can stay here tonight.' She said it airily, as if it were absolutely her province to give him permission. 'You can stay here tonight but you must go tomorrow. Or we'll make you go.'

He didn't once touch her. She didn't touch him. She left the house, unlocked the padlock on her bicycle chain and got on the bicycle. It's almost impossible for a practised cyclist to fall off a bicycle, but she did. She fell off in the road and the machine fell on her. He lifted the bicycle off her, put out his hand to help her up, pulled her to her feet. She jumped on the bicycle and rode off, turning round to call something after him but he didn't hear what it was. He returned to the house and thought that in the morning he'd go to the village and get into her parents' house, even if that meant breaking a window or kicking the door in.

In the morning the car was back. It was parked at the lake shore, the driver was David Stamford and the passenger Gillian Atkins.


If he went to the town and from there by the back way into the village, they would follow him. He had no doubt that they would physically prevent him from driving or walking along the lake shore road. It was harassment, their simply being there was harassment, but imagine telling this tale to the police, imagine proving anything.

Working on his translation was impossible. Attempting to find Susannah would be difficult, but he tried. He phoned the Peddars, Sandy Clements, the shop, the pub, Angela Burns. One after the other, when they heard his voice they put down the phone. It was deeply unnerving and after Angela's silence and the click of the receiver going into its rest, he stopped trying.

But there was some comfort to be drawn from these abortive phone calls. He'd been able to make them. They hadn't cut his phone line. It's some measure of the state he was getting into that he even considered they might. This negativity, this absence of some hypothetical action, told him there would be no violence used against him. He hadn't exactly been afraid of violence but he'd been apprehensive about it.

He sat down, in the back of the house where he couldn't see that car, and thought about what they'd done. Not so very much, really. They'd stopped him going to a wedding and followed his car and sent him to Coventry. Surely he could stick it out if that was all that was going to happen? If he had Susannah he could. He had to stay at Gothic House for her sake, he had to stay until he got her away.

'I thought of going out to them,' he said to me, 'to those two,

Stamford and the Atkins woman, and later on to the people who replaced them, the Wantages, Rosalind's parents, of going out to them and asking what they wanted of me. Of course I knew, really, I knew they wanted me to leave, but I wanted to hear someone say it, and not a child of fourteen. And then I thought I'd say, OK, I'll leave but I'm taking Susannah with me.'

By now he couldn't bear to leave his observers unobserved and he sat in the front window watching them while they watched him. He still hadn't been able to bring himself to carry out his intention. He just sat there watching and thinking of how to put his question and what words to choose to frame his resolution. In the middle of the afternoon a terrible thing happened. He had calculated that the Wantages' shift would end at four – that was the state he had got into, that he was measuring his watchers' shifts – and sure enough at five to four another car arrived. The driver was an unknown man, his passenger Susannah.

The car was parked so that its nearside, and therefore the passenger's seat, was towards Gothic House. He looked out into Susannah's eyes and she looked back, her face quite expressionless. There are times when thinking is dismissed as useless, when one stops thinking and just acts. He had thought enough. He walked, marched, out there, calling her name.

She wound down the window. The face she presented to him, he said, was that of a woman in a car of whom a stranger has asked the way. It was as if she had never seen him before. The man in the driving seat didn't even turn round. He was staring at the lake with rapt attention. He looked, Ben said, as if he'd seen the Loch Ness monster.

'Please get out of the car and come inside, Susannah,' he said to her.

She was silent. She went on staring as if he really was that stranger and she was considering what directions to give him.

'We can talk about all this, Susannah. Come inside and talk, will you please? I know you don't want to leave this place but that's because you don't know anywhere else. Won't you come with me and try?'

Slowly she shook her head. 'You have to go,' she said.

'Not without you.'

'I'm not coming. You have to go alone.'

She touched her companion's arm and he turned his head. From that touch, intimate but relaxed, Ben somehow knew this young fair-haired man was her lover as he had been her lover, and for a moment the sky went black and a sharp pain pierced his chest.

She watched him as if calculating all this. Then she said, 'Why don't you go now? You'll go if you've any sense.'

The young man beside her said, 'I'd advise you to leave before dark.'

'We'll follow you through the village,' said Susannah. 'Then you'll be safe. Pack your bags and put them in the car.'

'Shall we say an hour?' That was the young man, in his coarse rustic voice.

Ben went back into the house. He had no intention of packing but at the same time he didn't know what to do next. The idea came to him that if he could only get Susannah alone all would be well. He could talk to her, remind her, persuade her. The question was how to do that. Not at the hairdresser's, he'd tried that. She baby-sat for Jennifer Fowler one evening a week, an evening she'd never been able to come to him, a Wednesday – those few Wednesdays, how bereft and lonely he'd felt. Tomorrow, then, he'd somehow get to the village and Jennifer Fowler's house. They'd only kept up their surveillance till dark the night before and it would be dark by nine . . .

He sat inside the window watching Susannah for a long time. It was marginally better to see her, he'd decided, than to be in some other part of the house, not seeing her but knowing she was there. To gaze and gaze was both pleasure and pain. The strange thing was, he told me, that watching her was never boring and he couldn't imagine that applying to any other person or object on earth.

He also watched, in sick dread, to see if she and the man with her touched each other or moved towards each other or gave any sign of the relationship he had at first been sure was theirs. But they didn't. As far as he could tell, they didn't. They talked and of course he wondered what they said. He saw Susannah's head go back against the head-rest on the seat and her eyes close.

The afternoon was calm and dull, white-skied. Because there was no wind the surface of the water was quite smooth and the forest trees were still. He went into the back of the house to watch the sunset, a bronze and red spectacular sunset striped with black-rimmed thin cloud. These signs of time going by seemed to bring tomorrow night closer, Wednesday night when he could be alone with her. He began planning how to do it.

When he went back to the front window the car was moving, turning round prior to leaving. And no other had come to replace it. He began to feel a lightness, something that was almost excitement. They couldn't keep her from him if they both wanted to be together and if they could influence her, how much more could he? Any relationship between her and her companion in the car had been in his imagination. Probably, at some time or other, she had slept with Kim Gresham, but that was only to be expected. He had never had any ideas of being the first with her or even desired to be.

After a little while he poured himself a drink. Never much of a drinker, he had nevertheless had to stop himself having recourse to whisky these past few days. But at eight o'clock at night he could indulge himself. He began thinking of getting something to eat but he hadn't been outside all day except to speak those few brief words to Susannah and at about nine, when the twilight was deepening, he walked down to the lake.

Flies swarmed a few inches above its surface and fish were jumping for them. The water bubbled and broke as a slippery body leapt, twisted, gleaming silver in the last of the light. He watched, growing calm and almost fatalistic, resigning himself to the hard struggle ahead, but knowing that anyone as determined as he would be bound to win.

Because their lights were off and dusk had by now fallen, because they drove quietly and in convoy, he didn't see the cars until the first of them was almost upon him.

10

He went back into the house. He didn't quite know what else to do. They parked the cars on the little beach and on the grass, there were about twenty of them, and he said it was like people going to some function in a village hall and parking on the green outside. Only they didn't get out of their cars until he was indoors and then not immediately.

You have to understand that it was all in darkness, or absence of light, for it wasn't quite dark. The cars were unlit and so was the house. Once he was inside he tried putting lights on but then he couldn't see what they meant to do. He put on the light in the hall and watched them through the front room window.

They sat inside their cars. He recognised the Wantages' car and Sandy Clements's and of course John Peddar's white van. There was just enough light left to see that. He thought then of phoning the police, he often had that thought, and he always came to the same conclusion, that there was nothing he could say. They had a right to be there. For all he knew, they'd explain their presence by saying they'd come fishing or owl-watching. But by now he was frightened. He was also determined not to show his fear whatever they did.

The doors of the white van opened and the four people inside it got out, Susannah and her parents and one of the sisters. He stepped back from the window and moved into the hall. One after the other he heard car doors slamming. It seemed as if an hour passed before the front doorbell rang, though it was probably less than a minute. He breathed in slowly and out slowly and opened the door.

John Peddar pushed his way into the house, or rather, he pushed his daughter Julie into the house and followed behind her. Next came his wife and Susannah. Ben saw about forty people in the front garden, and on the path and the doorstep, and once he had let Susannah in he tried to shut the door but his effort was useless against the steady but entirely non-violent onslaught. They simply pushed their way in, close together, a body of men and women, a relentless shoving crowd. He retreated before them into the living room where the Peddars already were. He backed against the fireplace and stood there with his elbows on the mantelpiece, because there was nowhere further that he could go, and faced them, feeling that now he knew how it was to be an animal at bay.

My small front room was full of people. He thought at this moment literally that they meant to kill him, that as one they had gone mad. He thought, as I had thought in the wood, that the collective unconscious they seemed to share had taken a turn into madness and they had come there to do him to death. And the worst thing was, one of the worst things, that he grouped Susannah with them. Suddenly he lost his feeling for her, she became one of them and his passion evaporated with his fear. He could look at her, and did, without desire or tenderness or even nostalgia, but with distaste and the same fear as he had for her family and her neighbours.

At first he couldn't speak. He swallowed, he cleared his throat. 'What do you want?'

John Peddar answered him. He said something Ben couldn't believe he'd heard aright.

'*What?*'

'You heard but I'll say it again. I told you you could have my Carol, not my little girl, not my Julie.'

Ben said, his voice strengthening, 'I don't know what you mean.'

'Yes, you do. D'you know how old she is? She's not fourteen.' He was still holding the girl in front of him and now he pushed her forward, displaying her. 'See the bruises on her? See her leg? Look at that blue all up her arms.'

There was a murmur that seemed to swell all round him, like the buzzing of angry bees. His eyes went to Susannah and he thought he saw on that face that was no longer lovely to him the hint of a tiny malicious smile. 'Your daughter fell off her bicycle,' he said. 'She hurt her leg falling off her bicycle. The bruises on her arm I may have made, I don't know. I may have made them when I helped her to her feet, that's all.'

The child said in a harsh unchildish voice, 'You were going to rape me.'

'Is that why you've come here?' he said. 'To accuse me of that?'

'You tried to rape me.' The accusation, slightly differently phrased, was repeated. 'I fell over when I ran out of the house. Because you were trying to do it.'

'This is rubbish,' he said. 'Will you please go.' He looked at Susannah. 'All of you, please leave.'

'We've a witness,' said Iris. 'Teresa saw it all.'

'Teresa wasn't in the house,' he said.

'That's not true,' Teresa Gresham said. 'I'd been there an hour when Julie came. I expect you'd forgotten, there was a lot you forgot once you got to touch her.' She said to the Peddars, 'I came out of the kitchen and I saw it all.'

'What do you want of me?' he said again.

'We don't want to go to the police,' John Peddar said.

His wife said, 'It's humiliating for our little girl.'

'Not that it's in any way her fault. But we'll go to them if you don't go. You go tonight and this'll be the last you hear of it. Go now or we get the police. Me and Julie and her mother and Teresa. You can phone them on his phone, Iris.'

He imagined the police coming and his having absolutely no defence except the truth, which would collapse in the face of Julie's evidence and the Peddars' and Teresa's. If that weren't enough they'd no doubt produce Sandy Clements who would also have been there watching, cleaning the windows, perhaps, or weeding the garden. Sandy he could pick out of the crowd packed into the room, just squeezed in, leaning against the closed door beside his new wife.

'None of this is true,' he said. 'It's lies and you know it.'

They didn't try to deny it. They weren't interested in whether something was true or not, only in their power to control him. None of them smiled now or looked anything but grim. One of the strangest things, he said, was that they were all perfectly calm. There was no anxiety. They knew he'd do as they asked.

'This is a false accusation, entirely fabricated,' he said.

'Iris,' said John Peddar, 'phone the police.'

'Where's the phone?'

Teresa Gresham said, 'It's in the back room. I'll come with you.'

Sandy moved away from the door and opened it for them. The crowd made a passage, squeezing back against each other in a curiously intimate way, not seeming to resist the pressure of other bodies. Breasts pushed against arms, hips rested against bellies, without inhibition, without awkwardness. But perhaps that wasn't curious, perhaps it wasn't curious at all. They stood close together, crushed together, as if in some collective embrace, cheek to cheek, hand to shoulder, thigh to thigh.

Then Teresa went out of the room. Iris, following her, had reached the door when Ben said, 'All right. I'll go.'

He was deeply humiliated. He kept his head lowered so that he couldn't meet Susannah's eyes. His shame was so great that he felt a burning flush spread across his neck and face. But what else could he have done? One man is helpless against many. In those moments he knew every one of those people and those left behind in the village would stand by the Peddars. No doubt, if need was, they would produce other evidence of his proclivities and he remembered how, once, he had taken hold of Carol Peddar by the wrist.

'I'll go now,' he said.

They didn't leave. They helped his departure. He went upstairs and they followed him, pushed their way into his bedroom, one of them found his suitcases, another set them on the bed and opened their lids. Teresa Gresham opened the wardrobe and took out his clothes. Kathy Gresham and Angela Burns folded them and packed them in the cases. No one touched him, but once he was in that bedroom he was their prisoner. They packed his hairbrush and his shoes. John Peddar came out of the bathroom with his sponge bag and his razor and toothbrush. All the time Julie, the injured one, sat on the bed and stared at him.

Sandy Clements and George Whiteson carried the cases out of the room. One of the women produced a carrier bag and asked him if they'd got everything of his. When he said they had but for his dressing gown and the book he'd been reading in bed, she put those items in the bag, and then they let him leave the room.

If they were enjoying themselves there was no sign of it. They were calm, unsmiling, mostly silent. Teresa led them into the back room where he had worked on his translation, admitted him and closed the door behind him. Gillian Atkins – she was bound to be there, his nemesis – brought two plastic bags with her and into these they cleared his table of books and papers. They did it carefully, lining up the pages, clipping them together, careful not to crease or crumple. A man Ben didn't recognise, though his colouring, height and manner were consistent with the village people, unplugged his word processor and put it into its case. Then his dictionary went into the second bag.

Again he was asked if there was anything they'd forgotten. He shook his head and they let him go downstairs. Gillian Atkins went into the kitchen and came back with a bag containing the contents of the fridge.

'Now give me the door key,' Mark Gresham said.

Ben asked why. Why should he?

'You won't need it. I'll send it back to the present owner.'

Ben gave him the key. He really had no choice. He left the house in the midst of them. Their bodies pressed against him, warm, shapely, herbal-smelling. They eased him out, nudging and elbowing him, and when the last of them had left and turned out the hall light, closed the door behind them. His cases and bags were already in the boot of his car, his word processor in its case carefully placed on the floor in front of the back seat. He looked for Susannah to say goodbye but she had already left, he could see the red tail lights of the car she was in receding into the distance along the shore road.

They accompanied him in convoy through the village, two cars ahead of him and all the rest behind. Every light was on and some of the older people, the ones who hadn't come to Gothic House, were in their front gardens to see him go. Not all the cars came on, some fell away when their owners' homes were reached, but the Peddars and the Clementses continued to precede him, Gillian Atkins with Angela Burns continued to follow him and he thought the Greshams but he wasn't sure of that because he couldn't see the car colour in the dark.

After ten miles, almost at the approach to an A road, Gillian Atkins cut off his further progress the way a police car does, by overtaking him and pulling sharply ahead of him. He was forced to stop. The car behind stopped. Those in front already had. Gillian Atkins came round to his window, which he refused to open. But he'd forgotten to lock the door and she opened it.

'Don't come back,' was all she said.

They let him go on alone.

He had to stop for a while on the A road in a lay-by because his hands were shaking and his breathing erratic. He thought he might choke. But after a while things improved and he was able to drive on to London.

## 11

My key came home before he did.

There was no note to accompany it. I knew where it had come from only by the postmark. No one answered the phone, either at Gothic House or Ben's London flat. I drove to Gothic House, making the detour through the town to reach it, and found it empty, all Ben's possessions gone.

I phoned the estate agent and put the house up for sale.

A month passed before Ben surfaced. He asked if he could come over and, once with me, he stayed. The translation was done, he had worked on it unremittingly, thinking of nothing else, closing off his mind, until it was finished.

'Helen went back to her husband,' he said. 'He took her home to Sparta and she brought the heroes nepenthe in a golden dish, which made them forget their sorrows. My author got a lot of analytical insights out of that.'

'What was nepenthe?' I said.

'No one knows. Opium? Cannabis maybe?' He was silent for a while, then suddenly vociferous. 'Do you know what I'd like? I've thought a lot about this. I'd like them to build a road right through that village, one of those bypasses there are all these protests about. They never work, the protests, do they? The road gets built. And that's what I'd like to hear, that some town nearby has to be bypassed and the village is in the way, the village has to be cut in half, split up, destroyed.'

'It doesn't seem very likely,' I said, thinking of the forest, the empty arable landscape.

After that he never mentioned the place, so when I heard, as I did from time to time, how my efforts to sell Gothic House were proceeding I said nothing to him. I didn't tell him when I heard, from the same source, that old Mrs Fowler had died and had left, in excess of all expectations, rather a large sum.

By then he'd shown me the diary and told me his story. In the details he told me far more than I often cared to hear. He was still sharing my house, though he often talked of buying a new flat for himself, and one evening, when we were alone and warm and I felt very close to him, when the story was long told, I asked him – more or less – if we should make it permanent, if we should change the sharing to a living together, with its subtle difference of meaning.

I took his hand and he leaned towards me to kiss me absently. It was the sort of kiss that told me everything: that I shouldn't have asked or even suggested, that he regretted I had, that we must forget it ever happened.

'You see,' he said, after a few moments in which I tried to conquer my humiliation, 'it sounds foolish, it sounds absurd, but it's not only that I've never got over what happened, though that's part of it. The sad, dreadful thing is that I want to be back there, I want to be with them. Not just Susannah, of course I want *her*, I've never stopped wanting her for more than a few minutes, but it's to be with all of them that I want, and in that place. Sometimes I have a dream that I am – back there, I mean. I said yes to the offers, I was accepted and I stayed.'

'You mean you regret saying no?'

'Oh, no. Of course not. It wouldn't have worked. I suppose I mean I wish I were that different person it might have worked for. And then sometimes I think it never happened, I only dreamt that it happened.'

'In that case, I dreamt it too.'

He said some more, about knowing that the sun didn't always shine there, it wasn't always summer, it couldn't be eternally happy, not with human nature the way it was, and then he said he'd be moving out soon to live by himself.

'Did you manage to sell Gothic House?'

I shook my head. I couldn't tell him the truth, that I'd heard the day before that I had a buyer, or rather a couple of buyers with an inheritance to spend, Kim Gresham and his wife. Greshams have always liked to live a little way outside the village.

# Myth

It was a map of the Garden of Eden. The monk, who was also their guide, pointed it out to them under its protective glass and said something in Greek. The interpreter interpreted. Made in the eighth century AD by one Alexander of Philae, the map had been in this monastery for a thousand years, had been stolen, retrieved, threatened by fire and flood, defaced, patched up and finally restored to its present near-perfect condition.

The tour party crowded around to look at it. Rosemary Meacher, standing in front of her much taller husband, saw a sheet of yellowish parchment that looked as if coffee had been split over it, spindly-legged insects died on it and a child experimented on its mottled surface with a new paintbox. The monk made another short speech in Greek. The interpreter said that, if they were interested, on their way out they could buy postcards of the map at the shop.

'Or tea towels perhaps,' whispered Rosemary to her husband, 'or tablecloths with matching napkins.'

David Meacher made no reply. He had moved to a position beside her and was peering closely at the map. For the first time since their holiday began, for the first time, really, since he was made redundant, his face wore an expression that was neither bitter nor indifferent. He was looking at the map as if it interested him.

The monk and the interpreter moved on; through the library, through the refectory, out into the cloisters. The party followed. Flaking frescos and faded murals were pointed out, their provenance explained. The hot sun was white and trembling on the stone flags, the shadows black. Thankfully the party surged into the shop.

There were no tea towels or tablecloths or aprons or even calendars of the map of the Garden of Eden, but there were the postcards and life-size facsimiles. Framed or unframed.

'You don't really want one, do you?' Rosemary said.

'Yes, of course I do.' David had taken to barking at her lately, especially if, as now, she seemed even mildly to oppose his wishes. 'I think it's very beautiful, a marvellous piece of history.'

'As you wish.'

He bought a framed map and then, on second thoughts, an unframed map as well and four postcards. Back at the hotel he got her to pack the framed map, parcelled in bubble-wrap and their clothes, into their carry-on bag. The unframed map he spread out on the desk top, weighting down its corners with the ashtray, two glasses and the stand that held the room service menu. He sat down with his elbows on the desk and studied the map. After dinner, instead of going to the bar, he went back to their room and she found him there later, crouched over the desk. From somewhere or other he had procured a magnifying glass.

She was pleased. He had found something to take him out of himself. These were probably early days to think of a hobby developing from it, that he might begin collecting old maps, antiquarian books, something like that. But surely this was how such things began. She vaguely remembered hearing that an uncle of hers had started collecting stamps because a friend sent him a letter from Outer Mongolia. If only David would find an interest!

Since the loss of his job he had been a changed man, sullen, bad-tempered, sometimes savage in his manner towards her. And he had been very unhappy. The large sum of money he received in compensation, the golden handshake, had done nothing to mitigate his misery. He still spoke daily of the Chief Executive, a young woman, walking into his office, telling him to clear his desk and go.

'I'll never forget it,' he said. 'Her face, that red mouth like a slice of raw beef, and that tight bright-blue suit showing her fat knees. And her voice, not a word of excuse or apology, not a hint of shame.'

Rosemary saw to her horror that he had tears in his eyes. She thought it would help when the cheque that came was twice what he expected. She thought he might put those humiliating events behind him once she had found the beautiful house in Wiltshire and driven him there and shown him. But apathy had succeeded rage, and then rage came back alternating with periods of deep depression. He sat about all day or he paced. In the evenings he watched television indiscriminately. His doctor suggested this holiday, two weeks in the Aegean, before the move.

'I don't care,' he said. 'If you like. It's all one to me. I'll never get her voice out of my head, not a word of apology, no shame.'

He rolled up the map of the Garden of Eden and she packed it in his suitcase. What became of the postcards she didn't know until she saw him studying one of them on the plane.

They moved house two weeks after their return. It was only his second visit to the house, only the second time he had walked through these spacious rooms and down the steps from the terrace on to the lawn to look across at the seven acres which were now his. Wasn't this better than living in a north London terrace, taking the Northern Line daily to a Docklands office? She wasn't so tactless as to ask him directly. It put heart into her to see him explore the place, pronounce later that evening that it wasn't so bad, that it was a relief to breathe fresh air.

She busied herself getting the place straight, unpacking the boxes, deciding where this piece of furniture and that should go. Two men arrived to hang the new curtains. Another brought the chandelier, holland-wrapped, tied up with string. He hung it in the drawing room and he hung the pictures. David hung up his framed map of the Garden of Eden in the room that was going to be his study. Then he asked the man to hang a much bigger picture he had and which he wanted in the dining room. Rosemary saw, to her surprise, that it was the map again, but blown up to three times its size (and therefore rather vague and blurred) in an ornate gilt frame.

'I had it done,' David said. 'Last week. I found a place where they photocopy things to any size you want.'

She was overjoyed. If she felt a tremor of unease it was a tiny thing, brought about surely by her heightened nervousness and sensitivity to his moods. If she was ever so slightly disturbed by the spectacle of a man of fifty engrossed in a cheap copy of a map of some mythical place . . . But no, it was wonderful to see him returning to his old self, to interest and occupation. He even arranged the furniture in his study, put his books out on the shelves. By nine next morning he was out in the garden and later in the day off in the car to a nursery where there was a chance of finding some particular shrub he wanted.

After they had been in the new place a week she realised he hadn't once mentioned the Chief Executive or her mouth or her blue suit or her voice. So this, apparently, was the solution. Not the holiday or the doctor's drugs or even kindness but the move to somewhere new and different. His days, which had been empty, gradually became busy and filled. He followed a pattern, gardening in the morning and in the afternoon going out in the car and returning with books. Some came from a library, some he bought. She paid them very little attention. It was enough to know that he was reading again after not opening a book of any kind for months. Then one day he asked her if they had a Bible in the house.

She was astonished. Neither of them had religious leanings. 'Your old school Bible is somewhere. Shall I look for it?'

'I will,' he said, and then, 'I want to look something up.'

He found the Bible and was soon immersed in it. Perhaps he was about to undergo some sort of conversion. This house was his road to Damascus. Disquiet returned in a small niggling way and when he was outside mowing the lawn next day she looked at the library books and the books he had bought. Every one of them was concerned in some respect or other with the Garden of Eden. There was a scholarly examination of the book of Genesis, an American Fundamentalist work, a modern novel called *Rib into Woman*, Milton's *Paradise Lost* and several others. Well, she had hoped he would take up a hobby, that he would study something or collect something, and what it appeared he was studying was evidently – paradise.

Presumably, he would tell her about it sooner or later. He would say what the purpose of it was, what he meant to do with it, what he expected to accomplish. They had enough to live on comfortably, he had no need of an earned income, but perhaps he intended to write a book for his own pleasure. She watched him. She didn't ask. Her own life was less busy than it had been in London and it took concentration to find enough to do. She must become involved with village life, she thought, find charity work, develop her own interests. He didn't seem to want her to help in the garden. Meanwhile, she cooked more than she ever had, baked their bread, made jam from the soft fruit. She admitted to herself that she was lonely.

But when, at last, he did tell her, it came as a shock. She said, 'I don't understand. I don't know what you mean.'

'Just what I say.' He had stopped barking at her. He habitually spoke gently now, even dreamily. 'It's here. The Garden is here. This is where it is. It's taken me a few weeks to be sure, that's why I've said nothing till now. But now I am absolutely certain. The Garden of Eden is there, outside our windows.'

'David,' she said, 'the Garden of Eden doesn't exist. It never did exist. It is a myth. You know that as well as I do.'

He looked at her with narrowed eyes, as if he suspected her mental equilibrium. 'Why do you say that?'

'Believing in it as a real place is like saying Adam and Eve really existed.'

'Why not?' he said.

'David, I'm not hearing this. You can't be saying this. Listen, people used to believe in it. Then Darwin came along and his theory of evolution, you know that. You know that God, if there is a God, didn't make a man out of whatever it is . . .'

'Dust.'

'Well, dust, all right. He didn't take out one of his ribs and make a woman. I mean, it's laughable. Only crazy sects believe that stuff.' She stopped, thought. 'You're joking, aren't you, you're having me on?'

In a rapt, dreamy tone, as if she hadn't spoken, he said, 'It's always been believed that the site of the Garden was somewhere in the Middle East because Genesis mentions the river Euphrates and Ethiopia and Assyria. But, seriously, how could a garden be in Syria and Ethiopia and Iraq all at the same time? The truth is that it was far away, in a place they knew nothing of, a distant place beyond the confines of the known world . . .'

'Wiltshire,' she said.

'Please don't mock,' he said. 'Cynicism doesn't suit you. Come outside and I'll show you.'

He took the Bible with him and one of the postcards. The area of their land he led her to comprised the old orchard, a lawn and the water garden, through which two spring-fed streams flowed. She saw that the lawn had been mown and the banks of the streams tidied up. It was very pretty, a lush mature garden in which unusual plants grew and where fruit trees against the old wall bore ripening plums and pears.

'There, you see,' he said, referring to his Bible, 'is the river called Pison, that is it which compasseth the whole land of Havilah, where there is gold.' His eyes flashed. There was sweat on his upper lip. 'And the name of the second river is Gihon, and the third Hiddekel and the fourth river is Euphrates.'

She could only see two, not much more than trickles, flowing over English stones among English water buttercups. He turned and beckoned to her in his old peremptory way but his voice was still measured and gentle. His voice was as if he was explaining something obvious to a slow-witted child.

'There,' he said, 'the Tree of Life. Sometimes we call it the tree of the knowledge of good and evil.'

He pointed to it and led her up under its branches, a big old apple tree, laden with small green apples. When first she saw the house she remembered it had been in blossom.

'Mustn't eat those, eh?'

His smile and his short bark of laughter frightened her. She felt entirely at a loss. This was the man she had been married to for twenty years, the practical, clever businessman. How had he known those words, how had he known where to look for this – this web of nonsense? She put out her hand and touched the tree. She hung on to it, leaned against it, for she was afraid she might faint.

'I wondered, when I first discovered it,' he said, 'if we were being given a second chance.'

She didn't know what he meant. She closed her eyes, bowed her head. When she felt she could breathe again and that strength was returning she looked for him but he was gone. She made her way back to the house. Later, after he had gone to bed, she sat downstairs, wondering what to do. It couldn't be right for him to be left to go on like this. But in the morning when she woke and he woke, when they encountered each other on adjoining pillows, then across the breakfast table, he seemed his normal self. He talked about taking on a gardener, the place was too much for him alone. Would she like the dining room redecorated? She had said she disliked the wallpaper. And perhaps it was time to invite the neighbours in – if you could call people living half a mile away neighbours – have a small drinks party, acquaint themselves with the village.

She summoned up all the courage she had. 'That was a game you were playing last evening, wasn't it? You weren't serious?'

He laughed. 'You evidently didn't think I was.' It was hardly an answer. 'I dreamt of that bitch,' he said. 'She came in wearing that ghastly blue suit that showed her fat knees and told me to clear my desk. She was eating an apple – did I tell you that?'

'In your dream, do you mean?'

He was instantly angry. 'No, I don't mean that. In reality is what I mean. She came into my office with an apple in her hand, she was eating an apple. I *told* you.'

She shook her head. He had never told her that, she would have remembered. Next day the new gardener started. She was afraid David would say something to him about the Garden of Eden. When neighbours came in for drinks a week later she was afraid David would say something to them. He didn't. It seemed that conversation on this subject was reserved to her alone. With other people he was genial, bland, civilised. In the evenings, alone with her, he spent his time compiling a list of the plants indigenous to Eden, balm and pomegranate, coriander and hyssop. He took her into the fruit garden and showed her the fig tree that grew up against the wall, pointing out its hand-shaped leathery leaves and saying that they could stitch the leaves together and make themselves aprons.

She looked that up in Genesis and found the reference. Then she went to seek advice.

The doctor didn't take her seriously. Or he didn't take David's obsession seriously. He said he would review the tranquillisers he was already prescribing for David and this he did – with startling effect. David's enthusiasm seemed to wane, he became quiet and preoccupied, busied himself in other areas of the grounds, returned to his old interest of reading biographies. He joined the golf club. He no longer spoke of the Chief Executive and her blue suit and her apple. The only thing to disquiet Rosemary was the snake.

'I've just seen an adder,' he told her when he came in for his lunch. 'Curled up under the fig tree.'

She said nothing, just looked at him.

'It might have been a grass snake, I'm not sure, but it was certainly a snake.'

'Is it still there?'

There came a flash of the bad temper she hadn't seen for weeks. 'How do I know if it's still there? Come and see.'

Not a snake, but a shed snake skin. Nothing could have made Rosemary happier. She was so certain the snake was part of his delusion, but he had seen a real snake, or a real snake's skin. He was well again, it was over, whatever it had been.

The summer had been long and hot, and the fruit crop was spectacular. First the raspberries and gooseberries, then peaches and plums. Rosemary made jam and jelly, she even bottled fruit the way her mother used to. None of it must be wasted. David picked the pears before they were ripe, wrapped each one individually in tissue paper and stored them in boxes. The days were long and golden, the evenings mild and the air scented with ripe fruit. David often walked round the grounds at dusk but that was the merest coincidence, it had nothing to do with the Lord God walking in the garden at the cool of the day.

The big tree was a Cox, David thought, a Cox's Orange Pippin, considered by many even today to be the finest English apple. It was laden with fruit. They used an apple picker with a ten-foot handle but they had to put a ladder up into the highest branches. Rosemary went up it because she was the lighter of them and the more agile. He held the ladder and she picked.

If her fears hadn't been allayed, if she hadn't put the whole business of the map and the Garden of Eden behind her – and, come to that, the Chief Executive in her bright-blue suit – she might have been more cautious. She might have been wary. She had forgotten that cryptic remark of his when he said that they – meaning mankind? – might have been given a second chance. She had come to see his delusion as the temporary madness of a man humiliated and driven beyond endurance. So she climbed down the ladder with her basket of shiny red and gold fruit and, taking one in her hand, a flawless ripe apple, held it out to him and said, 'Look at that, isn't that absolutely perfect? Try it, have a bite.'

His face grew dark-red and swollen. He shouted, 'You won't do it a second time, woman, you won't bring evil into the world a second time!'

He lashed out at her with the apple picker, struck her on the side of the head, on the shoulder, again on her head. She fell to the ground and the apples spilled out and rolled everywhere. Her screams fetched the gardener who got there just in time, pulled David off, wrested the bloodstained apple picker out of his hands.

Rosemary was in hospital for a long time but not so long as David. When she was better she went to see him. He was in the day room, quiet and subdued, watching a game show on television. When he saw her he picked up the first weapon that came to hand, a table lamp, brandished it and flung himself upon her, cursing her and crying that he would multiply her sorrow. They advised her not to go back and she never did.

She stayed in the house on her own, she liked it. After all, she had chosen it in the first place. But she took the maps of the Garden of Eden out of their frames and gave the frames to the village jumble sale. In the spring she had the apple tree cut down and made a big fishpond where it had stood. Fed by the streams he had called Pison and Gihon, Hiddekel and Euphrates, it was an ideal home for her Koi carp which became the envy of the county.